WHY WE FIGHT

"Vanessa, you *can't* stake an entire star cluster's survival on holding them here, not if they keep coming like they have."

"Oh yes I can," she said, and he heard the ring of steel in her deadly-soft voice. "This time we *hold*. Not the Bugs, not the devil, not God Himself, is pushing me out of Sarasota. No more retreats. No more slaughtered children. No more parents who die knowing the Fleet abandoned them. *Not this time!*"

"But—"

"No." She cut him off again, more sharply, and a dangerous fire flickered in her eyes. "I know the risk, but there's a point where 'military logic' becomes irrelevant, and that point is right here, right now. There are a hundred *million* humans in this system, and I won't let these fucking monsters have it while I have a single starship or fighter to throw at them!"

ALSO IN THIS SERIES:

Insurrection
Crusade
In Death Ground

BAEN BOOKS by DAVID WEBER

Honor Harrington Novels:

On Basilisk Station
The Honor of the Queen
The Short Victorious War
Field of Dishonor
Flag in Exile
Honor Among Enemies
In Enemy Hands (*forthcoming*)

Mutineer's Moon
The Armageddon Inheritance
Heirs of Empire

Path of the Fury

Oath of Swords

BAEN BOOKS by STEVE WHITE

The Disinherited
Legacy
Debt of Ages

IN DEATH GROUND

DAVID WEBER
STEVE WHITE

IN DEATH GROUND

This is a work of fiction. All the characters and events portrayed in this book are fictional, and any resemblance to real people or incidents is purely coincidental.

A Baen Books Original

Baen Publishing Enterprises
P.O. Box 1403
Riverdale, NY 10471

ISBN: 0-671-87779-8

Cover art by David Mattingly

First printing, May 1997

Distributed by Simon & Schuster
1230 Avenue of the Americas
New York, NY 10020

Typeset by Windhaven Press, Auburn, NH
Printed in the United States of America

In difficult ground, press on;
In encircled ground, devise stratagems;
In death ground, fight.

Sun Tzu,
The Art of War,
circa 400 B.C.

BOOK ONE

Before the Thunder

The cruiser floated against the unmoving starfield with every active system down. Only its passive sensors were powered, listening, watching—probing the endless dark. It hovered like a drifting shark, hidden in the vastness as in some bottomless bed of kelp, and no smallest, faintest emission betrayed its presence.

"So, Ursula! Is the circus ready?"

Commodore Lloyd Braun grinned at his flagship's captain. Despite requests, HQ had decided Survey Flotilla 27 was too small for its CO to require a staff, so Commander Elswick had found herself acting as his chief of staff as well as his flag captain. She hadn't known that was going to happen when her ship was first assigned to Braun, but she had the self-confidence that came with being very good at her job, and now she cocked an eyebrow back at him.

"It is if the ringmaster is, Sir," she said, and he chuckled.

"In that case, what say we get this show on the road? Outward and onward for the glory of the Federation and all that."

"Of course, Sir." Elswick glanced at her com officer. "Inform Captain Cheltwyn we're about to make transit, Allen."

"Aye, aye, Sir."

1

"As for you, Stu," Elswick continued, turning to her astrogator, "let's move out."

"Aye, aye, Sir." The astrogator nodded to his helmsman. "Bring us on vector, Chief Malthus, but take it easy till I get a feel for the surge."

The helmsman acknowledged the order, and Commodore Braun sipped coffee with studied nonchalance as the plot's icons blinked to reflect his command's shift to full readiness. The fact that Captain Alex Cheltwyn, commanding Light Carrier Division 73 from the light cruiser *Bremerton*, was Battle Fleet, not Survey Command, had bothered Braun at first. The captain's seniority had made him Braun's second-in-command, and while Braun knew too much about the sorts of trouble exploration ships had stumbled into over the centuries to share the cheerful contempt many Survey officers exuded for the "gunslingers" the Admiralty insisted on assigning to even routine missions, he really would have preferred Ursula Elswick or Roddy Chirac of the *Ute* in Cheltwyn's slot. Both of them were Survey veterans, specialists like Braun himself, with whom he'd felt an immediate rapport.

Yet any reservations about Cheltwyn had faded quickly. Alex wasn't Survey, but he *was* sharp, and, despite Braun's seniority, he was also a far better tactician. Of course, a Battle Fleet officer *ought* to be a better warrior than someone who'd spent his entire career in Survey, but Alex had gone to some lengths to pretend he didn't know he was. Braun wouldn't have minded if he hadn't bothered, but that didn't keep the commodore from appreciating his tact. And, truth to tell, Braun was delighted to have someone with Cheltwyn's competence commanding the warships escorting his six exploration cruisers. Traditionally, Survey crews found boredom a far greater threat than hostile aliens, but it was comforting to know help—and especially *competent* help—was available at need.

The commodore blinked back from his thoughts as TFNS *Argive* edged into the fringes of a featureless dot in space, visible only to her sensors, and her plotting officer studied his readouts.

"Grav eddies building," Lieutenant Channing reported. "Right on the profile for a Type Eight. Estimate transit in twenty-five seconds."

Braun sipped more coffee and nodded. Survey Command had known the warp point was a Type Eight ever since the old *Arapaho* first plotted it during the Indra System's initial survey forty years back, but Survey considered itself a *corps d'élite*. Channing was simply doing his job as he always did—with utter competence—and the fact that he might be using that competence to hide a certain nervousness was beside the point . . . mostly.

Braun chuckled at the thought. He'd literally lost count of the first transits he'd made, yet that didn't keep *him* from feeling a bit of— Well, call it nervous anticipation. R&D had promised delivery of warp-capable robotic probes for years now, but Braun would believe in them when he saw them. Until he did, the only way to discover what lay beyond a warp point remained what it had always been: to send a ship through to see . . . which could sometimes be a bit rough on the ship in question. The vast majority of first transits turned out to be purest routine, but there was always a chance they wouldn't, and everyone had heard stories of ships that emerged from transit too close to a star—or perhaps a black hole—and were never heard of again. That was one reason some Survey officers wanted to rewrite SOP to use pinnaces for first transits instead of starships. Unlike most small craft, pinnaces were big and tough enough to make transit on their own, yet they required only six-man crews, and the logic of risking just half a dozen lives instead of the three hundred men and women who crewed a *Hun*-class cruiser like *Argive* was persuasive.

Yet HQ had so far rejected the notion. Survey Command lost more ships to accidents in *normal* space than on exploration duties. Statistically speaking, a man had a better chance of being struck by lightning on dirt-side liberty than of being killed on a first transit, and that, coupled with the enormous difference in capability between a forty-thousand-tonne cruiser like *Argive* and a pinnace, was more than enough to explain HQ's resistance to changing its operational doctrine.

A pinnace had no shields, no weapons, and no ECM. Because a *Hun*-class CL *did* have shields, it could survive a transit which would dump a pinnace within fatal proximity to a star. It could also defend itself if it turned out unfriendly individuals awaited it—something which might have happened rarely but, as Commander Cheltwyn's presence reflected, could never be entirely ruled out. And while its emissions signature was detectable over a far greater range than a pinnace's, it also mounted third-generation ECM. Unless someone was looking exactly the right way to spot it in the instant it made transit, it could disappear into cloak, which no pinnace could, and, last but not least, its sensor suite had enormously more reach than any small craft could boast. All in all, Braun had to come down on HQ's side. Things that could eat a "light" cruiser the size of many heavy cruisers were far rarer than things that could eat a pinnace.

"Transit—now!" Channing reported, and Braun's stomach heaved, just as it always did, as the surge of warp transit wrenched at his inner ear. He saw other people try to hide matching grimaces of discomfort, and his mouth quirked in familiar amusement. He'd met a few people over the years who claimed transit didn't bother them at all, and he made it a firm policy never to lend such mendacious souls money.

But that was only a passing thought, for his attention was on his display. For all his deliberate disinterest, this was the real reason he'd fought for Survey duty straight out of the Academy. Survey attracted those with incurable wanderlust, the sort who simply *had* to know what lay beyond the next hill, and the first look at a new star system—the knowledge that his were among the very first human eyes ever to see it—still filled the commodore with a childlike wonder and delight.

"Primary's an M9," Channing reported, yet not even that announcement could quench Braun's sense of accomplishment. A red dwarf meant the possibility of finding a "useful" habitable planet was virtually nonexistent, but that didn't make the *system* useless. Many an unpopulated star system had proved an immensely valuable warp junction, and—

"Sir, our emergence point's a Type Fourteen!" Channing said suddenly, and Braun twitched upright in his command chair.

"Confirm!" he said sharply, but it was only a reflex. Officers like Channing didn't make that sort of mistake, and his mind kicked into high gear as Plotting double-checked the data.

"Confirmed, Commodore. Definitely a Type Fourteen."

"Prep and launch the drone, Captain Elswick. Then go to Condition Baker, standard spiral." Braun made himself sit back once more, laying his forearms on the arms of his chair, and pushed the sharpness out of his voice. No need to get excited just because it was a closed warp point, he told himself firmly. They weren't all *that* uncommon.

"Aye, aye, Sir. Communications, launch the drone. Tactical, take us into cloak at Condition Baker and confirm!"

Braun frowned at his plot as *Argive* expelled a warp-capable courier drone to alert Cheltwyn and the rest of the flotilla then began to move once more, sweeping outward in a standard survey spiral, hidden by her ECM while passive sensors peered into the endless dark. A subtly different tension gripped her bridge crew, and Braun's frown deepened as he ran through his mission brief once more.

There'd been little pressure to survey the Indra System's unexplored warp point for forty years for two reasons. First, there'd been no human population within five transits of it until the first outposts went in in Merriweather and Erebor, so Survey had seen no pressing need to explore further. That, as Braun well knew, reflected budgetary constraints as much as anything else. The Corporate World-dominated Federal government was much more inclined to fund Survey's operations to maintain nav beacons and update charts for heavily traveled areas than to "waste" money on "speculative missions" in underpopulated regions of the Fringe.

But the second reason no one had attached any urgency to exploring Indra's single unsurveyed warp point was that nothing had ever come *out* of it. The nonappearance of anyone else's surveying starships had seemed to indicate there was no star-traveling species—and so no external threat to the Federation's security—on its other side.

But that comfortable assumption had just become inoperable. "Closed" warp points were far less common than "open" ones—or, at least, astrographers had traditionally assumed they were. It was hard to be positive, since the only way to locate a closed point was to come through it from an *open* one at the far end of the link, and the latest models suggested closed points might in fact occur much more frequently than previously assumed. Indeed, the more recent math predicted that the conditions which created such warp points in the first place would tend to put closed points at *both* ends of a link.

If true, there could be hundreds of undetectable warp lines threaded all through explored space, but what mattered just now was that the discovery that Indra's open warp point connected to a closed one here automatically upgraded SF 27's mission status. If no one could even *find* the thing, the fact that no one had come through it meant nothing, so the possibility of meeting another advanced species increased exponentially. Star-traveling races were rare. So far humanity had encountered barely half a dozen of them, but some of those encounters had been traumatic, and Survey Command's operational doctrine had been established as far back as the First Interstellar War. The first responsibility of any Survey ship was to report the existence of such a race before attempting to make contact, and the second was to see to it that no potentially hostile species learned *anything* about the Federation's astrography until formal contact—and the newcomers' bona fides—had been established. The best way to accomplish both those ends was to be sure no newly encountered race even knew the survey force was present until it had been observed at length, which was the reason the *Hun*-class mounted cloaking ECM.

"We've completed the initial sweep, Commodore." Braun looked up as Channing swiveled his own bridge chair to face him. "No artificial emissions detected."

"Thank you." Braun leaned back once more and crossed his legs, rubbing his chin as he glanced at Commander Elswick. "It looks like we're in clean," he said, and she nodded.

"Yes, Sir. The question is whether or not there's anyone out there to notice anything anyway."

"True. True." Braun pursed his lips, then shrugged. "You know the odds against that, but we'll play this strictly by The Book. Continue your spiral but hold your drive to no more than half power and maintain Condition Baker."

"Of course, Sir."

Elswick returned her attention to her own console, and Braun settled himself in his chair. It was going to be a longer watch than he'd anticipated.

"Well, that seems to be that, Sir," Commander Elswick observed.

"Um." Braun nodded slowly, his eyes still on the rough holo chart. The system they'd assigned the temporary name of Alpha One was thoroughly unprepossessing, with only eight planets, the innermost a gas giant seven light-minutes from its dim primary. *Argive* had been in-system for over six days now without detecting anything but lifeless worlds and what *might* be a second warp point just over three light-hours from the star. There'd certainly been none of the clutter star-traveling civilizations tended to leave lying about, like nav buoys or com relays. On the other hand, any star system was an enormous haystack. Scores of starships could be hidden in this one, and as long as they radiated no betraying emissions, they'd all be effectively invisible. *Argive* by herself had far too little sensor range to sweep such a huge volume for covert targets—assuming there were, in fact, any to be found—and Braun was eager to get on with the system survey which was his proper task.

The question was how he did so. SOP required him to bring his escorts through to cover the Survey cruisers, but Cheltwyn's "gunslingers" had no cloaking ECM. If Braun brought them up, the flotilla's presence would be obvious to any hidden watcher. The cloaked *Huns* might not be detectable, but the carriers and their screen would be, even under tight emissions control.

He snorted mentally at his own thoughts. If Ursula's scanner crews hadn't spotted anything, odds were there was nothing *to* spot, despite the volume to be searched, for *Argive* had a far better chance of detecting anyone else than they had of detecting *her*. Even the best sensors had an omnidirectional range of little more than seventy-two light-minutes against something as small as a starship's drive field, and given that their entry warp point had been a closed one five light-hours from the primary, no one could even have known where it was in order to keep a sensor watch on it. Not even the most eagle-eyed watcher could have detected their actual arrival, and they'd gone into cloak immediately, so for anyone to be out there and unseen, they'd have to be hiding just as hard as *Argive* was, and that was ridiculous. Why should anyone hide in his own stellar backyard, particularly when he thought the backyard in question held no unexplored warp points? It would take something more severe than mere paranoia to inspire that sort of behavior!

"All right, Ursula," he said finally. "Call Alex forward. We'll hold the gunslingers on the warp point under tight em-con and turn the rest of the squadron loose in cloak."

"Yes, Sir." *Argive*'s captain seemed to hesitate a moment, her eyes on Braun's face, and the commodore quirked an eyebrow.

"Something on your mind?"

"I was thinking about asking *you* that, Sir. I've got the feeling you're not entirely comfortable about something."

"Not comfortable?" Braun frowned at the holo, then

shook his head. "I'm not *un*comfortable. This isn't my first closed warp point—just the first one when I've been the fellow in command. I suppose I'm finally beginning to understand why the old fuddy-duddies I used to serve under seemed to take so long to get off the pot. But—" he shoved himself up with a grin "—that's why they pay me the big money, isn't it? Go ahead and get the drone off to Alex."

CHAPTER ONE

The Fate of the *Argive*

The drifting cruiser had missed Argive's arrival, but it stirred at last as a cluster of energy sources appeared where they had no right to be. Passive sensors reoriented on the betraying signatures of unknown starships, and a trickle of power sent it sliding closer to them, silent as the vacuum about it, a darker shadow in a lightless room. The newcomers were obviously practicing strict emissions control, but they were not cloaked, and the signatures of their standby drive fields betrayed them. The watching cruiser hovered, counting them, prying at their emissions to learn their secrets, and a com laser deployed. It adjusted itself with finicky precision, aligning its emitter on another patch of space—one as empty to any sensor as that which held the cruiser itself—and a burst transmission flicked across the light-hours.

There was no acknowledgment, but the watching cruiser had expected none. It had discharged the first part of its own function by sounding the warning; now it set about the second part of its duties, maintaining its stealthy watch upon the intruders . . . and waiting.

"Everything in order at your end, Alex?" Commodore Braun asked the face on his com screen.

"Yes, Sir. *Kersaint's* got the backdoor, and the rest of the flotilla's ready when you are."

"Good." Braun nodded in satisfaction. Detaching the single destroyer to cover the Indra warp point was almost certainly unnecessary, but standing orders were firm. *Kersaint* was the insurance policy. If anything nasty transpired, the destroyer would be clear of it, able to fire out courier drones to alert the rest of the Federation, whatever happened to the rest of SF 27.

Not that anything was likely to happen. They'd spent almost four months sweeping Alpha One without turning up a single sign of intelligent life. The survey had taken much longer than usual due to Condition Baker's requirement that the Survey cruisers remain permanently cloaked, and Braun knew his personnel were even more eager than usual to check out the two outbound warp points they'd plotted. If neither of *them* led to closed points, the flotilla could revert to normal operations and put all this stealthy creeping about behind it.

"Very well, then, Alex. We'll check back with you shortly."

"We'll be here, Sir," Cheltwyn agreed, and Braun waved a casual salute to the screen and glanced at Elswick.

"Once more into the breach, dear comrades."

"Yes, Sir. You have the con, Stu."

"I have the con, aye," the astrogator confirmed, and TFNS *Argive* crept forward into yet another warp point.

A dozen ships waited, hidden in cloak and spread to intercept any vessel bound in-system from the warp point, but the picket cruisers' reports had revealed a problem: many of the intruders were faster than any of the waiting defenders. The defenders couldn't overtake them in a stern chase, nor could the pickets send warning when the intruders made transit. The alien ships were clustered about the warp point, certain to spot any courier drone which might be sent through, and that would warn them to flee. The defenders thus found themselves forced to guess about the enemy's current maneuvers and plans, but they knew he was surveying. That meant he was bound to come through eventually, and so the ambush had been set. If the intruders were obliging enough to send their entire force through the warp point and into point-blank range, there would be no need to pursue . . . and if they declined to do so, perhaps they could be induced to change their plans.

The transit was a rough one, but Braun shook off his disorientation and nausea as *Argive*'s temporarily addled electronics sorted themselves out and Channing checked his readouts.

"System primary is a G0," the lieutenant reported.

Braun's display restabilized, and he grimaced. A starship's initial heading upon emergence from an unsurveyed warp point was impossible to predict. Grav surge could—and did—spit a ship out on any vector, and until a point had been thoroughly plotted, no astrogator could adjust for it. Of course, that seldom mattered much. Since he didn't know anything about what lay at an unplotted warp point's terminus, one vector was as good as another.

In this instance, however, the system's central star lay almost directly astern. The warp point was well above the ecliptic, giving *Argive*'s sensors an excellent look "down" at it, but her course took her steadily away from the primary, and Braun had just opened his mouth to order Commander Elswick to bring her ship about when Channing's senior petty officer spoke up.

"Emergence point is a Type Six," she announced, and Braun exhaled in satisfaction. A Type Six was open, so perhaps they could forget all this cloaked sneaking about and—

"I'm getting artificial emissions!" Channing snapped suddenly, and Braun whipped his command chair around to face Plotting.

"What sort?" he demanded.

"Clear across the spectrum, Sir." Channing's voice was flatter, but it was the clipped, hard flatness of professionalism, not calmness. "Looks like navigation beacons further in-system, but I'm also getting radar and radio."

"I'm showing unknown drive fields in-system," the tac officer said in the same clipped tones.

"How many?"

"Lots of them, Sir," Tactical said grimly. "Over a hundred, at least."

"Jesus," someone whispered, and Braun felt his own face tighten.

"Condition Able, Captain Elswick!"

"Condition Able, aye." Elswick nodded sharply to the tac officer, and the shrill, atonal wail of *Argive*'s General Quarters alarm whooped. Despite her size, the specialized equipment of her calling put a severe squeeze on the Survey cruiser's armament. She had barely half the broadside of Battle Fleet's *Bulwark*-class heavy cruisers, but her weapons crews closed up with gratifying speed as the alarm screamed at them.

"Update the drone. Append a full sensor readout and launch," Braun ordered through the disciplined chaos. *Argive*'s speed was so low the range to the warp point had opened to little more than a thousand kilometers, and the courier drone's drive was no more than a brief flicker across the plot as it streaked away at 60,000 KPS. The commodore watched it go, then turned his eyes back to the fresh icons appearing on the large-scale master plot as Plotting and Tactical worked with frantic haste to update it.

"Commodore, I've got something strange here." Channing sounded as if he could hardly believe his own sensors, and Braun raised his eyebrows at him. "Sir, this system has at least three planets in the liquid water zone. I've only got good reads on two of them from here, but— Sir, I'm picking up massive energy signatures from both of them."

"*How* massive?"

"I can't be certain from this far out—" Channing began, but the commodore chopped a hand at him.

"Give me your best guess, Lieutenant."

"Sir, I've never seen anything like it. *Both* of them look bigger than Old Terra herself."

Braun stared at him in disbelief. Humanity's home world was, by any measure, the most heavily industrialized planet in known space. Not even New Valkha came close.

"I'm sorry, Sir," Channing said defensively, "but—"

"Don't sweat it." Braun shook himself and managed a crooked smile. "Just be sure the stand-by drone gets a continuous update of your findings."

"Aye, aye, Sir." Channing sounded relieved by the mundaneness of the order, and Braun turned to Commander Elswick.

"Let's not get in too deep, Ursula. Come to zero-five-zero. We'll sweep the perimeter for a while and see if we can get a better feel before we move further in-system."

"They've found *what?*"

Captain Alex Cheltwyn looked at his communications officer in disbelief, then yanked his eyes down to the display at his elbow as the drone completed its download and a new star system appeared. Detail was sadly lacking from the preliminary data, but bright, scarlet icons glowed balefully in its depths, and his nostrils flared as he studied them.

Commodore Braun held the ultimate responsibility, but he was on the far side of the warp point. It was up to Cheltwyn to decide what to do with the rest of the flotilla, not just the escort, and his brain shifted into high gear.

Even *Argive's* preliminary info suggested the presence of a massive, highly advanced culture, and, unlike the link to Indra, both of this line's warp points were open—so why hadn't they seen any sign of these people on *this* side? There might not be any habitable worlds, but why weren't Alpha One's warp points even buoyed? It was possible its only other open point led to an equally useless cul-de-sac, which might explain the absence of navigation buoys, but Cheltwyn couldn't afford to assume that. Yet if that wasn't the case, then the absence of *any* spaceborne artifacts could only represent a deliberate decision on someone's part. Either that, or—

"Com, raise *Ute*. Advise Commander Chirac of *Argive's* report and instruct him to stand by to fall back on the Indra warp point with the rest of the *Huns*. Then get off a transmission to *Kersaint*. Download the full report and instruct Commander Hausman to relay to Sarasota."

"Aye, aye, Sir."

"Allison, bring us to Condition Able and have Commander Mangkudilaga arm *San Jacinto*'s squadrons for a shipping strike. We'll use *Sha*'s for fighter defense if we need them."

"Yes, Sir." His exec turned to her terminal and began inputting orders, and Cheltwyn stared back down into his plot and gnawed his lower lip. Something didn't add up here, and a worm of acid burned in the pit of his belly.

The fact that the intruder had emerged from an unexplored warp point headed out-system wasn't surprising, but it hadn't changed course to head in-system. Like all its other electronic systems, its cloaking ECM had fluctuated as it made transit, and the watching sensors had spotted it easily. With that head start and helped by its low speed, they tracked it with relative ease despite its cloak, but its heading took it directly away from the ships deployed to catch it. Worse, it had not summoned its fellows forward, and its sensors must be amassing more system data with every passing second. Minutes trickled past while the intruder continued to move away from them, and then, at last, six superdreadnoughts and six battlecruisers turned to pursue.

"Sir? I think you'd better take a look at this."

"At what?" Commander Salvatore Hausman looked up with a frown. Captain Cheltwyn's electrifying transmission had come in three hours ago, and Hausman had been deep in discussion of its implications with his executive officer.

"This, Sir." The tac officer tapped his display, and Hausman stepped closer to look over his shoulder. A vague blur of light flickered in the plot, and Hausman's frown deepened.

"What *is* that, Ismail?"

"Skipper, that's either a sensor ghost . . . or an active cloaking system at about thirty-six light-seconds."

"A *cloaking system?*" Hausman stiffened, eyes suddenly wide, and the tac officer nodded grimly. "How long has it been there?"

"Just turned up, Skip. If it *is* somebody in cloak, he's closing in very slowly. I make it about fifteen hundred KPS."

Hausman grunted as if he'd been punched in the belly, and his mind raced. It *couldn't* be a cloaked starship . . . could it? The very idea was insane, but Ismail Kantor wasn't the sort to make that kind of mistake.

The commander turned away and pounded his fists gently together. *Kersaint* was four and a half light-hours from the rest of the flotilla, and that meant Hausman was on his own. If that *was* a cloaked ship, it could only mean the people whose existence Commodore Braun had just discovered already knew the flotilla was here. But if they knew and hadn't even attempted to make contact, and now they were trying to sneak in close—

"Stay on it, Ismail," he said. "Don't go active, but get Missile Defense on-line. I want an intercept solution cycling ten minutes ago."

"Aye, aye, Sir."

"Com!" Hausman wheeled to his communications officer. "Record for transmission to Captain Cheltwyn."

"Recording," the com officer replied instantly, and Hausman faced the pickup.

"'Sir, Tactical has just detected what may be—I repeat, *may* be—a cloaked starship closing my position from—'" he glanced at his repeater display "'—zero-niner-two one-zero-three at approximately fifteen hundred KPS. I will initiate no hostile action, but if attacked, I will defend myself. Please advise me soonest of your intentions and desires.' Got that?"

"Yes, Sir."

"Send it Priority One," Hausman said grimly, and settled back in his chair as the light-speed burst transmission sped across the vacuum. His warning would take over four hours to reach its destination. Any reply would take another four hours to reach him, and, he thought grimly, if that signature *was* a cloaked ship, that would be at least six hours too long.

The picketing cruiser eased closer to the unsuspecting enemy ship that sat motionless on the warp point. Its active sensors and targeting systems remained on standby, but its missiles were ready, and its mission was simple.

Commander Elswick and Braun stood side by side, staring into the master plot, and *Argive's* captain shook her head as still more icons appeared. The range was far too great for detailed resolution, but Braun had decided to chance deploying a pair of recon drones. It was a risk, since the drones couldn't cloak, but their drive fields were weak. The chance that someone might notice them was remote, yet they extended *Argive's* sensor reach over a light-hour further in-system, and what they reported was incredible.

The system swarmed with activity. Drive fields tentatively IDed as freighters moved back and forth between its huge asteroid belt and the inner planets, and the RDs had long-range readings on the mammoth orbital constructs those freighters apparently served. Braun had once spent twenty months in the Sol System on a routine cartography update, and the spaceborne activity of *this* system dwarfed anything he'd seen there. He pinched the bridge of his nose, then looked up as Lieutenant Channing appeared beside him.

"Commodore, you're not going to believe this," the lieutenant said quietly, "but I've just gotten a look at the third orbital shell. It's not another habitable planet—it's *two* of them."

"Twin planets?"

"Yes, Sir. They're both around one-point-two standard masses, orbiting about a common center." The lieutenant shook his head. "That makes four of them, Sir. *Four* in one system."

"Lord." Braun shook his own head, trying to imagine

the sort of industrial base a star system with four massively populated planets could support. Survey Command had come across quite a few twin planets in its explorations, but he couldn't remember a single system with *this* much habitable real estate. Which raised an interesting question.

"This is a big system, Ursula," he mused. "If you were these people, wouldn't you feel a certain need to make sure nothing nasty happened to it?"

"Sir?" Elswick frowned, and he plucked at his lower lip.

"They've got four inhabited planets. From all the energy they're radiating, each of them must have a population in the billions, assuming our own tech base is any sort of meterstick. Shouldn't a nodal system like this have better security than we've seen?"

"But we don't *know* what sort of security they have, Sir," Elswick pointed out. "We're assuming all these drives—" her finger stabbed at the plot "—are freighters because there's no reason they should be anything else, but we're still way too far out to get any kind of look at what they may have in the inner system. I'll bet their inhabited worlds have orbital fortifications, and we didn't see any sign of them on the far side of the warp point. To me, that suggests they figure Alpha One's a cul-de-sac." She shrugged. "If the system's useless, there's no point maintaining fortifications or a standing picket to watch its warp point. For all we know, the points that *do* lead somewhere are crawling with OWPs and patrols."

"Maybe." Braun peered into the plot for another long moment, then turned back to his command chair. "Maybe," he repeated, shaking his head as he sat, "but I don't buy it. If Sol had more than one warp point, don't you think Battle Fleet would at least picket the second one, even if we 'knew' it didn't lead anywhere? Think about it. We know closed warp points exist—don't you think these people must know it, as well?"

"Well, yes, Sir. . . ."

"And if they know about them, why aren't they even remotely concerned? We've been sneaking around in their space for over ten hours now. If we were so inclined, we could sneak right back out and whistle up the entire Home Fleet."

"What are you getting at, Sir?" Elswick asked slowly.

"I don't know," Braun admitted. "It just doesn't make sense to me." He frowned for another moment, then shrugged. "Well, whoever these people are, it's time to leave. I don't want to sound paranoid, but I'd feel a lot more confident making a first contact with someone this big if at least half of Home Fleet *was* handy."

"Paranoia can be a survival tool, Sir," Elswick observed, and Braun snorted in agreement.

"Turn us around, Captain. Let's get out of here."

The pursuing starships had drawn their dispersed units into closer company, but they'd been unable to overhaul the intruder. It was just as fast as they, and its course had persisted in carrying it away from them, but now it had come about, and they slowed.

The intruder's new course would carry it directly back to its entry warp point, and, coupled with its failure to summon its consorts to join it, that was an ominous sign. It must have obtained sufficient data for its purposes. Now it was falling back to join the others, and the enemy's unwillingness to thrust all of its ships into an ambush was unacceptable.

The guardian starships halted, then the superdreadnoughts came to a new heading, bound for the invaders' entry warp point at their maximum speed while the battlecruisers waited.

Lloyd Braun made himself sit quietly, radiating calm. It was hard. He was even more aware of the gnawing tension than *Argive*'s crew was, for the ultimate responsibility was his. That was true of any commanding officer, but at a moment like this—

The sudden, shocking howl of an alarm jerked his eyes down to his display, and his face went white. Six drive fields had blinked into existence, appearing out of nowhere, directly ahead of *Argive*, and he swallowed an incredulous, frightened oath as their field strength registered.

"Six unknowns," Channing said in the flat, sing-song half chant of someone relying on training to keep him functioning in the face of shock. "Frequency unknown. I show battlecruiser-range masses. Bearing zero-zero-three, zero-one-zero. Range one-six light-seconds and closing."

"Wide-band emissions from unknowns!" Tactical weighed in. "Radar and laser. Battle Comp calls them targeting systems!"

"Com, initiate first contact protocols!" Braun snapped, but deep inside he knew the effort was futile. Those ships had appeared too suddenly, and they were too close, barely five light-seconds outside standard missile range and already well inside the capital missile envelope. Watching *Argive*—even stalking her—from cloak might have been no more than a sensible precaution, but uncloaking this abruptly and lighting her up with tracking systems without even attempting to communicate first was something else, and he looked at Elswick.

"Bring in the Omega circuit for continuous drone update, but do not launch."

"Aye, aye, Sir." Elswick jerked her chin at her com officer, passing on the order, but her attention was focused on Tactical. The rest of the flotilla was Braun's responsibility; the survival of her ship and crew was hers.

"Any response to our hail?" the commodore asked tautly.

"None, Sir." The com officer's voice was flat, and Braun's jaw tightened as fresh light codes flashed beside the red-ringed dots of the unknown battlecruisers. There were no Erlicher emissions to indicate readied force beams or primaries, but the energy signatures of activated missile launchers were unmistakable. Instinct urged him to launch the drone now, for his overriding responsibility was to get his data out, but the drone launch would almost certainly be construed as a hostile act. Unlikely as it might be that the newcomers' intentions were pacific, there was no way he could *know* they weren't until and unless those battlecruisers fired.

"Sir, there's something odd about their drive fields," Tactical said, and Braun and Elswick both looked at him as he tapped keys at his console. "They're too unfamiliar to be certain, but I think those may be commercial drives," he said finally, and Braun frowned.

Commercial drives? Why would anyone put civilian drives into *battlecruisers*? Commercial engines were more durable, more energy efficient, and required smaller engineering staffs than the units most warships mounted. Unlike military drives, they could also could be run at full power indefinitely, but they paid for that by being twice as massive, and their maximum speed was barely two-thirds as great. Freighter designers loved their durability and cost efficiency, but only a few special-purpose warships—like *Argive* herself, who spent most of her time moving slowly along surveying—could afford the mass penalty . . . or accept a lower combat speed.

But whether or not commercial-engined BCs made sense, it might give *Argive* a minute chance of survival, for it meant the alien vessels were no faster than *she* was.

"Still no response, Com?"

"None, Sir," the communications officer replied, and Braun nodded grimly.

"Go to evasive action, Captain."

"Aye, aye, Sir. Helm, come about one-eight-zero degrees!"

Braun stared into his display, watching the battlecruisers as *Argive* swung directly away from them. Her efforts to avoid them might be taken as the final proof her intentions were hostile, but he dared not let that much firepower into any closer range. *Argive* carried only standard missiles, but those ships were big enough to mount capital launchers. If they did, they were already well within their own range, and if they were inclined to—

"Missile separation!" Tactical snapped suddenly. "I have multiple missile separations! Time to impact . . . twenty-two seconds!"

"Stand by point defense," Ursula Elswick said harshly.

✧   ✧   ✧

The battlecruisers flushed their external ordnance racks, and forty-eight capital missiles screamed through space at .6 c, closing on the single alien ship like vengeful sharks.

Counter missiles raced to meet the incoming fire, but *Argive* was an exploration ship. Her defenses were far too light to survive that weight of fire, and Commodore Braun's jaw clenched.

"Launch the drone!"

The cruiser's ready courier drone blasted from its box launcher, streaking towards the warp point, and it seemed to take the enemy by surprise. None of them even tried to engage it as it flashed past them on a diametrically opposed vector, and Braun tried to take some bleak satisfaction from that, but he couldn't look away from the incoming fire.

Fireball intercepts began to spall the space between his flagship and her enemies. Each savage flash was one less missile for the close-in defenses to handle, but too few were dying. Thirty missiles broke through the counter-missile zone, and laser clusters swiveled and spat like coherent light cobras. More missiles died, but the rest kept coming, and then *Argive* lurched like a wind-sick galleon as the first warhead exploded against her shields. The explosions went on and on, battering the ship like the fists of a furious giant, and Braun clung to the arms of his command chair with fingers of iron until the terrible concussions ended.

"Seven hits, Skipper," Tactical reported. "All standard nukes."

"Damage?" Elswick snapped back.

"We've lost ninety percent of our shields and we've got some shock damage, but that's it." The tac officer sounded as if he couldn't believe his own report, and Braun didn't blame him. That many battlecruisers should have torn *Argive* to bits—not that he intended to complain!

He sat tense and still, waiting for the next salvo. There wasn't one, and he felt his muscles slowly unlock as he tried to figure out why. He punched a query into his plot with steady fingers that felt as if they were shaking like castanets, and his eyes narrowed. That salvo density was too low, unless. . . .

"Those were all from their external racks."

He hadn't realized he'd spoken aloud, but Elswick's head snapped around to face him, and he shrugged. "If they'd fired from internal launchers as well, there'd have been at least twenty or thirty more birds. So maybe they don't *have* any internal capital launchers."

"Maybe," she agreed. "I'm certainly not going to complain if they don't, anyway!"

"Me either," Braun replied, but something nagged at the back of his brain. He shoved himself back in his chair, mind racing while Engineering labored with trained haste to put the ship's shields back on-line, and his frown deepened. He tapped more commands into his display and watched the entire encounter replay in accelerated time, starting from the moment the battlecruisers uncloaked, and suddenly he stiffened. Dear God, had they—?

"Captain Elswick!"

"Yes, Sir?"

"I think they've suckered us. They *wanted* us to survive their first salvo!"

"I beg your pardon?" Elswick's eyes widened at his preposterous statement, and he shook his head sharply.

"They should have scored more than seven hits with that many birds. And why did they uncloak when they did? With luck, they could have closed the range another four light-seconds before we picked them up. We would've been almost into standard missile range if they'd waited. They couldn't have counted on that, but why *concede* that big an advantage?"

"But, Sir, why would—?"

"Because they *did* have pickets in Alpha One," Braun said flatly. "They've known we were there the whole time."

Dead silence filled the bridge. Every officer's eyes clung to the crimson-on-crimson light dots pursuing their ship, and the sick, hollow voids in their bellies mirrored Braun's.

"Commercial drives," Elswick said, and the soft words were a bitter, venomous curse.

"Exactly." Braun's fist clenched on the arm of his command chair, but he made himself speak levelly. "This wasn't an accident, Ursula. Not a failed communications attempt. They were stalking us from the get-go. But if *all* their ships have commercial drives and they did have pickets watching us, they must have realized the carriers and their escorts can outrun them. *That's* why they let us see them early—and why their targeting was so poor when they finally fired."

His eyes met those of *Argive's* captain, cold and bleak as death.

"We're bait, Ursula."

Six superdreadnoughts bored through space. A courier drone flashed almost directly through their formation, easily within engagement range, and they let it pass without a shot.

"Courier drone coming through, Sir!"

Alex Cheltwyn looked up from the memo board in his lap, then rose and crossed to the com officer's station to look over her shoulder as she queried the drone's memory. She tapped keys for a few moments, then jerked upright in her chair.

"*Argive* is under attack, Sir!" she exclaimed, and an icy fist squeezed Cheltwyn's heart.

"Download the tac data to Plotting!" he barked, and spun towards *Bremerton's* master plot. The data flashed, and he flinched as he saw the battlecruisers appear from cloak. He stood tautly, watching the plot, and someone gasped behind him as the angry light dots of capital missiles suddenly speckled the display. The drone had launched before impact, and he had no way to know how much damage that salvo had inflicted, but it looked bad.

Lightning thoughts flickered through his brain as the ambush played itself out before him, and his lips drew back in a snarl. The bastards had ambushed *Argive*, but they must not have counted on the rest of the flotilla's presence. Six BCs could tear any survey cruiser apart . . . but five *more* cruisers, especially with two light carriers in support, could more than return the favor.

"Communications! Transmit the drone download to *Kersaint*. Instruct Commander Hausman to make immediate transit to Indra and relay the data to Sarasota."

"Aye, aye, Sir," the com officer responded, and he wheeled to his exec.

"We're going through, Allison. *Callahan* will lead, then the carriers. The rest of the *Huns* will bring up the rear."

"Yes, Sir." The exec bent over her console, punching in orders, and Cheltwyn made himself return to his chair while Survey Flotilla 27 erupted into furious action.

The picket cruisers noted the courier drone's arrival, and, unlike Alexander Cheltwyn, they'd known it would be coming. Even before Bremerton's *com officer queried its memory, a com laser had already sent another message burst streaking across the system.*

TFNS *Callahan* raced through the warp point. Commander Chirac of the *Ute* had already worked up the sensor data from *Argive's* initial drone, and his rough calculations of the warp point's stresses made *Callahan's* transit far less violent than *Argive's* had been. It was still more than rough enough, but none of the destroyer's crew had time to waste on nausea. Their sensors were already sweeping the space about the warp point for any sign of the enemy.

There was none, and *Callahan's* skipper fired his own drone back to announce the all-clear.

The oncoming superdreadnoughts picked up the first alien ship's drive signature. The enemy had reacted more swiftly than expected, and the capital ships were still beyond effective engagement range. But they had no desire to engage until all the enemy vessels were into the system, anyway, and they altered course slightly, curling still further away from the system primary on a vector which would take them to the warp point well after the last enemy ship made transit. With the aliens' only avenue of retreat sealed, they would have no choice but to come to the superdreadnoughts on the defenders' terms, and speed would avail them nothing then.

Bremerton made transit, with *San Jacinto* and *Sha* on her heels, and Cheltwyn breathed a sigh of relief as the *Hun*-class cruisers followed them through. He'd been half afraid he was heading into an ambush, but the enemy had screwed up. They must have assumed *Argive* was operating solo, or they never would have let the rest of the flotilla into the system unopposed.

"Instruct Commander Chirac to launch recon drones," he said. "I want a light-hour shell up and maintained. Then tell Commander Mangkudilaga to hold his launch for my command."

"Aye, aye, Sir."

He shoved himself firmly back in his comfortable chair. There was no point advertising his full capabilities any sooner than he had to. It was remotely possible the opposition didn't have fighters—after all, the Thebans hadn't had any sixty-odd years ago. Even if it did, his own would prove far more effective if the bad guys didn't know he had them until they—

"Sir, we're picking up a loop transmission from *Argive!*"

"On my display!" Cheltwyn snapped, and looked down as Commodore Braun's grim face appeared on the screen beside his knee. The time display in the corner of the screen was a half-hour old, and the captain shivered at the thought that the man behind that face might well already be dead, but then that thought vanished as Braun spoke.

"Alex, if you receive this, turn around and get out of here," the commodore said harshly. "We've been mouse-trapped. These people have commercial—repeat, *commercial*—drives, and they're using *Argive* as bait. They were waiting for us, and they're probably waiting for *you*.

If you're not already engaged, you will be shortly, so get the hell out. That's a direct order." Braun paused for a moment, then forced a bleak smile. "Good luck, Alex. Get my people home."

The screen blanked, then lit once more, replaying the same message, and Alex Cheltwyn's blood turned to ice. He stared at the display, willing the transmission to change, to say something else, but it simply repeated, and he closed his eyes tight.

Braun might be wrong, and if he was—and if he was still alive— Cheltwyn's ships were *Argive*'s only hope. But he might *not* be wrong . . . and as the captain's brain ran back over the data from the drone download he felt sickly certain the commodore wasn't. And if he wasn't, there were only two possible reasons his own command wasn't already under attack. Either the enemy hadn't gotten to the warp point yet . . . or else he was waiting for Cheltwyn to move still further in-system before he sprang the trap.

Every instinct cried out to ignore Braun's order, to go to his commodore's rescue, but the cold, pitiless light of his intellect said something else, and he drew a deep breath.

"Bring us about, Allison," he said, and his iron-hard voice was a stranger's.

The cruiser which had crept stealthily closer to TFNS Kersaint for so many hours received the transmission from its sister. The enemy had advanced into the trap; now it was time to destroy the only vessel which might get word of the ambush out.

"Skipper, I'm picking up a transmission of some sort."

"What d'you mean, 'of some sort'?" Salvatore Hausman's nerves had wound tighter and tighter as he watched the light blur on his plot. It hovered on the very edge of the standard missile envelope now, and the agonizing wait turned his voice harsh. "Is it from Captain Cheltwyn?"

"No, Sir. I can't—" *Kersaint*'s com officer shook her

head. "It doesn't seem to be *saying* anything, Skipper. It's just some sort of electronic noise."

"Noise?" Hausman repeated sharply.

"Yes, Sir. It's almost like it's just a carrier. If it's got any content, my computers can't recognize it."

"Source?"

"I can't say for certain, but the bearing's about right to be from Captain Cheltwyn."

"Skipper, that bogey's moving again!" Lieutenant Kantor's crisp voice pulled Hausman's attention away from the com officer, and he darted another look at his display. The light blur *was* moving, and whoever was in command over there had to know he was at the edge of certain detection, cloaked or not, so why . . . ?

The transmission. It had to be the transmission, and if the bogey was still coming in rather than revealing its presence and attempting to communicate—

The picket cruiser slid still closer, and then, suddenly, the alien starship which had seemed so oblivious to its presence reacted. Targeting systems lashed out, locked on, and before the picket could respond, the alien opened fire.

"There he is, Skip!" Ismail Kantor snapped as his first salvo exploded. The range was long, but his passive sensors had been given over five hours to plot the bogey's movements. His targeting solution took full advantage of that data, and his external racks and internal launchers sent a dozen missiles streaking straight for it. Nine of his birds got through, and cloaking ECM was useless against active sensors at such short range. Light codes danced and flickered in the fire control display, and then the bogey glowed with the red-circled white dot of a hostile cruiser.

"She's a CL," Kantor reported as his second salvo went out, and Hausman bared his teeth. A light cruiser was thirty percent larger than his destroyer, but cramming cloaking ECM into something that small ate deep into weapons volume. Unless the bastard had some sort of weapons technology the Federation had never heard of, he and *Kersaint* were evenly matched.

Answering fire spat back, and Hausman's vicious smile grew broader as its weight confirmed his guess.

"Launch the drone!" he barked, and his com officer sent a courier drone streaking through the warp point for the Sarasota fleet base. Whatever happened here, the Federation would know *something* had happened . . . and the Terran Federation Navy would do something about it. The corner of one eye watched the drone disappear, but his attention was on the enemy's light dot.

"Come to zero-niner-zero, zero-zero-three! Let's close the range on this bastard!"

The shocked picket cruiser writhed under the attack. The fire's accuracy proved its target had seen it coming, known it was there, and the sheer number of missiles was a dismaying surprise. The first, stunning salvo ripped away its shields, breached its hull in dozens of places, and irradiated its external missiles into useless junk. The wounded ship belched wreckage and air as the alien vessel sprang into motion, speeding straight for it, but it made no attempt to flee. Instead, it accelerated to meet its foe.

Two missile-armed starships charged straight towards one another, their launchers in continuous rapid fire. *Kersaint* was handicapped by the TFN practice of carrying no antimatter warheads in peacetime lest a fluctuating containment field blow a ship apart. The enemy cruiser was under no such constraint, but at least it seemed to mount only first-generation AMs, not the vastly more destructive second-generation weapons. The range flashed downward, and both ships staggered as hits got through, but *Kersaint*'s initial salvo had given her a crushing advantage, and she exploited it savagely. A dozen more of her missiles scored direct hits, lacerating her enemy, in return for only three hits of her own, but the enemy cruiser didn't even try to break off. It came straight for her, and both ships went to sprint-mode fire as the range fell to five light-seconds. The missiles shrieked in at such high velocities point defense could no longer stop them, and Salvatore Hausman snarled as his ship staggered again and again. But he was winning. He could take the bastard, and then . . .

His eyes flared suddenly wide as the enemy cruiser altered course once more. It was only a small alteration, but—

"Hard a starboard!" he shouted. *"Hard a—"*

A savage fireball glared in the soundless depths of space as two starships met head-on at a closing velocity of .17 *c.*

The superdreadnoughts were still at extreme missile range when the aliens suddenly stopped advancing. They paused for just an instant, then reversed course, darting back the way they'd come, and the range was too great to stop them.

But it wasn't great enough to let them escape totally unscathed. The superdreadnoughts twitched as they expelled a lethal cloud of external ordnance. A hurricane of fire sizzled towards the enemy, and even as they fired, one of the superdreadnoughts activated a com laser. If there were no mice to be trapped, there was no longer any need to preserve the cheese, and a message flashed out to other cloaked ships.

A fresh alarm sounded, and Commodore Lloyd Braun looked down into his plot. More icons spangled it—dozens of them strewn across *Argive's* bow in lethal clusters of crimson. He watched identification codes blink beside them, and his mouth tightened. Not with surprise. Not even with fear. He'd known this was coming, and all he felt was a strange, singing emptiness as the proof appeared.

"I make it ten superdreadnoughts and at least twenty battlecruisers, Sir," Commander Elswick said softly, and he nodded.

"Do you think Captain Cheltwyn got out, Sir?" she asked quietly.

"I don't know, Ursula. I hope so. And he's good. Maybe

he did." The commodore looked down into his plot, and his eyes flicked to the six battlecruisers still clinging to his heels. He gazed at them for a long, silent moment, then drew a deep breath.

"Somehow I don't feel much like surrendering," he said almost calmly. He looked up and caught Elswick's eye, and the commander nodded. "All right, then. We can't do much against those big bastards in front, but those fellows behind us have been chasing us long enough. Perhaps it's time we let them catch us."

Ursula Elswick simply nodded, then raised her voice. "Allen, launch the Omega drones. Then purge the computers."

"Aye, aye, Sir," the com officer said quietly, and Elswick looked at her astrogator.

"Bring us about, Stu," she said. "We're going down their throats."

CHAPTER TWO

Storm Wind Rising

Alex Cheltwyn sat stiff and still as his display's lurid
damage codes confirmed Commodore Braun's worst
suspicions. His shell of recon drones had still been racing
outward when the first salvos roared in, and only the
extreme range and command datalink had saved his ships
from destruction. His RDs had gotten one good look at
the enemy vessels, despite their cloak, before *Bremerton*
fell back to Alpha One. No wonder the initial salvos had
been so heavy . . . and thank *God* they'd concentrated
on his escorting warships!

Survey ships were intended to *evade* enemies, but Battle
Fleet units were designed to survive the crucible of
combat, and *Bremerton*'s battlegroup command net fused
all the escorts into a single, multiship entity. Their offensive
fire functioned in fine-meshed coordination . . . and so
did their active defenses. The *Huns* were forced to rely
solely on their own on-board point defense, but the escorts
were able to bring the antimissile firepower of every ship
in the net to bear on fire directed against *any* of them.
The Survey ships had taken heavy damage, despite the
relatively light fire targeted on them, but his escorts had
survived virtually unscathed. Not, he reflected bitterly,
that there hadn't been enough wreck and ruin to go
around this bloody day.

The gunslingers had covered the Survey ships' retreat,

waiting until all the *Huns* had made transit back into Alpha One before they followed. All Cheltwyn had been able to do was grit his teeth and take it while he ran, for none of his shipboard weapons could even engage the enemy. His only long-range offensive power was his light carriers' strikegroups, but thirty-six fighters couldn't possibly have taken out six SDs, and he dared not linger in missile-range of capital ships to recover them, anyway. Launching them would have sentenced all of their flight crews to death, and so he'd done nothing but run, and he'd never felt so useless in his entire life.

TFNS *Ute*, the last Survey ship through, had taken a dreadful pounding before she could transit, but worse was waiting when Cheltwyn returned to Alpha One and discovered what had happened to the other Survey ships he was "protecting." *Cheyenne* had led the retreat . . . and run straight into the totally unexpected fire of two light cruisers. The effects of warp transit had put her defenses far below par, and the cloaked CLs' first salvos had come scorching in before she even knew they were there. Their fire had smashed her into an air-streaming hulk and killed two-thirds of her crew, and her sister *Sudanese* had taken almost as many hits before anyone else could assist her. *Myrmidon* and *Tutu* had at least managed to find the attackers, and, in combination with *Callahan*, their broadsides had been enough to destroy them, but not before *Callahan* had been pounded even harder than *Sudanese*.

Now he sat waiting, hands clenched in ivory-knuckled fists, while his com section worked frantically to sort out the bad news, and the bile of failure burned in his throat. *Argive* and all her people were gone. If they weren't dead already, they would be soon, and his soul would never forgive him for abandoning her. Now he had four more savagely wounded ships—ships he was supposed to *protect*—and it had been left to the exploration specialists, not their Battle Fleet escorts, to engage the enemy. He knew it wasn't his fault. Neither he nor Commodore Braun had been given any reason to suspect what was coming, and, under the circumstances, the survival of *any* of SF 27's units was near miraculous. He *knew* that . . . and none of it did a thing to reduce his crushing sense of guilt.

"Sir?" He looked up as Commander Nauhan appeared beside him. "*Cheyenne*'s a write-off, Skipper," she said. "She's lost all power—can't even blow her fusion plant to scuttle. We think we've gotten everyone off who's still alive, but—"

She shrugged helplessly, and Cheltwyn nodded in bitter understanding. With the cruiser's power down, dozens of people could be trapped in her ruined compartments, and there was no time for systematic rescue efforts.

"*Tutu* and *Ute*?" he asked harshly.

"Yard jobs, both of them." Nauhan met his gaze unflinchingly, and he saw the echo of his own pain in her brown eyes. "*Tutu*'s lost her ECM, and *Callahan*'s drive damage is even worse than theirs is. None of them can make more than half speed, Sir."

"*Damn*," Cheltwyn whispered. Then he shook himself. Those SDs had to be coming in pursuit, and he had no time for the luxury of grief. "All right, Isis. Tell Chirac, Sergetov, and Ellis to set their scuttling charges and abandon. We'll take them aboard *Bremerton* and the carriers for now and redistribute later."

"Commander Sergetov is dead, Sir," Nauhan said quietly. "Lieutenant Hashimoto's assumed command."

"*Hashimoto?*" Cheltwyn stared at her. Arthur Hashimoto was *Tutu*'s assistant engineer, *ninth* in the chain of command. Dear God in heaven, how heavy had her casualties *been*?

"I don't care who's in command!" he snapped, and knew his harsh voice gave him the lie even as he spoke. "Just get them aboard!"

"Yes, Sir." Nauhan's reply was carefully expressionless, and he clenched his jaw.

"*Bremerton* will stand by *Cheyenne*. As soon as we've got all the survivors transferred, we'll destroy the wreck by fire."

"Yes, Sir. Understood."

"All right." Cheltwyn shoved back in his chair and made himself think. With *Argive, Tutu, Cheyenne,* and *Ute* gone, there were only two survey ships left: *Myrmidon* and *Sudanese*. They were thirty percent slower than the escorts, but if the murderous bastards beyond that warp point did, indeed, mount commercial drives, they were still a third again faster than the pursuing superdreadnoughts. Adding them to the battlegroup net would slow his warships, but he could still stay away from the enemy if he could get out of range in the first place, and neither of them could hope to survive on their own if they *didn't* get out of range. Besides, he thought bleakly, with *Kersaint* detached and *Callahan* abandoned, he had two nice, empty slots to put them in.

"Get *Sudanese* and *Myrmidon* plugged into the net," he said heavily, and Nauhan nodded.

"Yes, Sir."

Cheltwyn nodded back, then turned to his tactical officer. "What do we know, Fritz?" he demanded.

"Not much, Skipper," Lieutenant Commander Szno admitted. "From the little data I have, it looked like the Commodore was right. They do seem to mount commercial engines, thank God. That's about all I can say with any assurance. I can make a few guesses based on the pattern of the engagement, but guesses are *all* they'll be."

"Call 'em any damned thing you like, but trot them out fast." Cheltwyn's mouth twitched in a bleak parody of a smile, and Szno tugged on an earlobe.

"I'd say we've got the tech edge, Skip. They were firing in three-ship groups, which probably means they don't have command datalink, and that *should* give us the advantage in any missile engagement. Or—" his smile was as bleak as his CO's "—it would if three superdreadnoughts didn't mount more internal launchers than our entire battlegroup."

"Understood. Is that the only reason you think we've got better tech?"

"No, Sir. This is more speculative, but sensors confirm they used only standard nukes and first-generation antimatter warheads."

Cheltwyn cocked his head with a frown, then nodded. "All right," he said. "I think you're onto something there. Anything else?"

"Not really, Sir, and I'm afraid to assume a bigger edge. Just because we developed systems in a given pattern doesn't mean they've done the same thing. Remember the X-ray laser. The Thebans' general tech base was well behind ours, but we'd never even thought of that one. These people may have surprises of their own."

"Point taken," Cheltwyn grunted, and turned his head as Nauhan reappeared.

"We've gotten everyone we could find off *Cheyenne*, Sir, and *Myrmidon* and *Sudanese* are tied into the net. We should have the last personnel off *Callahan*, *Tutu* and *Ute* in another ten minutes; the small craft are docking with them now."

"Then get us underway. The boats are fast enough to overtake us, and I want as much distance as possible between us and this warp point before the bad guys come through."

"Aye, aye, Sir." Nauhan nodded to *Bremerton*'s astrogator and the tattered survivors of Survey Flotilla 27 and its escorts began to move.

"Do you have lock on *Cheyenne*, Fritz?"

"Aye, Skipper." Szno sounded unhappy, and Cheltwyn didn't blame him. No one liked to destroy one of his own, but they couldn't let that hulk's data or technology fall into enemy hands.

"Destroy her," he said harshly, and the tac officer pressed the firing key. There was no drive field to interdict, and the Survey cruiser's shattered wreck vanished in a sun-bright boil as a single warhead took her dead amidships.

Cheltwyn watched the visual display as *Cheyenne* died, and his bitter eyes matched the hellish glare of her pyre. Then he made himself look away as Nauhan finished passing his orders to the small craft evacuating the other three ships. He beckoned to her and rose from his own chair to glower into the main plot.

"We'll try to run without engaging them, Isis. Fritz thinks we've got a tech advantage, but it's not enough to let us go toe-to-toe with capital ships."

"Yes, Sir."

"Have Mangkudilaga rearm his birds. Shipping strikes against that much firepower would be suicide, and we'll need them for a combat space patrol if they bring up carriers of their own."

"Yes, Sir. Should we launch *Sha*'s group now? They're already configured for intercepts."

Cheltwyn shook his head. "No. We should have enough warning to get the CSP off from standby before anyone can hit us, and I want maximum endurance on their life support when we do launch."

"Understood, Sir."

"All right. Once you've passed those instructions, get a fresh RD shell deployed. We don't have enough of them, so use them to sweep a sixty-degree cone along our line of advance. We'll just have to take our chances on the flanks."

"We could cover that with the recon fighters—" Nauhan began, then shook her head. "No. We'll need every bird we've got for self-defense."

"Exactly," Cheltwyn agreed. "Besides—" he gave another bleak smile "—I want to keep the fact that we've got them our little secret for as long as possible. It's unlikely these people don't have fighters of their own, but if they think *we* don't, they may come in fat and happy, and we need every edge we can get."

"Yes, Sir."

"As soon as we've gotten all that done," the captain went on, "run everything we got from Commodore Braun's drone and every sensor reading Tactical and Plotting got on the actual engagement through the computers. Add *Callahan*'s download from what happened here and put Battle Comp on it. See if they can improve on Fritz's guesstimate of their capabilities, then download the results and all the raw data to two courier drones. Send one to *Kersaint* so Hausman knows what's going on, and send the other straight to Sarasota."

"Yes, Sir." Nauhan gazed into the plot for a moment, then raised her eyes to her CO's.

"What does Sarasota have available, Sir?" she asked softly, and Cheltwyn sighed.

"Not enough," he admitted in an even lower voice. "Admiral Villiers is on maneuvers in K–45, but he's only got a light task group. The next closest force is Admiral Murakuma's, and she's clear up beyond Romulus. She'll need time to get here . . . and her heaviest unit's a battleship." He turned to face his exec squarely. "These people have one hell of an industrial base just in this one system. If they come after us, we're going to lose a lot of systems before we can get enough Fleet units in here to stop them, Isis."

Nauhan opened her mouth, then closed it, nodded, and walked towards the com section. Cheltwyn watched her go, and his thoughts were grimmer even than his face, for he knew what she hadn't said. There were only five thousand colonists in the Golan System, but there were eight million in Merriweather, another thirty million in Justin, over a hundred million in Sarasota, and more than a *billion* in the five inhabited systems of the Remus Cluster, and Alex Cheltwyn and the Terran Federation Navy were oath bound to protect them all.

He knew that. It was the highest calling he could imagine—the reason he'd first put on Navy black and silver and sworn himself to the Federation's service—and he knew the men and women of the Fleet would honor that oath or die trying.

But he also knew that unless the TFN had one hell of a technological advantage, this time it was a promise they couldn't keep.

CHAPTER THREE

The Stuff of Dreams

No one had ever really been able to account for the existence of warp points, least of all the humans who'd blundered onto the one in Sol's outer system by accident. Centuries ago, the great Orion astrophysicist Feemannow'hhisril predicted the presence of Khanae's warp points, but only by inference from their effect on that system's bodies; his work begged the question of causation. Everyone agreed they must in some way be related to the still-imperfectly-understood phenomenon of gravity, which shapes space—that much was clear from the grav surge that made them directly detectable. So the most popular theory held they must result from interruptions in a galactically vast pattern of gravitational interrelationships. Fortunately for this theory, most warp points occurred in association with the gravity wells of stars. Unfortunately for it, some didn't.

Starless warp nexi were as depressing for starfarers as they were frustrating for theorists. For it was only here that humans—or members of any other known species, for that matter—ever experienced the reality of the interstellar abysses they normally bypassed. Here, with no nearby sun to give a reference point, finite minds must confront infinity, and the bottomless void could swallow the soul of anyone who stared into it too long.

Rear Admiral Anthony Villiers knew the void well, for

he'd spent a goodly percentage of his life in space. He knew it was just as well that most of TF 58's personnel never needed to look beyond the bulkheads of their ships. The terror that could overtake even strong minds—the sensation of lostness, of awakening from a dream of cozy ordinariness into a horrifyingly incomprehensible reality—was a problem that had been outweighed in the TFN's estimation by the security advantages of conducting maneuvers in a starless nexus like K–45. Villiers wasn't altogether convinced.

But now he stood, ramrod-straight as usual, and stared into the flag bridge's view screen. None of the task force's other ships were visible, of course; even if they'd been close enough, what light was there for them to reflect? There was only an emptiness that mirrored what he felt inside as he listened to his chief of staff announce the unthinkable.

". . . and so Com was able to finish copying the message before the last of the drones transited to Justin," Captain Santos reported, plowing doggedly ahead despite the Admiral's lack of response. Could *nothing* take the starch out of that stiffness? "Captain Cheltwyn concludes his report to HQ by stating that he'll soon be transiting to Indra but doesn't intend to halt there. He'll proceed directly to Golan and assume a defensive posture. He requests that all available reinforcements—"

"Quite," Villiers cut in abruptly, turning on his heel to face Santos. "We will discontinue the maneuvers forthwith. All elements of the task force will proceed immediately to Golan at maximum speed, Commodore." In some segments of the TFN, the shipboard courtesy "promotion" of anyone holding the rank of captain, reserving the sacrosanct title for the skipper, was considered passé. Villiers upheld it with the same rigor he brought to the enforcement of the most traditional possible interpretation of uniform regulations. This surprised no one, least of all his staff, who now stood uncomfortably under the gaze of those pale blue eyes.

"But, Admiral," Santos said hesitantly, "we've received no orders to—"

"We scarcely need them, Commodore," Villiers clipped in that version of Standard English which, coming from that little island of Old Terra which had birthed the language, held a certain prestige-conferring rightness everyone else in the Federation recognized even as they resented it. "As the nearest force, we are not only authorized but required to respond to Captain Cheltwyn's request for reinforcements. Standing Order 347–A admits of no ambiguity in this matter."

Santos' brown face remained impassive, but Commander Frankel, the operations officer, hadn't been with Villiers long. He turned his head a few degrees toward Commander Takeda, the supply officer, and muttered, "Oh, yeah. The Orglon Scenario."

The lips under Villiers' micrometrically trimmed mustache thinned even more than was their wont, and he gave Frankel a glare beneath which the ops officer wilted. "I believe, Commander, that we can all identify the standing order in question without recourse to sensationalistic labels which the popular media have dredged up from cheap science fiction." Everyone tried to be as inconspicuous as possible, for Frankel had disturbed a particularly rampant bee in Villiers' bonnet. The real problem, of course, was that the "cheap science fiction" had been produced by a fellow TFN officer— not that Villiers would have willingly accorded Captain Marcus LeBlanc any such status. The maverick intelligence officer would have been anathema to Villiers even had he not used his spare time to write a novel almost as notable for its iconoclasm about the upper Fleet echelons as for its heterodoxy concerning potential alien threats. Still, LeBlanc's "Orglon Empire" had filled what seemed to be a widespread need after two generations of peace. Plausible menaces were hard to come by these days.

Santos came to Frankel's rescue by changing the subject. "You said 'maximum speed,' Sir. Did you mean that literally?"

"What, pray tell, might lead you to suspect I did not?" Villiers asked in a deceptively mild tone.

"But, Sir, if we run the drives flat out over that long a period, we're likely—"

"I am quite aware of the implications, Commodore." Villiers' cold gaze swept over the staff before he resumed in fractionally less glacial tones. "If there is any truth to Captain Cheltwyn's report—and I cannot believe he would be guilty of hysterical exaggeration—the urgency of this matter cannot be overstated. Both time and firepower are of the essence, and the task force *will* proceed at maximum. See to it, Commodore." Without another word, he turned away from the array of eyes with their varying degrees of resentment and gave his attention to the tactical display.

Presently the little colored dots that represented three battleships, seven battlecruisers, four light carriers, three heavy cruisers, two light cruisers and three destroyers began to curve around into courses that would take them to the warp point leading to Erebor and thence to Golan. He stole a glance at the view screen, where the stars were precessing as TFNS *Rattlesnake* altered heading.

It sometimes occurred to Villiers to imagine how one of the pioneering astronauts of four centuries ago would have reacted to the sight of spacecraft performing this kind of maneuver. Depending on temperament, the astronaut would probably have sought out either psychiatric counseling or the nearest bar. For in those days, reaction drives had been—and, the physics of the day had confidently asserted, would always be—the only way to get around in space. Today's reactionless drives slipped through a then-unsuspected loophole in the law of conservation of momentum, although they didn't really cancel inertia. Rather, a modern ship wrapped itself in a drive field which could best be described as an inertial sump, although the term caused the specialists to wince. Thus it had become possible to cheat Newton even before the discovery of warp points had made it possible to cheat Einstein.

But, like anything else, the drives could go wrong. . . . Villiers glanced back at the tac display and noted the tight formation as the task force accelerated to the maximum 25,000 KPS its battleships could maintain. Of course, how long it could continue to move at eight percent of light-speed was anyone's guess. Military engines allowed a higher tactical speed than any commercial engine could produce—the maximum speed of a battleship or SD with a commercial drive would be almost 10,000 KPS slower—but their higher power levels made them more failure prone. Running them at such high output for the entire voyage to Golan could have catastrophic effects, however good his engineers, and he knew it as well as Santos. Yet he'd spoken no more than the truth to the captain—indeed, rather less than the truth. His command was too weak to defeat the forces Cheltwyn had reported in a deep-space battle. His only real chance was to fight delaying actions until help reached him, and he could not afford to give up a single warp point without a fight. He could only hope the mysterious unknowns—the Orglons, some annoying imp whispered at the back of his mind—would continue surveying Indra until he reached Golan, and even at these ruinous power levels, the odds that he would arrive in time were low.

None of which mattered in the least as far as his responsibilities were concerned. For now, he wouldn't let himself think about it—or about the civilians at the Golan outpost, more civilians than he could possibly evacuate even if he packed them in like the cargo of some ancient slave ship. . . .

He stood at the notoriously misnamed position of parade rest, gazing into the view screen and thinking thoughts that none of the men and women on the flag bridge would have guessed. For he was thinking of the sixty years that had passed since the Theban War, and wondering if anyone ever recognized a golden age before it was over.

"Excuse me, Admiral."

Villiers looked up from the paperwork on his terminal as Captain Santos entered his briefing room.

"Yes?"

"I've just receipted a message from *Naginata*, Sir. Commander Plevetskaya's engineers have reported a serious harmonic in her Number Two Drive Room."

"How serious?"

"Bad enough they had to shut it down, Sir. Plevetskaya's got enough reserve speed to hold station for the moment, but her people report signs of collateral damage in Drive One. She's requested time to conduct diagnostics, but she needs to shut down Drive One to do it, so, with your permission, I'll instruct the task force to slow to let her—"

"Out of the question, Commodore. I will depart from my usual practice and repeat myself: all elements of the task force are to proceed at maximum speed for Golan."

Santos opened his mouth, then closed it with a click, nodded sharply, and withdrew. The hatch hissed shut behind him, and Villiers gazed at it for a long, silent second. Task Force 58 was barely halfway to Erebor, and he would be fortunate indeed if *Naginata* was the only ship which had to drop out of formation, yet he dared not slow. It was a cruel trade-off. If he maintained speed, he lost ships he might need desperately, but if he slowed down he lost something even more precious: time.

Perhaps that's why these buggers put commercial drives into their warships in the first place, he thought. *No Terran designer would accept such a tactical inferiority, but look at the strategic advantage it gives them. Their superdreadnoughts can actually move fifty percent faster than ours over any sort of long voyage.*

He gazed at the hatch for another endless moment, then sighed. *Well, I can't change what I have—and I suspect I shall be happy enough to have it once the shooting starts!*

He snorted a mirthless chuckle and returned his attention to his terminal.

As soon as possible after the task force's arrival in the Golan system, Villiers had the man he was relieving piped aboard *Rattlesnake*.

Ordinarily, Captain Cheltwyn knew, his haggardness would have drawn at least an unspoken rebuke from the admiral, whose standards of punctilio sometimes provoked muttered speculations about time travelers from the Victorian era. But Villiers greeted him with his very best attempt at warmth . . . not that it really mattered to Alex Cheltwyn at that moment. He'd seen most of his command die and then waited in this system, praying that reinforcements arrived before the attack that would obliterate his three effective ships with contemptuous ease. He could still function, but he would never again be young.

Now he sat facing Villiers and his staff in *Rattlesnake's* outrageously spacious—or so it seemed to a man accustomed to ships of heavy cruiser size or smaller—briefing room. The staffers' eyes told him they'd hoped for some sort of reprieve from him, some silver lining to the pall his courier drones had cast over their universe, and he felt an altogether irrational guilt because he had none to give.

His eyes sought the briefing room's view screen. Nothing could be seen save the star-blazing firmament. Golan B, this system's class-M secondary sun, lurked two hundred and fifty light-minutes away with its sterile brood of planets, not even visible as a ruby star. Golan A, the system primary, would have gleamed with a Sol-like yellow light calculated to awake memories imprinted in Cheltwyn's's genes, but it was in the wrong direction. So for lack of an alternative, his eyes wandered back to the troubled faces around the table.

Villiers, however, remained unruffled. Cheltwyn had never met the admiral, but so far he'd seen nothing to contradict his reputation as a man who would never enjoy widespread affection but who had a certain martinet style.

"Now, then, ladies and gentlemen," the admiral rapped, reasserting control of a meeting that had threatened to drift into despondent aimlessness, "first things first. Commodore Santos, have the pinnaces completed transit to Indra?"

"They have, Sir."

"Excellent." It had been one of Villiers' first priorities on arrival. Cheltwyn could fully understand why, after having waited in this system while an enemy of unknown but certainly overwhelming strength prowled on the far side of a warp point. He'd had to live with it; none of his surviving ships could be left behind in Indra, and none of them carried warp-capable pinnaces. Villiers' capital ships did, and he'd dispatched three of them at once. They would lurk in the outer reaches of the Indra System, probing stealthily inward toward the fire of Indra's sun to observe the enigmatic foe. They didn't carry courier drones, of course; they were little bigger than courier drones themselves. But they would always leave at least one of their number near the warp point, poised to dash through with word of any onrushing attack.

It was, Cheltwyn reflected, a classic problem. He who would defend a warp point knew exactly where his opponent must come from; but he normally could not know *when* the attack would come, and—contrary to the assumptions of journalists and politicians—no military organization can remain permanently at maximum alert. But Villiers' opponents hadn't yet settled into Indra and, indeed, probably hadn't yet surveyed the warp point that led to Golan, a fact he meant to exploit for all it was worth. He might face overwhelming numbers, but he would not be taken by surprise.

"Excellent," the admiral repeated, absently tapping the edge of the table with a light-pencil that he contrived to wield like an ivory-and-gold baton. "Now, as to our deployment, I know of nothing to invalidate the tactical conclusions which we reached en route, and of which I believe Commodore Cheltwyn has been apprised." He lifted one inquisitory eyebrow, and Cheltwyn nodded in confirmation. "Well, then, it's clear enough that a light battle-line such as ours can't hope to go toe-to-toe, as it were, with an opponent who can bring to bear the kind of tonnage Commodore Cheltwyn observed . . . especially in light of our lack of antimatter ordinance—"

"And," Frankel muttered, in tones just low enough to

be arguably short of insubordination, "in light of the fact that we haven't got *Naginata*."

Cheltwyn sucked in a breath and braced himself for an explosion. But none occurred, and he came to the realization that he was the only one who was shocked. Clearly, the ops officer had tapped into a deep pool of resentment. Even Santos' glare at his immediate subordinate seemed motivated more by outrage at violated proprieties than by any fundamental disagreement.

Villiers didn't allow the silence to stretch. "Commander Plevetskaya has personally assured me that she anticipates no great delay in solving her engineering problems since being left behind," he said mildly. "So *Naginata* should be rejoining us in short order. In the meantime, we will follow our preplanned operational dispositions. Our carrier group, including *Sha* and *San Jacinto*—" he inclined his head in Cheltwyn's direction "—will deploy so as to be able to cover the warp point. Our battle-line will hold back and offer long-range missile support." He turned toward Cheltwyn again. "Our fighters should come as an unpleasant surprise to an opponent who apparently lacks any knowledge of them—and still lacks it, thanks to Commodore Cheltwyn's courageous act in forebearing to reveal his fighter capability." Cheltwyn felt a glow of satisfaction at praise from a man to whom praise clearly did not come naturally.

"At the same time," Villiers continued, "this deployment will also minimize the enemy's opportunity to use boarding tactics like those of the Thebans. Admittedly, none of Commodore Cheltwyn's observations suggest that they employ any such tactics. Nevertheless, we want no surprises along these lines. We're ill-equipped to face boarders in the absence of our Marines."

Heads nodded around the table. After transiting from Erebor to this system, Villiers had first proceeded to Golan A II—a life-bearing planet, but no great prize from the standpoint of human habitability—and landed all his ships' Marine detachments there before proceeding on to rendezvous with Cheltwyn's survivors. The publicly announced reason had been to help the outpost's administration maintain order in event of panic. The real reason was known to everyone in the briefing room, but Villiers' next words brought it home to them anew, and Cheltwyn felt his depression come flooding back.

"This leads us to the matter of contingency planning for the evacuation of Golan A II," the admiral stated inexorably. "The chief engineer has prepared an estimate of how many civilians we can accommodate with the Marine berthing spaces freed up and by going to emergency life-support procedures. It is, of course, nothing like the outpost's entire population. But, on a positive note, it is a figure which we can realistically hope to embark in a short period of time, especially given the fact that the Marines are already planet-side and won't have to be debarked simultaneously." Villiers paused reflectively, evidencing no reaction to, or even awareness of, the seeming drop in the briefing room's temperature. Then he resumed with his customary briskness.

"The problem, of course, is one of choosing which civilians can be evacuated and which will remain. After studying the chief engineer's report and the local demographic data, I have decided that first priority will be given to children of age twelve and under, and second priority to pregnant women. We should be able—barely—to accommodate all members of these two categories."

Santos spoke impassively, breaking the silence. "One possible problem, Admiral. The separation of the members of these . . . categories from their families may cause difficulties. It could result in disruptions which we can ill afford, since any such evacuation will, by its nature, be subject to a tight schedule—if," he added, almost defiantly, "it takes place at all."

"A valid concern, Commodore. Before his disembarkation at Golan A II, I spoke privately to Major Kemal. He is fully aware of such potential problems, and is prepared to take whatever measures are necessary to assure the successful evacuation of those we are able to evacuate. He," Villiers continued, laying a slight stress on the pronoun, "is under no illusions as to our inability to save all the civilian population here, nor as to our duty to save those we can." He ran his cold eyes around the table, forcing each of them to meet his gaze. And some of them thought of that which he left unsaid: the fact that if they were forced out of Golan they'd be in the same position all over again in Erebor . . . except that this system held five thousand civilians and that one held over fifty. . . .

The chime of his bedside communicator, and the whooping of klaxons through the structure of the ship, awakened Villiers. He tried to speak, but had to swallow before he could address the machine. "Yes?"

"Admiral," came the voice of *Rattlesnake's* captain, "the pinnaces have transited back from Indra, broadcasting the alert. As per your standing orders, I've sounded general quarters."

"Quite right, Captain. I'll be on the flag bridge directly."

Odd, he thought as he swung out of his bunk. He should have been fighting a black tide of despair, because he'd awakened into his ultimate nightmare: the attack had come before any reinforcements had reached him. But he found he preferred that nightmare, even though there was no awakening from it, to the one from which the communicator had roused him—the one in which all the dying women and children had worn the faces of his wife and daughter.

CHAPTER FOUR

"What else would you have me do?"

Explosions and all other manifestations of violence, however cataclysmic, produce no noise in the vacuum of space. So there was nothing incongruous or eerie about the silence in which the events at the warp point linking Golan with Indra were transpiring. What *was* eerie was the silence on *Rattlesnake*'s flag bridge, where Anthony Villiers and his staff stood with shock-marbled faces and watched Ragnarok unfold.

The returning pinnaces had warned them of what to expect. But those dryly factual reports hadn't prepared them for the reality of a dozen mountainous superdreadnoughts emerging one after another from the warp point, intruding their brutal masses into the metrical frame of local space/time like malignant tumors.

Nevertheless, there had been enough warning for the six carriers, positioned to cover the warp point, to launch their full complements of fighters before the first of the mysterious hostiles materialized. And the invaders' vectors were randomized, as was inevitable on emergence from an unsurveyed warp point. So it was under optimum conditions that the fighters, laden with external FR1 close attack missiles, swooped down on those mammoth ships out of hell.

Sending them in against such odds with weapons as short-ranged as the FR1 had been a grim decision, yet there was little choice. The longer-ranged FM2 would have allowed them to attack from beyond the effective close-in envelope of most antifighter weapons, but an entire squadron could mount only twelve FM2s, and that throw weight was too little to saturate a superdreadnought's point defense. One or two would probably get through, but even if TF 58 had had antimatter warheads, the FM2 couldn't mount one. They needed the greater damage the heavy warhead of an FR1 could deliver, and the close-attack weapon moved at such high velocities as to be impossible for point defense to intercept. Villiers' pilots would pay a high price to get into range in the first place, but once they did, they would also inflict far, far greater damage.

Fortunately, it soon became apparent that Cheltwyn— now aboard *Sha* commanding the carriers—was right. No opponent with experience of fighters would have made so little effort to avoid letting those tiny craft slip into the blind zones that starships' space-distorting reactionless drives created directly aft of themselves . . . a conclusion reinforced by the ineffectual quality of the enemy's point defense fire. So almost all of the carriers' hundred and eight fighters survived to send their FR1s racing ahead, overloaded little drives piling acceleration atop the fighters' own vectors and suicide-compelled cybernetic brains seeking self-immolation.

It took seconds for the light of the explosions to reach Villiers' battle-line, hanging back at extreme missile range. The people on the flag bridge watched, faces bathed in the glare of nuclear warheads and the strings of secondary explosions that erupted as shields went down and bare metal sundered. They watched in silence as the readouts told a tale of devastation beyond their peacetime-conditioned imaginations—all of them but one. For Villiers, though appalled as any, forced himself to analyze the readouts beyond the raw totals of vaporized tonnage.

"Commodore Santos," he said after a moment. The chief of staff started, for the clipped voice had been almost like a gunshot in the hush. "If you will note, certain patterns appear to be emerging in the data."

"Patterns, Sir?" Santos moved to join the admiral while the others looked on. "You mean the enemy's apparent unfamiliarity with fighters?"

"Yes; Commodore Cheltwyn certainly stands confirmed on that point. But I'm thinking now of the response to our own missile fire." The battleships and battlecruisers had been supporting the fighters with missile fire, not very effective at this range. "Or, rather, the lack of any such response after the initial release of their external ordinance. This, combined with the volume of energy-weapon fire the fighters have reported—ineffectual fire, unsurprisingly given that ship-to-ship weapons aren't intended for an antifighter role—point to only one conclusion."

"You mean, Sir . . . ?"

"Precisely. Those superdreadnoughts are pure energy-weapon platforms, with no integral missile armament. So the enemy's possession of antimatter warheads is, at present, academic." Villiers' sharply chiseled features wore an annoyed expression. "Pity. We could have positioned ourselves at a more effective missile range from the warp point. But that's water over the dam, isn't it? At present, the fighters are retiring to rearm, and the enemy is still coming. We must engage them more closely at once. Captain Kruger," he spoke in the direction of a com pickup, addressing *Rattlesnake*'s captain. A series of orders were passed, and the battle-line began to advance.

"Sir," Santos spoke up, "superdreadnought-sized enemy units are still emerging from the warp point. Some of them, in the later waves, are bound to mount missile launchers. And they *do* have antimatter warheads. . . ."

"True enough, Commodore. But I call your attention to another pattern in the data. Please note these recurring figures in the fighters' reports of the volume of fire they encountered."

Santos studied the columns of figures, while others, including Frankel, peered over his shoulders. Slowly, the chief of staff's frown smoothed itself out into under-standing.

"Admiral, unless I'm misreading the data, those—" he caught himself before using a colorfully obscene term "—hostiles really *don't* have command datalink!"

"Exactly so, Commodore; Commodore Cheltwyn would appear to have been correct about that, as well. And, given that advantage in fire control technology, I am prepared to risk a missile duel with an antimatter-armed opponent—even without *Naginata.*" The battlecruiser had limped into Golan only four hours before the attack had begun, and was still toiling across the system at a speed not even Commander Plevetskaya's frantic determination could improve. "And now, ladies and gentlemen, I suggest that we let Captain Kruger fight her ship and concentrate on trying to discern further clues as to the enemy's capabilities and intentions."

Santos' "Aye, aye, Sir" was echoed by a rumble of agreement from the staff, including an unexpectedly emphatic contribution from Frankel.

Villiers' battle-line—so puny in tonnage compared to the procession of enemy SDs that continued to emerge into Golan space—closed to effective missile range, and the space-wracking release of energies escalated to a level that space itself seemed insufficient to contain.

It soon became apparent the enemy's fire control was, indeed, a generation behind the TFN's. Only half as many of those dark ships could link into a single entity for targeting purposes. Perhaps even more importantly, that applied to defensive fire as well as missile salvos, for after the first dozen superdreadnoughts had come others that *did* mount missile launchers, in the numbers possible only to hulls of such size. And they *did* have antimatter warheads for those missiles. But only occasionally could such a missile get through the lattice of defensive lasers from as many as six Terran ships. The few that did were enough to savage the battleships *Aigle* and *Culloden* and obliterate the heavy cruiser *Emanuele Filberto* and the destroyers *Lancer* and *Suleiman*—nothing less than a capital ship could withstand more than a very few hits from the fires of antimatter annihilation. But time and again six of Villiers' ships sent the entire output of their launchers to converge on a single target as though actuated by a single will. Their warheads, though limited to essentially the same merely nuclear energies that had seared Hiroshima and Bombay so long ago, would ignite simultaneously in a cluster of fireballs that grew, touched and blended together in a single glare of destruction that revealed an expanding cloud of gas and glowing debris when it faded. And Villiers, maintaining a mask of cold aloofness amid the whoops and shouts of triumph on the flag bridge, allowed himself for the barest instant to hope.

But *still* those ships came. There were no more super-dreadnoughts after the twenty-fourth of those Brobding-nagian vessels had emerged—to their deaths, in nine cases. But battlecruisers followed, one after another with night-marish repetition, and they were armed with missiles—full magazines of missiles. Villiers studied the dwindling totals of his own ships' depletable munitions with a concentration broken only by the report that the destroyer *Danton* had died. That brief, cruel moment of near-euphoria that had slipped past his defenses only made it worse.

The admiral drew himself up, armored in formality, and turned to Santos. "Commodore, it is now time to implement our contingency plan for evacuating this system. Have Com raise Commodore Cheltwyn for me."

The chief of staff, his brown face speaking silently for all of them, gave an order. Villiers looked into the face of Alex Cheltwyn, and past it at the tightly controlled excitement on *Sha*'s bridge as the light carrier prepared to send her rearmed fighters back into the struggle.

"Commodore Cheltwyn," he began without preamble, "it has become necessary for us to break off engagement. Our speed advantage should enable us to reach Golan–A II before the enemy. But if he presses the pursuit, he will arrive there in time to prevent completion of our evacuation plan. It is therefore imperative that the fighters cover our withdrawal, delaying the enemy's advance. Can you do it?"

"We'll try, Sir."

"Remember, your carriers are too valuable to be risked within missile range of the enemy. You're to avoid letting them close with you, while harrying them with fighter strikes."

"Understood, Admiral. We'll do our best."

"I'm sure you will, Commodore. You know, of course that much depends on it." Villiers made no direct mention of the civilians on Golan A II, nor did he need to.

The battlecruisers slid through space, pulling ahead of the ponderous superdreadnoughts. But not as far ahead as they might have, for the inexplicable little attack craft persisted in their stinging, irritating attacks, which had to be dealt with. The seemingly impossible performance data of their tormentors were not really a matter of interest, except on the level of tactical utility. Analysis would, of course, be left to Higher Authority. And, aside from minor tactical adjustments, no deviation from course was thinkable, for the main enemy force had broken off, fleeing towards the electro-neutrino spoor which betrayed a habitable world. Those battleships must not be allowed to escape . . . and if they were foolish enough to stand in defense of that world, so much the better.

At the outpost's longitude, Golan A was setting in a red glow all too suggestive of blood.

"No! Lydochka!" Ludmilla Igorevna Borisovna strained between the arms of two Marines and cried out to her daughter. Two-year-old Lydia Sergeyevna, blond hair whipping in the wind around a face congested with terror, screamed back as she was borne away across the spacefield, and Ludmilla struggled harder, heedless of her husband's efforts to restrain her.

Then a shadow fell across them and, from the height afforded by powered combat armor, a face looked down—a swarthy face with a hawklike nose and slitted dark eyes. The tribes of humanity had been united under the Federation since the days before they had ventured off

Old Terra into interstellar space, and ethnic distinctions meant nothing anymore. Of course. And yet . . . too many times, men with faces like that had ridden out of the steppes, looking on the Slavic tillers of the soil simply as another herd to be thinned.

But this man wore the insignia of a major of TFN Marines. And he looked down at them with a compassion that shone through his sternness.

"I'm sorry, Mr. and Mrs. Borisov," Major Mohammed Kemal said, "but the admiral's orders are clear. Children and pregnant women take priority. I must insist that you cooperate."

"*Chernozhopi!*" Ludmilla spat. Kemal blinked in incomprehension of the word—literally, "black ass"—that the Russians had used for his sort of people from time immemorial. She was about to say more, but a hand grasped her shoulder from behind as Irma Sanchez, maneuvering her swollen belly through the crowd, moved up from her place next in line.

"Let them take her, Ludmilla," she said urgently. "She'll be safe—I'll look after her, I promise. And you'll rejoin her. You heard the major's announcement earlier: the Navy will pick up everyone else before they leave this system. They *have* to—don't they, Major?"

"Of course, Ma'am," Kemal stated emphatically.

"You hear that, 'Milla?" Sergei Ilyich Borisov tried his clumsy best to be soothing. "Everything will be all right, you'll see. Now let's go."

Ludmilla stared fixedly ahead, but the blond head had vanished in the crowd just as the screams had been swallowed tracelessly by the general din, and she was denied a final look. "Lydochka," she whispered before letting her husband lead her away.

"Thank you, Ma'am," Kemal said quietly.

"Don't thank me, you motherless bastard," Irma Sanchez spoke dispassionately. "I did it for them, not to make it easier for you to carry out your goddamned orders. And the fact that those orders are *right* doesn't make you any less a liar." Head aloft, she marched out across the field towards the waiting shuttle without a backwards look.

Kemal stared after her, and everything that went into his makeup prevented him from shouting after her, as he wished to, *What else would you have me do?*

The last of the light carriers sailed out of the warp point into the sky of Erebor and Anthony Villiers allowed himself an inaudible sigh of relief. Less than a third of the fighters those ships had once carried were still aboard them—the others remained in the Golan System, either as impalpable clouds of infra-debris or as derelict hulks, now lifeless or soon to be, that had been beyond the hope of recovery as the task force fled Golan. But all six of the carriers had survived. And they'd done their job of delaying the enemy's advance. Villiers couldn't actually hear the weeping and moaning of the children and pregnant women crowded into *Rattlesnake*'s bowels, but he imagined he could.

It had been a near thing. The mysterious foe had come inexorably on, slowing to fight off their attackers but never allowing themselves to be swayed from their course, as though held by some wizard's geas to advance by the most direct route toward the nearest concentration of human life. Villiers had almost stopped trying to imagine what manner of beings crewed those silent engines of destruction, and he'd ceased reprimanding people who used the word "Orglons," for he had no better theory to offer.

Captain Marcus LeBlanc, wearing his novelist's hat, had tapped into a nightmare which had receded nearly to the vanishing point in the years of peace. He'd conjured the ultimate enemy, an alien empire that had been expanding for millennia through one warp point after another, growing like a melanoma in the body of the galaxy. His Orglons represented the obscene end-product of the unrestricted cyborging on which humankind had turned its back after some bad experiences in the twenty-first century: flesh and metal, neurons and silicon, blended into a soulless amalgam created long ago by a race that no longer knew or cared what its own original organic form might have been—if, indeed, that race could still be said to exist at all, after having merged its identity into that of its machines. Villiers had scoffed, but now, with the memory of those relentless attackers fresh in his mind, he wasn't so sure.

On impulse, he turned to the intelligence officer. "Commander Santorelli, you know Marcus LeBlanc, don't you?"

Lieutenant Commander Francesca Santorelli looked up from her terminal, surprised. "Why, yes, Admiral. I met him on my first deployment. He was chief intelligence officer aboard—"

"Well, Commander," Villiers went on, as though he'd barely heard her, "when you're preparing your summaries for the courier drones, I suggest you keep him, and the sorts of things he'd want to know, in mind. You see, I have a feeling he's going to be called in on this."

He turned away to face the tactical display and watched his task force—with its empty missile magazines and its two-thirds empty fighter bays and its refugee-crammed berthing spaces—deploy to meet the possibility he tried not to let himself think about: an immediate enemy advance through the warp point whose location they must know about, since they'd been within scanner range to observe his ships vanishing into it. No, he couldn't think about that just now—nor about the fifty-three thousand colonists on Erebor A II. For if those silent ships emerged from conquered Golan, laden with death, he'd have precisely one option: immediate withdrawal, without even thinking about trying to evacuate the colonists.

"Well," Commodore Augustino Reichman breathed as the disorientation of transit subsided and the sunless sky of Warp Nexus K–45 took shape in the view screen, "just one more transit and we'll be in Erebor. And Admiral Villiers knows we're coming, so he must have gotten the colony set up for rapid evacuation. *This* time there'll be no civilians left behind." Not on *my* watch, he didn't add.

"No, Sir," echoed Captain Yu. Most of the flag captain's

attention was on the tactical display, as one after another of Task Group 58.1's superdreadnought-sized *Flower*-class transports and *Dull Knife*-class assault transports, emerged with their six escorting light cruisers. The task group had been hastily assembled with the single objective of getting Erebor's colonists out of harm's way, for that system's puzzling reprieve couldn't last forever. Yu couldn't help thinking about it.

"I wonder why whoever-they-are have delayed so long, Sir? I mean, it's been almost a month."

"Who's to say, Wang? Maybe we're the first opponent they've ever met who's ahead of them technologically. From his report, Admiral Villiers must have given them a good shaking-up before he had to evacuate Golan."

There was a silence at the mention of Golan. Yu broke it diffidently. "Too bad about those civilians. What do you suppose . . . ?"

"Oh, I'm sure most of them're still all right." Reichman's voice was just a shade too hearty. "The enemy—whoever in God's name the enemy *is*—will want to keep them alive for forced labor, and maybe for their hostage value. Only makes sense, doesn't it?" He made a dismissive gesture. "Anyway, we can't let ourselves worry about that now. Our job is to make sure the same thing doesn't happen in Erebor on a larger scale."

"Yes, Sir," Yu agreed. "Believe me, I'm not complaining about the time the enemy's given us! And I imagine Admiral Villiers isn't either."

"You can be sure of that." Warships and ammunition colliers, faster than Reichman's lumbering transports, had already reached Erebor in the maximum numbers Fleet had been able to scrape up. "He's been heavily reinforced—especially since Admiral Teller should've gotten there by now. And he's been replenished with antimatter warheads, so if the enemy still think they've got a monopoly on those, they're in for a rude awakening! And, judging from that courier drone we passed in the Sarasota System, Admiral Murakuma's task force should be on the way. . . ."

❖   ❖   ❖

Those pre-space denizens of Old Terra who bequeathed Rear Admiral Vanessa Murakuma her married surname would have been shocked to know they had, for she was unmistakably *gaijin*. Generations of the 0.78 g gravitation and UV-poor sunlight of Truman's World had produced a fairness of skin that was rare indeed among Old Terra's grandchildren after so many centuries of racial blending. Her green eyes and the slenderness that made her seem taller than her hundred sixty-eight centimeters mingled with waist-length, flame-red hair to give her the look of one of the ancient *Sidhe* from the misty island whence Truman's World's original settlers had come. She also seemed too young to be an admiral, but that was an illusion conferred by the antigerone treatments the Federation supplied to its colonists. In odd contrast to the strong chin that redeemed her face from delicacy, she had dimples which appeared, to her annoyance, in moments of amusement.

They were not in evidence now.

"Did you get in my last addendum to the report, Leroy?" She paused in her pacing to glance again at the blip that represented the receding courier drone.

"Affirmative, Sir. I double-checked with Communications." Captain Leroy Mackenna, her chief of staff, wondered why the admiral was so antsy about her urgent request that Marcus LeBlanc be assigned to her staff. Of course, there *was* the rumor that she and the intelligence community's slightly aging *enfant terrible* had once— But even the juiciest versions of that rumor agreed that it had been a long time ago. Surely it couldn't be the reason. . . .

The admiral seemed to read his thoughts in that disquieting way she had, for her lips curved in a smile too slight to conjure even the ghost of a dimple. "I need his insights, Leroy. He's the only one who's done any thinking lately on the subject of unprecedented alien threats, however little some people—" (of course she couldn't name names, least of all that of Admiral Anthony Villiers) "— think of his speculations . . . or the way he went public with them."

Mackenna grinned. "Don't worry, Sir. There was plenty of time to amend the report before we fired it off."

She acknowledged with a distracted smile and resumed her pacing. TFNS *Cobra's* flag bridge was maintained at the TFN's statutory one standard Terran gee, but Murakuma, for all her light-world upbringing, paced with a determined stride for which the flag bridge seemed too confining. She was thinking of the unknowable that lay ahead . . . and of the courier drones that had already proceeded up the communications chain, and how far their reverberations must have reached by now. Indeed, they must have reached Old Terra itself by now. . . .

"But *surely* the Fleet could have *tried* to *communicate* with them! After all, *anyone* who can build spaceships must be *rational*, and *all* rational beings *must* want peace. . . ."

Sky Marshal Hannah Avram thought beautiful thoughts and tried to tune the whiny voice out. She didn't even waste the mental effort it would have required to wonder if the Honorable Legislative Assemblywoman had forgotten the genocidal Rigelians and the fanatical Thebans, both of which races had been all too capable of building spaceships and neither of which had subscribed to the philosophy the Honorable Legislative Assemblywoman, with a parochialism fit to shame a medieval peasant, assumed must be universal. She'd long ago given up hoping for anything better from Bettina Wister of Nova Terra and the rest of her mush-minded ilk. It wasn't that they were *incapable* of rational thought—Wister, for example, was a past mistress at servicing her constituents and managing the bureaucratic political machine which assured her continual reelection to the Legislative Assembly. They were simply too lazy, ignorant and self-absorbed to look beyond their own rice bowls, and attempting to hold them to a higher standard was pointless. Better to just let this Naval Oversight Committee meeting meander to its conclusion and try to catch up on her sleep.

But the nasal platitudes wouldn't go away. "And besides,"

Wister bleated on, "as *all* civilized beings recognize, violence *never* settles *anything*. . . ."

All at once, Avram decided she'd had enough. Carried beyond a certain point, stupidity was personally offensive to her. "Tell that to the Confederate States of America and the National Socialist German Workers' Party, Assemblywoman Wister," she cut in. "If, that is, you can find them."

Wister looked blank—the Liberal-Progressive Party that ruled Nova Terra had long since reduced the teaching of history to an elective. Obviously Wister had never so elected, and she had no idea what Avram was talking about. But some others in the committee room failed to altogether smother their laughter, and no one reprimanded the Sky Marshal. Hannah Avram could get away with quite a lot by trading on her record; her fame from the Theban War stood second only to that of Ivan Antonov, now rusticating in retirement on Novaya Rodina. Avram chuckled inwardly at the memory of some of the things Ivan the Terrible had said out loud in this place. Wister would be hiding under the table if *he* were here! The thought encouraged her to exploit the pause she'd created.

"I invite the committee to recall Captain Cheltwyn's report: Commodore Braun implemented full com protocols despite the unarguable fact that the aliens had deliberately lured him into a trap. In fact, such protocols are automatic in first-contact situations—and cover the entire spectrum of possible frequencies. But, by definition, it takes two to communicate. At no time have these unknowns evinced any response other than automatic, unreasoning, and lethal hostility. Under the circumstances, the on-scene commanders have behaved in the only manner possible, and I stand squarely behind their actions." Her eyes scanned the entire committee, finally settling on the chairman.

Agamemnon Waldeck of New Detroit peered back at her from between rolls of fat. He had the features that typified his clan of Corporate World magnates, almost obscured in his case by blubber. "All very well, Sky Marshal," he rumbled. "But what about Admiral Villiers' loss of Golan? Shouldn't he have been able to hold a warp point against an anticipated attack?"

"Yes!" Wister honked. "We should set up a . . . a special subcommittee to investigate the Military Establishment's *inexcusable* failure to defend our citizens. Mister Chairman, the people have a right to know the facts behind this, and no coverup can be permitted to—"

Avram's attention didn't stray from Waldeck's porcine little eyes. Wister was merely contemptible, but the chairman rated a certain respect as a villain. He knew perfectly well that Howard Anderson himself couldn't have held Golan; he was just pandering to the electorate's need to believe that any bad news from the front could only be the result of uniformed incompetence. So when she spoke, addressing him directly and ignoring Wister, she didn't even bother to mention the impossible circumstances and overwhelming odds Villiers had faced.

"Aren't we forgetting something, Mister Chairman?" Her voice was of normal volume, but something in it cut Wister off in mid-vaporing. "Aren't we forgetting the time lapse involved?"

"I'm afraid I don't quite follow you. . . ."

"Then permit me to spell it out. Only *twelve standard Terran days* elapsed between the attack on Survey Flotilla 27 and the fall of Golan. In other words, what invaded Golan—two dozen superdreadnoughts, for starters—was this enemy's idea of a *quick-reaction force*."

Waldeck's normally florid face paled. "You mean . . . ?"

Avram nodded. "Yes, Mister Chairman. We have to ask ourselves what we'll be facing when the enemy has *mobilized*." She let the silence stretch before adding, "In fact, for all we know, Admiral Villiers may already be facing it."

"Transit completed, Sir," Captain Yu reported as the sky of Erebor settled into focus.

Commodore Reichman nodded complacently. "Good crossing time for these tubs, Wang. Shape a course for planet A II—but, of course, check in with Admiral Villiers at once."

"Aye, aye, Sir. Admiral Villiers has a picket just off this warp point; should only be a short time delay in hailing her and receiving acknowledgment."

While Yu turned aside and spoke to his com officer, Reichman studied the system display. Erebor A's Type K orange companion-sun was fifty light-minutes away—this wasn't a very widely-separated binary, and it was lucky to have planets. Equally lucky was that a system so young—component A was a Type F—had given birth to life. In fact, it had done so twice, though component B's heavy, dense-atmosphered second planet was no place for humans. The little orange secondary sun was ignorable, as was the system's third warp point, leading to the cul-de-sac system of Seldon, for the outpost there had already been eva-cuated. His goal lay ahead . . . the white glare of Erebor A, moving into the center of the view screen. . . .

"Commodore." Yu's voice brought him abruptly out of his musings. "We've contacted the picket. And . . . and, Sir, there's already a battle going on here."

CHAPTER FIVE

Buying Time

Admiral Villiers had gotten his first surprise when the enemy emerged into Erebor.

He'd been sitting on *Rattlesnake*'s flag bridge. The flagship had happened to be among the third of his units that were currently at GQ; there'd be no pinnaces to warn of an attack this time, and TF 58 had been on rotating general quarters for a Terran month. So there'd been a full bridge crew on hand as he'd studied the tactical display and wished for the thousandth time for the minelayer support he'd repeatedly and urgently requested. With fields of mines—actually cheap homing missiles with only a "dash" capability—covering the warp point, he would have slept a lot better lately. As it was, he had to struggle to keep haggardness from encroaching on his almost dandyish norm.

Still, he couldn't complain about the support Fleet had managed to push through to Erebor. His task force was now up to seventeen battleships and battlecruisers, ten light carriers, and eighteen cruisers and destroyers. An impressive augmentation of his strength by any standard except the one that mattered: the numbers and tonnage he knew he would have to face.

So he and Rear Admiral Jackson Teller, who'd arrived in Erebor a week ago, had settled on a variation on the delaying tactics he'd used at Golan. Once again, the carriers with their escorting battlecruisers and lighter units were positioned to cover the warp point with their fighters, which now numbered one hundred and forty-nine—not full complements for his ten *Shokaku*-class light carriers, but still better than what he'd had in Golan. And better armed, for the antimatter munitions he'd received had included the far more lethal FRAM variant of the FR1. After they'd inflicted the maximum possible destruction on the leading attack waves, Villiers would advance with his battle-line to extreme missile range. It was a terrifying gamble, for he would be facing superdreadnought-sized leviathans, and analysis of the sensor data from Golan had told him things he didn't want to know about their armament. Some could hurl equivalents of the TFN's capital missiles, superior to any of his in range and destructive capability; others mounted capital-ship force beam projectors that could reach out to missile ranges with wrenching, disrupting tractor beams that oscillated between positive and negative attraction in microsecond bursts. But Villiers, relying on his superior fire-control technology, would duel with his mammoth opponents until his magazines were empty, then use his superior speed and the harassment value of his fighters to beat a fighting retreat across the system to Erebor A II—which, he devoutly hoped, would stand empty, its colonists already evacuated by Commodore Reichman's transports, which ought to be arriving any time now. . . .

With the thought came, unbidden, the memory of his address to the Golan refugees just before their departure to what he still dared hope was the safety of the Sarasota System. He hadn't wanted to do it—he never felt comfortable dealing with civilians. But his officers' eyes had told him clearly enough what they thought of his avoidance of the massed human misery in the lower decks, and when the transports had come he'd said a few words to the children and pregnant women who were being taken off his hands. He'd wanted to be reassuring but knew beyond any possibility of self-deception that he hadn't been. As he forced himself to remember the scene, his recollections narrowed to a single face, a face in which Castillian blended with Aztec. The pregnant young woman had stood holding a blond, blue-eyed toddler that couldn't possibly have been her own, and her face had worn an expression Villiers could not forget. . . .

It was in his mind's eye at the instant the alarm klaxon sounded.

He thrust that face out of his mind, along with the leaden thought, *Reichman's not here yet*, and stood up with the briskness of invincible habit. He turned to face Santos . . . and the expression on the chief of staff's face stopped him with his mouth half open.

"Sir," Santos said with the kind of impassivity that set off alarm bells in anyone who knew him, "I think you'd better have a look at the readouts from the pickets."

Villiers did so. At first, what he was seeing didn't even register. When it did, his immediate thought was, *Instrument malfunction*. But a lifetime's mental discipline didn't let that denial reflex survive for even an instant. He knew that what he was seeing was an accurate report of what was happening at the warp point that led to Golan and hell.

The forces that roil in the maelstrom of a warp point have never been fully understood, but their *effects* are understood all too well. In that vortex of the unknowable, conservation of momentum loses its meaning, which means there can be no such thing as "formation flying" through a warp point. Ever since the dawn of interstellar flight, the first principle of safety—indeed, of sanity—had been that ships transited one at a time. Simultaneously transiting ships could emerge in any sort of relationship to each other—including that of *occupying the same space*. This, of course, was impossible . . . and people who commit impossibilities tend to come to *very* bad ends. Villiers, like every naval officer, took the principle so completely for granted that for that first split second his mind simply rejected what the sensors and his eyes had reported.

Light cruiser-sized ships—*thirty-six* of them—materializing simultaneously in that Type One warp point. Of course, not all of them *remained* material for very long. . . .

"Eight hostiles interpenetrated on emergence, Sir," Santos reported in a monotone. He didn't waste words describing what had happened to those eight ships. Villiers scanned the readouts of the energy releases involved, and wondered what those four explosions—what an inadequate word!—had done to the communications and sensor capabilities of the other twenty-eight hostiles.

"They must be robots," Frankel breathed. At any other time, Villiers would have slapped him down for uttering rot. The early computer age's forecasts of artificial intelligence, like those of direct neural interfacing, had proven overoptimistic to the point of giddiness. Time and again, autonomous robotic combat units had lasted precisely as long as it had taken them to come up against opposition directed by a trained and motivated sentient brain. Villiers, like the rest of the military, had long since written off as chimerical the dream—nightmare?—of eliminating the human (or equivalent) element from war. But surely no living beings could have crewed those ships!

He forced himself to concentrate on studying the overall tactical picture while resisting the temptation to fire off signals that would only distract people who had their orders and knew their jobs. And they were doing those jobs as well as could be expected, considering the stunning surprise that had been heaped atop the fatigue of a month spent alternating between general quarters and mere "alert" status. The fighters of the combat space patrol swooped in and launched as the invaders tried to bend their randomized vectors into some kind of organized formation. Ships as small as light cruisers had no business trying to absorb the fury of antimatter warheads; one after another, they died in that hellish glare . . . but not without taking toll, for the foe had learned from what had happened in Golan. The antifighter fire, while still far short of TFN standards, had improved significantly enough for the difference to fairly leap out of the raw data. More fighters were dying than even Villiers' worst-case estimates had allowed for at this stage of the battle. Before the last of the invasion's vanguard had been destroyed, the surviving fighters had exhausted their missiles—and much of the task force was still struggling to come to full readiness. The admiral gazed at the columns of figures and the swarming lights in the master plot's holo tank, and saw his plan lying in ruins.

The CSP's survivors had just turned to return to their carriers to rearm and the other carriers were not yet prepared to launch when the first superdreadnought emerged from the warp point. It was alone—evidently not even this enemy could afford to treat those huge ships as expendable, and there were no more lunatic simultaneous transits—and Villiers turned to Santos and proceeded to exceed even his usual capacity for studied understatement.

"We appear, Commodore, to be faced with an unanticipated gap in our fighter coverage of the warp point. We must therefore make adjustments to our plan. The battle-line will advance."

The Assault Fleet had done its work. As the super-dreadnought oriented itself, its sky-sweeping sensors revealed that the anticipated little attack craft had exhausted their armament in reducing the light cruisers of the initial transit to the handful that survived, and were now withdrawing to their tenders. The enemy battle-line—the same sort of ships as before, little more than two-thirds as massive as a superdreadnought, but more of them this time, as was to be expected—was closing to within standard missile range.

It would be necessary to induce them to narrow the range even more.

Villiers' outward impassivity, so habitual as to be unconscious, was now a dike holding back a rising flood of despair.

His battle-line's finely orchestrated salvos of antimatter missiles had done fearful damage to the oncoming superdreadnoughts. But those implacable behemoths continued to come, and come, and come . . . and each of them mounted massed arrays of point defense that made it a difficult target even without the ability to coordinate its antimissile fire with that of its fellows. And these enemies were of the class that mounted capital force beams. Those weapons' destructiveness was attenuated at this range, but there were a lot of them, and Villiers' battleships began to take damage that felt like a rending and tearing at his own guts.

After an interval that seemed far longer than it was, the reserve carriers finally began to launch their fighters. A small cheer arose on the flag bridge at the news, and Santos cursed the young jackasses under his breath and braced himself for thunderbolts from the admiral's station. A full heartbeat passed before he realized that they hadn't come.

Suddenly concerned, the chief of staff turned and stared at the admiral, who hadn't moved. Concern growing, he stepped over to Villiers' side.

"Sir . . .?"

Villiers turned his command chair to face him. For a shocking instant Santos saw behind that face, saw the full depths of the hell in which the admiral's soul now dwelt. And he spoke as he'd never thought he'd live to speak to Anthony Villiers.

"It's not going to be enough, is it, Sir?"

A tiny smile caused Villiers' mustache to twitch upward. "No, it isn't, Raoul." At any other time, the use of his first name would have sent Santos into shock. Now, like so much else, it didn't seem to matter very much. "The fighters will do a lot of damage. But I think I'm learning how these . . . beings think. They send in what they *know* will be an overwhelming force and accept whatever losses it takes to secure the objective. They sent two dozen superdreadnoughts into Golan and we gave them a good fight—so they'll send in at least two or three times that here. They'll just keep coming and coming. . . ." He shook his head slowly. "Our options have narrowed to withdrawing now or . . ." His voice trailed to a halt, and Santos wondered what he was thinking. "Of course," Villiers resumed, "the decision would be an easy one if only Commodore Reichman had gotten here—"

"Sir!" The cry from the com station seemed to shatter a glass case around Villiers and Santos. "The picket at the K–45 warp point reports that Commodore Reichman's ships have begun to enter the system!"

Once again there was a muted cheer. Villiers and Santos stood apart from it. But then Villiers stood up straight. He seemed to slough off his despairing indecision, but Santos, eyeing him narrowly, saw that only the indecision was gone; the despair was still there.

"Well," the admiral spoke with a ghastly caricature of his old briskness, "that settles that, eh? Have Com raise Admiral Teller."

"Sir, you don't have to do this!"

Rear Admiral Jackson Teller forced himself to sit through the delay as his blurted appeal sped across the light-seconds to *Rattlesnake* and back again. All he could do was stare at the com screen, at the face of the man who'd just condemned himself to death.

Finally, the reply came. "My mind is made up, Admiral Teller. The weight of point defense those SDs mount individually is canceling out our fire-control advantage—especially in light of the fact that our datalinked point defense is useless against their capital force beams. So I am resolved to take point defense out of the equation entirely by taking the battleships in to ranges where their missiles can be used in sprint mode."

"Sir . . . they've already put a dozen superdreadnoughts into this system, and there's no sign they've stopped coming. You can't stop them!" Ordinarily, he wouldn't have dreamed of saying that to Anthony Villiers, but times had ceased to be ordinary.

"Of course not, Admiral Teller." Villiers' time-lagged response came in a shockingly mild tone. "With the forces we have available, the idea of stopping them cannot enter our tactical calculations, can it? My objective is to inflict the maximum possible damage on them—hopefully enough to make them pause in their advance. Your responsibility—" (*After succeeding to overall command*, he did not add) "—will be to gain Commodore Reichman enough time to complete the evacuation of planet A II. And now," he concluded, "I'll sign off. Good luck, Admiral."

"Good luck, Sir." Teller barely had time to make the meaningless noise before the screen went dark. Then he turned to the tactical display's swarming points of light. The green ones representing Villiers' battleships were crawling towards the purple circle that denoted the Golan warp point, still expelling the red dots of enemy super-dreadnoughts in a kind of horrid ejaculation.

"Admiral." Francesca Santorelli interrupted his thoughts. The intelligence officer had been here aboard the command battlecruiser *Sorcerer* when the attack had begun and was now an ad hoc addition to Teller's staff. "These latest superdreadnoughts to emerge are a new class, judging from some subtle differences in their energy signatures."

"A 'new class,' Commander?" Teller queried, preoc-cupied.

"Yes, Sir. The first dozen belonged to one of the classes we encountered at Golan—what we've seen of their weapons mix confirmed our initial identification. But these coming now are . . . something else."

"Give those conclusions to the computer, Commander. I want this different class tagged so they show up in the plot."

"Aye, aye, Sir." Presently, thin red circles appeared around the newly arriving dots. And as Villiers' battle-line closed in, Teller began to notice something. The survivors of the earlier superdreadnought waves continued to target the battleships with their force beams. But from the haloed newcomers, no fire came.

Worried, Teller turned to a small screen flanking his command chair's shock frame. It showed the exterior view from a pickup on Villiers' flagship. As usual, not much could be seen of space combat, such were the distances across which it was waged. But the coming clash of capital ships, at what passed for point-blank range, promised to be more visually stimulating than most. Here and there were the flashes of detonating warheads as Villiers' missiles smashed at their targets in uninterceptable sprint mode. Lasers were, of course, invisible in vacuum, as force beams were anywhere. Glancing at the tac display, Teller saw that the battling heavyweights were passing very close indeed now. In fact, the dots of *Rattlesnake* and a hostile were almost brushing against each other on the plot. He looked back to his private screen and thought, with a faint prickling of the neck, that the stupendous enemy ship would be visible were there light from a nearby sun for it to reflect. . . . There! Maybe that was it, occluding a tiny segment of the dense star-fields. . . .

Almost too swiftly for Teller to catch, what looked like coherent lightning flashed from the enemy ship to a point just to the left of the pickup, not far away on *Rattlesnake*'s hull. As Teller blinked his dazzled eyes, the universe as revealed by the pickup shook and lurched violently and then went out.

Teller's stunned silence lasted less than a heartbeat. "Com!" he roared. "Raise *Rattlesnake* at once!"

"No can do, Sir," came the com officer's harried voice. "They must have taken a serious hit—their communications array is out."

"Keep trying." Teller whirled on Santorelli. "What in God's name *was* that thing?"

"Unknown, Sir." The intelligence officer sounded as shaken as Teller imagined he himself did. "It happened too fast for any kind of analysis. But . . . we're getting reports from some of the other battleships, and some of them are downloading some meaningful data." She studied that data while Teller watched with horror as one after another of the green dots in the tac display began to flicker and then vanish.

"Sir," Santorelli reported after a time, "we've got enough readouts now—that weapon has a hellacious emissions signature—for some tentative conclusions. What we're looking at seems to project a bolt of plasma contained in an electromagnetic bottle."

"But that's crazy!" blurted Teller's own staff spook. Lieutenant Tranh's feelings about being shouldered aside by a visiting lieutenant commander made him even more argumentative than the theory itself would have. "That mag bottle couldn't hold together for more than an infinitesimal amount of time after leaving its generator."

"'Infinitesimal' might be a little strong, Lieutenant," Santorelli retorted. "But in essence you're right. Still, the fact that it's near light-speed makes it workable as a short-range weapon. And within that range . . . it must be almost like a directional fusion bomb."

"Couldn't point defense disrupt the mag bottle?" Tranh asked in a more subdued tone.

"In theory, yes. But it would be like shooting at a missile in sprint mode. Easier to detect, granted—but also even faster, hence even less tracking time. In fact—" Santorelli fell silent, staring at the tac display. Teller followed her gaze and saw the flickering green dot that represented *Rattlesnake*—and all the friends she must have aboard her—had vanished.

"I think you're in command now, Sir," she whispered.

Teller tore his eyes away from the holo tank and its tale of disaster and addressed the com officer levelly. "Com, I want you to patch me through to all the carriers, and all the presently deployed fighters you can reach. Tell the carrier skippers to put me on intercom."

"Aye, aye, Sir." It didn't take long, and Teller only had a moment to gather his thoughts as he watched the three battleships still able to do so swing away in an attempt to escape. The ringed scarlet sigils of enemy super-dreadnoughts moved in pursuit, as still more of the behemoths continued to emerge from the warp point, and emerge, and emerge. . . .

"Ready, Sir," Com reported.

"This is Admiral Teller speaking. Since Admiral Villiers is unable to communicate—" (*True, as far as it goes,* some ghastly voice gibed inside him) "—I am assuming command

of the task force. I will be blunt with you. Our objective—
the *only* objective we can allow ourselves to even contemplate achieving—is to delay the enemy as long as
possible. Every minute we can buy for Commodore Reichman means hundreds of civilian lives. I intend to press
home fighter strikes to the limits of our ability while holding
the carriers just outside capital missile range on a vector
designed to draw the enemy away from planet A II." He
paused for breath, then started to say more . . . but what
more do you say to pilots you've just declared a forlorn
hope and carrier crews you've just declared bait? "That is
all," he finished.

*The Fleet completed its destruction of the enemy battle-
line and shook down on its new vector. The small attack
craft were no surprise this time, and the Fleet had learned
much from its previous encounter with them. It knew
they must come to it—and that it lacked the speed to
overtake the mother ships from which they operated. The
Fleet could not reach their bases, and so it made no
attempt to. It would kill the attack craft as they closed,
accepting its own losses to wear them away. And in the
meantime, the plethora of com signals and powerful energy
sources clustered around the life-bearing planet ahead
of the Fleet whispered that a better target than ships it
could not kill awaited it.*

Flight after flight of fighters struck, returned to rearm,
and struck again. They soon learned the enemy's plasma
weapon was deadly to fighters, yet they couldn't stay
beyond its limited range. The enemy capital ships carried
too much point defense for FM2s to penetrate; that left
them the sole option of flying into the throats of those
hell-weapons in order to strike home with the FRAMs
no point defense had time to stop.

And they did it. Over and over, they did it.

Teller watched from *Sorcerer's* flag bridge, and nausea
warred with pride as he saw those splendid young people
spend themselves, trading their lives for whatever damage

they could do to an enemy they couldn't even visualize, an enemy that seemed but a faceless essence of elemental, inexplicable malevolence. Their losses sickened him, as did the fact that they'd been unable to prevent the destruction of the last of the battleships. Villiers' gallant gesture had sunk without trace in a bottomless pit of futility.

But what sickened him most was the fact that the invaders refused to be sucked into pursuing his carriers and battlecruisers. Like monstrous insects drawn to light, they made their implacable way sunward towards the warmth that might shelter life.

"Their course is gradually pulling them away from us, Sir," Santorelli observed.

"I see it is," Teller growled, then ordered himself not to take it out on the intelligence officer. "We'll have to follow them; otherwise the range will widen to the point where we won't be able to conduct fighter strikes. But we'll stay out of missile range. . . ." He seemed to reach a decision, and turned to face his ops officer. "Commander DeLauria, I want a general order sent out to all carriers. The fighters are to spread out their attacks."

"Spread them out, Sir?"

"Right. Instead of concentrating on one ship and pounding it to pieces, I want to hit as many as possible, inflict just enough damage to slow them down." He smiled faintly. "I know it goes against the fighter jocks' training and temperament—they want to go for the kill. But it's as I told them earlier: our job is to buy time."

"They'll understand, Sir." DeLauria was a former fighter jock herself. Orders began to go out.

Teller couldn't keep his eyes off the serene blue-marbled loveliness of Erebor A II that curved below him, even though he knew it was a lie. The truth was in the screens that showed the endless lines of refugees moving slowly towards the shuttles. At least they were orderly. Too orderly. Even the children seemed subdued as they shuffled along clutching favorite toys. Their faces showed little more bewilderment than their parents'.

Teller shared their feelings. He could hardly have felt a greater sense of unreality if the screens had shown sacrificial victims being led towards a blood-drenched altar, or Jews being herded into gas chambers disguised as showers. Things like this weren't supposed to happen anymore.

The truth was also in the com screen that showed Augustino Reichman's face. The full-fleshed commodore was generally an embodiment of good-living solidity. Now his haggardness brought home to Teller what was happening in a way the anonymous thousands in the screens could not.

"Jackson, I've *got* to have more time! I can get them all off this planet—I have the berthing capacity." Reichman took a deep breath. "Sorry; I know your people have already done all that was humanly possible to slow them down. But . . . look, maybe we could speed things up if I could get more people down to the planet. I've got volunteers lined up!"

Teller shook his head slowly. His idea for slowing the enemy advance had worked—and as he contemplated the eighty-five percent of his fighters he'd lost, he couldn't bring himself to feel the least stir of self-satisfaction. But the two hundred-plus pilots who'd flown those one hundred and twenty-seven fighters had bought more time with their lives than he'd dared hope, forcing the enemy fleet to slow its pace to that of its cripples. Teller's battlecruisers and carriers had swept around them in a wide arc just outside missile range and proceeded to this planet, where Reichman now had sixty-six percent of the colonists aboard his transports, or else in shuttles en route to orbit or ready to lift off.

But still the enemy came on. They came slowly, but they came. And Teller, with four battlecruisers, ten nearly-empty light carriers, and thirteen light combatants (including Reichman's) faced a situation materialized from sheer nightmare.

Jackson Teller had never thought of himself as a particularly brave man. Indeed, he'd often wrestled with doubts about the adequacy of his courage. So he'd long ago forced himself to face all the likely ways in which he might be called on to sacrifice his life on the altar of duty. For he was, above all else, a conscientious man, and he needed to know he would be able to call on something to serve in place of whatever quality people meant when they spoke of "dash." He'd confronted all his demons, and felt he'd stared them down.

Now he realized how inadequate his efforts to imagine demons had been. For the decision he must now make rendered the hazarding of his own life almost banal by comparison.

He shook his head again. "No, Augustino. I've got only twenty-three fighters left, and almost no munitions. And as soon as these . . . creatures realize an evacuation's underway, they'll send their undamaged superdreadnoughts ahead at full speed—they must know I can't even put up a pretense of fighting them. And slow as they are, they're as fast as your transports. So if you don't get a head start on them, *nobody* will be saved." He took a deep breath. "We have to depart for K–45 as soon as we can recover the shuttles now en route or on the ground—and the ones on the ground have to lift at once."

Reichman's round face paled. "No, by God! A third of the colony's still down there! We can't —"

It seemed to Teller that someone else spoke, in a voice other than his. "You will abort the evacuation *now*, Commodore, and prepare for immediate departure from this system. That is a direct order, which you may have in writing if you wish."

For a full heartbeat, Reichman seemed about to say the unsayable. But the moment passed. "That won't be necessary, Admiral," he said expressionlessly.

Teller turned away, for he didn't want to look at Reichman's face any longer. And he *definitely* didn't want to be looking at the view screens when the crowds on the planet's surface heard the announcement that no more passengers would be accepted.

"Commander DeLauria—"

"Yes, Admiral?"

"Get with Com and Engineering. As we proceed to the K–45 warp point, I want to lay a chain of com buoys. I also want you to patch me through to whoever's in charge on the ground down there." Teller wasn't looking at DeLauria. He seemed to be listening to the low, ugly roar over the pickup audio—the refugees must have heard the announcement. "You see," he continued quietly, "I want the ground stations to keep broadcasting as long as they can. I want them to report everything they can possibly tell us about whoever or whatever is doing this."

CHAPTER SIX
Slow Them Down

"Attention on deck!"

Vanessa Murakuma's green eyes swept her collected flag officers and squadron commanders like fire control lasers as she entered TFNS *Cobra*'s main briefing room with Leroy Mackenna, Ling Tian and Marcus LeBlanc on her heels. The dark-complexioned captain had never bothered to do anything about his receding hairline—not even Murakuma had ever figured out whether he was simply too busy to bother with such inconsequentials or whether his baldness was its own affectation—but the neatly trimmed beard he'd grown in compensation was an expression-shielding asset for any intelligence officer. *Especially today,* she thought, as she studied her senior officers' faces. Most were grim and strained, but her own was composed, almost serene. No one had to know how hard it was for her to keep it that way.

She crossed to the head of the table and took her seat while her three staffers stood behind the chairs to her right and left.

"Be seated, ladies and gentlemen." Her soprano was as calm as her face, and a quiet rustle filled the briefing room as her subordinates sat. She tipped back her chair and laid one fine-boned hand on the tabletop. None of them had yet seen the official reports from Erebor, but

80

their faces said they'd heard the rumors, and she drew a deep mental breath.

"I'll come straight to the point," she said. "The enemy—whoever and whatever they are—have taken Erebor." Someone inhaled at the confirmation. "We anticipated that. What we did *not* anticipate was the destruction of Admiral Villiers entire battle-line." A sort of electric shock ran around the table, and she continued in that same, quiet voice. "Captain LeBlanc and Commander Ling will bring you up to speed on our best current information in a moment, but I want each of you to understand what this means."

She paused a moment, as if to let them brace themselves, then continued flatly.

"The Federal government has activated the mutual assistance clauses of our treaties with the Orions and Ophiuchi Association. Both of our treaty partners have promised assistance and begun redeploying their own units, but neither they nor any substantial numbers of our own units can reach us for many weeks. In short, we're it . . . and we're out of time.

"As you know, our original orders were that, while Admiral Villiers screened the approaches, we were to hold station here in Sarasota to assemble our entire assigned order of battle before advancing. That's no longer possible. We must advance now—immediately—to K-45 to cover the evacuation of Merriweather. All indications are that it will be at least another two months—possibly three—before we can be sufficiently reinforced to think about actually stopping the enemy. What we *can*, and must, do is slow him down. Sky Marshal Avram's instructions are unequivocal: we *must* buy time to evacuate as much of the Merriweather and Justin populations as we can, yet we must do so without suffering crippling losses of our own. We're all there is, ladies and gentlemen, and you all know how hard it's been to scrape up even this many ships. If we allow ourselves to be destroyed, the reinforcements currently en route will, in all probability, be too little to stop the enemy short of Romulus or even

Belkassa, and it will be at least *another* two months before follow-on units can reinforce *them*. Which means—" she turned her head, sweeping them all with cold, still eyes "—that if it becomes a choice between heavy Fleet losses or abandoning populated worlds, we will have no choice but to withdraw."

An almost-sound of protest swept the table, but those dark jade eyes froze it back into stillness. Every officer in that compartment knew the TFN tradition: the Fleet died before it abandoned civilians. That wasn't policy; it was a matter of duty, honor, and pride . . . but they also knew she was right. That wouldn't save them from the poisonous guilt they would feel, but they knew she was right.

"Very well, then." She let her chair slip forward, laid both hands on the table, and looked at her ops officer. "Commander Ling?"

"Yes, Sir." Ling was the most junior officer present, but her dark eyes met those of the assembled admirals, commodores and captains levelly as she brought her terminal on-line.

"We have a reasonably complete report from Admiral Teller," she began. "Most of his carrier group and its escorts survived, but his strikegroups took catastrophic losses. Of the one hundred and forty-nine fighters with which he began the engagement, twenty-three survived."

Rear Admiral Waldeck, Murakuma's second-in-command, flinched visibly, but Ling continued in her most clinical voice.

"The good news, such as it is, is that the enemy still has not employed fighters, SBMs, SBMHAWK missile pods, or second-generation antimatter warheads. Coupled with our more sophisticated datalink, we continue to hold an overwhelming advantage in long-range actions. With anything approaching equality of forces, we should be able to stop these people cold. As it is, we estimate the tonnage loss is as much as four-to-one in our favor, and they still keep coming. Captain LeBlanc—" she nodded at the intelligence officer "—will address this point, but my own concern is with the immediate operational consequences rather than the enemy's motives."

Her eyes dipped to her terminal screen, then rose once more.

"The bad news is that the enemy *has* demonstrated both a new tactic and a previously unknown weapon which, in combination, brought about the destruction of Admiral Villiers' battle-line. Without SBMHAWKs, he seems to have adopted another approach to assaulting a warp point: a simultaneous transit. Captain LeBlanc and I are still analyzing the record, but it appears the enemy has built an entire fleet component of cruiser-sized vessels expressly to mount mass transits to clear his battle-line's way. Obviously, his losses from interpenetration will be considerable, but it allows him to introduce a massive amount of firepower quickly.

"No one in TF 58 anticipated such a tactic. When it was actually employed, Admiral Villiers felt he had no option but to close . . . at which point he discovered the existence of the enemy's new weapon system. For want of a better name, we're currently calling it a 'plasma gun.' Our tech people don't yet know how the enemy projects a containment field to hold it together, but they estimate that it must be quite short-ranged compared to conventional energy weapons. Unfortunately, it's also extremely powerful, and from the numbers of plasma guns a single SD apparently mounts, it must be considerably less massive than our own energy weapons. We're trying to formulate doctrine for dealing with it, but it combines the nastier features of a sprint-mode missile and an energy weapon: high accuracy over its range, massive destructiveness, and a velocity too great for effective point defense engagement. At the moment, the only real advice we can give is to stay out of its envelope."

She paused and flicked her eyes over her terminal once more, then looked back up.

"I've prepared a download of Admiral Teller's data for you and your staffs. My assistants and I are continuing our own analysis of it. By the time we arrive in K–45, we should be prepared to discuss it in much greater detail, but any additional input will be most appreciated."

She sat back, and Murakuma looked to her left.

"Captain LeBlanc?"

"Yes, Sir." The newly arrived intelligence officer produced a crooked smile. "What we seem to have here, ladies and gentlemen, is something out of a bad novel." One or two officers actually surprised themselves with barks of laughter. Even Murakuma smiled briefly, but then LeBlanc leaned forward, and there was no humor at all in his deep-set brown eyes. "Even with this new plasma weapon, our technological advantages are surely as evident to the enemy as they are to us. As Commander Ling just pointed out, the loss ratio is overwhelmingly in our favor and seems likely to remain so, yet the enemy continues to throw superdreadnoughts at us, and now he's added this assault fleet component. All humor aside, I never actually expected to run into the Orglon Empire, but that seems to be exactly what's happening. To date, we haven't been able to examine any enemy wreckage or databases to get any idea of his psychology, so all we can do is make inferences from his tactics, and those inferences aren't good."

The briefing room was deathly still, and he cocked his chair back slightly.

"First, and of the greatest immediate concern, he's far less sensitive to losses than we are. I submit that no Terran admiral would continue to advance this aggressively after suffering such heavy—and one-sided—casualties. Quite aside from morale damage, the cost in terms of lost hardware would make it unthinkable. I suppose we might postulate that this sort of behavior reflects how close we are to what must be one of their most important star systems, if not their home system itself. If Sol were under threat, no doubt Home Fleet would be willing to accept mammoth losses to push the enemy back, and it's possible these people are driving so hard to build defensive depth before we can bring up our main strength. Tempting as that explanation may be, however, I do not believe it to be correct. Or, to be more accurate, the second salient point about their operations convinces me it's not the *entire* answer."

"Second point, Captain?" Waldeck asked quietly.

"Yes, Sir. These people never even attempted to communicate with Commodore Braun before opening fire. Not even the Rigelians began a full-fledged war against the Federation without at least attempting to evaluate us first; these people simply started shooting. By our own standards, or those of any other race we've previously encountered, that sort of reaction is insane, which suggests the xenologists are going to have a hard time figuring out what makes them tick. Obviously, an inability to understand what motivates them will make it extremely difficult to project their probable actions, but it's very tempting—so far, at least—to assume that this violent aggressiveness, more even than our proximity to a nodal system, underlies their strategy to date.

"Perhaps even more to the point, we have this assault fleet component. Think about that for a moment. As Admiral Murakuma herself pointed out to me years ago, no reasonable race would sacrifice hundreds of capital ships in headlong assaults on a succession of defended warp points. Against warp points they *knew* were critical to their opponent, yes; perhaps they *would* do that if it was the only way to break through. But simple mathematics would make that unthinkable as a *routine* tactic. It takes us the better part of two standard years to build an SD. Completely ignoring the question of training a capital ship's crew, no one can afford to expend that big a chunk of industrial output without a good reason.

"*These* people, however, seem to have found an approach they think *is* cost-effective. There's no way to prove it—yet—but Commander Ling's initial analysis agrees with mine: the ships they used for that simultaneous transit were purpose built. Whatever we *don't* know about our enemies' psychology, we've been given very convincing evidence that they're willing to accept massive losses in light units—which can be replaced in a much shorter time frame—to clear the way for their heavies. To me, at least, this suggests we can expect to see suicide tactics on the Rigelian or Theban model, and I advise all of you to be on the lookout for them.

"Finally, I'd like to return to the losses in capital ships which they *have* so far accepted . . . which suggest we have to assume an industrial base *at least* as large as our own." Someone made a sound of disagreement, and LeBlanc smiled grimly. "I realize we're accustomed to considering the Federation's industrial capacity as unmatched in the galaxy. To date, we've had every reason to think just that, but could *we* expend so many SDs to capture what are obviously colonies, not core systems? Let me stress once more that, however ferocious he may be, the enemy still has to build the starships he's using up. More, he has to realize we're still redeploying to meet him—that we may have a much greater strength to throw at him than he's seen yet. In similar circumstances, *our* response would be to use probing forces we could afford to lose. We certainly wouldn't cut our mobile forces to the bone in offensive operations that left us unable to meet counterattacks. While we dare not assume our own idea of logic governs these people, I find it very difficult to believe we're *that* different. And if we aren't, their losses to date must represent an *acceptable* loss rate. Which, in turn, suggests they have enormous reserves of capital ships, and for that to be true, they have to have an industrial base capable of building them in the first place."

LeBlanc shrugged, and more than one of the grim faces around the table paled. The enemy's insensitivity to losses had been a tactical concern, but the Federation's status as the most productive civilization in galactic history was so fundamentally accepted—by nonhumans, as well as humans—that few of them had gotten around to considering what LeBlanc had just said. It simply wasn't possible for anyone to outproduce them . . . was it?

Murakuma let them live with the implications for a few moments, then cleared her throat.

"We can't know if Captain LeBlanc is correct, but the consequences of overestimating an enemy are certainly less likely to be fatal than those of *under*estimating him. And whether he's correct or not, *our* concern has to be slowing these people down until the rest of Battle Fleet can respond."

Several people nodded, and she smiled a thin, cold smile.

"Very well, then. Since we do seem to possess the technological edge at the moment, I suggest we decide how best to use it. Commander Ling's current analysis of the Erebor action is available on your terminals. Please take fifteen or twenty minutes to peruse it. After that—" her smile was colder and thinner than ever "—the floor will be open for suggestions."

Vanessa Murakuma sat in her palatial day cabin and watched a display with empty green eyes. K–45 was no more than an empty spot where three warp lines met, and the massed ships of Task Force 59, Terran Federation Navy, held station on TFNS *Cobra* as she floated in that emptiness. It was a powerful force—twelve battleships, twenty battlecruisers, and twelve light carriers, plus escorts—and she supposed she should be excited to have it under her flag. Yet she felt no elation. She'd fought all her life to exercise an authority just like this one, and now, as she faced the hideous decisions that authority was about to force upon her, all she felt was a sick, gnawing need to pass it to someone—*anyone*—else.

She killed the display, blanking away the light dots of the thousands of human beings waiting to live or die at her orders, and her face twisted as her eye fell on the innocent-looking data chip on her desk. She stared at it, bile churning in the back of her throat, then drew a deep breath and made herself look away as her cabin's entry chime sounded.

She squared her shoulders, forcing the sick despair from her expression, and pressed the admittance stud. The hatch slid open, and the officers she'd asked to join her walked through it. Rear Admiral Teller led the way, followed by Demosthenes Waldeck, Leroy Mackenna and Marcus LeBlanc. The four of them sat in the comfortable chairs facing her desk at her gesture, and she made herself pick up the data chip.

"Thank you for coming, gentlemen." Her flat voice sounded over-controlled even to her, but it was the only one she had. "I assume you've all viewed the visual records from Erebor?"

Heads nodded, and she felt a stab of sympathy for Teller's haunted eyes. It wasn't his fault. He'd gotten everyone he possibly could out, yet it made no difference to his bitter self-loathing, and Murakuma understood only too well. Just as she knew it would make no difference to her own when the time came. She studied his face for a moment, then cleared her throat.

"Before we continue, Admiral Teller, I'd like to thank you for your efforts in Erebor." Dull surprise flickered in the junior admiral's eyes, and she faced him directly. "I can only imagine what you're feeling, Jackson," she said quietly. "I'm very much afraid that will change shortly, and I'll be honest with you—with all of you—" she let her eyes sweep over the others "—and admit that terrifies me. It terrifies *all* of us now," her hand tightened on the data chip, "but we can't admit that. We have to put it away somewhere deep inside and pretend it isn't there, because if we don't, if we let it show and affect our personnel or, even worse, paralyze *us* . . ."

She shook her head. The others looked back without speaking, but Waldeck nodded curtly. Demosthenes Waldeck came from one of the most powerful of the Corporate World dynasties which ruled the Federation, and many of Murakuma's fellow Fringers, including her own chief of staff, were prepared to hate him for that. Despite the Federation military's long-standing tradition of political neutrality, the festering hatred between the Fringe, which produced an ever growing percentage of the Fleet's total manpower, and the Corporate Worlds had spilled over into the Navy, and that saddened Murakuma.

She understood it, and watching the Corporate World politicos' cynical manipulation of political power disgusted her, yet she felt something precious and irreplaceable slipping away from the Fleet. It was like virginity, she thought sadly. That sense of something special and almost holy—of being a fellowship of arms whose dedication to protect and preserve placed it above political factionalism and pettiness—could never be regained once it was lost.

Even worse, it sowed distrust, and that was something the human race simply could not afford. She and Leroy Mackenna had come as close to a shouting match over that as they ever had, for Mackenna was from Shilo, whose economy had been devastated fifty years back for daring to defy a major Corporate World shipping line. The Liberal-Progressive Party had enacted special legislation to "clarify" the dispute between the system government and Trans-Stellar Shipping, and Mackenna's family was one of the many who'd been paupered by its provisions. Expecting him ever to forgive the Corporate Worlds for that was not only unreasonable but wrong, yet Murakuma had no option but to insist that he put it aside in his new position.

Especially, she thought, *in this case.* For all the Waldeck clan's immense power, it was also one of those confusing families whose members sometimes refused to fit neat stereotypes, and Demosthenes' branch had a habit of producing outstanding naval officers. His grandmother, Minerva Waldeck, "the mother of Terran carrier ops," had been a heroine of ISW–3, one of the greatest officers ever to wear the TFN's black and silver. Murakuma had known Demosthenes for years, and none knew better than she that he was cut from the same cloth as his grandmother. Even Mackenna was coming to accept that, almost against his will, and after Teller's, Waldeck's face was the grimmest in her cabin. The massive Waldeck jaw clenched tight, and his eyes were shadowed, but his deep, measured voice was level when he spoke.

"You're right, Sir. We *can't* allow this to paralyze us . . . but with all due respect, it has to affect our planning. I realize we can't afford to take heavy losses, but we're talking about millions of lives. We've *got* to slow these bastards down enough to get as many out as we possibly can."

Mackenna's strong-nosed black face wore a strange expression as he looked at the admiral. Under other circumstances Murakuma would have been pleased to see Leroy realize Demosthenes was as determined to save Fringers as he would have been to save Corporate Worlders, but there was no room in her for pleasure this day.

"Agreed," she replied, "and that's why I'm so grateful to Jackson. If he hadn't preserved his command, we'd have only four carriers, not twelve. And if he hadn't laid the comsat chain from Erebor, we wouldn't know what was happening to the people we didn't get out." She looked back to Teller, and her voice was soft. "I realize pulling out of Erebor was a hard decision. I know it's going to haunt you, and I know a lot of second-guessers who weren't there and didn't have to make the call will suggest all sorts of clever ways you could have avoided it. I happen to believe you did exactly the right thing, and I've so advised Sky Marshal Avram."

"Thank you." Teller's tenor was low and hoarse. She heard the genuine gratitude in it, but she also heard the strain, and his hands trembled visibly before he gripped them together in his lap. "If I'd had even a few more fighters left . . . or maybe if they hadn't been bringing up still more SDs . . ." His voice trailed off, and his nostrils flared as he inhaled deeply.

"You did the right thing," she said again, stressing the measured words, then leaned back with a sigh and dropped the chip on her desk. "Nonetheless, Demosthenes is also correct. We know what the stakes are now."

All of them nodded this time, and Murakuma shuddered as her mind insisted on replaying the chip yet again. Some of the Erebor ground stations had survived long enough to transmit footage of the enemy's landings and . . . activities via Teller's chain of comsats. They'd seen the enemy now, and she'd felt a shiver of pure, atavistic horror at her first sight of them. They looked, she thought, like some obscene alloy of spider and starfish—eight-limbed, hairy monstrosities that moved with a hideous, flowing, tarantula-like gait. Humanity had encountered other life forms at least as strange to human eyes, but none of them had ever awakened such a sense of instant, instinctive hatred as these creatures did. It was as if they resonated somehow with humankind's darkest phobias, and their behavior on Erebor only validated that hatred.

The xenologists had dubbed them "Arachnids," and the current best guess was that they were carnivores. It was only a guess, but whether they were pure meat-eaters or not was beside the point. The Federation would never know who'd been behind the camera which transmitted the horrifying footage, for the transmission had ended with terrifying abruptness as one of the aliens loomed suddenly before the lens, but humanity owed whoever it had been a debt beyond any price, for he'd caught them feeding. Without that footage, mankind would not have known that *these* aliens regarded humans as a food source.

Vomit rose in her throat once more, and she wondered if the government would dare release the imagery. A part of her hoped it would be forever sealed, but she knew better. Sooner or later it would be released, or leaked, or stolen, and every living human would know what she knew now. For all their long, segmented, spiderlike legs, the aliens massed no more than half again as much as humans . . . and they preferred their food living. That made *children* just the right size for—

Vanessa Murakuma clenched her fist and thrust the memories violently aside, then made herself look at Mackenna and LeBlanc.

"I've just received a response to our dispatch to Sarasota," she said as normally as she could. "They agree with our assessment. In order to evacuate the maximum possible numbers from Merriweather and Justin we'll have to use Sarasota as the collection point. We simply don't have enough lift capacity to take them any further back, and even stopping at Sarasota we're never going to get everyone out."

"How soon can they get additional transports to us, Sir?" Mackenna asked quietly.

"Not soon enough." Murakuma's voice was flat, and she pinched the bridge of her nose. "What Reichman has now is everything in the sector. Even for a hop as short as the one to the Sarasota Fleet Base, we simply don't have enough personnel lift. Admiral Eusebio has authorized me—" she smiled bleakly "—to use my discretion in utilizing what we do have most effectively."

LeBlanc made a harsh, disgusted sound, but Murakuma shook her head.

"I don't blame him. I'm the commander on the spot, and making decisions like that comes with the job."

"With all due respect," Waldeck began hotly, "you've got enough on your shoulders fighting the damned battle without having to accept resp—"

"I said I don't blame him, Demosthenes," Murakuma said flatly. He closed his mouth with a snap, and she smiled more naturally and squared her shoulders.

"At least knowing what we now do simplifies our priorities, gentlemen. Leroy, I want you and Tian to get with Commodore Reichman and his staff as soon as his transports return from Sarasota. We have to establish hard guidelines on who we evacuate and in what order. We'll begin with minor children and pregnant women. Whenever possible in two-parent families, I want one parent included, as well. After that, we go with second parents and the elderly."

"The elderly, Sir?" Mackenna asked with a careful lack of expression, and Murakuma smiled bitterly. She knew what he wasn't saying—and what someone else most assuredly would. The elderly, after all, had already lived full lives and had less to contribute to the war effort. She loathed the people who could make that argument, but they existed . . . and whatever she decided would be wrong in their eyes. How would it feel, she wondered mordantly, when they started calling *her* a monster—and a coward—for "saving herself" by "abandoning civilians to their fate"?

"The elderly," she repeated, trying—and failing—to hide her pain. "We owe them that . . . and their age will make them more of a liability for the people we can't get out."

"A 'liability' in what way, Sir?" LeBlanc asked.

"There are no noncombatants in this war, Marcus." Murakuma's voice went harsh. "Admiral Eusebio is stripping Sarasota of infantry weapons and sending them up with Reichman. He'll drop them off at Justin, and while Leroy and Tian are conferring with the Commodore on ship movements, *you*, Marcus, are going to be working with General Servais on deployment plans for Marine garrisons on Justin, Harrison and Clements."

"*Garrisons?*" Waldeck looked at her in disbelief, and she raised an eyebrow. The other admiral hesitated for a moment, then gripped the nettle. "Sir—Vanessa—if we can't keep the enemy from taking the system, how can we possibly justify sending in *ground* troops? Once the enemy controls the high orbitals, they'll be in a deathtrap!"

"'*We*' aren't justifying it; *I* am," Murakuma said flatly. "Everyone else on those planets will already be in a deathtrap unless we can somehow fight our way back in. We can't fool ourselves here, Demosthenes. These . . . *creatures* don't distinguish between military personnel and civilians. Anyone we leave behind won't just be killed— they're going to be *eaten*, and I will *not* simply abandon them. We may not be able to save them, but we can at least give them the weapons and advisers to make the bastards *pay* for them!"

Flaming green eyes pinned her subordinates in their chairs, and her voice was a sliver of soprano ice.

"This war is going to be for *survival*, worse than ISW– 3 ever was. We've grown out of the habit of thinking that way, but *this*—" she slammed the heel of her hand on the data chip "—says we'd damned well better remember how. And, gentlemen, starting right here—right now— we are going to teach these fucking monsters humans don't come cheap!"

CHAPTER SEVEN

To Face the Hurricane

"The Admiral is on the bridge."

Officers looked up, but Murakuma's wave sent them back to their tasks as she crossed to her command chair, settled into it, and fiddled with her plot's contrast controls. She adjusted it to her satisfaction, then looked up and beckoned to Commander Ling, and the ops officer gathered up her memo pad and crossed to her side.

"Good afternoon, Admiral." The commander was ten centimeters shorter than Murakuma, but she was also a native of Old Terra—one of the very few native Terrans, relatively speaking, in TF 59—and for all her petite slenderness, she looked almost stocky beside the taller admiral.

"Tian," Murakuma acknowledged, then pointed at the memo pad. "Did you and Admiral Teller reach the same conclusions I did?"

"Yes, Sir." Ling set the pad on Murakuma's console and switched it on. Its tiny holo unit projected its display before the admiral, and Ling highlighted a block of characters in amber. "You were right," she said. "*Akagi, Bunker Hill, Cabot, Emperor* and *Kuznetzov* didn't want to admit it, but analysis of their operations indicates pilot fatigue's become a definite problem for them."

"Not surprising," Murakuma murmured, studying the numbers. Sarasota had been able to make good the enormous hardware losses of Jackson Teller's strikegroups by sending forward every reserve fighter in inventory, but Admiral Eusebio had been unable to replace their dead flight crews. It was a hellish choice, for Sarasota depended heavily on fighters for its own defense, and Eusebio *could*, in fact, have brought Teller's groups back up to strength . . . but only by sending up enough pilots to critically reduce his own capabilities. As it was, the Fleet Base's squadrons were at barely sixty percent strength, and he refused to deplete them still further.

Murakuma couldn't fault him for that. What had happened in Erebor was grim proof of the sort of casualties TF 59 might suffer, and if that happened, Eusebio's fighters were all he'd have. But understanding made her own problems no less pressing, and she frowned at the uncaring numbers.

Teller's staff had done its best to redistribute its available pilots, but fighter squadrons were intricately meshed organisms whose members worked together almost as much by instinct as order. Breaking them up or introducing newcomers, however well trained, degraded effectiveness until the replacements had time to settle in, and no one knew how much time they had. They knew only that TF 59 would be heavily outnumbered when the time came, and the Federation's apparent monopoly on the strike-fighter made those fighter groups pearls beyond price. They *had* to be as efficient and deadly as possible, so Teller, with her approval, had left the groups of the four newly arrived carriers untouched, and mixed and matched to rebuild those of the Erebor survivors as best he could.

They had sufficient personnel to operate all their fighters, but fighter ops were the most physically demanding duty the TFN offered. They were also among the most dangerous, as Vanessa Murakuma knew only too well, for Lieutenant Tadeoshi Murakuma had died on routine ops exactly three days after their second daughter was born. But it was the fatigue factor which worried her now. A carrier normally carried twice as many crews as fighters, so it could rotate its personnel, but the groups of the five carriers Ling had listed were at barely forty-two percent strength, and most were scratch-built out of bits and pieces from Sarasota after the complete replacement squadrons had been distributed to other ships. The strain of shaking down as combat-capable entities while simultaneously pulling their weight in TF 59's routine patrols showed, and pilot fatigue was rising rapidly towards unacceptable levels.

"All right," she said finally. "I want those groups stood down for at least forty-eight hours—have Admiral Teller redistribute patrol assignments to adjust. Once they've had a couple of days to recuperate, he can reintegrate them, but I want his primary emphasis to be on getting them shaken down, not scouting duties. After all—" she smiled thinly "—we know where the enemy will be coming from."

"Yes, Sir." Ling tapped a note into the memo pad, and Murakuma crossed her legs.

"The minelayers completed their operations on schedule?"

"Yes, Sir." Ling's reply was as calm as ever, and Murakuma surprised herself with a brief chuckle. She'd been an ops officer herself, and Tian's unflagging courtesy couldn't fool her. The commander didn't have to say "of course" for Murakuma to hear it anyway.

Ling arched a graceful eyebrow, but Murakuma only shook her head. Bad enough that she was fretting over routine details without admitting she *knew* she was.

"That's all for now, Tian," was all she said, and smiled fondly at the commander's back as Ling returned to her station. Then her smile faded, and she steepled her fingers under her chin as she gazed back down at her icon-frosted plot.

Classic warp point defense doctrine was to hit the enemy as he made transit in the old wet-navy equivalent of catching him as he emerged one ship at a time from a narrow strait. Sixty years ago, before the Theban War, the defender's advantage had been so crushing the mere thought of a full-scale warp point assault could turn any admiral gray, but the pendulum had shifted in the attacker's favor with the SBMHAWK. The warp-capable missile pods were expensive, both to build and in terms of freighter lift, but enough of them could gut any close-in defense . . . as Ivan Antonov had proved almost exactly fifty-nine years before at the Fourth Battle of Lorelei.

But this enemy didn't seem to have SBMHAWKs, which made a close defense far more appealing—or would have, without his assault fleet. Murakuma couldn't afford to expose her lighter battle-line to a mass simultaneous transit that was almost certain to enjoy the advantage of surprise, however briefly. Even light cruisers could tear battleships apart if enough of them caught the capital ships when they weren't at battle stations.

Yet she did have one huge advantage Villiers had been denied in Erebor. The minelayers had emplaced every antimatter mine and laser buoy Sarasota could scrape up around the enemy's entry warp point. There weren't as many as Murakuma could have wished, and neither mines nor buoys could be placed directly atop an open warp point, since the grav tides of an open point would suck in and destroy anything that small. But they could be placed *around* the point, and Ling's patient report confirmed that hundreds of them had been.

No doubt most of the single-shot buoys would expend themselves on the simultaneous transit rather than its betters, but the mines behind them should at least pen the big boys up until they could be cleared. It was tempting to hold her full force—or at least the ones armed with strategic bombardment missiles—in range to batter them while they fought to break through the mines, but the enemy would have an enormous advantage in launchers, and the fact that he hadn't used the extended range SBMs yet didn't *prove* he didn't have them. Worse, Sarasota's R&D staff still couldn't give her a definitive estimate on the range of those damned plasma guns. She dared not assume their envelope was as tight as R&D *thought* it was, and even if it was, they knew the enemy had the capital force beam. Add capital missiles from his missile-heavy SDs, and sheer volume of fire would quickly cripple her lighter battleships if she met him head on.

No, she told herself again. A conventional defense was out of the question. She had to concede the warp point—bleed them on it, yes, but let them have it—and make it a running fight in deep space, where her speed and tech advantages could be exploited to the maximum. If she'd had any chance at all of stopping them dead, she would have accepted the losses of a close defense to do it, but she didn't. All she could do was mount a fighting retreat that inflicted the maximum attrition . . . and pray the people trapped in Merriweather when she finally withdrew wouldn't haunt her dreams with the horror she knew they would.

"All right, Marcus. Give me the bad news."

Captain LeBlanc sighed. His recliner was cocked back at a comfortable angle, one hand held a tall, iced drink, and he'd kicked his boots off—something he never would have done if anyone else were present—but his eyes belied his relaxed posture.

"It's not good, Vanessa," he admitted. "Commodore Reichman's working wonders, but it's going to take at least six more round trips to get everyone out."

"What if we detached our destroyers?" She leaned forward in her own chair, left hand squeezing the fingers of her right. "The *Johnstons* are too small to be really combat effective, and—"

"Vanessa." LeBlanc interrupted her more firmly than a captain should interrupt an admiral, and she looked up from her hands. "It wouldn't matter," he said. "They don't have enough life support to make any difference. Even if you let Reichman have all seven of them, they couldn't squeeze more than two thousand people aboard."

"But—" Murakuma chopped herself off, then sighed and rubbed her face with her palms. "You're right." Her hands muffled her voice, but he heard the pain in it. "I'm dithering, aren't I?"

"In a word," he said gently, "yes. God knows I don't blame you, but would giving up those ships really save enough colonists to justify dropping them from your order of battle?"

"No," she said. "It's just knowing what those fucking Bugs are going to do. . . ."

She broke off with a shudder she would have let no other member of her staff see, and his mouth tightened. Forty years had passed since the demands of their service careers terminated their Academy affair. He didn't know if anyone suspected they'd once been lovers, and it wouldn't have mattered to him if they had, but at this moment a tiny, ignoble part of him wished he knew Vanessa less well. She needed *someone* with whom to share her inner strain, and, in many ways, he was honored to be that someone. Yet in at least one way he was just like any of her other officers; his own desperate fear needed the rocklike strength she radiated in public, and knowing how savagely her responsibilities were wounding her frightened him. She looked so delicate—"bird-boned," his mother had called her the time she came home with him for a visit. He knew better than most that appearances could be deceiving, but how in God's name could the determination to meet something like *this* be packed into such a frail-looking package?

"They aren't really insects, you know," he said as lightly as he could. "I know it's tempting to reach for a Terran analogue. Even the xenologists did that when they tagged them as 'Arachnids,' but if you start ascribing insect behavior to them—"

"They're bugs," she said flatly. His eyes flicked back up to her face in surprise at the cold, vicious hatred in her voice. "They're not Orions, not even Tangri. They're filthy, vile, crawling *bugs*, and we are by God going to *exterminate* them like the vermin they are."

"Vanessa, I—" he began, but she cut him off with a bark of laughter.

"Don't worry. I'm not losing it yet, Marcus. But I mean it. There won't be any treaties after *this* war—not once the Assembly sees the Erebor footage. We're going to dust off General Directive Eighteen, and we're going to wipe these monsters from the face of the universe."

Her cold, flat, absolute certainty sent a shudder through

LeBlanc. Intellectually, he knew she was almost certainly right, and his own emotions agreed with her, but hearing so much icy, distilled hatred from Vanessa frightened him, and he cleared his throat.

"I never thought you would 'lose it.' I only wish it hadn't landed on you."

"If not on me, then on someone else," she said more normally, and shrugged and reached for her own drink. "Whoever else it was would still—"

The sudden, raucous scream of *Cobra*'s GQ alarm ripped across her voice. She jerked as if she'd just grabbed one end of a live wire, then whirled to her com terminal.

"Status!" she barked even before the officer of the watch's image solidified on the screen.

"Tsushima." The stress-flattened word was harsh, and her face tightened. "Simultaneous transit, Sir. Plotting makes it—" the woman on the screen paused to consult her plot "—fifty-plus bandits in a single wave."

"Understood. Activate Plan Able."

"Yes, Sir!"

Murakuma released the key and spun away from the terminal, already unsealing her tunic. Her vac suit closet had opened automatically when the alarm went, and she bounded across the carpeted cabin towards it.

"Marcus—"

"Already gone." She darted a glance at him and felt a hysterical urge to giggle as he snatched up his boots and headed for the cabin hatch in sock feet. "See you on Flag Bridge."

The hatch closed behind him before she could reply, and she reached for her suit, eyes automatically checking the tell-tales even as her mind reached out to the horde of starships coming to kill her.

Sixty light cruisers erupted into normal space in a single massive wave. Twelve vanished in sprawling boils of plasma as they interpenetrated, and more died under the laser buoys' fury. The bomb-pumped lasers consumed themselves in the instant they fired, stabbing immensely

powerful beams straight through electromagnetic shields
to shatter armor and hull members, but their pro-
gramming spread their fire among all the cruisers. They
inflicted crippling damage, yet only a handful of intruders
actually perished.

The wounded, air-streaming survivors paused, searching
for enemies, but no one was in range to attack them. They
hesitated a moment longer, and then—one-by-one—headed
away from the warp point . . . and straight into the waiting
mines. Savage explosions pocked space as the hunter-killer
satellites lunged at them in eye-tearing flares of detonating
antimatter, yet they accomplished their goal.

Vanessa Murakuma's pitiless face was stone as she
watched the last enemy cruiser die.

"They're going to break clear of the mines sooner than
anticipated," Mackenna said, and she nodded. It didn't
really matter, given the battle plan she'd evolved, but it
was fresh proof of the terrifying difference between the
beings who'd crewed those ships and humans. Even
allowing for the mines' antimatter warheads, the fields
hadn't been *that* heavy. Sarasota hadn't had enough to stop
capital ships, but these people—these *Bugs*—hadn't even
tried to sweep them normally. What kind of psychology
could see the deliberate self-destruction of ships they could
have saved, if only for future use, as a *reasonable* alternative
to minor damage to minesweeping capital ships?

"It doesn't matter," she said aloud, and looked up from
the master plot. "How long since we sent Commodore
Reichman the alert message?"

"Ten minutes, Sir."

"Um." Murakuma cocked her head and considered K–45's
geometry. The warp point to Erebor lay "below" the two
leading to Merriweather and Justin, distributed like the
points of an angled right triangle. The distance from the
Erebor point to Justin was only five-and-a-half light-hours—
sixty-five hours' transit time for her battleships—but the line
from Merriweather to Justin formed the triangle's hypo-
tenuse, and Reichman's transports were in Merriweather.

Her alert would reach him in seven hours, but his transports were slow; they'd need fifteen hours just to get back to K–45, then another eighty to reach the Justin warp point. She wasn't worried about their being intercepted in deep space—they were as fast as anything the enemy had, and all they needed to do was stay beyond missile range—but even if Reichman pulled out the instant her warning reached him, he'd still need a minimum of a hundred and two hours to escape to Justin.

That defined how long she *had* to hold the enemy's attention. She had to lead those superdreadnoughts outside their detection range of Reichman and away from the Justin warp point for at least five standard days, keeping them in play until she was certain the transports were clear, before she could fall back herself. Of course, the Bugs were so slow they'd take a hundred hours to reach the warp point even on a least-time course, but she dared not cut things that close. If anything delayed Reichman in Merriweather and the Bugs reached his exit point first, he and all the evacuees packed aboard his ships would be hopelessly trapped.

"Anything on their battle-line's composition?"

"Plotting's on it now," Ling replied. "So far, they make it forty-two superdreadnoughts, but they're still coming through. We think the lead element were either *Augers* or *Acids*, but we're seeing at least some *Archers* in the follow-on waves."

"Any sign of the *Avalanches* yet?"

"No, Sir, but we're still not sure we can distinguish them from the *Augers*."

Murakuma nodded, walked slowly to her command chair, and racked her helmet on its side while she thought. They wouldn't know anything about the enemy's technology until they managed to stop the bastards and examine their wreckage, but they'd assigned tentative reporting names, based on observed armament, to some of his classes. The *Augers, Acids* and *Avalanches* mounted almost pure energy armaments. Analysis suggested the *Augers* had heavy primary beam outfits, and the *Acids* carried those damned plasma guns, but it was the *Avalanche-* and *Archer*-class ships which worried her. The *Archers* were pure missile platforms, with massive capital missile batteries, while the *Avalanches* mounted equally heavy capital force beam armaments.

The *Augers* were potentially deadly, since no known defense could stop a primary beam. If they had capital primaries, which hadn't been confirmed but seemed likely, they'd have an effective range of almost nine light-seconds, and they'd punch straight through anything they hit. But they'd also be slow-firing, and the ships which mounted them were forty percent slower than her slowest unit. The only way they'd get into range of her would be if she *let* them.

No, it was the *Avalanches* and, especially, the *Archers* she had to sweat, and she looked up at Mackenna.

"We'll go with Tsushima Six, Leroy." Her calm voice gave no indication of the tension twisting in her belly, and the chief of staff nodded with matching control.

"Aye, aye, Sir. Tsushima Six."

"Have Admiral Waldeck com me as soon as he has everything in motion."

"Yes, Sir."

Mackenna turned to begin passing orders, and Vanessa Murakuma watched her repeater plot as her ships deployed.

The Fleet moved out through the minefield gap, advancing on the light dots of the enemy at five percent of light-speed. The Fleet knew nothing about this warp junction's astrography. Its ships were slower than its enemies, and by now it knew about many of the enemy's technological advantages, but that didn't matter. It had the firepower to crush him, and for all his superior speed, he had only two choices: engage it or abandon the nexus without a fight.

The oncoming superdreadnoughts would settle for either.

✦   ✦   ✦

"All right, Demosthenes," Vanessa Murakuma said quietly to the face on her plot. "Let's do this right the first time."

"Agreed." Her battle-line commander bared his teeth. "Husac is coming up on her firing position now."

"Good." Murakuma nodded to the pickup, then turned back to her plot and made herself keep her mouth shut as TF 59 executed Tsushima Six.

She'd split her force into two task groups—59.1 under Jackson Teller, who commanded her carriers and their screen from the battlecruiser *Sorcerer*, and 59.2, the battleline units, under Waldeck in the battleship *Pit Viper*. Delegating authority had always been hard for her, and it was even harder when so much depended on the execution of *her* battle plan, yet she had no choice. She might hold overall command, but it was Jackson's and Demosthenes' job to execute her plan while she monitored and adjusted for anything that went wrong, and if she yielded to her penchant for back seat driving it would only make them think she questioned their competence.

Rear Admiral Jennifer Husac's two battlegroups of *Dunkerque*-class battlecruisers were TF 59's rearmost units, trailing astern of the battle-line as it fell steadily back before the advancing superdreadnoughts, leading them away from the Justin warp point. The *Dunkerques* were smaller and more lightly protected than battleships, but they were Murakuma's long-range snipers, with heavy capital missile batteries, and despite their smaller size, their superior datalink meant they could actually throw heavier salvos than the missile-armed SDs. Plotting's analysis was tentative, but it suggested that the opposing *Archers* outnumbered them by at least fifty percent. That was an awesome edge in launchers, but she didn't expect Husac to take out the enemy all alone. Hurt him, yes. That much she expected, but Husac's real purpose was to positively identify the missile ships by drawing their return fire.

"All right," she said quietly as the range from the

Dunkerques to the enemy fell. "Let's see what these bastards have."

"Coming into extreme range . . . now," Commander Trang said

"Stand by." Jennifer Husac watched her display intently as TFNS *Endymion*'s tactical officer made his tense announcement.

"Good luck, Sir," Trang added, and Husac's lips quirked in a humorless smile. Trang wanted to open fire *now*, as soon as his internal launchers had the range, and she didn't blame him. Her twelve ships were a preposterously frail force against seventy-plus superdreadnoughts, and any intellectual awareness of superior technology ran a poor second to visceral awareness of the odds. On the other hand, the enemy had yet to demonstrate any equivalent of the missiles she was about to fire at him. Only a handful of the Terran ships he'd yet engaged had carried strategic bombardment missiles, and none had really had the chance to use them as doctrine dictated, but Husac was about to change that. Each SBM ate up twenty-five percent more magazine space than a regular capital missile, so Terran ships never carried pure loads of them and Sarasota had had too few in stores to provide Husac's ships with full load-outs, but she intended to make best use of the ones she had. Their poorer ECM made them easier point defense targets than capital missiles, but they had a full five light-seconds more range, and Trang wanted to use it all. But one of Husac's objectives was to confirm whether or not the enemy had the weapon, which meant she had to make sure she was well within its envelope. Besides, every light-second she closed gave *her* birds a better chance of scoring.

"Eighteen light-seconds," Trang said. More endless seconds crept away as the two forces continued to close. "Seventeen . . . we're in range for the external birds, Sir."

"Let the range fall to sixteen light-seconds," Husac said softly.

❖   ❖   ❖

Murakuma chewed her lower lip. It was hard to believe the Bugs didn't have the SBM, yet Husac was three full light-seconds inside its range, and not a shot had been fired. If the Bugs *didn't* have the weapon now, it shouldn't take someone with their evident tech capability long to develop it once it was used on them, but in the meantime . . .

"Sixteen light-seconds," Trang said flatly, and Husac nodded.

"Hold us at this range, Helm," she said, then— "Engage the enemy, Commander Trang!"

Twelve battlecruisers sent a hundred and sixty-four missiles slashing through space as both battlegroups flushed their external racks and opened up with their internal launchers as well. Not a single shot replied, and Jennifer Husac's eyes glowed with hellish delight. *That answers one question; if the bad guys had them, they'd sure as hell use them now!*

Her eyes blazed still brighter as the massive opening salvos roared down on just two SDs, and countermissiles began to explode. The bastards' early-generation datalink left each of those ships on its own against the incoming fire, but no single ship could stop *those* salvos, and a snarl ran around *Endymion*'s flag bridge as they struck. The fireballs were eye-watering even at this range, but Husac refused to look away, and when the glare died, both of her targets had vanished.

"Two down," someone said, and the admiral nodded.

"Let's add to that," she said grimly. "Make them count as long as they last, Commander."

The Fleet ground steadily onward, despite the missiles battering it from beyond its own range. The enemy battlecruisers' first salvos had exhausted their external ordnance, and the follow-on broadsides were thirty percent lighter, but they continued their deliberate pounding in overpowering waves of thunder that smashed through all active defenses by sheer weight of numbers. Shields flared and died, shattered armor fumed away in vapor, skeins of atmosphere trailed behind, and some ships fell out of formation with damaged drives. They could have fallen back—no enemy was in range to prevent them— but each wounded leviathan simply kept coming. No ship could stand more than three of those devastating salvos, but each targeted ship made the enemy expend those missiles upon it.

"SBMs are running dry, Sir," Trang said tautly. "We've got two more salvos, then we're down to CMs."

"Confirmed kills?" Husac demanded.

"We make it eight with . . . two more badly damaged. We *think* they were all *Archers,* but our ID criteria are pretty tentative. Until they return fire, we can't positively identify them."

"Understood." Husac watched the last two SBM salvos roar from her internal launchers. The enemy continued to advance, accepting the slaughter she'd wreaked on him without flinching, and a primitive corner of her mind gibbered that *nothing* should wade into such fire when it couldn't even shoot back. It was like fighting the insensate violence of a hurricane, not living, thinking beings, and that primitive part of her whispered they *were* an unstoppable force of nature. But it was only a tiny part, and she bared her teeth. "All right, Li-Dong. Phase Two."

"Admiral Husac's exhausted her SBMs," Demosthenes Waldeck announced from Murakuma's com screen. "She's closing to capital missile range now."

"Understood." Murakuma turned to Ling Tian. "Warn Plotting. They'll be returning fire shortly, and I want every one of those *Archers* fingerprinted the instant it opens up."

The battlecruisers began to close once more. They were entering the Fleet's reach now, and targeting systems watched them come.

❖   ❖   ❖

"Fifteen light-seconds," Trang reported. "Coming into— Missile launch! Multiple hostile launches! One hundred twenty plus inbound. Impact in two-seven seconds from— mark!"

"Return fire!" Husac snapped, and locked her command chair shock frame as the enemy's missiles scorched towards her.

The bastards had taken a page from her own book and concentrated all their fire on a single target. They obviously couldn't tell her *Thetis*-class command ships from the *Dunkerques*, or perhaps they didn't realize there was any difference to look for. If they didn't have command datalink, then they had no way to know only a single ship in each battlegroup mounted the master systems that tied them together. Yet what they knew or didn't know made no difference to TFNS *Goeben*, and she watched the ship go to violent evasive action.

But unlike Husac's targets, *Goeben* wasn't alone against the storm. *Endymion*'s datanet wove a deadly, fine-meshed net of warheads and spitting lasers, ripping the incoming missiles apart, and the enemy's cruder command and control systems split his fire into smaller salvos that couldn't saturate the battlegroup's defenses.

Point defense stopped ninety-five percent of the incoming fire short of *Goeben*, yet simple probability theory said at least *some* birds had to get through, and the battlecruiser heaved as they wiped away her shields and tore at her armor. Husac's fists clenched as damage reports chattered over the net, and her face was grim. They'd done well to stop that many incoming, but well or not, another exchange like that would blow the ship apart . . . and she had only twelve ships.

"Hit the bastards!" she snarled, and *Endymion* bucked as she threw fresh fury at her foes.

"*Goeben*'s been hit hard, Sir," Commander Ling said, and Murakuma nodded curtly. Battlecruisers were too light to face SDs, however superior their datalink, but she had no choice. The *Dunkerques* and *Thetises* were the only

CM-armed ships she had; they *had* to engage the *Archers*—and be engaged in return—if only to identify the missile ships for her.

"IDs on the *Archers*?" Her voice was flat, and Ling nodded.

"Tracking is confident, Sir. Two more salvos and we'll have them nailed."

The superdreadnoughts shuddered under the battle-cruisers' fire, but the odds were evening. Even with the enemy's heavier salvos and more destructive warheads, he needed three salvos to guarantee a kill, but the Fleet's projections indicated that each battlecruiser could survive no more than two like the last one.

Another superdreadnought vanished in an expanding ball of fire, but the enemy had an iron lock on *Goeben*, and this time the other SDs flushed their external racks in support. The battlegroup's point defense performed brilliantly, but three more missiles got through. Men and women died as concussion and flame and radiation came for them, atmosphere streamed from breached plating, and Jennifer Husac's voice was harsh.

"Get her out of it, Li-Dong!"

Orders flashed over the net, and *Goeben* turned away. She'd lost an engine room, but she was still twice as fast as the oncoming superdreadnoughts. She swung away from them, fleeing their fire, and their targeting systems shifted to her sisters.

"*Goeben*'s breaking off," Waldeck said. "Looks like they're shifting to *Nevada*, but Husac took out another of them first."

"Understood." Murakuma watched the wounded battlecruiser accelerate clear of the Bugs' envelope, but even as a part of her cheered the ship's survival, another cursed bitterly. If only she had a few missile SDs of her own! The battlecruisers were fighting magnificently, but their superior systems were overmatched by their opponents' sheer toughness. The *Archers* were still dying, yet *Goeben*'s withdrawal diluted the weight of her battlegroup's next salvo—and the effectiveness of its point defense—by a sixth.

"Instruct Admiral Teller to launch his strike," she said.

"Launch!"

Twelve light carriers twitched as mass-drivers hurled fighters through their drive fields and into space. Two hundred and sixteen small, deadly craft, heavy with external ordnance, curved up and away at .2 *c*, shaking down into formation, turning for the enemy, and Commander Anson Olivera watched the continuous tactical update spill across his command fighter's display. Admiral Husac was taking a fearful pounding—her own battlegroup was down to only three ships and falling back behind its consorts—but only five confirmed and one possible *Archer* remained.

"Target designation." His strain-flattened voice was clipped as he tapped keys on his console. "Paired group strikes. Commander Renquist has *Archer* One. Slattery takes Two, Sung takes Three, and Takagumi and Marker take Four and Five. We'll take the last two strikegroups in to clean up the survivors ourselves. Confirm input."

"My board confirms," his tac officer called back, and Olivera switched to the central net. Sweat beaded his hewn-granite face, but he made his words come out even, almost jovial.

"Go get 'em, boys and girls. Last one back to the barn buys the beer."

The fighters swept past Husac's battered battlecruisers. The *Dunkerques*' magazines were down to thirty percent, and her own group had been gutted. All its ships survived, but *Goeben*, *Nevada*, *Barham*, and *Jean Bart* had been driven out of action with heavy damage. Yet the enemy's concentration on only one of her battlegroups was the first real mistake he'd made; he'd crippled one of them, but the second was untouched.

"Pass tactical command to Commodore Suchien." Her

voice was vicious with mingled loss and satisfaction as she watched the fighters. "Tell him the force advantage is about to shift."

Targeting priorities changed as the small, fleet craft hurtled into the Fleet's midst. They were fast and agile, squirming in wild evasion maneuvers even as they lined up on their targets, but a hurricane of close-in fire met them. One died, then another. Two more. A fifth. Dozens of fireballs glared as point defense lasers or force beams or missiles ripped into them, but still they came on, charging into the teeth of their own destruction. They tore into the missile SDs like demons, spitting deadly quartets of short-ranged missiles, and scores of antimatter warheads erupted against shuddering shields and the alloy they protected.

Banshee howls of triumph erupted from the speakers as Teller's flagship relayed his strikegroups' voice telemetry to *Cobra*. Those howls and the fireballs that spawned them were thirty seconds old by the time Vanessa Murakuma heard and saw them, and she clenched her jaw as all too many jubilant shouts chopped off in sudden silence. Of the two-hundred-plus fighters she'd committed, only a hundred and seventy fell back on their carriers, but they'd done their job. All remaining *Archers* and two suspected *Avalanches* were gone, and despite the anguish of her own losses, her brain ticked smoothly, efficiently within its protective cocoon of professionalism.

So far she'd lost only four badly damaged battlecruisers and fifty-two fighters to kill sixty light cruisers and seventeen superdreadnoughts. That outmassed her entire task force, but the bastards were still coming, and a shudder very like the one Jennifer Husac had felt coursed through her. How in God's name could *anything* keep coming after a pounding like that?

But they *were* coming . . . and they had fifty-eight SDs left.

The surviving battlecruisers, unopposed now by any

capital missile, closed to the very edge of the standard missile envelope, battering their enemies, but their magazines had to be almost dry, and she might well need them even more later. She looked at her link to *Pit Viper.*

"Have Husac fall back to the colliers and reammunition, Demosthenes."

"Yes, Sir."

"Once she's clear, move the battle-line into extreme missile range. It's *our* turn to have a go at the bastards."

"Aye, aye, Sir." Waldeck's voice was taut, but there was savage satisfaction in it, as well, and Murakuma nodded with a grim smile.

All right, you fuckers, she thought coldly. *We've pulled your missile ships' teeth. Try bringing your goddamned energy armaments into range* now!

Rear Admiral Vanessa Murakuma crossed her legs and leaned back in her command chair as twelve battleships of the Terran Federation Navy advanced against their overpowering foe.

CHAPTER EIGHT

Options and Obligations

Major General Xavier Servais looked up as Colonel Mondesi entered the compartment. The colonel's great-great-grandparents had migrated from the island of Haiti to the Fringe World of Christophe, and his face was the color of obsidian . . . and utterly expressionless. Which, Servais thought as he stood behind his desk, meant Mondesi had already heard about his orders.

"Colonel." Servais offered his hand, and the younger man clasped it firmly. "Sit, please." Servais gestured at a chair and waited until Mondesi obeyed his polite command before he reseated himself. He pulled a pipe from his pocket and took his time stuffing it. It was an archaic affectation, but he sometimes found it a useful bit of stage dressing, and he used the delay to study Mondesi.

He liked what he saw. The colonel had posted a superb record in the specialized world of the Marines' Raiders, and despite whatever he'd already heard, he returned the general's measuring gaze levelly. That argued for more than his fair share of intestinal fortitude . . . and he was going to need all of that he had.

"I wanted to see you to discuss a special operation, Colonel," Servais said once he had his lit pipe drawing. "We're calling the overall plan Redemption, and you've been tapped to command one component of it: Operation Citadel. The good news, such as it is, is that you're being

113

breveted to brigadier for the op, but I won't sugarcoat
things. The odds of your living long enough to have the
rank confirmed aren't good."

He paused for Mondesi's reaction, but the colonel simply
nodded and said, "May I ask what this operation will
consist of, Sir?"

"You may." Servais leaned back, caressing the polished
bowl of his pipe with one hand. "Now that the enemy—
the 'Bugs,' as Admiral Murakuma calls them—have K–
45, it's only a matter of time until they hit Justin. The
Fleet hurt them badly, but they got in their own licks,
and the Admiral's staff estimates we have no more than
three weeks before they resume the advance."

Raphael Mondesi nodded again. Most space battles were
both violent and brief. When fleets threw antimatter
warheads at one another, it seldom took long for the weaker
side to be annihilated or run, but the Battle of K–45 had
been different.

TF 59 had done what it set out to do and mauled the
enemy brutally, but at a price. With the *Archers* eliminated,
TG 59.2's battleships' superior datalink had let them hold
their own, but their mixed missile and force beam batteries
had compelled them to come into range of the enemy's
Avalanche-class SDs. They'd learned the hard way that the
Acids did, in fact, mount missile launchers to back their
plasma batteries, but their salvos had been too light to
break through Murakuma's point defense, and the only Bug
energy weapon with the range to reach her had been the
Avalanches' force beams. She'd taken a pounding from
those beams, but she'd ignored the *Acids* and coordinated
the fire of her battle-line's shipboard weapons with strikes
by carefully hoarded fighters to pick off as many *Avalanches*
as possible, then broken off. But this time it hadn't been to
withdraw. She'd disengaged just long enough to carry out
emergency repairs to her own ships, then resumed the
action.

No one had ever seen a battle like it. For five full *days*,
Vanessa Murakuma had played matador, smashing away at
her overwhelming opponents with ever dwindling numbers,

drawing them ever further from her exit warp point. She'd battered ship after ship into wreckage, and as each mangled hulk fell out of formation, her surviving fighters pounced upon it and finished it off. She and Demosthenes Waldeck had reorganized their battlegroups on the fly—mixing and matching as damage drove individual units out of action, pulling out ships with empty magazines to race back to the colliers and reammunition. Damage control crews had labored till they dropped, fighting the mounting tide of crippled systems, and not a single unit of her own battle-line had escaped unhurt. When she finally disengaged for good, she'd lost eighty percent of her fighters, a battleship, three battlecruisers, two heavy cruisers, and five destroyers, with eight more capital ships—including the battleships *Conquistador* and *Héros*—so damaged they'd barely been able to limp back to Sarasota. But she'd destroyed fifty-three super-dreadnoughts first.

It was, by any measure, the most one-sided victory in naval history . . . and it hadn't changed a thing, for yet another wave of Bug capital ships had entered K–45 even as Murakuma disengaged. Her superior speed had let her break contact, preventing the Bugs from tracking her to her exit warp point, so they'd have to find it the hard way, but when they did . . .

"I understand, Sir," the colonel said. "May I assume Citadel has something to do with what happens when they do arrive?"

"You may." Servais' voice was much grimmer than before. "In the absence of direct divine intervention, they're going to push us out of Justin. We managed to evacuate eighty-five percent of the Merriweather colonists . . . but that left over a million behind. And while the transit time from Justin-A to Sarasota is less than twenty percent that from Merriweather to Sarasota, there are four times as many people in the system, and we've got, at best, a month. That means we're going to have to leave at least nine million more people behind. Admiral Murakuma feels—and I agree—that we cannot simply write those people off, and that's where you come in."

He pinched the bridge of his nose, then sighed.

"I don't like last-man battles," he said, "but that's exactly what this war's going to demand. We can't negotiate civilian surrenders, because we don't have the least idea how to communicate with these Bugs. And, judging by the Erebor transmissions, there's no point trying to figure it out. They see us as food sources, Colonel. All we can do is give them the worst case of bellyache they ever had, and civilians don't have the training or the firepower for that."

"But Marines do," Mondesi said.

"Marines do," Servais confirmed. Their eyes met for a long, silent moment, and then the colonel nodded once again.

"What's the plan, Sir?" he asked quietly.

"We'll concentrate on evacuating Justin A." Servais activated a holo display of the Justin Binary System above his desk. "Justin and Harrison"—the third and fourth planets of Component A flashed as he named them—"have much larger populations than Clements"—Justin B II lit in turn—"and with the Sarasota warp point associated with Justin A, the transit time is seventy hours shorter. Admiral Murakuma's already instructed Clements to shut down all emissions and go bush. There are less than a million people on the entire planet, scattered around in very small settlements, so they may be able to conceal their presence from anything but a very close scan.

"But we can't do that for Justin-A, so Admiral Eusebio's sent up every rifle, mortar and HVM he can find. Your job, Colonel, is to distribute those weapons to the civilians of Justin and Harrison. I've already contacted General Merman, the system Peaceforce CO, and we're organizing quicky classes to bring his people up to speed on front-line equipment. We're also combing out our Marine contingents, and I estimate we can give you the equivalent of a light division."

Servais paused, looking into Mondesi's steady eyes, and raised one hand, palm uppermost.

"Even with the Peaceforcers to back you, a light division could never stand off an invasion, Colonel, but that isn't your job. The Navy's going to reinforce as quickly as possible, and it's our intention to retake Justin at the earliest possible moment. I wish I could tell you how soon that will be. I can't. All I can tell you is that it's *your* job to organize and lead a guerrilla resistance for as long as you can—hopefully until we *can* retake the system. In the meantime, Admiral Murakuma's staff is organizing a plan for Redemption, a raid to be launched in the event the Bugs offer us an opportunity to mount it. They will designate refuge areas, landing zones from which we will attempt to lift out anyone we can if we're able to fight our way back in even temporarily, but don't count on that happening."

The grim-voiced general held the colonel's gaze and spoke very quietly.

"I have never before sent an officer into a situation in which I *expected* him to die, Colonel Mondesi. In this case, however, I have no choice but to do precisely that. Admiral Murakuma truly thinks she may be able to relieve you. I believe she'll make every humanly possible effort to do just that . . . but I expect her to fail. Which means you and all your people will be on your own. I won't insult you or them by pretending otherwise to stiffen your morale. I will simply remind you that you are Marines and that you will be defending nine million civilians."

Servais stood and held out a data chip to the officer he'd just condemned to death.

"Your official orders and full data on Justin and Harrison are on the chip. Under the circumstances, the least I can do is give you complete freedom in planning your own operations. Anything my staff or I can do to assist you is yours for the asking."

"Yes, Sir." Mondesi slipped the chip into his pocket. "We'll remember we're Marines, General," he said.

"I never doubted it, Colonel." Servais extended his hand once more, and Mondesi gripped it as firmly as he had when he first entered the compartment. "God bless, Colonel," the general said very quietly, and Mondesi nodded, released his hand, and walked through the hatch.

❖   ❖   ❖

Captain Andrew Foote Prescott of the battlecruiser *Daikyu* came to attention as the delicate, red-haired woman by the holo tank straightened and turned to face him. Her black-and-silver uniform set off her coloring with a perfection any HD producer would have killed for, and she stood tall and straight, but there were lines of strain on her oval face.

"Captain Prescott." Prescott was of only average height and build, yet he found himself taking the hand she extended gingerly, as if he feared a firm grip would shatter the fragile bones. The skin around her weary eyes crinkled, and a faint smile dimpled her cheeks, as if she was used to the reaction, but she squeezed hard.

"Admiral," he said, and found himself smiling back. For all her fatigue and obvious strain, this woman still radiated an indefinable serenity and a very definable aura of command.

"Thank you for coming so promptly," she said, and gestured at the tank. "Have a look."

He quirked an eyebrow, then stepped closer to the tank. It held a small-scale display of the Justin System, centered on the F8 furnace of Justin A. Justin B, its G0 companion, lay the better part of five light-hours distant, barely visible at the edge of the tank, but what caught his eye were five crimson dots scattered about the Justin B asteroid belt at its closest approach to Justin A. He gazed at them for a moment, then looked inquiringly at his admiral.

"Those are—or shortly will be—the locations of hidden supply ships, Captain. Yours."

"Mine, Sir?"

"Yours," she repeated. She pointed at a chair and folded her hands behind her to consider him as he slid into it and laid his cap on the table.

The Prescott family had served the Fleet well. It ought to have, for naval service was bred into its bone and blood. A Prescott had served Prince Rupert of Bohemia aboard the *Royal James* at the Four Days Battle. Others had died on the decks of the brig *Lawrence* in the Battle of Lake Erie and the *Cumberland* at Hampton Roads, and yet another had sailed into Manila Bay aboard the cruiser *Olympia*. His grandson had flown from the deck of the carrier *Yorktown* at the Battle of Midway, and when the Federated Government of Earth merged the old national militaries, the Prescotts had taken their tradition into the Federation's Navy. Murakuma was only the third member of her family to don naval uniform, but this man's naval lineage stretched back for over six standard centuries. That was one reason she'd chosen him, and she could almost feel his ancestors' silent presence at his shoulder as he looked calmly back at her.

"I intend to hold this system if at all possible, Captain," she said finally. "I think I have a chance to do so, but it isn't a good one. Whatever we do to these creatures, they simply keep on coming, and without reinforcements—"

She shrugged, and Prescott nodded. This woman had just won one of the greatest naval victories in history. Some officers in her position would have hidden their fears for the future behind pride in the past, but Vanessa Murakuma didn't, and her composure—and frankness to a relatively junior captain—impressed him.

"Because it seems likely we will, in fact, fail to hold Justin," she went on, "it is incumbent upon me to plan for the worst. That's where you come in."

She took one hand from behind her back to gesture at the holo tank.

"We're going to leave a lot of civilians behind, and the decision to withdraw will be mine. I, Captain Prescott, will personally sentence nine million human beings to death." He opened his mouth to dispute her cruel self-accusation, but she shook her head. "No, Captain. I realize I'll have no choice, and my orders from the Admiralty are clear. The Justinians must be considered expendable, and I am specifically forbidden to risk the destruction of my command to save them. But I also intend to move heaven and hell to get as many of them out as possible. Perhaps it's only a sop to my conscience or a whimsical gesture, but I will not sacrifice a single human being I can save to these monsters, whatever my orders!"

Prescott stiffened in his chair as bared steel clashed behind her serenity, and her exhausted eyes flickered with a hard, dangerous light.

"I want you to understand something, Captain Prescott," she said softly. "What I intend to do could be construed as a violation of my own orders from Sky Marshal Avram. I cannot order you to accept the responsibility I'm about to ask you to shoulder. I can only ask you to volunteer, and if you do so, your chance to succeed—or survive— will be slight."

"What, precisely, do you want me to volunteer *for*, Sir?" Prescott asked in a level voice.

"I'm asking you to accept an extremely hazardous assignment." She folded both hands behind her once more and looked into his eyes. "Your ship's a *Broadsword* class, with cloaking ECM. If and when we're forced to withdraw, I want to detach *Daikyu* as part of a scouting force which will remain in Justin to observe the enemy."

"To what purpose, Admiral?" Prescott asked after a moment.

"It will be some time before Battle Fleet can reinforce us sufficiently to take the offensive. It is remotely possible, however, that before that time comes, the chance to raid Justin from Sarasota will arise. My staff is currently planing for just such an operation under the codename 'Redemption,' but we've come up against one problem again and again. For an inferior force to raid a superior one, it *must* have accurate information on its enemies' strength and deployments."

"I see." Prescott looked down at his cap for a moment, stroking its braided visor with a forefinger, then looked back up at his admiral. "I can think of several difficulties, Sir," he said calmly, "but I'm sure we can figure out a way around most of them if we put our minds to it."

CHAPTER NINE

They Just Keep Coming

It was late as Vanessa Murakuma prowled Flag Bridge. She ought to be in bed. Her wakefulness and inability to sit still only advertised her edginess and might well shake her subordinates' nerve, but she couldn't help it. It was harder each day to project the composure and certainty her personnel needed, and her ignorance of the Bugs' activities only made it worse.

She wheeled back to the master plot and glowered into it. Each of the twenty-two days since the Battle of K-45 had added its weight to her millstone tension, yet each had also been a priceless treasure. Sarasota had done wonders with the ships she'd sent back to it, and a few desperately needed reinforcements had arrived, as well, headed by five fleet carriers and three *Matterhorn* missile SDs, but she was grimly certain the Bugs had been reinforced even more heavily.

Certain, yet unable to confirm it. She'd tried sneaking pinnaces through to K-45, but the cost had been too high. Over eighty percent had been picked off before they could reverse course and escape. Volunteers continued to come forward, but there was no possible way to justify sacrificing them, particularly when she knew the enemy was heavily equipped with cloaking ECM. Enough of her people were going to die when the Bugs finally attacked; she wouldn't send them to their deaths in efforts to spy on an enemy who could hide so much of his strength, anyway.

Perhaps another admiral could have done it. Perhaps it would even have been justified in the cold, brutal math of war. She couldn't, yet the strain of waiting in ignorance twisted her nerves, and her nights were haunted by nightmares whose existence she dared admit to no one, even Marcus, though she suspected *Cobra's* chief surgeon guessed. He hadn't argued when she finally went to him to demand something to help her sleep, at any rate.

It wasn't her fault. She knew that, and she'd tried to accept that lack of options absolved her from guilt. But she'd learned more about herself in the last three months than in all her previous sixty-seven years, and there was a flaw at her core. The very one, she knew now, which had sent her into uniform in the first place: responsibility. It was her *job* to protect civilians, to stand between them and their enemies. To die, if that was the only way to save them. Most of them never spared the Navy a thought in peacetime. Of those who did, many complained bitterly about funds the Fleet diverted from other expenditures, but that changed nothing. It was her job to keep them safe enough they could afford to feel that way about her, and she'd never fully realized how deep her sense of responsibility cut until she'd been forced to abandon millions of them to horrible death. Now she did, and she wondered, in the night while she waited for the nightmares to come, how many more worlds she could abandon before she broke.

She gazed down into the plot for endless minutes, searching for an answer. But no answer came, and, at last, she drew a deep breath, turned, and walked from the flag bridge to her cabin.

The light cruisers of the Assault Fleet formed up. It had taken the survey ships less time than usual to locate the warp point—the enemy's attempts to use small craft as spies had helped—but the staggering losses the Fleet had so far suffered had delayed its timetable. Yet it was ready now, and its ships floated silently in space, ready to resume the advance at last.

The alarm's wail yanked her from her sleep, and she jerked upright even as one hand reached automatically for the inhaler. She fumbled it to her face, then squeezed the button and gasped as a fiery pinwheel exploded in her brain. The stimulant was as brutal as the surgeon had warned it would be, but it smashed the drugged fog from her mind, and she shook herself fiercely.

She tossed the inhaler aside and activated her bedside com.

"Talk to me!"

"They're coming through, Sir." It was Leroy Mackenna's grim voice, and she wondered what he was doing on Flag Bridge at this hour. Was he having as much trouble sleeping as she?

"Strength?" she demanded, shoving the blankets aside.

"Only their light cruisers so far," Mackenna said tensely. "Plotting makes it seventy-five-plus of them. I expect we'll see the big suckers shortly, Sir."

"Understood. On my way." She cut the com circuit and climbed into her vac suit, wincing in pain as she made the plumbing connections with ruthless haste. There was a preternatural sharpness to her thoughts—a gift, no doubt, from the stim—yet even with that edge (if edge it was), she couldn't understand the Bugs' tactics. Surely K–45 had taught them she wouldn't risk a point-blank defense! And if none of her ships lay within the cruisers' engagement envelope, taking losses from interpenetration was pointless.

She snatched up her helmet and headed for the hatch at a run. Maybe the bastards were simply slaves to The Book. Despite herself, her lips quirked as she pictured a Bug admiral with The Book open in front of him, eyestalks cocked as he ran the tip of a tentacle down the type, but the smile vanished quickly. That many light cruisers might indicate a commensurate increase in capital ships, and there was nothing at all humorous about that.

◆　　　　◆　　　　◆

Ninety cruisers made transit. Seventy-one survived the experience, and their sensors scanned the space about the warp point while courier drones raced back to confirm transit. There were none of the mines that had cost their fellows so dear in the last battle, and they moved outward, englobing the warp point at one light-second's range.

Mackenna and Ling Tian were bent over the master plot when Murakuma stepped onto Flag Bridge, and Demosthenes Waldeck looked down from a bulkhead com screen. Jackson Teller's face filled another screen, and Rear Admiral John Ludendorff, who'd arrived with the *Borzoi-* and *Kodiak*-class fleet carriers, occupied another from the bridge of TFNS *Polar Bear.* Although senior to Teller, Ludendorff had readily agreed to serve as the junior admiral's exec rather than shake up TF 59's command team.

Mackenna started to speak as Murakuma strode quickly to the plot, but her raised hand stopped him long enough for her eyes to devour the icons. The Bug CLs had spread out about the warp point, and a long, lethal line of superdreadnoughts had begun to flow through in their wake.

"Is Admiral Kuzak ready?" she asked him then.

"Yes, Sir. She's standing by for your order."

"Good." Murakuma watched the display a moment longer, then nodded. "Tell her to do it," she said flatly.

"Yes, Sir," Ling Tian replied, and Murakuma racked her helmet on the side of her command chair and watched her repeater plot as she seated herself.

Her ships' icons blinked from the amber of standby to the flashing brilliance of General Quarters, and the ready fighters spat from her carriers' catapults, but her eyes dropped to the light codes representing the five OWPs which had orbited Justin A III until she'd demanded enough *Turbine*-class fleet tugs to move them to within ten light-seconds of the warp point. *Turbines* were more powerful than civilian tugs, able to give the "immobile" OWPs a velocity equal to any Bug ship's. Just as importantly, they mounted light shields, point defense . . . and datalink. They could be brought inside the OWPs' datanets, and their skippers had orders to keep their ponderous charges between them and the enemy. In effect, Murakuma had turned the forts into a mobile support force, and her lips skinned back at the thought. Each of those OWPs was the size of a super-dreadnought, and none of its hundred and eighty thousand tonnes were devoted to the engines an SD required. Four were pure missile platforms—with standard missiles, not capital launchers, unfortunately—and the fifth was the command base, with a pure energy armament to support its master datalink and deep space control systems. Its hetero-dyne lasers were powerful weapons, but she doubted she was going to get much use out of them. Which didn't bother her. Given the unorthodox strategy she'd evolved, the command base was about to prove worth its weight in any precious substance someone cared to name, and each standard base had the offensive missile power of an entire battlegroup of *Belleisle*-class battleships. She'd had to break them into two battlegroups and use Admiral Kuzak's *Cotton-mouth* as the second group's command ship, but they'd be able to throw an awesome number of missiles once they engaged.

For the moment, however, her attention was on the command OWP. She'd exhausted her supply of mines in K–45, but someone up the logistics pipeline had scraped up something even better for this fight. One hundred small buoys floated in a thin shell, six light-seconds from the warp point. There were so few of them, and they were so widely dispersed, the Bugs might not have picked them up at all. Even if they had, they'd probably assumed they were laser buoys—a threat, but an acceptable one. Only they weren't laser buoys; they were independently deployed primary beam platforms, and the command base had just ordered them to engage.

Four seconds passed while the order sped to the nearest buoys, then another twenty while they waited until their more distant brothers received the command base's targeting setup and confirmed their readiness to the master buoys. And then, in one terrible instant, one hundred primary beams stabbed out in a single, deadly salvo.

The lead superdreadnoughts staggered as unstoppable stilettos stabbed through shields and armor with contemptuous ease, and the SDs—safely outside the enemy's range—had made no effort to take evasive action. Over seventy primaries scored direct hits on the ten lead ships. The narrow-focus weapons punched tiny holes, little more than five centimeters across, but they punched those holes through anything . . . including magazines.

The beams ripped into the stored warheads. Containment fields ruptured, matter met antimatter, and a deadly chain reaction tore through every warhead aboard the targeted ships.

"Yes!"

Leroy Mackenna's exultant hiss filled *Cobra's* flag bridge as fireballs glared on the warp point, and Murakuma's fist slammed down on her command chair's armrest. She'd hoped to hurt the bastards, but her most optimistic prediction had fallen short of this! Ten clear kills—*ten!*—in the opening salvo! By God, she might be able to stop them after all!

"Ready Jackson?" she asked, looking up at Teller's com screen.

"Ready, Sir!" The carrier admiral's fierce exultation matched her own, and she nodded.

"Send them in," she said, and glanced at Waldeck. "Engage the enemy, Admiral Waldeck."

For just a moment, even the Bugs seemed paralyzed by the destruction visited upon their battle-line's van. Then the first Terran missile salvos began to rip into them even as their sensors detected the closing signatures of two hundred and sixty strikefighters, and the globe of light cruisers moved closer to the warp point to screen the emerging line of superdreadnoughts.

✧   ✧   ✧

"Jesus! *Look* at that bastard!"

Commander Olivera nodded grimly. He was the backup strike commander this time, and that gave him too much leisure to observe the light cruiser Lieutenant (JG) Carlton Hathaway had centered on his display. The damned thing must mount nothing *but* point defense, because it was putting out three times the defensive fire of a *Belleisle*-class BB, and that was bad. Very bad.

"How many of them do you see?" he asked tautly.

"I make it at least fifteen, Skip—probably more. What the hell *is* that thing?"

"How the fuck do *I* know?" Olivera demanded harshly, then shrugged. "Hell, maybe it's a minesweeper—if it matters!" He glanced at Lieutenant Malachi, his command fighter's pilot. "I hope you're feeling agile, Jane."

"As a weasel, Skip." Malachi was the quintessential fighter jock; her voice only got calmer as the tension rose, and Olivera managed a tight smile, then looked back at the tac officer.

"Punch up the alternate command net, Carl."

Hathaway nodded in grim understanding. Gloved fingers danced across his panel, and Olivera bent over his own, setting up a running download from the strike leader in case he had to take over.

"We've got a new light cruiser class, Sir!" Ling Tian's voice was clipped, but sudden worry burned in its depths. "It appears to be an antimissile ship or minesweeper. Whatever it is, it's got at least fifty percent more point defense than a *Dunedin!*"

Something inside Murakuma flinched. The *Dunedin*-class escort light cruisers were antimissile platforms designed to bolster the defenses of light carrier or battle-line battlegroups. CLEs were fragile compared to a capital ship but mounted enormously powerful point defense for their size, which made them extremely efficient at killing missiles . . . or fighters.

"Switch the *Matterhorns* and OWPs to them!"

"Aye, aye, Sir."

Murakuma bit her lip as Ling's acknowledgment came back to her. She hated taking her bases and handful of superdreadnoughts off the Bug heavies, yet those CLEs would wreak havoc among her fighters, and the OWPs and *Matterhorns* were her best chance to take them out. The bases had the sheer volume of fire to saturate their defenses and the penetration aids of the *Matterhorns'* capital missiles might just let them sneak through, and it wouldn't take many hits with second-generation AM warheads to blow a light cruiser apart.

She bit her lip harder. Should she recall the strike, wait until she'd had a chance to whittle away at this unanticipated threat? The casualties her strikegroups were about to take said yes, but if she pulled back now she lost her best—possibly her only—chance to actually *stop* the bastards. The warp point was a holocaust of exploding warheads, ripping at the incoming capital ships. She'd already killed ten, and half a dozen more were bleeding air. If she could just hit them hard enough, savage them terribly enough, surely even *Bugs* would break off!

Her long-dead husband's face flickered before her, and she closed her eyes, fighting Tadeoshi aside while options and costs and possibilities cascaded through her brain. Even if she pulled them back now, they might take equally heavy losses later, she told herself. If she backed off on the strike, let the capital ships make transit in strength, the defensive fire would be almost as terrible even if every CLE were blown apart. But the decisive factor, the one she simply could not ignore, was timing, the possibility of getting the fighters in quickly enough, in sufficient strength, to stop the enemy dead and save nine million civilians.

She opened her eyes once more and watched the fighter icons streaking towards the holocaust and said nothing.

"It's gonna be a rough ride, Skipper," Hathaway said flatly, and Olivera nodded. Whatever their designed purpose, the Bug cruisers' defenses made them missile sponges. They were soaking up enormous volumes of fire

. . . and diverting TF 59's fire from the Bug battle-line when its transit-destabilized units were at their most vulnerable.

"Entering their envelope in fifteen seconds." The tac officer's voice was flatter than ever, and Olivera felt his guts tighten.

The fighters slammed into the Bugs' defensive globe, and Vanessa Murakuma's face went white as every light cruiser opened fire simultaneously. The CLEs were the most effective, but the class Ops had codenamed *Carbine* was almost as bad. They didn't have the AFHAWK, thank God, but they didn't really need the specialized antifighter missile—not when they had enough sprint-mode standard missiles to go around. The Bug cruisers had to be extremely austere designs, she thought almost calmly, without the support systems Terran designers included as a matter of course. If they were regarded as expendable throwaways, that actually made sense . . . and it also meant the tonnage they *didn't* use for self-protection could be diverted to offensive purposes. The *Carbines'* missile broadsides were twice as heavy as a TFN light cruiser's, and she watched in horror as they ripped into her fighters.

"Coming up on our final turn, Skip!" Hathaway's voice was jagged with tension, and nausea swirled in Olivera's belly as Malachi went to full power and evasive action and a savage fist crushed him back in his couch. No one had ever figured out how to build a fighter inertial compensator with the efficiency of a starship's or even a larger small craft's. Fighters were the smallest, fastest, most agile deep-space craft ever designed, and the engineers had been forced to accept some fundamental compromises to offset the acceleration effects which would otherwise have turned any human passenger into gruel. In effect, a fighter's inertial sump was shallower than that of anything else in space. It worked . . . but it didn't work as *well* as those of larger units, and that was what made fighter ops so physically punishing when they went to full power.

Malachi took them into the teeth of the enemy's fire at .8 *c*, and Olivera felt another, colder nausea twist his gut as fighters began to die.

I should have called them back. The icy thought burned in Vanessa Murakuma's brain as dozens of Terran fighters exploded. *I should have called them* back!

But she hadn't, and her hands locked on her command chair's armrests like talons as her bleeding squadrons continued to close.

"Captain Brigatta's gone!" Hathaway barked, and Olivera nodded.

"Rampart Strike, this is Rampart Two," he said over the net while the giant's fist crushed him back and antiacceleration drugs fought his body's abuse. "Maintain profile. We're going in."

Half the fighters were already dead when the survivors broke through the cruisers, and more died as they charged across the final light-seconds towards their targets. Clumsy, waddling superdreadnoughts tried to turn aside even as their own weapons lashed at their attackers, but this was what Rampart Strike had come for. It would not be denied, and broken bits of squadrons bucked and bounced through the curdled space in the SDs' wakes. The warp point was a mad confusion of fishtailing fighters and swerving capital ships; Bug jammers overpowered squadron datanets; light cruisers turned to follow them into the madness, point defense firing furiously while the Terran missiles it was ignoring roared in to kill them; and even as Rampart Strike closed, fresh superdreadnoughts continued to make transit into the maelstrom. No computer could have sorted it all out, but that no longer mattered. Rampart Strike's survivors swerved into the blind spots of their victims, and Olivera knew there would be too few left for a second strike like this. They had to get close—so close not a shot missed, for it was the only pass they were going to get.

"Visual range!" he barked over the net. *"Visual range launch!"*

"Holy Mary, Mother of God, blessed art thou among women . . ." Carlton Hathaway whispered as an enemy superdreadnought loomed on his targeting screen. The range was less than a hundred thousand kilometers, and it flashed downward like lightning with the fighter's overtake velocity as Malachi lined up. The tac officer's hand rested on the control panel built into the armrest of his flight couch, and the ball of one gloved thumb reached for the big, red button.

". . . pray for us sinners at—"

The SD appeared suddenly on his visual display, and his thumb jabbed.

"Birds away!" he screamed, and threw up into his helmet as Jane Malachi redlined her drive in a vicious hairpin turn. Four antimatter-armed close attack missiles blasted from the fighter, roaring down on the SD, and eight more missiles followed them in from the only other two survivors of Olivera's original squadron.

All twelve scored direct hits. There was no wreckage.

Vanessa Murakuma's bleak, frozen eyes watched the fragments of Jackson Teller's fighters fall back to their carriers. They'd killed sixteen SDs, and Plotting estimated that they'd inflicted heavy damage on six more, but they'd paid for it with almost seventy percent of their number, and it was her fault.

She stared into her own soul, loathing what she saw, then made herself accept it and set it aside. There would be time to face her dead later.

She drew a deep breath and looked back into her plot. They'd put the next best thing to thirty superdreadnoughts out of action, but that many more were already in-system, and more were making transit as she watched. It was unbelievable. Whatever she did, however many she killed, however brutally she smashed them, they just kept *coming*, and with her fighter strength decisively blunted, she couldn't stop them. Perhaps she couldn't have stopped them anyway. Perhaps her hope of doing that had never been anything more *than* a hope, no more than a desperate need to believe she could do it. But whatever it had once been, it was only one more failure now.

She inhaled again, nostrils flaring, then looked up at Ling Tian and Leroy Mackenna.

"Go to Charlie Seven," she said, and her own calm, even voice as she ordered her task force to begin its long retreat astonished her.

"Yes, Sir," Mackenna said softly, and she looked at Teller's ashen face on the com screen.

"Consolidate your squadrons, Jackson. I'll give you as much time to reorganize as I can."

"Yes, Sir." There wasn't a trace of condemnation in his voice, and she wanted to scream at him. But she stopped herself. Somehow she stopped herself.

"Once you've consolidated, detach any carrier without at least two squadrons on board," she said flatly. "Send them back to Justin and Harrison to evacuate every civilian you can pack aboard. You're authorized to redline your environmental systems."

"Yes, Sir," Teller said once more, and Murakuma nodded. She leaned back in her command chair, watching the ravaged light dots flashing back towards their carriers, and her mouth twisted.

At least she'd just made sure they'd have lots of spare life support for the civilians, she thought bitterly.

Chapter Ten

"We *can't* wait!"

One inescapable consequence of the physics of the reactionless drive was that the instant a drive field went down, any velocity it had imparted went with it. The energy shedding process as the immense forces concentrated in the surface of the field's "bubble" dissipated was spectacular but harmless, and the ability to decelerate virtually instantaneously from $.1\,c$ to whatever a starship's relative motion had been at the moment the drive was engaged could be invaluable. There were, however, circumstances under which the velocity loss required some inventiveness.

And this, Andrew Prescott thought sardonically, watching *Daikyu*'s master display with what he hoped was an air of calm confidence, *is one of them.*

The battlecruiser slid stealthily through the system's outer reaches, creeping along (for her) at barely 15,000 KPS under cover of her ECM while passive sensors probed the vacuum like a cat's quivering whiskers. Her course carried her directly towards the Justin-Sarasota warp point, but that invisible dot lay two billion kilometers ahead, and she had no intention of approaching it any more closely than she must. While a coward would never have let himself be "volunteered" for his present mission, Andrew Prescott was no fool. He was confident he could spot and evade any enemies which weren't cloaked, but even though

his scanners hadn't found any, the presence of cloaked
Bug pickets was a certainty, and logic suggested there
were more of them than there were of him.

He looked around the bridge once more, and his mouth
quirked at the duty watch's tense body language. The
last three weeks had been nerve-wracking for his subordinates, but those same weeks had held another, even
deeper strain for him. The others were concerned primarily
only with surviving; he was responsible for the success of
his mission, as well.

His half-smile vanished at the thought, for if *his* ship
had evaded all enemies, her consort *Longsword* hadn't.
He couldn't be certain, but he suspected Captain Daulton
had gotten too close to the warp point—either to probe
it or in an effort to get a courier drone to Sarasota—five
days ago. Whatever his intention, *Longsword* had been
detected, ambushed and destroyed with all hands. *Daikyu*
had been just close enough to catch the omnidirectional
Code Omega which confirmed her destruction, and
Andrew Prescott was determined the Bugs would not get
his ship, as well. *Daikyu* had a job to do, and to do it,
she must survive.

But she also had to know what was going on and—
trickier still—whether or not what she knew was important
enough to report. Just securing the data was hard enough,
as his present elaborate maneuvers illustrated, but it was
easier than deciding when that data was vital enough to
risk passing it on. He'd made up his mind at the outset
not to make any reports that *weren't* vital, and *Longsword's*
destruction reconfirmed his determination, for there was
no way the Bugs could miss a transiting courier drone.
Even assuming they didn't manage to backtrack it to
Daikyu, its mere existence would tell them *Longsword*
hadn't been the only spy left to watch them, and their
efforts to find *Daikyu* would redouble if they knew
positively that she was there to be found. Worse, it might
cause them to rethink whatever deployment had inspired
him to send the drone in the first place, and unless he
was in a position to see any changes they made—*and*

report them to Sarasota—those changes could turn his original message into a trap.

The same considerations applied to recon drones. An RD was a low-signature object, with every built-in stealth feature the TFN could devise, but even the stealthiest drone's drive field could be spotted under the wrong circumstances, especially at close quarters, and he needed to get his RD right on top of the warp point. Redemption couldn't be risked on questionable data; he had to reduce the uncertainty factor to the absolute minimum. The problem was to somehow get the damned thing to point-blank range *without* using its drive, and he and Fred Kasuga, his exec, had wracked their brains to find a way. The actual suggestion had been Kasuga's, but like everything else, the final responsibility for its success— or failure—was Andrew Foote Prescott's.

He grimaced at the familiar thought, then sighed. There were times he wished he'd told Murakuma to hand the stinking job to some other captain, but *someone* had to do it, and he'd accepted it because it had to be done. And, he admitted privately, because deep down inside he was convinced *he* could do it better than anyone else.

Well, Mister Wonderful, if you're so hot it's about time you prove it, he thought, and glanced at his astrogator.

"On profile?" he asked quietly.

"Yes, Sir. Coming up on release point in—" Lieutenant Commander Belliard glanced at the countdown ticking away in a corner of his display "—eight minutes."

"Good." Prescott looked at his tac officer. "Status on the bird, Jill?"

"Just completed the final diagnostic, Skipper." Lieutenant Commander Cesiaño popped a chip out of her console, loaded it into a message board, and handed it to him, and he glanced over it. Every system checked—as he'd expected from Cesiaño—and he handed it back with a nod.

"Outstanding. Now if everything works, we may even get away with it."

The tac officer grinned, and he smiled back at her as he

felt the rest of the bridge crew respond to his wry tone. *Funny how even really bright people can be amused by stupid jokes,* he thought, and settled into his command chair to watch the final minutes limp into eternity.

"Stand by for release," Cesiaño said finally, and Prescott tipped his chair back and steepled his hands across his flat belly. All he could really do at a moment like this was try even harder to radiate confidence, and—

"Drone away!" Cesiaño said, and Prescott's eyes narrowed. The RD's low-signature materials made it all but invisible even to *Daikyu's* sensors, and it radiated no active emissions at all. Even its drive was down—indeed, Cesiaño's missile crews had physically disabled it, just in case—and it stopped dead as it penetrated *Daikyu's* drive field. But a readied tractor jerked it instantly back into motion. It couldn't accelerate without a drive of its own, but the tractor tugged it bodily along, imparting the momentum of *Daikyu's* velocity. It couldn't maneuver or change course, but it also offered no betraying energy source to warn anyone it was coming, and its present heading would take it directly past the Sarasota warp point in almost exactly thirty-six hours at a range of less than fifteen light-seconds. And in the meantime . . .

"Execute breakaway," he said.

"Aye, aye, Sir," Belliard responded. "Executing now."

Cesiaño cut the tractor, and *Daikyu* looped up and away from the drone. The range opened gradually, and Prescott inhaled in satisfaction as it vanished from even *Daikyu's* ken four minutes later. It was unlikely in the extreme that anyone would see it coming, but that left the trickiest parts still to accomplish. First, *Daikyu* had to up her speed (and consequent chance of detection) enough to circle round the warp point to catch the drone at the appointed rendezvous on the far side, and then—

And then, Andrew Prescott told himself, *I have to decide if the result of the exercise is worth breaking silence to inform Sarasota.* He grimaced again and looked at the chronometer. Three days. The time, he knew, was not going to pass quickly.

✧   ✧   ✧

"They're coming over us! *They're coming over us!*"

An explosion roared over the link, and the voice in Acting Major Frieda Jaëger's earbug went from a tenor shout to a soprano scream. The link brought the terrible concussion right into her command vehicle with her, slamming her head aside in involuntary reflex as her mind pictured the carnage with masochistic clarity, and her hands fisted. Somehow the transmitter at the other end had survived the explosion, and she heard the scream collapse into a horrible, high-pitched, endless sound of agony before her com officer could cut the circuit.

Jaëger drew a deep breath and shook herself. Lieutenant Furness wasn't the first to die since the Bugs came to Justin. *He won't be the last, either,* her mind said grimly, but he'd blown hell out of the Bug point before they called in the heavy stuff on him.

She dropped her eyes to the map display. So far, the Bugs didn't seem to have sorted the recon satellites out of all the other orbital junk, but Colonel—*No,* Brigadier *Mondesi,* she corrected herself—wasn't taking chances. A sneaky opponent might opt for planting scanners around the satellites to track their whisker laser transmissions to whatever was receiving them, so Mondesi had them reporting to widely dispersed (and unmanned) remote ground stations, and aside from short-range tactical traffic, all transmissions were compressed into burst transmissions and then bounced off anything *but* one of the recon or surviving comsats. Transmission quality might suffer, but there was almost always some handy piece of space junk, manmade or natural, to get the message through, and the tight beams were virtually undetectable.

Which was good, because hiding things like Jaëger's Asp command vehicle from an enemy who controlled the high orbitals was hard enough without radiating "Oh kill me now!" emission signatures. In fact, she would have preferred to command her "battalion" of Marines, Peaceforcers, and civilians from her battle armor and a hole in the ground that gave the Bugs nothing at all to spot. Unfortunately, she had too many civilians and Peaceforcers and too few armored Raiders to make that practical. Worse, her force was spread so thin and so widely dispersed that she needed all the command and control capability she could get, and in that respect an Asp was vastly superior to anything even a Raider "zoot" could provide.

For what it was worth.

She glared at the display as the Asp's computers turned Furness's position from green to crimson. The Bugs' operational doctrine sucked, and they didn't appear to have any equivalent of the Corps' zoots, but the bastards were incredibly fast and strong even without it. The intelligence pukes' best guess was that they came from a high-grav world, though none of the planets *Argive* had reported had been massive enough to account for it. That was an unsettling thought. Jaëger had seen the population estimates Intelligence had formed based on Commodore Braun's report, and if that many Bugs lived in a star system that didn't even contain their home world—

Jaëger snarled at her own wandering thoughts. *Fatigue. I've got to find a way to get at least some shut-eye, or my brain's going to go straight to mush. But how the hell am I supposed to do that when the bastards keep coming this way?*

She forced her mind back to the present. Wherever their home world was, the Bugs' strength let them carry weapons almost as heavy as a zooted Raider's, and they could scuttle through even close terrain with dreadful, flowing speed. Man for man (though applying the term "man" to a Bug, however obliquely, made Jaëger gag mentally), they were far better armed than most of her non-Marines, and much faster. Without zoots or vehicles, it was desperately difficult for any of the Justin Defense Force's units to disengage and break contact. Worse, these bastards were perfectly willing to launch frontal assaults and accept incredible losses to get in among her positions, and once they did, their firepower made them hideously effective killers.

But that same attack mentality could be used against them. For all their individual firepower, they were only sparsely equipped with support weapons, and Mondesi's Marines had quickly taught their hodgepodge of police and civilians to show them targets in order to suck them into prepared fire sacks. If they took the bait, the support squads lurking in ambush could inflict massive casualties, and their own aggressiveness kept them coming when any Terran unit would have broken off, which only increased the body count. The defenders had managed to destroy more than one attack force down to the last Bug—*which,* she thought grimly, *seems to be the* only *way to guarantee breaking contact.* Furness, unfortunately, hadn't, and she'd been unable to reinforce in time to save his platoon. Not, at any rate, without committing her zoots or handful of remaining assault skimmers, and she had to be extremely careful how she moved those. The energy they radiated moving at speed was painfully visible from orbit, and the defenders had learned the hard way that the Bugs were perfectly willing to nuke any juicy target they saw.

But at least Furness had drawn the attack onto his own unit, and its fight to the death had diverted the Bugs from the refugee camp long enough for its occupants to scatter into the hills. Some would be caught by the clumsy helicopters which seemed to be the Bug's only tactical aircraft, but the Bugs had learned—also the hard way—what happened to any chopper that encountered a Marine with an HVM. The man-portable hyper velocity missile moved at ten percent of light-speed, giving them energy-weapon accuracy over any tactical range, and the kinetic energy released when they struck their target was far worse than merely devastating.

"Have Blocker One-One move down the valley to here," Jaëger said, and dropped an icon into the display. "Blocker One-Five and Back-Up Zero-Four can cover them from overwatch here and here." Two more icons appeared atop hills flanking the valley. "Inform Lieutenant Harpe that his mission is to *delay* the Bugs. He's buying time for the refugees to get clear, not trying to wipe the bastards out, so tell him I'm going to rip him a new asshole if he forgets it."

"Yes, Sir." Her com officer bent over his own panel, inputting the orders and instructing his systems to compress them for burst transmission and consult the Asp's orbital catalogs for suitable bodies to bounce the signals off. Furness left the ex-Peaceforcer to the task and looked over her shoulder at Master Sergeant Helen McNeil. The sturdy, auburn-haired Raider had been bumped to acting sergeant-major of Jaëger's makeshift battalion, and the look in her eyes matched the one in her CO's. Harpe was a hotshot who was almost as good as he thought he was, and he'd already pulled off two successful ambushes. Jaëger and McNeil both knew he was just aching to make it three and that they couldn't afford the losses they'd take if he screwed it up. That was why Jaëger hated to use him at all, but his were also the only troops close enough to turn the trick, and Jaëger had lost too many civilians already. She would *not* lose a single additional life she could save—even if it meant putting Harpe into the line.

Brigadier Raphael Mondesi watched his own display as Major Jaëger's overstretched battalion fought desperately to hold the Bugs, and his face was ebon iron. His HQ's camouflage would have made even a Marine instructor smile in approval, and all his communications went by secure, undetectable land line to one of eight remote transmission sites . . . which only made him feel even more guilty. It was an irrational guilt—the Justin Defense Force's CO *had* to have a secure command center—but that didn't make it any easier to live with. Whatever his collar insignia said, he still felt like a colonel, and a colonel's place was with his regiment.

"What's close enough to support Jaëger?" he asked harshly.

"Nothing." His executive officer's voice was just as harsh, and Mondesi looked up quickly. He opened his mouth to dispute the single, flat negative, then closed it with a snap. General Simon Merman was a cop, not a Marine, but he'd learned a lot in the last two terrible weeks, and half Jaëger's troops were his Peaceforcers. If anything had been in position to support the major, he would have moved heaven and earth to get it there.

"Damn." The Marine sighed, and his ramrod-straight spine sagged just a bit.

"At least they're still scatter-gunning us," Merman said.

Mondesi nodded. He'd hoped his SigInt sections might manage to at least track the Bugs' tactical traffic, but as the Navy had discovered against their starships, Bugs didn't seem to *say* anything to one another. The signal intelligence types had picked up lots of transmissions—the Bugs seemed to rely primarily upon easily intercepted omni-directional radio—but none of those transmissions carried anything his people could even identify as communications. They had to be carrying *something*, but the most painstaking analysis couldn't *find* anything!

It was maddening—and dangerous. If they'd even been able to tell which transmissions were addressed to military units, Mondesi's people would have been in a far better position to estimate what the Bugs were up to; as it was, he could only guess in the dark. The Bugs had landed troops in and around all the larger cities and slaughtered every human they found (or, worse, collected them for later consumption), and they had sizable forces in the field, yet there seemed no discernable pattern to their operations there. More than half Mondesi's hastily camouflaged refugee camps weren't even threatened; others had been hit in overwhelming force and wiped out to the last man, woman, and child, but it was almost as if they attacked only those targets they happened to stumble across, and his total inability to predict their intentions made it all but impossible to adjust his own deployments to meet them. But at least Merman was right, and the brigadier tried to feel grateful. The Bugs' attacks might be virtually random so far as he could tell, but they *had* left the majority of his camps unhit. Unfortunately . . .

"They may be 'scatter-gunning' us, Simon," he said, "but look at this." He punched a command into the holo unit, and patches of scarlet flashed. Each formed a rough wedge, reaching out from the invaders' main concentrations in no apparent pattern—certainly none were angled to meet one another—but three aimed almost arrow-straight at a trio of small, green shuttle icons.

"See?" the Marine asked quietly.

Merman stared at the holo for a long, silent moment, then inhaled sharply.

"Shit," he said, and Mondesi nodded again.

"Exactly. In about—" he glanced at the estimate his ops officer had put together that morning "—twelve more days, they're going to reach three of our alpha sites."

"Can we adjust?" Merman asked tightly.

"Some. But we placed the original camps in relation to the planned evac sites. If we start moving large bodies of refugees around, the Bugs are almost certain to spot at least some of them. If they do, they'll attack in force . . . but if we *don't* move them, they won't be able to reach any of the other evac sites in time to be picked up without one hell of a lot more notice than the Fleet's going to be able to give us."

"Which means?" Merman was a policeman, but his tone said he already knew what Mondesi was going to tell him. Unfortunately, he was right.

"Which means," the Marine said heavily, "that if the Navy doesn't launch Redemption within the next ten days, we'll have only two choices. Move the refugees anyway and hope at least some survive to reach a backup site, or leave them where they are. And if we do that, at least twelve thousand people we *might* have been able to get out won't have any place to get out *to*."

Andrew Prescott sat in his command chair once more. The last three days had been more nerve-wracking than usual, for there were even more Bug scouts swarming about the warp point than he'd feared, and their courses carried them further out from it than he'd anticipated. At one point, he'd actually had to shut down everything— including *Daikyu*'s drive field—and imitate a drifting hunk of rock, and his forehead had been a solid sheet of sweat as the prowling light cruiser passed within less than eight thousand kilometers of his ship. If it had seen her and popped off a broadside while her drive was down, a single hit would have vaporized his command.

As it happened, it *hadn't* spotted *Daikyu*, but the delay had put them twelve hours behind schedule to collect the RD. Given the fact that they knew its exact course, that *shouldn't* pose any problem, but the damned thing would be so hard to spot on passive, even for the people who'd launched it, that he couldn't help sweating every minute until it was safely back aboard, and—

"Contact." He sat up straight as Lieutenant Commander Cesiaño's quiet announcement broke the stillness. "Zero-zero-two by zero-zero-five. It's definitely the drone, Skipper."

"*Very* good, Jill," Prescott said, equally quietly, then looked at his exec. "Nudge us a little closer, Fred. I want the weakest tractor we can generate to pull it in."

"Aye, aye, Sir." Kasuga nodded to Belliard, and *Daikyu* moved to match vectors with her offspring. It took another fifteen minutes of slow, careful maneuvering, and then Cesiaño stabbed the drone with a tractor.

"Got it, Skip!" she announced, and a quiet rustle of approval ran around the bridge.

"Well executed, everyone," Prescott said sincerely as Belliard altered course without orders and took the ship away from the rendezvous point on the prearranged vector. The captain watched his plot a moment longer, then rose, crossed to Cesiaño's station, and frowned as data began to scroll across the bottom of her display. Most of her screen was occupied by a map of the warp point's immediate environs, which showed the dense clouds of mines he'd expected. But something else had been added, and he leaned over her shoulder to tap the sphere of small red dots which represented individual starships just outside the minefields.

"Are those what I think they are?" he asked, and Cesiaño nodded.

"Definitely those CAs we saw earlier, Skipper."

"Um." Prescott rubbed his chin. They'd spotted a bevy of commercial-drive, heavy-cruiser-sized vessels moving across the system at a suspiciously low speed, even for Bugs, two weeks earlier, and he'd decided to risk coming in close for a better look. They already knew the Bugs used military drives, not civilian ones, in the light cruisers of their "Assault Fleet," probably because the less massive military units let them devote more mass to weapons in units which were, after all, designed to be expended in action.

The fact that the mystery CAs used commercial engines had thus suggested they, at least, weren't intended for the assault role. While low top speeds wouldn't be much of a problem for a simultaneous transit—they wouldn't have far to go—such slow units could hope neither to catch an enemy nor to run away from one under normal combat conditions. That suggested they were another specialized unit, and their present deployment certainly appeared to confirm his original guess as to what their purpose was.

Makes sense, too, he thought grudgingly as he watched still more data appear. *We haven't used SBMHAWKs yet, so they may not know we can send missiles through a warp point, but they have to know we could use our own Assault Fleet. These suckers may be tactically slow, but fitting them with commercial engines gives them a decent strategic speed, and that lets them build 'em back home, then send them forward under their own power and save the time we spend putting OWPs together in forward systems. They're smaller than most forts, but enough should still do the trick, and if all they have are weapons and defenses . . .*

He shook free of his thoughts and looked back up at Cesiaño.

"Any sign of heavy units in close to the point?"

"No, Sir," the tac officer replied, and her tone mirrored the cold satisfaction of her eyes as she looked up at her CO. "In fact—"

She tapped a function key, and Prescott smiled a shark's

smile as he watched her display. The drone had caught a cluster of over thirty superdreadnoughts falling back from the warp point once the cruiser sphere was in place.

"Looks like these fellows—" Cesiaño tapped her display "—are pulling back to join the rest of their battle-line."

"So it does," Prescott murmured. He patted her shoulder and walked slowly back to his chair while his mind raced. It appeared the Bugs had at least one thing in common with humans: *they* couldn't remain at general quarters indefinitely, either, and they'd been rotating their battle-line units on the warp point ever since taking the system. As one group of units reached the end of its GQ endurance, it fell back to over two light-minutes, well outside the weapons envelope of any attacker, and another replaced it. It was a reasonable move to protect their capital ships from surprise attack, but if they'd turned responsibility for the close-in defenses over to the CAs . . .

He settled into the chair, tipped it back, and rested his heels on his repeater plot as he thought. Before detaching his ship, Murakuma had brought him up to speed on her anticipated reinforcement schedule. Assuming it had been met, she wouldn't have received much in the way of additional ships yet, but she *should* have received at least the first wave of SBMHAWKs. If she had, and if the second-generation AMBAMs had also arrived, the Bugs' shift in deployments might just offer her a chance to mount Redemption after all.

Unfortunately, she didn't know that, and if he used a courier drone to tell her, the Bugs would know he had. Would they revert to their original dispositions and back up the CAs with capital ships once more? *He* certainly would, but the Navy had already learned that human-style logic could be no more than a way to screw up with confidence where Bugs were concerned.

He pursed his lips as he considered another point. If Murakuma's munitions *hadn't* arrived, she'd be unable to do anything with his data even if it got through to her, in which case he'd have risked warning the Bugs to change their strategy (and, incidentally, risked *Daikyu's* own detection and destruction, as well) for nothing.

It was tempting to wait, but Brigadier Mondesi was still getting transmissions out from Justin-A III. The brigadier didn't know where they went after they hit the stealthed comsats, and since setting out to deploy the RD, Prescott had been unable to tap his own end of the satellite chain which brought the transmissions back from the support freighters in Justin-B, but the Marine CO's reports made grim reading. If Redemption wasn't launched within the next week to ten days, there wouldn't be much of anyone left to rescue.

Captain Andrew Prescott scowled as he faced the decision he had to make, then sighed, sat up straight, and looked at his com officer.

". . . so that's the situation, ladies and gentlemen," Leroy Mackenna said.

Marcus LeBlanc sat quietly, showing no sign of his own worry, as Mackenna and Ling Tian finished their presentation to the task group and battlegroup COs. Murakuma nodded to them, and they put the holo of the Justin-A System on hold and resumed their seats. She gazed at the display, then looked around at her assembled flag officers.

"Captain Prescott's done an outstanding job," she said. "Now it's up to us to do ours."

A sort of ripple run through the admirals and commodores. Jackson Teller, John Ludendorff, and Demosthenes Waldeck, as her senior officers, looked at one another, and then Waldeck cleared his throat.

"Should we assume from your statement that you intend to launch Operation Redemption on the basis of this information, Sir?" he asked carefully.

"I do," she said flatly.

Waldeck might have winced, but he said nothing. Neither did Ludendorff, but Teller leaned forward to make eye contact with Task Force 59's CO.

"I appreciate your desire to get as many people out as

possible, Sir," he said quietly, "but I must point out that we haven't received a single additional starship, while Captain Prescott's report clearly indicates the Bugs have been heavily reinforced."

"I realize that." Murakuma laid her fine-boned hands on the table and squared her frail-looking shoulders. "We have, however, repaired our damages and received the munitions we were promised, and your strikegroups have been brought back up to strength."

More than one officer quailed before her soprano voice's icy tonelessness, yet Jackson Teller was made of sterner stuff. He was junior to both Waldeck and Ludendorff, whatever the table of organization might say, but it was his fighter crews who'd suffered the heaviest proportionate casualties in the last two engagements.

"I realize we can blow our way into the system," he said in that same, quiet voice. "I also realize their decision to pull their battle-line back should give us the chance to use our speed and range advantages to full effect in deep space. But if they close the point behind us, we'll still have to come to them to fight our way back out. And while my strikegroups are *officially* back up to strength, less than ten percent of my squadrons can really be considered combat ready. Most are still shaking down replacements. If I commit them to close action, they'll take catastrophic losses."

He'd been careful not to say "again," but something inside Vanessa Murakuma winced anyway, and then Waldeck spoke up.

"Admiral Teller's made a valid point, Sir, and there's another one. We'll have twelve more superdreadnoughts and six additional fleet carriers within five days. With those reinforcements, we'd be in a much stronger position to—"

"I realize that." Waldeck's eyebrows rose, for it wasn't like Murakuma to break in on one of her subordinates and her voice was flint. "I *also* realize, however, that we don't have the luxury of waiting. As Captain Prescott pointed out, the mere fact the Bugs know he's reported to us may cause them to alter their dispositions, in which case even the reinforcements you've mentioned would find it extremely costly to break into the system. Either we attack now—immediately—or we give up what may be the only chance we'll ever have to mount Redemption, and the people dying in Justin even as we sit here are *civilians* we—*I*—had no option but to leave behind."

She glared around the table—as if, LeBlanc thought uneasily, the briefing room were filled with Bugs, not her own officers. There was a dangerous, brittle quality to her, one he'd never seen before, and he felt a sudden chill. He understood her argument, yet there was something more behind it. A personal something that pursued her like the Furies' whips, and he wondered suddenly if she'd somehow slipped over the edge without his noticing. He started to open his mouth, then changed his mind. Anything he said was unlikely to change her decision; that much was painfully obvious, whatever was going on in her head. And if she *was* starting to lose it (and God knew she had a right to!), he couldn't afford to antagonize her into seeing *him* as an enemy.

"The question of whether or not we attack is not debatable," she said in that same frozen scalpel of a soprano. "We *can't* wait, whatever the arguments in favor of doing so. The task force will attack within the next twelve hours, so I suggest we all turn our attention to our ops plan."

She hadn't raised her voice, but Waldeck and Teller closed their mouths and sat back without another word. She ran those flinty eyes around the conference table one more time, then sat back in her own chair with the harsh ghost of a smile.

"Good," she said softly. "In that case, Admiral Waldeck, we'll start with the battle-line."

CHAPTER ELEVEN

Recall

"Of course we *all* agree that the visuals—assuming they can be relied upon—are *horrifying*. But at the same time, there must be some *rational* basis for their actions, some *misunderstanding* that could *surely* have been avoided if it hadn't been for the Military Establishment's vested interest in having an enemy to justify its own existence. . . ."

Hannah Avram smiled grimly as she listened to Bettina Wister's strident bleating from across the presidential reception room and watched the embarrassed maneuvers of people trying to get away from her. The evidence of what the Bugs—the term was rapidly achieving universal use—did to occupied planets' inhabitants had discredited Wister's viewpoint in all but the most hopelessly blinkered of eyes. But she was still a member of the Naval Oversight Committee, and it had been impossible to avoid inviting her to this reception for the newly arrived Orion representatives to the Grand Allied Joint Chiefs of Staff.

The formal speechifying had ended earlier, and at least that had been done on a higher level than Wister's—or even Prime Minister Quilvio's. President DaCunha had spoken for the Federation, for his office still remained its visible embodiment. Despite all the unnatural acts that had been performed on the Constitution, it was only proper that mankind's highest elected official speak for humanity on such an occasion as the reactivation of the

149

Grand Alliance that had crushed the Rigelians. The other parties had responded with every evidence of good grace. Privately, they might take a "better thee than me" attitude towards humanity's current troubles, but they'd learned from experience that such troubles were best squelched as early as possible.

Avram's grin widened as she watched Agamemnon Waldeck succeed in disengaging himself from Wister's diminishing audience. He might be a son-of-a-bitch, but he and his Corporate World fellows could be counted on to support the military, which kept the Federation's commerce safe from the Tangri, renegade Orions and other predatory types. It was a persistent fissure in their alliance with the Heart Worlds—which had been too rich and too safe for too long—and their one patch of common ground with the despised Fringers.

She sipped her white wine—something stronger might have helped her get through this reception, but with advancing age she found alcohol did less and less for her— and felt depression close in as it always did when she contemplated the political dislocations of the Federation that held her loyalty. The human race had expanded outward in three waves, punctuated by wars. First the Heart Worlds had received Federation-subsidized colonies, ethnically balanced to the nicety mandated by twenty-first-century notions. Then, in light of the expense of the wars with the Orions, expansion had shifted to the private sector under the auspices of megacorporations which farsightedly seized the "choke point" systems with multiple warp nexi, the gateways to the universe beyond. Then, after the Third Interstellar War had made Federation and Khanate allies and removed the Rigelian threat, the impetus for colonization had been provided by ethnic, national, cultural and other groups seeking to preserve identities they saw vanishing tracelessly into cosmopolitan sameness. The result was a vast number of newly settled worlds with small—albeit fast-growing—populations.

The Corporate World magnates were incapable of seeing the Federation as anything more than one of their own tame planetary governments writ large—an engine for maximizing profit. Avram despised the game they played, but she couldn't deny the skill with which they played it. They'd amended the Constitution into a parliamentary cabinet system, reducing the President—still elected by direct Federation-wide popular vote, ever more difficult even with modern communications and data processing—to a figurehead. Besides, for all their power, the Corporate Worlds alone could deliver too little of the popular vote to control the election of the presidency. On the other hand, the Prime Minister who held the real power had to command the support of a majority of the Legislative Assembly, which the Corporate Worlds effectively controlled by virtue of their own single-mindedness and dense individual populations, the Heart Worlds' disunity and philosophical confusion, and the Reapportionment of 2340. The reapportionment plan had been bitterly resisted by the Fringe Worlds for a very simple reason: Corporate World populations averaged close to 1.75 billion, while the average Fringe World was fortunate to have a total population of thirty to forty million. The Constitution guaranteed every Federated World at least one representative in the Legislative Assembly, but the Reapportionment had pushed the qualifying population base for each additional representative up to ten million. A particularly populous Fringe World thus might boast five or six representatives, while a planet like Galloway's World was entitled to over two *hundred*. Given the centralized cooperation of the Corporate Worlds' Liberal-Progressive Party, that kind of concentrated Legislative bloc gave politicos like Agamemnon Waldeck enormous power . . . and they knew it.

They see themselves as the lords of creation, Avram thought, looking across the room at Waldeck, conversing with a knot of his cronies. *The hell of it is, they're right.* Morosely, she raised her left arm—the prosthetic one, legacy of the Theban War (at times she found herself forgetting which was which)—and took another sip of Chablis.

She became aware of motion beside her and turned

with a smile of greeting. The senior Orion representative to the Grand Allied Joint Chiefs of Staff evidently didn't share her aversion to booze. Nor did most members of his species, which alcohol affected in much the same way it did homo sapiens. Indeed, the Khanate had become a major importer of bourbon. In that respect, Kthaara'zarthan was atypical; his glass held straight vodka, and Avram had observed him sprinkle a pinch of pepper into it, something she'd never seen on Old Terra west of Minsk or east of Vladivostok.

"Lord Talphon," she greeted him formally. "I hope you're enjoying yourself." Uncontrollably, a chuckle bubbled up. Kthaara raised one tufted ear, signifying inquiry. "Oh, I was just recalling the response a great playwright of ours, George Bernard Shaw, made to precisely that question, under similar circumstances: 'That, madam, is the *only* thing I am enjoying.'"

Kthaara emitted the deep purring cough of Orion laughter. Aside from rare individuals with *extremely* flexible vocal apparatus, the two species couldn't produce the sounds of each others' languages, but they could learn to understand them. That understanding represented a triumph over the gulf that yawned between completely alien evolutions. As always, Avram had to remind herself that the human characterization of Orions as "felinoid" was worse than simplistic. The resemblance was purely coincidental; a Terran lizard, or oak tree, was more closely related to Terran cats than was the urbane being who stood before her, unconsciously smoothing out his spectacular whiskers. His pelt was the midnight-black of the oldest Orion noble families, now acquiring a silvery frosting that indicated advancing age to those who knew what to look for. *Well,* she reflected, *none of us are getting any younger.* She'd met Kthaara late in the Theban War, when he'd been serving under Ivan Antonov in his quest for vengeance against his cousin's murderers. The Orions lacked humanity's antigerone treatments, and despite their century-and-a-half natural life spans . . .

"Ah, yes," Kthaara broke in on her thoughts. "I

remember Zhaaaw. A classic example of the way literary brilliance can coexist with political imbecility." He gave a teeth-hidden carnivore's grin. "And speaking of the latter, how do you manage to put up with her sort?" He indicated Wister. "Or perhaps the question I am really asking is *why* you put up with them."

"Well, Lord Talphon, some humans tend to believe that the further removed a political philosophy is from reality, the more morally pure it must be."

"Why?" Kthaara's perplexity was manifest. "I know you better, Sky Marshal"—the title he really used was "First Fang"—"than to think you yourself believe anything of the kind."

"You're quite right. But I'm trying to explain the biases of the civilization which initially gave form to the Federation. That civilization's dominant religion—which I myself don't subscribe to, by the way—was heavily influenced in its formative years by a philosophy called Gnosticism, which held that the world as reported by the senses was inherently corrupt and deceptive. Given that assumption, the only reliable source of knowledge was correct doctrine, and the attitude lingers on in secularized form. Demonstrated unworkability in the real world merely proves a belief system's 'higher truth' in the eyes of its true believers."

Kthaara's ears twitched in the slow movement that conveyed incredulity as he listened to her explanation. "I shall never understand your species, First Fang." He sighed.

"Just as well, Lord Talphon." Avram grinned. "We'll never understand ourselves either!"

They sipped their respective drinks for a few moments in a silence which wasn't destined to last, for the Ophiuchi and Gorm representatives to the Joint Chiefs approached.

"Ah, Ssssky Marssshallll," Admiral Thaarzhaan said, "I sssee the ssseniorrr memmmbers of our ressspective partnersssshipsss are deep in dissscussion. Sssurely a good ommmen forrr the smmmooth fffunctioning of the Grrrannnd Alliannnce, is it nottt?"

Fleet Speaker Noraku, the Gorm representative, was

the tallest person in the room (when he stood fully upright), but Thaarzhaan came in second by a safe margin. Terra's traditional Ophiuchi allies were no more "birds" than her old enemies and recent allies the Orions were "cats." The number of forms a viable tool-making animal could take, while numerous, were finite, however, and coincidences were bound to occur in a galaxy of four hundred billion suns . . . especially in the vanishingly rare cases where a species specialized in two different things— in the case of the Ophiuchi, flying and tool using.

Still, Avram sometimes caught herself being surprised that Thaarzhaan didn't exhibit a certain . . . well, *apprehension* in Kthaara's presence. She shouldn't have, of course. Orions might be felinoid carnivores and Ophiuchi might be among the galaxy's more pacific races— now—but Thaarzhaan and his people were hardly oversized canaries. They had evolved from raptors which, like the Orions themselves (or, for that matter, humans), had stood at the top of their planet's food chain, and the tall, down-covered, hollow-boned Ophiuchi retained the massive, crested heads and wickedly hooked beaks of their ancestors. *And*, she reflected, *the fact that they're the only known race that make even better fighter pilots than the Tabbies doesn't hurt*.

That predilection for fighter ops was also one of many reasons the Ophiuchi Association Defense Command was so prized by its Terran allies. The Association had been a Terran treaty partner ever since ISW–2, when they'd allied against the Khanate, and over the centuries the Ophiuchi had proven utterly reliable. Less militant even than humans, far less Orions, they were determined, gallant and pragmatic when military action became unavoidable. Perhaps *especially* pragmatic. The Association had exhausted its open warp points. Faced with an inescapable physical limit on interstellar expansion and physically uncomfortable with population densities humans or Tabbies found acceptable, the Ophiuchi had stabilized their planetary populations at relatively sparse levels which limited the size of the navy they could build or maintain, but their technology was among the galaxy's best and their units routinely exercised as integral parts of TFN formations. Any Terran admiral regarded their carrier strikegroups as pearls beyond price, yet the almost emaciated-looking Ophiuchi projected an undeniable appearance of frailty.

The Gorm, on the other hand, could hold their own physically with just about anyone, Avram thought as she watched Fleet Speaker Noraku advance with the almost prancing gait allowed by Terra's low gravity. His facial features were unsettlingly humanlike (aside from the triple eyelids and extremely broad nose), but there was no chance of confusing the Gorm with any Terran evolutionary branch. Descendants of hexapods, the grayish, armor-hided beings generally moved on their rearmost pair of limbs alone, as Noraku was doing now; but the middle limbs with their dual-purpose "handfeet" could be used as a second pair of legs if greater speed was desired. Or if the ceiling were lower. Heavy-grav life forms tended to be either very small or very large, and the Gorm inclined toward the latter. Noraku stood just under three meters in height when fully erect, and he was not a particularly tall member of his race.

That size was one reason the Gorm, unlike the Ophiuchi, made extremely *poor* fighter pilots. Squeezing that much body mass into a strikefighter was hard enough, and their hexapedal body form only made it worse. Gorm "chairs" were more like saddle-like couches, supporting their length to just above their mid-body shoulders, which left them poorly adapted to the g forces a fighter's "shallow" inertial sump couldn't fully damp. There *were* some Gorm fighter jocks, but by and large, they preferred to leave such duties to their Orion fellow-citizens.

She was relieved to note that the Fleet Speaker seemed to be breathing normally. Native to a 2.68 g planet whose partial pressures of the standard atmospheric gasses would have killed an unprotected human and wishing to avoid the nuisance of the full helmets his race normally used to equalize pressures, Noraku had volunteered to help field test an experimental implanted respirator during his extended stay on Nova Terra, where the Joint Chiefs were expected to establish themselves.

Avram was never quite sure how to characterize the Gorm's relationship to the Orions. The Gorm were a subject race . . . sort of. But though they were subjects of the Khan, the Empire of Gormus was an autonomous, self-governing entity within the Khanate, whose dominance by the Orion race and culture was undeniable and undenied. There were several reasons for that. One was the way their outnumbered navy had come within a hair of kicking the Tabbies' butts in the Gorm-Khanate War of 2227–2229, which had earned them tremendous respect from the Orions. Another was their heavy-grav origins, for the Gorm had spread throughout the Khanate's vast sphere to colonize planets whose atmospheres would have been lethal to the Tabbies, and people who could turn worlds like that into revenue-generating propositions were far too valuable *not* to be granted special status.

They were also as unlike the Tabbies philosophically as they were physically, yet they got along remarkably well with the prickly Whisker-Twisters. They might make poor fighter pilots, but they were just as pragmatic as the Ophiuchi and even more stubborn than Terrans. They were almost too logical to make good analysts (as far as Avram knew, no Gorm in recorded history had *ever* played a hunch), and their lack of any formal system of permanent naval or military ranks sometimes confused their imperial partners . . . or, for that matter, anyone else. Noraku's own title of "Fleet Speaker" was as close as any Gorm would ever come to "Chief of Staff," yet it was only a temporary, acting rank. For purposes of getting along with other navies they assigned their personnel equivalent seniorities, but the fact of the matter was that not even the Tabbies truly understood how the consensual Gorm picked their military officers. No doubt *minisorchi*, the mysterious Gormish telepathic ability, played a part, but whatever the process, a Gorm who commanded a super-dreadnought this week might have moved over to head the tactical section of a battlecruiser next week. Such instability would have made a shambles of any human chain of command, yet it worked for the Gorm. Precisely *how* it worked was something Avram had never understood, but no one could doubt its efficacy. The Gorm Space Navy's tacticians were among the best in the business, and the high tactical speed of their starships made them especially valuable to the KON by providing it with the fastest battle-line in the galaxy.

Nevertheless, Avram often wondered how they had managed—or been allowed—to retain their distinctive character, free from any foredoomed attempt to culturally assimilate them. And she was intellectually honest enough to doubt that humans could have managed matters so sensibly in either race's position.

She shook free of her bleak thoughts and addressed herself to Thaarzhaan's question. "Of course, Admiral, even as it is encouraging that associates of the Federation and the Khanate such as yourself and Fleet Speaker Noraku work together in such obvious harmony." All three aliens gave their races' equivalent of sonorous nods. Avram hated being put in the position of arbiter—it was inevitable, inasmuch as the Federation was the galaxy's acknowledged first power, but she was still uncomfortable with it. At least she wouldn't have to deal with it much longer. "Of course, my own connection with the Grand Allied Joint Chiefs of Staff will be indirect."

"Ah, yes," came Noraku's basso profundissimo. Unlike Thaarzhaan, whose beak gave his consonants an odd, drawn out sibilance, the fleet speaker's vocal apparatus could manage Standard English almost as well as a human's. Which, Avram reflected, was a vast relief, since it would obviate the need for yet another echelon of interpreters at their working meetings.

"We're still awaiting the arrival of our Human member," Noraku continued, and glanced at Kthaara. Everyone knew Lord Talphon's appointment to represent him on the new allied military command had been widely seen as an earnest of the Khan's commitment to fulfilling his treaty obligations. And it was an appointment that all but mandated who the Terran representative must be. . . .

Assuming, Avram reflected, *that he accepts the job.*

Aloud, she was all smooth assurance. "Even as we speak, Fleet Speaker, a liaison officer has been sent to brief him and arrange his journey to Nova Terra."

Skimmers were no longer strictly military and emergency vehicles, for steady improvements in the low-powered version of the reactionless space drive had brought them within reach of the private sector. But on a relatively young and not-too-affluent Fringe World like Novaya Rodina, it was only official business that brought one of the vehicles swooping soundlessly across the sky.

Captain Midori Kozlov gazed through the transparency at that sky, whose tinge of orange she doubted she could ever have become used to. She knew all about the harmless airborne microorganisms that caused it, but it still seemed wrong. Her eyes strayed downwards to the plains, where endless fields evidenced a degree of agricultural inefficiency that she, child of the resolutely rationalized culture of Epsilon Eridani, found even harder to get used to than the sky's color. But that was fine with the colonists. Their grandparents had come here to preserve a bit of Russia, or of what Russia had once been, or might have been, or *should* have been, and no vision of Russia, however idealized, could ever include much in the way of efficiency.

All of which ruminations, Kozlov realized, merely served the purpose of distracting her from thinking about her mission here. Her belly annoyed her by tightening, and she felt an odd envy of her pre-space ancestors. *They* hadn't had to worry about meeting their legends in the flesh, for in those days people generally hadn't lived long enough to *become* legends before they were decently dead.

The skimmer went feet-wet over the Ozero Kerensky—Novaya Rodina was a world-continent with landlocked seas, not a world-ocean with island-continents like most

Earth-like planets. The waters sped beneath the skimmer for what seemed a short time as Kozlov tried to organize her thoughts. Then a coastline backed by low, villa-dotted hills appeared ahead and swiftly grew. The skimmer homed unerringly on a particular *dacha* and settled onto a landing area outside a gate in a low outer wall.

Kozlov thanked the pilot and emerged into the summer warmth, smoothing nonexistent imperfections out of her black-and-silver uniform. She looked around at the landscape, which she'd heard was about as similar as you could get on this planet to a peninsula of Old Terra called the Crimea. The smell of roses suffused the air; the man she'd come to visit had occupied his retirement with developing a subspecies that would grow in these latitudes of Novaya Rodina. She stood before the gate and let its security sensors scan a face that reflected more ethnic strains than just the Japanese and Russian that her name suggested.

"Identify yourself, please," the gate finally requested.

She cleared her throat and spoke with the clarity and distinctness that were advisable when addressing robots. "Captain Midori Kozlov to see the Sky Marshal." Though the *dacha* owner's permanent rank was that of Admiral of the Fleet, he was entitled to be addressed for life by the title he'd held at the time of his retirement. "I believe I'm expected."

A moment passed in silence, just long enough for the entirely human bass rumble to be startling. "For God's sake, don't call me by that damned title! Come on in. My secretary will meet you."

The gate swung silently open. In the absence of further instructions, Kozlov followed a graveled walkway around the left side of the *dacha*. A man stood waiting—*not* the man she'd come to see. This man looked late-middle-aged (she'd have to see him move before deciding whether his apparent age was natural or the result of antigerone treatments) and contrived to wear his entirely civilian clothes like a uniform. Kozlov recalled what she'd been told of a very senior enlisted man who'd followed his admiral into retirement, and the sense of walking into a historical novel—which had been growing on her for some time—intensified.

"Good afternoon, Captain," the secretary said in faintly accented Standard English. "Please follow me."

They were rounding the rambling *dacha* when a man came stumping around a corner—a white-bearded man whose massive solidity made him seem shorter than he was. He wore an anachronistic-looking smock and carried gardening tools in his big, grimy hands . . . and Kozlov felt her body, acting for her without orders, come to the position of attention.

Ivan Nikolayevich Antonov glared at her from under shaggy white eyebrows. That glare gave her an instant to take in more of his appearance. He was certainly in good shape for a man of one hundred and forty-five standard Terran years. But, she recalled, he'd committed himself by contract at a relatively early age to emigrate after retirement, and thus obtained access to the antigerone treatments long before he would have gotten them anyway by special act of the Legislative Assembly as victor of the Theban War. The Federation had a long-standing policy of encouraging colonization by providing colonists with the anti-aging technology that was available on the inner worlds only to those who somehow obligated society to them. And in a sudden flash of insight she wondered if the willingness of Heart Worlds like her own native Odin to be passive accomplices in the Corporate Worlds' political sodomizing of the Fringe Worlds might have less to do with all the well-known rationalizations than with simple, elemental, unadmitted envy.

Antonov's bass broke in on her uncomfortable thoughts. "Thank you, Kostya," he addressed the secretary in what Kozlov suspected was his very best attempt at a mild tone. "Please excuse us."

"*Da*, Nikolayevich," the man responded. Memories of grandfather Kozlov, combined with her orientation briefings, enabled her to recognize the "affection" and "respectful affection" modes of address in that exchange.

The latter was old-fashioned, very uncommon, and *not* an automatic prerogative of superior military rank. But then Kostya was gone and the living legend turned his glare on her again.

"Well, I agreed to see you, so I suppose I have to be civil, even to a headquarters *zalyotnik*." She knew that the idiom—literally, "butterfly"—wasn't exactly a flattering one. "So come inside and have a drink, Captain Kozlova."

She recalled the conversation she'd had with Hannah Avram just before departure, and the Sky Marshal's advice on how she must respond at this point. So she took a deep breath and commanded her voice to steadiness and her eyes to a level gaze. "Excuse me, Sir, but that's 'Captain *Kozlov*.' My Russian ancestors—I'm only one-eighth Russian, by the way—emigrated to Epsilon Eridani in the early twenty-second century. It's been generations since the family used the Russian language or Russian naming conventions, including feminine forms of surnames."

For a moment, Antonov's brows drew together and almost met, and Kozlov was reminded of fissionable material reaching critical mass. But she wouldn't let herself flinch. Then, all of a sudden, the bearlike former Sky Marshal expelled a bark of laughter, rather like a volcano venting its force harmlessly. The chuckles that followed were like seismic aftershocks.

"Well, that's the first time since the Theban War, when Angelique Timoshenko . . ." Antonov shook his head and chuckled again. "I see you don't frighten easily, Captain. That's good. Maybe you're not a complete butterfly after all. Let's get that drink."

It was early in the day for her, but she quoted platitudes about Rome and the Romans to herself. "Very well, Sky Marshal."

"I thought I told you not to call me that!" Antonov's scowl was back as he led the way into the glass-walled loggia that faced the sea. "I'm Ivan Nikolayevich." He stomped over to the bar. "Vodka?"

She detested the stuff, but— "Certainly, Sk . . . Ivan Nikolayevich."

"Better," Antonov rumbled as he brought the drinks and waved her towards a leather-bound armchair. He then settled into the chair's mate and raised his glass. "*Za vashe zdorovye.*" He tossed back his vodka with a rapidity that made Kozlov's stomach lurch at the mere sight of it.

"So," he said after a moment, "you come from Hannah Avram. How is she?"

"She's well, Sir. Although, of course, the situation now—"

"Yes, yes; I've been following it." He reached for the vodka bottle and refilled his glass. He scowled at Kozlov's glass, at which she'd been sipping. "*Ty chto mumu yebyosh?*" he growled. Then he suddenly seemed to remember himself, and the broad muscular face wore an incongruous expression of embarrassment. "Er, it means 'Drink up,'" he explained. Then he intensified his scowl as though to make up for his lapse. "Well, this new war is Hannah's problem. She was fool enough to accept that damned 'Sky Marshal' title they dreamed up for me after the Theban War. By now she must have found out what it really means: having to deal day in and day out with those *tarakani* in the Legislative Assembly. Well, she can have it! I'm retired. You couldn't pay me enough to dive back into that cesspit! 'Reactivating my commission,' eh? Well, you can tell them I said to take my reactivated commission, complete with the stiffest shoulder boards they can find, and shove it up their—"

"Oh, I think you misunderstand about your reactivation, Sir." Antonov stopped and gave her the look of a man unused to being interrupted. She hurried on. "You're not being recalled as Sky Marshal. As you yourself pointed out, that's a special rank, invented for the military commander-in-chief of the Fleet. You'll be back on the active list under your permanent rank of Admiral of the Fleet, as the Terran member of the Grand Allied Joint Chiefs of Staff."

For a heartbeat of utter silence, Antonov seemed to expand slightly, as though building up to an explosion. "You mean," he said in a tone whose quietness wasn't even meant to be deceptive, "I'd be *subordinate* to Hannah Avram?"

"Well, Sir, that might be an oversimplification of the relationship. After all, you'd be functioning outside the normal TFN command structure, on the Joint Chiefs of which you . . ." Kozlov paused. She'd been about to say, "Of which you will undoubtedly be chairman," but she had a pretty good idea of how this man would react to anything that even smelled like flattery. So she fell back and regrouped. "On which you will be serving with Kthaara'zarthan, among others."

The air seemed to go out of Antonov. "What? You're telling me that Kthaara Kornazhovich is the Khan's representative on this Grand Allied boondoggle?"

"Yes, Ivan Nikolayevich. Your *vilkshatha* brother is on Old Terra even now." She smiled inwardly, for Hannah Avram had told her of the bastard Orion-Russian patronymic Antonov had bestowed on the Orion who'd admitted him to the oath of *vilkshatha* that made two warriors members of each others' families—the first non-Orion in history to be so admitted. It annoyed Kthaara almost as much as the even more bastardized diminutive "Kthaasha." Aloud, she continued in a neutral tone. "In fact, I spoke with Lord Talphon before my departure. He sends his best regards. Also, in connection with your reluctance to accept the reactivation of your commission, he asked me to memorize a certain Russian phrase and convey it to you." Her brow creased with puzzlement. "Oddly enough, it was the same one you translated a few minutes ago as 'Drink up.' But according to him, it means 'Why are you fucking a cow?'"

For an anxious moment, she thought Antonov was going to have a stroke. But then she saw that he was really struggling to contain a gargantuan guffaw. He finally released it as a kind of gasping cough. "Well, er. . . you see, that's the literal translation," he explained when he'd gotten his breath. "It can be used in any context to mean 'get a move on' or 'get the lead out.'" He shook his head and chuckled. "Old Kthaasha . . . ! Well, I suppose this wouldn't be the worst foolishness I've ever gone along with." He deployed his scowl again. "All right, maybe I'll do it . . . but on one condition. I want you on my staff."

Kozlov almost spilled her still half-full vodka glass. "Sir?"

"Yes. You've got ba— er, guts. I like that. I'll need an Intelligence officer—I'm not so old I can't read your insignia. And Winnie Trevayne is too damned senior now," he added, naming the Director of Naval Intelligence—who, Kozlov recalled, had been his staff spook in the Theban War. "Well?" he barked.

She tossed off the remainder of her vodka. It felt like an expanding sun going down her gullet. She hardly noticed until she tried to speak. "Ah. . . of course Sir, if. . . well, Sky Marshal Avram would have to approve my going on detached duty from her staff. . . ."

"Oh, Hannah will come around," Antonov rumbled. He reached out and refilled her glass. "And now, unless I'm mistaken, you have a classified briefing for me. All I know is the news any other old *muzhik* can get."

"Yes, Sir," she said, still wheezing a little and gazing with dismay at the refilled glass.

"Good." Antonov topped off his own glass and raised it. "*Nalivay!*"

CHAPTER TWELVE

What Price Redemption?

The heavy cruisers floated about the warp point. The time to resume the advance would come, yet the losses already suffered dictated that any new attack wait until more reinforcements reached this system. For now, the cruisers waited—forty-eight of them, screened by thousands of mines—rotating through their readiness cycles as they guarded against any threat.

Andrew Prescott swore with silent venom as another drive field appeared on his sensors. There were three now—light cruisers all, moving in a search pattern which could only mean they'd gotten a sniff of *Daikyu*. It couldn't have been a clean sensor hit, or they wouldn't still be searching, but they'd managed to pin down her rough location.

He made himself cross his legs and consider his options. *Daikyu* had the firepower to kill all three of those ships, but the Bugs probably *wanted* him to go after them, given how openly they were operating. For all he knew, a dozen cloaked battlecruisers lurked just below his sensor horizon, waiting for their beaters to drive him into their sights— or for his own fire to reveal his position. One of his ancestors, a submarine commander back on Old Terra, had once been hunted for three days by a Japanese antisubmarine flotilla, and now he knew exactly how that long-dead Prescott must have felt.

But great-great-whatever-granddad got his ass out of it, he reminded himself. *All I have to do is be as good as he was.*

"Come to zero-three-zero, one-zero-five," he said quietly.

"Aye, Sir. Coming to zero-three-zero, one-zero-five," Daryl Belliard replied, and Prescott watched his display alter as Commander Kasuga stepped back from the master plot.

"We're too close to the warp point, Sir," Kasuga said too softly for anyone else to hear. Prescott nodded in curt agreement, but he refused to be driven any further from it. He'd used no less than five courier drones to alert Sarasota, and it was as well he had. Only two had gotten past the OWP CAs, and, as he'd known they must, they'd alerted the enemy to *Daikyu's* presence.

The Bugs' most obvious response had been to race for the drones' origin point to mount an intensive search, but he'd programmed the CDs' nav systems for delayed activation before dropping them, and he'd been over a light-minute clear when their drives came on-line. That had given him some margin to play with, yet it was essential he stay close enough to the warp point to spot any move to reinforce it. If that happened, he'd be forced to send fresh drones to Admiral Murakuma. That would almost certainly bring the Bugs straight in on him, yet Task Force 59 *had* to know if the situation changed.

He didn't know if the Bugs realized his intentions. If they did and threw up a shell of scouts well outside the warp point then simply swept inward, they were bound to get lucky eventually. In the meantime, his course turned *Daikyu's* stern—the most vulnerable aspect for any cloaked vessel—away from all known searchers. It wasn't much, but—

"Pods transiting the warp point!" Jill Cesiaño's abrupt, half-shouted announcement smashed through the tension, and Prescott whirled to face her. "Dozens of them, Sir— hundreds!"

The plot flashed as clouds of diamond-bright icons

exploded from the warp point, and Prescott throttled a whoop of delight as he recognized the SBMHAWKs.

One moment all was serene; the next, a horde of tiny, robotic spacecraft burst into being. Some vanished in the star-bright boils of interpenetration, but only a small percentage, and the waiting cruisers had no idea what they were. They were too small for warships, yet they must represent some threat, and the ready-duty cruisers began tracking. But there were too many pods; they saturated the defenders' fire control, and less than ten more had been destroyed before the cruisers found out exactly what they were.

The Terran Navy had invented the Strategic Bombardment Missile, Homing All the Way Killer pod for the Theban War, but the latest-generation SBMHAWK was deadlier than anything dreamed of during that war. It carried more missiles, its guidance and tracking systems were more accurate, and each warhead was vastly more destructive. Now scores of them adjusted their attitudes as sensors located their targets. Passionless computers ignored the fire beginning to destroy their fellows while they considered targeting criteria and ordered their launch queues.

And then they fired.

The CAs' designers had never contemplated the volume of fire which screamed in upon them. Each ship was the target not of dozens but of scores of second-generation antimatter warheads. Point defense might stop the first three, or five, or seven, but the others got through, and no heavy cruiser could survive direct hits of such power.

One minute after launch, every cruiser had been wiped from the face of the universe, and even as they died, superdreadnoughts and battlecruisers made transit on the pods' heels.

No mine could be emplaced directly atop an open warp

point, and that gave TF 59's warships a small space in which to deploy. The surrounding mines confined them to the limited clear zone, but that was why the TFN had produced the Anti-Mine Ballistic Missile. The new, internally-launched AMBAMs were big, ugly mass hogs, eating up magazine space which might have been devoted to antiship missiles, but Vanessa Murakuma didn't care, and her green eyes flamed as her capital missile-armed ships began to launch.

The AMBAMs sped out—slow and clumsy by missile standards, but fast enough for their task—and deployed with ungainly precision, then belched spreading shoals of independently targeted antimatter warheads that coated her plot like diamond dust, invading the minefields. Then they exploded, and for just one instant, space flamed like a star's transplanted heart. The perfectly synchronized detonations merged into a torrent of heat and blast and radiation, and the mines caught in that riptide died. The sheer volume of space was too vast for many to suffer outright destruction, but their control systems were irradiated, blinded, burned into so much useless junk, and Murakuma smiled a shark's smile as her AMBAMs ripped a hole clean through the dense minefields and her starships charged into it.

The superdreadnoughts and battlecruisers were over two light-minutes from the warp point. By the time their light-speed sensors reported the enemy's arrival, every defending cruiser was dead and the totally unexpected AMBAMs had blasted a path through the mines, but their crews knew what to do, and the entire vast force wheeled ponderously towards the invaders.

"Their battle-line's moving, Skipper. They're heading straight for Admiral Murakuma."

"Understood." Prescott watched his plot, forcing his face to remain calm, but exultation boiled behind his eyes. *Daikyu* had done it! They'd actually *done* it, and TF 59 was in clean!

"Picking up three battlecruisers!" Cesiaño said abruptly, and Prescott's eyes narrowed. The bastards *had* been waiting for the CLs to drive him into their arms, but the fresh threat had changed their minds. They'd gone to full power, turning to race towards TF 59, and he bared his teeth.

"Bring us around behind them as they pass, Daryl," he said.

"Aye, aye, Sir!" Anticipation edged Belliard's acknowledgment, and Prescott turned that hungry smile on his tac officer.

"They're giving us a nice, clean shot into their blind spots, Jill. Let's make it count."

The trio of battlecruisers sped towards the invaders. Despite reckless power settings, they were far beyond any range at which the oncoming starships' sensors could pierce their ECM. They could never hope to stop so much firepower, but if they got into a suitable ambush position, they could make the enemy pay heavily to kill them.

They continued on their course, their original mission forgotten in the face of this greater threat, and never noticed the silent, stealthy killer sliding in behind them.

"Firing . . . *now!*"

Jill Cesiaño closed the master key, and TFNS *Daikyu* went instantly to rapid fire. Her five standard launchers lacked the range and massive striking power of a *Dunkerque*'s capital missile batteries, but they fired far more rapidly, and she was in her targets' blind spots, hidden beyond the distortion their own drive fields created. They'd never guessed she was back there, and even if they had, point defense couldn't engage missiles it couldn't even see.

Prescott's fire streaked in with deadly accuracy, and he slammed a fist down on his chair arm as the warheads struck. *Just like stamping on a spider,* he thought with cold, savage hatred.

✧   ✧   ✧

"Tracking reports antimatter detonations, Sir."

Murakuma blinked at Tian's announcement. Then her darting eyes found the explosions in her plot, and her brow furrowed for a moment before she nodded sharply.

"It's Prescott," she said. "It must be—whoever it is is shooting up at least three targets . . . and kicking the hell out of them, too," she added respectfully as one of the Bugs suddenly blew apart. "Warn the screen he's out there, Tian—we don't want any misunderstandings when he's done so well this far—then launch the RDs."

Commander Olivera settled firmly into his couch as TFNS *Dalmatian* prepared for action. His command fighter shuddered as the tractors deposited it in the big fleet carrier's number three catapult, and he flicked his eyes over his panel while he tried to ignore how dry his mouth was.

He didn't know how he and his crew had survived K–45 and First Justin, and a fatalistic part of him accepted that he was living on borrowed time. But at least he had a better chance of hurting the bastards this time. Strikegroup 47's survivors had been transferred to *Dalmatian* as the core of her rebuilt attack group, and he had twice as many fighters under his direct command.

"Launch status Alpha," a voice said in his earbug.

"Alpha confirmed," he replied, and punched a button. "Computers cycling."

"Green board," PriFly responded. "Tac feed on-line. Give 'em hell, Commander."

"We've got them on the drones, Sir," Commander Ling reported. "Battle Comp's IDs match *Daikyu*'s figures for their main force, but we're missing several picket CLs."

"Cloaked," Mackenna said, and Murakuma nodded. No doubt some of those hidden light cruisers would try to duplicate Prescott's ambush, but it was unlikely they could penetrate her drone shell. If they did, that was why capital ships had escorts, and she turned her attention to the main Bug force. There were ninety-two superdreadnoughts, eighteen battlecruisers, and over a hundred and twenty light cruisers over there—six times as many ships as she'd brought with her, and God only knew how vast the Bugs' tonnage advantage was. If *she'd* had that sort of edge, she would have been perfectly willing to let a faster, longer-ranged enemy stooge around the system however he chose. After all, if she moved directly to the warp point and sat on it, he'd be forced to engage on *her* terms, not his, when he tried to go home again.

But the Bugs weren't doing that, and she gave LeBlanc a fierce, satisfied smile. The intelligence officer returned it with interest, and her mind whirred with detached ferocity as she looked back at the display. They might not know how these monsters' strategic doctrine worked, but at least they seemed to follow predictable *tactical* patterns. They were charging after her at their best speed, precisely as they'd done in their earlier engagements. They'd still have a chance to intercept on her withdrawal, despite their lower speed, as long as they stayed between her and the warp point, but that was fine with her. In fact, it was exactly what she *wanted* them to do.

Still, it wouldn't do to give them too much time to consider other options. . . .

"Launch!"

Dalmatian's catapults spat thirty-six heavily armed fighters into space, and Anson Olivera grunted as a familiar lead boot kicked him in the stomach. He grunted again as his bucking fighter rammed through the CV's drive field, but his eyes clung to his display.

The Bug CLEs which had wreaked such havoc in Justin, glared crimson within the enemy's formation, but there weren't many, and he bared his teeth in satisfaction. He didn't know how the Bugs could be stupid enough not to have brought more forward—unless their own lack of fighter experience kept them from realizing how effective they were?—but he didn't much care.

"I make it only eighteen *Cataphracts*, Carl. Do you confirm?"

"Affirmative, Skip." Lieutenant Hathaway sounded

equally satisfied, and Olivera punched into the strikegroup command net.

"All right, people—listen up! We stay the hell away from the *Cataphracts* and leave the *Cleavers* and *Cannons* to Commander Yeung and Commander Abbot. *We* want the *Carbines*."

"Lucky us," someone muttered, and despite his tension, Olivera smiled. The intelligence pukes who'd coined the reporting names for the Bug cruisers had a sense of humor. The *Carbines* were missile ships, while the *Cleavers* carried pure primary armaments and the *Cannons* packed heavy plasma gun broadsides. Primaries were useless against targets as maneuverable as fighters, and plasma guns had too little reach to engage them beyond FRAM range, but if the Bugs had cooked up an equivalent of the TFN's AFHAWK anti-fighter missile, his people would take a pounding from the *Carbines*. Still, they hadn't shown anything like it yet. . . .

The first attack wave scorched towards its targets, and the cruisers obliged by forming a screen to intercept it short of their main force. Under normal circumstances, that was a smart move; given the plan Admiral Murakuma's staff had evolved, it was a recipe for disaster.

"Coming up on Initial Point," he murmured over the group net, and spared a glance for Jane Malachi. His pilot was completely focused on her controls, eyes glued to the red cursor of the initial point as she sped towards it and SG 47 held formation on her. Despite their losses and the short time they'd had to work up their replacements, the group was steady as a rock, and Olivera felt a fierce pride in his men and women.

"IP . . . *now!*" he snapped. The group whipped through a sharp turn, arrowing straight for its assigned targets while Bug tracking systems locked them up for the close-in defenses to slaughter, and he grinned savagely. *That's right,* he thought. *Keep your point defense configured to shoot us, you bastards. We've got a little surprise for you.*

"Launch in seventeen seconds," Hathaway said flatly. "Fifteen. Ten. Five. *Launch!*"

The command fighter shuddered as it launched its missiles from five light-seconds, and Olivera's eyes flamed with vengeful delight. The FM2 fighter missile had a lighter warhead than a FRAM, but it also had five times the range . . . and the Bugs had never seen it before. They'd expected the Terran squadrons to close to knife-range once more, and they'd configured their point defense to shoot at *fighters*, not missiles. His group's fire streaked in virtually unopposed, and if his warheads were lighter, enough of them would do the job just as well.

Leprous light boils spalled the Bug formation. Someone howled gleefully as the first light cruiser belched air and debris, and Olivera wanted to howl himself as four more followed. SG 47 sent seventy-two missiles into its targets, and most scored direct hits. None of the ships were dead, but all fell out of formation, crippled and lamed, and the Bugs' pursuit of Murakuma's starships left them behind. That was fifteen percent of their total *Carbines*; it looked as if the other groups had done even better against their targets; and TF 59 hadn't lost a single fighter!

"All right, people—back to the barn," Olivera said. "You did good; now let's come back and do better."

"The first strike nailed eighteen," Ling Tian reported. "The second wave's going in now."

Murakuma nodded. Light cruisers were trifling targets compared to superdreadnoughts, but she had no intention of throwing her fighters against an unshaken wall of fire again. First she would whittle away at their most vulnerable screening elements, taking the easy kills and blooding her green pilots. Every cruiser she killed would weaken the close-range defenses, and then . . .

"They're still pursuing, Sir," Mackenna said quietly, "but they're dividing their forces."

He used a light pencil to indicate the twenty-odd SDs and escorting light cruisers splitting off from the main Bug formation. It left the main force more than enough firepower to deal with TF 59—assuming it could catch the Terrans—but the second force was dropping back

to cover Murakuma's most probable vector for a return
to the warp point. Despite their slower speed, the two
formations could "herd" her further and further from her
only way back to Sarasota if they tried, but that was fine
with her.

"As long as they keep concentrating on us," she
murmured softly, and watched the first fighter strike race
back towards its carriers to rearm.

*Formations shifted as the infernally fast little attack
craft poured missiles into the light cruisers. The escorts
drew in closer to the capital ships, seeking to shelter under
the umbrella of the battle-line's fire, for however expendable
they were, there was no point in spending them for no
return. Yet the move was little help. The attack craft
couldn't throw dense enough salvos to overwhelm a
superdreadnought's point defense, but they didn't try to.
They ignored the bigger ships to continue pounding the
cruisers, and only the Cataphracts had sufficient missile
defenses to stave off their fire. At last the surviving cruisers
actually moved inside the battle-line's globe, concealing
themselves from the enemy, but only thirty-one of them
lived long enough to hide.*

"Well, we're done shooting fish in a barrel." Mackenna
grimaced as the last light cruiser vanished into the midst
of the Bug formation, and Murakuma nodded.

"Distance from the warp point?"

"Just over twelve light-minutes for Bug Two," Ling Tian
replied. "Bug One is at fifteen light-minutes; we're at
seventeen."

Murakuma nodded again and glanced into the com
screen linking her to TFNS *Pit Viper*. Demosthenes
Waldeck looked back at her, and she raised one hand.

"Execute Able Three," she said.

TF 59 slowed, letting the range close, and fresh fighter
strikes went in as the *Matterhorn* superdreadnoughts and
Dunkerque battlecruisers began to fire. The *Dunkerques*

carried almost pure SBM loads, keeping their lighter shields and weaker point defense beyond the range of any return fire, but the *Matterhorns* carried the smaller, shorter-ranged capital missiles, for they had the strength to stand up to counterfire and they could cram far more CMs into their magazines. The fireballs of heavier warheads began to blaze, this time concentrating on the Bugs' similarly armed *Archers*, but the starships' salvos were carefully timed to coincide with the fighter strikes. The incoming missiles forced the Bugs to split their point defense between them and the fighters, weakening the antifighter barrage as the Terran squadrons streaked in to point-blank range at last.

Despite the covering fire, they took losses this time. Almost five percent of the attacking fighters were killed short of launch, but those who made it rippled salvos of FRAMs, and powerful warheads pounded the enemy brutally. More starships fell out of formation, and they were no longer light cruisers. The Bug battle-line trailed air-bleeding wrecks in its wake, and Murakuma nodded to Commander Ling.

"Alert Mondesi and launch the drones."

"Sir! Sir!"

Raphael Mondesi swore and snatched for a towel as the young Peaceforce lieutenant charged into the head, waving a message board in one hand, and skidded to a halt.

"What?" Mondesi asked sharply, killing the water with one irritated hand while the other tried awkwardly to whip the towel about his waist. He was not amused, but Lieutenant Jeffers seemed unaware of that as she thrust the message board at him.

"It's Redemption, Sir! *They're mounting Redemption!*"

Mondesi forgot all about showers and jerked the board from her hand. He darted a lightning glance over the display, then threw the board back to her, knotted the towel in place, and ran barefoot for his command center.

❖   ❖   ❖

"Drone coming through, Sir."

Commodore Reichman looked up quickly, and the light cruiser *Ashigara's* com officer pressed her earbug more firmly against her ear as she listened to the downloaded message.

"Execute Redemption!" she announced, and Reichman nodded to his ops officer.

"You heard the admiral, Al."

"Yes, *Sir!*" Commander Alvin Lopez grinned as hugely as if he were headed for one of his beloved jai alai games rather than an excellent chance of getting himself killed and began transmitting orders to Task Group 59.3's thirteen *Dull Knife* transports and the three CVLs and nine light cruisers of their escort.

Frieda Jaëger jerked as a hand pounded her shoulder. She blinked sleep-crusted eyes and reached instinctively for her com console as adrenaline flooded her exhausted body, but she wasn't in her Asp. She was in her bedroll under it, and she reached up to catch Sergeant Major McNeil's wrist before the noncom could pound her again.

"What the *hell*—" she began sharply, but McNeil broke in on her.

"Redemption, Sir! We just got the alert—Admiral Murakuma's launching Redemption!"

Jaëger rolled out from under the Asp, irritation forgotten. She stared at McNeil for a fleeting moment, then bounded to her feet.

"ETA?" she snapped.

"Two hours," the sergeant replied, and Jaëger winced. She'd known warning would be short, but the original plan hadn't counted on having a Bug division less than forty klicks from the Edward Mountain evacuation site. The refugees immediately behind her battered battalion were well concealed, but she had to start them moving within ninety minutes if they were going to be on-site when the shuttles arrived. Yet the Bugs were almost certain to spot them the instant she put them in motion. Worse, their movement towards the LZ would point the Bugs at *that*, as well.

"Any orders from HQ?"

"Your discretion, Sir," McNeil said grimly, and Jaëger mouthed a silent curse. She couldn't fault HQ's decision—she *was* the senior officer on the spot—but the crushing responsibility for five thousand civilian lives slammed down on her like a boulder.

She stared into the moonlit night and rubbed her hands up and down her thighs as she tried to balance imperatives and possibilities. She *had* to get those people moving, but what was left of her battalion could only hold the Bugs off so long. . . .

"Seventy minutes," she said abruptly, and turned to face McNeil. "Find Captain El-Hamna. Have him pass the order to stand to. As soon as the civilians start moving, all hell is going to come down on us. We'll go with Stonewall."

"Aye, Sir!" McNeil dashed off into the darkness, and Jaëger bent to pick up her uniform jacket, wishing she hadn't given up her own zoot to help equip her small mobile reserve.

She had a feeling she was going to need it.

Commodore Reichman's task group scorched through the warp point at its best speed. The big, vulnerable transports slowed it, but the main Bug units were too far away to intercept, and he stared fixedly at his plot, hoping they stayed that way. The *Dull Knifes* were big enough to read as battleships to any hostile sensors, and if the Bugs thought they really *were* battleships, they might well wheel to go after them.

But it didn't look like they were going to. His CVLs launched recon fighters to sweep ahead while recon drones covered the flanks, and the battle between Murakuma's main body and its pursuers redoubled in intensity as she pounded them harder than ever. It was her job to draw the enemy onto her own force, luring him away from the transports, and she was paying a price to do it. Scanner

resolution was poor at this range, but her superdreadnoughts were taking a beating, and now her handful of
shorter-ranged battleships were closing to support them.

*The sudden appearance of still more invaders surprised
the Fleet. The new force was less numerous than the first,
but it contained twice as many battleships. Added to the
force already engaged, it might have had a decisive effect,
yet it was running away from the engagement. The Fleet's
doctrine offered no explanation for its purpose, but if
those ships wished to abandon their consorts to destruction,
that was acceptable.*

"Got something, Skip. Looks like a cloaked *Barfly*."

Commander Alice Depogue, CO of the light carrier
Amir, glanced at her plot and nodded.

"Got it, Frank," she told her exec, and studied the data
relayed from the recon fighter. It certainly looked like
one of the cloak-capable picket cruisers, and it seemed
to be maneuvering to ambush TG 59.3. *Gutsy move,* she
conceded silently, *but stupid.* The TFN had amassed
enough data to know the *Barflies* were easy meat for
fighter strikes, and she bared her teeth.

"Have the recon birds stay clear. If they don't know
we've seen them, keep it that way."

"Aye, Skip." *Amir*'s com officer nodded, and Depogue
looked at her fighter ops officer.

"Pass the word to Commander Sinkman, Etienne. Full
group launch—I want that bastard killed in a single pass."

Reichman watched *Amir*'s strikegroup blow the lone
cruiser to vapor and nodded in approval as the victorious
squadrons wheeled quickly back to rearm while the recon
fighters continued their search for prey. But there was
tension under his satisfaction. The smaller of the two Bug
forces was dropping back. It was still closer to Murakuma
than to him, but it might not *stay* that way, and he had
only fifty-four fighters of his own. If the bastards came
in on him . . .

He twitched his shoulders. There was nothing he could do but wait and see, and he was already closing on the planet. The Bugs had placed a dozen missile platforms around it—not to engage attacking starships, but to support their ground troops with orbital strikes—and he had to kill them before they spotted the evacuation sites, whatever the risk to TG 59.3.

"Instruct *Akagi* to launch her strike," he said harshly, and a full third of his limited fighter strength went scorching off towards the distant sapphire on his visual display.

"Holy shi—!"

The expletive in Major Jaëger's earbug chopped off with sickening suddenness as whoever had started to utter it died. Her camouflaged Asp sat in the saddle of a steep ridge, and the night below her was hideous with explosions and small arms fire. The Bugs were coming in on her even harder than she'd feared, and her support squads were running short of ammo. Here and there Bug thrusts had gotten into her positions, and deadly firefights raged as her people fought frantically to beat them back again.

She wrenched her eyes to the display, and her fists clenched on her console. Her main line was buckled, but it was holding. Barely, perhaps, and at hideous cost, but holding. Yet while it held, a Bug pincer was sweeping out around her flank. No doubt it meant to curl into her rear and smash her, but one of the refugee columns lay squarely in its path. She bit her lip so hard she tasted blood as she thought of the five hundred terrified men, women and children struggling through the darkness, and her voice was harsh.

"McNeil!"

"Aye, Sir!"

"Tell Lieutenant Harpe—"

"Harpe's dead, Skipper," the zooted sergeant interrupted, and Jaëger cursed.

"All right. Get over there and take command. There's a Bug thrust coming around Captain Thaler's flank. Hit them at the river and hold their asses."

"Aye, aye, Sir!"

McNeil vanished in a whine of exoskeletal "muscles," and Jaëger stared after her for a moment. They both knew what the sergeant was going into, and she suddenly wished she'd taken time to say good-bye.

"They're pounding Jaëger hardest," Simon Merman said, "but they're going after the Lake Anderson site almost as hard."

"I know." Mondesi stared at the display, fingers drumming on the edge of his console, then nodded grimly. "Send Major Ashman to support Lake Anderson," he said harshly.

"But Jaëger—" Merman began, but Mondesi cut him off.

"Jaëger's gone, Simon." Loss and helpless rage filled his grating voice. "She's too weak, and we can't get there in time. If we try to reinforce both sites, we'll only lose them both."

"But we're talking about five *thousand* civilians!" Merman protested in raw anguish, and Mondesi closed his eyes.

"I know," he repeated, "but we can't reinforce failure. If we try, we lose *ten* thousand." He stared into the plot, unwilling to meet Merman's eyes. The blur of combat chatter muttered from the com section behind him, and the Peaceforcer barely heard his final words. "Jaëger's on her own, God help her," Brigadier Raphael Mondesi said softly.

The second enemy force launched attack craft at the planet, blotting away the fire support stations, and the smaller of the defending forces reacted at last. It curved away from the main engagement, swinging back towards the planet as the threat to its own ground forces finally registered. If those battleships wanted to, they could sterilize the planet with a saturation bombardment, paying the trifling price of their own noncombatants to wipe out every warrior on its surface. That could not be permitted, but the enemy was foolishly reluctant to sacrifice his starships in combat. A threat in sufficient strength might deflect him from his mission, and the massive superdreadnoughts forged ahead at their best speed to present that threat.

"They're coming in on us, Sir."

Reichman looked at Tactical's display. Twenty-three SDs and the tattered remnants of forty CLs bore down on his rear, and he studied the time estimates closely. The Bugs were slower than he. He could break off and evade them with ease, but if he continued with his mission, they'd be able to range on him within forty-five minutes of the time he entered orbit. He bit his lip for a moment, then punched a com stud.

"General Servais?"

"Yes, Commodore?"

"The enemy is diverting a heavy force after us. That means our window just got a lot narrower, but I think we've swept the area between us and the planet clear of Bug starships, and the little we're getting from planet-side sounds like Mount Edward and Lake Anderson are under heavy pressure. I recommend you launch your shuttles now, Sir."

"Agreed." The confirmation came back immediately, and the assault shuttles of four fresh battalions of Terran Marine Raiders, every man and woman of them a volunteer, spat from the transports *Hasdrubal, Insula* and *Viracocha*. They raced for the planet, stark naked if the fighters had missed a single Bug cruiser, and Reichman watched them go, then looked at his ops officer.

"Turn the escorts around," he said quietly. "We've got to buy the transports some time."

"We can't hold 'em, Skipper!" Helen McNeil's voice burned in Jaëger's earbug, and the major's face was beaten iron as the thunder of combat came to her over the link. Her main position had been breached frontally in two places, and the force battering McNeil's hopelessly outnumbered Raiders was less than five klicks from the refugee column.

"We're down to fifteen zoots," McNeil continued, "and—"

"Buy me some more time, Helen!" Jaëger heard the desperation in her own voice and hated herself for asking the impossible.

"We're trying, Skip, but—"

McNeil's link went dead, and Jaëger's heart twisted in anguish. It was all coming apart. Her entire position couldn't hold fifteen more minutes. Even now, less than half her people could possibly disengage, and if she didn't start pulling back now—

"Edward Mountain, Edward Mountain. This is General Servais. I have two Raider battalions twenty minutes out. Send drop coordinates. Edward Mountain, Edward Mountain, I say again. Two battalions with shuttle air support twenty minutes out. Send coordinates now."

Jaëger twitched as the totally unexpected voice rattled her earbug. For just an instant, hope flared, but then it died. Her people couldn't hold twenty more minutes if God Himself ordered it. She could fall back, but with Bugs already in among her positions, the chances of disengaging were minute. And even if she pulled it off, she would have abandoned five hundred civilians, and she couldn't do that. She simply couldn't. Even if she could, it was unlikely she could stand again anywhere short of the evacuation site itself, and air support or no, if Servais' raiders had to drop into a landing zone under direct enemy fire—

Her nostrils flared, and she closed her eyes. Then she opened them once more, and they were very still as she punched the transmit button.

"This is Edward Mountain. Your LZ is the evacuation site, General."

"We can reinfor—" Servais began, but she shook her head, almost as if he could see her.

"I say again, your landing zone is the evac site," she said flatly, and switched frequencies.

"Lieutenant Haldane."

"Aye, Sir!"

Weapons thundered in the valley below as the commander of her last four surviving assault skimmers replied. Jaëger watched the holocaust grinding up the slope towards her and knew Haldane expected her to send him into it in a desperate bid to hold the enemy while she disengaged. But that wasn't what she intended. A fighting withdrawal wouldn't work, yet there was still one way she might manage to divert the Bugs from the evac site.

"We've lost our right flank," she said almost conversationally, "and the Bugs are closing on Reitner's refugee column at Alpha-Six. Get over there. Hit the bastards with everything you've got and open a hole for him, then cover him to the evac site. Understood?"

There was a moment of silence, and then Haldane cleared his throat.

"Understood, Sir, but . . . what about the battalion?"

"Just get Reitner's people out, Jeff," Jaëger said softly. She tapped one last frequency change into her console, patching into the all-channels com net of her dying battalion, and stood. She shimmied into the access trunk of the Asp's turret, settled herself in the fighting chair, and placed her hands on the grips of the single multi-barreled autocannon which was the lightly armored vehicle's sole offensive weapon, then keyed her boom mike.

"All units, this is Jaëger," she said. "Fresh forces are dropping on the LZ in—" she glanced at her chrono "—seventeen minutes. It's up to us to make sure there's an LZ for them to land on, and that means sucking the enemy away from it. Attack. I repeat, attack. Break into the bastards. Make them worry about *us*, not advancing . . . and God bless."

She closed down the com and looked at the small screen that held her driver's face.

"Let's go, Sandy," she said quietly, and the Asp lurched downslope into the inferno.

CHAPTER THIRTEEN

"You *know* I can't tell him that!"

Alpha Centauri A was at midmorning height, and its yellow light streamed at a forty-five degree angle through the conference room's tall windows. Alpha Centauri B, the orange companion star, was too far away in its highly eccentric orbit to complicate the day-night dichotomy. And the late-M type third component was, as always, invisible without the aid of powerful telescopes. Midori Kozlov recalled that component C—distinctly second-rate even as red dwarfs went—had been discovered in the twentieth century and dubbed "Proxima Centauri" because it had possessed the one lonely distinction of being Old Terra's closest stellar neighbor. (Except, of course, for Sol, which didn't count.) Nobody had thought of it for generations, least of all the inhabitants of Nova Terra and Eden, the twin planets that occupied Alpha Centauri A's second orbit and constituted humanity's oldest, richest and most populous extrasolar colony.

Gazing around at the austere, understated elegance of the chamber, Kozlov thought it had been good of Nova Terra's planetary government to provide these facilities, for there was certainly nothing so nice in the TFN reservation. The footage from Erebor had shocked the mush-minds who governed this planet into an awareness of which universe they were living in. They'd doubtless recover from their temporary attack of common sense, but for the present they were cooperating with the military in exemplary fashion. And right now, like everyone else, they were euphoric over the news of Operation Redemption. Murakuma had lost a battleship, three battlecruisers and six lighter units, but she'd inflicted the customary disproportionate losses and snatched 48,000 civilians from the teeth, or whatever, of the Bugs.

Like all the staffers, Kozlov sat with her back to the chamber's walls, well back from the oval table—well back, but readily available at call. They didn't have long to wait before the Grand Allied Joint Chiefs of Staff began to file in and take their places at the table, where only they might sit. Ivan Antonov stationed himself before the chair directly in front of her, while his three colleagues moved to their specially designed chair equivalents. Last to enter was Hannah Avram, who moved to a chair midway along one side of the table.

"Please be seated, ladies and gentlemen," the Sky Marshal said. The form of address was automatic, even though all four of the Joint Chiefs were males of their respective species. And, Kozlov reflected, at least it was a nice gesture from the standpoint of the females among the spear-carriers lining the walls. Avram waited a couple of heartbeats after everyone was settled before resuming.

"On behalf of the Terran Federation Navy, I formally declare this meeting convened. I am gratified that the work of establishing Allied Grand Fleet Headquarters is going smoothly, and that everyone concerned came so readily to agreement that the Alpha Centauri System was the logical location for it—"

"Especially considering the alternative," a mischievous voice whispered into Kozlov's left ear. She turned a slantwise glare on the speaker, but Ensign Kevin Sanders' blue eyes lost none of their twinkle and his grin made his sharp features look even more foxlike than usual. The fresh-caught snotty must have attracted somebody's attention at the Academy, for he'd gone directly to work—albeit in a very junior capacity—for the Sky Marshal's staff spook. And although he was a little too irrepressible for

Kozlov's tastes, she'd taken him along to Antonov's staff. These days, with so much to deduce about the Bugs from so little data, a capacity for original thought covered a multitude of sins.

And, she reminded herself, he was right. It would have been out of the question to headquarter Allied Grand Fleet in the Solar System, where it would have looked entirely too much like a Federation agency for alien sensibilities. Alpha Centauri might be only one warp transit from Sol (and an insignificant four-and-a-third light-years in realspace, though nobody but astronomers thought in those terms anymore), but that one warp transit placed it at a symbolically important remove from the Federation government's seat on Old Terra.

Still, the choice made military as well as political sense. In addition to being an economic powerhouse, Alpha Centauri possessed no less than eight warp points—one of which connected with Sol's solitary one. This system had been humanity's gateway to the galaxy, and from the security standpoint its location deep in the heart of the Federation was unbeatable. Where could the Grand Alliance's top brass be any safer than here?

She dragged her attention back to Hannah Avram's words, for the Sky Marshal had begun getting down to practicalities. "As you're all aware, my status as convening officer of this initial meeting is simply a formality, consequent upon my position as commanding officer of the 'host navy.' Rest assured that the Terran Federation Navy intends to function as a coequal member of the Grand Alliance, under the overall operational direction of the Joint Chiefs of Staff—that is, of this body. As soon as you have organized yourselves, I will revert to my regular duties as commander of a component navy of the Allied Grand Fleet. I therefore open the floor to nominations for chairman of the Grand Allied Joint Chiefs of Staff."

Less than a human heartbeat passed before Fleet Speaker Noraku rose to his full height. Kozlov was prepared to entertain the possibility that he'd never considered the psychological advantage that height conferred. His ability to form the sounds of Standard English unaided also helped.

"I submit," came the almost subliminal bass, "that there is only one possible choice: the only living being who has exercised fleet command in a large-scale war, and led his star nation's forces to total victory in that war. The being whose campaigns have set the standard for our profession since before many in this room were born. The being, moreover, who represents the star nation actually under attack. I refer, of course, to Admiral of the Fleet Ivan Antonov, TFN. I nominate him for chairman of the Grand Allied Joint Chiefs of Staff."

An affirmative murmur ran around the room, and Kozlov commanded herself not to grin as matters took their prearranged course, played out for the benefit of the news media. Kthaara, as Antonov's *vilkshatha* brother, could hardly nominate him. Neither could Thaarzhaan; as representative of a Federation ally which was clearly a junior partner but was resolved to maintain its independence, he was unsuitable from all standpoints. That left Noraku.

Kthaara rose as the Gorm resumed his seat. "I second the nomination." All of the Joint Chiefs understood the Tongue of Tongues, and interpreters translated for those staffers who didn't—or would have done so if any translation had been necessary.

"The nomination is made and seconded," Hannah Avram spoke formally. "The floor is open for discussion."

Thaarzhaan unfolded himself from the uncomfortable-looking framework "chair" his race favored. "Sssssky Marshhhhhhal, I move thattttt the ssssselection be by accccccclamation."

"The motion is made and seconded," Avram said after Noraku's rumbled second had ceased reverberating. Then she smiled and seemed to relax from her formality. "There appears to be no need for further discussion. Admiral Antonov, I'll ask you to assume the chair."

❖   ❖   ❖

"*Davai glaz nalyom!* Let's put one in the eye!" Antonov sighed deeply as he settled into his armchair and loosened the collar of his uniform.

Hannah Avram grinned crookedly at him. "Not bad enough you should steal my staff intelligence officer, Ivan Nikolayevich; you also have to be a bad influence on me, as usual. Oh, well. *Le chaim!*" She raised her vodka glass. Then her mood darkened even before it reached her lips. "A good toast these days, no? Life—our kind of life, anyway—seems to be getting scarcer."

"Ah, don't be so gloomy Hannah—you're not even Russian." He tossed off his vodka. "*Ty chto mumu yebyosh?*"

She drank a moderate sip and grinned again. "I may not be Russian, you old reprobate, but my ancestors lived there a long time ago . . . and I know a few phrases of the language, including that one."

"Oh." Antonov took on a philosophical look. "Amazing the number of people I meet whose ancestors *left* Russia at some time or other. I wonder why that is?"

"Think about it," she suggested archly.

They both chuckled, then sat in companionable silence for a time. Alpha Centauri B was visible tonight, a superlatively bright orange star, and it shone through the broad window of Antonov's office, banishing most other stars even though the night was clear and moonless. Of course, *all* nights of this hemisphere of Nova Terra were moonless; the giant "moon" Eden hung perpetually over the antipodes of this planet, whose rotation it had long ago halted. The inhabitants of *that* hemisphere's island chains—mountaintops, really, that were all the ocean's fixed tidal bulge had left above water—had the permanent spectacle of an Earth-like planet filling a good portion of their sky. They could never make sense of the expression "once in a blue moon."

No question about it, Nova Terra was a lovely place. If it had a fault, it was the inconvenient day-night cycle as the twin planets revolved around their common center of mass in slightly over sixty-one standard hours. Avram's stay here hadn't lasted long enough for her to adjust to it. But at least, she thought, recalling a five-and-a-half-centuries-old quotation about "an equality of dissatisfaction," it was an adjustment that all four of the Alliance's member-races, coming from worlds with more typical diurnal periods, had to make.

Antonov finally broke the silence. "So, Hannah. How is your charming family?"

"Fine—I think." Avram's tone carried a carefully metered edge of genuine bitterness. "Dick is back out at Galloway's Star, up to his hip pockets in that slime pit. God knows I'd like to see more of him, but we *need* someone riding herd on those . . . those—"

Words failed her, and she bit her lip for a moment. Her husband had attained senior flag rank himself, but in BuShips, not one of the combat arms. Unlike her, he'd been able to retire with a clear conscience almost twenty years ago and become a highly sought after defense consultant. His relationship to Sky Marshal Avram would have barred him from any lobbying employment, but it was the military itself, not the contractors, who valued his expertise, and that was exactly why he'd been sent to Galloway's Star. The Corporate World industrialists of Galloway's World had a nasty reputation for intentional cost overruns and generally inventive bookkeeping, and it was Dick's job to keep them honest.

A task, she reflected, *not unlike that of a gentleman named Hercules and a certain stable. Or Sisyphus, perhaps.* She gave herself a mental shake.

"At any rate, he's fine, even if we're both feeling sorry for ourselves over the separation, and at least most of the kids had the sense to avoid service careers. Josh is the only one with any real aptitude for it, and he just made captain." She grinned. "At the risk of sounding prejudiced, I think the young sprout may actually be ready for it—not that I intend to tell *him* that!"

"Hannah, Hannah!" Antonov gave another seismic chuckle. "*You've* certainly changed from the young commodore—*arguably* a commodore, at least—who came to report to me after Second Fleet relieved Danzig."

Six decades rolled away, and Avram recalled every step she'd taken through the superdreadnought's passages as she'd marched to meet Ivan the Terrible and face the consequences of her own actions. It had not been a cheerful exercise for an officer who'd used Federation Marines to seize dictatorial control of an entire star system on the basis of a more than questionable legal opinion. But she'd survived the meeting, and her memory continued marching, through the subsequent battles that had cost part of her body and all that remained of her youth to the long years of peacetime service and the political infighting that was so much more exhausting than combat ops. She gave her head a shake, stirring hair that was now iron-gray. "Yes, I've changed, all right: less young— and less slender! Antigerone treatments aren't magic, you know."

"No, no, it's more than that. You've grown up in a lot of ways, Hannah. You've become . . . not 'cynical' or 'world-weary,' nobody will ever be able to call you that. Your ideals, the things that make up your essence as a person, are unchanged. But you've seen more of the ways life can frustrate those ideals, and still not lost them. Those who *do* lose them become less than they were. You've become more."

For a moment, Avram felt something akin to embarrassment, for there couldn't be many to whom Antonov spoke in this way. Then, in the wake of a score of generations of ancestors, she took refuge in levity. "Hey, dealing with politicians this many years would do it to anybody! You of all people ought to know that."

"Ha! Did I ever tell you how glad I was when you became Sky Marshal? I had to laugh at the thought of those *svolochy* wetting their pants every time they looked at you and remembered how you dealt with your *local* politicians in the Danzig system."

"Oh, come on, Ivan Nikolayevich! The circumstances there were extraordinary. Unique, even. And I had legal precedents for my actions."

"*Da, da.* I know. Your legal officer must have been a *pyzdobol*—a real piss-artist. And your little coup was upheld in the end. Still . . ." He chuckled again, with pure pleasure. "Nothing improves a politician's character like fear."

"You're incorrigible!"

"So Howard Anderson used to tell me," Antonov acknowledged. "For some reason, he felt I lacked sufficient respect for properly constituted civilian authority."

Avram emitted a fairly ladylike snort. "Where do you suppose he ever got *that* idea?" Abruptly, her mood darkened again. "Speaking of politicians, I've been unable to prevent some uniformed ones from accompanying Admiral Murakuma's reinforcements."

Antonov scowled. "That's always the way, isn't it? There are always a certain number of *zalyotniki* who make careers out of being somebody's eyes and ears in the Fleet." Then his scowl smoothed itself out into a look of something resembling fatalism. "Well, at least we *are* getting reinforcements to Sarasota finally."

"Personally," Avram said bleakly, "I'm even more pleased we've gotten all those piled-up refugees *out* of Sarasota. They're far enough back now they may actually be safe, and we're starting to make progress on evacuating Sarasota itself."

"*Da.* And the first Ophiuchi elements should be arriving there soon, with the Orions and Gorm not far behind. By the time we're ready to upgrade Murakuma's task force to a full fleet, it won't just be an organizational fiction."

"And that leads to another political problem," Avram said grimly. "Certain highly placed people think this new Fifth Fleet ought to be commanded by an officer of 'appropriate seniority' rather than a mere rear admiral. They're bringing pressure on me to replace Murakuma."

"What?" Antonov shook his head ponderously. "*Eto polneyshaya yerunda.* That's rubbish. They must know what Murakuma's accomplished. She's destroyed over ninety superdreadnoughts outright, and intelligence estimates she's sent another fifty-odd to the repair yards.

God alone knows the losses she's inflicted in the lighter ship classes. And, more importantly, it's because of her we've gotten the time to bring her forces up to fleet level. She won that time for us with her raid into Justin. Aside from the civilians she got out, she must have rocked the Bugs back on whatever they use in place of heels, and made a shambles of their timetable for the next offensive against Sarasota." He shook his head again, this time with a chuckle. "I remember her—not too well, I'm sorry to say—from her days on the faculty at the War College. She must be quite a lady, Hannah. Maybe I've been a little too hasty with some of the things I've said about the younger generation of officers."

"Unfortunately, some people don't see it that way. Like Agamemnon Waldeck." Avram paused, slightly apprehensive. So far, Antonov had taken all this very quietly—suspiciously so, in fact. She waited for him to erupt with full-throated fury at the mention of the Naval Oversight Committee's chairman. But no volcanic activity came, and she pressed on. "He thinks the Justin raid was reckless. For that reason, as well as her lack of seniority, he wants her replaced. He even has a replacement in mind: Vice Admiral Mukerji." She hurried on, hoping to forestall a reaction she expected would cause permanent hearing loss. "Yes, yes, I *know* about Mukerji. He's like . . . well, I can't even come up with a comparison. But one of my more history-minded staffers mentioned somebody named Marshal Bazain. . . ."

"That's actually an insult to Bazain," Antonov remarked with a mildness far more startling than the expected eardrum-bruising roar would have been. "Other names occur to me. General Elphinstone, for one."

Avram was beginning to be alarmed. It was all very well to joke about the limitations of the antigerone treatments. But was the Grim Reaper finally catching up with Antonov? Could he be—God forbid—*mellowing?*

"Well," she challenged, "what do you suggest I do? Given Waldeck's position, I can hardly ignore him."

"No, you can't. But it's a situation you'll have to handle,

Hannah. I and my colleagues are responsible for overall strategic direction of the war, but TFN personnel assignments are a matter for the TFN. And, if you really want my advice, that's what you should tell Assemblyman Waldeck: that this is a military decision, best handled within the legally appointed chain of command." Avram's concern mounted, but Antonov continued in the same mild tones. "Of course, there are a few other steps you can take. First, you can light a fire under the board and get Murakuma promoted to vice admiral—it should have been done already, and it will dispose of the argument that she lacks seniority. Second, you can tell Legislative Assemblyman Waldeck that, while the Grand Allied Joint Chiefs of Staff have no intention of meddling in a purely internal TFN matter, you've been assured by the chairman of that body that Terra's allies have full confidence in Admiral Murakuma and would view with concern a change of command at such a crucial juncture. And, third and finally . . ." He suddenly grinned, and his high cheekbones squeezed his eyes into slits through which the twinkle was barely visible. "You can tell Legislative Assemblyman Waldeck to fuck himself—if he can find the place to do it, in all that blubber."

Avram had just raised her vodka glass to her lips. Now she spluttered a good portion of the contents onto her lap. "Well," she gasped when she'd gotten her coughing fit under control, "you certainly had me going, you . . . you . . ." Once again, if for very different reasons, words failed her. "Damn it, Ivan Nikolayevich, you *know* I can't tell him that!"

"Pity. But the important thing is that you keep Murakuma in command of Fifth Fleet." Antonov's eyes took on a distant look. "Believe it or not, Hannah, there have been one or two politicians in human history who weren't total wastes of space. One of them—an American, of all things—was once urged to dismiss a general who'd run up a hefty casualty list. He replied, 'I can't spare this man; he fights.'" Then the grin was back. "You know, I believe I'd like to renew my acquaintance with Admiral

Murakuma. And I have a feeling that Kthaara Kornaz-hovich would like to meet her. I wonder . . . yes. After things are running themselves here, I think he and I need to conduct an inspection tour to get a feel for conditions at the front. Don't you?"

CHAPTER FOURTEEN

"This time we *hold*!"

Vice Admiral Vanessa Murakuma stood once more on her flag deck and studied the master plot. *Cobra* floated over five light-minutes from the Justin warp point, surrounded by the mobile units of her newly renamed Fifth Fleet, and she folded her hands behind her as she considered their precise formations of icons.

The promised heavy units had arrived . . . fortunately. Everyone else was euphoric over the success of Operation Redemption, but as one of Murakuma's favorite pre-space statesmen had once observed, "Wars are not won by retreats," and the cost in destroyed and damaged ships—especially the light cruisers screening Reichman's transports—had been excruciating. For all the damage she'd inflicted in return, she was privately certain that if the Bugs had kept coming she would have lost Sarasota, as well.

The thought sent a chill through her, and she closed her eyes. The transports had lifted out every civilian who'd lived to reach an evacuation site, yet she'd not only lost over eight thousand Marines and God alone knew how many Peaceforcers and civilian volunteers but reduced TF 59 to near impotence to save them. In the cold math of a war against a seemingly limitless foe, that had to be counted a questionable bargain, especially when it had left Sarasota so exposed.

She'd confidently expected Sky Marshal Avram to relieve her, and a part of her desperately wished Avram had. None of her staff—except, perhaps, for Marcus—seemed to realize how little she had left inside. Even Mackenna thought she should be delighted by her successful rescue mission, yet proud as she was of her personnel, forty-eight thousand was such a tiny number beside the millions she *hadn't* gotten out. They haunted her dreams, wearing the faces of people she'd known and cared for, and the knowledge that over a hundred million more of them waited behind Fifth Fleet's frail shield weighed upon her soul like a neutron star.

I can't survive another retreat, she thought numbly. *I just can't. I have to stop them this time. I tell everyone it's because I'm sure I can do it, but it's a lie. Not confidence—desperation. Dear God, I am so tired of death! And if they knew the truth, if they guessed all my "confidence" and "determination" are no more than a need to evade more guilt even if it kills us all. . . .*

She drew a deep breath and reopened her eyes, staring at the icons once more, seeing the ships beyond them, and her hands fisted behind her. She was stronger than she'd ever been, with a solid core of sixteen superdreadnoughts, nine battleships, twenty-five battlecruisers, eleven fleet carriers, and seven CVLs, plus their escorts, the five fortresses of Sarasota Sky Watch and the enormous, heavily-armed orbital Fleet Base, and over six hundred fighters. She had minefields, laser buoys, primary buoys, and SBMHAWKs. It was a massive force, as powerful—given the advances in weaponry—as any Terran admiral had ever commanded, yet she cringed whenever she thought of the Bug squadrons she knew were massing against her. By Marcus and Tian's most conservative estimate, the Bugs' losses to date were half again the TFN's *entire* pre-war battle-line, yet each attack force so far had been bigger and more powerful than the last. What *conceivable* kind of navy could absorb that loss rate and keep *coming* like this?

She wasn't fighting a navy. She was fighting an elemental

force, something forged in the bowels of Hell to smash anything in its path, and she was afraid. So afraid. Not of dying—death would be welcome beside abandoning still more civilians—but by the hideous conviction that she faced Juggernaut . . . that she would both die *and* fail the civilians she was sworn to save.

She knew she would, but it was knowledge she hid behind the confidence she showed her subordinates, for it was her duty to lie to them and lead them all to death in her hopeless cause.

She heard a sound and drew a deep breath, then turned as Demosthenes Waldeck, Jackson Teller, and John Ludendorff arrived for their conference. Leroy Mackenna, Ling Tian, and Marcus LeBlanc stood behind them, along with her subordinates' chiefs of staff, and she bared her teeth in a cold, confident smile as she checked the bulkhead time display.

"Right on time, I see," she said. Her smile grew broader as they nodded back, and she raised one slender hand to gesture at the briefing room hatch. "In that case, ladies and gentlemen, let's get to it. We've got some Bug ass to kick."

Marcus LeBlanc sat in his quarters, fingers occasionally flicking his keypad, but even as his eyes scanned the neat blocks of characters, his mind was less on the ops plan before him than on the woman who'd created it. He came to the end of a section, sighed, and sat back, rubbing his face with both hands, and wrestled with his dilemma.

Vanessa was losing it. He knew she was . . . he simply didn't know what to do about it. No one else seemed to realize the ragged thread by which her stability hung, but they didn't know her as well as he did. Even Mackenna and Waldeck—that ill-assorted pair who worked so closely with her—were blinded by the magnificent job she'd done so far. They knew her pain cut far deeper than she let them see, but like everyone else, they were mesmerized by the losses she'd inflicted on the enemy. By any meterstick, no admiral in history—not just human history, but *anyone's*—had ever wreaked such one-sided havoc on a foe. Their own losses, however savage, paled to insignificance beside the enemy tonnage Vanessa had smashed into glowing wreckage.

Yet none of those other officers were in command, and none of them—except, perhaps, Jackson Teller—could truly understand the crushing psychic wounds her authority had inflicted upon her. But LeBlanc did. He'd seen them growing deeper for weeks, for he was the only one with whom she'd dared drop her mask, and there was so pathetically little he could do. He could only be there, listen, share her pain, try to find some way—*any* way—to ease it. Old feelings he'd thought had transmuted into simple friendship long ago complicated his efforts, yet this was no time to think about such things, especially when it was his job to remain her clearheaded analyst, and so he'd shoved them back down, pretended they didn't exist. But he'd known about her pain.

He saw the ghost of every butchered civilian in her green eyes, felt the despair in her soul, and he knew she was a woman with her back to the wall. One who couldn't—not wouldn't, but literally *could not*—abandon still more people to death. That was the true reason she'd made no contingency plans for a withdrawal this time; because another retreat, however desperately the military situation demanded it, simply was not an option for her.

For *her*, Vanessa Murakuma the woman, not Vice Admiral Murakuma.

He rubbed his face harder, wondering yet again if he should speak to Waldeck. It would be a personal betrayal of someone he'd once loved—*still* loved, if he was honest with himself, or perhaps loved again—but it was also his duty. If Fifth Fleet fought to its own destruction, the Federation would lose not only Sarasota but the entire Romulus Cluster. Surely his responsibility to prevent that outweighed his loyalty to Vanessa!

But—

The door chime sounded, and he lowered his hands

and pressed the admittance button, then snapped to his feet in surprise as Vanessa stepped through the hatch.

"Good evening, Marcus." Her eyes flickered to the ops plan on his display, then back to his face, and she smiled. There was no humor in that smile, and he wondered uneasily what his own expression might have betrayed before he got it back under control.

"Hello, Vanessa," he replied after a moment, and watched her sink into a chair, cross her legs, and clasp her hands on her raised knee while she surveyed him.

"To what do I owe the honor?" He tried to make his voice light and knew he'd failed when her lips quirked again.

"To the fact that you think I'm losing my grip," she said softly, and he winced.

"Vanessa, I—"

A raised hand stopped him in mid-protest, then rejoined its companion on her knee.

"Don't." She sat deeper in the chair, jade eyes dark. "I didn't want to discuss this with anyone, especially you, but you've been watching me too closely. You know, don't you?"

"Know what?" he asked as neutrally as possible.

"Please, Marcus. We've known each other too long for lies."

He winced again at her voice's quiet, infinite weariness, then bowed his head to stare down at his own hands. He longed to pretend he didn't know what she meant, but she was right. They *had* known each other too long, and so he nodded slowly, without looking up at her.

"Why haven't you said anything?"

"Because—" He stopped and inhaled deeply, then shrugged. "I don't know why, really. I'm your intelligence officer. I know what will happen if we lose Fifth Fleet, and this—" he looked up at last and gestured at his display "—is a very good way to do just that if we don't hold them. Vanessa, it's my *duty* to point that out, but—" He shrugged again.

"I thought so," she said so softly he hardly heard her,

and stared deep into his eyes for a long, still moment. Then she leaned back, crossing her arms below her breasts, and smiled with a dreadful, aching whimsey.

"Poor Marcus," she murmured. "You know I'm losing my grip, and the officer in you needs to tell someone, but the man in you . . ." She shook her head sadly. "You're a good man, Marcus LeBlanc. Too good to be caught in a disaster like this. But, then, I suppose a lot of good people are caught in it with us, aren't they?"

"Vanessa, please," he leaned towards her, extending one hand. "You've done a brilliant job. God knows, if anyone in this universe has a right to lose her grip you're her, and I don't want—*God*, how I don't want!—to dump anything else on you. But we both know you're right. You can't take much more of this. You *know* you can't."

"What do you want me to do?" she asked in a bleak, terrible voice. "Request my own relief? Dump the responsibility on Demosthenes? Go back to the rear and say, 'Well, you gave it your best shot, Vanessa. Now let someone else shoulder the guilt'?"

He flinched, then shook his head.

"You're not God. None of this is *your* fault, and, intellectually, you know that. But this battle plan . . ." He shook his head again. "Vanessa, you *can't* stake an entire star cluster's survival on holding them here, not if they keep coming like they have."

"Oh yes I can," she said, and he heard the ring of steel in her deadly-soft voice. "This time we *hold*. Not the Bugs, not the devil, not God Himself, is pushing me out of Sarasota. No more retreats. No more slaughtered children. No more parents who die knowing the Fleet abandoned them. Not this time, Marcus!"

"But—"

"No." She cut him off again, more sharply, and a dangerous fire flickered in her eyes. "I know the risk, but there's a point where 'military logic' becomes irrelevant, and that point is right here, right now. There are a hundred *million* humans in this system, and I won't let these fucking monsters have it while I have a single starship or fighter to throw at them!"

She paused, glaring at him, then drew a deep breath and made her voice calm.

"Oh, you're right—if I dig in to hold to the last ship, I can lose it all, but have you really considered what happens if I *don't* dig in? How many systems can we write off out of 'military necessity' without devastating not only our own morale but our allies', as well? The first Ophiuchi units are only two weeks out, with the first Orions right behind them. We're stronger than we've ever been, reinforcements are on their way, and Remus is right behind us. If we lose that system, we lose the entire cluster, and this is the last place we can stand short of it. If we don't fight to the last ship *here*, what does that say to the *next* CO . . . or the civilians of the next system on the Bugs' list? They just keep coming, Marcus—not like a navy, but like some pestilence or forest fire. You've seen how desperate our people are. You know why they *have* to regard Redemption as a major victory. If they don't, they have to admit it's hopeless, and if we ever admit that, what happens to our will to fight? No." She shook her head sharply. "We have to stop these monsters somewhere, whatever it costs, and that somewhere is here. This time, we *hold!*"

LeBlanc sat back, staring at her while madness edged her voice, and knew, with absolute certainty, that she'd made her decision for all the wrong reasons. All her arguments, however logical, were no more than afterthoughts to her own bleeding need to die before she fell back again. Yet that didn't necessarily make them *wrong*, and he wondered, suddenly, how many of history's great stands had been fought by people who simply couldn't make themselves do anything else. Leonidas and the Three Hundred, Maccabeus and Masada, Zizka and his war wagons, Castle Saint Elmo and the Siege of Malta, Hougemont and La Haye-Sainte, Travis and Bowie, Gordon and Khartoum, Leningrad, the Warsaw Ghetto, First Tannerman, Second Redwing—the list went on and on, and if all too many of those desperate stands had ended in death and defeat, a handful had not. And even the ones which *had* weren't always in vain. . . .

"'They shall not pass,'" he murmured. Murakuma blinked at him, and he smiled sadly. "From another war, Vanessa. From another war." He cocked his head, and a faint edge of true amusement edged his smile's sadness. "Sometimes it takes a madman—or woman—doesn't it?"

"Am I mad?" she asked with almost childlike wonder, and he shook his head.

"Maybe you are, but your secret's safe with me." Her shoulders twitched with relief, and he smiled again. "Go fight your battle, Vanessa. And, do you know, I think you may be right. We may just hold this time after all."

CHAPTER FIFTEEN

In Good Company

Losses to date, though much higher than projected, were acceptable in light of the systems captured and the size of the Reserve, and the enemy was either far weaker or else so sensitive to losses he was unwilling to press attacks home. Only his technological advantages made him dangerous, and those advantages would not last. Already the first new weapons had reached the Fleet, and the serried ranks of waiting superdreadnoughts would be far more dangerous. No doubt many would still die— probably far more than they killed. But there were far more of them . . . and this time the Fleet knew how to force the enemy to stand and fight.

One moment all was calm in the Sarasota System; in the next a lightning bolt of starships erupted from the warp point. But this wasn't *quite* a simultaneous transit— the Bugs spent all of thirty seconds sending their ships through, which reduced the kills from interpenetration.

Reduced, but did not eliminate, and as alarms wailed and men and women rushed to battle stations, searing explosions announced Juggernaut's arrival as laser buoys and primary platforms added their fury to the blazing cauldron pent within the minefields. Over sixty cruisers were blown apart and a score more were reduced to wrecks, but that left seventy, and Vanessa Murakuma's eyes flicked to the tactical sidebar scrolling down her plot.

Unlike Second Justin, the Bugs had brought along a solid phalanx of those damnable *Cataphracts*. More, they'd held them back, phasing their transits to decrease their losses. It was hard to be certain from this range, but it looked like at least thirty of them had survived. That promised agonizing losses for her fighter jocks, yet the Bugs' failure to send their light units crashing into the mines was almost more ominous.

Assault Fleet had accomplished its mission to secure the warp point. It was unfortunate the enemy had once more declined to deploy within reach of its weapons, but aside from the mines and energy buoys, its cruisers were beyond his range, as well. Courier drones returned to Justin, announcing success, and the superdreadnoughts and their escorts began to make transit.

"Here come the big boys," Mackenna murmured.

Capital ships came steadily, deliberately, through the warp point, like some nightmare pre-space freight train, and Murakuma's belly tightened. Forty. Fifty. Sixty. They kept on coming, flowing into existence in an endless stream of alloy, shields and weapons, and she fought the urge to lick her lips. Every instinct screamed to hit them *now*, but she couldn't contest the warp point without crippling her own fleet too early. She had to let them in, give them room to deploy, and pray her speed and range advantages were enough to stop them once she had.

If you can stop them, her mind whispered mercilessly. *If they haven't learned enough, adapted enough. If they haven't figured out some way to offset your advantages. If—*

She strangled the whisper and checked her display again. The computers were losing track—with so many ships packed into so small a volume mutual interference made it impossible to generate an accurate drive field count—but Plotting estimated there were already ninety-plus Bug

SDs in the system, and Fifth Fleet's total order of battle was only a hundred and seventeen ships, twenty percent of them tugs or antimissile escorts without a single offensive weapon. The odds were even more daunting than she'd feared, and she toyed with the seal of her vac suit.

Transit was complete, and the superdreadnoughts and battlecruisers settled into precise formation while the cruisers advanced into the waiting mines. Pre-war doctrine had assigned that task to the CLEs, but those ships had proved too valuable against the enemy's small attack craft, and two-thirds of them were held back while the remainder, with their more vulnerable consorts, moved forward. Those consorts were easy targets for the hunter-killers, for they lacked the CLEs' point defense batteries, but that had been anticipated. They might kill relatively few mines before they died, but they would draw them down upon themselves, tricking them into wasting themselves on what were, after all, expendable units.

"Damn. I expected the mines to do better," Mackenna muttered, and Murakuma shrugged.

"They're still scoring a lot of kills."

"Yes, Sir, but only on cruisers. We're not getting any big boys at all."

"I'll take what I can get." Murakuma's voice was so flat Mackenna looked up in surprise. She was staring too intently into her plot to notice, and he glanced at LeBlanc. The intelligence officer was watching her closely, and the chief of staff felt a sudden stab of worry. Something about the admiral's fixed, unyielding glare and LeBlanc's anxious eyes made him wonder if he'd missed something. LeBlanc knew the admiral far better than he, and if *he* looked so worried—

"They've cleared a lane." Ling Tian's quiet announcement snapped Mackenna's attention back to his own display. "Plotting makes their losses close to ninety cruisers, but they're in, and it looks like they're heading directly for the planet."

"The SBMHAWKs?" Murakuma asked without looking up.

"They've receipted their programming, Sir."

"Good." Murakuma brooded at her plot a moment longer while her thoughts whirred. SBMHAWK replacements hadn't fully replaced Redemption's expenditures, but she'd placed the ninety she had near the warp point. She'd hoped the Bugs would lose more heavily to the mines, but she'd been convinced they'd settle for clearing a single lane. Given the way they "swept" mines, they had little choice; their assault units might be expendable, yet their numbers were finite. Not even *Bugs* could throw away enough cruisers to clear multiple lanes.

But a single lane would give the SBMHAWKs their best chance. They wouldn't engage as the Bugs passed through it inbound, for there were too many starships out there. The pods relied on saturating an enemy's point defense, and the sheer numbers of targets would spread their fire too thin. But if Operation Thermopylae worked, the Bugs would be in a situation they hadn't faced yet. Despite their losses, they'd taken their objective in every previous battle; if they *couldn't* take this one, even they might withdraw. And if they did, the SBMHAWKs would be waiting on the flanks of the cleared lane. With far fewer targets to spread themselves among, a totally unexpected ambush in what was supposedly a safe zone . . .

A small, savage smile curled Vanessa Murakuma's lips. Something hot and primitive with vicious hate boiled within her, and she embraced it.

"Demosthenes," she glanced at her second-in-command's com image, "are you and John ready?"

"As we can be," Waldeck replied from TFNS *Amazonas'* flag deck.

"All right. We'll go with Thermopylae Four, Jackson." Her eyes flicked to her carrier commander. "Roll them out."

Anson Olivera wished Strikegroup 47 hadn't done *quite* so well last time, and he remembered his favorite instructor from his days at Brisbane. "Old pilots," the grizzled veteran had said, "got that way by never flying with anyone braver than them and *never* letting the brass know how good they really were." Given that Commander Hidachi had earned so much fruit salad it wouldn't all fit on his tunic, Ensign Olivera had figured it was just a line old sweats used to impress newbies. Now he understood. If the brass decided you were really, really good, guess who got dropped into all the deepest crap?

He grimaced and settled himself in his couch. His was the command fighter for the entire first strike, twenty-five full-strength squadrons, and at least he wasn't required to close with the *Cataphracts*. Not yet, anyway.

"All right people," he murmured. "Stay loose. We've got plenty of time to work on them."

No one replied, but he hadn't expected them to, and he punched up his master display as Jane Malachi led Fifth Fleet's first thrust towards the enemy.

Tracking systems locked on, but this time the Fleet knew about the small attack craft's longer-ranged weapons. Only the CLEs configured their fire control for close engagement, for they had point defense and to spare to both kill enemies and stop missiles. All other units reserved their point defense solely for missile intercepts and waited while the attack swept in.

"They're holding course for the planet," Ling Tian reported, and Murakuma nodded. She'd been afraid of that. These creatures clearly made detailed plans, then stuck to them come Hell or high water, and they'd let themselves be pulled after her faster warships in every previous engagement. But that didn't mean they couldn't learn, and they weren't letting themselves be diverted this time. If she wanted to stop them, *she* had to come to *them*, and that meant, sooner or later, that she was going to have to enter *their* engagement envelope.

Maybe I will, she conceded, *but I can sure as hell bleed the bastards first.*

She raised her eyes to John Ludendorff's screen. The neatly bearded rear admiral commanded her two least orthodox battlegroups, and he already knew what she was going to say.

"Once the fighters have worked on them for a bit, it's going to be up to your OWPs to open the ball, John. Watch your ammo. If these bastards keep coming for the planet, you may be able to break off and rearm." *Unlike First Justin, where they just kept right on chasing us.* "If they're willing to give us the chance, *I'm* willing to take it."

"Understood, Sir," Ludendorff replied, and she nodded and looked back at her plot. His task group's superdreadnought flagship and six OWPs with their individual tugs moved steadily forward through her formation, settling down on the edge closest to the Bugs, as the fighters streaked towards their targets.

"Here we go, people! Make 'em count!"

Olivera smiled thinly. The bastards must know what was coming this time, but that wasn't going to help them, because none of Olivera's chicks were ever going to enter their range . . . unless, of course, they'd managed to develop the AFHAWK since the last time.

They hadn't. Each squadron volleyed its missiles in a single, synchronized salvo. Not all of their missiles caught their wildly evading targets at this range, and many of those which might have were killed by point defense. But Olivera's attack plan had allowed for that, and he concentrated his entire assault on a mere five targets. He didn't kill all of them, but the two survivors fell astern, streaming debris and atmosphere, and he grinned viciously.

"Good job, troops! We do this good a few more times, and there won't be any of 'em left by supper! Now back to the barn. Let's see what Captain Janowski's strike can do."

Squadron commanders acknowledged and wheeled for their hangar bays, but Olivera knew his blithering optimism hadn't fooled anyone. They were taking the easy kills, clearing the way to the ships they really wanted, but sooner or later they had to go in after the *Cataphracts*, and they'd need FRAMs to get through their point defense.

There were going to be empty bunks in Flight Country tonight . . . lots of them.

Wave after wave of Vanessa Murakuma's fighters launched from just beyond the Bugs' range. It was like watching army ants gnaw at the hide of an elephant or rhino, each taking one more tiny bite without ever threatening its vitals. But every ship killed was one less threat when her battle-line had to close, and even if it hadn't been, the hatred in her soul exulted as she pictured thousands of Bugs withering in flame.

Die, you bastards! The venomous thought crackled in the back of her brain as still another cruiser died. *Goddamn you to Hell,* die!

The range of the enemy's weapons made efforts to withdraw the more vulnerable cruisers deep within the main formation useless. It was impossible to spread the formation far enough to force him into its defensive envelope, but that had been accepted when the plan was devised.

Besides, it wasn't as if those ships were important.

"We've nailed most of the regular CLs and CAs, Sir," Jackson Teller reported. "My evaluation people make it about fifty ships. That leaves the *Cataphracts*. From here on, we'll have to go in after them."

"We'll see if we can't help you out a bit first, Jackson." Murakuma looked at Waldeck and Ludendorff. "Gentlemen, our fighter jocks would appreciate a little assistance."

Five huge, ungainly Type Five OWPs, never intended for mobile warfare, dropped further back in Fifth Fleet's formation, accompanied by their superdreadnought flagship. *Mekong* would probably draw the most fire, but her presence was necessary; only one of the forts carried a datalink master installation, and it was vital that their tugs be brought under their point defense umbrella. But unlike First Justin, four of *these* forts mounted capital missile launchers—a *lot* of launchers: twice as many as a *Matterhorn*-class SD and six times as many as a *Mount Hood*. The command base mounted a primarily energy armament, but the sixth was a pure antimissile/antifighter platform, and that base was tucked into the "battlegroup" closest to the enemy.

The fortress crews knew their jobs, and Plotting had worked overtime to give them precise data. They knew the Bugs had thirty-six of their *Archer* missile superdread-noughts, and they opened a heavy, deliberate SBM bombardment from beyond capital missile range. Jennifer Husac's ten *Dunkerques* joined them, pouring in their own SBMs, and *Archers* began to die. Not quickly or easily, for they were tough, but steadily.

Murakuma watched them die and bit her lower lip. They were going, but she *still* didn't have enough SBMs to fill her magazines with the longer-ranged missiles. What her ships had now were all they had for the entire battle; once they were gone, it would all be up to the capital missiles, and the Bugs *could* match *their* range.

Husac's BCs exhausted their SBMs and turned to race for the ammunition colliers. The fortresses, with their larger magazine space, didn't. They still had plenty of CMs left, and it was time to start using them.

Ludendorff let the range fall still further and shifted his targeting. The first answering fire spat back from the surviving *Archers*, and Murakuma watched it come. She hated to take her fire off those ships, but she *had* to hammer those CLEs back for her fighters, and capital missiles were the hardest birds to stop. At least some of them would get through even a *Cataphract*'s point defense, especially with salvoes that dense, and—

Four *Cataphracts* died in the opening salvo, but then the first Bug capital missiles arrived, and Vanessa Murakuma went white as one of them got through against a fort. The single hit smashed a twelfth of the OWP's shields flat, and she heard Ling Tian suck in air.

"That was a second-generation warhead, Sir!" The ops officer tried to hide her own shock, but Murakuma knew Ling was as dismayed as she was. God, those bastards were quick off the mark if they'd already figured out how to put AAMs into production!

"Forget the cruisers, John!" she snapped. "Kill as many *Archers* as you can—the fighters are just going to have to deal with the *Cataphracts* themselves."

"Aye, Sir." Ludendorff's voice was grim, for he, too, understood what those warheads meant. Powerful as his forts were, they couldn't stand up to many AAMs—and their tugs could stand even less. Murakuma's plan to kill the escorts so her *fighters* could go after the Bug missile platforms had just gone out the airlock; she had to nail those *Archers* as quickly as possible.

"Permission to support?" Waldeck asked tautly, and she didn't hesitate. His SDs could stand less damage than the forts, but they carried another eighty launchers.

"Granted," she snapped, and Waldeck's battle-line sped towards the enemy. She was putting it in far sooner than she'd planned, but she had no choice.

The missile ships shuddered under the enemy's pounding, but at last he had to come within their reach, and they poured back fire. Their individual salvoes were lighter, but there were a great many of them, and the new warheads performed exactly as predicted.

Anson Olivera stood in his squadron's ready room, watching dry-mouthed as the ops plan came apart. None of Admiral Ludendorff's forts had been destroyed yet, and the Bugs seemed not to realize that killing the tugs would immobilize them, but the sheer weight of fire was awesome. Point defense intercepted hundreds of missiles, but some got through, and three of the forts had already lost their shields. They'd killed five more *Archers*, but now each hit ripped into their armor. They weren't knocking down shields now; they were killing people and weapons.

A tone beeped, and he turned to the com screen.

"Saddle up, Commander," TFNS *Dalmatian's* captain said grimly. "You're going in."

A fort exploded as something reached its magazines, and Murakuma bit her lip so hard she tasted blood. Ludendorff's *Mekong* was shields-down, as well, and she wanted desperately to order him back, but she couldn't. She needed that ship where it was, holding its net up, and—

TFNS *Mekong* blew apart. There were no life pods. There was barely even time for her automatic transmitter to begin her Omega transmission. One instant she was there; the next she was an expanding cloud of plasma, and her datanet went with her.

"Get them out!" Murakuma barked, but it was too late. Stripped of their interlinked antimissile defenses, not even Type Five OWPs could stand that battering. Missiles ripped down on targets now totally reliant on their own, individual defenses, and she watched sickly as two tugs and a fort exploded. Life pods littered the display, proving at least some of their people had gotten out in time, but *Mekong's* entire battlegroup died within two minutes of its command ship, and Vanessa Murakuma closed her eyes in agony.

"Shall I order the other battlegroup to withdraw?" Ling Tian asked quietly, and instinct screamed to say yes, but Murakuma shook her head.

"No," she said flatly. "They went for *Mekong* because they could pick her out. Unless they get the command fort by sheer coincidence, they can't knock her net down."

She didn't look up from her plot, but she felt her flag bridge crew's eyes on her, and her soul cringed from what she might have seen in them had she looked.

Fifth Fleet's fighters launched. The big fleet carriers held back a small reserve, but every other fighter went. SG 47 lead the wave, and Olivera watched his tactical feed from *Dalmatian* as seven hundred and fifty fighters screamed towards the enemy. Only fourteen *Archers* remained in action, though three more had fallen astern, yet the Bugs had wiped out over half the OWPs, and the battle-line had taken a battering of its own. As Olivera watched, TFNS *Borah* pulled out of line, limping away with half her launchers out of action, and two more superdreadnoughts bled atmosphere. The remaining *Archers* were hurting, too—they *had* to be—but Bugs didn't break off. They went right on firing until they died, and they were hurting Fifth Fleet badly.

But not for much longer, Olivera told himself grimly. He and his people were going to take savage losses, but they had the strength to kill the bastards, and—

He blinked as a sudden cascade of tiny lights speckled his display. What in God's name—?

"Sir! The Bugs have just launched small craft!"

"Small craft?" Murakuma stared at Ling Tian in surprise, then looked at LeBlanc.

"Yes, Sir. We've got over two hundred *cutters* coming at us." Ling sounded as confused as Murakuma felt, but LeBlanc's face tightened in instant, instinctive understanding.

"Kamikazes," he said flatly. Murakuma looked at him blankly for a moment, then paled. If those cutters were loaded with antimatter—

"Divert your strike, Jackson!" she snapped, wheeling to Teller's com screen.

"But, Sir, the *Archers*—"

"Get the cutters! We think they're kamikazes!"

"Kami— Dear God!" Teller whirled to his own com officer, and Murakuma slammed a fist down on her command chair's arm. The Bugs could not have launched at a worse time. She *needed* those fighters to take the pressure off Demosthenes, and it was terribly tempting to send them on in. After all, her ships were designed to kill fighters; their defenses ought to have a field day against *cutters!* But she didn't know how much antimatter could be crammed aboard. They didn't have much cargo capacity, but they wouldn't *need* a lot, either.

✧   ✧   ✧

Olivera's jaw clenched as *Dalmatian* changed his mission. *Kamikazes?* No one had used them since ISW–3! But they should have guessed the *Bugs* would, and he started snapping orders.

The small craft fanned out, spreading far and wide. If they could get through to their targets, well and good, but it would be almost as satisfactory if they simply diverted the enemy's more capable attack craft. And that was precisely what they were doing.

The battle-lines' fire grew more vicious as the wounded survivors smashed one another in an orgy of mutual destruction, and Murakuma knew the exchange was in the Bugs' favor. If they destroyed Waldeck's missile-armed SDs, even at the cost of every one of their *Archers*, they won the round, for aside from Husac's battlecruisers, they were the *only* heavy missile ships she had.

The massive fighter strike had dissipated in wild confusion as its squadrons raced after the suspected kamikazes, and she swallowed a curse as she checked the large scale plot of the entire system. The Bugs were driving straight for Sarasota. They hadn't reached it yet, but they would.

"*Korab, Kerintji* and *Toubkal* are Code Omega, Sir. *Borah* and *Apo* have disengaged successfully, but they're out of it. Only one missile fort is still in action."

"Understood. The Bugs?"

"Seven *Archers* left, Sir. They're all damaged; we don't know how badly."

"Admiral Husac?"

"Rearmed and returning. ETA seventeen minutes."

Murakuma nodded and looked back up at Waldeck's com screen.

"Pull the SDs back. We'll have to let Husac handle them."

"Agreed." Waldeck's voice was as bitter as her own thoughts.

"Can what's left of John's command get free?"

"I think so. They don't have much firepower left anyway."

"Then pull them out. We might as well save *somebody*," she said harshly.

"Sir, it's not your fault," Waldeck said quietly. "No one could have—"

"Just pull them out, Admiral," Vanessa Murakuma said flatly, and turned away.

The battle raged on. The Fleet's missile ships were gone, but the enemy had suffered heavily. All his missile superdreadnoughts and five of his battlecruisers had been driven out of action or destroyed. Neither side now possessed an extended-range missile capability, but the Fleet retained a solid core of forty-eight superdreadnoughts, screened by twelve battlecruisers . . . and if the enemy wanted to engage them, he would have to come into their range.

Murakuma paced savagely about her briefing room. The Bugs had been reduced to a bare third of their initial strength over the last seventy-nine hours, but that third was still coming. Her fighters had hunted down all but four of the cutters, and those four had been easily picked off by her starships' defenses, but the huge fireballs as they died confirmed Marcus' suspicion. Only heavy loads of antimatter could account for them, yet knowing she'd been right to divert her fighters made her feel no less a murderer. She'd left her missile-armed battle-line to fight unsupported, and it had been battered into uselessness, and the fact that it had done the same to the Bugs' missile ships was scant comfort, given how damned many *other* SDs they had left.

She took another turn around the compartment, like an exhausted, goaded animal. She'd battered the Bugs viciously, slashing in with coordinated fighter strikes and pounces by her short-ranged missile ships, but they were still *coming*, and—

The admittance chime sounded, and she whirled towards

the hatch. For one moment, her lips drew back in a snarl, but then she closed her eyes and drew a deep, shuddering breath.

"Enter," she said flatly, and Marcus LeBlanc stepped into the briefing room.

The intelligence officer looked worn and worried, but unlike her, he'd actually managed a few hours' sleep, and she wanted to curse him for the concern in his eyes. Concern for her.

"Well?" she said sharply.

"I—" LeBlanc shrugged. "Tear my head off if you want, but someone has to say it. You need rest."

Murakuma opened her mouth to flay him, but then she made herself stop and turned her back, fists clenching as she stared at the holo display above the conference table.

The planet Sarasota hung there, and her exhausted, bloodshot eyes clung to the huge Fleet Base in orbit around it. That base was as heavily armed as twenty superdreadnoughts. Against any rational foe, she would have backed it to handle every battered capital ship still headed for it, but if even a single Bug superdreadnought managed to penetrate its defenses and ram, it would die.

"I *don't* need rest," she grated. "The stims are holding."

"Like hell," LeBlanc said. "Damn it, Vanessa, you're killing yourself!"

"Why not?" Hysteria edged her jagged laugh. "That's what I'm best at, killing people."

"It's not your fault! Damn it to hell, you're not *God!*"

"This discussion is closed." She wheeled back to him, and he recoiled from her raw fury.

"No it isn't." He tried to keep his voice calm and rational. "Someone has to say it, and none of the rest of your staff will—"

"I said it's closed! Or do you need a little brig time to remind you what a direct order is?!"

He opened his mouth again, then closed it. She truly meant it, he realized shakenly.

"All right," he said finally, his tone leached of all

emotion. "But whether you're willing to rest or not, you have to make a decision. You've done a hell of a job, but they're still coming, and for all we know, there's a hundred more SDs right behind them."

"There aren't," she said flatly. "If there were, they'd already have called them forward."

"Why?" he shot back. "Because *we* would?" He barked a laugh. "The one thing I can tell you for absolute certain is that these things sure as *hell* don't think like we do! Maybe they're expending this entire force just to grind us up so they can send in a reserve for the kill!"

"No." She shook her head so violently she had to catch herself on a chair as her exhausted body staggered. "No, this is it. All they have. And they're not taking this system away from me."

"It's over, Vanessa," he said softly. "No one could have done more, but it's over."

"No it isn't." She shoved herself back upright and glared at him.

"But—"

"*It isn't over!*" He stepped back involuntarily as she shouted at him, and then she stormed past him onto the flag deck. He followed quickly, mind racing for some argument, *any* argument, that might get through to whatever rationality remained under her exhausted desperation.

"Get me Admiral Teller," she told her com officer, and turned to the screen as Teller's face appeared. "How many fighters do we have left?" she asked without preamble.

"About two hundred, plus the Fleet Base's group. Call it three hundred."

"Call the base's fighters forward. We'll stage them through your bays."

"That will leave the planet without any fighter cover," Teller began, "and—"

"I know that. Just do it—now."

Teller's eyes widened. She saw them dart over her shoulder, as if seeking someone else, and deliberately stepped between him and LeBlanc. The movement wasn't lost on the other admiral, and after a moment, he nodded.

"Yes, Sir," he said quietly. "May I ask what I'll do with them once they arrive."

"You may." Murakuma punched a stud, bringing Demosthenes Waldeck's worn face up on another screen, and faced them both. "Demosthenes, we're calling in the base's fighters. Once they've arrived and our own groups have had time to reorganize, activate Leonidas."

Waldeck's face stiffened, and, for just an instant, she felt the protest hovering behind his eyes. Leonidas was the last-ditch option, a headlong attack into the enemy. It had been devised as a contingency plan, one to be activated only after the Bugs had been decisively weakened, and she recognized his desperate concern for his battered battle-line. His remaining ships were heavily out-massed by the surviving Bug superdreadnoughts, and Leonidas would commit them to a fight to the death within the enemy's weapons envelope.

"Sir, are you certain about this?" he asked quietly.

"I am. I know they outmass us, but they're hurting, too. And they don't have any fighters. You'll coordinate with Jackson and we'll go in together, fighters in tight. We'll hold them there till we're into energy range, then throw them in the bastards' faces."

It was a council of desperation, and she knew her subordinates knew it, but Waldeck said nothing for a moment. And then, to her exhausted astonishment, he nodded slowly.

"It might just work," he said, and Leroy Mackenna looked up from his console in disbelief as the Corporate Worlder nodded again.

"It better," Teller said grimly. "We won't have anything left to try again if it *doesn't*."

"Sir, have you considered waiting just a little longer?" Ling Tian asked hesitantly. "We're still wearing them down, and—"

"And they're wearing *us* down," Murakuma cut her off. "The odds aren't going to get any better, and we can't

let things that use starships for projectiles get close enough
to ram the base."

"We won't be in any shape to stop a follow-up attack,
Sir," Waldeck cautioned, but his tone was that of a man
considering all options, not a protest.

"We'll worry about that then," Murakuma said flatly.
"Now let's get moving."

". . . and that's the plan," Anson Olivera told Fifth Fleet's
three surviving strikegroup COs. Given the plan he'd just
briefed them on, he didn't expect to survive much longer
. . . and neither did they. It was against the fighter jock's
code to ever sound less than breezily confident, however
tough the mission profile, but all four of them were having
trouble pulling it off this time.

"That's *it*?" Lieutenant Commander Beachman asked.
"We just go right down their throats with the battle-line
and shoot anything that moves?"

"That's it," Olivera confirmed, and managed a thin smile
as the other three stared at him. "The battle-line will be
shooting the whole way in, so how can we predict which
targets'll be left for us? There's no way to set this one up
neatly. We'll be tied into the Flag for the approach,
and Admiral Murakuma's staff will try to give us targeting
updates, but no one can guarantee that."

"Jesus," Beachman muttered, shaking her head. " 'Go
shoot a superdreadnought—*any* superdreadnought.' They
never put *that* one in the Brisbane syllabus! We're going
to have all kinds of targeting conflicts. What if we screw
up and mob three or four of them and let the others
by us? We're going to lose command and control the
instant we mix it up with these bastards. What are our
squadrons supposed to do if we can't even tell them who
to go after?"

"I asked Admiral Murakuma more or less the same
question," Olivera agreed.

"And she said?" Commander Liracelli asked.

"She paraphrased an ancient wet-navy order." The
others looked at him blankly, and he actually felt himself

smile. "She said, 'Something must be left to chance. No pilot can do very wrong if he fires on the enemy.'"

"Sounds like the prelude to the biggest cluster-fuck in history," Beachman grumbled. "Who the hell ever gave an idiot order like that?"

"Horatio Nelson," Olivera told her. "And if it worked at Trafalgar, it might even work here."

Vanessa Murakuma looked up as a shadow fell over her console, and her mouth tightened. Marcus LeBlanc looked at her for a long silent moment, and she hunched an impatient shoulder.

"We're going in in ten minutes," she said. "If something's on your mind, say it quick."

"I was just thinking about the fellow you named this operation after," he said quietly.

"Leonidas? What about him? Or—" her eyes hardened dangerously "—is that a not so subtle reference to what happened to *him*?"

"I suppose it was," LeBlanc said in that same, quiet voice, "but not the way you're thinking." He saw the surprise in her exhausted eyes, and under it he saw the grim death grip she'd fastened on herself. The absolute, total determination—the *fanaticism*, for that was the only word which truly fitted now. He looked down at her for a moment longer, and then he squeezed her shoulder gently, oblivious to all the flag bridge's watching eyes.

"'Go, stranger, and to the listening Spartans tell, that here, obedient to their laws, we fell,'" he quoted softly. "Whatever happens, you're in good company." He squeezed her shoulder again. "God bless, Vanessa."

"And you, Marcus." She smiled, and somehow that gentle smile looked completely right on her exhausted, warrior's face. Then she nodded at his console. "Take your station, Captain."

"Aye, aye, Sir." LeBlanc slid into his couch, and as he adjusted his shock frame, he heard Vanessa Murakuma's voice—a voice that had somehow shed its exhaustion and uncertainty and fear.

"All units, this is the Flag. The Fleet will advance!"

CHAPTER SIXTEEN

"We're going back."

The Orion cutter drifted through the monopermeable force field into TFNS *Cobra*'s boat bay, and Vanessa Murakuma watched it settle to the deck, then nodded to the lieutenant who headed the side party.

"'Ten-*shun!*" The side party snapped to attention as the cutter's hatch opened into the squeal of bosun's pipes, and Murakuma offered up a silent prayer that someone had warned her guest, for Orion hearing was far more acute than Terran. She had no idea how a bosun's pipe might sound to a Tabby, but she suspected it didn't sound *good*.

If it didn't, the tall, tan-furred being who stepped from the cutter gave no sign of it. Fifty-Sixth Fang of the Khan Anaasa'zolaath, Khanate of Orion Navy, was well into his seventh decade, but there was little silver in his pelt. His jeweled metal harness flashed with what seemed barbaric splendor, but the furred Tabbies, who went unclothed in normal environments, invested all the effort humans expended on tailors on their metalsmiths, and by Orion standards, Anaasa's harness was downright modest.

The Orion came to his race's version of attention and touched his right hand first to his *defargo* honor dirk and then to his chest in salute until the pipes stopped wailing, then spoke. It sounded like an angry, basso-profundo tomcat to Murakuma, but the translator listening in over the boat bay intercom whispered through her earbug.

"He asks permission to come aboard, Sir."

"Permission granted," Murakuma said clearly, and the big Tabby smiled the polite, teeth-hidden smile of his carnivorous race and yowled something else.

"He says thank you, Sir."

Anaasa stepped forward, extending his right hand in the human gesture of welcome, and she took it. She'd tried for years to acquire at least enough mastery of Orion to understand it—as Anaasa had obviously mastered Standard English, given his lack of any earbug—but her tone deafness had defeated her. But it hadn't kept her from learning all she could about Orion culture, and Anaasa's smile broadened as she squeezed his right hand, then raised her left, fingers clawed, and slapped her nails lightly against the side of his face. His own hand came up, needle-sharp (and still highly functional) claws bared, and brushed her own cheek with equal care. Once that exchange had been quite different, with each warrior slashing his claws in with all the speed he could and stopping at the last possible instant. It had been a tremendous loss of face to draw blood, but an even greater one to flinch from the strike, and the Tabbies had lost more than one high-ranking officer to the duels clumsy greetings had inspired. That was why Liharnow the Great had insisted his warriors adjust to more civilized ways a hundred and fifty Standard Years ago.

"In the name of my government and people, Fang Anaasa," she said clearly, "I welcome you to Sarasota. The speed with which your Khan has met his treaty obligations does honor to him, who sent you, and to you, who have come."

"Honor comes to he who acts with honor," Anaasa yowled back through her translator. "When *farshatok* call, their war brothers must answer, for if my claws guard not your back, whose claws shall guard mine?"

Murakuma bowed, then gestured politely for Anaasa to accompany her to the intraship car. The Tabby padded gracefully along at her side, silent in the open-toed sandals his people wore in place of the TFN's boots, and his shoulder-wide whiskers quivered with interest as his bright eyes compared *Cobra* and her company to his own battlecruiser flagship. The two of them stepped into the car together, and Murakuma felt as if an enormous weight had been partly lifted—not completely, but partly—from her shoulders as she pressed the button.

The rest of Fifth Fleet's senior officers and their staffs rose as Murakuma and Anaasa entered the briefing room. There were more of them now, and she felt a pang as she looked at the woman beside Demosthenes Waldeck. Rear Admiral Carlotta Segram was a fine officer, but she'd stepped into John Ludendorff's slot, and every time Murakuma looked at her she saw an expanding cloud of gas she should have withdrawn sooner.

She gave herself a savage mental shake, banishing the image, and walked to the head of the table with Anaasa. It was fortunate that the Tabby was junior to Demosthenes Waldeck but senior to every other Allied officer present, for his five fleet carriers, eight battlecruisers, and five heavy cruisers were the largest Allied contingent yet to reach Sarasota. More, the Khanate of Orion was the Federation's only true peer as a Galactic Power, and his rank made him the natural commander for her third task force—which was good, since TF 53 would consist entirely of *his* ships. In a way, she would have preferred to integrate his units into her other two task forces, but the Tabbies' datalink wouldn't interface with the TFN's.

The same was not true, fortunately, of Rear Admiral Saakhaanaa's Ophiuchi ships, for the Ophiuchi Association Defense Command's units were specifically designed to fight in joint TFN-OADC battlegroups, and Murakuma glanced at Saakhaanaa as she and Anaasa seated themselves. The Ophiuchi and his staff were the tallest people in the briefing room, but they probably weighed no more than Ling Tian. Murakuma guessed they *did* outmass her own low-grav-adapted body, though it couldn't have been by much.

She finished seating herself and smiled as she watched Anaasa and Saakhaanaa project matching airs of physical comfort neither felt. Orions preferred a damper, more humid—and warmer—climate, while Ophiuchi preferred drier worlds. Orion atmospheric pressures also ran well above Terran norms, while the Ophiuchi preferred lower-grav worlds with proportionately lighter pressures. Ophiuchi could survive aboard Orion ships, and vice-versa, but neither could have functioned efficiently there, whereas humans could adapt to either. And, as this widely assorted gathering demonstrated, both allied races could adapt to Terran conditions. In a way, she mused, that summed up what made her own species so successful. Both Ophiuchi and Orions did some things better than humans, but Man remained the known galaxy's ultimate generalist.

"Thank you all for coming," she said, and knew her alien allies recognized the stark, simple honesty of her gratitude. "With your help and the fortifications being emplaced on the Justin warp point, I now feel confident of holding Sarasota against any fresh offensive. Indeed, we may be in a position to take the battle to the enemy at last."

A small stir ran around the table, and she flicked a sidelong glance at Marcus LeBlanc. Only he, Mackenna and Ling Tian had known she intended to say that, and she knew he retained strong reservations. The tension between them had eased, but he was still unconvinced she truly had herself back together. *And,* she admitted, *he may have a point. But all I can do is the best I can do.*

She returned her attention to her assembled officers. "Since you've just joined us, Fang Anaasa, I felt we should begin with a complete briefing. I realize you've seen our reports to GHQ, but the Centauri System's far enough back there's bound to be some com lag. More to the point, this will give you a chance to ask any questions which may have occurred to you en route. Please feel free—as should all of you—" she added, eyes sweeping over the other officers "—to stop us at any time for clarification or expansion. It's essential that we develop a firm, shared appreciation of the situation, and I welcome any input from a perspective other than my own."

She paused until Anaasa and Saakhaanaa indicated assent, then gestured to LeBlanc.

"Captain LeBlanc, my intelligence officer, and Commander Ling, my operations officer, have prepared a brief for us. Captain LeBlanc will begin with what we have so far learned, deduced, and guessed about the enemy, after which Commander Ling will update us on our own strength and deployments. Captain LeBlanc?"

"Yes, Sir." The captain activated a holo unit, and the image of a charging Bug warrior, captured on a Marine's zoot scanners and firing on the run, appeared above the table. Murakuma felt Anaasa tense beside her and heard a faint hiss as he bared his fangs in instant, instinctive challenge. *Interesting. He seems to react to it exactly the way humans do. And so did Saakhaanaa, the first time he saw the imagery. I wonder how much of that stems from what they know about the Bugs' actions and how much of it is just plain instinct?*

"This, ladies and gentlemen, is an Arachnid," LeBlanc began in his most clinical tones, and Murakuma leaned back in her chair to listen.

"I still think you're pressing too hard." LeBlanc's voice was carefully professional, and Murakuma felt the effort with which he strained all personal feeling from it. It was hard on both of them, and she wondered if she'd been right to request him in the first place. He was undoubtedly the best man to have at the sharp end of this particular intelligence stick, but was he the right intelligence officer for *her*? They meant too much to one another for either to listen to the other with total, detached professionalism, and it was a source of tension which wore upon them both.

"I realize that," she said, and looked at the others she'd invited to this small, private meeting. LeBlanc and Mackenna were the only staffers present, but Waldeck,

Teller and Anaasa, as her task force commanders, and Saakhaanaa, as Fifth Fleet's senior Ophiuchi, sat in chairs designed for their respective species. Saakhaanaa nibbled on a *sharkü* stick, crunching the dried, jerky-like delicacy quietly, and Anaasa nursed a flagon of *chermaak*, the spicy, slightly alcoholic beverage his race used instead of coffee and beer alike, while Demosthenes—in what was undoubtedly the most bizarre habit of all—puffed on a black briar pipe. At least he'd been careful to place himself directly under a ventilator and as far from Anaasa's sensitive nose as possible!

"I realize that," she repeated, keeping her own voice neutral, "but perhaps we *need* a little pressing. So far, they've lost almost two hundred SDs, and even *they* have to run out of capital ships eventually. But how can we know if they have unless we at least probe for information?"

Saakhaanaa cocked his head in an Ophiuchi gesture of agreement, but his eyes narrowed. That indication of curiosity was one of the few expressions his race and humanity shared, and she wondered if he wondered why she was arguing with a mere intelligence officer. The TFN didn't usually do that, and he knew it. Anaasa, on the other hand, seemed completely at ease. Well, it wasn't unheard of for even a junior member of an Orion commander's staff to argue violently with him. It must make staff meetings lively, but the Khanate's size was proof it worked.

"I agree their losses are catastrophic by the standard of any other race we've ever met," LeBlanc conceded. "At the same time, they appear almost totally insensitive to casualties. The way they didn't even attempt to break off here in Sarasota is the clearest possible indication of that. And because they are, I must stress again my belief that they must have an enormous reserve strength. We, on the other hand, while substantially reinforced, *also* suffered heavy losses, and we're unlikely to see any additional large reinforcements for another two or three months. If we lose still more ships and the enemy *isn't* running out of superdreadnoughts—"

He shrugged, and Murakuma nodded, hiding her wince at the words "heavy losses." Leonidas had stopped the Bugs, but the cost had been as dreadful as she'd feared. By the end, Fifth Fleet had lost seven hundred fighters, three out of five OWPs (with the others so shattered Fortress Command had written them off rather than rebuild them), eight superdreadnoughts, twelve battle-cruisers, and over thirty percent of its screen. Demosthenes' surviving battle-line had been battered into near impotence, and only Teller's carriers—with a bare hundred fighters embarked—had escaped undamaged.

She'd known, as she surveyed her shattered command, that Marcus had been right. If the Bugs had put in a second attack—even a weak one—they would have rolled right over what was left of Fifth Fleet. *But they didn't, and that's the point. If they'd had them to put in, they* would *have*.

"Captain LeBlanc has a point," Mackenna said diffidently. "With the new mines and energy buoys—not to mention the OWPs—we've got a mighty strong stopper in the bottle. If we move into Justin, we expose ourselves to heavy starship losses we can't really afford, but if we wait another sixty days, enough additional heavy stuff will arrive to mean we *can* accept losses."

"And while we wait," Murakuma said very quietly, "anyone left in Justin is being eaten."

Mackenna winced, and LeBlanc shut his mouth firmly as he heard the echo of her desperate guilt, but Anaasa looked up from his *chermaak*.

"You raise an important point, Ahhhdmiraahl," he said while her earbug translated. "We are warriors. It is our function to protect and defend civilians, whatever race those civilians may belong to, against such menaces as the Baahgs."

"Exactly!" Murakuma looked at Waldeck and raised an eyebrow. "Demosthenes?"

"Of course it is," the Corporate Worlder said simply. "Captain LeBlanc and Commander Mackenna have both raised valid arguments, but the bottom line is that if we have the firepower to take the battle to the Bugs, we clearly have to do just that. *If* we have the firepower."

"And do we?" Murakuma challenged.

"I don't know," Waldeck said frankly. "Captain LeBlanc's right about the implications of their willingness to take losses, but you have an equally valid point in their failure to try Sarasota a second time when they have to know how close they came the first time. Certainly no Terran— or Orion or Ophiuchi—" he added with a courteous nod to the two aliens "would give an opponent any longer to fort up than he had to when he knew he'd had him on the ropes before. Under the circumstances," he tilted his head back for a moment, then shrugged, "I'd have to come down on your side of the analysis. But, as you say, the only way to *know* is to go look."

"Admiral Saakhaanaa?" Murakuma asked.

"I am forrrced to agree withhh Admiral Waldeckk," the Ophiuchi said. "Ifff we can take the warrr to the Buggsss, we mussst do ssso."

It was odd, Murakuma thought, that different as all their vocal apparatuses were, all of them could manage a form of "Bug" that was at least recognizable.

"In that case, I think we can consider the decision made," she said, and met LeBlanc's eyes with a hint of challenge. "Leroy, please inform Tian that Operation Salamis is a go. Gentlemen, we're going back to Justin!"

CHAPTER SEVENTEEN

"I saw what I wanted to."

Captain Anson Olivera frowned at the reports on his terminal. His new promotion should have taken him out of a cockpit. Normally, a fighter jock had to move onto something more "important" than squadron or even strikegroup command to advance beyond commander, but the Navy had decided to take a page from the Tabbies' book. The Orions—arguably the best (and certainly the most enthusiastic) strikefighter practitioners—were far less rigid in their personnel career tracks, and it wasn't uncommon for an Orion pilot to reach the rank of small claw or even claw—roughly equivalent to a TFN commodore—while still drawing flight pay. Indeed, the present Lord Talphon, had made it all the way to small fang before they pried him out of a cockpit, though that was a special case.

Olivera grimaced. It irked him to admit it, but the Tabbies were better than Terrans at fighter ops. For that matter, they were better even than the Ophiuchi. Their equipment wasn't—in fact, it wasn't as good—and their individual pilots were less capable than Ophiuchi. But unlike the TFN, the KON was uncompromisingly carrier oriented. The Federation Navy was a "balanced" fleet in which the battle-line and carrier forces were coequals. That had proved a lifesaver on occasions when carriers accidentally strayed into range of enemy capital ships, and carriers were ill-suited to things like warp point assaults. They were meant to stay away from hostile starships while their fighter "main batteries" went out and killed the enemy, not to mix it up with capital ships, minefields, or energy buoys. That sort of silly operation was the purview of the battle-line.

The Tabbies didn't see things that way. For them, the only truly honorable form of combat was between *individuals*, which had made the fighter a gift from the gods for them. Unlike the TFN, the KON relegated the battle-line to a purely supporting function except in warp point assaults. The fighter was *the* decisive weapon for the Khan's fangs, one they'd learned to wield with more elan and skill than any other navy in space, and Olivera suspected the seniority their active-duty pilots could attain was a major part of the reason.

Admiral Murakuma seemed to agree. She and Admiral Teller had reorganized their carriers on a distinctly Orion pattern, and that was why Olivera and what was left of SG 47 had moved to the carrier *Orca*, flagship of Carrier Division 503. Admiral Teller had opted to retain the battlecruiser *Sorcerer* as his flagship, but Admiral Rendova, his second-in-command, flew her lights in *Orca*, and she'd wanted Olivera where he was handy, because Ms. Olivera's little boy Anson had just become the TFN's first *farshath-khanaak*. The Orion term translated roughly as "lord of the war fist"—a somewhat poetic way to describe an entire task force's or fleet's senior pilot. Except in purely administrative matters, Olivera's group and squadron COs reported to *him*, not the skippers of whatever carrier they happened to fly from. He would not only lead them in combat but represent them at the highest levels, and unnatural as it seemed, he had almost as much clout on the ops end as Admiral Teller did.

Which was all very well, but didn't change how expensive those ops were proving. Fighter jocks always had lower combat life expectancies than battle-line personnel, but the glitz and glamor of the deadly little strikefighters kept attracting the hot dogs—like, Olivera admitted, himself—anyway. And from a cold-blooded viewpoint, it made sense. A fighter squadron consisted of only thirty or forty people, including alternate flight crews, and fighters were cheap compared to starships. Any group CO sweated blood to bring all his people back every time, but fighters were fragile, ultimately expendable weapons, and the people who flew them knew it.

Oh, yeah, we know it, Olivera thought grimly, *but we've taken at least eighty percent losses in every battle to date except Redemption, and sooner or later these bastards are going to come up with their own AFHAWK. Nobody who's ever tried to penetrate their close-in defenses is dumb enough to think they're stupid, whatever their SOP looks like. They know how badly they need a long-ranged fighter killer, and once they develop it, we're going to get hurt even worse.*

He shook his head irritably. Of course they were getting hurt, but that was largely because of the odds they faced! Doctrine called for using numbers to saturate the enemy's defenses, and they hadn't been able to do that . . . yet. But Fifth Fleet now boasted the most powerful carrier component assembled in sixty years—since the First Battle of Thebes—and there were enough long-ranged heavy hitters in the battle-line to take a lot of pressure off them. He wasn't going to indulge in any foolish optimism, but—

He inhaled deeply, shook himself, and returned to his paperwork. One way or another, they'd learn how effective those changes were in about forty-seven more hours.

Vanessa Murakuma stood on *Cobra's* flag bridge, hands clasped behind her, and watched the master plot. Demosthenes and Jackson were exasperated with her for retaining her battleship flagship now that sufficient superdreadnoughts were available, and she understood their frustration. A battleship was a fragile place for a fleet commander to fly her lights, but *Cobra* had been her flagship for over two years. Her tactical and plotting departments were a smoothly functioning extension of her own staff, and she wasn't about to spend the time breaking in a new flagship in the midst of a campaign this furious.

Besides, we've taken less damage than any other capital ship in the fleet. Who was it who said "I'd rather be lucky than good"? Her mouth flickered in a small smile at the thought, but then the smile vanished and her eyes narrowed. It was time.

The Justin warp point's environs had changed drastically in the last two months. The huge Fleet Base had labored—was *still* laboring—to repair her damaged units, though the worst hurt ones had been sent further up the line. But while the Base's yard modules dealt with her warships, hordes of construction ships were busy assembling powerful, prefabricated OWPs drawn from Fortress Command's peacetime stockpiles. They'd put them together well away from the warp point and any pounce the Bugs might engineer, but now a solid shell of twenty had been towed into position. Another ten were almost ready, and still more were being thrown together at top speed. Coupled with the dense minefields and energy buoys which were finally available, they had the firepower to handle even one of the Bugs' simultaneous transits. Even if she couldn't retake Justin, it would no longer be necessary for her to concede the warp point.

But at this moment, her attention wasn't on the forts or minefields. It was on thirty-six tiny icons, each representing a single pinnace. A lot of the volunteers crewing those small craft were about to die, but she *had* to have some idea of the Bugs' deployment, and until the R&D types got off their asses and put the promised warp-capable recon drones into production, those pinnaces were the only way to get it. If she threw enough through in a single transit, the odds said at least one or two would get back with the data she needed.

She brooded over the plot, watching the clock tick down, and bit her lip, hating herself for what she had no option but to do. She and her staff had assembled ten different ops plans, each predicated on a different Bug deployment. Ten minutes after the surviving pinnaces returned and uploaded their data, one of those plans would go into effect.

Forty-eight heavy cruisers floated amid the minefields. There might have been more, but the enemy's last attack had proved he could destroy them any time he chose, and the Fleet had decided not to expose additional units. But that had not deprived the cruisers of a mission, and they waited to perform it.

A sudden shoal of small craft sped out of the warp point. A few interpenetrated, but most survived, and they swept outward while augmented sensor suites probed the warp point's environs. The mines ignored such small, agile targets, as did the laser buoys seeded among them, but the ready-duty cruisers opened fire instantly. Another half dozen pinnaces died, but the range was long, they were difficult targets, and the heavy cruisers were far too slow to pursue them. They could only engage any foolish enough to enter their envelope, and over half the pinnaces survived to dash back through the warp point to safety.

The cruisers watched them go. They had done their duty . . . and the trap was set.

Ling Tian waited patiently. She knew *Cobra*'s Combat Information Center would upload the information as soon as all the pinnaces' reports had been collated, and she forced her face to remain serene while she waited.

Ah! Her display blinked, and a forest of light codes appeared. Her trained eyes skimmed them quickly, and she allowed a small smile to flaw her serenity.

"We've got the first run, Sir," she called. Admiral Murakuma walked towards her, and she went on speaking. "We make it forty-five to fifty of those OWP cruisers right on the warp point, with another, larger force just over one light-minute out. They seem to be in standby mode."

"Numbers?" Murakuma rested a hand on Ling's shoulder and bent over her display.

"Even with their sensors augmented, that's long range for pinnaces, but we've got a tentative count. It looks—" Ling punched a button and watched the sidebar change "—like forty-two SDs and forty-five to fifty CLs. We can't pick the *Cataphracts* out at this range."

"Any breakdown on the superdreadnoughts?"

"Negative. We can't tell an *Archer* from an *Avalanche* until they bring up their systems."

"True." Murakuma rubbed her lip, but her green eyes flamed. She'd been right—they *had* hurt the bastards badly. Only forty-two superdreadnoughts and *no* battlecruisers . . . no *wonder* they hadn't put in a second attack on Sarasota! Fifth Fleet had only twenty-five SDs of its own, but she had eight battleships and almost fifty battlecruisers to support them. Even without any fighters at all, *she* finally had the force advantage.

And I do *have fighters*, she thought viciously. *Over a thousand of them!*

She nodded sharply and turned to the screens linking her to her task force and battlegroup commanders. "It looks like their dispositions are tailor made for Salamis Four," she said crisply. "Demosthenes, we're transmitting the target profiles now. Update your birds; we'll go through on their heels, and I want to hit them before they can redeploy!"

The heavy cruisers which had been at standby brought their systems to full readiness. It would do no good in the long run, but if the enemy were cunning enough to send through more pinnaces as observers, he might wonder why they didn't even attempt to defend themselves.

Eighty SBMHAWKs flashed into Justin. The defenders poured fire into them, and killed nineteen before they could launch, but sixty-one *did* launch, and three hundred-plus SBMs roared down on the cruisers. Point defense stopped almost a quarter of them; the other two hundred and thirty reduced forty-three heavy cruisers to glowing wreckage.

The five Bug survivors were drifting, toothless hulks when the first Terran starships came through, but they hadn't been the warp point's only defenders. Laser buoys attacked instantly, and the first three ships were ripped and torn. Massive armor blew apart, atmosphere fumed into space, and men and women died, but superdreadnoughts were tough. They survived, and they'd drawn all the buoys' onto themselves. Undamaged consorts moved past, already firing AMBAMs into the mines, and TFNS *Antifola, Erciyas* and *Hsinkao* turned to limp back into Sarasota while damage control and rescue teams fought to save trapped and wounded crewmates.

Their battle had lasted all of ninety seconds.

Murakuma set her teeth against the nausea of transit, then waited impatiently for her plot to steady. *There!*

She peered into it, and her eyes burned hotter. The Bug battle-line was only beginning to move in on the warp point, and all of Waldeck's TF 51 had already made transit. They were still bunched within the confines of the mine-free zone, but the AMBAMs were doing their job, and Demosthenes' lead battlecruisers were already probing forward through the lanes. Battleships and superdreadnoughts moved in their wakes, and she bared her teeth as the Bugs suddenly stopped advancing. They hung there for a moment, and then they began to fall back. They fell *back*. They were retreating! For the first time in eight months, the bastards were *retreating!*

"We've got them," she whispered. "By God, this time we've *got* them!"

"The enemy appear to be withdrawing at maximum speed, Sir." Ling Tian couldn't have heard Murakuma's whisper, but her confirmation was perfectly timed, and the admiral heard her ops officer's own exultation behind the professionalism of her report.

"They can run, but they aren't fast enough to hide," Murakuma said flatly, and looked at Waldeck's com screen. "Go get them, Demosthenes! Jackson can follow at his best speed. With a little luck, he'll be ready to send in his first strike about the time your SBMs range on them."

"Aye, *aye*, Sir!" Waldeck's smile was almost as hungry

as her own, and Fifth Fleet's battle-line went to maximum power as it thundered after its slower foes.

Jackson Teller prowled TFNS *Sorcerer's* bridge deck like a caged Old Terran tiger while the rest of Fifth Fleet pursued the Bugs. He had even more reason than Waldeck to even the score. He *wanted* their asses, wanted to watch them die, wanted to be there personally when they paid for the civilians they'd butchered. And he *would* be there. It took time to pass thirty carriers and light carriers, seventeen battlecruisers, and their escorts through a warp point, but his slowest unit was twice as fast as a Bug superdreadnought, and his fighters were even faster. He'd catch the bastards, and then he and Demosthenes would kill every fucking one of them.

His last unit made transit, and he turned to his com section as his task force started through the cleared lanes. Captain Olivera looked tense but eager on the small screen linked to the cockpit of his command fighter, and Teller bared his teeth as their eyes met.

"Launch your birds, Captain. Get the recon fighters out to cover the flanks, then take your strike forward. With any luck, we'll finish these things off in a single pass."

"Sir, that sounds good to me," Olivera agreed, and switched to his command net. "All units, we will launch in succession. Launch order Alpha One. I say again, Alpha One."

Acknowledgments came back, and then *Orca's* catapult kicked him in the belly.

Teller watched the first fighters appear on his display. Under emergency conditions, he could have flushed full decks and put every fighter into space in a single launch, but there was always a risk of collision when carriers in close company did that. The congestion of the cleared lane through the mines only made that worse, and he had plenty of time, so—

"*Incoming fire!*" someone screamed. "Missiles in acquisition, bearing one-seven-three, zero-two-seven! Impact in seventeen seconds—*mark!*"

Teller wheeled to *Sorcerer*'s master plot, and his face went white. Dozens of missiles, scores—*hundreds!*—of them had just appeared out of nowhere. They must have been launched from cloak, and now they streaked in from dead astern—*straight out of his blind spot!*

"Expedite launch!" he shouted. "Get them off—*get them off!*"

His carrier commanders tried to obey, but the missiles were coming in too fast, and Teller's face went even whiter as he realized those were SBMs. The Bugs had *SBMs*, and that was why they hadn't been spotted. Because they'd been able to hide in cloak further from the warp point than anyone had suspected and still engage.

His *Dunedin*-class CLEs swung wildly to open their broadsides. If they could get around, acquire clear tracking data, his carriers could still engage the incoming fire with datalinked point defense. But there wasn't time for *that*, either. Just one of his four heavy carrier groups managed to acquire; the other three were defenseless as the missiles shrieked in, and only the accuracy penalties imposed by the extremely long range at which the Bugs had fired saved any of them.

Fireballs ripped through TF 52's heart. TFNS *Airedale* and *Beagle* blew apart, and four thousand men and women—and seventy-two priceless fighters—went with them. More ships staggered as the missiles screamed in, and *Coachdog*, *Dalmatian*, and the Ophiuchi carriers *Zirk-Bajaamna* and *Zirk-Kohara* died. And then a massive salvo roared down on *Sorcerer*, and she and her entire company—including Vice Admiral Jackson Teller, TFN—vanished in an incandescent cloud of gas.

"Dear God." Vanessa Murakuma's whisper hung in her own ears as the Bugs massacred her carriers. They were seventy light-seconds astern, far beyond any range at which she could intervene, and the frantic crackle of battle chatter washed over her as men and women fought for survival. Three of the *Dunedins*, still maneuvering hard in an effort to get their point defense into action, strayed into the minefield and were blown apart, but at least some of her ships were managing to defend themselves against the last few salvoes.

"A decoy." She turned her head, green eyes shocked, and saw savage comprehension on LeBlanc's face. "Those fucking CAs were *decoys*—Judas goats! They *wanted* us to blow our way in over them. They *deliberately* sacrificed fifty cruisers for *bait!*"

Horror crackled in his voice, and a detached corner of Murakuma's brain realized why. He'd stressed the Bugs' willingness to take losses over and over, like some stuck recording. If anyone in Fifth Fleet had grasped that point, it was he . . . yet the minds of beings who could condemn fifty starships and their crews to death simply to lure an opponent into ambush were too fundamentally inhuman, in every sense of the word, for even Marcus to have seen this coming.

And I didn't either. I saw what I wanted to see. I saw them running, and I saw a chance to kill them, and I took it, and, oh, dear God, how many of my own people have I just killed?

"Sir, the first force is turning back. They're coming in to engage!" Ling Tian, alone, seemed unaffected. She wasn't. She was simply doing her duty—burying herself in it to escape her own horror—but Murakuma wanted to spit curses at her. The admiral clenched her fists and shook herself savagely. Somehow she had to get her people out. She was an incompetent, little better than a murderer, but she was still in command, and she reached out to the terrible weight.

"Com, prepare to record for courier drones," Vanessa Murakuma said, and her soprano voice was calm, almost even.

The Fleet achieved only that single, devastating firing pass before the enemy managed to adjust formation. His lighter escorts swung around, tacking back and forth across his bleeding formation to clear their sensors, and despite his surprise, his point defense knocked down the follow-up salvoes with relative ease. But the fire had concentrated on the ships that carried his attack craft. Most were damaged, one was an immobile hulk, and ten had been destroyed outright. At least half the attack craft had been destroyed in their launch bays, and the Fleet charged forward, still cloaked. It would overrun the warp point and crush the cripples, then cut the rest of the enemy off from retreat.

Fifty-Sixth Fang of the Khan Anaasa'zolaath raged about his flag deck like a wounded *zeget*, and officers flinched aside as he swept down upon him, claws flicking in and out, in and out of their sheaths in a combat instinct he could not overcome. Sixty thousand years of instinct screamed to rush to his human commander's aid, but her own orders held him here, waiting. He understood her reasoning, and even in his fury a part of him felt enormous respect for her cool calculation, but every dragging minute tore at him like white-hot pincers.

"Sir, the pods—"

He wheeled with such a furious snarl Claw Renassaa recoiled. The fang's ears flattened with shame at his ops officer's response, and he fought himself back under control.

"Yes, Renassaa?" He made the words come out calmly, and the claw straightened.

"The pods have been programmed, Sir," he said, and Anaasa gave an approving ear flick.

"Good, Renassaa. Good." He rested a clawed hand lightly on the other's shoulder for a moment, then forced himself to walk slowly to his command chair. He settled himself in it and leaned back, for there was nothing else he could do.

The three worst damaged of Teller's surviving CVs were also closest to the warp point. They managed to turn and run, trailing atmosphere like blood. More missiles screamed in on them, but they vanished back to Sarasota before the warheads struck. TFNS *Lexington* was less fortunate, and the helplessly crippled light carrier vanished in another eye-tearing boil of fury.

The rest of TF 52's survivors were too far from the warp point; they could only run towards TF 51 at the best speed they could still manage. *Sorcerer* had died, but at least the rest of their command ships had escaped, and the nets were still up. As long as any member of any net could track the incoming fire, they could defend against it, and Admiral Ellen Rendova's *Orca* led them as they ran desperately for the doubtful cover of the trapped battle-line.

Damage reports flooded *Orca*'s command deck, and Rendova winced at the litany of disaster. Two-thirds of her fighters had been destroyed in their bays or were trapped aboard ships too damaged to launch them, and the Bugs had SBMs. Fifth Fleet's range advantage had been stripped away, and without her fighters to redress it—

"Got 'em, Sir!" She whirled to her ops officer. Commander Houston stared into a display tied to the recon fighters sweeping back along the incoming missiles' tracks for the enemy turn. She saw his shoulders tighten, and then he looked up at her. "Seventy of them, Sir," he said. "Twenty-four battlecruisers and forty-six superdreadnoughts. Looks like only twelve are *Archers*; most of that first wave must have come from the others' XO racks."

"Position?" Rendova snapped.

"They'll reach the warp point in six minutes," Houston said flatly.

The force TF 51 had been pursuing had turned. It was sweeping back, and already its first SBMs crossed with Murakuma's. *At least we've still got better point defense*, she thought bitterly, but that was her only remaining advantage, and it wasn't going to be enough against so many launchers. She could still take the first group of Bugs, but they'd beat Waldeck's battle-line to scrap in the process, and then that second force would sweep up the pieces.

But only if I let them! she told herself fiercely, and looked up at Waldeck's com screen.

"Ready, Demosthenes?"

"Yes, Sir." The burly Corporate Worlder managed a grim smile. "I sure hope this works."

"It'll work—I just don't know how well." Murakuma made herself draw a deep breath, buttressing herself against guilt and despair while her flashing brain rechecked her desperate plan for flaws. She found none—but, then, the situation was too grim for complicated maneuvers.

"Very well, Demosthenes. It's up to you. Bring us about."

The enemy's battle-line reversed course, rushing back to succor its wounded companions, and that was the stupidest thing he had done yet. He was faster than the Fleet. He should have run for it, drawn out of range, tried to maneuver his way around the defenders, instead.

His new course was headed directly for the warp point, as if he thought he could blast his way through the waiting superdreadnoughts and battlecruisers, but he was wrong. Com lasers whispered across the gulf between the Fleet's separated battle-lines, and the second component slowed. It would move just past the warp point, maneuvering to stay between the enemy and his only way home, and wait until its fellows drove him into its tentacles.

Anson Olivera gathered his battered strikegroups astern of the carriers. He didn't know exactly what Admiral Murakuma planned, and the thought of leading his pilots into that much firepower turned his belly to lead, but he knew she had no choice, and his earlier thoughts about expendability jeered at him. If the destruction of every surviving fighter got even a single division of superdreadnoughts out of the trap, the exchange would be completely worthwhile . . . which wasn't much comfort for the human and Ophiuchi pilots about to sacrifice themselves.

The pursuing Bugs swept past the warp point and slowed. They came to a halt, backs to the warp point, targeting systems tracking his fighters, and he swallowed.

He sat tense and still, waiting for the order, and a corner of his brain noted the courier drones flashing past him.

"Fang Anaasa!" Anaasa looked up at his com officer's shout. "The drones!" the officer said sharply, and Anaasa bared his fangs.

"*Go!*" Olivera's command crackled over the net, and two hundred fighters streaked straight down the Bugs' throat. Every one of those pilots knew—didn't think; *knew*—he or she was going to die. But they were doomed anyway, and they rammed their power through the emergency gate, for if they had to die, at least they could kill a few more enemies first.

Olivera's vision grayed as Malachi took them in at a velocity so far beyond design limits he couldn't believe the bird was holding together, and he bared his teeth—then jerked in surprise, despite the crushing power of the drive, at Carl Hathaway's shriek of delight.

"Beautiful! Oh, *beautiful!*" the tac officer screamed. "Look at 'em, Skip! *Look at those fucking Tabbies go!*"

One moment, the second Arachnid force had the situation completely under control; the next, an insane explosion of violence ripped into it as TF 53—the *Orion* task force the Bugs had never seen, never suspected had been held back—flashed through the warp point into its rear. No one in the galaxy was better at fighter ops than the KON, and Fang Anaasa's deck crews set a new all-Navy record for launch speeds. Two hundred and ten fresh fighters charged straight up the Bugs' blind spots as *their* missiles had charged up TF 52's, and they weren't alone, for the SBMHAWKs Murakuma hadn't used in her initial bombardment came with them. There'd been no need to use them to kill a mere fifty cruisers; now seventy fresh pods belched missiles into the astonished Bugs, and the fighters screamed in behind them, ripple-salvoing their FRAMs.

It was the most devastating fighter strike in history.

Twenty Bug superdreadnoughts were blown apart in sixty shrieking seconds, and eighteen battlecruisers went with them. Almost every surviving ship was damaged, many badly, and the Tabby pilots closed in, accepting brutal losses from the survivors' point defense to strafe with their onboard lasers. Less than forty seconds later, Anson Olivera's fighters came howling in from dead ahead, taking their own losses but slamming a fresh wave of FRAMs down the Bugs' throats.

The twin strike couldn't kill them all, but it hurt them, and the ships which had lured Murakuma into pursuing them had fallen too far astern of TF 51 to help them. Demosthenes Waldeck's battle-line flashed past TF 52's wounded carriers, and Rendova's ships reefed around in the hairpin turns of inertia-canceling drives to follow in their wake. But it was up to the heavies to clear the way, and Waldeck and Vanessa Murakuma took them straight into the Bugs' teeth as though *superdreadnoughts* were so many more fighters.

It was insane, a violation of every manual ever written . . . and the only path to salvation. Every one of Anaasa's carriers and battlecruisers was within the Bug's weapons envelope; if TF 51 *didn't* close, they would be annihilated, despite the shocking damage they'd inflicted, and Murakuma *had* to break through before the Bugs pursuing her could overhaul. The enemy knew it, too, and detached his faster cruisers in a desperate bid to assist their fellows on the warp point. But the cruisers had to get past TF 52, and Rendova launched her surviving escorts into them in a savage, short-ranged hammering match that kept them off Waldeck's back . . . at a price.

Yet furious as that fight was, it was a sideshow, and Murakuma sealed her helmet as TF 51 slammed into the Bugs. Launchers went to sprint-mode, spitting standard missiles and the heavier, far more destructive, CM-sized close assault missiles. Answering fire smashed back, and *Cobra* heaved as fists of flame hammered her shields flat. Force beams, primaries, plasma guns, hetlasers, and Ophiuchi particle beams snarled at ranges as low as eight hundred kilometers, and armor ripped like tissue. Damage alarms screamed, two of her superdreadnoughts blew apart, a Bug battlecruiser rammed a Terran battleship head-on, two more battleships vanished in massive fireballs, and then something smashed into *Cobra* like the hammer of Thor. She felt her flagship heave, heard the scream of escaping air, saw Ling Tian torn in half by a flying axe that was once a bulkhead. And then something exploded into the side of her own command chair, and her universe vanished in an instant of agony too terrible to endure.

The last Bug superdreadnought blew up under the fire of three Terran superdreadnoughts and sixty fighters, and TF 51's survivors turned at bay. They faced the remaining enemy force, holding it off until the last damaged carrier made transit. Of the five hundred fighters which had actually launched, two hundred and six escaped aboard Anaasa's carriers and the only three unhurt Terran CVs, and then the rearguard retreated to Sarasota, still smashing sullenly at its foes.

Eight superdreadnoughts, seven battleships, fourteen battlecruisers, eleven carriers, five heavy cruisers, and eighteen light cruisers remained behind forever.

"M-Marcus?" Vanessa Murakuma didn't recognize her own hoarse whisper, but Marcus LeBlanc bent over her instantly. She lay under crisp sheets, staring up at a pastel overhead, and she could feel nothing from the waist down.

"Hi," LeBlanc said softly.

"T-Tian?" she whispered, and he flinched. Then he shook his head gently, and she turned away in agony. Her tears blotted the pillow, but LeBlanc's gentle fingers cupped her chin, making her turn back to him.

"You got them out, Vanessa," he said quietly.

"But how many?" Her voice was stark and wounded, her green eyes dark, bottomless wells of pain, and he blinked his own eyes as tears stung.

"More than anyone else could have," he said. Her mouth twisted, and he bent lower over her. "Damn it,

Vanessa, it's true! All right, they suckered you. Well, they suckered me, Waldeck, Teller, Anaasa—even Tian! *No one* could have seen that coming . . . and no one *else* could have gotten us out of it. Don't you *dare* think otherwise, or . . . or—"

"Or what?" She expected it to come out with savage bitterness, but to her astonishment it came out soft, almost chiding.

"Or as soon as you're out of that bed, Sir, I'll put you over my knee, peel down those trousers, and whale the living shit out of you!" he told her fiercely, and a soft ghost of a laugh gurgled in her throat. Her eyes softened, and she raised an arm which felt far heavier than even a full standard gravity could account for to touch the side of his face.

"Oh, Marcus," she whispered. "I should have listened to you, love."

"Why? You thought I was arguing just because I was worried about *you* . . . and I was," he admitted. He sank into a chair and caught her hand as it started to fall, cradling it against his cheek. "I guess maybe that's why Regs frown on people who love each other in the same chain of command, isn't it?" he said gently.

"Maybe. But you were still right."

"It's my job to be right, and sometimes I manage it. But it's *your* job to win battles, not take counsel of your fears. Or mine." He smiled and stroked red hair back from her forehead.

"How bad is it?" she asked after a moment, gesturing at her lower body with her free hand, and he smiled again.

"It looks terrible," he said frankly, "but the doctors are delighted with themselves, and they say you should be up and around again within six or seven weeks. You'll have to take it easy for quite a while, but you're going to be fine, Vanessa. Really."

"Well, at least I'll have time to 'take it easy,'" she said with a trace of bitterness, and he raised an eyebrow. "Come on, Marcus! You *know* they're going to relieve me after *this* fuck-up!"

"You have a strange way of describing a battle in which you kicked the bad guys' ass, Admiral Murakuma," LeBlanc said, and she snorted her opinion of his judgment. "No, I mean it. The Bugs lost a hundred and thirty-nine ships. That's a better than two-to-one ratio in hulls, and the tonnage balance was even more decisive. Sky Marshal Avram is very pleased with you—and she's going to be even more pleased when she hears what happened yesterday."

"Yesterday?" Murakuma repeated blankly, and he nodded.

"The Bugs tried to bounce Sarasota. I guess they figured they'd hurt us badly enough to make it easy, and they brought up reinforcements. But Demosthenes and Leroy—and, Lord, how I *wish* you'd seen that pair working together!—got reorganized with Anaasa and put Leonidas Two into operation exactly as you'd planned it. They lost every cruiser and the first twenty-five SDs that tried to follow." His eyes blazed, and he stroked more hair from her forehead. "They broke off, Vanessa! You finally stopped the bastards so cold they *knew* they were licked!"

"You mean Demosthenes did," she whispered, but her own eyes glowed, and LeBlanc shook his head.

"Woman, you aren't allowed any more doubts. After all—" he grinned wickedly "—that's why *I'm* here, right?"

She laughed again, softly, and then he bent still closer and kissed her.

CHAPTER EIGHTEEN

"Welcome along, Sir."

The powered walker whined softly as Vanessa Mura-kuma "walked" from the intraship car into the boat bay. The muscle feedback-controlled walker was less responsive than the direct neural-feed prosthetics used to replace lost limbs, which made her progress more than a little clumsy, but she wasn't complaining. She didn't *want* permanent replacement parts, however efficient, and the surgeons promised her legs would be good as new in time. They were talking about six months, though she intended to make it in four, and this wasn't even the first time she'd had to use a walker, for her home world prepared its people poorly for the planets most humans lived on. She'd spent three years exercising her Truman-bred muscles before reporting to the Academy, but New Annapolis' 1.25 gravities had still been a hideous ordeal. The medical staff had insisted she stick with the walker for her first semester, and the aching cramps protesting a body weight sixty percent greater than the one she'd been bred to had made her perfectly willing to obey.

Now she maneuvered herself into position in TFNS *Euphrates'* boat bay and tried to suppress a pang of grief for her last flagship as another cutter docked. *Cobra* had been luckier than many of Fifth Fleet's ships, but she'd still taken a fearsome pounding. She'd only returned to service last week, and two-thirds of her tactical department were squeaky-new replacements for men and women who'd died in Justin. Murakuma no longer had a logical reason to oppose shifting her lights to one of the better-protected *Mekong*-class SDs—and, she admitted, she no longer wanted to. Seeing all those new faces in place of the ones she'd come to know so well . . .

She shook off the thought as a hatch opened and the side party's two separate honor guards—one of Terran Marines, gorgeous in black-and-green dress uniform, and a second of even more gorgeously bejeweled Orion Marines—snapped to attention.

The first person through the hatch was a human. He was of little more than average height for his race, but despite the snow-white hair and beard, he radiated a sense of purposeful mass which made him seem much bigger. His Orion companion's night-black pelt was liberally threaded with silver, yet the Tabby carried himself with a springy predator's grace, only slightly stiffened by age. No one, however, would have described the human as "graceful." He certainly wasn't *clumsy*, but he moved with a burly, unstoppable momentum which dared any object to intrude into his path . . . and promised no quarter for anything foolish enough to accept the challenge.

"Grand Fleet, arriving!" the intercom announced through the twitter of the bosun's pipes, and *Euphrates'* captain nodded to the side party.

"Preeee-sent, *arms*!"

The barked command was in Standard English, since *Euphrates* was a human ship, but both Marine contingents snapped to their version of present arms with the simultaneous precision of careful practice. A corner of Murakuma's eye noted the perfection of the maneuver, yet her attention was focused on the two visitors as they saluted the Federation banner on the boat bay's forward bulkhead, then turned to salute Captain Decker as well.

"Permission to come aboard, Sir?"

"Permission granted, Sir," Jessica Decker said.

The visitors crossed the line on the deck, formally

boarding the ship, and Murakuma's walker whined as she stepped forward and saluted.

"Admiral Antonov, Fang Kthaara. Welcome to Fifth Fleet."

"Thank you, Admiral Murakuma." Antonov's deep, bass rumble hadn't gotten any frailer since his retirement. She'd met him several times during her stint as a War College instructor, and she felt a bit odd addressing him as "Admiral," since he'd been Sky Marshal at the time.

"It's good to see you again," Antonov went on, and waved a hand at the tall Tabby. "I don't believe you've met Lord Talphon?"

"No, Sir." Murakuma turned to the Orion with a polite, tooth-hidden smile of greeting. Ninth Fang of the Khan Kthaara'zarthan, Lord Talphon and *Khanhaku'a'zarthan*, had been a pilot's pilot in a service where the fighter reigned supreme. He was also the ninth ranking active-duty officer in the Khan's service and almost as legendary—in TFN service, as well as the KON—as Antonov himself, and Murakuma's small, Orion-style bow of greeting was deeply respectful. "I've certainly heard a great deal about you, however, Sir. I'm honored to meet you at last, and my carrier pilots have asked me to extend their invitation to a small party aboard *Orca*. I believe they want to offer you an, ah, traditional welcome to the Fleet."

The big Tabby's whiskers twitched as he gave her a small, answering bow of acceptance.

"I would be honored, Ahhhdmiraal," he yowled as her earbug translated, "although a warrior of my advanced years may find it somewhat difficult to do full justice to their invitation."

"Ha!" Antonov snorted derisively. "No doubt they'll offer you bourbon or some other anemic substitute!"

"No, Sir," Murakuma murmured. "Least Fang Anaasa has informed us Lord Talphon prefers vodka, and I understand a suitable supply has been laid in."

"*Khorosho!* Good! Perhaps we'll civilize our flight crews yet!"

"We'll certainly try, Sir," Murakuma agreed, then waved towards the intraship car. "In the meantime, I've asked the Fleet's senior officers to assemble in Briefing Room Three. If you and Fang Kthaara would care to accompany me—?"

"Of course, Admiral." Antonov nodded briskly to the side party and honor guards, and he and Kthaara adjusted their pace to that of Murakuma's walker as they crossed to the waiting car.

Murakuma steered the walker into her cabin and allowed herself to sigh with relief as the hatch closed behind her. She worked her way behind her desk, maneuvering carefully in quarters designed for people with two good legs, and parked at her terminal. That was the only word for it. Handy as her artificial suspension was, it was a pain to climb in and out of, but at least, she reminded herself with a weary grin as she brought up Fifth Fleet's current order of battle, it was also the right height to let her work at her desk without a chair.

Just as well, too. The way the paperwork keeps piling up, I'll be stuck here for hours. Don't think I'll complain, though. The problems I've got now beat the crap out of the ones I had two months ago!

She studied the order of battle with deeply grateful satisfaction, for despite the reaming her command had taken in Third Justin, she was stronger than ever before, and the trickle of reinforcements flowing down through the Romulus Cluster was about to become a torrent.

We did it, she thought almost wonderingly. *We actually did it. We held the bastards long enough for the Alliance to get organized . . . and now*—her face turned suddenly grimmer—*it's time to turn this thing around and kick their asses the hell out of Justin!*

She ran her eyes down the OB. Additional units had come up from every Allied navy: Terran, Ophiuchi, Orion—even the first Gorm ships. She was particularly glad to see the latter, for the high tactical speed of Gorm starships made them especially valuable. More to the point, perhaps, the GSN had the furthest to come to reach Sarasota, and the arrival of its first units had been an enormous shot in the arm for Fifth Fleet's morale.

Not that their contribution was solely symbolic. Fifth Fleet now counted over a hundred and twenty starships, headed by eighty-one capital ships (including six GSN superdreadnoughts and five GSN battlecruisers) and supported by nineteen fleet and eight light carriers. Its Task Force 54—commanded by the newly promoted Rear Admiral Reichman since his return to active duty— consisted of twenty-nine massive fortresses, with almost eight hundred fighters embarked, and still more forts were under construction. Fifth Fleet's mobile units could put over nine hundred more fighters, almost half of them Orion, into space, and for the first time, Vanessa Murakuma was absolutely confident of her ability to stop any Bug offensive cold.

But the point isn't to stop them, she reminded herself, green eyes momentarily bleak.

She studied the numbers a moment longer, then punched a combination into her com panel, and the screen lit almost instantly with the face of a painfully young female lieutenant.

"Intelligence, Lieutenant Abernathy," the young woman announced, then stiffened to a sort of seated attention as she recognized Fifth Fleet's CO. "How can I help you, Admiral?"

"Is Commodore LeBlanc there?"

"No, Sir. He's in CIC."

"Would you ask him to join me in my quarters? I'd like to see Captain Mackenna and Commander Cruciero, too. Please run them down for me and ask them to accompany him."

"Of course, Sir."

"Thank you." Murakuma cut the circuit and leaned back. Antonov's decision to inspect the front meant he and Lord Talphon would be looking over her shoulder, but both of them had earned reputations as aggressive, hard-hitting COs in the Theban War, and nothing indicated they'd changed since. She was confident she could convince them to authorize the operation . . . assuming she could convince her own staff she hadn't lost her mind.

"You want to do *what?*"

LeBlanc hadn't raised his voice. In fact, he sounded more resigned than incredulous, and Mackenna simply sat back in his chair with a sigh. Commander Ernesto Cruciero, Ling Tian's replacement as Murakuma's ops officer, was another matter. His hawk-nosed, dark face was well suited to concealing strong emotion, yet he couldn't quite hide his shock. He looked back and forth between his seniors for a moment, then cleared his throat.

"Excuse me, Sir," he said diffidently, "but we don't know a thing about what the Bugs are doing on the other side of the warp point, and we *do* know at least one of their major systems is far closer to Justin than we are to our own core systems. Given the fleets they've thrown at us so far, don't we have to assume they must have reinforced at least as strongly as *we* have?"

"Certainly," Murakuma agreed, and smiled thinly at the commander's expression. "I understand your point, Ernesto, but the transit times for our reinforcements—and theirs— aren't going to change. If we decide we can't risk action as long as they can reinforce faster than we can, we'll never take the offensive at all."

"No doubt, Sir," Mackenna put in, "but our first responsibility has to be keeping them out of Sarasota, not battering ourselves against *their* defenses."

"Agreed." Murakuma nodded, but there was no give in her expression. "That's why we have TF 54 and the minefields covering the warp point. The purpose of fixed defenses, however, is to *free up* mobile forces, not anchor them in place. With Admiral Reichman to mind the store, we can afford to take some chances with our striking force—and I remind you all that there are still Terran civilians trapped in Justin. If our first responsibility is to protect Sarasota, surely our next highest obligation is to save as many Justinians as we can."

Mackenna and Cruciero glanced at each other. There was no possible counter for that argument, but clearly they both remembered Fifth Fleet's last venture into Justin. Murakuma watched them for a moment, then looked at LeBlanc.

"Marcus?" Her tone was neutral, but she held his eyes, and, after a moment, he shrugged.

"Leroy and Ernesto both have valid points, but so do you. And while I agree that they've probably reinforced even more heavily than us, there's an element no one else has mentioned." He sounded like a man who didn't like the point he was about to make, but he made it unflinchingly. "We may have the technological edge, but we've already seen how quickly these things put both second-generation antimatter warheads and SBMs into production. Since they had neither when they started shooting ten months ago, the fact that they have them *now* indicates their R&D is quick off the mark. Which—" he looked at Cruciero "—means that the longer we wait, the more chance there is of losing our current advantages, and that would put pressure on us to hit them as quickly as possible even if they were only in a position to *match* the tonnage we can deploy."

"So you think we should attack?" Murakuma pressed.

"No—I only think we *have* to," he said unhappily. There was a moment of silence, and then Mackenna twitched his shoulders.

"Marcus is right, Sir," he said flatly. "I shouldn't have let myself overlook that aspect."

"But even if they *do* duplicate our systems, they still have to put them into production." Cruciero's tone was respectful but persistent, and Murakuma noted it with approval. She didn't know him well yet—Mackenna had selected him while she was still in hospital—but he'd already demonstrated his competence, and it took courage for a commander to argue against the united opinion of an admiral, a commodore, and a captain. That was good. The last thing she wanted was an ops officer who rolled over and played dead.

"Maybe so," Mackenna said now, "but we can't afford to mirror-image them. We know how long it takes *us* to introduce new hardware, but they may be faster. Worse, we don't know how far their R&D has to go, and we won't know they've closed the gap on us—if they do—until they get around to using any new systems against us. That means we have to hit them as hard as we can while we do hold the edge. And, as the Admiral says, we've got an obligation to take Justin back while at least some of its people are still alive."

Cruciero sat back, eyes hooded, then nodded, and Murakuma hid a sigh of relief. They'd come around more quickly than she'd expected, and she suddenly wondered why she'd thought they wouldn't. Was it a leftover from the terrible pressures of her retreat to Sarasota? Or was it because *she* knew how dreadfully Fifth Fleet could get hurt in Justin? Had she been projecting her own inner doubts onto her staffers?

She shook the thought aside and leaned towards them.

"All right, then. Marcus, I want you and Leroy to bring our appreciations and projections up to date. I know they're all tentative, but they're all we've got to work from. Once you've done that, I want the four of us to work out several rough ops plans. I don't need a lot of detail yet, but I want something tangible in hand before I sit down with the Allied COs. I don't expect anyone to question the necessity of the operation; I only want a clear, definite basis for discussion."

"With your task force commanders, or with Admiral Antonov?" LeBlanc asked with a slight smile, and Murakuma looked at him innocently.

"Why, Marcus! Whatever makes you think I'm concerned by the Admiral's presence in our midst?" Her subordinates chuckled, and she smiled back. "All right, gentlemen—go put it together. I want your preliminary efforts on my terminal by 0900 tomorrow morning."

"A most audacious plan, Admiral Murakuma."

Ivan Antonov's deep voice was thoughtful as he gazed

at the holo above the conference table. Ernesto Cruciero may have had his doubts about Operation Navarino, but the half-dozen alternative ops plans he'd put together were impressively aggressive and made maximum use of the Alliance's tactical advantages. Now Antonov studied the display, conscious of the eyes watching him with carefully hidden tension . . . and of the youth behind those eyes. Even Murakuma was less than half his age, and the near veneration of her younger staffers made him uncomfortable. That unquestioning sense of awaiting the oracle's response was one of the reasons he'd retired in the first place. The antigerone treatments, unlike flashy gadgetry such as reactionless drives and faster-than-light travel, had changed the human condition in a fundamental way—the first such change since convenient contraception had broken the immemorial link between reproduction and sexual jollies. Now, a species selected by evolution to get out of the way of its adult children had the dubious blessing of living fossils like himself, as though Black Jack Pershing had lived on to command Operation Desert Storm.

On the other hand, he reminded himself, *perhaps a Pershing who'd kept himself technologically current wouldn't have been such a bad thing. At least he'd have had the experience to know what happens when you call a campaign off early!*

He shook the thought aside and used a light pencil to highlight the transport echelon which the holo showed following in the wake of Fifth Fleet's warships.

"I don't recall GHQ's having provided you this many Marines, however," he rumbled mildly. "According to this, you're planning on using a full corps—just over thee divisions."

"We are," Murakuma agreed, and nodded to Mackenna.

"We've checked the numbers, Admiral Antonov," he said confidently, "and we can make them up if we strip the Fleet Base, comb out all our shipboard Marine detachments, *and* combine Terran and Orion Marines in composite regiments. We'll have some problems with equipment and doctrine compatibility, but General Mondesi and Least Claw Thaaraan believe they can overcome the difficulties if we give them a couple of weeks."

"I see." Antonov glanced at his *vilkshatha* brother, and Kthaara gave a small ear flick of agreement. The admiral returned his eyes to the holo, his face giving no hint of the thoughts behind it, and sat in silence for another endless ninety seconds, then nodded slightly.

"Your plan seems sound, given what you know, Admiral Murakuma," he said slowly. "The problem, of course, is what you *don't* know, and omniscience is possible only for the Almighty. You have sufficient SBMHAWKs for the break in?"

"We believe so, Sir. Fang Anaasa's fleet train is bringing forward Orion pods in some numbers. They won't link with ours, but we intend to split the targeting assignments. Our birds will go for one type of unit—probably the heavy cruisers, if they've deployed as before—and the Orions' will go for any superdreadnoughts sufficiently close to the warp point."

"And if there *are* no capital ships?"

"Then we'll simply have to send them through in two waves and hit them with successive salvos. Or, if we have sufficient TFN pods, we can hold the Orion SBMHAWKs in reserve to cover our retreat in the event we're pushed back."

"I see." Antonov cocked his chair back, still gazing at the holo, then shrugged. "Fifth Fleet is your command, Admiral. *I* never enjoyed having some rear echelon gas bag second guess *me*—" Kthaara gave a deep, purring chuckle, which Antonov ignored "—so I suppose I should grant you the same freedom I enjoyed."

"Then you approve the operation, Sir?"

"Fifth Fleet is your command," Antonov repeated, "and you enjoy my fullest confidence. I would appreciate the chance to review your final ops plan, but, yes, I approve the operation." He smiled suddenly. "I only wish I could see the politicians when *they* hear about it!"

"I knew we would hear about politicians eventually, Vaanyaa!" Kthaara laughed.

"Ha! If you'd had to put up with all the officious shit *I've* had to endure, you'd have a more respectful attitude, Kthaara Kornazhovich!" Antonov shot back. "Do you remember how the *pizdi* were all shitting their pants before Parsifal?"

"Those were the days, were they not?" the big Tabby yowled regretfully. "But we were younger then—and you! You were a *zeget* with a broken tooth!"

"And you weren't?" Antonov snorted, then shook his head. "But you're right. We've grown too old. At last I truly understand how Howard Anderson must have felt." He looked at Murakuma, and his deep voice was soft. "Remember this moment, Admiral. The most horrible lesson a commander ever learns is that people die following his orders. However good he is, however carefully he plans, however brilliantly he leads them, they die. I realize you've already learned that, yet at least you have this much: you risk your own life with them. You have not yet come to the point at which you must send them to their deaths from safety."

It was as if he and she were alone in the briefing room, and Vanessa Murakuma stared into the eyes of a legend— of the man still known as "Ivan the Terrible," who'd fed his ships into the meat grinders of Parsifal, the Fourth Battle of Lorelei, and the Battle of Thebes without a tremor. There was pain in those eyes, and a grief utterly at odds with the ruthless image of the legend, and she felt strangely moved that he would lift his mask, however briefly, to share it with her. To tell her, she suddenly realized, that she was not alone against her nightmares or the crushing weight of her responsibility, for they were nightmares and a weight he, too, had faced.

"You and Fang Kthaara aren't that old yet, Sir," she heard herself say equally softly, "and there's an extra command chair or two aboard *Euphrates*." She felt LeBlanc and Mackenna staring at her in horror, and she knew they were right to feel it, but it made no difference as she watched Ivan the Terrible sit straighter in his chair. His dark, deep-set eyes brightened, cored with a fire that hadn't touched them in decades, but he shook his head.

"Prime Minister Quilvio would have me shot at dawn," he rumbled, yet there was a yearning note in his voice, and Kthaara laughed suddenly.

"Oh, *shaarnulk* to the politicians! Or would you tell me you have begun to worry about the reactions of *droshokol mizoahaarlesh* at this late date?" The Orion turned his slit-pupilled eyes to Murakuma. "For myself, Ahhhdmiraal Murrrrakuuuuma, I will take one of those chairs you have so kindly offered. Warriors should die in battle, not in bed!"

Murakuma smiled at him, but her attention was on Antonov, and the white-bearded fleet admiral glanced back at the holo, then at her face, and shrugged.

"Very well, Admiral Murakuma. Make that *two* command chairs."

"Of course, Sir." Murakuma beamed while her staff looked on in stunned disbelief, then reached across the table to extend one slender hand to the military commander-in-chief of the Grand Alliance. "Welcome along, Sir," she said, and he laughed as his huge hand enveloped hers.

CHAPTER NINETEEN
"I beg to report . . ."

Vanessa Murakuma stood in her walker, seeming frailer than ever with Ivan Antonov's massive presence on one side and Kthaara'zarthan's sable menace on the other, and watched as CIC's interpretation of the scouting pinnaces' data coalesced on Cruciero's display. The pinnace losses had been even heavier than she'd feared, and she understood why when she saw what she'd sent them into, but she shoved that guilt into the back of her brain and bent to study the data.

"Well," she sighed, "it appears they *do* have normal OWPs to back those CAs."

"Yes, Sir," Cruciero agreed, but his tone was quite different. He touched a function key, and his hawklike face creased with predatory satisfaction as eighteen superdreadnought-sized vessels flashed on the plot. "They've got forts, Sir, but they aren't very smart about how they emplace them. These aren't warships—look at the energy readouts. They're construction ships."

"*Construction* ships?" Murakuma looked at the light codes glowing beside the flashing ships, and her eyes narrowed. "They're actually *assembling* forts right on top of a warp point?"

"Exactly, Sir," the ops officer gloated. "It looks like they've got the shields on-line, but not one of those forts even tried to pot a pinnace. They would have if their point defense was operable, and look here."

He entered another command, and a visual replaced the icon-studded schematic. One of the pinnaces had made a close pass on an OWP, and the fort was studded with leprous patches of naked girders. A clumsy construction ship hovered nearby, and the imagery had actually caught its tractors transferring a capital missile launcher from its own holds to the base for installation, and Vanessa Murakuma bared her teeth in a smile her Orion allies would have understood perfectly.

"By God, we caught them with their pants down," she murmured. *And thank God we did! If they'd had time to get those things on-line . . .*

She felt Antonov's presence, yet he'd made it clear this was her show. No doubt he would offer advice if she asked for it, but he had no intention of second-guessing her decisions, and she was grateful. She stood for a moment, thinking hard, then nodded sharply.

"All right, we'll go with Navarino Six. Our SBMHAWKs will take the cruisers and the forts—if their point defense isn't up, we shouldn't need many to take them out—and TF 53 will hold its pods in reserve. The construction ships can't be heavily armed, so we'll take them out with shipboard weapons. But be sure they're designated as primary targets. I don't want any of them getting away in the confusion."

"Yes, Sir. And their main force?"

"Ignore them. They're too far out for clean kills, and they might decide not to chase us if they have cripples."

"Yes, Sir."

"Set it up quickly, Ernesto," she told him, squeezing his shoulder to emphasize her urgency. "They know we're coming."

The Fleet raced to readiness as the last pinnace vanished back into the warp point. The enemy had chosen a bad moment. Even a few more days would have seen enough fortresses on-line to stop him; as it was, his missile pods could sweep them all away. The construction ships turned about, fleeing at their best, lumbering speed, and the massed superdreadnoughts of the picket force gathered their escorts close. They turned towards the warp point, but it was no part of their plan to enter the radius of the enemy's pods. Had the forts been ready they might have been able to kill enough pods before they could fire; as it was, they could but wait to strike the enemy when he presented himself, and at least they were present in overwhelming strength.

"Execute!" Ernesto Cruciero snapped, and the TFN's SBMHAWKs slammed through the warp point, locked their targeting systems . . . and fired.

The forts couldn't maneuver at all, and the slow-footed heavy cruisers were almost equally immobile. Point defense did its best, but only thirteen of the cruisers escaped destruction, and losses were even heavier among the fortresses.

Demosthenes Waldeck's TF 51 crashed through the warp point on the pods' heels, led by twenty Terran super-dreadnoughts. The Bugs had seeded their minefields with laser buoys, but they had fewer of them than a Terran admiral would have employed, and none at all of the far more lethal primary buoys.

Unfortunately, Cruciero had been wrong about the OWPs. Or, more precisely, he hadn't been entirely correct, for five were fully operational. They'd been mauled and battered, but they were as big as the TFN's OWP-6s. Half-destroyed as they were, each of them retained the missile power of a *Matterhorn*-class SD, and they poured close assault missiles into TF 51's teeth. For all intents and purposes, the CAMs were sprint-mode capital missiles, virtually impossible for point defense to engage, and the stress of transit had reduced their targets' systems efficiency, as well. TFNS *Fuji San*, *Gunnbjørns* and *Grand Paradiso*, leading the Terran assault, blew apart under the pounding, but their consorts answered their deaths with massive, vengeful broadsides, and the forts were already badly damaged. That single, agonizing salvo was all they got off, and the Terran superdreadnoughts turned their missile batteries on the minefield even as their energy armaments massacred the frantically fleeing construction ships.

AMBAMs blew their lanes through the mines, and the rest of TF 51—and the Terran and Ophiuchi carriers of Vice Admiral Saakhaanaa's TF 52—formed up behind the battle-line.

The enemy had learned. He made no effort to lunge after the deep-space picket through the gaps his missiles had blown in the mines. Instead, he waited, bringing forward all of his units and launching his small attack craft to cover them. The small, fleet vessels fanned out, ignored by the hunter-killer satellites, but there were fewer of them this time. The last battle's ambush had killed many of the ships which carried them, and that was good. It meant they would be less able to swarm over the defending starships, and the enemy seemed to realize it as well, for they did not rush to the attack. Instead, they swept the space about the warp point, assuring themselves no additional units of the Fleet lurked in cloak to ambush them once more.

The Fleet hesitated, but then its light-speed sensors began to report. They identified only eight of the attack craft mother ships, and the laser buoys must have done better than projected, for many enemy superdreadnoughts streamed atmosphere in proof of heavy hull breaching. More than that, several had suffered drive damage, as well; their emissions were far weaker than usual, promising that they could be but little faster than the Fleet, and the picket force accelerated towards the warp point once more.

"They're coming in." Commander Cruciero's voice was grimmer. He was the one who'd first assumed none of the OWPs were fully operational, and Murakuma heard his sense of guilt. But she'd leapt to the same conclusion, and she rested a slender hand on his shoulder once more.

"Good," she said. "It looks like your little brainstorm is working, Ernesto."

The ops officer looked up at her, then smiled almost shyly and bobbed his head in thanks for her reminder, and she turned her walker to cross to the command chair. She parked beside it, reaching out to rest her right hand on the helmet racked on its side, and watched the master plot.

She and Cruciero had spent hours putting their surprise together, and she smiled thinly at the sensor readouts. Half her SDs had shut down anywhere from half to two-thirds of their shield generators and opened personnel locks to vent atmosphere. With their drive power reduced, they presented a chillingly realistic appearance of heavily damaged units, even to her, and her smile grew still thinner as she glanced at Saakhaanaa's carriers. All nine of his Terran CVs had their ECM in deception mode, and they showed on her plot as battlecruisers, not carriers. Two could play the decoy game, she thought viciously, and glanced at her com officer.

"Are the drones ready?"

"Yes, Sir. All we need is the sensor data from Plotting."

"Good." The AMBAMs had completed their mine clearing duty, and Murakuma nodded to the com screens linking her to Demosthenes Waldeck and Saakhaanaa's command decks. "You know the plan, gentlemen," she said. "Now suck these bastards in and kick their asses."

The enemy moved at last, flowing through one of the cleared lanes towards the system's habitable planets. Clearly he intended a fight to the finish this time, for his wounded ships came with him rather than fleeing to safety, and that was good. Not only would it bring them out where the Fleet could reach them, but it indicated he was weaker than anticipated. From his previous tactics, he would have sent them back . . . unless they were all he had and he needed them here.

"They're splitting up, Sir," Cruciero reported. "Most are coming after us, but it looks like— Yes, Sir. They're peeling off a dozen SDs and their escorts to close the warp point."

"Good." Murakuma glanced at Antonov, and the burly admiral nodded in grim approval. The main Bug force retained a solid core of ninety-six superdreadnoughts and twenty-four battlecruisers, but every little bit helped. Besides, it would make Anaasa happy.

"Composition of the detachment?"

"They look like *Acids*, with *Carbines* and *Cataphracts* attached to cover them."

"Makes sense, Sir," Mackenna observed quietly. "The *Acids*' plasma guns to kill anything that tries to get past them either way, with the cruisers to cover them against fighter strikes. The main force probably figures it's got the point defense to handle fighters without them."

"Then Admiral Saakhaanaa and Captain Olivera will just have to show them the error of their ways. Com, update the alert drones and get them off. I want them out of here before the enemy's close enough to see them past our drive signatures."

"Aye, aye, Sir. Update downloaded and locked. Launching—now."

Two courier drones separated from *Euphrates*. There was no need for more with no one to shoot at them as they vanished back through the warp point, and their emission signatures were lost in the background of Fifth Fleet's drive fields.

"Come to one-one-five, Demosthenes."

Fifth Fleet altered heading, curving away on a wider arc, and the main Bug force shifted its vector to cut a chord across it. The maneuver let it simultaneously make up distance and get behind Murakuma's ships, edging between them and any retreat while its detachment headed directly for the warp point as insurance. Thanks to her superdreadnoughts' "drive damage," the Bugs were actually a bit faster for a change. They were making the most of it, and she smiled thinly. The Alliance might still be unable to figure out what made the bastards tick, but it was nice to know they could be manipulated on a tactical level.

The enemy continued on course. No doubt he would eventually realize he could not defeat the Fleet's battle-line with so few attack craft to support his wounded ships. When he did, he would turn to flee as he always did, but the blocking force would hold him in play and the pursuit force would crush him against the warp point like a hammer.

The blocking units slid into position, and the pursuit force turned directly after him.

"Launch the execute drones!" Murakuma snapped, and hordes of courier drones—a torrent so vast the Bugs had no hope of stopping it—streamed through the warp point, and even as they launched, Admiral Saakhaanaa's cloaked carriers dropped their deception. Hundreds of additional fighters, the Terrans configured for antishipping strikes and the Ophiuchi as a combat space patrol, streamed from their bays, and as they went out, the superdreadnoughts which had been masquerading as cripples switched shields and drives to full power and stopped venting air.

TF 52's carriers accelerated away to keep clear of the battle, but TF 51's battle-line turned back upon its enemies as the first jaw of Vanessa Murakuma's trap sprang . . . and then the *second* jaw struck.

The sudden wave of courier drones completely surprised the blocking force. It opened fire as they flashed into their teeth, but only out of reflex, for the Fleet had only begun to consider what their purpose might have been when it found out.

These courier drones carried no message; their appearance *was* their message, and Fifty-Sixth Fang of the Khan Anaasa bared his fangs in predatory delight. He hadn't liked his secondary role as first explained, but he was too experienced a warrior to argue. After all, the humans' weapons and defensive technology were superior to his own, and system incompatibilities left his Orion and Gorm ships unable to integrate directly with their allies. And while he might dislike his own role, he admired the plan itself. It was more Orion than human in concept, for the TFN believed in simplicity. Small Claw LeBlanc had tried to explain "the demon Murphy" to Anaasa over most of a bottle of bourbon, and the fang had listened politely, but his own people preferred a more subtle approach which emphasized carefully timed converging strokes. If pressed, he would admit the human insistence on minimizing complexity had its own virtues, but he was an Orion, not a human, and the more he saw of Vanessa Murakuma, the more he liked her.

Now he yowled a terse order that sent seventy Orion SBMHAWK pods through the warp point, programmed with the targeting criteria Murakuma's first drones had provided, and six superdreadnoughts of the GSN led fourteen battlecruisers through on their heels.

The guardian superdreadnoughts shuddered in agony as the pods spawned behind them. The enemy's missiles ignored the escort cruisers; instead, they concentrated on the capital ships and missile CLs, and a wave of antimatter fury crashed over them. All the targeted cruisers died, the superdreadnoughts were savagely mauled, and even as the Fleet reeled under the unexpected blow, fresh capital ships charged through the warp point at impossible speeds.

Class for class, Gorm warships were the fastest any navy had ever built. The Gorm world was a harsh place, with brutally high gravity and background radiation levels higher than those of any other known sentient race's home planet. That environment had produced the Gormish philosophy of *Synklomus*, which enshrined the responsibility of every adult Gorm to protect all members of the *lomus*, or "household," from harm as his primary and overriding duty, but it had also produced a species which was incredibly tough. The Gorm were not only physically strong, with the blinding reaction speed their gravity well imposed;

they also had a radiation tolerance no other species could match . . . and their starships took advantage of that tolerance.

The fundamental technology of the enhanced drive system was common knowledge, but few navies were willing to pay the price the "tuners" imposed. It was nice to be able to build a superdreadnought as fast as anyone else's battlecruisers, yet the torrents of radiation the tuners produced were too much to expose one's personnel to. Unless, of course, those personnel were Gorm, who could endure far higher radiation levels than anyone else.

GSNS *Hazak* led her consorts through the warp point at a speed which would have had any Terran crew vomiting on the deck plates, and her capital missile launchers spat CAMs as she came. Only seven *Acids* had survived the SBMHAWK bombardment, and their battered defenses were no match for the massive fire of their undamaged foes. Only *Nirtanahr*, the third ship in Force Leader Darnash's battle-line took any hits in return, and her heavy shields shrugged the pair of missiles aside almost contemptuously.

None of the *Carbines* had survived, and the *Cataphracts* were suddenly helpless. They were minesweepers and antimissile ships, fearsome opponents for any fighter but without a single weapon capable of damaging a starship. They turned on their foes, trying to ram, but the Gorm and their escorting Orion battlecruisers were too maneuverable. They evaded the kamikaze attacks, pouring energy fire into the cruisers while they dodged, and within four minutes, every unit of the blocking force had been destroyed without the loss of a single Allied unit.

It was a trap.

The blocking force was gone, and even as it died, torrents of small attack craft streaked from the "battlecruisers" accompanying the enemy's "crippled" battle-line even as still more carrier starships emerged from the warp point behind the impossibly fast superdreadnoughts.

The Fleet came to an abrupt halt, and then, for the

first time since the war had begun, it turned to flee. It had no option, for it could neither overtake its foes unless the enemy chose to be overtaken nor stand off such massive waves of attack craft. Its starships launched antimatter-loaded cutters in efforts to divert the attack craft, but this time the enemy refused to be diverted. Only a few attack craft swerved aside, engaging the cutters with lethal efficiency; the others bored straight in, and waves of additional craft came howling up from the warp point in support.

Vanessa Murakuma watched with eyes of ice-cored jade as her fighters smashed into the Bugs. Dozens of them died, but they rammed their attack home, and the first strike was decisive. The Ophiuchi combat space patrol swarmed over the kamikaze small craft, piloted by the finest dogfighters in space, and the Terran and Orion pilots sent a tsunami of FRAMs into the superdreadnoughts. They didn't attempt to kill their targets; instead, they concentrated on battering down the shields and armor of the *Archer*-class missile ships, pounding each ship just hard enough to be *certain* they'd destroyed its fragile, first-generation datalink. They reduced the Bugs' entire missile component to individual units, incapable of synchronizing their fire, and then they broke off, their losses incredibly light compared to earlier engagements, while Waldeck's battle-line closed in from one side and Force Leader Darnash swept in from the other.

It wasn't totally one-sided. A few Bug missiles were bound to get through, despite the *Archers'* catastrophic damage, and they ignored the fire pouring in on them to concentrate everything they had on one or two Allied ships at a time, yet they were doomed. Waldeck and Darnash had an overwhelming advantage, and they used it ruthlessly. They smashed the *Archers* into wreckage, then pulled back beyond standard missile range, pounding the shorter-ranged survivors with utter impunity, and the Bugs broke. Enveloped by faster, longer-ranged enemies in deep space, they scattered in a desperate effort to save at least a few ships by forcing the Allied capital ships to choose which ones they would pursue and kill.

But that was what Saakhaanaa and Anaasa had been waiting for, and their rearmed, reorganized squadrons swept down on the Bugs as they fell out of mutual support range. Entire strikegroups drove in on single, isolated superdreadnoughts, taking their losses from the close-in defenses to streak in and blow them out of space. Once the Bugs broke, it *was* one-sided—a massacre—and Vanessa Murakuma watched with cold, hating eyes as, one by one, the Bug leviathans died under the stings of her deadly swarms of wasps.

It took less than two hours, and when those two hours ended, not a single enemy starship survived in the entire Justin System.

"All right, Demosthenes," she said then. "Secure the K–45 warp point. You can send a few pinnaces through for a look, but don't take any chances."

"Yes, Sir." The embers of battle still smoked in Waldeck's eyes, but he nodded soberly.

"Com," Murakuma looked over her shoulder, "inform General Mondesi that he can proceed against the planets."

"Aye, aye, sir." The communications officer dispatched another courier drone to the transports in Sarasota, and Murakuma's walker whined softly as she turned to face Ivan Antonov.

"Sir," she said very quietly and formally, "I beg to report that Fifth Fleet has regained control of the Justin System."

CHAPTER TWENTY

Ashes of Victory

"It's confirmed, Sir—they never even landed on
Clements!"

"I'll be damned." Major General Raphael Mondesi,
TFMC, Lion of Terra, Grand Solar Cross, shook his head.
He'd never believed—never *let* himself believe—Admiral
Murakuma's order to go bush would work, but the entire
population of Justin B had eluded the Bugs. *It wouldn't
have worked against humans*, he thought. *We're too
damned curious. Someone would've landed, if only to
see what was there. But the Bugs didn't. Interesting—
and possibly useful. If they're that much less curious than
we are, we may just be able to use it against them.*

He nodded, but he had little time to ponder the
thought, for his assault force was closing on the planets
of Justin A. After lengthy discussion, he and Least Claw
Thaaraan, Fang Anaasa's senior Marine, had concluded
they had no choice but to hit Justin and Harrison in
succession. Neither liked it, and their troopers were going
to be enormously outnumbered anyway, however they
operated, but this time Mondesi had the assets to equalize
the odds. His transports' assault shuttles would make
mincemeat out of any Bug helicopter foolish enough to
contest the air, and their escorting starships would be
available for fire support. They could lay conventional
precision-guided munitions in right on his own positions

at need, and the Fleet Base had diverted enough of its capacity to build sufficient support weapons to arm the Allied contingents with Terran mortars, heavy grenade launchers and HVM.

He turned to the holo Fleet had already generated from radar and optical mapping, and his eyes were bleak. That detailed, space-eye look at the terrain was invaluable, but it also revealed what had happened to the planets he'd tried to defend.

What had been cities were wastelands churned by high explosives, incendiaries . . . even nukes. The humans of Justin and Harrison had known what would happen to them, and those who'd been unable to make it to the refugee camps had stood and fought with the ferocity of despair. Now their hopeless fight had ground to its ghastly conclusion, and the shattered ruins told him what he was going to find.

He glared at the glass-floored crater which had once been Justin's capital, and hate boiled at his core like lye. This deliberate mass slaughter of noncombatants said there not only would not but *could* not be any question of quarter or negotiated peace. As Admiral Murakuma had said so many months before, when this war ended, there would be only the victors and the dead, and so Raphael Mondesi embraced his hatred, for if a species must die, it would not be his.

The Terran transports slid into orbit, and grim battalions from three different races filed into their assault shuttles. The handful of Marines aboard the Gorm ships wouldn't be used—they lacked powered armor, and the planet would have been a hostile environment for them—but the Ophiuchi and Orions had provided the equivalent of two and a half more brigades of Raiders. The Tabbies' armor wasn't quite as good as the Federation's, but the Ophiuchi's was actually better. Even so, Mondesi was going to have to use a lot of people in regular battle dress. That was a losing proposition against Bugs, but he had a plan to reduce the odds, and as part of that plan, he'd picked spots for his spaceheads just beyond weapons range of the Bug's main concentration. Now the shuttles swooped into atmosphere to land their troops and heavy lift shuttles brought in Terran assault skimmers, artillery, and air-defense batteries manned by drafted Navy technicians. And even as the troops dug in, the assault shuttles howled back aloft. Half were tasked to bring in the follow-up waves, but the other half were armed with external ordnance to provide air support.

In any peacetime exercise this size, Mondesi reflected, there would have been massive confusion, even without the need to cooperate with nonhuman allies. There'd simply been too little planning time for any other outcome. But there was very little muddle now, and draconian orders sorted out any that *did* arise ruthlessly. In less than three hours, each of his divisions had a two-brigade force down and dug in, ready for any Bug counterattack.

Not only ready, but praying for it. This time *they* had the firepower, and every Bug that died discovering that fact would be one less they'd have to hunt down later.

"What's the latest?" the general growled, settling into the padded chair aboard his Cobra divisional command vehicle. His ops officer dumped the data from her own panel to his display, and he bared his teeth as he saw Bug forces rolling towards his LZs. He'd hoped the compact target of the spaceheads—far enough apart to offer the temptation of crushing them in detail, yet so close they invited envelopment—would draw a massive response, and it had. Seven separate columns advanced with the obvious intention of launching simultaneous converging attacks. But first they had to get into position, and a lot of them weren't going to.

"Still nothing but those choppers?" he asked, checking his display sidebar.

"Not so far," Major Windhawk replied. "Orbital recon of their main facilities shows what could be atmospheric fast-movers at Alpha and Tango, but they're staying put. If they try to lift, the fire support ships will nail them from orbit."

"Good." Mondesi studied the display a few minutes longer, bringing up specific areas in high-order magnification for closer examination, then looked at his fire support officer.

"All right, Varnaatha. We'll start with Bravo and Charlie, then take out Golf."

"Yes, Generaaal." The Orion FSO punched keys, highlighting the designated Bug columns on her display. Mondesi had had a few doubts about accepting an Orion on his staff—not because he doubted the Tabbies' capabilities, but because of the language problem—but Daughter of the Khan Varnaatha'shilaas-ahn's sheer professionalism had won him over. Least Claw Thaaraan swore she was the best fire support officer in the Orion Atmospheric Combat Command—the equivalent of the Terran Marines—and an allied operation's command staff *had* to be integrated. Besides, Varnaatha was the Orion equivalent of a "Tabby specialist." She understood not only Standard English but the colloquialisms which baffled many Orions, and she never forgot Mondesi was a human. Despite a two-year intensive languages course, his command of Orion was much poorer than her ability with English, and she spoke slowly and distinctly to avoid any confusion.

She also, Mondesi suspected, chose the simplest possible way to express herself, but that was fine with him.

"Shall I utilize the support ships?" she asked now.

"No. We want the other columns to stay bunched until we get around to them, and they're likely to disperse if they figure out we've got starships to back up the shuttle strikes."

"Understood," she yowled, and he watched his display sidebar shift and flow as the computers projected the results of her instructions to the shuttles. He doubted he would entirely wipe out any of the columns he'd designated—there had to be fifty or sixty thousand Bugs in each—but he could hurt them. *Besides, if I kill all of 'em, the others'll just disperse and—*

"Orders acknowledged, Generaaal," Varnaatha

announced. "First strike will commence in five Standard minutes."

"All right—now we take the bastards!"

Captain Apollo Greene, TFMC, led the transport *Sequoia's* assault shuttles in a sweeping turn. The "column" known as Alpha was actually many smaller columns, each about the size of a Terran brigade, and the air above them was thick with the armored helicopters Bugs used for air support. Greene had studied the data Operation Redemption's ground component had paid so high a price to obtain, and he respected those clumsy choppers' firepower. But they were out of their league against his squadron, and he grinned in wolfish anticipation.

"Boomer, your section takes right flank. Bucky, you're on the left. Anything in the middle belongs to me."

"Aw, hell! You *always* get the easy shots!" "Boomer" Weintraub grumbled in the resonant bass which had earned him his call sign. "Look how those buggers are piled together in there—you couldn't miss 'em if you tried!"

"Be nice, Boomer," Annette Sherman—known, for reasons Greene had never figured out, as "Bucky"— chided. "He has to take something he can hit, after all."

"Stow it," Greene growled around a grin, and checked his instruments. The squadron shook down into two sections of five and one of six shuttles each and fanned out, and his grin vanished. "Commence your runs and make 'em count!"

He put the nose down, and the squadron leapt from high subsonic speed to mach five. Targeting computers aboard each shuttle considered the constantly changing pattern of the enemy helicopters, murmuring to one another and sharing the targets out among themselves, and then the squadron screamed into attack range and the HVMs began to launch.

A hyper-velocity missile had no seeking system, and it needed none. At ten percent of light speed, no atmospheric target could move far enough between launch and impact to generate a miss if its initial targeting was on . . . and very few targets could survive a direct hit.

The Bugs had already met the infantry version of the HVM. If it had occurred to them that the Federation had a vehicle-launched version, they must have known what would happen to their helicopters, but they went to violent evasive action anyway. Perhaps they thought they *could* generate misses, that some small percentage of their aircraft could survive long enough to salvo their shorter-ranged missiles back. If they did, they were wrong.

The HVMs carved incandescent tunnels of superheated air like some pre-space concept of death rays, and fireballs glared above the Bugs Varnaatha'shilaas-ahn had marked for death. Staggering concussions marched across their airspace in boots of flame, and Greene's squadron howled past above it. The sixteen shuttles killed fifty-eight helicopters in that single pass and lifted their noses, screaming back towards space to rearm, and exultant chatter filled Greene's earbug.

"Lord, did you *see* that!" Bucky Sherman shouted. "Like shit through a—"

Her voice chopped off, and Greene's eyes darted to his plot in horror as the icon of her shuttle flashed from green to scarlet. He wrenched his head around, staring at the visual, and his face went cold and deadly as the fireball fell away astern. Somewhere in that column below, a Bug missile crew had managed to get at least one bird off, and its explosion strewed Apollo Greene's friend and her crew across four square kilometers of jungle.

"Jesus," someone whispered, and Greene looked away from the falling fire.

"Back to the ship," he grated, and punched for the priority com circuit. Bug SAMs were better than projected, and he buried his grief and hatred under the cold formality of his report.

Lieutenant Sherman wasn't the only pilot lost in the opening air strikes, yet overall losses were minuscule. Aerial superiority missions swept the sky clean, and the ground strikes came rumbling in on their heels. Ripple-salvoed HVMs tore the hearts out of the designated formations, and other shuttles sowed the jungle around them with lethal cluster munitions. Surviving Bugs, those on the fringes of their columns, raced into the jungle, seeking safety in dispersal, but their flight took them directly into the waiting antipersonnel bomblets, and Varnaatha bared her fangs at her display as flame seeded the jungle and orbital observers tallied the results of her first attack.

"Seventy-six-plus percent kills over all, Generaaal! *Seeequoiaaa* reports a complete sweep on Alllphaaa-Two!"

"Good, Varnaatha. Tell them well done—and to get back down here and do it again!"

The massed air strikes continued pounding the Bugs, and despite his own experience, Mondesi found it hard to believe they were actually proceeding with their plan. Surely their columns were in communication with one another! Yet their sole concession to his aerial flail was to break up into smaller groups, each about the size of a TFMC regiment. But dispersal only slowed the destruction; it couldn't *stop* it, and the killing went inexorably on.

But perhaps they had no choice, Mondesi thought. They were on their own, beyond any hope of support, and if they couldn't surrender—and, it appeared, they couldn't— the only other thing they *could* do was attack.

The first three columns were virtually annihilated short of their jump-off points, but three more got through, and Mondesi switched his aerial attacks onto them. This time Varnaatha sent every shuttle in on a single target, slamming down on it with a hammer of HVMs, napalm and cluster bombs that tore a thousand square kilometers into a smoking moonscape. The Bugs had reconcentrated for their attack, which made her task easier, but it also massed their SAMs, and her pilots paid for their success with five more shuttles.

Yet the column's destruction goaded the two survivors on. They seemed to have been waiting for the seventh and last force to reach its attack point, but they waited no longer. Instead, they launched something no Terran commander had seen in over two centuries: a mass charge.

Over a hundred thousand sentient beings burst from the jungle, hurling their unarmored bodies into the teeth of a prepared fire zone, and Mondesi's ground forces opened up with every weapon while orbiting warships poured in missiles from above. The jungle writhed, kilometer-wide expanses of vines and giant, spreading ferns exploding in a maelstrom of high explosives and HVMs, and *still* the Bugs came on! They didn't die by scores, or even hundreds—they died in *thousands*, yet even as they died, their own support troops opened fire, and nuclear-armed missiles shrieked through the carnage.

Navy air-defense teams fought back desperately. The Federation had long since abandoned surface-to-surface missiles slower than HVMs, for energy weapons doomed anything that moved slowly enough to be tracked. Yet there was one way they *could* get through, for enough of them could saturate the defender's tracking or firepower. Only one or two might break through, but if those one or two missiles carried nuclear warheads, they might well be enough.

Raphael Mondesi sat silent at his console as his support elements saturated the jungle with destruction and his antiair teams waged their battle against the missiles. There were more of them than he'd expected, and the Bugs' frontal assault had diverted his main firepower from their launchers. He could kill missile teams or he could kill infantry, and for all he knew, the infantry carried nuclear charges of their own. That would be of a piece with the rest of their apparent tactical doctrine, and if they did, he had to kill them as far from his own positions as possible. Which meant the air-defense crews were on their own, and he prayed they were good enough.

They almost were. A single Bug missile—just one— got past, and a fresh fireball glared as it scored a direct hit on the two companies of Terran Raiders holding the center of Landing Zone Two's northern perimeter.

The kilotonne-range explosion was a ground burst. The Raiders directly in its path died instantly, but the men and women on their flanks were in combat zoots that shielded them from the radiation and initial thermal bloom. Vaporized vegetation, soil and humans mushroomed from the detonation, and the blast front ripped out like an enraged fist. It picked up entire trees, tore them to splinters, and hurled them outward in a shearing wave of "shrapnel" not even zoots could stop. More men and women died, and then the firestorm crashed over the survivors.

Some lived through it. Their zoots were smaller, faster and more heavily armored than the old Theban War equipment, and if they were very, very lucky, they were in a depression or the lee of some small swell of ground. One squad less than five thousand meters from ground zero actually made it through without losing a man, for their veteran sergeant had goaded them into digging their foxholes deep, driving them into what turned out to be a reverse slope at a sharp angle. But they were the exception. Two hundred Marines died in the explosion, with another three hundred wounded or incapacitated. For all intents and purposes, an entire battalion had been wiped out, and the dazed ten-man squad crawling out of its collapsed holes into a smoldering slice of Hell found itself all alone, directly in the path of the charging Bug infantry.

Raphael Mondesi swore viciously as LZ-Two's reserve—two platoons of Terran assault skimmers supported by two companies of Orion Raiders—rushed forward, for some of the Bugs had actually gotten through his supporting fire. It was impossible. *Nothing* could have lived in that inferno, but over six thousand of them had. They were shattered and broken, any trace of unit organization gone. They weren't an army; they were a mob, but they were an *armed* mob, and as long as any Bug remained on its feet, it continued to charge forward.

❖   ❖   ❖

The isolated squad saw it coming. They were dazed and disoriented, suffering from dangerously high radiation doses, but their screaming sergeant cursed them into action. They hit their jump gear, bounding back to their alternate position, and each of them carried a full automatic flechette launcher. No unarmored Bug could survive a direct hit from their weapons, and they wreaked fearsome execution on the enemies streaming past the warhead's blast zone.

The enemy barely seemed to notice them. No one knew enough about how Bugs thought to know why, but perhaps their own disorganization was to blame, for no race, however ferocious, could have coordinated its efforts after the pounding the attackers had endured. They came out of the smoke and dust and thunder on six evil, segmented legs, like nightmares given flesh. They were unarmored, and the radiation of their own warhead sleeted through blood and bone. They had to know they were doomed by such a massive dose, but it didn't matter, and they lunged forward in total, terrifying silence, killing anything in their path.

Wounded Marines, or those merely trapped in disabled armor, died screaming for help no one could give as Bugs fired into them at point-blank range, and the single intact squad cursed and shouted their hate, weeping as they poured fire into that swirling madhouse. Some of the Bugs noticed them at last and turned on them, but they, too, attacked as individuals, and the squad shot them down. It walled its position in their ripped and torn bodies . . . and watched in horror as Bugs with one and two and even three limbs blown away kept thrashing forward. More got in behind the squad, firing into its rear, and men and women who'd survived the fury of a nuclear warhead died as armor-piercing rounds riddled their zoots. Two went down, then a third. Two more. The five survivors rallied around their sergeant, firing desperately, knowing they were doomed, but the madness was upon them, too. They were as crazed as the Bugs, and they held their ground in the thunder and smoke, screaming their defiance, *daring* the Bugs to kill them as they blazed through their ammo.

A single Bug flung itself into their position in an impossible, prodigious leap. They couldn't shoot it without killing one of their own, and the sergeant dropped his launcher. His armored hands closed on the Bug's weapon. Exoskeletal muscles whined as he ripped it away, and the alien hurled itself upon him bodily, rearing high on two limbs to smash at him with the others. His zoot shrugged off the pounding attack, and he opened his armored arms to embrace its central body pod. The entire surviving squad heard his bellow of primal hate as he squeezed, and the Bug writhed in agony. Yet even as the sergeant's arms crushed its pod, even as fluids and splintered bones and crushed internal organs erupted like obscene fruit, *still* it was silent.

The sergeant hurled the corpse away. He snatched for his launcher once more as another Raider went down and swung it in an arc, hosing the Bug who'd fired, and then he shouted again—a wilder shout, of disbelief, not hate—as the first Terran assault skimmer whined through the smoke, bow guns blazing. Another came behind it, and another, and Tabby Marines swept forward with them.

Raphael Mondesi sagged in his chair, saturated with sweat. *Dear God,* he thought shakenly, *if this is how they fight on a captured colony world, what's going to happen if we ever have to hit one of their worlds?*

It was a terrifying thought, but he felt his staff's eyes upon him, sensed the shock which had shaken even Varnaatha's Orion militancy. That single warhead had hurt them badly—he doubted more than ten percent of the battalion it had hit had survived—but it was the only point at which his perimeter had broken, and their attackers were finished. Search and destroy teams were moving forward, covered by assault skimmers, and even as they moved out, Varnaatha's shuttles and orbiting starships turned their attention to the seventh and last column.

His plan had worked. That *had* to have been the bulk of the Bug combat troops on the planet. He'd sucked them out into a killing ground and annihilated them, and grievous as his losses might be, they were trifling compared to the enemy's. He told himself that firmly, almost fiercely, and he knew it was true, yet there was little comfort in its truth.

It's them, he thought. *It's the way they just keep coming, as if it doesn't even matter to them whether they live or die. We're not fighting soldiers; we're fighting something none of us ever truly believed existed. It's like trying to kill a hurricane, and, God help me, no exchange rate is "acceptable" against something like this!*

He drew a deep breath, then made himself turn to his staff with a fierce smile.

"All right, people, we've got the bastards now. We've proved we can stop anything they throw at us, and they can't have much left to throw. Angie," he looked at Major Windhawk, "instruct Least Claw Thaaraan to begin his drop north of Murphysville. We'll move out from LZ-Three to meet him, then reconsolidate and move east on New Cornell. In the meantime—"

He went on talking, brisk and confident, every inch the military commander who'd just scored a crushing victory, and felt the confidence flowing back into his staff.

Now if only *he* could feel it.

"Are you positive, Marcus?"

Vanessa Murakuma stared at her intelligence officer, and her shoulders sagged as he nodded grimly. *Dear God. Dear sweet God, we left over* six million *people on this planet. Marcus* can't *be right. He* just *can't!*

But he was, and she turned away as she saw her own horror in his eyes.

Eight thousand. Eight thousand one hundred and three. That was it—the *total* count of survivors on the planet Justin. Eight thousand brutally traumatized, filthy, terrified, human-shaped animals who'd been herded into holding pens and watched hopelessly as all the others who'd been herded in with them were marched away and *eaten*.

She closed her eyes and buried her face in her hands, and her body shook. Her fault. It was all *her* fault. *She* was the one who'd pulled out, left them, abandoned them to this atrocity.

"Vanessa." She shook her head fiercely, but the gentle voice refused to be rejected. "Vanessa!" it said more sharply, and hands gripped her wrists. They pulled her own hands down, and Marcus' face swam through her tears as she stared at him in mute anguish and *your fault, your fault, your fault* tolled through her brain.

"You couldn't help what happened," he said, kneeling before her walker. "No one could."

"I . . . I should've come back. Come back sooner. Gotten in here and—"

"You *did* come back." His voice was fierce. "My God, you came back *three times!* You damn near got yourself *killed* coming back, and you know as well as I do that you *couldn't* have retaken this system a day sooner than you actually did!"

"I should have found a way," she whispered. "There *had* to be a *way!*"

"There wasn't," he said more softly, and her tear-soaked face pressed into his shoulder as he put his arms about her. He hugged her close, alone with her in the briefing room, and if Regs said lovers couldn't serve together, then Regs could go to Hell. One hand stroked her red hair, and his own tears—tears of grief, of shared, irrational shame, and of anguish for the woman he loved—flowed down his cheeks as he murmured to her. "There wasn't a way, love. I wish there had been, but there wasn't. You did everything you possibly could—more than anyone else could ever have done—but there wasn't a way you could stop it."

"Then what use am I?" She clung to him, and the words choked her like slivered glass.

"You didn't stop it here," he told her, still stroking her hair, "and you didn't stop it on Harrison, no. But you *did* stop it on Clements, love. And in Sarasota and Remus and New Prague and Vernon and Walker. You stopped it when you ignored me before First Sarasota. We lost fourteen million people here and in Merriweather and Erebor, but you got *twenty-four* million out, and you saved another hundred million in Sarasota alone."

"It's not enough," she whispered.

"Of course it isn't," he said gently. "It'll never be enough. But it's what you've got, and horrible as it is, it's a magnificent achievement." She twisted in his arms with an ugly sound of vicious rejection, but he held her until her struggles eased, and he smiled through his tears.

"You'll never see that," he told her. "Oh, Vanessa! You're the one person in the galaxy who won't see it, whatever I tell you. But that doesn't change what it is . . . and it doesn't change what you have to do now."

"What?" she asked hopelessly, and he kissed her ear.

"You have to go on," he said quietly. "You've kicked these monsters out of Justin; now you have to *keep* them out, and after that, you have to go on leading fleets and commanding in battles. Do you remember what you told us before K–45? About the way this war would end?" She nodded against his shoulder, and he held her tighter. "Well, you were right, and you're going to be there to the bitter end, Vanessa Murakuma. You're going to be out in front of us, showing us it can be done, leading us—kicking us in the ass and by God *dragging* us forward—because we need you. Because we can't let you hand the job off to anyone who'd do it one iota less well."

"I can't," she whispered in horror.

"You can, and you will. Not alone—trust me, there'll be grief enough for a hundred admirals before this is over—but you'll go on. The only way the Bugs will stop you is to kill you, love, and the only way you'll let *yourself* stop will be to die, because, God help you, it's what you *have* to do and because we need you so desperately."

She clung to him, and the dreadful truth of his words crushed her like the weight of the murdered world her flagship orbited. He was right. She had to go on. She couldn't *not* go on, for she owed it to fourteen million ghosts, and she could not fail them again.

She drew a deep breath and nodded against his shoulder, then gave him one more fierce hug and pushed him away. She straightened in her walker and scrubbed her face like a child, wiping away her tears, and took the tissue he gave her with a watery smile. She blew her nose and took another breath, then turned her walker towards the hatch without another word.

Her staff was waiting on Flag Bridge. They needed her to tell them this holocaust was a triumph, and Marcus was right, God help her. It *was* a triumph. She knew it was—now she simply had to make herself believe it and transmit that belief to her officers.

It sounded so simple for something so agonizingly hard, yet she had no choice, and as the briefing room hatch hissed open, Vice Admiral Vanessa Murakuma smiled at her staff while her walker carried her forward into the ashes of victory.

CHAPTER TWENTY-ONE

The Xenologists' Best Guess

". . . so they've authorized a complete resurvey." Marcus LeBlanc grimaced on Murakuma's terminal. Her own expression mirrored his, and not simply because of what he was saying. Marcus had been recalled to Nova Terra as Ivan Antonov's resident Bug expert before she was out of that damnable walker, and she resented it. Not that she'd been about to explain to Ivan the Terrible that his desire to "frock" Commodore LeBlanc to rear admiral and assign him critically important duties had put a monumental kink in her love life!

She felt her grimace smooth into a small, fond smile. At least Antonov had let her keep Marcus until Estelle Abernathy was fully up to speed as his replacement. They'd had time to say a lot of things that needed saying . . . and for her to begin to accept that just perhaps Marcus was right. Given the challenge she'd faced, perhaps she *hadn't* done too badly.

She realized the letter had gone on playing while she gathered wool, and she ran it back.

". . . resurvey," Marcus said again. "Of course, it's kind of hard to blame them, but just between us, Admiral Antonov considers it pure PR. The Justin death toll hit civilian morale hard, and a lot of other worlds seem convinced there could be an unknown Bug warp point right next door to *them*, as well. This way the Powers

That Be can convince the electorate they're Doing Something to keep them safe."

He grimaced again, then sighed.

"Maybe I'm being too cynical. Lord knows a lot of survey data needs updating—some of it's over two hundred years old—and just one unplotted warp point near any core world could make what happened to Justin look like a pillow fight. The problem is, any points like that are almost certain to be closed, or we'd have found them by now. And if they *are* closed, we're not going to find them anyway, and all the ships we've got busy looking for them could be better employed pushing out into unexplored space to find a flank route into *Bug* space."

He paused for a moment, then shrugged.

"Still and all, we might as well spend our time doing that. We're still gearing up, and it's going to be a while before we're ready to mount any offensives. And speaking of gearing up, you should *see* what the Nova Terra yards are turning out! I haven't been out to Galloway's Star, but I hear the yards out there are working even harder. It's going to be a while yet before you start seeing much new construction out there at the sharp end, love, but when you do, it'll knock your vac suit off. The new assault carriers are beautiful, and R&D's pulled out all the stops to get the new shields and armor into service. Well, you know they have, of course. By the time you screen this, you'll have started seeing some of the refits."

He paused and leaned back, smiling into the pickup.

"Enough shop talk—we've got more important things to discuss. And I wish we *could* 'discuss' them directly. You remember that little hotel at Crawford's Point here on Nova Terra? The one where we spent midterm break? Well, it's still there, and I'll be damned if old Matsuoka isn't still running the place! I mentioned you to him, and he remembers our visit—or pretends he does, anyway. In fact, he's invited us back if you ever get a long enough leave." He wiggled his eyebrows in his very best leer, and Murakuma surprised herself with a bright, sunny laugh—the sort of laugh she hadn't laughed since the

Battle of K–45. "You're out of that walker by now, so figure out how to get back here for a visit. You could always confer with GHQ's planning staff or something during the day, and then during the night we could get to the *important* things.

"I hope you like the kimono," he continued more seriously. "Nobiki picked it out." Murakuma's eyebrows quirked at that. She hadn't quite had the nerve to mention Marcus to her children. They'd known him all their lives, but only as "Mother's friend, Marcus," and if they got the notion she was picking up an old affair which had predated her love for their father—

"She gave me a pretty hard time when she handed it over," Marcus went on with a wry grin. "Seems she and Fujiko think we're a bit slow—due to our extreme old age, no doubt. According to Nobiki, they've had a pool going on how long you'd take getting back together with Oji-san Marcus for over ten years now!"

"Attention on deck!"

The assembled officers rose as Murakuma, Anaasa, Saakhaanaa, and Force Leader Darnash entered *Euphrates'* largest briefing room. The hatch was a tight fit for Darnash, and Murakuma had been prepared to allow him and his staff to attend the conference electronically. Not only was the briefing room claustrophobically confining for someone his size, but his clear, globular helmet, while a masterpiece of engineering, didn't look any too comfortable.

Yet Darnash had politely refused the offer. He was one of her officers; he would attend her meetings, and do so in person. That, as far as he was concerned, was that.

Now the massive Gorm made his cautious way around the table to the spot where two chairs had been replaced with a Gorm-style couch and lowered himself onto its saddle with every indication that he was completely at ease.

Murakuma gave him a small smile as he settled into position, then looked at her other officers. The haunted desperation which had been so much a part of earlier meetings had eased. Most of her officers—human and non—still looked grim, but they'd smashed a Bug fleet, driven the enemy from Justin, and held it without more than half-hearted sparring at the warp point for over three months. More to the point, the fortresses on the Sarasota side of the warp point had been reinforced to the point of near impregnability, and every single noncombatant had been evacuated. They could afford to fight their kind of battle if—when—the Bugs tried a comeback, and if they had to, retreat entirely out of the system without abandoning civilians to the enemy. It was, Murakuma thought more grimly, a sign of the sort of war this was that knowing they could "afford" to give up a star system with three habitable planets was actually a source of relief.

"All right, ladies and gentlemen," she said. "As you know, we've just received our first echelon of refitted TFN starships, and Rear Admiral Teschman brought along GHQ's latest update. My staff has evaluated it, and I'd like to begin with their reports. Captain Mackenna?"

"Yes, Sir." Leroy Mackenna stood behind the lectern against the briefing room's after bulkhead and brought up a huge holographic chart of the local warp lines.

"As you know, ladies and gentlemen, we now hold Sarasota in strength," he said, and the Sarasota System blinked. "As of this morning, we have fifty-two OWPs on the warp point, with a total fighter strength in excess of two thousand, and the minefields and energy platforms are being heavily reinforced on an ongoing basis. In short, we may now consider our rear secure."

Assuming, Murakuma thought, *that* anything *is "secure" where Bugs are concerned.*

"With that in mind, GHQ has reconfirmed our basic mission profile. Until we've fully reequipped with updated units, we're to stand on the defensive, retaining control of the Justin System, but we are authorized and directed to fall back on Sarasota rather than risk heavy losses. My understanding is that the fact that we *can* fall back is the reason we have not yet been more heavily reinforced.

Our current strength is sufficient for a fighting withdrawal against any opponent, and GHQ's decision to send us only refitted units rather than committing additional *un*refitted ones will impose an unavoidable delay on offensive ops."

One or two officers frowned, but Murakuma wasn't one of them. Like any CO, she wanted as many ships as she could get, yet GHQ had a point. Fifth Fleet's order of battle now counted thirty-four fleet carriers and twelve CVLs, backed by thirty-two superdreadnoughts, eleven battleships, and thirty-four battlecruisers. That was sufficient, given their monopoly on fighters, for any deep-space engagement, and she was entirely in favor of refitting the ships she would have to lead into battle. The new third-generation shields and advanced armors had been available even before the war—they simply hadn't been fitted because the civilians had balked at the cost. Now they *were* being fitted . . . and now the same civilians who'd screamed about the cost were screaming about the Navy's "inexcusable" delay in not having fitted them earlier!

Well, I can live with their stupidity as long as they let me have ships that can survive, she thought with a trace of bitterness. *And thank* God *they agreed to reconfigure the* Belleisles!

That refit was the most drastic so far proposed, and her own recommendations had been the deciding factor. None had come forward yet—the refitted battleships she'd so far received had simply been given shield and armor upgrades—but the *Belleisle-B*s would give up their entire energy armament for a massed battery of standard missile launchers. They couldn't live in close combat with Bug superdreadnoughts anyway, and while they would still lack the range of the capital missile-armed ships, they'd be able to lay down devastating fire from outside the enemy's effective energy envelope. And if they *were* forced to close-range combat, a broadside of twenty-four sprint-mode missiles with AAM warheads would take the starch out of *any* opponent.

"—in the meantime," Mackenna was saying, and she shook herself back to attention. "Given the civilian death toll in Justin, GHQ has concluded there are no survivors in any of the Bug-occupied systems between here and Indra, and Admiral Antonov has no intention of sacrificing warships—and lives—to retake empty real estate. Fifth Fleet's function thus becomes that of holding Justin as our forward point of contact and as a security buffer for Sarasota while our accelerated survey activities seek additional points of contact. According to the theoretical astrophysics sections of both the Terran and Orion survey commands, the odds are high that we'll find some, given the general pattern of the warp lines in this sector. Should we do so, it will give us a second axis of advance and force the Bugs to divide their forces against more than one threat. Should we *fail* to do so," Mackenna's voice turned much grimmer, "we'll have no option but to reinforce Justin to the maximum possible extent and attack from here."

He said no more on that point, but every officer present knew how hideous casualties would be if the Alliance had to hammer straight ahead down a single, predictable line of advance.

"With your permission, Admiral," Mackenna continued with a glance at Murakuma, "I'll turn the lectern over to Commander Abernathy for a few moments, then let Commander Cruciero bring us up to date on our own dispositions."

Murakuma nodded—*exactly,* she thought, *as if we hadn't discussed it ahead of time*—and the newly promoted lieutenant commander who'd replaced LeBlanc as her staff spook rose. She looked ridiculously young— like a golden-haired schoolgirl in uniform—and her hands fidgeted a bit as she faced the briefing room full of senior officers, but her voice was clear and level.

"Admiral LeBlanc and the GHQ intelligence staff have put together a comprehensive briefing on the results of their examination of the material captured here in Justin," she began. "I've prepared copies of their complete download for each of you, so I'll simply hit the high points here. Please stop me if you have any questions.

"First, we've finally gotten some feel for the Bugs' technology. For the most part, they're somewhat behind us, as we'd surmised. That's the good news. The bad news is that they aren't *far* behind us. Based on known rates of R&D for our own races, GHQ estimates they'll need no more than eight months to duplicate our command datalink, even assuming they captured no intact installations to give them a leg up in any previous engagement."

A stir went through the briefing room. Not of surprise— it was a given that the Bugs realized how much their cruder datalink hurt them and were working to redress the balance—but at the thought of losing their greatest advantage in a missile engagement.

"The most puzzling aspect of the captured material, however, concerns the enemy's databases," Abernathy went on. "As you know, we secured several intact computers, both here and from destroyed enemy fleet units and dispatched them to Centauri, where Allied technicians and xenologists could examine them properly."

What Abernathy meant, Murakuma reflected, was that they'd been sent back to let *Orion* techs at them. In general terms, Terran hardware tended to be the best in space, but the Tabbies persistently—and irritatingly, for some humans—produced the galaxy's best cyberneticists. If anyone could tickle the Bug computers into giving up their data, it was the Whisker-Twisters.

"Unfortunately," Abernathy said, "they've been unable to generate any meaningful output. They—" She paused as Anaasa raised a clawed hand. "Yes, Fang Anaasa?"

"They have generated *no* output?" The Orion demanded. "None at all?"

"I didn't say that, Sir. I said they've been unable to generate any *meaningful* output. They're convinced they're generating *something*, but no one's been able to figure out what it is."

"That's preposterous," Waldeck muttered. His face reddened as he realized he'd spoken aloud, and he shrugged. "What I mean is, if they're generating anything at all, the xenologists should be able to make *something* of it. They've got enough filters and computers to run it through, after all—and surely *some* of it is simple visual imagery!"

"I'm sorry, Sir, but it isn't—visual imagery, I mean," Abernathy said respectfully. "So far as anyone can tell, it's just so much electronic noise." Waldeck looked at her like a man who wanted to disbelieve, and she shrugged. "According to Admiral LeBlanc, Doctor Linokovich of the Xenology Institute hypothesizes that they're telepathic, and medical forensics may offer some corroboration. According to the autopsies, the Bugs are mute."

"*Telepathic?*" Carlotta Segram stared at Abernathy, then shook her head. "This is like some bad holodrama. You're telling us these things are *mind readers*, too?"

"No, Sir. That's the point. As you know, we've never been able to demonstrate reliable telepathy in humans. The Gorm—" she nodded to Darnash "—do have a telempathic sense, but though their *minisorchi* talent's existence has been conclusively demonstrated, no other race has ever been able to perceive it. The current theory is that the Bugs operate on a unique mental 'frequency' which they've managed to convert into electronic storage. Our problem is that we simply can't 'see' it. As Admiral LeBlanc puts it, we're like blind people trying to understand pink. But at least if we can't read *their* records, it seems unlikely they can read *ours*."

"I wouldn't bet on that," Admiral Rendova murmured. "Our data outputs are all some form of visual information, and mute or not, we know these things have eyes."

Abernathy started to reply, but Murakuma's raised hand stopped her.

"That's certainly a point to bear in mind, Ellen. For now, however, all of this can only be considered an unproved theory. We'll just have to stick to our standard procedures for purging all databases which may fall into enemy hands and hope."

Rendova nodded soberly, and Murakuma waved for Abernathy to resume.

"For the moment," the lieutenant commander said, "the

most immediate consequence is that, despite all the data we've apparently captured, we've been unable to learn a thing about the enemy except by direct observation. We still have no idea how large his imperium is, how his warp lines are laid out, or what his ultimate industrial and military potentials are. What we *do* know is that the Bugs aren't organized like any other species any of our races have ever met. They seem much more specialized by function, for example. The medical teams report distinct physiological differences between what GHQ is calling 'the warrior caste' and the other Bugs we encountered on Justin and Harrison. The 'warriors' are larger, stronger and tougher than the 'workers,' almost as though they were genetically engineered for combat."

"Lord! It gets stranger and stranger." Segram sighed. "Is GHQ saying they really *are* bugs? That we're up against some kind of hive race? Some sort of communal 'over mind'?"

"GHQ doesn't think so." Abernathy shook her head. "Our own ground forces' observation indicates they react as individuals. Not as individuals of any race we've previously met, perhaps, but still as individuals. The med teams' best guess—and it's only a guess, at this point—is that this species preselects individuals for societal roles at a very early point in life. It would appear the species differentiates physically as some Old Terran insects do: if fed one diet, they become workers; fed another they become warriors. If that's true and their society does preselect for function, then presumably it feeds them the diet and tailors their training to enable them to fill their selected roles most efficiently. The xenologists tend to agree, especially since both the 'warriors' and 'workers' we've seen so far are neuters. Xenology's best hypothesis to explain the Bugs' tactics is that this race has taken specialization to an unprecedented height. The *only* function of their warriors appears to be to fight; they have no other value to the race, since they can't procreate. That doesn't require that they be part of any 'hive mind,' and it doesn't prevent them from being imaginative—as they demonstrated in their Third Justin tactics—but it does mean they may regard themselves as completely expendable in the interest of their race."

"Perhappps they are notttt *necessssarily* unimaginatttive," Admiral Saakhaanaa put in, "yett they woulddd appearrr to *acttt* ass ifff they are."

"They certainly seem to stick to a plan once they've made one," Waldeck agreed.

"True, but they're not unique in that," Murakuma pointed out. "Humans are pretty flexible, but there've been enough humans who insisted on 'sticking to the plan' even when it obviously wasn't working. Think about the Japanese military in World War Two—or the Communists in the old Soviet Union, or the 'social engineers' the West turned out in the twentieth century. Every one of them rode 'the plan' down in flames instead of changing it."

The various Allied officers looked puzzled, but they let it pass when Waldeck nodded. After all, everyone knew Humans were the galaxy's most complicated—and confusing—race.

"At any rate," Abernathy concluded, "research is continuing. No one expects any sudden breakthroughs, but anything they do come up with will be passed on to us as soon as possible."

"And in the meantime, *we'll* be the main laboratory," Murakuma agreed. She nodded for Abernathy to be seated and glanced at Cruciero. "Ernesto?"

The ops officer replaced Abernathy at the lectern and punched up a fresh hologram, this one a detailed breakdown of Fifth Fleet's order of battle.

"As you see, ladies and gentlemen," he began, "we're in much better shape these days, and GHQ informs us that industrial rationalization is proceeding as planned. Within another three months, Terran industry will be turning out expendable munitions—missiles and mines—designed for universal compatibility. Within another six, we'll be producing launchers and energy weapons which can be mounted aboard any unit of any Allied navy, as well. We'll pay a slight mass penalty for the additional control runs, but it should simplify our logistics tremendously."

Everyone nodded—or whatever his or her race used to indicate agreement—though there were some slightly sour expressions. The non-human officers found it irritating that Terran industrial productivity eclipsed their own by such an enormous margin that the Federation was the logical arsenal of the Alliance. Concentrating only on shipbuilding while the Federation produced their weapons would vastly simplify their own problems, but some of them—and particularly the Orions—resented humanity's industrial dominance. Yet some of the *humans* in the briefing room—like Leroy Mackenna—looked almost equally disgusted, for it was the industrial might of the Corporate Worlds which made it possible. Fringers like Mackenna might be grateful that capacity existed, but that made them no less angry over how the Corporate Worlds had manipulated the Federation's economy and laws to *create* it.

"In the meantime," Cruciero went on, "our own posture remains unchanged. As you can see from the holo, the Seventh Battle Squadron—"

He went on speaking, and Vanessa Murakuma tipped her chair back, expression attentive. The big news of the briefing had already been presented; all that remained now was the discussion of the nuts and bolts and their chance to display their confidence to one another. Those things were important, of course, and she would give them her full attention when the time came, but now, as Cruciero reported details she already knew only too well, she let herself concentrate on planning her next letter to Marcus.

Chapter Twenty-Two

"What *are* those things?"

Vice Admiral Murakuma closed her eyes and held the saki cup between her palms to inhale its sharp aroma. She'd been a sad disappointment to Tadeoshi's parents, despite her determined efforts to understand their culture. They'd welcomed her as warmly as they could, yet they'd never quite been able to forget she was *gaijin*. The fact that she'd asked them to raise her daughters after Tadeoshi's death rather than drag them from duty post to duty post with her had helped, but still that slight taint of the foreign barbarian lingered in their eyes.

Which made her father-in-law's gift all the more precious, for she *knew* how hard they'd tried to accept her . . . and how difficult that had been.

She opened her eyes and raised the cup to the holocube—the one of a laughing Tadeoshi on the Brisbane flight line—and then to the sheathed *katana* thirty generations of Murakuma *samurai* had borne. That blade was only in her keeping, to be passed to Nobiki on her thirtieth birthday as Tadeoshi had requested, and her eyes misted as they rested upon it. Then she sipped, and the saki burned down her throat, seeming to evaporate before it ever reached her stomach.

She savored the fiery taste which had come five hundred light-years from the planet Musashi. It was fitting that it should have been bottled on a planet named for Japan's greatest *samurai*, for she drank it in remembrance of warriors. Of her husband, who'd died training for the battles he never fought, and of those who'd perished in the First Battle of Justin one year ago today.

She sipped again, alone with the holocube and the sword which represented so much, and promised herself that blade would go to her daughter with its honor unstained.

"They're up to something." Mackenna frowned across the conference table at Murakuma. "I *know* they're up to something."

"Demosthenes?" Murakuma said, and the Corporate World admiral shrugged.

"Leroy's right," he said, and Mackenna nodded vigorously. *Interesting*, she thought. *Once it was only "Captain Mackenna" and "Admiral Waldeck." I wonder if either of them even realizes how much his attitude has changed?* "They're burning too many pinnaces probing us," Waldeck continued, "and I can only think of one reason to do that."

"With all due respect, Admiral Waldeck, I'm not certain we can assume that," Ernesto Cruciero said politely. "It's been seven months since we kicked them out of the system. They haven't made a serious attempt to take it back yet, and we know how close one of their core systems is to us. If they planned an attack here, surely they could *already* have reinforced to launch it, and we've had similar upsurges before when no attacks were launched."

"Not to this extent," Mackenna countered. "Look at it—they've sent three waves of fifty-plus through in just the last two weeks. The CSP killed ninety percent of them, too. Even for Bugs, that's a lot of pinnaces to throw away if they're not planning *something!*"

"I don't categorically say they aren't, Sir. All I'm saying is that we shouldn't *assume* they are. As Admiral LeBlanc keeps saying, these things just don't think like we do."

Murakuma looked from one face to another. As a rule, she preferred to let subordinates debate without committing herself, for she got the fullest exposition of their views by letting them argue with one another rather than work, however unconsciously, to *her* viewpoint. But in this case they'd begun to rehash old positions, and all eyes snapped to her as she cleared her throat.

"Your point's valid, Ernesto," she said, "but Leroy and Admiral Waldeck have a pretty convincing argument. And the bottom line is that we're better off going to an enhanced readiness state when they're not about to attack rather than failing to do so when they *are*."

"It's the SBMHAWKs and energy platforms that concern me, Sir." Cruciero's tone was diffidently stubborn. "We could put a lot of time on their clocks for an attack that never comes."

"That's true enough," Waldeck murmured, and Murakuma nodded. Energy platforms were maintenance-intensive compared to minefields. They tended to get temperamental if they were held too long at full readiness without periodic overhaul, and the same was true of the two hundred SBMHAWK pods deployed to cover the warp point.

"I know," she said, "but the first OWP strikegroups will be ready in five weeks. Once they're on-line, we'll be far less reliant on the platforms. I think we can stretch them to cover that five-week gap, then shut down for complete maintenance once the forts are in place."

Her juniors cocked their heads in consideration. Now that the Sarasota fortress shell was complete, the construction ships were assembling still more prefabricated bases in Justin. Given the Bugs' mass transit tendencies and the possibility of their developing their own SBM-HAWKs, Murakuma had argued that Justin's forts should all be fighter-armed Type Fives or Type Sixes. They mounted no offensive weapons, but each OWP-5 could put seventeen fighter squadrons into space, while an OWP-6 could launch *twenty-seven*, and she intended to deploy them well back from the warp point and use their strikegroups to swamp any attack. Ten Type Fives were already operational, but she had no intention of exposing them to attack until she was confident of their ability to hold, for she refused to abandon their crews if her mobile units were forced back. Her five-week deadline would see another ten forts—all Type Sixes—on-line . . . and put the equivalent of seventy-four more fleet carriers into her defensive order of battle.

Until they were ready, however, and—especially—until their strikegroups had worked up, Fifth Fleet's mobile units had to shoulder the burden. And to do that, they needed the energy platforms and SBMHAWKs on-line the instant any attack came through.

"The platforms would be good for that long," Cruciero agreed. "They won't go much longer before effectiveness degrades, but they should make five weeks. The pods won't, though."

"They won't have to," Murakuma replied. "I want their tasking changed."

"Change their tasking?" Waldeck echoed, then his eyes narrowed. "You want to take them out of independent mode?"

"Exactly. If we slave them to the battle-line's fire control, they'll never go on-line at all unless we send the Fleet to general quarters."

"You'll cut way down on salvo density," Cruciero pointed out.

"Not really," Mackenna said. "We'll pick up anything we lose with better targeting. A *Matterhorn* can control up to ten pods—that's a fifty-missile salvo, enough to saturate the point defense of any ship without command datalink."

"And you've got twenty-five SDs, Demosthenes," Murakuma pointed out. "We can pound hell out of them in one firing pass even without a mass launch."

"I like it," Waldeck agreed.

"In that case, I think we can consider the matter decided. Ernesto, I'd like you to have the new fire plans to me by dinnertime."

The Fleet was ready once more.
The delay between offensive operations had been far longer than pre-war planning had visualized, for the

Fleet's doctrine was based upon seizing and maintaining the momentum, but the time had not been wasted. The last engagement had taught a lesson about underestimating the enemy, and the effectiveness of his attack craft— especially when used in numbers—had taught another. This attack force had barely eighty percent as many superdreadnoughts as the one which had been annihilated in the last engagement, but two-thirds of those it did have had been refitted with improved shields and armor, and they were only the beginning of the refit and construction programs, for less than forty percent of the Reserve had yet been mobilized. Every unit which was activated would receive the latest updates as it was taken from mothballs, and the Fleet had already begun laying down entirely new types to further redress its disadvantages. New battlecruiser classes, every bit as fast as the enemy's vessels, would soon be available, as would new and heavier battle-line units designed to bolster the long suffering super-dreadnoughts. And, of course, there was the other new type designed to answer the enemy's small attack craft.

Enough new and refitted units had come forward to make a fresh attack worthwhile, and even if it failed, the warp point linking this starless nexus to their target system had been so heavily fortified that no conceivable counterattack could take it. It was time to evaluate the new technologies in combat, and the massed ranks of capital ships came to full readiness behind the light cruisers of the Assault Fleet.

The two-toned priority signal warbled while Murakuma was working at her terminal. She opened a window to take the call, and Captain Decker appeared on her screen.

"Yes, Jessica?"

"We've got another pinnace transit, Sir—a big one," her flag captain said. "CIC makes it over a hundred, and they're hanging around for detailed scans, not making an immediate turn back for the point. The CSP's taking a lot of them out, but we're not going to get them all."

"Send the Fleet to battle stations," Murakuma said

instantly. "Activate Alpha One and launch the ready squadrons. Then tell Leroy and Ernesto I'll be on Flag Bridge in five minutes."

She cut the circuit and wheeled from her terminal. *Two more weeks,* she thought bitterly. *All the bastards had to do was wait two more weeks, and I'd've had the forts in here, too!*

But they hadn't waited, and she opened her vac suit closet.

The twelve surviving pinnaces broke back to rejoin the Fleet and beamed their data to the waiting starships. Evaluation was rapid, for the enemy had made few changes since the last probe, and the positions of the ships which mothered the small attack craft were noted. Only then were orders passed, and the Assault Fleet began its advance.

The light cruisers came through just as Murakuma dashed out of the intraship car into Flag Bridge. There was no time to give any orders, but that was why Fifth Fleet had battle plans, and Alpha One sprang into operation even as she jogged across to the master display. She stood with her helmet in the crook of her arm, and her jade eyes were intent as icons blinked in the tank.

Just under a hundred light cruisers flashed into existence. Fifteen exploded *out* of existence just as quickly, and the others spread out past the fireballs, deploying in the clear zone about the warp point. But this time Murakuma had the firepower for a classic warp point defense, and she intended to fight just that.

The primary beam platforms seeded among the mines held their fire—they were tasked for bigger fish—but a hundred and fifty laser buoys lashed out at just thirty enemy cruisers, and none of their targets survived. Nor were the lasers alone, for Fifth Fleet had twelve hundred fighters, and its heightened readiness state had increased the standing combat space patrol on the warp point to forty squadrons. Now the deadly little craft roared in, and Anson

Olivera's *farshatok* had their priorities right. The *Cataphracts* were their natural enemies, and they peeled off to kill them while their transit-addled point defense fought to stabilize.

Degraded or not, the sheer volume of fire killed almost fifty fighters, but that was too little to stop Fifth Fleet's pilots. They rammed their attacks home, ripple-firing FRAMs at pointblank range, then pulled sharply away. The Bugs had sent twenty-four *Cataphracts* through the warp point; when the CSP broke off, two of them survived.

Murakuma's eyes flamed as two-thirds of the Bugs' assault wave was annihilated. Too little of it survived to clear lanes completely through the dense minefield, though they thinned it dangerously in two places, but the mine barrier was still intact when the last died, and she bared her teeth at the status boards. Waldeck had brought the waiting SBMHAWKs on-line, and she settled into her chair with hungry anticipation as she awaited the first Bug superdreadnoughts.

Assault Fleet courier drones told a disturbing tale. Despite its previous experience, the Fleet had underestimated the efficiency of the enemy's attack craft against ships whose systems were degraded by transit and which could not maneuver in the confines of the mines. But the purpose of this battle was largely to test the Fleet's new systems and its analysis of enemy capabilities. There could be no question of breaking off until those objectives had been attained.

"Here come the heavies," Cruciero said flatly, and Murakuma nodded. The Bugs were coming through dangerously tight—some superdreadnoughts actually made simultaneous transits, though this time the luck favored them and none were destroyed—and there were a lot of them.

"Bring up the jammer buoys," she replied, and thirty-five buoys, without a single weapon among them, came to life. They were pure electronic platforms with only one function: to jam Bug datanets. And even as they roused, the primary-armed energy platforms opened up. A hundred unstoppable beams ripped effortlessly through shields and armor, and fifteen riddled Bug superdreadnoughts blew apart as their magazines exploded.

The warp point was a cauldron of dying ships, and as the first wave of Anson Olivera's main strike came shrieking into it, Demosthenes Waldeck's battle-line began to fire.

Twenty of his superdreadnoughts controlled ten SBM-HAWK pods apiece, feeding the pods targeting data from their vastly superior fire control. A single six-ship datagroup could—and did—send a perfectly synchronized salvo of three hundred missiles straight down the Bugs' throat before their defenses could stabilize, and more small, terrible suns glared. Terran *Dunkerque*, Orion *Prokhalon* and Gorm *Bolzucha*-class battlecruisers added their SBMs to the holocaust, and more FRAM-armed fighters swooped in. Desperate Bug point defense stopped some of the missiles, killed some of the fighters, but it couldn't possibly stop them all, and human, Ophiuchi, and Orion howls of triumph echoed over squadron com nets as still more capital ships blew apart.

It was a massacre. Not even the *Archers* could reply effectively, for the jammer buoys smashed their datanets back, forcing each to fight alone, splitting their fire into individual salvos the Allies' datalinked point defense brushed aside with contemptuous ease.

The battle was disaster made flesh. The battle-line reeled, and even as it staggered, the enemy's shorter-ranged missile ships closed in to add their fire to the holocaust. For only the second time in the Fleet's history, orders went out to halt the advance before all of the battle-line had even made transit, for no starship could live in that vortex of warheads, beams and attack craft. But the enemy had closed to concentrate his fire, and even as the battle-line fell back, the third wave streaked through in the opposite direction.

❖   ❖   ❖

"What the——!" Carl Hathaway blinked as four hundred fresh lights spangled his display. They were far too small for starships, but their emissions were stronger than some corvettes, and they slashed through the carnage at incredible speed. "What the fuck *are* those things?" he blurted.

"Sir! We've got a new vessel of some sort!"

Murakuma's head whipped around at Cruciero's announcement. She looked down at her repeater plot, but the explosion of icons swamped its detail, and she shoved herself up to look at the master tank as the newcomers dashed into the minefields. Whatever they were, their emissions were powerful enough to attract the mines, but they were also impossibly fast. The mines were catching some, but most survived to streak straight towards her starships.

Anson Olivera took one look at the readouts and keyed his mike.

"Abort your runs!" he barked over the command circuit while Hathaway fought to get him data on the fresh threat. "All units, this is Ramrod. I say again, abort your runs! Leave the warp point to the battle-line and get on the new bogies!"

Hundreds of fighters acknowledged, but the newcomers were fast. Slower than fighters in clean condition, but far faster than they were with external ordnance mounted.

He glared at his display, watching the new threat run away from his pilots. They'd have to jettison. It was the only way to catch the bastards, and he opened his mouth to give the order.

"Sir!" Hathaway caught him before he could speak, and he darted a look at his tac officer. "These things' emissions are strong enough my missiles can lock them up!"

Olivera's eyes flashed, and he keyed his mike again.

"Ramrod to all units! Jettison FRAMs. I say again, jettison *FRAMs*, but any fighter with missiles attempt a missile engagement."

✧   ✧   ✧

"Well?" Murakuma snapped. She knew she sounded angry, for she was, but not at Cruciero. He simply had the misfortune to be the man on the spot, and he shrugged helplessly.

"I don't know, Sir. They're bigger than fighters, but smaller than anything else with such powerful signatures. They're obviously warp capable, but their power levels are much higher than a pinnace's. It looks like a whole new drive system—something that crosses the line between small craft and starship drives. I'd guess they can run it flat out at settings that would burn out any other small craft's systems."

"What—" Murakuma began, then closed her mouth as the new vessels began to fire.

"Jesus Christ!" Olivera muttered. What the hell *were* those things? They weren't firing fighter missiles—they were firing full-sized standard ship-killers from ten light-seconds out!

But they weren't firing many of them, and his eyes narrowed. It looked like they could carry only four birds each, and the jammers were knocking back any datalink they mounted. That forced them to fire as individuals, which gave them a snowflake's chance in hell of getting through battlegroup point defense. But they seemed to realize that almost instantly. It was as if the first to fire had done so only to prove it wouldn't work, and half of them suddenly swerved straight in on TF 51's battle-line.

Demosthenes Waldeck shoved further back into his command chair and clamped his jaw as the small Bug warships charged his superdreadnoughts. They were far bigger targets than fighters—indeed, they could be killed by weapons which could never have engaged a fighter—but they were also lethally fast and a total surprise. No one had expected such a threat, and—his jaw clamped tighter as the readouts flickered—unlike fighters, they mounted point defense. That made them highly resistant to missile fire, and his missile-heavy battle-line was weak in energy weapons.

Half the Bugs howled down on his capital ships, but the other half broke suddenly towards TF 52. They seemed to ignore Anaasa's TF 53, but Saakhaanaa's Terran and Ophiuchi carriers were obviously priority targets. Yet the carriers were also well back, and carriers and their escorts were fast. The new Bug ships had no more than a fifty percent speed advantage, and Saakhaanaa had wheeled his ships almost instantly, racing away from the threat, slowing the closure rate while reserve squadrons spat from his catapults. Anaasa's fighters were launching, as well, cutting in from one flank while Olivera's antishipping strike charged up from astern.

But Waldeck had little time to watch, for the Bugs who weren't chasing carriers were lunging straight at *him*. Energy weapons and point defense blew dozens out of space, and fighters killed still more. The Bugs' point defense took toll of the fighters who closed with their onboard lasers, but the fighters were harder targets and the kill ratio was entirely in their favor.

Yet favorable kill ratio or no, they couldn't stop them all in the time they had . . . and neither could TF 51's energy batteries. At least forty survived everything Fifth Fleet could throw at them and hurled themselves headlong upon the capital ships. They didn't attempt to fire the missiles they carried; instead they rammed, delivering their antimatter warheads—and their own ships—in shattering concussions of flame and death.

There weren't enough to be decisive, thank God. They couldn't kill many of his ships, but they could—and did—wound them cruelly. TF 51 staggered under the blow, yet the Bugs' decision to split their attack between the battle-line and the carriers was crucial. "Only" three superdreadnoughts and a pair of battlecruisers were actually destroyed, and had they thrown everything at TF 51, they *would* have killed many of its units; Waldeck was certain of that. As it was, they'd failed . . . and they were failing against the carriers, as well.

He wrenched his eyes away from his plot's appalling damage sidebars and snarled vengefully as shoals of Allied fighters closed in. Saakhaanaa's turn away had bought just enough time for them to mass, and they tore into the Bugs like demons. Dozens of Allied flight crews died, but the Bugs shriveled like spiders in a candle flame, and TF 52's escorts fell back astern of the carriers to pick off any Bug who leaked through the fighters.

A shaken Vanessa Murakuma sat in her command chair once more, watching her plot. She knew her victory had been decisive, but it would be a while before her emotions accepted that. The Bugs had lost their entire light cruiser force and over sixty superdreadnoughts before they broke off, yet their new weapon had crippled half of Demosthenes' battle-line, and her fighter losses were over two hundred. That might be far lower than the disastrous casualties they'd taken in the early days of the war, but it was still seventeen percent of her total fighter force.

So much for our "uncontestable" tech superiority. We had every conventional advantage there was. We should have annihilated their starships for minimal losses, and we did, but Lord God did they hurt us after that. And Battle Comp says some of those SDs had third-generation shields, too. She shook her head, eyes bitter as preliminary damage and casualty reports continued to crawl across her terminal. *They don't seem to do things the way we do, but the bastards are no slouches. Those gunboat things aren't as good as fighters, but we never thought of anything like them, and I can see some advantages to them. But the real point is how fast they got them into production. They couldn't have had them when the shooting started, or we'd already've seen them. Did they cook them up from some pre-war R&D program? Were they already close to producing them then, or are they a response to our fighters?* She shivered. *God, I hope they were working on them pre-war! If they weren't— if they actually developed an entire new weapon system from scratch in barely sixteen months—what else are they going to hit us with?*

She stared at the steadily scrolling reports and found no answer.

BOOK TWO

BOOK TWO

CHAPTER TWENTY-THREE

All We Can Do

TFNS *Euphrates'* Marine detachment, Vanessa Murakuma reflected, had had more practice than most at receiving exalted VIPs on inspection tours. Still, the Terran Marines—no Orion ones, for this visitor—came to attention in an exceptionally perfect line of black trousers and green tunics as the shuttle's hatch opened.

The woman who stepped through that hatch was known by sight, but not at all socially, to Murakuma, who'd been out of the War College and back in the Fleet before she'd become Sky Marshal. Hannah Avram lived on in her memories as a tall, slender sword-blade of a woman. Nowadays, middle-aged solidity had begun to make inroads despite all that antigerone treatments could do, but the image of a sword still came to mind, for she was still a living weapon, to be wielded against humankind's enemies.

Murakuma stepped forward and saluted with great formality. "Welcome to *Euphrates* and to the Justin system, Sky Marshal."

Avram returned the salute with equal punctilio, but there was no warmth in her dark eyes. "Thank you, Admiral. Now, perhaps we could find a place to talk in private."

Murakuma felt the bottom drop out of her elation at meeting one of the heroes of the Theban War. "Certainly, Sky Marshal. Please come this way."

✧   ✧   ✧

"Now then, Admiral Murakuma," Avram began as soon as they'd detached themselves from the cloud of hangers-on and settled into the sanctum of *Euphrates'* flag quarters, "there are certain matters we need to address." She dropped with evident relief into one of the comfortable chairs, laying her attache case in her lap, and continued in the same clipped tones. "First, congratulations are in order. You've managed to reverse the course of this war by holding the Bugs and pushing them back, out of this system."

Murakuma felt a thawing of the chill Avram's manner had induced in her gut. "Thank you, Sky Marshal. That means a great deal to me." She indicated the well-equipped bar. "Would the Sky Marshal care for a drink?"

"Thank you, no. And secondly," Avram resumed in exactly the same tone, "just what the *hell* did you think you were doing, hazarding the persons of two members of the Grand Allied Joint Chiefs of Staff—one of them the chairman?" She raised a hand to forestall a defense Murakuma hadn't even formulated. "Oh yes, I know. Boys will be boys, and there's no fool like an old fool. And now that we've gotten those two platitudes out of the way, the fact remains that you had every right to turn down their doubtless piteous pleas to come along—turn them down with a Marine 'escort,' if necessary! That wasn't just your right, Admiral Murakuma—it was your *duty!*" She paused, looking annoyed with herself, and lowered her voice back to its original decibel level. "I know how Ivan Nikolayevich can be. But you could have told him to take any complaints to me. I'd have told him to grow up—some would say it's about time! He would have told me to stop being a Jewish mother, but that's not your problem. The point is that you should have realized, even if he doesn't, that he's got no business risking his life in combat operations."

Murakuma surprised herself with her voice's firmness. "May I speak, Sky Marshal?"

"Say your say," Avram grunted.

"First of all, I didn't yield to any entreaties or bullying on Admiral Antonov's part. It was *my* idea to invite him and Lord Talphon along."

Avram's dark brown eyes locked with her jade-green ones. "Well, Admiral Murakuma, I'll say this for you: you're not a bore." The Sky Marshal settled back and spoke conversationally. "So, you claim full responsibility for the idea of risking Admiral of the Fleet Antonov, and also Lord Talphon, a relative of the Khan—if *he*'d gotten killed in this little escapade, we might have had a *second* war on our hands." She cocked her head. "Care to explain why, Admiral?"

Murakuma drew a deep breath. "It was something Admiral Antonov said to me when we presented the ops plan for his approval. The people I'd already lost were . . . haunting me. He seemed to sense it, and he spoke directly to me, as though he and I were the only ones present who belonged to a kind of horrible fraternity—the only ones who could possibly understand."

"Yes, I know he can be like that, too," Avram murmured, almost to softly to be heard.

"And then," Murakuma continued "he said something that brought all my self-pity into perspective. He reminded me I still had the option of taking the risks I order others to take." (Unnoticed, and unconsciously on her own part, Avram shifted her left hand and fingered that which had replaced her right arm.) "So I still have something he lost a long time ago. And I felt a sense of obligation—a need to let *him* share it once more." She shook herself and gazed directly at the Sky Marshal with green eyes that had gone almost mischievous. "That's really all I can say in mitigation, Sir. Except perhaps for yet another platitude: all's well that ends well."

Avram held those eyes, unblinking, for so long that they almost wavered. But then a twinkle banished the Sky Marshal's glare, although nothing below the eyes softened. "I can perhaps understand your feelings, Admiral. But the fact remains that you took an unjustified chance with the lives of very important people. The consequences could have been very grim. More to the point, those consequences could have fallen on *me!* Don't you *ever* expose me to a risk like that again! Do I make myself clear?"

"Perfectly, Sir," Murakuma replied in a small voice.

"Good. And now, a couple of final points that could have been communicated to you through regular channels . . . but, since I was coming out here anyway—" The twinkle was back, this time accompanied by a very slight smile. Avram fumbled in her attache case and extracted an official-looking folder. "You're a full admiral now. We'll make the official announcement later." She allowed herself a moment to savor Murakuma's expression, then made a great show of having an afterthought and reached back inside the attache case. "We'll also make this official later." She extracted a small, flat box, deep-blue edged with gold, and casually tossed it to Murakuma, who seemed to come out of shock just in time to grab it out of the air.

The newly promoted admiral forced her maelstrom of emotions to subside—dear God, she'd only been a vice admiral for . . . how long?—and opened the box. The light caught the twenty-four karat gold of what lay within, but that wasn't what dazzled her as she gazed at the royal beast suspended from the multicolored ribbon. The Lion of Terra—highest decoration the Federation could bestow on its sons and daughters, conferring on its holder the right to take a salute from anyone in uniform who didn't possess it, regardless of rank.

After a time, Murakuma remembered where she was and lowered the box, revealing Hannah Avram, smiling an odd little smile. "I believe, Admiral," the Sky Marshal said, "That I'll have that drink now. Have you got any white wine?"

Murakuma's smile started out tremulously, but didn't stay that way. "Sure you won't make it Irish, Sir?"

Rear Admiral Marcus LeBlanc leaned back, propped his feet on the desk, and ran a hand over the top of his head from front to back in a habitual gesture of weariness. The surviving hairs were insufficient to mar the sleekness, and for the thousandth time he wondered if that was because of wry realism, misplaced pride, sheer damned stubbornness, or just a lifelong aversion to putting himself in the hands of the medical profession.

"Are these the last of the reports?" he asked the offensively young ensign.

"Yes, Sir," Kevin Sanders responded, with more energy than he had any right to show this late in the working day. "We had to practically extort a final draft out of Dr. Kovac. But they're all here, ready to be correlated."

"Too damned late in the day to start doing it now," LeBlanc muttered. His gaze shifted to the window. They were at that point of their work-cycle where the end of the working day actually corresponded to the setting of Alpha Centauri A. As usual at this time of year in this particular part of Nova Terra, it was dipping behind the pale blue curve of Eden that loomed over the oceanic horizon like some titan-emperor's floating pleasure dome. LeBlanc's ad hoc organization of Bug specialists had been isolated here for reasons which he'd at least found good for a cynical laugh. The Powers That Be could stress "security" all they wanted, but they were far less concerned over Bug spies disguised as humans or fanatical human adherents of Bug-ism than that their citizenry might get wind of his team's . . . disturbing theories. Yet he couldn't deny that the island of New Atlantis was a lovely place, with its dramatic topography and the subtropical Terran vegetation that had pretty much pushed aside the less-evolved local stuff. Maybe too lovely; where reality presented such a gentle aspect, it was almost possible to forget what was happening in the universe beyond the white-sand beaches and regard the beings they studied as some fascinating abstract problem in xenology. Periodically, LeBlanc made himself view the tapes from Erebor.

Sanders followed his gaze. "Beautiful island, isn't it, Sir? I don't know about the name, though. I mean, there never was an *old* Atlantis!"

LeBlanc grinned. Sanders should know, coming as he did from Old Terra, which made him something of a *rara avis* in the TFN. He'd been working for Admiral Antonov's staff spook but had contrived to get himself detached to LeBlanc's outfit. The new-minted rear admiral was glad to have him; he had the kind of irreverent originality this project needed, and he was the sort to fit in well with this oddball half-military and half-civilian crew. In particular, he seemed to resonate well with the Tabbies, of whom there were quite a few here, along with a fair number of Ophiuchi and a couple of Gorm. Besides, LeBlanc liked him in the way people generally like those in whom they unconsciously recognize their own younger selves.

"Take a load off," the admiral said, gesturing at a chair. "Sorry you had to deal with Kovac—I know he can be difficult." He stretched hugely. "Late as it is, I suppose I need to try and make some sense of these reports tonight. The Director is sure to want a briefing." The Director of Naval Intelligence had arrived on Nova Terra less than a local day ago. So far she'd been kept busy at Allied Grand Fleet Headquarters, a quarter of the way around the globe. But she was bound to show up at New Atlantis, sooner rather than later.

"There's not much you can tell her about the databases, Sir," Sanders said as he settled into the chair. "We're still where we were when Dr. Linkovich had his initial insight. The Gorm have been trying to construct a model for electronic—'psychotronic'?—storage of psionic data patterns by analogizing from what they know of how their *minisorchi* operates. They're *sure* there must be such a model. But . . . Well, Gorm don't scream and smash the furniture. Not their style. But I can tell that that's exactly what they'd be doing if they were human.

"Trouble is, not even they have a 'unified field theory' relating psi to matter and energy. We humans don't have a clue; we've never had any real reason to be interested. So until some genius comes up with such a theory—which the Bugs must already have—we're just pissing into the wind."

LeBlanc stretched again, and rubbed his eyes. "Well

then, we'd better concentrate on areas where we have a chance of accomplishing something. Like these new attack craft Admiral Murakuma encountered."

"Oh, yes." Sanders brightened, oblivious to the pain that had crossed LeBlanc's face at the mention of Admiral Murakuma. "That was what Kovac was working on. He gave me a running discourse while his flunkies were getting his 'extremely tentative and incomplete conclusions' printed out. I think I've got a pretty good—if elementary— idea of what he's driving at."

"Well, summarize for me. I'd like to hear the 'elementary' version before I tackle the full report."

"I fancy I'd like to hear it too, Ensign."

The clipped, British-accented voice from the doorway had a remarkable effect. LeBlanc was on his feet, fumbling to fasten his collar, while Sanders, who wasn't all that far removed from the Academy, was too busy trying to brace a bulkhead that wasn't there to be concerned with the state of his uniform.

"Why, er, Admiral Trevayne," LeBlanc stammered, "we weren't expecting . . . that is, we didn't know you were . . ."

Winnifred Trevayne waved a dismissive gesture, and occupied an empty chair. "Please be at ease, Admiral LeBlanc and Ensign . . . Sanders, isn't it? I remember you from your time on the Sky Marshal's staff." She steepled her fingers and gazed over them, sighting along the bridge of her keel-straight nose. Her coloring was dark, but that was the only vestige of the Jamaican fraction of her ancestry. "I suppose I should have given you some notice of my arrival. But I've only just been able to get away from Grand Fleet Headquarters. Besides, I couldn't face one more well-prepared reception." Her eyes surveyed the none-too-tidy office, finally settling on LeBlanc and Sanders, and her lips formed what in anyone else might have been suspected of being a smile. "Something rather refreshing about this place, actually. And now, Ensign Sanders, you were starting to say when I interrupted . . . ?"

Sanders took a deep breath. "Well, Admiral, our staff's

concluded that the Arachnids have found a somewhat different approach to applying classic drive theory to small craft. We've always had a problem in applying the technology to smaller packages, because of the 'shallowness' of the inertial sump associated with small craft." The ensign was rapidly returning to his chatty norm. "For example, the version that made fighters possible paid for its compactness with a sump that was so much less deep that fighter performance, unlike that of starships, is degraded when carrying external ordinance, and—"

LeBlanc cleared his throat nervously. "I believe the Director is already conversant with these matters, Ensign."

Sanders had the grace to blush. "Er, sorry, Sir. We have a lot of xenologists around here who have to have things outside the biological and social sciences explained to them, and you sort of get used to . . . Well, let me cut to the chase. The data from Fifth Fleet suggests that the Bugs have developed a kind of intermediate drive for these 'gunboats,' too large for most small craft but with a sump almost as deep as a full-sized starship's. Their maximum speed is lower than an unloaded fighter's, but they can carry external ordinance without being slowed down."

"They must pay some sort of penalty," Trevayne mused.

"Oh yes, Sir. The penalty comes in the form of a high power requirement, with a correspondingly strong emissions signature. This, combined with its large size—for a small craft—means a gunboat can be targeted by ship-to-ship weapon systems. And it's not large *enough* to absorb the kind of damage those weapons dish out."

"That suggests it ought to trigger mine attacks as well," LeBlanc put in. "Actually, there's another piece of good news, as well. Analysis of the observational data confirms the supposition that, being larger than other small craft, gunboats can't use internal bays. Instead, they seem to be carried externally on ships. So rearming them must be an EVA operation, and it doesn't take much imagination to see how awkward *that* must be."

"For openers," Sanders piped up, the other two's exalted ranks momentarily forgotten, "it means the mother ship's drive field has to be deactivated while they're doing it. The radiation would deep-fry somebody in a vac suit!"

He seemed about to say more, but Trevayne raised a hand. In the ensuing silence, she looked from one of them to the other and then back again.

"I'm afraid you're missing the point, gentlemen. You see, all the points of 'good news' you've adduced are outweighed by the one very large item of *bad* news." She met their eyes again, even more gravely than before. "The one, single advantage we've had up to now has been our somewhat superior technology. And we've assumed that that state of affairs will continue, that their tactical inflexibility must be accompanied by a lack of inventiveness. We can no longer make any such assumption. Since encountering our fighters, they've developed, produced and deployed a countervailing system. I'm not certain we could do so well in so short a period."

In the dead silence that followed, LeBlanc's quiet voice seemed almost raucous. "Uh, Sir, Admiral Murakuma speculated that the gunboats could perhaps be the end result of some R&D program they already had underway before the war."

"That, Admiral LeBlanc, is a classic example of whistling in the dark. It would be sheer folly for us to rely on it. Instead, we must assume there are more surprises in store. You and your people here must try and foretell what those surprises are going to be. You must try to deduce, on the basis of past experience, what they find most threatening in our technological tool kit and how they'll seek to counter it." All at once, her trademark crispness wavered, and she held a hand over her eyes as though to shield them, even though the office was only dimly illuminated against the twilight. "It's all we can do," she said, addressing someone other than LeBlanc and Sanders. "We really have no way of knowing what lies in wait."

Outside the window, the slow rotation of the twin-planet system sent the last light of Alpha Centauri A vanishing behind Eden. The sister planet shaded abruptly from sky blue to ultramarine, and the heavens grew dark.

CHAPTER TWENTY-FOUR

Broken Claws

Fourteenth Great Claw of the Khan Zhaarnak'diaano glowered into the small holo tank of his repeater plot. The worthless planets of the uninhabited Telmasa System orbited their K4 primary with a bland uselessness which mirrored his own mood all too accurately. Clan Diaano had once been famed for the warriors it produced in the Khan's service, but that had been before the Wars of Shame. It was not his clan's fault no chance had arisen to win back the honor lost in those disastrous wars, yet every one of his ancestors seemed to prowl the back of his mind, muttering balefully over their descendant's failure to seize glory by the throat in *this* war. For more than a full human year—almost two Orion years—it had raged, and *still* he sat tethered as a "rear area security umbrella" designed only to reassure civilians!

He growled and kneaded his claws in and out of his chair's padded armrests. Of course, very few of the Khan's warriors had so far been given the chance to measure themselves against these new foes—these "Bugs." Fang Anaasa and his pilots had won enormous renown for their rescue of the Human Fifth Fleet in the Third Battle of Justin, but no more of the KON's units had been rushed forward . . . for reasons which were one more ember in Zhaarnak's seething disgust.

Technology. Technology and experience. The Humans'

R&D had—once more—outpaced the *Zheeerlikou'valk-hannaieee's*, and so they were better equipped than the Khan's Navy. They had begun the war with better shields, better armor . . . better weapons. Even now their *technical missions* were busy throughout the Khanate, working to upgrade the KON's technology as if the *Zheeerlikou'valk-hannaieee* were cubs who must be led by the hand. And though the Federation's last major war was an Orion century old, it remained more recent than anything the *Khanate* could claim. Antipiracy operations, the suppression of a slaving outbreak in the Khithaar Sector, the short confrontation when District Governor Maashaar defied the present Khan's sire . . . those were all the "wars" the KON had fought since the Third Interstellar War, and so the Grand Alliance had agreed the Humans should lead the battle in the Romulus Cluster.

The great claw bared the tips of his fangs. Deep inside, a part of him acknowledged that it was the Humans who had first been attacked. Their warriors' blood had been the first shed, their civilians the ones butchered, and so it was right that they be given the honor of facing the foe. Yet another, deeper part of him could not accept that. Humans were *chofaki*. They *had* no honor. They were clever, yes, and skilled in the cold blooded execution of maneuvers, yet they lacked the warrior's fire. He had heard the arguments—*Valkha*, but he had heard them!—since the Theban War. *Minisharhuaak!* Of *course* they had shouldered their obligations in that war, but they had done so out of *fear*, Zhaarnak thought. It was they who had given the crazed Thebans technology in the first place, and they'd feared Liharnow the Great would loose the Navy upon them if they did not "step forward." And they had shown themselves *chofak* yet again in this war. What true warrior would have fallen back again and again, abandoning millions of his own civilians to certain death— to being *eaten* like so many *marhangi*?

He made his claws retract, and his mind replayed the official briefings like some endless, meaningless chant. The Humans had had no choice but to fall back. They had fought again and again, and not even Zhaarnak could deny the damage they had inflicted—assuming the reports were accurate. Yet that was the point. If the reports *were* accurate, then *why* had they been forced back? Almost four hundred superdreadnoughts—that was how many capital ships the Humans' Fifth Fleet claimed to have destroyed. *Four hundred!* The entire Orion *Navy* contained only four hundred and six starships, including even *destroyers!* Was he to believe the Humans had destroyed thirty times the KON's total tonnage without even *slowing* their enemies?

Ridiculous! Such inflated claims were the proof they were *chofaki*, dirt-eaters, beings so lost to honor they could not even recognize it as a concept! According to those same intelligence packets the Humans' ships were faster, their weapons longer ranged, their defensive technologies and datalink superior, *and* they had fighters! If they had destroyed so many ships, if they held such a tremendous tactical advantage, then why were *they* on the defensive? Oh, true, they had retaken Justin—finally, with Fang Anaasa's help—yet did they truly expect Zhaarnak to believe any opponent could absorb such losses and continue to *attack?*

He shook himself and rose. *Softly, Zhaarnak,* he told himself. *Softly. Whatever you may think, it is your duty not to show your officers your disgust. And be truthful. Would you be so ready to believe them* chofak *had they not brought such dishonor upon your clan?*

He twitched his ears brusquely, angry with that last thought, yet he could not quite reject it. His clan fathers had charged into battle in the Orion way in the Wars of Shame . . . and the Humans had slaughtered their commands in the *chofak* Human way. Perhaps the Terran Navy *had* taught the KON how wars were won, but what of *honor?* What of the battle sagas chanted when warriors were laid to rest? The Wars of Shame took those things from his clan, and even the meager redemption Clan Diaano had won in the Third Interstellar War had come on Human terms. It was the Humans who shared the strikefighter technology with the Khanate even before the Rigelians turned on the *Zheeerlikou'valkhannaieee*. It was the Humans whose industrial might had built entire *starships* for the Khan. Even Varnik'sheerino, the greatest fang of the last three centuries, had been forced to dance to Human terms, coordinate his plans with theirs!

Be honest. Be honest, Zhaarnak. Chofak Humans may be, yet what you truly hate is that they never let your clan regain honor from them—only with them. There is no Human blood upon your claws, and you hate them for it.

Well, perhaps that was truth, but truth was a bitter herb, and whatever cause he had to hate them, their showing in *this* war was cause enough for contempt.

He snorted and stepped into the intraship car. If he could not take his battlegroup to war, at least he would not sit here on his flag bridge like some clawless cub and watch an empty plot!

Least Claw of the Khan Shaiaasu'aaithnau sighed in relief as his six *Lahstyn*-class light cruisers headed for the warp point. Under other circumstances, he would have enjoyed exercising his first squadron command, but the Shanak System was and always had been as useful as a screen door on an airlock. It was lifeless, a cul-de-sac accessible only via a single closed warp point, whose sole claim to importance was that it lay adjacent to the *extremely* useful Kliean System. Unlike Shanak, Kliean boasted two habitable planets and an immensely rich asteroid belt. It was one of the Khanate's oldest and wealthiest inhabited systems . . . and the only reason Shaiaasu and his ships had just spent a thoroughly boring month resurveying Shanak.

He let himself relax as his lead ship entered the warp point, and lazy thoughts chased about his brain. He understood the panic behind his orders. If the rumors from the Human's Justin System were true, even the potential for a similar threat to a system like Kliean must be terrifying to the Khan's administrators. And, he admitted, the survey data on Shanak *had* been over four Orion centuries old. Improved instrumentation *might* have discovered a second warp point—it had not, but it might have—yet that had made the mission no less boring, and he felt abandoned so far from the front. Not that *Lahstyn*-class cruisers would have been much use in combat.

He purred a chuckle at the thought of his little survey ships leading a life-or-death attack. He had seen one of Humans' *Hun*-class cruisers. Now *there* was a survey ship! But the Federation was wealthy enough to build such vessels for survey work, and the *Zheeerlikou'valkhannaieee* were not. Indeed, he took a sort of perverse pride in his command's austerity. Humans might need big, comfortable ships; Orions did not. Not, he admitted, that he would refuse one!

He chuckled again, then braced himself as his own ship entered the warp point. *Acutar* seemed to twitch around him in the familiar stress of transit, and he carefully did not grunt in relief as the brief nausea eased. He gazed longingly into his plot at the blue dot of the planet Masiahn. He had relatives down there—and he wished he had time to visit them. Masiahn was one of the jewels in the Khan's crown, a beautiful world of mountains, forests, and swift, white-foaming rivers. The planet had an enormous tourist trade, and Shaiaasu would have loved to spend a few weeks there. The *jahar* hunting was excellent, and not many could mount one of the needle-tipped antler racks on his wall or claim he'd taken the beast with no weapon but his own claws.

But it was not to be. His squadron had completed this component of its mission, and he knew Great Claw Zhaarnak's reputation. The 109th Survey Squadron was an independent command, but the great claw was responsible for covering its operations, and Zhaarnak must be like a *zeget* with a thorn in its paw. Any mere least claw who wasted a single hour longer than necessary would regret giving him a target for his ire!

✦   ✦   ✦

The cloaked cruiser watched the last enemy vessel disappear. It had been astounded when the enemy first appeared, for this system had always been useless. Reachable only via a closed warp point and with no outbound warp points, it had never attracted any attention. Yet doctrine was inflexible: any star system, however useless, must be picketed, and so this one had.

Now the cruiser waited, making absolutely certain of the coordinates of the second closed warp point through which the enemy vessels had vanished before it fired its courier drone home.

Zhaarnak looked up from his paperwork as his com buzzed. He activated it, and Least Claw Daarsaahl'haairna-ahn, his battlecruiser flagship's CO, looked out of it at him.

"Yes, Daarsaahl?"

"Least Claw Shaiaasu has reported, Sir," his flag captain—a term the KON had borrowed from the Humans, Zhaarnak thought sourly—twitched her ears derisively. "Having found nothing in Shanak, he is en route to Thraidaar. He will pass through Telmasa within the next two days."

"So he found nothing. Why am I not surprised?" Zhaarnak's ears mirrored the flag captain's sour humor. If Shanak had been cleared, the battlegroup would shortly be moved from Telmasa to Sak to cover the choke point there, and would *that* not be exciting?

He cocked his head in thought. Shaiaasu's message was for his information only, for the least claw was not technically under his command, but Zhaarnak *was* a great claw . . . and bored.

"Very well, Daarsaahl. Let me know when he arrives. We may as well run a tracking exercise on him. In fact, set up a few days of maneuvers. He can delay his Thraidaar survey that long, and we have been too long idle. Whether they let us fight it or not, there *is* a war on!"

"Of course, Great Claw."

"Good. In the meantime—" Zhaarnak surprised himself with a chuckle of true amusement "—I have more than sufficient paperwork to keep me occupied for the next several hours. Invite Theerah to join both of us for supper, and we can discuss the exercise plans over a haunch of *zeget*."

The freighter *Sellykha* was no swift *thirahk*. In fact, she was big, ugly, ungainly, and about as maneuverable as an over-age asteroid, but her captain loved her. The resource extraction ship had never been out of Kliean. She made her routine trips between the asteroid belt and the orbital smelters, earning her owners a steady if unspectacular profit, and if it was a boring berth, well, Shipmaster Faarsaahl'ynaara had *earned* a bit of boredom in the autumn of his life.

Still, it *was* a welcome diversion to be ferrying the small prospecting team to Shaylka's single moon. The outermost planet of the system was a typical ball of ice, but its moon was much more interesting. Its eccentric orbit had been noted during the original system survey, yet only in the last few years had anyone gotten around to taking a closer look at it. No one was prepared to suggest where it had come from or how Shaylka had captured it, but it appeared to be rich in transuranic elements, and *Sellykha's* owners had gotten in the first claim on its mineral rights.

Faarsaahl padded down the bridge access tunnel—no intraship cars for work-a-day *Sellykha!*—while he wondered how much his employers would earn from those rights. It might all come to nothing, but there was at least the chance of a fat bonus, and his son-in-law and daughter had just presented him with his seventh, eighth and ninth grandcubs. Their home on Masiahn would need additional rooms, and he planned to give them a new wing for Jaathnaa's birthday.

He stepped onto the bridge, crossed to his command chair, and paused to check the engineering readouts. Number Two engine room had reported the recurrence of that irritating harmonic, and he wanted a detailed record for the yard techs. "Engineer's imagination" indeed! *This* time he would make those *thaarkoni* admit there was a problem and *do* something about it.

"Shipmaster?" He looked up at his fourth officer's call. The youngster's ears were half-flattened, and he waved at his display. "Could you look at this, Sir?"

Faarsaahl crossed the bridge, wondering what fresh totally prosaic discovery Huaath had made. *You were young once yourself,* he chided himself, but the cub was so shiny and new Faarsaahl kept looking for milk on his lips.

"What is it?"

"I am not certain, Sir." Huaath peered intently into his display as his claws ticked gently over his panel. "I seem to be picking up some sort of drive field."

"A drive field? Out *here*?" Faarsaahl tried to keep the incredulity out of his voice.

"Yes, Sir. Its frequency matches nothing in our database, however." Huaath waved at his display. "Look for yourself."

Faarsaahl peered over the youngster's shoulder, and his spine stiffened, for there *was* a drive field out there. *Sellykha*'s sensors fell far short of Navy standards, but the signature burned clear and sharp, and Faarsaahl felt his claws slip from their sheaths in sudden, terrible suspicion.

"Its vector?" he asked quietly.

"It appears to be inbound from Shanak," Huaath said, and Faarsaahl's belly knotted. He stared at the display for one more moment, then turned sharply to his communications officer.

"Get your transmitter on line!" The com officer blinked in surprise, and Faarsaahl bared his fangs. "Quickly! Alert Masiahn and Zhardak that unknown starships have entered the system!"

The com officer stiffened, whiskers aquiver in sudden understanding, and bent over his panel with frantic haste. Faarsaahl watched him, then turned back to his fourth officer and laid a clawed hand on the confused youngster's shoulder.

"Inform them that Fourth Officer Huaath'raamahl spotted them," he told the com officer quietly. "See to

it that they know it was only his alertness which let us
get the warning off."

"Aye, Shipmaster," the com officer said equally quietly,
and Faarsaahl squeezed Huaath's shoulder. The cub still
hadn't realized, he thought sadly. *Sellykha* had only a
freighter's speed, but at least he could insure that Clan
Raamahl knew it had a new father-in-honor.

Zhaarnak'diaano stared at his flag captain.

"What strength?" he demanded.

"The Governor had little data when he transmitted the
alert," Daarsaahl replied flatly. "*Sellykha* was destroyed
within minutes of sending her warning. Shipmaster
Faarsaahl continued sending updates to the last, but he
had seen only twenty or thirty light cruisers at that time."

"*Valkha*," Zhaarnak whispered. At least the message
had reached him quickly via the interstellar communication
network comsats that relayed light-speed transmissions
between warp points, but his thoughts seemed frozen.
Shanak. They had come from Shanak, but how——?

"They tracked Shaiaasu," he said softly. "They must
have. But how did they *get* there?"

"There must be a second closed warp point." Daarsaahl's
ears went flat as she spoke. "*Minisharhuaak!* Our own
survey showed them the way!"

Zhaarnak shook off his paralysis and spun to his com
section.

"Emergency priority, Juaahr! All units are to form on
Dashyr for transit to Kliean. Then set up a conference
link with the carrier commanders. Request an immediate
update on squadron readiness states from *farshathkhanaak*
Derikaal. Then send our own alert up the ICN. Request
any available support—utmost priority." The com officer
nodded, and Zhaarnak wheeled to his operations officer.
"If this is only a probe, we may be able to stop it, Theerah.
Configure Derikaal's squadrons for an antishipping strike.
If we can destroy them or drive them back on Shanak,
we have a chance to delay them long enough for someone
else to get here."

"Who, Sir?" Son of the Khan Theerah'jihaal asked quietly.

"*Anyone!*" Zhaarnak snapped, then flicked his ears in apology. His fear and anger were not the ops officer's fault. Oh, no. It was the four *billion* civilians in Kliean who woke the terror at his heart, and he turned back to his console as the first carrier commander appeared on his com.

The Fleet continued its advance. Two more freighters had been destroyed. Both appeared to have been moving towards the Fleet, perhaps in an effort to acquire more data. If so, that was a good sign—an indication there were no enemy warships to oppose the attack.

Sensors continued to report. Both targeted planets blazed with the emissions of densely populated, high-tech worlds, and those same sensors had already detected the system's massive asteroid-based industry. That, too, was good. It indicated the wealth of resources waiting for the taking. Once its planets had been cleansed, this system would be a valuable prize.

Great Claw Zhaarnak's battlegroup raced through the warp point. Least Claw Shaiaasu's light cruisers screened the main force: six battlecruisers and an equal number of *Mohrdenhau* light carriers. That was it. All Zhaarnak had. Twelve starships and one hundred and seventy-six fighters, and the great claw felt the agony of his own inadequacy as Zhardak and Masiahn glowed in his plot. Four billion. The number repeated again and again, tolling through his brain, and his eyes dropped to the icon of Shaiaasu's ship. He wanted to hate the least claw for letting this happen, yet Shaiaasu had only followed orders. He should have been more careful, but he had obeyed procedures. *And perhaps he, as you, saw his mission only as a distraction from his true duty. From his chance to win honor. And if he did, what does that say of you, Zhaarnak'diaano?*

"Transmission from Zhardak, Sir!" The com officer

listened for a moment, and his ears went flat. Zhaarnak glared at him, part of him wishing Juaahr would suddenly be struck mute, yet he had to know. "Zhardak reports at least nine battlecruisers and an unknown number of superdreadnoughts," the com officer said in a dead voice.

"*Shiaaahk!*" Daarsaahl whispered the savage oath, and Zhaarnak's claws drove deep into his armrests. This was no probe . . . and his battlegroup could never stop it. The light dots of the inhabited worlds drew his eyes like a black hole, and the same black hole sucked his soul into its maw as his earlier thoughts about warriors who abandoned civilians mocked him.

"Very well," he said after a moment, and the calmness of his own voice astonished him. "Update your force appreciation, Theerah." He looked down at the com link to his senior pilot. "Inform your squadrons, Derikaal," he said quietly. "Tell them—" He paused, searching for the words. "Tell them we are warriors. What we can do, we must, as the Khan expects of us."

"Yes, Sir," the *farshathkhanaak* said softly, and Zhaarnak looked at his flag captain.

"Take us to meet them, Daarsaahl."

The Fleet's sensors picked up the attack craft first, then the ships which had launched them, and the light cruisers fell back on the main force. There were no gunboats to cover them, for this was a rapid reaction force, with none of the new units. But the enemy was still weaker, with less than two hundred attack craft and nothing heavier than a battlecruiser to support them.

Eighty-Third Small Claw of the Khan Derikaal'zohkiir's fighters neared the enemy, and the *farshathkhanaak's* blood ran cold as he saw their true strength at last. Twenty-seven superdreadnoughts—a small force beside the ones waging such titanic combat on the Justin front, yet impossible odds for a single light battlegroup—were screened by nine battlecruisers and thirty-three light cruisers, including a dozen of those the Humans had codenamed *Cataphract*. His fighter squadrons were a cub's toy against such power, but they were all Kliean had, and he forced his voice to remain calm as he designated targets.

"Ignore the cruisers," he told his pilots, knowing even as he did how many of them those cruisers would kill. "Mass on the lead superdreadnought division."

Acknowledgments came back, and he took his place at their head—the post of greatest honor and danger— as they shook out behind him. His two-man command fighter was more austere than its Human counterparts, without a separate pilot. He remembered the arguments in which he had maintained the superiority of the Human arrangement, the times he had stressed how the extra position eased a strike commander's load, but today he was glad the controls were in his own claws . . . and it was not as if it would have mattered.

His pilots streaked into the Bugs' engagement envelope, and fireballs pocked their ranks. Fighter after fighter blew apart, but they held their course, howling down their enemies' throat in an attack they knew could only be futile. Yet it was an attack they had to make. They were Orions, and four billion civilians lay behind them.

A quarter of the enemy attack craft were destroyed short of the Fleet, but the survivors shrieked in on the leading superdreadnoughts, closing through everything the Fleet could throw at them, and salvoed their deadly FRAMs. Four SDs blew apart, and the attack craft tore through the formation, strafing with their onboard lasers, ripping at the Fleet in desperate fury.

Of the hundred and seventy-five who had attacked, eighty-one broke free to rearm, and the Fleet rumbled onward. Losses were higher than projected, but over half the attack craft had been destroyed. Their next attack would be weaker . . . and the one after that weaker still.

Zhaarnak sat bitterly in his command chair as the remnants of his third strike broke off. Derikaal had lived to lead the second, but the last had been led by a mere

cub of the Khan, for no more senior officer had survived.
Now his remaining fighters—all sixteen of them—fell back
to their carriers . . . and the enemy continued remorselessly
onward. Ten of his pilots had ignored orders and rammed
capital ships, but it was useless. Useless. Their suicide
runs had not even dented their targets. Only seven
superdreadnoughts had been destroyed, and his battlegroup
was hopelessly inadequate to stop the survivors.

"The fighters are rearming, Sir," Son of the Khan
Theerah said, and Zhaarnak fought the need to scream
curses at him. The fighters were *rearming*. What did
Theerah think less than three squadrons could *do* against
such firepower?

Every instinct shrieked to attack. That was the
Farshalah'kiah, the Warrior's Way, which required him
to die before he let these creatures murder his
people's worlds, yet reason knew his battlegroup's death
could not save Kliean. The system was doomed, unless
reinforcements could somehow take it back, and there
were no reinforcements. Kliean was too far from what
all had assumed was the front. The bulk of the Fleet
was busy deploying towards the known fighting or
refitting for future deployment; only light forces like
his were available, and if the enemy had massed so
heavy a fleet this quickly, at least one of his main
bases must lie in close proximity.

It should not be so, he thought bleakly. *We are caught
like the Humans themselves, struck where we never
expected it and naked under the enemy's claws. Yet there
is* one *difference. The Humans had only colony worlds to
defend . . . we* have *the entire Idnahk Sector.*

His blood was frozen. Four billion in Kliean, yes, but
another billion and a half in Hairnow, yet another in
Alowan, and over *thirty* billion within six transits of Sak.
He looked upon the greatest disaster in the *Zheeerlikou'valkhannaieee's* history, and he could not stop it. Gods
above, *he could not stop it!*

"Fall back, Theerah," he said.

"Sir?" The ops office stared at him, and Zhaarnak closed

his fists, extended claws sinking a centimeter deep into his palms.

"Fall back," he repeated. His ops officer continued to stare at him, and Zhaarnak made himself meet that stare. "We cannot stop them," he said, wondering how he could speak so flatly while his soul died, "but we are the only force available. We must fall back to Telmasa. We cannot sacrifice ourselves here when our ships may make the difference in a warp point defense there."

"But, Sir, the planetary defense centers! If we fell back, joined with the PDCs—"

"The PDCs are antiques," Zhaarnak said, and his voice was no longer flat. It was harsh and ugly with despair and self-hate. "They lack even datalink! What they can do, they must, but our support would add nothing to their capabilities. We must fall back on Telmasa, where we *may* make a difference, not sacrifice ourselves where we know we cannot."

Theerah stared at him, still unable to believe what he was hearing, and Zhaarnak slammed a clawed, bleeding fist on the arm of his chair.

"*Minisharhuaak!* Must I repeat myself yet again? *Fall back*, Son of the Khan! We have an entire sector to consider!"

"I—" Theerah closed his mouth, then nodded curtly. "As you command, Great Claw." His voice was ugly, but the ugliness was directed less at Zhaarnak than at the knowledge that the great claw was correct, and Zhaarnak let it pass. Who was he to task another for the dishonor of insubordination when he had just abandoned four billion people to death?

Least Claw Shaiaasu listened in shock. *Fall back? Abandon the system? No!*

He stared into his own plot, seeing what Great Claw Zhaarnak saw, and knew what the great claw knew. The system was doomed—*doomed because of* you, *Shaiaasu'-aaithnau*—and all the battlegroup could hope for now was to hold the Telmasa warp point until relief forces arrived.

But it couldn't. There were enough fighters in Hairnow and Alowan to replace the carriers' losses, but even with full hangar bays, they could never stop the Bugs—not in Telmasa, not in Alowan, not in Sak . . .

Humans had a word for what he had unleashed upon his people; they called it Juggernaut.

"Sir?" His exec's eyes met his, as sick as his own, and he looked past her, looked about him at his bridge officers, pictured all the other officers and ratings of *Acutar's* company and the dishonor he had brought upon them all.

"No!"

Zhaarnak lunged upright as KONS *Acutar* changed course. She darted straight for the enemy, and as he watched, *Kilokharn* and *Kurv* wheeled to follow her, then *Faulhi*, *Nabahstahr* and *Zairoh*, until Shaiaasu's entire squadron streaked for the Bugs behind its flagship.

"Raise Least Claw Shaiaasu!" Zhaarnak roared, and his com officer punched keys. The great claw waited, watching in fury as his entire light cruiser element charged to its own destruction, and then Juaahr looked up.

"Acutar does not respond, Sir," he said.

Zhaarnak sank back into his chair, and to his watching officers, it was as if he aged a century before their eyes. He gazed into his plot, watching the first missiles streak towards the light cruisers—light cruisers which lacked even command datalink—and his ears were flat. *Curse you, Shaiaasu,* he thought numbly. *Curse you for doing what I long to do!*

Acutar staggered as the first missile slammed into her shields. Another followed, and a third. Her shields went down, and vaporized hull plating streamed astern, yet she never slowed, never hesitated. Her own launchers fired back as she entered their range, but they were pinpricks. The Bug leviathans shrugged them aside and poured a butchery of fire into Shaiaasu's squadron.

Kilokharn blew up, then *Zairoh*, but their sisters held their course, and Zhaarnak raised his open, blood-streaked hand. He thrust it towards the display, then closed it once more, digging his claws into his lacerated palm in salute even as his soul railed at the officers who had defied his orders. *Kurv* vanished, and beams began to fire, as well. *Nabahstahr* exploded, but *Acutar* and *Faulhi* continued their mad charge. They were broken wrecks, yet their drives survived, and they hurled themselves upon the enemy. A Bug light cruiser accelerated to meet *Faulhi*, and the two ships were blotted from the universe as they struck. Another light cruiser lunged at *Acutar*, but somehow Shaiaasu's ship evaded it. One ship—a single ship, out of an entire squadron—charged the massive target of its foes, and Zhaarnak looked up, watching the visual display, as *Acutar* struck her target and an enemy superdreadnought blew apart in a shroud of flame.

My claws are broken, Zhaarnak thought. *My honor is no more. I have failed my Clan Fathers and those who will follow me. I have failed my Khan. But in my dishonor, I may yet shield my farshatok.*

"Claw Daarsaahl."

"Yes, Great Claw?" his flag captain's voice was quiet, and Zhaarnak kept his eyes on the visual display's fading ball of fire.

"Make an entry in the log, Claw Daarsaahl. The decision to withdraw is mine and mine alone. I did not discuss it. I did not seek the concurrence of any other officer."

"But, Sir—" Daarsaahl began, only to stop as Zhaarnak raised a forestalling hand.

"Make the entry," he said softly.

CHAPTER TWENTY-FIVE

"May our claws strike deep."

"All right." Rear Admiral Raymond Porter Prescott looked at his subordinates with grim hazel eyes. "We reach Alowan in eighteen hours, and the Tabbies still hold it. Our job is to make sure they *continue* to hold until Great Fang Koraaza gets here."

Commodore Diego Jackson, commanding Task Force 23's light carriers, shook his head. "That's a tall order, Sir," he said quietly.

"Maybe, but that's the mission," Prescott said, and looked at his intelligence officer. "Bring us up to speed, Eloise."

"Yes, Sir." Commander Eloise Kmak had her notes on her terminal, but she didn't look at them. No doubt, Prescott thought bitterly, they were indelibly graven into her mind.

"The real surprise," she began, "is that there're any KON units *left* in Alowan. Given the Orion honor code—and, especially, his own record—I'm amazed Great Claw Zhaarnak fell back at all. The fact that he's managed to preserve his battlegroup essentially intact is even more astounding.

"As far as we can tell, he bled the Bugs badly in Telmasa, but they punched a simultaneous transit into his face. He got a little too close—that's how he lost the ships he did—but for the most part he used only his fighters. That was smart, Admiral. Very smart. They're his most replenishable resource; he was able to make good his losses in Kliean from Hairnow, and the Alowan Fleet Base was able to replace those he lost in Telmasa. According to our latest reports, he has six Orion and three Gorm BCs, six CVLs, and eight *Gharbahg*-class CLs. That's not a lot, but the Tabbies did well to scrape up even that much after being surprised this way. GHQ and Idnahk Sector Command are trying to keep us updated on what else they may be able to find, but the situation's so confused no one's certain what is or isn't available. Essentially, we've sent out an 'all ships' signal. We'll take what we can get, but for now, we—and Zhaarnak—are it."

Prescott nodded slowly, for Kmak was right. It also meant his ten battleships, nine light carriers, nine battlecruisers, five light cruisers and five destroyers represented a far heavier force than Zhaarnak's. *Not that it's heavy enough,* he thought, and his mouth twisted as he remembered the two battleships he *didn't* have. TFNS *Mars* and *Triomphant* had both lost too many engine rooms to keep up on the desperate, high-speed voyage from New Bristol, and he had no idea how the battle-cruisers *Ranseur* and *Pikeaxe* had managed to keep *their* drives on-line.

Maybe these bastards have a point using commercial engines. They may suck wind in a tactical *sense, but—*

"Given the larger strikegroups Tabby carriers carry and the partial squadrons they put aboard their capital ships, he actually has about sixty more fighters than we do," Kmak went on. "Our combined force will be able to put over three hundred into space, but we're very weak in capital launchers and, of course, we have no SD element. If we have to fall back on the Pairsag twin planets, we'll pick up another hundred and twenty fighters plus the Fleet Base's and PDCs' capital launchers, but that will also mean letting the Bugs range on the planets."

"We're not supposed to tie ourselves down, Sir," Commander Kenneth "Zulu" Sosa, Prescott's chief of staff, said.

"I'm aware of my orders, Zulu." Prescott didn't raise

his voice, but most of his staff found someplace else to look. Every one of them knew it would be at least two months before Fang Koraaza'khiniak could reach Alowan. They also knew Zhaarnak and Prescott were under direct orders to continue falling back until he did. What they didn't know was whether or not Prescott intended to *obey* those orders, and he let the silence linger, then waved for Kmak to resume.

"My best appreciation is that things are going to get rougher, Sir. Bug doctrine is clearly to keep pouring it on until they hit something so hard they *have* to stop, and the Kliean population size has to've told them they're into the Tabbies' core systems. Claw Zhaarnak's been lucky so far in not facing any gunboats, but it's unlikely they won't bring them along for an attack on Alowan.

"The only good news is that they may not yet realize the Hairnow System is there. The connecting warp point's a Type Two, so it won't be too hard to find, but it's over five light-hours out, and they've only had a couple of weeks to look for it. More importantly, Zhaarnak managed to destroy the ICN link to the system, so there're no comsat 'bread crumbs' to lead them to it. Additionally, they know where he went—he deliberately let them track him to the Alowan warp point—so we can at least hope they've concentrated on following him up."

"That was gutsy," Jason Pitnarau observed. Prescott's flag captain was short and stocky, and his almond eyes narrowed. "There's what—a billion people in Alowan?"

"Yes, Sir. But at least Alowan has some fixed defenses." Kmak's shrug was bitter. "Sak and Alowan are supposed to be the only way into the Kliean Chain; that's why both of them were fortified in the first place. But Hairnow was supposed to be covered by Alowan, so it has no local defenses, and there are a billion and a *half* civilians in that system."

"I didn't say it was *wrong*, Eloise, only that it took guts. He could've waffled and broken contact—left it to the luck of the draw. And if he loses Alowan, *someone* will damned sure blame him for 'leading the Bugs to it.'"

"He wouldn't still have a battlegroup if he were the waffling sort," Prescott said. "Eloise is right—it's amazing he managed to hold his command together at all."

"Yes, Sir." Kmak paused for a moment, then cleared her throat. "Ah, there are a couple of points to consider about the command structure, Sir," she said carefully.

"Such as?"

"Well, you're senior to Zhaarnak, and, well . . ." The intelligence officer drew a breath. "Sir, according to ONI, Zhaarnak *hates* Terrans. He may not react well when you supersede him."

"I'm aware of Zhaarnak's attitude, Commander." Prescott's tenor voice was toneless, but it was unlike him to use formal rank titles in staff meetings, and Kmak shut her mouth.

Prescott let his eyes circle the table, then spoke very slowly and deliberately.

"We're not going to tell him I'm senior." Several people stiffened, whether in surprise or from a desire to protest he didn't know, nor did it matter. "This officer has been, and remains, under tremendous strain. He's compromised his own honor to do the right thing—the smart thing. Fang Koraaza's approved his actions, and no doubt GHQ will, too, but he's a Tabby. An *Orion* from a clan whose honor has already taken a beating and who left four billion of his people on their own rather than dying in their defense, and you can bet your pensions there are *other* Orions who'll spit on his shadow for that. All right, he doesn't like Terrans. Well, some Terrans don't like *Orions*. I don't happen to be one of them, but I understand their attitude, and it's up to us to understand his. The smooth functioning of this task force in the defense of Alowan— which, I remind you, is also an *Orion* system—is our sole priority. If I can make it function more smoothly by letting him retain command, I'll do it . . . and given Orion traditions, I *can't* do it if he knows I'm senior. So understand me. Who's senior to whom stays right here in this compartment. It will not be discussed, even in casual conversation, with any other persons. Is that clear?"

Heads nodded soberly, and he waved a hand at Commander Alexander LaFroye.

"In that case, Alec, let's get to the nuts and bolts. I want contingency plans based on Zhaarnak's probable tactics so we can slot into *his* plans with the minimum of confusion."

"Yes, Sir." The ops officer brought blocks of information scrolling up his terminal. "In that case, Sir, the first thing to look at is the compatibility of our carrier elements, and—"

Great Claw Zhaarnak stalked out of the flag bridge intraship car into dead silence. He crossed to his command chair, hands folded behind his back, and stood beside it, glaring down into the repeater tank at the light dots of his reinforcements.

Humans, he thought almost despairingly. *What more can the gods do to me? Not enough to take my honor, not enough to fill me with nightmares of slaughter. No. Now they send the very* chofaki *who first destroyed my clan's honor as my "reinforcements."*

The thought burned like acid, and his stubborn self-honesty's insistence that he should be burning incense sticks for *any* reinforcement only made the it worse. It was the sheerest fluke that this Human great claw—this Prescott—had been close enough to respond. The Idnahk Sector had been colonized centuries ago, yet the Humans had found a closed warp point within it twenty of their years before. The protocols between the two imperiums had ceded it to the Khanate, since it lay in *Zheeerlikou'valkhannaieee* space, yet it linked the sector to *Human* space. Given the warp lines' crazed ingeodesics, the Human base at New Bristol was actually closer than any Orion base to Alowan, and this was the result. The KON was scrambling frantically to scrape up anything it could, but this task force—this *Human* task force—was the only organized unit available.

Zhaarnak watched it sweep closer and tried to feel some spark of hope, some belief that, with its aid, he might hold Alowan. But there was no spark. There was only the cold, drear sense of failure which had filled him since Kliean.

He shuddered, mind filled with the ugly imagery the Kliean comsats had delivered to Telmasa before the Bugs drove him from it. The horrifying images of feeding Bugs, proving that the *Zheeerlikou'valkhannaieee*, too, were food for them. He closed his eyes, soul twisting in the icy wind at his center, and the stillness behind him made that wind even colder.

Do they hate me, my officers? Do they feel contempt for the coward who fell back rather than die? Do they understand why I did it? Or do they even care why? My dishonor covers them, shields their names and their clans' names, but do they fear the taint which clings to mine?

He turned away from his plot. The Human commander would arrive aboard *Dashyr* within the hour, and he must be in the boat bay to greet him.

Zhaarnak walked from Flag Bridge, and Son of the Khan Theerah watched him go. The great claw's spine was ramrod straight, yet Theerah sensed his despair and wished he knew how to fight it. He had been shocked by the order to abandon Kliean, and he understood the horror which haunted his commander, but the great claw had been correct. Theerah knew that now. Yet the way of the *Zheeerlikou'valkhannaieee* offered no way to *tell* Zhaarnak that, and so he watched the great claw in silence even as his heart burned to speak.

Raymond Prescott stood as his cutter's hatch cycled. He and his staff had changed into summer-weight uniforms in anticipation of the Tabbies' shipboard temperatures, and he flicked imaginary lint from his perfectly tailored cuff. A faint, fond smile curled his lips as the mannerism woke memories of his kid brother. Andy was twenty years younger . . . and totally unable to pass up any chance to tease him for the personal vanity he'd never quite overcome. And ever since Andy had attained captain's rank he'd taken to teasing Raymond over his "stalled career," too. Of course, promotion always slowed once an officer reached flag rank. Actually, Raymond had made captain earlier in his career than *Andy* had, and he was on the short list for vice admiral, but Andy had always been the feisty one, and teasing or no, Raymond wished he were here now.

No you don't—you want him to live. He felt his smile vanish into a grim, hard line, then inhaled deeply and stepped forward with Commodore Jackson and Zulu Sosa at his heels.

The Tabby side party snapped to formal salute, and a wild, swirling keen washed over him in place of the TFN's bosun's pipes. It was inevitable, Prescott thought, that a race whose language was often described as "a cat fight set to bagpipes" would develop *real* bagpipes as the favored instrument for its martial music. *Oh, well. At least it makes a change!*

He saluted the russet-furred great claw, and Zhaarnak returned his human-style courtesy with a stiff, formal Orion salute. It was always hard to read alien facial expressions, especially when the face in question featured a blunt muzzle, shoulder-wide whiskers, and a covering of soft, plushy fur, but Prescott sensed the exhausted belligerence behind that salute.

"Permission to come aboard, Sir?" he asked—and saw Zhaarnak's whiskers twitch as the request came out in High Orion. He knew he hadn't gotten it quite right, for human vocal cords simply couldn't hit the language's higher notes, but Prescott had the rare combination of perfect pitch and the ability to imitate almost any sound, and he waited while Zhaarnak grappled with the sheer shock of hearing a human speak the Tongue of Tongues.

"Permission granted, Ahhhdmiraal," he replied after a moment, and Prescott lowered his hand from the salute and gestured to his subordinates.

"Allow me to present Commodore Diego Jackson, my senior carrier division CO, and Commander Sosa, my chief of staff," he said in Orion. Zhaarnak bowed to each of them in turn, then rested one hand on the shoulder of the slender female officer beside him.

"Ninety-Sixth Least Claw Daarsaahl'haairna-ahn, my flag captain," he said, and waited while Sosa translated for Jackson, whose grasp of Orion was poor, to say the least. The flag captain returned Prescott's bow, and he reminded himself that a KON flag officer's flag captain was also his chief of staff. He was unfamiliar with Clan Haairna—no non-Orion could keep their sprawling clan structures straight—but Daarsaahl's pelt was the sable of the oldest Orion nobility, and she also wore the starburst of the *Valkhaanair'zegaair*, the equivalent of the Solar Cross, along with several lesser decorations. *Not just an aristocrat, but a good one*, he thought. The Orion patriarchal culture had persisted well into its interstellar stage, and even today, female Orion officers, regardless of birth rank, had to be a cut better than their male peers if they expected to advance. Daarsaahl, it appeared, was no exception to the rule.

"If you would accompany us," Zhaarnak said, "my staff is waiting to brief you." He paused, then continued more stiffly. "I regret that there is insufficient time to greet you with a proper meal, Ahhhdmiraal, but—" He broke off with an ear-flick shrug, and Prescott nodded.

"I understand, Sir," he said, and followed Zhaarnak and Daarsaahl to the intraship car.

"—so while we are not positive of the enemy's strength or plans," Theerah'jihaal finished his brief, "the addition of your carriers will let us mount a much stronger combat space patrol on the warp point. We do not know if we will be able actually to hold this system. Certainly we intend to try. The Sak fortresses rely upon the Pairsag Twins for support and maintenance; if we lose Alowan, we lose that support. More to the point, there are a billion civilians on the Twins. And, of course, every system we lose is one more we must retake before we can relieve Kliean."

Zhaarnak kept his expression impassive as he watched

his new allies' flat, naked faces. For the first time in his life, he wished he had made a serious study of them. He suspected this Admiral Prescott was skilled at evaluating *Orion* expressions, and that irked him. Human faces were far more mobile than he had previously appreciated, yet he was unable to interpret their mobility.

He watched Commodore Jackson as Sosa murmured a translation of Theerah's remarks into his flat, round ear and felt another flicker of resentment as the commander's translation reemphasized Prescott's ability to speak the Tongue of Tongues. It was convenient, but what business had a *chofak* learning the tongue of warriors? And why had he bothered? It could not have been easy, given the differences in their vocal apparatuses, so why take the trouble?

Now Prescott glanced at Jackson and raised an eyebrow. The commodore nodded, confirming his understanding of Theerah's presentation, and the admiral looked at Zhaarnak.

"I believe I understand your intentions, Sir," he said—still in the Tongue of Tongues, curse it, "and we can adjust our operations to conform with them. Commander Sosa has brought along chips detailing our current readiness states and com procedures. We will, of course, adapt our own protocols to yours, and, with your permission, I will send Commander LaFroye, my own operations officer, to *Dashyr* for more detailed conversations with Son of the Khan Theerah."

Zhaarnak flicked his ears in approval, but then his eyes narrowed as Prescott leaned back. Familiar with Human body language or not, the great claw recognized the look of someone about to suggest changes, and something inside him bristled in instant resentment. But he made himself wait. *Chofak* or no, this Human's task force was more powerful than his own. If Prescott wished to make suggestions, Zhaarnak had no option but to listen, however stupid they might be.

"One point which has not been discussed," Prescott said, "is that of equipment compatibility. As you know, our datalink is unable to mate with your own. This is unfortunate, and I understand your R&D people are working with our own to correct the problem, though it will not help us here. The point I would like to offer for your consideration, however, Sir, are the differences in our munitions and, particularly, our fighter ordnance."

Zhaarnak felt a fresh prickle of surprise at the Human's calm, respectful tone and raised one hand, palm uppermost and claws retracted, to invite him to continue.

"A support echelon from New Bristol will join us here as soon as possible, but the yard ships and freighters are slower than our warships and left later. They will not arrive for three more of our weeks, and the ordnance currently on hand is all we will have for that time. We were aware this would be true, so we have filled our own cargo holds with additional missiles which I would like to tranship to your Fleet Base. That would get them out of harm's way, and we can reammunition from the space stations following any engagement."

He paused, and Zhaarnak flicked an ear in agreement. That much, at least, was simple enough, but the Human was not yet done.

"Turning to the matter of fighter ordnance, our carriers can recover and launch one another's fighters. We cannot rearm your fighters, however, nor you ours. What I would suggest is that we redistribute our ordnance and life-support modules. If we were to transfer, say, half of our missiles, FRAMs, and life-support pods to your carriers and replace them with *your* hardware, it would be possible for any carrier to support any fighter squadron. Not only would this increase our tactical flexibility, but it would give us greater platform survivability through redundancy."

It was all Zhaarnak could do to keep his jaw from dropping. The Human's Orion was not perfect—he seemed incapable of reaching the proper notes for full emphasis, and his grammar was overly formal—yet that meant nothing beside what he had just suggested. The great claw glanced at Daarsaahl, seeing his flag captain's surprise—and approval—at the offer, and wondered why it had not occurred to him to make the same suggestion.

Perhaps it was because you let hatred blind you, he thought unwillingly. *Yet the offer has merit—great merit.* He gathered himself to speak, but before he could, Commodore Jackson leaned forward. His speech was incomprehensible to the great claw—*I must learn to understand them after all; chofaki or not, they are our allies, and it seems they may have something worthwhile to say after all*—and he waited while his own earbug translated.

"There's one other point I'd like to mention, Sir," the commodore said. "The Pairsag Fleet Base has a powerful fighter component, and it occurred to us during our discussions en route to Alowan that it might be worthwhile to consider staging those fighters through our carriers. With tenders and full life-support loads, they could make the flight to us well outside their theoretical range, and we could arm them once they arrive."

Zhaarnak looked at Theerah. His ops officer and he had discussed the same possibility but without a decision. Their carriers would have been badly overextended trying to support so many fighters, but if they adopted Prescott's suggestion about ordnance loads, it would be possible. It would also strip the Pairsag Twins of local fighter defenses, yet it would increase his own fighter strength—and hence his chance of actually holding the system—by almost fifty percent.

Theerah looked back, then flicked his ears, and Zhaarnak returned his gaze to Prescott.

"I believe these suggestions have merit, Ahhhdmiraal." It irked him that he still sounded faintly begrudging, and he made himself add, "It is a generous offer, and I thank you for it."

"'If my claws guard not your back, then whose claws shall guard mine?'" the admiral said softly, and Zhaarnak experienced yet another flicker of surprise at this Human's command of the Tongue of Tongues. How many years must he have studied the *Zheeerlikou'valkhannaieee* to have attained such insight into them? And, again, why had he bothered?

The great claw felt a nagging suspicion he would not like the answer to that question if he knew it. Not because Prescott had done so with sinister intent, but because . . . because . . .

He shook the thought aside. There would be time to consider it later—assuming any of them survived—and he pushed his chair back on its powered track and stood.

"Very well, Ahhhdmiraal," he said. "I approve your suggestions. Son of the Khan Theerah and Least Claw Daarsaahl will hold themselves in readiness to discuss the details with your Commaaaander LaaaFroyyye. In the meantime—" he hesitated, then made himself extend his hand in the Human manner "—welcome to Alowan. May our claws strike deep."

"May our claws strike deep," the Human agreed, and gripped his hand firmly.

CHAPTER TWENTY-SIX

"There are no *chofaki* here."

Zhaarnak looked up as his intelligence officer entered the briefing room. Nineteenth Least Claw Uaaria'saalath-ahn was young for her rank, especially as a female, but Zhaarnak had specifically requested her. She was a bit of a maverick, which scarcely endeared her to some superiors, yet she was also brilliant and the daughter of an old friend. And, he admitted with what he knew was old-fashioned sexism, she was most pleasant to look upon, as well. But now her expression caused him to put his display on hold, halting the play of the latest tactical plan Theerah and the Human LaFroye had worked out.

"Yes, Uaaria?"

"I have just learned something which should be drawn to your attention, Great Claw," she said with rather more than normal formality, and his ears pricked. "As you know, I requested background files on Ahhhdmiraal Pressscott and his senior officers from the Eyes of the Khan."

"I remember. Not that they told us much."

"No, Sir. But my request was bucked up to GHQ in Centauri, and the Humans provided the information we lacked."

"They did?" Zhaarnak was surprised. It remained difficult not to think automatically of Humans as *chofaki*, though he was being forced—to some extent—to modify his opinion as Prescott's task force shook down as TG 37.2

of the Grand Alliance's newly designated Task Force 37. Even so, he would not have expected their navy to provide such data.

"Yes, Sir." Uaaria almost seemed to squirm, then sighed. "Great Claw, he is senior to you."

"He—?" Zhaarnak sat as if struck to stone. Senior to him? The Human was *senior* to him? Impossible! Surely he would have said something! But Uaaria did not make such mistakes.

"Are you positive?" he asked finally.

Uaaria's ears flicked, and Zhaarnak's thoughts floundered. If Prescott was senior, why had he not said so? Why had he always addressed Zhaarnak as "Sir" and accepted *Zhaarnak's* plans?

He looked back up at Uaaria. Young or no, she was a shrewd judge of character, and, unlike Zhaarnak, she *had* studied Humans as part of her intelligence training.

"Have you any theory as to why he has not told us so? Could he be unaware of the fact?"

"I doubt his ignorance, Sir," Uaaria said carefully. "Ahhhdmiraal Pressscott is clearly a student of our people. I feel certain he requested *your* dossier before reporting to Alowan."

"Then why?" Zhaarnak asked, and his eyes narrowed as the least claw hesitated. "Speak your thoughts, Least Claw," he said firmly, and she sighed once more.

"Great Claw, I think he knows your feeling for his people," she said softly. "I believe he chose to accept your authority because of it."

Zhaarnak leaned back in a welter of chaotic emotions. Astonishment. Confusion . . . and shame. If Uaaria was right, Prescott had deliberately renounced a command authority to which he was entitled. One of the *Zheeer-likou'valkhannaieee* might do such a thing, but only under very special circumstances which did not apply here. Part of the great claw longed to put it down to cowardice, to a *chofak's* desire to avoid responsibility, yet he had been forced to work too closely with Prescott over the last ten days to believe that.

No, he knew what the truth had to be: Prescott had done what he himself could not. The Human had sacrificed honor to the prejudices of another, accepting a lesser role, obedient to one he had the right to command, because he knew his legal subordinate hated his race. And he had not done so openly lest it underscore the great claw's prejudice and so dishonor *Zhaarnak*.

"I am sorry, Great Claw," Uaaria said, "yet I thought you should know. I—"

"No, Uaaria," Zhaarnak said quietly. "You did well in this. It is *I* who have done poorly."

"You have much on your mind and spirit," the least claw protested in his defense.

"Not enough to excuse insult to an ally," Zhaarnak replied, and fresh surprise filled him as he realized he meant it. That it was not simply the mouthing of a formality.

"There is no insult, Sir," Uaaria argued. "There would be insult only had you known."

"Which I now do," Zhaarnak pointed out. He looked back down at the frozen display and sighed. "Very well, Uaaria. Thank you. I shall com Ahhhdmiraal Pressscott and—"

He never finished the sentence, for even as he spoke the alarms began to scream.

"They're coming through, Sir!" Sosa reported as Prescott charged onto Flag Bridge. "Simultaneous transit—forty-plus CLs, but they seem weak in *Cataphracts*."

"Thank God for small favors, Zulu," Prescott muttered, and his mouth tightened as his plot confirmed Sosa's estimate. It also showed him something else, and his mouth tightened further as the first gunboat icons began to appear.

"Claw Zhaarnak's activated Alpha-Three," LaFroye said. That wasn't what the Tabbies called it, of course, but it was a designation humans could pronounce, and Prescott nodded.

"Acknowledge." He punched a stud and Diego Jackson's face appeared on his screen. "Alpha-Three, Diego," he said without preamble, wishing yet again that it had been possible to integrate TF 37's com net more fully. "Roll 'em out."

The Assault Fleet made transit with the leading gunboats. There were no energy buoys to flail them this time—a fringe benefit of pressing the enemy so hard— but there were sufficient mines to delay the light cruisers which survived transit. The enemy attack craft came slashing in, intent on killing the CLE's before their systems stabilized, and the gunboats went to meet them.

The gunboats were bigger, more vulnerable targets, but this time there were no jammer buoys to break their datanets, and while the attack craft were more heavily armed, their internal energy weapons could bear only directly ahead of them. The gunboats' internal lasers, however, had a command of over 270°, and their point defense systems had even more coverage. A dozen of them died in the first pass, but four-ship squadrons fired back at the attack craft driving in on them. Coupled with the cruisers' weapons, they killed at least as many enemy units for the loss of only seven CLEs, and that was a worthwhile exchange. The enemy had more carriers this time, yet none of his larger ones. He could not have many attack craft to expend.

"Their gunboats are more effective than expected, Great Claw," Theerah reported tersely. "Our CSP has lost heavily, but we have accounted for all but two *Cataphracts*."

"Here come the Humans, Sir," Daarsaahl said. Zhaarnak's eyes flicked back to his plot. Jackson's squadrons swooped past the survivors of his CSP, armed with missiles, not FRAMs. They opened fire from beyond the Bugs' range, and Zhaarnak snarled as fireballs glared. The gunboats' point defense might make them resistant to missile fire, but not resistant enough!

"The cruisers are moving into the mines," Theerah said, and then the ops officer's ears went flat. "Here come the superdreadnoughts."

❖   ❖   ❖

The superdreadnoughts made transit in a tight chain. There were but thirty-eight, for the Fleet was still redeploying to exploit this axis, yet there were no enemy superdreadnoughts. Once his attack craft were gone, the battle-line would roll forward unstoppably.

Prescott watched Jackson's squadrons tear into the gunboats, but the cruisers were clearing the mines. There simply hadn't been time to emplace enough of them, and it looked like at least some light units would survive to screen the main force.

"The Tabbies are launching their reserve strike," LaFroye reported.

"Has Zhaarnak alerted the Fleet Base, Zulu?"

"Yes, Sir. The message went out—" Sosa checked a time display "—eight minutes ago."

Prescott grunted in approval, not that any of the Fleet Base fighters could reach them in time to stop the enemy from making transit. The Pairsag Twins were currently on the far side of Alowan from the warp point. It would take the alert message four hours to reach the Fleet Base, and the fighters would have needed a full day to make the flight out. That was beyond their range even with full life-support loads, but Theerah and LaFroye had arranged a resupply point with the orbital base's tenders. *All* they could do was replenish the fighters' life support, but that doubled their range. By the time TF 37 fell back to them, they'd be ready to stage through the carriers.

And we're going to have plenty of spare hangar space, the admiral thought grimly as the Tabbies hurtled in to attack the leading superdreadnoughts and the flashes of dying fighters speckled the visual display. The Orions broke through to salvo their FRAMs and five *Archers* blew up, yet their consorts caught the Tabbies in a crossfire between their own weapons and the gunboats, and Zhaarnak's pilots paid heavily for their success.

"They've cleared a lane, Sir," LaFroye said flatly. "They're breaking out."

❖   ❖   ❖

The Fleet uncoiled directly towards the enemy starships, and those ships gave ground. They retreated steadily, remaining beyond missile range and sending in their attack craft again and again, but the battle-line forged remorselessly ahead. Battlecruisers and the remaining light cruisers screened the superdreadnoughts against the attackers, and the enemy shifted targeting. He had no choice, for he must blow a gap through the screen just to reach the battle-line.

"They are no longer sending gunboats to meet our fighters, Great Claw."

Theerah sounded concerned, and Zhaarnak understood. The Bugs were saving their gunboats until his fighter strength was blunted. His pilots were his best defense against them; only after his strikegroups had been whittled away would the enemy commit them against his starships.

"Fighter losses?" he asked sharply.

"Forty-two percent for our own carriers. The Human loss rate is somewhat lower. I estimate they have lost perhaps thirty percent."

Zhaarnak flicked his ears in acknowledgment. The Human losses might be lower, but not because they were avoiding action. Their squadrons had not been harrowed by his own earlier losses in Kliean and Telmasa, and their experience showed. Even his carrier commanders admitted they were as good as any KON strikegroups, and they were spending themselves more wisely than his own *farshatok*, yet they fought as furiously as if it were *Human* worlds they defended.

If only the Bugs had fewer screening units! His strikes were costing their escorts dear, yet aside from that initial pass, only three superdreadnoughts had been destroyed.

"Inform *farshathkhanaak* Liaahk that he is to maintain a reserve of at least twenty percent. We dare not reduce our CSP below that."

"Yes, Great Claw," Theerah replied, and Zhaarnak looked at his com officer.

✧   ✧   ✧

"Message from the Flag, Sir." Prescott turned his command chair at the com officer's announcement and waited. "Tango-Three-Delta, Sir."

"Acknowledge." Prescott looked at LaFroye. "Pass the order, Alec."

Fourteen battlecruisers—three Orion, three Gorm, eight Terran—advanced against the enemy. The Gorm and Orion BCs were TF 37's only true capital missile ships, for the Terran *Broadswords* were configured primarily for closer action. They were attached solely to support and protect their longer-ranged allies, and as they closed, a fresh fighter strike went past them. Massed squadrons, half Terran and half Orion, tore down on the surviving Bug screen, and this time a heavy fire of SBMs came with them from the Allied battlecruisers' external racks. The Bugs could use their point defense to stop missiles or fighters, not both, and ship after ship blew apart, yet the success came with a price. Another forty fighters were blasted out of space, and the battlecruisers' attack had brought them in reach of the surviving *Archers*.

Missile salvos roared back and forth, matching super-dreadnought shields and armor against the frailer battle-cruisers' superior point defense, and then a fresh wave of fighters slashed in. This time some of the gunboats came out once more, but not to engage fighters. Instead, they hurled themselves straight at the battlecruisers, and cursing Orion and Terran squadron commanders diverted from their antishipping strike to claw around in pursuit.

They caught a dozen, but the rest got by. The battle-cruisers went to evasive action, firing furiously, and the Terran ships maneuvered between the gunboats and their allies, for the missile ships were weak in energy weapons. Two-thirds of the Bugs were blown apart; the other third got through, and they brought a surprise with them. They didn't have FRAMs, but their R&D *had* produced the cruder nuclear-armed FR, and a gunboat carried three times as many as a fighter.

TFNS *Arrow, Ranseur* and *Partisan* died as the

gunboats poured fire into them. *Scimitar* and the command ship *Constitution* took heavy damage of their own, and despite all they could do, GSN *Bahlziak* fell astern, crippled and lamed.

Great Claw Zhaarnak watched the icons vanish. Once he would have felt only vengeful satisfaction at Human deaths; now he watched them dying like *farshatok*, deliberately drawing the enemy onto themselves to protect Orion ships. Dying under the orders of an Orion who was not even truly the senior officer of TF 37.

What now, Zhaarnak? The question seared through him. *Who knows the truth of honor? Those who die to defend their people . . . or those who die to protect another's?*

The Fleet ground onward. The enemy's battlecruisers had suffered heavily. They had finished off the Fleet's battlecruisers and two more superdreadnoughts, as well, yet three missile superdreadnoughts survived, and nothing the enemy had left could engage them. The rest of the Fleet formed around them, continuing its remorseless advance, and the enemy's attack craft came in in ever weaker waves. Soon it would be time to commit the gunboats once more.

Raymond Prescott scrubbed a hand across exhaustion-sore eyes. The battle had raged for almost two days, and losses were heavy on both sides. Heavier for the Bugs, but losses were *always* heavier for the Bugs . . . and never seemed to stop them. So far, TF 37 had destroyed sixty-three cruisers and battlecruisers and eleven superdreadnoughts—but that left twenty-seven superdreadnoughts, including those damned *Archers*. TF 37's fighters had been too weakened to get through to them, and even if they hadn't, killing them at this point would do little good. The whole point in killing *Archers* was to clear the way for Allied capital missiles and SBMs, and of TF 37's missile ships, only two Gorm *Bolzuchas* were still combat capable.

Their strikegroups had suffered too heavily to take more losses trying for the *Archers* now, anyway, for their original three hundred and forty fighters had been reduced to eighty-eight, only fifty of them Terran.

He checked the time display again. Eleven more hours. The Fleet Base's fighters were already en route, and in about eleven hours, the Bugs were going to get a surprise when a hundred and fifty fresh fighters exploded into their faces.

It was time. The enemy's attack craft strikes had all but ceased. His strength must be nearly exhausted, and the order went out.

For just a moment, the exhausted plotting officers didn't believe their own instruments. But they had to, and frantic orders crackled as two hundred and thirty Bug gunboats and small craft screamed towards the Allied starships. Scratch-built squadrons, assembled out of the remnants of TF 37's original strikegroups, launched to meet them, but the attack roared in, and only Zhaarnak's order to maintain a reserve gave TF 37 a chance. The strength of his carefully husbanded fighters took the Bugs by surprise, and gunboats and kamikazes which had been targeted on battleships were diverted to the carriers lest still more fighters launch from them.

The Allied pilots were exhausted, their original squadron organizations long since wrecked. Pilots flew with whatever wingmen they could find, and Terrans and Orions streaked into the enemy together, flushing missiles into the gunboats, then closed with their lasers. They carved a river of fire through their enemies, but the Bugs outnumbered them more than three-to-one. Half died in the first pass, and even as they looped back, the remaining gunboats abandoned the slower antimatter-loaded cutters to streak ahead under maximum power.

Zhaarnak saw it coming, and there was nothing he could do. The Human carriers were better protected, for their smaller fighter groups and more advanced shields let them build in twice the defensive firepower of an Orion CVL, and Prescott's task group included a dozen CLEs and DDEs. But those escorts could not datalink with the Orion carriers. They did their best to protect their allies, yet good as it was, their best was not enough.

Defensive fire killed dozens of gunboats, but others tore through the formation, ignoring its battleships. More than half went after the Terran *Shokakus*, but only a handful of those got through. Four of the TFN carriers were damaged, yet none were hurt critically.

Not so the KON. The Bugs broke through their lighter defenses in strength, salvoing their close-attack weapons and following their missiles in to ram. *Bhutnothin*, *Burkhan* and *Falkyrk* were destroyed outright, and *Bathyr* and *Firmiak* took heavy damage. Every Orion carrier was hit, most badly, and engine rooms became infernos as kamikazes sent power surges ripping through abused drive fields. They fell out of formation while frantic engineers fought their damage, and Zhaarnak stared at the ruin of his carriers. His own task group had been gutted. Only its light cruisers and three battlecruisers remained combat capable, and that was far too little to stave off the Juggernaut rolling down on his lamed carriers. The surviving fighters—all thirty of them—finished off the kamikazes before they completed the CVLs' destruction, yet he knew what he must do. He fought against it, but he had no choice, and he opened his mouth to order Prescott to abandon the doomed carriers and take his own command to meet the Fleet Base's fighters.

"The Tabby carriers are hurt bad, Sir." Alec LaFroye's fingers pressed his earbug as if to screw it bodily inside his head, and he grimaced. "Damage control's on it, but they need at least twenty minutes to get back enough drive rooms to stay away from the Bugs."

Prescott stared into his plot, eyes hard as the mind behind them whirred. Only eighteen Terran fighters survived, and his carriers hadn't gotten off unscathed. They had about eighty bays left, but over a hundred and fifty fighters were coming in from the Fleet Base. More to the point, those fighters were *Orion*, and, despite the transfers, his carriers were desperately short of Tabby ordnance after two exhausting days of battle. If they lost the surviving Orion fighter platforms, they wouldn't have the weapons to arm the Fleet Base's fighters once they got here.

"We've got to buy those ships some time," he said flatly.

"Sir, we don't have any orders from the Flag," Sosa pointed out. Prescott glanced at him, and the chief of staff looked back. The ex-fighter jock didn't like saying that, but it was his job to serve as his admiral's tactical conscience.

"I realize that, Zulu," Prescott said softly.

"Sir! Great Claw! The Humans!"

Zhaarnak's head snapped around at the semi-coherent shout, and his jaw dropped in disbelief. TG 37.2 was moving—not to break off as he had intended to order, *but to interpose between the Bugs and his carriers!*

It was insane! Prescott's battleships mounted only a single capital missile launcher each, and that only to deploy defensive missiles. He could engage the enemy only from within the Bugs' own weapons envelope, and he had *battleships*, not superdreadnoughts!

Even as he watched, the first missiles roared out, and capital force beams began to fire. The Humans' datalinked point defense blunted the missile salvos, but it could do nothing about energy weapons, and shields flashed and died as the suicidal pounding match began.

"Juaahr! Order Pressscott to break off!"

"Yes, Great Claw!" The com officer spoke urgently into his pickup, then stiffened. "Sir, Ahhhdmiraal Pressscott refuses!"

"Give me a direct link!" Prescott's face appeared on Zhaarnak's com screen instantly, and the great claw forced his voice to come out flat and level. "Break off, Ahhhdmiraal."

"I must respectfully decline, Sir," Prescott replied, and actually *smiled* as Zhaarnak's ears flattened in consternation. The image flickered as missiles and beams pounded the admiral's flagship, and Prescott shook his head in the Human gesture of negation. "You need those carriers. My own have too few weapons to support the Fleet Base's fighters."

"This is madness! You sacrifice your ships for nothing!"

"'My claws are yours, and your cause is just,'" the Human said softly. "'There is no dishonor in death—and no honor in flight.'"

Zhaarnak could not hide his shock as Prescott quoted the Warrior's Way. They were the final words of Shaasaal'hirtalkin, he who first formalized the *Farshalah'kiah*, second only to Craana'tolnatha among the fathers in honor of the *Zheeerlikou'valkhannaieee*, and even as Zhaarnak stared at him, the Human cut the circuit.

The great claw dropped his eyes to the plot, and his fists clenched as the outnumbered, outgunned Humans engaged their foes. Shields flashed and died, warheads and beams ripped at hull plating. Prescott's battle-line was trapped in the heart of a furnace, and *still* it held its ground, drawing the enemy's fury down upon itself while the carrier crews fought to repair their drives.

A battleship died, then another. A battlecruiser followed them, and Prescott's flagship shuddered as her own shields went down. Armor shattered under the pounding beams, yet no Human ship turned away. They stood and died at their admiral's side, thundering back at their massive enemies for five minutes, eight, ten. . . . For twelve endless, terrible minutes they held alone, until the surviving Orion carriers were able to get back underway.

Then, and only then, they, too, began to pull away from the enemy once more, but four battleships and three more battlecruisers of the Terran Federation Navy had died. Every surviving ship was damaged, some critically, yet Raymond Prescott had done what he set out to do . . . and Zhaarnak'diaano would never think of Humans in the same way again.

❖   ❖   ❖

The Fleet continued its pursuit until a sudden infusion of fresh attack craft assailed it. The enemy battleships had inflicted damage out of all proportion to their relatively small size, and the fresh attack craft struck at the worst possible moment. There were few gunboats left, and the Fleet—busy reorganizing its crippled data-groups—was caught unprepared. Six already damaged superdreadnoughts succumbed to a blizzard of FRAMs, several of those which survived were badly wounded, and the Fleet called off the pursuit. It knew where the enemy was headed, after all . . . and it also knew reinforcements were en route.

"The scanner buoys confirm it, Great Claw," Least Claw Daarsaahl said wearily. "Twenty-four additional superdreadnoughts have joined the enemy. At present rate of advance, they will enter range of the Twins in seventy-one hours."

"Escorts?" Zhaarnak'diaano asked.

"Thirty battlecruisers and approximately fifty light cruisers," Daarsaahl said flatly. "They appear to be accompanied by many additional gunboats, as well."

"I see." Zhaarnak drew a deep breath, and closed his eyes. Five days had passed since the first attack withdrew, and he'd let himself hope. Now that hope died.

"Has Ahhhdmiraal Pressscott been informed?"

"They were his sensor buoys, Sir," Daarsaahl said with a flicker of weary humor, and Zhaarnak's own ears twitched in bittersweet amusement. *Human technology,* he thought. *Must they* always *be better than we?*

"Your orders, Great Claw?" his flag captain asked, and Zhaarnak shrugged.

"There will be no retreat this time," he said. "Lord Khiniak will not arrive for another month. If Great Claw Eaarnaah's fortresses can hold Sak until he arrives, his force should be powerful enough to retake Alowan. But if the Bugs can take Sak first, or even mount a warp point defense of Alowan in strength, he will pay heavily to break in. I know only one way to weaken them for him, and I doubt the enemy realizes how powerful the fixed defenses are. Between us, the bases and our ships can cripple this force before we are destroyed—perhaps even inflict sufficient delay to prevent an invasion of the Twins before Lord Khiniak relieves them."

"And the Humans?" Daarsaahl pressed in a gentle voice.

"I will not insult their honor," Zhaarnak said softly. The flag captain gazed at him a moment longer, then nodded, saluted, and withdrew without another word.

Zhaarnak returned to his terminal, staring sightlessly at the reports which had just become so meaningless, then cleared the screen and brought up a visual of TF 37's battered remnants.

Eleven wounded light carriers, only three of them Orion, hung in orbit about the twin planets, supported by six damaged battleships—all Human—and eleven battlecruisers—three of them Human. With the missile batteries of the Fleet Base and the PDCs, they would give a good account of themselves, yet they were doomed. Zhaarnak knew it, and he knew Prescott knew it, but the Human had not even suggested the withdrawal of his units. *Horned Viper* had been hit hard in her stand against the enemy battle-line. Commander Sosa was dead, Commander Kmak was badly wounded, and Prescott himself had suffered minor wounds to the head and leg. Many of his other ships had been damaged, as well, and unlike Zhaarnak's ships, none of them could tie into the massive point defense nets provided by the PDCs.

It did not matter. The Human support ships had not yet arrived, yet Prescott's exhausted crews had torn into their repairs with what limited help the Fleet Base technicians could provide. Most of their shields had been restored, many of their weapons had been put back on-line, and the munitions Prescott had off-loaded earlier had sufficed to refill their surviving magazines. Yet their armor was riddled, and their repairs were fragile. It would take little fresh pounding to put them back out of action, but Raymond Prescott would not abandon the Pairsag Twins. As Zhaarnak, he knew relief could not arrive in time . . . but that every enemy ship destroyed killing his own vessels would be one less to bombard the Twins or contest Lord Khiniak's entry into Alowan.

And, like me, he cannot abandon still more civilians. A warrior could do worse than die with such "chofaki," the great claw thought wearily. *And as Prescott himself said, "There is no dishonor in death—and no honor in flight."*

"Here they come, Sir," Jason Pitnarau said softly, and Prescott nodded. His flag bridge was a shambles, but his only other command battleship had been destroyed outright, so he'd moved himself and Alec LaFroye onto *Horned Viper's* command deck.

Now he rubbed the bandage on the shaved half of his skull, watching the master plot's ominous icons, and pictured the civil defense plans springing into purposeful—and ultimately futile—action on the Pairsag Twins. He doubted the Bugs even began to suspect how powerful the local defenses were, but when they found out, it was going to be ugly.

No doubt the PDCs would draw a heavy bombardment, which was why the Federation seldom mounted offensive weapons on inhabited worlds, and once the Bugs realized what they faced, they would abandon any plan to come in piecemeal and throw everything they had straight at the huge, heavily armed Fleet Base . . . and what was left of TF 37.

Glad you weren't here after all, Andy, he thought, then smiled crookedly at *Dashyr's* icon. *For a bigot, you're not too shabby, Zhaarnak'diaano. I suppose a man could do worse.*

"How long, Alec?" he asked.

"Seven hours," LaFroye replied, and Prescott astonished himself with a chuckle.

"Right on our original projection," he observed. "Remind me to congratulate CIC."

"Of course, Sir," Pitnarau said with a small smile of his own, and they returned their attention to the plot as the minutes leaked away. The Bugs slid closer and closer, inching towards engagement range—and then, suddenly, they stopped.

Prescott straightened in his chair. He hissed as his wounded leg protested the movement, but it was a distant pain. There was no reason for them to stop. They'd advanced across the system for days, and the one thing Bugs *didn't* do was hesitate about committing to action!

But they *were* hesitating. And then, as abruptly as they'd stopped advancing, they turned away! *All* of them turned away—gunboats, cruisers, superdreadnoughts, the entire fleet!

"What the *hell*?" Pitnarau was staring into the plot in disbelief, and Prescott shook his head. A part of him was actually angry at the Bugs for stopping when he'd made up his mind to die. *Get in here and get it over with, you bastards! Isn't it enough for you to kill us without screwing around this way?!*

But they were still moving away—moving away at maximum speed. They—

"Sir! The buoys are picking up— My God, Sir!"

"*What?*" Prescott snarled, taking out some of his confusion on the hapless lieutenant who'd just spoken. The young woman shook herself and punched commands into her console.

"Look at your repeater, Sir," she said, and Prescott dropped his gaze to the display.

"Holy Mother of God!" he whispered.

Thirty-four fresh Orion ships were headed in from the Sak warp point. And not *just* ships. Over a hundred fighters led the way, a combat space patrol sweeping the way for twenty fleet carriers and fourteen superdreadnoughts!

"It can't be," he said softly. "Koraaza's still over a month out, and he doesn't have anywhere *near* that much firepower to begin with! Those people can't *be* there!"

"Well, for people who don't exist, they look mighty good to me!" Pitnarau said jubilantly

In fact, Prescott was right. That huge relief fleet not only couldn't be there, it wasn't. Or, rather, it wasn't what it looked like. The massive task force was actually only three battleships, five CVs—*not* twenty—and five CVLs, and twenty-one battlecruisers and heavy cruisers. They weren't part of Lord Khiniak's force. Indeed, many weren't even combat ready. They were simply everything the Tabbies could scrape up—convoy escorts, training ships, vessels snatched out of the Bureau of Repair's hands, *anything*. None of the CVLs had any fighters, the battlecruisers' magazines were less than two-thirds filled, and two battleships still had repair techs aboard, but they all mounted third-generation ECM, and the Tabbies had it on-line in deception mode.

A bluff, Prescott thought two days later as he stood in *Horned Viper's* boat bay. *The whole thing was a colossal bluff! I don't think I'll ever play poker with a Tabby.*

He smiled at the thought, then straightened, leaning heavily on his cane, as the Orion cutter settled into its cradle and the side party came to attention.

Great Claw Zhaarnak'diaano stepped out into the twitter of bosun's pipes. He saluted sharply, and Prescott ignored the pain in his leg as he came to attention and returned the courtesy.

"Permission to come aboard, Sir?" the Tabby yowled to Captain Pitnarau.

"Granted, Sir," Pitnarau replied, and Zhaarnak stepped over the line on the deck.

The pipes fell silent, and deafening quiet filled the bay as Zhaarnak crossed to Prescott. He stopped and gazed into the admiral's eyes for a moment, then drew his *defargo*, the honor dirk of an Orion warrior. The wickedly keen blade gleamed in his hand, and he spoke quietly.

"When I was told Human ships had arrived to support me, Ahhhdmiraal Pressscott, I accepted them only because I had no choice, for such aid was an insult to my honor and that of my clan. Any allies were better than none, yet I swore to my clan fathers that the day I no longer needed your assistance I would spit upon your shadow. I would not challenge you as I would one of the *Zheeer-likou'valkhannaieee*, for I knew you would not accept challenge if I offered it, and it would only insult my honor further if you had."

Prescott's mouth tightened, but he said nothing. He simply stared into Zhaarnak's slit-pupilled eyes, waiting, and the Orion moved his ears slowly back and forth.

"Humans are cowards and *chofaki*, Fang Presscott. I did not *think* they are; I *knew* they are, as surely as I know my own name . . . but what I knew to be true was a lie, and black dishonor to your people." He flipped the *defargo* to extend its hilt to the Terran, the formal gesture of a liege man to his lord, and his eyes met Prescott's unflinchingly. "There are no *chofaki* here, Clan Brother. There are only *farshatok*. Your honor is our honor, and if ever Clan Diaano can serve you or yours with treasure or blood, we are yours to command."

CHAPTER TWENTY-SEVEN

"It *is* about honor."

The command balcony of the great orbital station looked out over an expanse of control consoles and computer terminals. Beyond them was a great, curving transparency showing the sun of Idnahk, its glare suitably stepped down. It was by the reflected light of that sun that Tenth Great Fang of the Khan Koraaza'khiniak, *Khanhaku* Khiniak, could see with naked eyes the ships of his command— that which was to be the Grand Alliance's Third Fleet.

Those ships had been straggling in since shortly after the ships of the enemy the Humans called *Bugs* had entered the Kliean System with their cargo of nightmare. The Navy had begun assembling all available ships here at the sector capital immediately after Zhaarnak'diaano sent forth the alarm. Then, with the delay built into all interstellar communications, had come the response of the Grand Allied Joint Chiefs of Staff. They'd recognized at once that the war had acquired a second front even more squarely within the domain of the *Zheerlikou'valk-hannaieee* than the original one was within Human space. So a new Fleet—a fleet of the Khanate, just as Admiral Murakuma's was a fleet of the Federation—had been added to the Alliance's organizational structure, and the Khan had honored Koraaza by entrusting him with its command.

Still, he reflected, it would have been nice if Third Fleet

had been anything more than an organization chart when he arrived here. The ancient Terran military theorist Sun Tzu—who had finally won acceptance in Koraaza's service despite the seeming contradictions between his precepts and *Farshalah'kiah*—had observed that numbers alone confer no advantage in war, and the ever-increasing number of ships whose flanks reflected the light of Idnahk's sun had built up to an impressive total—essentially everything in the sector capable of movement—but had never functioned as a fleet before. His hastily assembled staff would have been lucky to get all of them moving in the same direction on the same day, and any sort of coordinated maneuvers would have been impossible without the merciless exercises Koraaza had laid on. But those indispensable exercises had required still more time, and time was precisely what Zhaarnak'diaano—and, to an even greater extent, the civilians of Hairnow and any surviving Telmasans—did not have.

It was, thought Koraaza, who was something of a military history enthusiast, a lesson the Terrans had taught the *Zheeerlikou'valkhannaieee* in the Wars of Shame. His people, too long accustomed to expanding at the expense of unworthy opponents and therefore inclined to take the old hero-sagas literally, had thought of ships as individual swords to be wielded by the champions who commanded them. They had forgotten the long-term coordinated training necessary to provide the fleet and squadron organization which was to a navy as tempering was to a blade.

The thought of Terrans brought a smile to Koraaza's lips. He knew Zhaarnak'diaano, and when he'd heard that the first, crucial reinforcements that could be gotten to the great claw were *Terran* units, he'd seen disaster looming. Zhaarnak might not be quite so reactionary as his father in most things, but he seemed determined not to excel the old *Khanhaku* Diaano in unreasoning hatred of Humans—which would have been impossible—but to equal him. Koraaza had known, with a horrible sinking certainty, that Zhaarnak would not only bring about military

calamity but also dishonor the Khan by insulting an ally.
The latter had worried the great fang almost as much as
the former, for however much he consciously rejected the
narrow and rigid *Farshalah'kiah* of his ancestors in favor
of modern rationalism, he could no more free himself of
it than he could free himself of those ancestors' genetic
legacy.

So it had been with incredulous relief that Koraaza
had read Zhaarnak's last few reports, with their steady
change in tone. He was looking forward to meeting this
Human great claw (or *rear admiral* as they called it in
their unpronounceable tongue) who had brought about
that which he would once have unhesitatingly declared
impossible, and in little more than three local days, he
and Third Fleet would set out to do just that.

The communications officer broke in on Koraaza'a
thoughts. "Your pardon, Great Fang," said the young son
of the khan (*lieutenant commander*, Koraaza thought, his
mind continuing to crank out title equivalencies in the
outlandish Terran rank structure), "but Governor Kaarsaahn requests a moment of your time."

Koraaza's whiskers twitched with annoyance. As long
as Third Fleet was located within the Idnahk Sector, and
most especially while it was assembling at the sector's
capital, a degree of jurisdictional friction between the fleet
commander and the sector governor was inevitable. In
this case, differences in temperament made the situation
worse than it had to be. He turned resignedly to face
the holo imager, and moved within the pickup. "Put him
on," he ordered, and the governor of the Idnahk Sector
seemed to flash into existence.

"Governor Kaarsaahn," Koraaza greeted, touching
clenched fist to chest in salute.

The huge orbital station could accomodate the bulky
holo imager for which warships had too little space to
spare, but it was in geostationary orbit around Idnahk.
About a quarter of a second passed while the message
came and went, imposing a delay which was barely
noticeable, yet spoiled the illusion that Kaarsaahn was

here on the command balcony rather than in his palace on the surface. He responded to Koraaza's salute with a courtesy that verged on unctuousness.

"Greetings, Great Fang. I have no wish to disrupt your busy schedule, but I have not yet received confirmation that you have dispatched to Great Claw Zhaarnak the orders we agreed on. I'm sure you have done so . . . as we agreed," he added with pointed repetition. "But I felt obliged to confirm it personally."

Koraaza sighed inwardly. He *had* agreed, albeit with a reluctance that had caused him to put off actually keeping his promise. "Your pardon, Governor, but the press of my duties has prevented me from actually sending the dispatch. I have, however, prepared the necessary orders to Great Claw Zhaarnak: stand on the defensive in Alowan, attempting no counteroffensive before I arrive." He drew a breath. "Governor, I will of course send the orders if you insist on holding me to my promise. But perhaps we should reconsider. Remember, every day the enemy is left undisturbed inTelmasa is another opportunity for him to discover the Hairnow warp point. Some aggressive raiding, at Zhaarnak's discretion, might distract the enemy from survey activities."

Kaarsaahn's habitual blandness was beginning to look a little frayed around the edges. "As I argued at our previous discussion, Great Fang, we have no way of knowing that the enemy has not already discovered the Hairnow System. More to the point, until Third Fleet arrives in Alowan, Great Claw Zhaarnak's force is the sector's only defense. It cannot be hazarded on premature adventures. And, while I have hesitated to raise this point before, I fear Zhaarnak's 'discretion' cannot be relied on in this matter." He hastily raised a clawed hand. "Yes, I know you are honor-bound to defend a fellow officer. It does you credit. But consider: his withdrawal from Kliean and Telmasa flew in the face of his temperament as well as *Farshalah'kiah*. The fact that he had no choice cannot possibly compensate in his own mind. He is bound to be biased towards reckless displays of courage, seeking to wipe out the stain—however illusory—on his honor. Under the circumstances, the knowledge that your command will soon depart Idnahk may well goad him into such an action—independently—rather than encourage him to hold fast."

Koraaza opened his mouth to hotly declare that Zhaarnak, like all officers of the Khan, was well aware of his paramount duty to defend the race's inhabited worlds . . . then snapped it shut. For Kaarsaahn, damn him, had a point. Zhaarnak *was* aggressive by nature, and any imagined disgrace *would* make him even more so. He might not do anything culpably stupid, but he might well overestimate his own strength in order to rationalize his need for action. And according to the latest reports, that strength was insufficient for any serious attempt on Telmasa.

No, Zharnaak's guilt over the worlds he had been forced to leave to their deaths could not be allowed to imperil still more worlds. It was a truth to which the *Zheerlikou'valkhannaieee* had never really become reconciled: the higher one climbed on the ladder of rank, the more often honor had to be sacrificed on the altar of duty. Koraaza himself had yet to accept it gracefully.

"Your points are well taken, Governor," he said leadenly. "I will send the orders."

Raymond Prescott began to rise, struggling with his wounded leg, as Zhaarnak'diaano entered the briefing room, but the great claw waved him back.

"Sit, Great Claw." The Orion title came more naturally to Zhaarnak than the Terran one, and he smiled a fang-hidden smile as Prescott sank back. "After all," he added dryly, "it is *I* who should rise when *you* enter."

"Nonsense," Prescott said. "The task force is overwhelmingly *Zheeerlikou'valkhannaieee* and Gorm—and the fixed defenses are *wholly* Orion. If only because of communication problems, you must retain command."

"You are a strange being, Great Claw," Zhaarnak said. "Are all Humans like you?"

"We humans are a pretty confusing lot," Prescott replied with a smile. "But, yes. I think most of my people are much like me where it matters."

"Then it is my loss that I have not made myself more familiar with them." Zhaarnak's tone was serious, not a polite formula, and Prescott bobbed a small Orion-style bow. Then Zhaarnak inhaled sharply and lowered himself into a chair.

"You have seen Least Claw Uaaria's report?"

"I have."

"And your opinion?"

"I believe she may have a point," Prescott said after only the briefest hesitation. "While any rational foe might have avoided action against Claw Daairaah's apparent fighter strength, the Bugs have appeared willing to date to accept total annihilation in order to inflict attritional losses. And even if they believed Daairaah's force was overhwelming, they could have forced *us* to engage on their terms—or abandon the Twins and the Fleet Base—before he intervened."

"True." Zhaarnak tipped his chair back, claws kneading its armrests gently. "So why decline to attack? Unless, of course, Uaaria is correct."

Prescott nodded, wishing fervently that Eloise Kmak were still available. But while she was expected to recover fully, she would be out of action for months. He'd borrowed Lieutenant Commander Cruikshank from Diego Jackson to replace her, but Cruikshank was less comfortable with the Orion language. He also lacked Kmak's unorthodox imagination, and Prescott had always preferred intelligence officers who thought outside the boxes of conventional wisdom. He missed Eloise badly . . . but it seemed Least Claw Uaaria had the same ability.

He cocked his own chair back in thought. As Zhaarnak said, the Bugs had to have known they could carry through against the Twins. Based on every other battle they'd fought, that was precisely what they *ought* to have done, and Uaaria had been the first to ask why they hadn't.

The only answer she'd been able to come up with was

that, for some reason, *this* time they were unwilling to risk crippling losses. That was very unlike them, yet they couldn't have *expected* to contact the Alliance in Shanak, which suggested one possible explanation. If this contact had been as unexpected for them as for the Alliance, then they must have attacked with whatever was available. And if it was all an opportunistic response to an unanticipated opening, they might well have broken off because there were no—or very few—additional mobile units behind them. And if that were so . . .

"I think we must assume, tentatively, at least, that Uaaria *is* correct," he said finally. "If she is, it might also explain why they have not reinforced and attempted Alowan a second time."

Zhaarnak flicked his ears in agreement. Over a Terran month had passed since the enemy had pulled back, and during his inactivity Lord Khiniak's forces had completed assembling. They would reach Alowan within two weeks, and more reinforcements had arrived in the meantime than Zhaarnak had believed possible. Orion, Gorm—even a few additional Human starships had come in, and some, like the Gorm superdreadnoughts *Clerdyng* and *Dathum*, had been totally unexpected. They had been beyond New Bristol, in Human space, when the call went out, and communications had been so chaotic no one had realized they were responding. Which was probably as well. If anyone *had* realized, they would no doubt have been diverted to Idnahk.

The Human support ships had also arrived and labored mightily. Zhaarnak was deeply impressed by how rapidly they had put the wounded Human ships back into action, yet the other thing they had achieved was almost more important. The joint Human-Orion R&D teams had finally determined how to make TFN and KON command datalink interface, and the Humans' mobile shipyards had worked out jury-rigged field modifications. No doubt the "official" version would be much neater, but the Human techs' crude version worked. The ships under Zhaarnak's command could now be formed into battlegroups on a tactical basis rather than being forced to operate as separate national units, and the value of that would be difficult to exaggerate.

He was not certain he could have stopped a full-scale warp point assault, but Idnahk and New Bristol had sent up sufficient fighters to refill every hangar in Alowan. With that much fighter strength, backed by his hybrid battle-line and, if necessary, the fixed defenses, he felt confident he could hold the system, even if he were forced to concede the warp point.

And that is why Uaaria's theory is so convincing. The Bugs must realize we are straining every sinew to reinforce, and they would not have given us time to do so unless they had to.

"If," Zhaarnak said very carefully, "the enemy is, indeed, too weak to attack us, is it not possible he might be weak enough for *us* to attack *him?*"

He watched Prescott's face. He was learning, gradually, to interpret Human expressions, but nothing he had so far learned was of much help at the moment, and he wondered how Prescott would have fared across the *eschaai* table. *Probably quite well. I doubt even another Human could tell his thoughts just now.*

"I suppose," Prescott said after a moment, "that the possibility must exist. Of course, if we suggested as much, our superiors would no doubt find the evidence insufficient . . . particularly with such heavy reinforcements en route. I suspect they would order us to hold our position until relieved rather than risk our ships on any such hypothetical speculation by a mere least claw."

"Your command of the Tongue of Tongues is most impressive, Great Claw Pressscott," Zhaarnak remarked, "and your assessment of Sector Command's probable reaction is astute. We are, of course, merely discussing possibilities, and I feel sure Lord Khiniak would be more, ah, *adventurous* than Governor Kaarsaahn. Unfortunately, it is Kaarsaahn who holds final authority."

"I see." Prescott pursed his lips. "My people are not unfamiliar with such situations," he observed, "and we have a saying we sometimes use. 'What your superiors do not know about, they cannot countermand.' The translation is not exact, but I believe the meaning comes through."

"Indeed?" Zhaarnak gave a purring chuckle. "Interesting. There is a similar saying among the *Zheeerlikou'valkhannaieee*: 'Actions taken *without* orders are not taken *against* them.'"

"Perhaps our peoples are more alike than most think," Prescott replied, then met Zhaarnak's eyes levelly. "But however that may be, what we are considering constitutes a grave risk. Not simply to our commands, but to Alowan. If we attempt Telmasa—" Zhaarnak's ears twitched at the confirmation that they *were*, in fact, thinking the same thing "—and take heavy losses, we may expose this system to a *Bug* counterattack."

"Truth," Zhaarnak said seriously. "And I cannot and will not order you to support me in this. Not only are you my superior, despite your willingness to allow me to retain command, but the risk to your ships and personnel would be great—as would the risk to your career." Prescott made a dismissive gesture, but Zhaarnak continued in the same earnest tone. "Do not make light of it, Great Claw Pressscott. I think Human and *Zheeerlikou'valkhannaieee* admiralty boards are alike in that much. Success justifies all, yet failure blots out even past accomplishments."

"There is a time to consider careers," Prescott said, "and one to consider duty."

"You speak truly," Zhaarnak said. "And you are also correct about the risk to Alowan. Yet I cannot forget Kliean . . . or Hairnow. We do not know if the enemy has discovered Hairnow exists. Even if he has, he may not yet have had time to wreak much damage there, but he has been in possession of Kliean for over three of your months, and there are four billion of my people in that system. If we could retake Telmasa before Lord Khiniak arrives here, he would begin his own operations only one warp point assault from Kliean, not two. And if the enemy has not, in fact, learned of Hairnow's existence, we would protect another billion and a half of my people. Those are the prizes against which we would hazard our commands."

Prescott leaned back, eyes hooded, and considered the Tabby's quietly impassioned plea. And plea it was, he thought. The Alowan Fleet Base had produced a few dozen SBMHAWKs, but it was only now getting into full production. Yet New Bristol had stripped its own magazines bare and rushed the weapons forward. Over two hundred *TFN* pods had reached Alowan, and only the lavish use of those pods could possibly get them into Telmasa intact. Without Prescott's support, Zhaarnak couldn't possibly attack; even with it, the odds against success would be high.

Yet Zhaarnak was also right about Kliean and Hairnow. Every day that passed could be the literal difference between life and death for millions of Orion civilians, and he suddenly realized there was one argument Zhaarnak *hadn't* made.

Honor. Zhaarnak'diaano had pulled out of Kliean and Telmasa rather than fight to the death. His successful defense of Alowan might have vindicated his decision, yet honor and vindication weren't necessarily the same thing—particularly to a Tabby. But if he fought his way back into Telmasa, that, coupled with the Battle of Alowan, *would* cleanse his honor.

Yet he hadn't made that argument, and, as he looked into Zhaarnak's eyes, Prescott realized he *wouldn't* make it. Not because he felt it would have no impact on a Terran, for by now he knew how intimately Prescott had studied Orion culture and the *Farshalah'kiah*. He knew Prescott would understand the centrality of honor—his clan's, even more than his own—to any Orion, but his concern was with lives, billions of them. Orion or no, Zhaarnak'diaano had set his honor aside. Indeed, he was risking even greater dishonor, for if he made the attempt and *failed*, all too many of his fellows would consider him a total, feckless bungler. Very few Terrans would have understood the immensity of the self-sacrifice he was prepared to embrace . . . but Raymond Porter Prescott was one of them.

"'Death is lighter than a flower, but duty is heavier than a mountain,'" he said softly. Zhaarnak's ears cocked questioningly, and Prescott smiled. "A saying from Old Terra, Great Claw, from some of my people I think you would have understood."

"This is not about honor," Zhaarnak said quietly, but Prescott shook his head.

"No, Great Claw. It *is* about honor . . . and duty. One may sometimes clash with the other in the eyes of others, but it is *our* eyes we must consider here."

He held the Tabby's slit-pupilled eyes for a moment, then punched a code into his com without looking down. A moment passed, and then a voice spoke from the terminal.

"Yes, Sir?"

"Great Claw Zhaarnak and I are in Briefing Room A, Alec," Prescott said. "Please collect Cruikshank and join us. We have an operation to plan."

CHAPTER TWENTY-EIGHT

A Good Day for It

*The Fleet waited far behind its heavy cruiser screen,
for it was uneasily aware of its exposure. Pre-war doctrine
would have moved its entire strength into range of the
warp point; as it was, the decision to defend the system
at all had come hard. The Fleet was too weak to risk a
conventional deployment against missile pods, and the
temptation to fall back to the first system it had seized
was great. Yet the advantages of holding here—if it
could—were also great. At best, it would win time for
its reinforcements to arrive; at worst, the enemy still had
no idea where the second closed warp point in the contact
system was . . . and if the Fleet had not yet received the
warships it needed, it had received the new missiles to
support its gunboats.*

This time it was an Orion show, and Raymond Prescott
leaned on his cane on *Horned Viper*'s patched up flag
bridge as Task Force 37 headed for the Telmasa warp
point.

He and Zhaarnak had agonized over their timing, for
if they failed and Uaaria's theory was wrong, Alowan would
certainly be counterattacked. The Fleet Base's fighter
strength had been tripled, and tenders were prepared
to ferry fighters from Sak to Alowan to replace losses,
which should give the base a chance against whatever

the Bugs had left after destroying TF 37, yet neither Prescott nor Zhaarnak could free themselves of concern for the system. That was why they'd waited almost another week. Lord Khiniak must be en route now, and despite their burning need to relieve Hairnow, they'd delayed to buy a little more time for him to arrive. They were still cutting it close, but if, in fact, the Bugs hadn't yet discovered Hairnow, the risk was worth it.

And whatever happened, he thought grimly, TF 37—and especially its Tabbies—would take a lot of killing before it went down. Of the eighty-plus ships in his display, sixty-two percent were Orion. It had taken the assistance of his mobile shipyards to get them all ready in time, but thirteen of TF 37's twenty-one carriers and fourteen of its twenty-one battlecruisers were Orion. Combining their battle-line units' light fighter components with their carrier strikegroups, the Tabbies also accounted for eighty-three of the task force's hundred and ten fighter squadrons, and they'd managed to scare up four battleships, as well. Of course, KONS *Ambrych* had repair techs onboard even now, but the battleship's captain insisted she was ready to fight, just as the COs of the CVLs *Rohrdenhau* and *Vohlghar* insisted *their* ships were. Neither carrier had had a single fighter embarked when she arrived, and two of *Vohlghar*'s catapults were iffy, but no Tabby was going to sit this one out. They'd seen the imagery from Kliean. They *knew* what was happening there—and might be happening in Hairnow, as well—and the Devil himself wouldn't stop them.

Prescott understood that, and he was glad he'd insisted Zhaarnak retain command. The Battle of Alowan had earned his personnel enormous respect from their Orion allies, but as he'd told the great claw, TF 37's composition made it unthinkable for him to demand command authority. Not only was it a predominately Orion force, but he himself was the only one of his officers who could actually speak Orion, and he'd been hard pressed to find enough Orion-cognizant personnel just to fill the critical communication slots aboard his ships.

But Zhaarnak had done a little reshuffling of his own personnel when he reorganized his task groups. Prescott's TG 37.2 had given up its CVLs, its surviving battlecruisers, and two of its DDEs, to Zhaarnak's TG 37.1. It made sense to combine all the carriers in one force, and the *Broadswords'* energy weapons and short-ranged missile batteries would be more useful covering the fighter platforms against gunboats than going toe-to-toe with *Archers*. And Prescott couldn't complain about what he'd gotten in return: two GSN superdreadnoughts—*Gormus*-class ships with heavy energy batteries and no capital missiles, perhaps, but still formidable units; four Orion battleships; seven Orion and Gorm battlecruisers (all missile ships); and seventeen Orion heavy and light cruisers to supplement the four *Swiftsure*-class CAs New Bristol had scared up. Despite the pounding his original command had taken, his new task group was far more powerful, and every one of its allied ships had at least one com officer who understood Standard English.

Even so, I'm glad I reminded my tac officers to stay away from contractions, he mused. Contractions and homonyms, neither of which the Tongue of Tongues used, could give English-cognizant Orions enormous trouble, and with their emotions running as high as they were—

Of course, our emotions are pretty high, too. I probably should have looked closer at Mexicano's *readiness report— I'm pretty sure Captain Trayn did a little creative editing to get in on this one—but a battleship's a battleship, and we need everything we've got.*

He limped from the plot to his command chair, and settled back with a sigh of relief. A yeoman hung his cane on the shock frame for him, and he brought up his link to CIC. The senior plotting officer looked up as it came on-line, but Prescott only nodded to him. Commander Huyler nodded back and returned his attention to his own console, and Prescott checked the time.

Thirty-two minutes.

"Very well, Great Claw Pressscott," Zhaarnak said formally. "Engage."

"Yes, Sir." Prescott looked at Alec LaFroye, his acting chief of staff as well as his ops officer, and nodded. "Launch your birds, Alec."

"Aye, aye, Sir!"

LaFroye punched a stud, and one hundred and twenty Terran SBMHAWK pods carried six hundred AAM-warhead SBMs into Telmasa in a single mighty wave.

None of the Orion pinnaces which had probed Telmasa had survived, which suggested a massive gunboat CSP beyond it, and Least Claw Theerah had suggested programming at least some pods to go after those gunboats, but LaFroye had countered that they didn't know for certain that the pods would track on them. Even if they would, it would have required at least one full pod to insure the destruction of each gunboat, which could easily spread them too thin.

The TFN pod techs swore their birds would home on gunboats, but they had to admit they couldn't prove it, and LaFroye was right about the dispersion effect. More, he and Theerah agreed the Bugs would have used their heavy cruiser "OWPs" to cover the warp point, and the Terran had successfully argued in favor of targeting the pods on them. In return, Zhaarnak had decreed that only half their total SBMHAWKs would be used in the first strike. Six hundred missiles should account for the cruisers, especially when surprise was (hopefully) complete; the remaining pods would be held back to cover a retreat at need.

Now the SBMHAWKs vanished, and TG 37.2, Grand Alliance, accelerated towards the warp point on their heels.

The sudden eruption of missile pods caught the Fleet unaware, for the enemy had ceased expending reconnaissance pinnaces six days ago, and the Fleet had taken his inactivity to indicate he had no thought of an attack.

The gunboat CSP was only thirty units strong, and many were out of position to intercept before the pods stabilized. Less than a dozen pods were picked off before the survivors fired, and most of the cruisers were still rushing to general quarters when the missiles came in.

In direct contravention of normal tactics, Zhaarnak and Prescott had chosen to send TG 37.2's lighter ships through first. They had no choice, for they had too few capital ships to expose them to the first, terrible embrace.

Only eleven of the Bug cruisers Allied intelligence had codenamed *Danger* survived the opening bombardment, and all were damaged. Four had not yet brought their offensive weapons on-line when the first Allied cruiser appeared, but the other seven opened fire instantly, and each mounted no less than sixteen of the short-ranged plasma guns. TFNS *Ammiraglio di St. Bon* and *Peder Skram* died without getting a shot off, and TFNS *Eidsvold* and KONS *Debniha* fired only a single broadside apiece before following them into destruction. But each of those broadsides finished off an active Bug CA, and their consorts flooded forward, firing savagely. Within ninety seconds, every Bug starship on the warp point was dead.

Yet that left the gunboats Theerah had wanted to target. They came slashing in with heavy loads of close-attack missiles, driving in through the thunder of the Allied missile launchers to launch at point-blank range, then closed to ram. Only a few got through, but a few were too many. KONS *Athnak, Noizuwha, Vhertygho* and *Pilko* were destroyed outright, and the air-bleeding wreck of TFNS *Voltaire*, the only Terran CA to survive, turned to limp back to Alowan.

"The cruisers have cleared the warp point, Sir," LaFroye reported, and Prescott nodded grimly. Returning courier drones tallied the dreadful price his lead waves had paid, but they'd done their job, and their sensors confirmed that the nearest superdreadnought was over two light-minutes out. That was good, because he needed all the time he could get to clear lanes through the mines. Only the TFN's ships could fire the internally launched

AMBAM, yet each of his battleships mounted only a single capital missile launcher. Designed to deploy decoy enhanced-drive missiles as a defensive measure, those seven launchers were all he had to fire AMBAMs, and if the Bugs had been close enough to hammer his battle-line while it was still pinned down on the warp point, the entire operation would have had to be scrubbed.

But they weren't, and he nodded to Captain Pitnarau's com image.

"Take us through, Jason."

It was disturbing that the enemy had finally realized it made more sense to lead attacks with expendable units, for that indicated he was evolving better tactics, but the battleships which followed suggested he had no super-dreadnought element of his own. In turn, that suggested he had not been strongly reinforced. If that was true, the new missiles should make it relatively easy to hold this system after all, and the Fleet launched its ready-duty gunboats in a solid wave.

"They're moving in on us, Sir. Looks like they're sending in the gunboats first."

"Understood." Prescott acknowledged LaFroye's report almost absently. It was the ops officer's job to make it, but there was nothing Prescott could do about it. The *Belleisles* were clearing mines as fast as they could, but they were taking much longer than *Matterhorn*-class superdreadnoughts would have. "Have all the cripples cleared back to Alowan?"

"Yes, Sir. *Doushai* and *Juzavahn* didn't want to go, but they're clear."

"Good." Prescott watched his escorts form up to screen the battle-line and shook his head. *Tabbies! Neither of those ships had more than two launchers left, and they still* wanted *to stay!*

"Three more salvos and Alpha Lane will be through the field, Sir," Pitnarau reported.

"Beta and Charlie?"

"They're badly behind," Pitnarau admitted, and Prescott frowned.

"Forget them, then. We need maneuvering room. Move us out through Alpha now."

The enemy's units—including a mere two SDs—streamed through the minefield gap before the gunboats could attack. Some of his ships launched attack craft, but there were no more than thirty of them, and eighty gunboats streaked to meet them.

"Here they come," LaFroye said, and *Horned Viper* twitched as TG 37.2 belched missiles. The understrength fighter squadrons from the Tabby battleships and battlecruisers raced towards the gunboats as well, and fireballs pocked the Bug formation. But the kill numbers were lower than they should have been against such fragile targets, and the strike came on grimly. *That damned point defense of theirs*, Prescott thought bitterly, and looked at Pitnarau.

"Zulu Four, Jason."

"Aye, aye, Sir. Executing Zulu Four."

TG 37.2 turned away from the gunboats, maneuvering to hold the range open while missiles and Tabby fighters tore into them. The vector shift seemed to surprise the Bugs; they lost precious seconds correcting, and the defenders used those seconds well. Only twenty-one attackers broke through, and they flung themselves upon the two Gorm leviathans which dominated Prescott's formation. But a *Gormus*-class was a dangerous opponent for anyone, especially something the size of a gunboat. Heavy energy batteries and shoals of missiles exploded into the Bugs' faces, backed by the point defense of the entire battle-line. GSNS *Dathum* lost most of her shields and took some armor damage, but she and her sister, supported by the four Orion battleships datalinked to them, blew the gunboats into vapor before they could ram.

"All right!" someone shouted from CIC, but Prescott's

face was carved iron, for another wave was coming in, and this one was three times as strong.

"Looks like we find out if the techs were right, Alec," he said quietly, then raised his voice. "Zulu Five, Captain Pitnarau!"

The first mass strike was a disappointment, but it seemed to have confused the enemy. He recoiled, turning still further away, foolishly circling around behind the warp point. If he meant to retreat, he should have reversed course down his cleared lane and escaped the system entirely. Surely he did not expect the Fleet's own mines to deter its gunboats!

Apparently he did. He was trying to use the mines as a shield, and no doubt they would kill a few gunboats. At their speed, IFF gear was not fully reliable, and some mines were likely to attack them. But not enough to make any difference, and once they reached the warp point, they could block the enemy's retreat and swamp any additional enemy starships if they tried to make transit to support the units already in the system.

"Launch!" Prescott said, and a dozen courier drones flicked through to Alowan just as the gunboats hit the minefield. Six or seven were blown apart by their own mines, but the others screamed across the field to attack TG 37.2, and this time more got through. Most of the Tabby fighters were destroyed in a wild melee amid the mines, but they took out another forty gunboats first, and the Allied battle-line's missiles and energy weapons met the survivors furiously.

The Bugs slashed in, ignoring the screen to go after battleships, and once more, the two superdreadnoughts acted as magnets for their fury. But before they could reach their targets, a fresh wave of SBMHAWKs erupted from the warp point behind them.

The timing wasn't perfect. The pods were supposed to have caught the Bugs before they penetrated TG 37.2's perimeter, and they launched late. But the techs had been right. They *could* target gunboats, and the delayed launch actually increased their effectiveness, for gunboats, too, had blind spots, and the missiles drove straight up them.

One entire flank of Prescott's formation was a solid wall of glaring detonations as SBMs chased the Bugs in among his starships. Two of his battlecruisers got in the way of their own SBMs and took hits that shook them to their keels, but their shields held, and their tactical officers went right on pouring fire into the Bugs.

Dathum's last shield went down, and two gunboats got through with ramming attacks, as well, damaging her drive and ripping at her hull. Her armor buckled, but she shook off the damage, holding her station. KONS *Fikhar* was less fortunate. A tornado of missiles battered the Tabby battle-ship's shields flat, smashed her armor, and tore deep into her hull. She staggered *in extremis*, and her agony drew the attention of other gunboats. They howled in, ramming again and again, and suddenly one of them reached her magazines. Every antimatter warhead detonated at once, and the fireball licked away another half dozen Bugs as she died.

Fikhar was gone, and three of Prescott's battlecruisers were mangled wrecks, but the combination of TG 37.2's defensive fire and the unexpected SBMHAWKs proved decisive. The remnants of the Bug strike broke off, fleeing back to its own battle-line, and Prescott drew a deep, shuddering breath. He'd been hurt, but the core of his task group was intact and that *had* to have been the bulk of the Bugs' gunboats.

Of course, he thought as the enemy superdreadnoughts started forward, *that leaves the* rest *of their damned fleet!*

"Damage report from *Dathum*?" he demanded.

"She's lost an engine room, but she's still as fast as we are," LaFroye replied. "Damage control is bringing her shields back up now. Her armor's a sieve, but most of her weapons are in one piece, and Captain Haarmak says he's still combat capable."

"Good. We're going to need him. Com, send the second-flight drones."

✧   ✧   ✧

The gunboats had proved less effective than anticipated, and the proof that the missile pods could target them had grim implications for future actions. But the enemy remained too weak to meet the Fleet's battle-line head on, and thirty-eight superdreadnoughts and three battle-cruisers started forward, screened by their light cruisers.

"Great Claw Pressscott has done well," Zhaarnak purred, studying the drone readouts. He and his Human ally had structured TG 37.2 as a mace to smash through the shell of the defenses, but TG 37.1 was a rapier, and it was time to bring it into play. "We will advance, Theerah."

Twenty-one carriers and their escorts scorched into the warp point at max.

The Fleet paused as fresh enemy units suddenly materialized and began launching attack craft. The gunboats were still fleeing back to the twelve battlecruisers detached to rearm them, and the Fleet could not reach the warp point before these new enemies completed transit. It could neither seal the point against them nor afford to be destroyed if the new missiles proved ineffective, so it turned ponderously away, retreating until it saw how well the new technology worked. There would be time to return to the warp point if the missiles fulfilled predictions.

Raymond Prescott heaved a surreptitious sigh as Zhaarnak made transit, molested only by a handful of gunboats. Stragglers from the last Bug strike tried to penetrate to the carriers, but the old cliché about the snowflake in Hell came to mind as the Tabby squadrons pounced on them.

The task groups made rendezvous, and Prescott scratched the unshaven side of his head as he studied the plot. The Bugs were moving slowly *away* from the warp point rather than trying to close. They'd never done that before, and something seemed to crawl down the back of his neck as minutes dragged past without a single offensive act out of them. Zhaarnak held his own force on the warp point while his recon fighters swept outward to assure him no cloaked Bugs waited to pounce, but somehow Prescott was sure none did. Yet if not, what *were* the bastards up to?

"Great Claw Pressscott?" He turned from the plot to his com as Zhaarnak appeared on it.

"Yes, Sir?"

"My pilots have swept a light-minute sphere without contact. Least Claw Theerah and Commmodorrre Jaaacksssson agree it is time to launch the next phase. Do you concur?"

"Of course, Sir. However . . ." Prescott paused a moment, rubbing his upper lip, then shrugged. "I urge caution," he said. "They are not reacting in usual fashion, and I distrust an enemy who does exactly what *I* want him to do."

"Most surprises represent only misinterpretations of known data," Zhaarnak agreed. "Yet if they wish to stand, we can only attack and discover what it is they wish us to misinterpret."

"Truth, Great Claw. Strike deep."

The enemy was finally ready, but his delay had been helpful. The gunboat's greatest tactical limitation was its inability to dock internally. To rearm, it must return to its mother ship's external rack, and the mother ship must shut down her drive to reload its ordnance racks. The enemy probably had not learned that—yet—but his tardiness was still of immense value.

Though not, it was to be hoped, as much value as the new missiles.

The *Zheeerlikou'valkhannaieee* would launch the first strike. It was less a matter of honor than of practicality, for there were far more Orion fighters, and the chance of confusion between pilots who couldn't speak one another's languages had to be minimized. The less numerous Terrans were detailed as the task force's covering

CSP for the opening phase. Once the Bugs had been hammered a time or two and their gunboats had been finished off, Commodore Jackson's strikegroups could be used to help complete their destruction.

Besides, there would be more than enough action to go around.

Raymond Prescott watched three hundred Tabby strikefighters arrow into the attack. Least Claw Theerah and Zhaarnak had studied Fifth Fleet's combat reports intensively. They knew how dangerous the *Cataphracts* were, and they'd taken a page from Admiral Murakuma's book: their pilots would go for the screen, using longer-ranged FM2s to pick off the *Carbines, Cannons, Cleavers* first, then go for the *Cataphracts* with FRAMs.

It was a good plan—and it came apart the instant the fighters tried to execute it.

The attack craft flashed closer. Their targets were obvious, and the screen adjusted its formation slightly. There were only eighteen Cataphracts, *and two dozen* Carbines *formed a solid wall between them and the enemy, daring him to waste his fire upon them.*

Farshathkhanaak Iaouusa'hairniak led the attack. Gee forces drew his lips back, baring his fangs, and his eyes glowed as the Bugs shifted formation. The *dairshnahki* were actually moving his designated targets out where he could get at them!

Wait! What was th—?

Iaouusa never finished the question as the very first Bug AFHAWK ever used in action scored a direct hit on his fighter.

Prescott slammed his fist down on the arm of his command chair. AFHAWKs! The bastards had *AFHAWKs!* No *wonder* they hadn't tried to attack! They'd been waiting to spring their ambush when *Task Force 37* attacked!

Surprise was total. It shouldn't have been. He and Zhaarnak should have allowed for the possibility, but so little time had passed since the Battle of Alowan that such a radical shift in the tactical balance hadn't even occurred to them, and Zhaarnak's pilots paid a fearful price. The missile-heavy *Carbines,* suddenly infinitely more dangerous than the *Cataphracts,* poured devastating fire into the lead squadrons, and the fighters had *known* they were beyond threat range. None had even taken evasive action . . . and seventy-one died in the first, terrible salvo.

The survivors reacted like the elite pilots they were. They broke instantly, in apparently total confusion, only to drop into the Orion version of the TFN's "Waldeck Weave." They twisted their base vectors together in a tangle of competing target sources to confuse the enemy's fire control, and despite their shock, carried through against their targets. Some managed to break lock, maneuvering hard against the AFHAWKs which had acquired them; others were less fortunate, but none turned aside, and the survivors salvoed their missiles into their briefed targets.

The Bug screen writhed as the Orion fire struck. Half the *Carbines* were destroyed outright, and most of the rest were damaged. But *none* were supposed to have lived, and the kills had cost three times the projected losses. Worse, the cost of killing the *rest* of their fleet would be still higher, for the entire Bug battle-line was belching AFHAWKs.

The Orion survivors broke off to rearm—and reorganize around their casualties—and the Bugs waited until they had been recovered for rearming . . . then sent all two hundred remaining gunboats in to kill the carriers while they were helpless in their bays. But Diego Jackson's CSP charged to meet them. The carriers' escorts and the battle-line raced to interpose between them and the gunboats, raking the incoming strike with fire, but it was Jackson's outnumbered fighters who broke the attack's back.

They paid for it with sixty-one Terran fighters, and they didn't stop them all. That was perhaps the most terrifying thing about a mass suicide attack. When the attackers were intent on dying anyway, some *always* got through. The leakers slammed into TG 37.1 like hammers, and the Tabby fleet carriers were their primary targets. *Ytarible* tore apart under a hurricane of missiles and kamikazes, and *Celshakhan* and *Itumahk* were hit hard, especially *Itumahk*. Half the big carrier's hangar bays were reduced to ruin, taking their fighters with them, yet she was luckier than the CVLs *Ghiurdauni* and *Rymanthhus*. Both light carriers disappeared in the terrible glare of nuclear fusion, and the Terran *Bonhomme Richard* went with them.

But agonizing as the personnel casualties were, fighters losses were worse. Coupled with the effect of that first, dreadful AFHAWK broadside and the CSP's dogfight, half of TF 37's total fighter strength had been written off in less than twenty minutes . . . and those fighters had been Zhaarnak's main battery. His entire plan had been based on staying beyond shipboard range and battering the enemy to death with fighter strikes, but if the Bugs had AFHAWKs . . .

"I fear we must increase our fighter loss projections by at least a factor of two in light of the enemy's possession of the AFHAWK, Great Claw," Least Claw Theerah said heavily. He sat with his commander before a subdivided com screen which held the faces of Diego Jackson and his ops officer as well as Raymond Prescott and Alexander LaFroye. "Given the losses we have already suffered," he went on somberly, "I cannot guarantee success if we continue the attack."

"Wait a minute, Theerah." It was a sign of the least claw's concern that he didn't even wince as Jackson's atrocious Terran accent mangled his name. "We're hurt, sure, but we're not out of this yet. Your boys and girls kicked hell out of their *Carbines*, and *my* people finished off virtually all their gunboats. We can still take these bastards!"

Theerah let his earbug translate, then sighed. "I admire your spirit, Commmodorrre, but I am not certain I share your confidence. Our surviving strikegroups are badly disorganized. It will take hours to restore their efficiency . . . during which the enemy will reach the warp point.

The prudent course would be to withdraw to Alowan to reorganize, yet I fear that is impractical."

"Truth, Least Claw," Prescott said. "We have exhausted our SBMHAWKs. Without them, we cannot force a return to the system once we retreat."

"On the other hand," LaFroye pointed out, "we *have* knocked hell out of their gunboats. If nothing else, we've insured that they can't take Alowan before Lord Khiniak arrives."

"I didn't come here to lose, Alec," Prescott harshly. "I came here to relieve Hairnow!"

Zhaarnak hid a flicker of bitter amusement. *How odd. Humans say we do not know how to give ground, yet it is Theerah who counsels caution and Humans who reject his words!*

"Damn right," Jackson growled. "I have *had* it with these things, and I *want* their asses!"

"I realize that, Sir." LaFroye said respectfully, reminding himself Jackson was a fighter jock by training and inclination. "I'm simply pointing out that we've already achieved our minimum objective."

"You are correct, Commmannderrr LaaaFrrroye," Zhaarnak said, "as are you, Theerah. Yet as Great Claw Pressscott says, I did not come here to lose. So I ask you. Is Commmodorrre Jaaackssson correct? *Can* we complete the enemy's destruction?"

The least claw sat silent for several seconds, eyes straying to the plot on which the Bug battle-line advanced towards the warp point. If TF 37 meant to retreat before the enemy's missiles could command the point, it must begin its withdrawal within the next fifteen minutes.

Theerah disliked being the voice of caution. It felt unnatural and somehow sordid, yet it was also his job, and he closed his eyes and thought furiously. Then he sighed.

"I do not know, Great Claw," he said finally. "Certainly we can do them great damage, but to *destroy* them will require our battle-line to accept action. We cannot do it with fighters alone."

"We can hack that," LaFroye said, "but only if we take their SBMs and capital missiles out of the picture. They only have nine *Archers*. Can the fighters get in and kill them first?"

"Commmodorrre?" Theerah asked quietly, and Diego Jackson bared his teeth.

"We can do it," he said confidently. "It'll cost us, but we can do it."

"In that case, Great Claw, I think we can do it," LaFroye said. "They don't mount CMs in anything else, and we've got nine capital missile battlecruisers. We send the fighters in to kill the *Archers*, then empty the battlecruisers' magazines into them from outside their range. Instead of outright kills, we concentrate on knocking down their datalink, then the battle-line pounds them with standard missiles from outside effective energy range and closes with the fighters in tight, like Admiral Murakuma did in Leonidas, and kicks their guts out from the inside."

"Theerah?" Zhaarnak asked.

"It should work, Great Claw," the least claw said. "Yet casualties will be very heavy, and for us to attempt it, we must first complete our strikegroups' reorganization. That will require us to allow them to reclaim the warp point, so if it does *not* work, none of our ships will escape."

"Lord Khiniak will reach Alowan in six days," Zhaarnak murmured as if to himself. "Even if we are destroyed, his strength will hold the system, and if we do sufficient damage to the enemy, he will retake Telmasa with ease." His eyes flicked to the icon of the Hairnow warp point, and his ears flattened. He gazed at it for several seconds, then inhaled sharply.

"Very well, Commmannderrr LaaaFrrroye, you have convinced me. We shall send our worst damaged ships back to Alowan and attempt your plan with the remainder. And if we fail," he raised one clawed hand, palm uppermost, and closed it slowly into a fist, "then we shall end like *farshatok*." He smiled thinly. "It is a good day for it, war brothers."

CHAPTER TWENTY-NINE
The Tips of Our Claws

Tenth Great Fang of the Khan Koraaza'khiniak, *Khanhaku* Khiniak, CO Third Fleet, stood behind the side party in KONS *Ebymiae*'s boat bay and watched the cutter dock. It was a Human cutter, and Lord Khiniak found that entirely fitting as he glanced about the cavernous boat bay at the officers and ratings of his new flagship. He had shifted his lights to *Ebymiae* only six days before, on his arrival in Telmasa, for she was the sole Orion battleship to survive Second Telmasa. She *deserved* her status, and he felt a pride in her which only the *Zheeerlikou'valkhannaieee* could fully have understood.

Or perhaps not, he told himself, thinking of the officer he was about to greet.

The hatch opened, and the pipes skirled. They did not offer the KON's normal honors; instead they played *Suns of Splendor*, the anthem of the Terran Federation.

Two officers walked forward into that music. One was a tall, russet-furred Orion; the other a shorter, battered-looking Human who leaned heavily on a cane. His uniform bore the brand-new insignia of a TFN vice admiral, but one side of his shaven head showed a freshly healed, cruel-looking scar, and his immobilized left arm hung useless. He moved slowly, in obvious pain, and the Orion at his side tried not to hover attentively over him.

"Task Force Thirty-Seven, arriving!" the intercom

announced. That, too, was not usual Orion protocol, and Lord Khiniak saw surprise—and pleasure—in the Human officer's face.

The newcomers halted, and the Human looked down at his cane, then gave a crooked Human smile and braced painfully erect. He handed the cane to his companion, who took it gingerly, and saluted the son of the khan at the side party's head.

"Permission to come aboard, Sir?" he said in the Tongue of Tongues, and the son of the khan's salute would have done the Khan himself proud.

"Permission granted, Fang Pressscott!" he replied loudly, and Lord Khiniak stepped forward as Zhaarnak returned Prescott's cane. Lord Khiniak carefully did not note the Human's relief—or his small sound of pain—as he reclaimed his prop, but the great fang neither saluted Prescott nor offered his hand in the Human greeting his guest could not return while leaning upon it. Instead, he gave a much deeper Orion bow than usual.

"I am most pleased to meet you, Fang Pressscott," he said. "And to greet you once more, Great Claw." This time he did extend a hand, and Zhaarnak took it. They brought their free hands flashing to one another's faces in a warriors' salute, and Lord Khiniak smiled. "You bring great honor to us all, both of you. In the name of all the *Zheeerlikou'valkhannaieee* and of my Khan, I thank you."

Raymond Prescott watched Zhaarnak from the corner of one eye. The Tabby actually looked embarrassed, and Prescott waited for him to speak. But the cat seemed to have Zhaarnak's tongue—despite the pain of his wounds, the cliché made Prescott smile—and so he cleared his own throat.

"Honor comes to those who act with honor, Great Fang," he said for them both, "and it was our *farshatok* who brought honor to us all."

"Well said, Fang Pressscott," Lord Khiniak approved, then looked up. He clicked his claws, and a gorgeously bejeweled least claw stepped forward with a small, gem-crusted casket. Lord Khiniak took it in his own hands, and for all the solid weight of its precious metals and jewels, it seemed far too light for what it held as he turned back to his guests.

"Fang Pressscott—" no Orion would ever again greet this Human by his TFN rank "—Great Claw Zhaarnak, I bring you these as token of the honor you have earned. I speak in this as *hirikolus'ni'hami*, with the mouth of my Khan, and my hand is his hand."

Prescott and Zhaarnak stiffened and squared their shoulders almost in unison. Technically, every member of the Orion military was *hirikolus'ni'hami*, oath-sworn to the *Khan'a'khanaaeee*, but Lord Khiniak's formal emphasis carried another, deeper meaning. It was the ancient meaning, that of a liege man and war captain who, in this moment, literally *was* the Khan, a physical avatar for his distant warlord and hence for every Orion who had ever been or would be born.

He opened the casket reverently, and Prescott heard air hiss between Zhaarnak's fangs as Lord Khiniak lifted out a ribbon of deepest midnight blue, the imperial color of the Khanate. A magnificent golden starburst hung from it, broad as a Terran coffee cup yet delicate, exquisitely wrought like living, dancing flame, and a huge, blood-red ruby glittered at its heart.

The great fang returned the casket to his aide, who held it on open palms while his superior turned once more to face the Terran.

"Fang Pressscott, in the name and stead of my Khan, I beg you to accept this in the name of all the Human warriors who so valiantly perished defending the *Zheeerlikou'valkhannaieee*." Khiniak paused, then allowed a very small flicker of amusement to flaw his solemnity as he added softly. "We have consulted with your Navy and government, though we asked them not to inform you of our request and spoil our surprise, and they have approved."

"I—" Prescott paused to clear his throat. "I would be honored, Great Fang."

"Good." Lord Khiniak settled the ribbon about his neck,

then slapped him gently on the cheek with his claws. "In all our history, only two warriors not of our own race have received the *Ithyrra'doi'khanhaku*, and both were of our Gormish *farshatok*. Your name will be added to the Khan's own clan fathers in honor, and you are no longer human alone, Raaaymmonnd'pressscott. By the blood you have shed and the lives you have saved, you are *Zheeerlikou'valkhannaieee*, as well, *Khanhaku* Pressscottt, and while our people endure, we shall not forget."

Prescott bowed deeply, but he said nothing. He wasn't sure he could have trusted his voice if he'd tried to, nor was it the Orion way to indulge in flowery speeches. Few words but heartfelt ones were the Orion ideal. The more profound the occasion, the less they spoke of it, and he felt Zhaarnak quivering with emotion beside him.

Lord Khiniak gazed at him for a moment. Then his hand dipped into the casket once more for a smaller, equally beautiful copy of the star about Prescott's neck. This one was sized to fit an Orion officer's harness, and the great fang turned to Zhaarnak.

"As Fang Pressscott, so you, Great Claw," he said quietly. "You are named no longer Zhaarnak'diaano in the records of our clans, but Zhaarnak'telmasa, First Father of Clan Telmasa, and our Khan has personally charged me to welcome you to his fathers in honor."

Zhaarnak gripped his *defargo's* hilt so hard the tips of his claws emerged as Lord Khiniak removed the golden starship which marked him as an officer of the KON and snapped the star into its place. He would never again wear that starship, for the *Ithyrra'doi'khanhaku* would serve in its place . . . just as it would forever answer any slur upon his honor for retreating from Kliean.

Lord Khiniak finished affixing the medal, then stood back with a bow.

"And now, war brothers, join me in my flag briefing room. I would hear our situation from your own mouths."

"—and so we did," Zhaarnak finished quietly. "Commmannnderr LaaaFrrroye was correct; we did have the firepower . . . and as Theerah had warned, the cost *was* heavy."

Lord Khiniak flicked his ears in slow agreement, pondering the vagaries of Fate. His tardy order to stand fast had reached Alowan seven hours *after* TF 37 launched its attack. Had he sent it when Governor Kaarsaahn first instructed him to, the task force would neither have attacked nor suffered such casualties. And Third Fleet would have paid an even more terrible cost when *it* discovered the enemy's AFHAWKs.

He glanced into the repeater plot at the icons which been added to his own order of battle. They were agonizingly few, for ninety percent of Zhaarnak's and Prescott's fighters had died in Second Telmasa, and their battle-line had been savagely battered. The superdreadnought *Dathum* had perished . . . along with the battleships *Ambrych*, *Fikhar*, *Colossus*, *Mexicano* and *Umaghoz*. Virtually every surviving capital ship was little more than a wreck—Prescott's *Horned Viper* had barely survived, and her flag bridge had been reduced to an abattoir. TG 37.2's battlecruisers had been almost as heavily hammered, and the entire task force had been reduced to impotence.

But in return, TF 37 had destroyed every Bug starship in Telmasa . . . before the enemy discovered the warp point to Hairnow. A billion and a half civilians had been saved, and his own command faced only a single warp point assault to reach Kliean once more.

"You should not have done it, war brothers," he said softly at last. "You should not have, knowing I was coming. Yet it is well you did—very well, indeed. Thank you."

"We could not have done it without our Human *farshatok*," Zhaarnak said, and Lord Khiniak nodded, hiding his amusement at hearing such words from an old-line fire-eater such as he who had been Zhaarnak'diaano. He could hardly wait for Zhaarnak*telmasa's* next interview with *Khanhaku* Diaano. Clan lord or no, the old man would find cold welcome from Zhaarnak if he started on one of his anti-Human harangues now.

"Truth, Great Claw," the great fang said, and turned

to the human. "I am glad your own Navy has rewarded you with promotion, Fang Pressscott, and deeply regret that your fresh wounds will prevent you from serving with us when we return to Kliean. I trust they are less severe than original reports indicated?"

"The leg will be fine in time," Prescott replied. "As for the arm?" He gave a human shrug. "The surgeons have not yet given up hope, but I fear they have little to work with. And it may be as well if I leave *Horned Viper* . . . I seem to attract too much fire for her good."

Lord Khiniak gave a purring chuckle at his wry tone. It was amazing how well this Human spoke the Tongue of Tongues. Given Zhaarnak's original prejudices, the gods had smiled upon the *Zheeerlikou'valkhannaieee* indeed when they sent this man to them.

"We shall hope she suffers less in Kliean," he replied, "but I shall be honored to have her with us, and from all I have heard, Ahhhdmiraal Jaaacksssson will lead your *farshatok* well."

"Diego is a good man," Prescott agreed, "and he certainly deserves the promotion."

"Yes. Well." The great fang stood. "I thank you both for the briefing. Now I have other duties to attend to before we dine. Please remain here as long as you wish. Should you have any needs, my aide will remain on Flag Bridge and will be happy to attend to them."

He waved them both back into their chairs as Prescott struggled to rise, then left with a graceful bow.

Zhaarnak rose and crossed to the holo display, gazing at the ships which spangled it. A hundred and twenty starships, led by eighteen Gorm superdreadnoughts and eleven Terran and Orion battleships, glowed in its depths, supported by eight fleet carriers and thirteen CVLs. Over seven hundred fighters rode those icons—fighters which now knew the enemy had AFHAWKs and would not be surprised again, and that knowledge, he knew, was almost as important to the Grand Alliance as the relief of Hairnow. It was a mighty force beside the one he and Prescott had led into Telmasa, and still more warships were en route. The Idnahk Sector had been saved, and as he stared at the lights, he felt the Human who had truly made that possible behind him.

"We did it, war brother," he murmured. "We truly did . . . and I never thought we could."

"Indeed?" Prescott's chuckle turned Zhaarnak from the display, ears cocked, and the Human laughed. "You hid your doubt well, Great Claw. Did I hide mine equally well?"

"Well enough *I* never saw it," Zhaarnak replied. "But the price, my friend. Gods, the price was high!"

"By the tips of our claws," the Human agreed more somberly. He pushed himself up and limped over to the holo on his cane. "We did it by the tips of our claws," he repeated softly.

"Truth." Zhaarnak turned his head, studying Prescott while the Human looked into the display, then cleared his throat. "There is something I would ask of you, Fang Pressscott."

"Ah?" The Human's round-pupilled eyes looked at him from their flat, alien face, and Zhaarnak flicked his ears in agreement.

"We have seen much, you and I, and in the seeing, I have learned even more. About your people, and about myself. I have not enjoyed my lessons, yet learn them I have, and it is my honor to have learned from one such as you." The Human's face darkened with the blush Zhaarnak had learned indicated embarrassment, but he went on quietly. "Many years ago, I met Lord Talphon at a conference, and, to my shame, I regarded him with contempt, for he had sworn *vilkshatha* with a Human. Yet I know now why he did so, and so I ask this of you, little though I deserve it after so many years of foolish hatred." He drew a deep breath. "War brother, will you swear *vilkshatha* with me?"

CHAPTER THIRTY
Blind in the Dark

"I have grown to hate my work."

Son of the Khan Shaairal'haairaa looked up as Small Claw Maariaah'sheerino spoke. Survey Flotilla 80's commander was tipped back in his chair while he nursed a beaker of *chermaak*. He flattened his ears in an expression of abject misery the most skilled actor could not have bettered, and Shaairal purred a soft chuckle.

The Orion term *maavairahk* was not one of approval when it was borrowed from humanity in ISW–3. That remained true for the majority of the KON's officers even now, but it certainly fitted Maariaah. Yet maverick or no, he was also one of the best survey officers the KON had ever produced, which explained his rank at such a young age. Well, that and his status as the great-great-grandcub of one Varnik'sheerino, the greatest First Fang in Orion history. Personally, Shaairal suspected Maariaah had deliberately developed his iconoclastic persona *because* of his lineage, for it could not be easy to bear such a name. Besides, Varnik himself had been a *maavairahk* in his day, even if the Tongue of Tongues had not then boasted the word.

But whatever the small claw's motives, Shaairal recognized a cue when he heard one.

"And why is that, Small Claw?" he asked respectfully.

"Because it is so *boring*," Maariaah said plaintively.

Other ears cocked on *Harkhan*'s bridge as Shaairal's officers and the small claw's staff listened. The KON's survey crews were a tight-knit fraternity in which officers such as Maariaah inspired a sense of camaraderie rare outside the strikefighter community. "We go through the warp point, we look around, we hunt for fresh warp points, and, if we find one, we go through *it* and start all over again. Think of it, Shaairal. If we had but reactor mass enough, we could sail forever without ever reaching the end of it all." The small claw quaffed *chermaak* and shook his head mournfully. "There is too much emptiness in the universe, and I have already seen half of it."

"Perhaps so," Shaairal made his voice as sympathetic as he could, "but you should not think of it in that way, Sir. Instead, think of all the emptiness you may yet be the first to see."

"Oh, *thank* you, Son of the Khan! You have a gift—indisputably, a gift!—for encouraging your commander."

"Thank you, Sir," Shaairal replied as a chorus of chuckles ran around *Harkhan*'s bridge.

"You are welcome."

The small claw let his command chair swing upright and set his *chermaak* aside, satisfied the byplay had taken some of the tension out of Shaairal's bridge watch. Not all of it—a little tension kept people on their toes—but enough that he could now put it aside and get down to business. *And*, he thought, *it could be very serious business, indeed*.

"Are we prepared, Son of the Khan?" he asked the flag captain.

"We are, Sir. The escort and fortresses are all at action stations."

"In that case, proceed to that fresh emptiness you promised me."

Shaairal began giving orders, and Maariaah left him to it. His own eyes strayed to the master plot, and he felt his claws try to ease from their sheaths. Survey Flotilla 80's eighteen cruisers were almost lost amid the multihued lights of their escorts, and like every other person aboard

Harkhan, Maariaah devoutly wished those icons were somewhere far, far away.

But they were not. Four months—*No, three* standard *months*, he reminded himself, for the Grand Alliance had decided to use Human date conventions—had passed since Lord Khiniak's reconquest of Kliean demonstrated the consequences of the botched Shanak survey. Four billion dead, an entire star system's habitable planets reduced to so much useless, irradiated wasteland. It was a lesson the Alliance would not forget, and what had begun as a war of honor to succor an ally had become something else for the Orion Navy . . . which had no equivalent of the Human concept of "turning the other cheek." The fury the Kliean Atrocity had waked was impossible to exaggerate, and the consequences for the race which had wreaked it would be unimaginable.

But Kliean had also shaken the Alliance to its core. The millions who had perished in the Romulus Cluster had been bad enough; the death toll in Kliean was obscene, and a wave of panic had washed outward from it. If it could happen to Kliean, it could happen *anywhere*. It could not, of course. Maariaah knew that, but few civilians truly grasped the realities spacers took for granted. All they knew was that the planets of Kliean would lie lifeless for thousands of years.

Maariaah understood their fear, but he hated how the war had slowed as governments strove to calm the panic. Every nook and cranny was to be fortified; minefields were to be sown about every warp point, however far from the front; and massive covering forces were to be organized at nodal positions. It all amounted to an enormous diversion of industrial effort and priceless warships from offensive duties, and the impact on future operations would be profound.

And it is all so pointless, he thought moodily. *Even if the fears are correct, the sheer size of the fleets these Bugs commit will make a mockery of our efforts. We cannot fortify every system sufficiently to stop them, and so all our efforts will do nothing but divert desperately needed strength into public relations activities which ultimately accomplish nothing.*

Maariaah was not alone in his feelings. Both the Human Antonov and First Fang Ynaathar had protested the new directives, but in vain. The political leaders—*Zheeerlikou'valkhannaieee* and Human alike—refused to heed them, and even in the Khanate, warriors had no choice but to obey orders.

And in this particular case, Maariaah conceded unhappily, those directives actually made sense, for the warp point SF 80 was about to explore was in a terrifying location. It lay in the Rehfrak System . . . a sector capital with a population even greater than Kliean's had been.

The small claw's lips wrinkled with disgust as he considered the long dead commander of the original Rehfrak survey. Type Eleven warp points were elusive, but the instruments of the time had been quite capable of locating them. It would have required a considerable investment in time, however, and Claw Faairnaas had been in a hurry. He had skimped on the survey—a cursory reading of his log made that plain—and this was the result: an open, unsurveyed warp point at the heart of one of the Khanate's oldest, wealthiest and most heavily populated sectors.

Well, at least Rehfrak, unlike Kliean, had been fortified for over three Orion centuries. Once the initial panic passed, three dozen powerful OWPs had been towed to cover the newly discovered warp point, and the KON had assembled over a hundred warships to support them.

Quite an escort for one lowly survey flotilla, Maariaah thought, then tensed as *Harkhan* began to move towards the invisible hole in space. Soon enough, they would know if all this military might was no more than the wasted effort Maariaah devoutly prayed it was.

The transit surge passed, and Maariaah's ships vanished into cloak. After Shanak and Kliean, the Alliance had no choice but to assume the Bugs maintained pickets in every explored system, however useless. Henceforth, every survey force would operate only in cloak, which made sense but was expensive in both equipment wear and time. A cloaked vessel could not use active sensors, which cut its sensor reach by seventy percent, with a consequent increase in the time required to cover a given volume. Using larger survey forces could offset some of that, yet every ship added to a flotilla also increased the odds that it would be detected, despite its ECM.

And, of course, a Bug picket in precisely the right place might pick them up on transit, before they could bring their cloaking systems up, setting all their efforts at stealth at naught.

But in this case, Maariaah decided, it was unlikely any picket was present. Their entry warp point was a Type One five light-hours from the G8 component of a binary system. Component B was a dimmer K8, almost six light-hours from Component A and five hundred light-minutes from *Harkhan* as the light cruiser emerged from warp. But the important point was that Component A had a planet at six light-minutes, well within its liquid water zone. It also boasted a large asteroid belt at twenty-one light-minutes, with all the industrial advantages that offered, yet there were no artificial emissions, and the Bugs would surely have developed such prime real estate . . . had they known of it. No one, least of all Maariaah'sheerino, was going to assume anything—not with the bleeding wound of Kliean so fresh—yet he felt an undeniable easing of the tension about him as his officers worked their way to the same conclusion.

"All units' ECM is up, Small Claw," Shaairal reported, and Maariaah flicked his ears in approval.

"Well executed, Son of the Khan. Transmit my thanks to all units—discreetly, of course."

"Certainly, Sir."

"And while you are about it, set up our initial spiral," Maariaah added. "We will proceed cautiously, but the sooner we begin, the sooner we can move on to still more emptiness."

❖   ❖   ❖

Survey Flotilla 80 prowled stealthily about Component A. The warp points of a binary system were invariably associated with the more massive star, moving in their own, fixed relationship with it. The math which described the phenomenon always made Maariaah's head ache, but he was grateful for the way it reduced his survey area. By his most conservative estimate, however, the task would still consume at least two months, and more probably three, and he bent his attention on ways to keep his personnel alert as they settled in for the duration. What had happened to Kliean made that easier, but nothing could fully offset the sheer, mind-numbing tedium of their task. No one who had never participated in a first survey could truly appreciate the sheer immensity of any star system, and warp points were elusive prey.

Days passed, then weeks, and the cloaked ships continued their methodical activity, winnowing space for the tiny gravitational eddies which might indicate yet another warp point.

Maariaah was sound asleep when the alarm wrenched him from dreams of his wife and cubs. He lurched upright on his sleeping mat, stabbing for the com button even before his eyes opened, and light flared in his darkened cabin as his terminal came on-line.

"Bridge," a taut voice said, then changed as the officer of the watch recognized the small claw. "*Chaarkhan* has just reported detection of what may be an unknown starship, Sir!"

"*May?*" Maariaah repeated sharply.

"Yes, Small Claw. If it is, it, too, is cloaked."

An icy fist squeezed Maariaah's stomach, and he made himself pause. It would do neither his image nor the crew's nerve any service to appear flustered, and so he kept his voice level.

"Location?"

"Thirty-one light-minutes from *Harkhan* at zero-six-three, two-five-one, Sir."

"Do we have a vector?"

"No, Small Claw. It appears to be stationary."

Either that, or the dairshnakhu *saw* Chaarkhan *and went dead,* Maariaah thought grimly. *If he truly exists at all, he is pretending to be a hole in space and waiting for us to make a move.*

"Is Son of the Khan Shaairal there?"

"I have just arrived, Small Claw," Shaairal's voice said, and *Harkhan's* captain's face replaced that of the duty officer. "The flotilla has implemented standing orders, Sir."

"Good. I am on my way. Do nothing but observe until I arrive."

Maariaah's mind raced as he killed the com, scrambled from his mat, and reached for his harness. *Chaarkhan* might have detected only a sensor ghost, but he dared not assume anything of the sort. Yet how should he proceed? His standing orders had brought the entire flotilla to a halt, which reduced its drive signatures to a bare minimum and made its cloaking systems far more effective, but ships which did not move could not close to obtain better data.

The one thing he absolutely could *not* do was send word back to Rehfrak. Courier drones could not cloak, and a drone's vector would give the Bugs—if there *were* any Bugs!—a bearing on the flotilla's entry warp point. No, he must somehow determine whether or not the enemy was present, first. Then, if he had the firepower, he must destroy any pickets before *their* drones reported *his* presence. If he could not destroy them, he must somehow break contact with at least one of his ships and send it back to Rehfrak with word of the danger.

Whatever he did, the next few days would not be pleasant.

"There it is again, Sir," Observer First Cheraahlk said.

Maariaah raised a hand, stopping the flotilla's senior engineer in mid-report, and watched Cheraahlk lean forward. The observer babied his passive sensors and computers as he worked the elusive contact, and then his ears flattened in disgust.

"*Shiaaahk!*" He looked up, expression apologizing for the oath, but Maariaah waved it off. The last six days had been even less pleasant than anticipated. The unknowns—and there was no longer any doubt *someone* else was in the system—were fiendishly elusive, and Cheraahlk was his best sensor officer . . . and more than entitled to an occasional curse.

"Did you get any more on him?"

"Not much, Small Claw," Cheraahlk said apologetically.

"Anything at all will be welcome," Maariaah assured him.

"Observe your plot, please, Sir," Cheraahlk requested, and a crimson icon appeared on the small claw's repeater display. The observer replayed his entire brief track on it, and Maariaah watched it slide across the very edge of the sensor envelope and then vanish once more. "His instrumentation must be at least as good as our own," Cheraahlk said. "He knew we were here—not our precise location, but our general position—and came in for a closer look, then broke back out before we got a good lock. I think it was Unknown Three this time, Sir, but it could have been one we have not seen before."

Maariaah flicked his ears and keyed a replay command. The icon slid across the display once more, and there was something damnably familiar about it. Its maneuver was not one a ship of the *Zheeerlikou'valkhannaieee* would have employed, yet he had the maddening sense that he had seen it—or one like it—before.

He replayed it again and muttered a mental curse of his own. That sharp yet graceful turn *was* familiar . . . and Cheraahlk was right. The unknown's scanners must be at least as good as *Harkhan*'s. Probably better, for she had not picked it up until it was well into its sensor run.

Any cloaking field leaked a little energy, and the emission patterns which oozed through it were distinctive, and so far, Survey Flotilla Eighty had made tentative IDs on at least five unknowns. Their antics demonstrated that they knew Maariaah's command was present, yet they had launched no attacks, and every battle report Maariaah had seen suggested that the Bugs *should* have attacked by now, if only to draw his fire. Such a maneuver would almost certainly result in the destruction of the attacking unit, yet it would absolutely confirm the presence of his own units and give hard locations on the ships which fired. Given the enemy's willingness to sacrifice starships, Maariaah had anticipated just such an attempt for days now.

Yet it had not happened . . . and there was that nagging sense he had seen such a maneuver before. But where? Try as he might, he could not recall, and it was driving him mad.

He leaned back in his chair and folded his hands across his belly, tapping his claws together while he thought. There was a limit to how long he could let this game of hunt the *marhang* continue. Whether the Bugs knew it or not, *he* knew they posed a deadly threat to Rehfrak, and his overriding responsibility was to alert the sector capital.

He thought a moment longer, then beckoned Shaairal to his side and spoke quietly.

"Cheraahlk is correct, Shaairal. Whoever this is, his instrumentation is excellent. We are unlikely to pin him down without assistance, and we must warn Rehfrak. We dare not use a courier drone, so we must use one of our ships."

"Risky, Small Claw," Shaairal murmured. It was not a protest, simply a consideration of the difficulties, and Maariaah flicked his ears in agreement.

"Truth, Son of the Khan, yet I see no option. We will detach *Fraikhal*, *Mhote*, and *Shergha*. *Shergha* will be our courier, and the other two will accompany her to the warp point and screen her. She will hold position just clear of the warp point while they run a sweep around it, and she will make transit only when they report all clear."

"With your permission, Sir, I will add *Jhusahk* and *Timkhar*," Shaairal replied. "Daughter of the Khan Deaara has the next best observer after Cheraahlk himself, and I trust her judgment."

"An excellent thought," Maariaah agreed, "and—"

"*Communication laser!*"

Both officers whirled to the com officer in shock. The young cub of the Khan raised a hand, cupping his ear bug as if to somehow hear better, then looked up in total disbelief.

"Someone is lasing us, Small Claw! It— Sir, it appears to be a standard Alliance com protocol!"

An *Alliance* protocol? Maariaah looked at Shaairal, and the son of the khan gave an ear flick of helplessness. Was it possible the Bugs had somehow cracked a captured Allied database when the Alliance had persistently failed to crack theirs?

"Put it on intercom," he ordered, and a voice rattled the speakers. Maariaah read Standard English, but his understanding of the spoken language was poor, and he looked at Shaairal for a translation.

"He says 'Unknown vessel, this is the Terraaan vessel *Maaashhaaanaaa*. Identify yourself or be fired upon.'"

"*Maaashhaaanaaa?*" Maariaah repeated. "What sort of ship name is that?"

"Sir, I have her on our shipping list," Shaairal's tactical officer reported. "According to the file, she is one of their *Hun*-class survey cruisers."

"*Hun*-class, is it?" Maariaah wished—not for the first time—that all TFN ships could have such easily pronounced names rather than the clumsy sounds Humans kept inflicting on the poor things. But the thought was only a flicker on the surface of his mind, for the *Huns* were survey ships, like his own *Harkhan*. Was it truly possible—?

"Sir, the challenge is repeating," the com officer said nervously, and the assistant tactical officer spoke almost in the same breath.

"Captain, I am picking up fire control emissions from at least five sources!"

"Very well," Maariaah said far more calmly than he felt. "Com, reply 'This is the *Zheeerlikou'valkhannaieee* cruiser *Harkhan*,'" the cub of the khan acknowledged and

Maariaah looked at the tac officer. "If this is a ruse, he will fire the instant he receives our reply. Be ready."

"Aye, Small Claw."

A moment of intolerable tension hovered, and then the voice came from the speakers again. It spoke much more slowly this time, slowly enough even Maariaah could follow it.

"*Harkhan*, this is Captain Josepha Vargas, TFN, commanding Survey Flotilla Two-Five- One. You've had us worried," it said.

CHAPTER THIRTY-ONE

Hell's Gate

Small Claw Maariaah watched his plot's icons and tried—unsuccessfully—not to feel envious. His *Lahstyn*-class cruisers represented the best compromise the Khanate could afford: well equipped to avoid detection, yet extremely austere, without even command datalink. The KON simply could not divert sufficient funding to build the numbers of survey ships it required if it opted for any more sophisticated design, but the Terran Federation could . . . and had.

Maariaah was senior to Captain Vargas, the Human survey force commander, yet his ships, for all their numbers, made a poor showing beside her command. TFNS *Belisarius*, her flagship, was one of the new *Guerriere-B* command battlecruisers, with the control systems to provide a datanet for her entire flotilla, and her actual survey ships were all *Hun-Bs*, refitted with military engines. It reduced their strategic speed but gave them the tactical fleetness to outrun any Bugs they happened across—just as *Belisarius*' datalink gave them an excellent chance of outfighting any picket cruisers which crossed their path. And what Maariaah envied most of all, perhaps, was TFNS *Caravan*, an armed freighter built on a converted *Dunkerque*-class battlecruiser hull and equipped with cloaking ECM as well as a light missile battery. *Caravan*'s cargo capacity was the final support element which allowed the TFN to mount long-ranged, sustained survey operations which the KON simply could not match.

And the crowning element in Maariaah's ignoble envy were the eighty brand-new second-generation recon drones in *Caravan's* capacious holds. The Humans had finally gotten warp-capable drones into production, and the all but invisible robots let Vargas probe warp points at greatly reduced risk of detection . . . and without exposing her own ships to hostile action.

It was, he thought, a lesson in the advantages of affluence, and not even the fact that the Humans were shipping thousands of the new RD2s to the Khanate completely eased its sting.

Yet for all that, Vargas had reached the system Maariaah had named Zaaia'pharaan, in honor of his maternal granddam, only after his own flotilla. Zaaia'pharaan lay at the extreme end of a frontier warp line Vargas had been engaged in extending, and so was of far less value to the Federation than to the Khanate. No doubt the Humans would have ceded it to their allies for that reason alone, but under the Treaty of Mattar, a system belonged to whoever reached it first, and Vargas had readily acknowledged the *Zheeerlikou'valkhannaieee's* prior claim on Zaaia'pharaan.

Still, they were allies, and they were here, and he and Vargas had decided to operate in concert. Once they had realized they were playing catch-as-catch-can with allies rather than enemies—*or, rather, once* Vaaargaaas, *with her superior instrumentation, realized it*, the small claw reminded himself sourly—they had not taken long to complete their sweep of the system. They had found no sign of enemy vessels, but they *had* detected two additional warp points, and they would soon make the first move to explore them.

In the meantime, Rehfrak had been brought up to date. Vargas' relief at having a powerful fleet in support distance had been unmistakable, but the Human least claw had also realized why Maariaah was so nervous. She had no more desire than he to show the Bugs the way to Rehfrak, and it was she who had suggested that the fleet element remain in the sector capital rather than advance to Zaaia'pharaan. Under the circumstances, it was more important to keep the Rehfrak connection secret than to protect the survey ships. In the event that the enemy was encountered and managed to track them, the Humans had agreed that their combined force would fall back on *Human* space, leading the Bugs away from Rehfrak. Given that no inhabited Human system lay within twelve transits, the Federation had far more depth to play with. As to who held title to any additional systems they jointly discovered, that would be up to the diplomats, although Maariaah suspected the Khanate's possession of Zaaia'pharaan would give it the inside track.

"Caaaptain Vaaargaaas reports that she is prepared to deploy the first drone flight, Sir," Shaairal reported, and Maariaah flicked an ear in acknowledgment.

"Instruct her to proceed," he said.

"All right, Mal," Josepha Vargas said. "We've got an audience of Tabbies just waiting to see how well our new toy works. Let's not embarrass ourselves."

"I think that can be arranged, Sir," Commander Malcolm Klesko replied, "but please remember these things are still on the temperamental side."

"I'll be totally sympathetic," she assured him. "Right after I skin you out and salt down the hide."

"You're so understanding," Klesko sighed, but he grinned as he spoke. The RD2 was his baby, for he'd been assistant project officer on the team which finally got it into production. That was why Vargas had specifically requested him, and getting her request granted was a major coup for her. Yet they both knew he was right. The new drones were—or would be, once they got the kinks out of them—an enormous boon to Survey Command, but they were still a new system, and the conditions under which they had to operate were harsh.

Although larger than courier drones, they were smaller

than anything else which had ever been capable of making even a single transit, and single transits were useless for survey missions. They had to get through the warp point, look around, *and* come back. So far, about one in three was getting home, but only one survivor in ten brought back any useful data; the internal systems of the other nine were hopelessly addled by the brutal stress of a first-transit through an uncharted warp point. R&D promised the failure rate would drop, but the most optimistic success rate projected, even for the fully matured technology, was no more than forty to fifty percent.

"Just do your best," Vargas said, and Klesko nodded before he keyed his boom mike.

"Final systems check," he said crisply.

"All green, Sir," Ensign Michaelson replied instantly.

"Very well. Activate the first flight."

"Activating now," Michaelson confirmed, and Klesko watched his display.

The RD2s were too large to launch from XO racks. Instead, they had to be deployed from a cargo hold, preflighted in space by vac-suited technicians, and then sent on their way. It was all very complicated, but Klesko felt a glow of satisfaction as the first ten drones brought their drives on-line, headed for the warp point in a chain of glittering icons, and one by one vanished.

"Telemetry lost," Michaelson reported, exactly on the tick, and Klesko nodded and tipped his chair back to keep an eye on the time. All they could do now was wait.

"Those are very difficult sensor targets, Small Claw," Observer First Cheraahlk said in tones of deep respect.

"Good," Maariaah grunted. "Perhaps the enemy will find them equally difficult to detect," he added, and other officers flicked their ears in sober agreement.

"I wonder if Caaaptain Vaaargaaas would sell us a few?" *Harkhan*'s tac officer mused.

"I shall ask her," Maariaah assured him with a purring chuckle. "Of course, we would also have to rent *Caravaaan* to haul them around for us!"

"I have nothing else to spend my exorbitant salary on, Sir," the tac officer replied, and a wave of laughter rippled around the bridge.

Malcolm Klesko checked the time—again—and nodded. Assuming the warp point didn't lead to a black hole or something equally drastic, he should see something just . . . about . . . *now*.

"Transit beacon!" Ensign Michaelson sang out, and Klesko grinned. "I've got another one— No, wait . . . Correction, Sir. I have a total of four beacons!"

"Outstanding!" Klesko replied. A forty percent return rate was the highest they'd managed yet, but he reminded himself not to start celebrating too soon. The mere fact that his babies had returned didn't mean they'd come home coherent, and he began inputting commands.

The first drone was a disappointment; his techs *might* be able to overhaul the systems for reuse, but the memory core was a compete write-off, and he moved on to number two.

Aha! *That* was better. The second-stage astro data was shot, which meant the drone could provide no information on whatever lay beyond the warp point, but first-stage memory was intact. That gave him a readout on the grav stresses, and even if the other two drones contained no data at all, he'd be able to program the second flight for a much gentler transit, which would enhance the chance of obtaining recoverable data by at least a factor of ten.

He tapped a key, downloading the grav data to Plotting, and let the astrogation techs play with it while he moved on.

Drone three was a complete write-off. He doubted there was even much point in trying to salvage components, but he handed it off to Michaelson's crew anyway. They might get *some* use out of it, and the things were expensive enough to make the effort worthwhile.

Despite the blank on number three, Klesko felt

decidedly cheerful as he turned to number four. The grav readout alone justified all the hard work R&D had put in on the system, and—

His thoughts broke off as the drone's memory downloaded to his display. He stared at it for a moment, trying to convince himself he was really seeing it, then looked over his shoulder.

"Captain," he said very, very quietly, "I think you'd better look at this."

The tension hit Small Claw Maariaah and Son of the Khan Shaairal like a fist as Josepha Vargas' exec led them into TFNS *Belisarius'* briefing room. Neither was particularly skilled at reading human expressions, but their hosts' taut, unnatural stillness required little skill.

"Thank you for coming, Small Claw," Vargas said quietly, rising to greet the visitors.

"No thanks are necessary, Caaaptain," Maariaah replied after Shaairal had translated. "Your vessel's data systems are far better suited to processing and displaying this information."

Vargas dipped her head in a small bow and waved the two Orions to chairs. She waited until they were seated, then nodded to Klesko.

The commander cleared his throat—he was more accustomed to dealing with machinery than Tabbies, and he was very much the man on the spot—and brought the holo unit up. A small-scale display of the system beyond the warp point appeared, and he picked up his light pencil and spoke slowly, allowing Shaairal time to translate for the small claw.

"As you can see, gentlemen, we don't have much detail," he began. "The drones' sensors are the best we can build into such a small package, but they aren't very powerful compared to a full-sized starship's. Nonetheless, I think the imagery speaks for itself."

He used the light pencil to pick out the icon of the drone's entry warp point.

"This is a Type Fourteen closed point. That's the good

news. *This*—" the light pencil moved to the two innermost orbital shells of the G3 primary "—is the *bad* news."

The Human, Maariaah thought, had a distinct talent for understatement. The planets lay at six and ten light-minutes respectively, well within the liquid water zone, and they were a solid glare of high-level emissions. Worse, the closed warp point lay little more than a light-hour out, well below the system ecliptic. That had given the drone an excellent look "up" at its environs, and the space between the star's asteroid belt and those planets was heavy with drive fields.

Bug drive fields.

The small claw shivered. Undoubtedly, most of those drives belonged to freighters and resource ships, but there were over two hundred. Gods alone knew how many the drone had *not* seen, and, for the first time, Maariaah realized emotionally, not just intellectually, how massively the enemy exploited star systems. That many ships suggested an industrial base *at least* five times as great as that of any Orion system he had ever seen . . . and it lay two transits from Rehfrak.

Fathers of Sheerino, he thought numbly. *The very thing every Allied strategist dreams of finding, a closed warp point in the very heart of an enemy core system, and it lies* here.

"It's an El Dorado, gentlemen," Klesko said, "and I wish to God it was anywhere else."

"Truth, Commaaander," Maariaah said softly.

"Small Claw, this system belongs to the Khanate," Josepha Vargas said. "Whatever the Joint Chiefs ultimately decide, the immediate decision must be yours. Shall I send the second-flight drones through or suspend operations pending the decision of higher authority?"

Maariaah gazed at the holo—at the priceless axis of attack which was also the very gate of Hell for Rehfrak—and knew the Human captain was right. The decision *was* his.

"How confident are you that your drones have not been detected?" he asked.

"Mal?" Vargas said.

"I'm totally confident that no one actually observed their transit, Small Claw," Klesko replied. "This drone's systems came through in remarkably good shape. If anything had been close enough to spot such a small signature, the drone would have picked it up, even if it was cloaked. But we lost six drones somewhere in-system. The odds are vanishingly small that *we* could ever find them once power exhaustion takes their telemetry links off-line. The only way I could be sure of finding them would be to trigger their homing beacons, and the Bugs can't do that without the access codes. But there *is* a chance someone could literally stumble over them."

"Not a high one, I should think," Shaairal put in. "There appears to be no traffic near this warp point—not surprisingly, given how close to the primary it lies. One does not find many warp points so close in, and it also lies below the ecliptic. Surely there is only a very small chance any of their ships would come close enough to it to pick up such low-signature objects."

"No doubt you're correct, Sir," Klesko agreed, "and that's exactly what we designed the drones to accomplish. But 'unlikely' isn't 'impossible.' There *is* a chance, however slight."

"And if we insert additional drones, we increase that chance," Maariaah observed.

"True." Vargas sighed. She leaned back in her chair, one hand toying with a lock of short brown hair, and let her worried eyes sweep her own officers, then looked directly at Maariaah.

"Small Claw, there's going to be enormous pressure to use this warp point as soon as possible—especially from my people," she said flatly. "We've been totally on the defensive from Day One, and so far we've taken far more damage than we've inflicted. No doubt some of your own fangs will feel the same way, but you and I both know what a double-edged sword this is." Maariaah was unfamiliar with the metaphor, but he grasped the implications instantly when Shaairal translated, and he gave a vigorous human-style nod. "Is your Navy in a position to guarantee Rehfrak's security if this operation goes sour?" she asked bluntly.

"No." Maariaah's reply was equally blunt. He disliked admitting that, but it was only truth, and the stakes were too great for anything less.

"Neither can we," Vargas said. "We're a long way from the closest Terran naval base, and our covering force is no more than a heavy task group." She looked around once more, then nodded sharply. "Under the circumstances, I recommend against deploying the second flight."

"I concur, Sir," Shaairal said, and Maariaah flicked his ears in agreement, profoundly relieved by the human's attitude.

"I think that wise," he said after a moment. "We can always send more probes through later, and I would feel much better with powerful support forces in position first."

"As would I." Vargas looked back at the holo and sighed. "I've been looking for exactly this since the war started. Now I've got it, and I wish to hell I didn't. Or that it was somewhere out back of beyond. But at least this time we found *it* instead of them finding *us*, Small Claw."

"Truth," Maariaah said again, and bared just the tips of his fangs. "It is nice to be on the finding end for a change, is it not?"

"As long as it doesn't turn around and eat us after all, Small Fang," Vargas said very quietly, eyes still on the holo. "As long as it doesn't turn around and eat us."

CHAPTER THIRTY-TWO

Questions of Command

Kthaara'zarthan gazed at his *vilkshatha* brother, and shook his head slowly in what he'd learned was a gesture reflecting sorrowful contemplation of the depths of Human evil.

"I fear you have let it go to your head, as you Humans say, Eeevahn'zarthan."

Ivan Antonov grinned at him. Kthaara's pronunciation of his first name certainly came closer than the butchery—roughly, EYE-van—committed by native speakers of Standard English. "Come, Kthaara Kornazhovich," he said in a mollifying tone. "You know me better than to think I'd let my head be turned by this 'Grand Alliance Commander in Chief' nonsense. The only advantage it has is that, because some people *are* stupid enough to take it seriously, it lets me cut through the bureaucratic shit and get some things done more expeditiously than I used to as simple chairman of the Joint Chiefs of Staff."

"Like appointing yourself to command the offensive to be launched from Zaaia'pharaan," Kthaara accused.

Antonov smiled. "Be honest, Kthaasha. Is it the Khan's agreement to cede Zephrain?" (He used the human compromise with the impossible handle Maariaah'sheerino had given the system.) "Is that what's really bothering you?"

"It is not my place to question the Khan's decisions,"

Kthaara huffed. Then he relaxed with the suddenness that could still catch Antonov by surprise after sixty years. "And besides, I have to admit that this one makes sense. It is just so . . . well, unprecedented."

Antonov nodded, understanding Kthaara's feelings. The Orions were a conservative lot. And the agreement *was* extraordinary. But so was the dilemma the Khan and his advisers had found themselves in. Their very genes—to say nothing of the white-hot memory of Kliean—had cried out to them to use Zephrain for an offensive into what was clearly part of the Bug industrial heartland. But with the thought of Kliean had come the chilling realization of what could happen if a Bug counterstroke penetrated to Rehfrak. And the Khanate, unlike the Federation, could not spare the industrial capacity to undertake a massive new program of defensive construction.

So the Khan had stunned his Terran allies by offering to cede Zephrain to them in fee simple, in exchange for their pledge to fortify it—and also Rehfrak itself—beyond any reasonable possibility of danger should the offensive go awry. The Federation had accepted, and agreed to postpone the attack until the work of castramentation was complete. And so the freighters had begun to ply the route to Zephrain, laden with modular components of Fortress Command's prefabricated orbital weapons platforms and with the myriads of cheap but lethal mines that would envelop the crucial warp points with clouds of death. Those freighters' databases, like those of all Allied ships that would operate in Zephrain space, were innocent of all knowledge of the warp link to Rehfrak; secrecy, as much as firepower, would shield the Khan's subjects.

The titanic project was by no means complete, but it was far enough along for Antonov and his staff to begin planning the offensive that would set out from an impregnable Zephrain. And to name that offensive's commander . . .

Antonov smiled again. "Don't mope, Kthaasha. You

know I wouldn't do it if I didn't have you to leave here as acting chairman of the Joint Chiefs. As it is, I know I won't have anything to worry about." (Kthaara gave the brief low-pitched growl that was the equivalent of a human snort.) "And besides, you ought to be happy with my choice for a battle-line commander."

The ebon Orion brightened slightly. "Ah, yes: Least Fang Raaaymmonnd'pressscott—or Raaaymmonnd'*telmasa,* as he is now entitled to be known. A most impressive officer . . . for a Human. And one with whom you should feel something in common."

"True. Not every human has sworn *vilkshatha.*" In point of fact, aside from Antonov himself, Prescott was the *only* one who had. That had been just before he'd left for Alpha Centauri, to recover from his wounds and provide Grand Fleet with the benefit of his experience. So, unlike his *vilkshatha* brother, he'd missed the brutal slugging match of Second Kliean, when Lord Khiniak had retaken the system . . . and a remark Antonov had made during the Theban War had come back to haunt him. "Even a small planetary population is hard to completely extirpate, short of rendering the planet uninhabitable," he'd said, and the Bugs evidently agreed, because that was precisely what they'd done—and the population of Kliean had been far from small. All at once, the Khanate of Orion had lost interest in counting the cost. The Bugs had found that out when they'd returned to Kliean two and a half months later.

Third Kliean had been a see-saw exercise in mutual slaughter, with Third Fleet stopping the attempted reconquest and following the defeated Bugs back to Shanak. The Gorm, no less than the Orions, had felt the need to avenge the ghosts of Kliean; they had volunteered to take their first newly produced gunboats into Shanak in simultaneous transits—the first time the Allies had used that mad tactic. But Third Fleet, weakened by short-range plasma-gun fire and wholesale suicide attacks, had lacked the strength to seize Shanak and hold it against newly arriving Bug reinforcements. So the war in the Kliean chain had settled into the kind of standoff that Vanessa Murakuma already knew only too well.

There was no longer any serious debate in the Grand Alliance over the reimplementation of General Directive 18—the genocide directive that had been invoked only once before. The screech of static that had answered Third Fleet's communications hails in Kliean had put an end to *all* such debate in the Khanate, and the few human dissenters like Bettina Wister were now isolated even within their own Liberal-Progressive Party. The only problem had been the lack of any apparent way to effectuate the directive with the war stalemated on both fronts . . . until the discovery of Zephrain.

Antonov shook free of his thoughts. "*Da*, you're right. Vice Admiral Prescott and I share something unique among humans. And we also share something else: frustration. You know how much it's galled him to be absent from the battles at Kliean."

"Naturally." Kthaara nodded—a Human habit that had become second nature to him. "Anyone worthy of being asked to swear *vilkshatha* can only feel like a caged *zeget* when wounds or duty keep him from his *vilkshatha* brother's side in a desperate battle."

"There's more to it than that," Antonov said grimly. "He felt his place was at the head of his own personnel at Second Kliean. When he learned Rear Admiral Jackson had died there . . . well, there's a common phenomenon called 'survivor's guilt.'"

"It is not unknown among my own race," Kthaara remarked. "But we tend to deal with it by seeking vengeance against the killers of whomever we feel somehow died in our place. Least Fang Pressscott should find no lack of opportunities for vengeance when we launch our offensive from Zaaia'pharaan against these . . . these . . . I will not even call them *chofaki*, for it does them too much honor and dilutes a perfectly good insult." The Orion's voice remained so controlled that few humans would even have realized he was controlling it. But Antonov did, and he didn't interrupt the few heartbeats of silence that followed. Then Kthaara smiled his teeth-hidden carnivore's smile. "And now, back to business. I believe we are due at the staff conference soon."

"Attention on deck," Raymond Prescott said quietly, as senior officer in the conference room.

"As you were," Antonov rumbled as he and Kthaara moved to their seats. He looked around the table and at the holo dais where the image of Marcus LeBlanc had come to attention and was now resuming its seat as the actual Bug expert was doing in New Atlantis. "Admiral LeBlanc, I believe I saw you in deep discussion with Captain Kozlov a moment ago. I trust this means you have completed your analysis of the observational data from Second Kliean."

"Yes, Sir," LeBlanc affirmed. "In essence, we've confirmed the surmise of Lord Khiniak's people. The Bugs have learned to launch antifighter missiles from their gunboats. It surprised Third Fleet, which was the principal reason for our heavy fighter losses." (Prescott, outside the holo pickup and thus unnoticed by LeBlanc, winced.) "There's nothing mysterious about it; we've known all along that the gunboats could mount standard missiles as external ordinance, so there's no real engineering obstacle to fitting them with AFHAWKs. It's just one more indication that the Bugs are capable of more flexibility and inventiveness than we'd like them to have."

"That doesn't worry me as much as the sheer damned determination with which they fought," said Antonov's chief of staff. Captain Blanton Stovall was a scion of one of the TFN's "dynasties": families, mostly Russian or North American (like Stovall's) in origin, but including a fair number of Europeans in which Federation service had been a tradition for as long as there'd *been* a Federation. A stocky, sandy-haired type, he was as stolid and imperturbable as he looked.

"You can't really use terms like 'determination' or 'courage' in connection with the Bugs, Captain," LeBlanc admonished. "They're not applicable—"

"Indeed not," Kthaara muttered, unheard by anyone but Antonov.

"—because for virtues like those to have any meaning, there has to be the option of *not* acting that way."

"Oh, yes, I understand all that, Admiral LeBlanc. It just disturbs me that whatever they use as a substitute seems to work altogether too damned well."

Antonov cleared his throat. "This is aside from the point, gentlemen. I wish to defer consideration of Admiral LeBlanc's conclusions until later. First, we need to take up an organizational matter. The command structure for the offensive from Zephrain is now complete, with one exception: a commander for the carrier component. None of the possibilities we've discussed to date have been satisfactory, for various reasons. The floor is open to suggestions."

"I have one, Sir," Raymond Prescott said quietly. The newly named commander of Task Force 21 was flanked by his chief of staff, Captain Anthea Mandagalla—a very tall, very black woman from the planet Christophe—and Commander Jacques Bichet, his ops officer. "From any number of standpoints, I believe the best possible choice would be Least Fang Zhaarnak'telmasa."

Antonov gave Prescott an intense look. The visible signs of his wounds were now mostly gone. His hair—prematurely iron-gray, shading to nearly white at the temples—had grown back enough for a haircut that was short but even. And he had so adjusted to his prosthetic arm that it seemed as entirely natural to others as it usually did to him. There was still the barest hint of a limp when he walked. But when, as now, he was seated, it was easy to forget that he had been seared by forces of a kind that normally left no survivors, however scarred.

"Some might argue, Admiral Prescott," Antonov spoke mildly, "that yours is not an altogether unbiased recommendation."

"I'm aware of that, Sir. But my special relationship with Least Fang Zhaarnak doesn't alter the facts. His record in Alowan and Telmasa speaks for itself. And even if it didn't, the *Ithyrra'doi'khanhaku* would." Of course, Prescott didn't mention the blue-and-gold ribbon nestled among the rows of colorful cloth on his own left breast. The Orions didn't use ribbons to represent medals on service dress uniforms, and the TFN had had to hastily design one for a decoration it had never expected to see awarded to a human. "Furthermore, Sir, I would ask you to consider his more recent record. I refer in particular to the great moral courage he displayed during the Third Battle of Kliean . . . as Lord Khiniak himself has acknowledged."

Everyone present understood what he meant. Koraaza'khiniak had decided to withhold a considerable percentage of his SBMHAWK inventory from the initial strike into Shanak, looking ahead to the problem of securing the warp point after his fleet had transited. Zhaarnak had protested, respectfully but vehemently, doubting the adequacy of a first SBMHAWK wave that should have been ample against a normal enemy. Events had proven him right.

A cleared throat broke the silence, and Antonov turned to his ops officer. "Yes, Commander?"

Armand de Bertholet leaned forward with the eagerness, tinged with impetuosity, that he seemed to bring to everything he did. He was a younger son of one of the noble families of Durendal, and while cosmopolitan experience had long since worn away whatever aristocratic affectations he might have once possessed, he was inescapably a product of a culture that embodied a romantic worldview and valued dash. Not all Fringe Worlds had been settled by groups with roots sunk deep into pre-space Terra's ethnic topsoil. Some of the pioneering societies had been frankly artificial ones, cultures built around an idea rather than a sociopolitical reality. Antonov sometimes thought they *all* were, in greater or lesser degree; but some, such as the neo-feudalism of Durendal, were more obvious about it than most.

"If I may, Sir," he said, "I'd like to add another argument to Admiral Prescott's. It is essential that the tactical command structure for our offensive include representation of our allies of the *Zheeerlikou'valkhannaieee*." He wasn't as much of a "Tabby expert" as most of Antonov's staffers, but he made a creditable effort at pronouncing the name. "And what better field for that representation than the fighter operations at which they are admittedly pre-eminent? At the same time, Least Fang Zhaarnak has demonstrated an ability to work in close conjunction with humans—a necessity in what will, inevitably, be a predominantly human expedition."

"Commander de Bertholet has a point, Sir," said Midori Kozlov. It was unusual for the staff spook to outrank the ops officer, as Kozlov outranked de Bertholet, in the TFN, and the fact that intelligence officers were restricted line—specialists outside the direct chain of command—further muddied the waters. If Kozlov and de Bertholet had been the only two officers left alive aboard a ship, he would have been in command, and she made it a point not to stomp too hard on his toes. "Least Fang Zhaarnak's adaptability to cooperating with humans is all the more remarkable in light of what we know of his lifelong attitudes." She gave Kthaara a half-apologetic look.

"We are all adults here, Captain Khozzloff," the Orion said with a smile. "As such, I doubt if any of us are shocked by the fact that intelligence services take an interest in their allies as well as their enemies. I would be surprised if you did *not* have dossiers on senior officers of the Khan."

"Your attitude is much appreciated, Lord Talphon," Kozlov replied, trying to match his suavity.

"And furthermore," Kthaara went on, "you are absolutely right. Least Fang Zhaarnak has indeed demonstrated a capacity for growth—one which I doubt you can fully appreciate, not being directly acquainted with those of my race who belong to his father's school of thought." He turned to Antonov. "I concur: Least Fang Pressscott's suggestion is eminently sound. Zhaarnak would be an ideal choice for carrier commander."

"Lord Khiniak won't want to lose him," Antonov rumbled. "In fact, we won't need courier drones to hear him bellowing. Still, he'll have to admit Zhaarnak could do more good in a war of movement, which is what we have a chance of turning this one into when we attack from Zephrain. He's wasted on a deadlocked front. Yes." He brightened. "As I was saying earlier, Kthaara Kornazhovich, this 'Grand Alliance Commander in Chief' business has its uses when it comes to getting things done. Of course, I'll go through First Fang Ynaathar." The Khanate's senior officer had, of necessity, been named second in command when Antonov had gotten his new title. "But yes, we'll have him report here as soon as possible."

He gave Raymond Prescott a sideways look and noted the seemingly intensifying life in that face. Yes, he reflected, Zhaarnak would make an excellent carrier commander. But, just as importantly, Prescott would make an even better battle-line commander with Zhaarnak present. Antonov knew full well what it meant to have one's *vilkshatha* brother guarding one's back, and as he gazed surreptitiously at the one human with whom he shared that knowledge, he knew that whatever enhanced that man's attainment of his full potential was very much worth doing.

CHAPTER THIRTY-THREE

"Security is relative."

Commander Nobiki Murakuma had found that being the older daughter of one of Battle Fleet's rising captains—and then of one of its more respected junior admirals—was a burden for someone determined to make her career on her own, but being the daughter of Vice Admiral Vanessa Murakuma was worse. The newsies had dubbed her mother "The Savior of Sarasota," and every time Nobiki turned around some fresh infernal busybody wanted a "background interview." And the *questions* they came up with!

She shook her head as she checked the status boards in Sky Watch One, the massive orbital station which coordinated the Centauri System's fixed defenses. She loved her mother, but truth to tell, she'd seen more of her since joining the Navy than she had as a child. Vanessa Murakuma's daughters were Navy brats, and they'd learned early that an officer went where she was sent. They'd understood there was seldom any way to take children along, and no one could have given them a more secure (if sometimes confining) childhood than their grandparents. Their mother's slender, very un-Japanese beauty, long absences, and infrequent appearances had imbued her with a sort of glamorous magnificence which joined with the Murakuma tradition to make it inevitable they would follow her into uniform, and both of them were proud of her, yet they had few of the mother-daughter childhood memories civilian families seemed to take for granted.

The newsies appeared unable to grasp that. They kept plaguing Nobiki for background when, frankly, they could have gotten better information from the public record! Fortunately for Fujiko, her Survey Command duties put *her* safely beyond their reach. Nobiki had no such luck. She wished Captain Hammani would let her tell them where to go, but someone from Public Information had gotten to her CO and stressed the necessity of cooperating with the press, and—

An anomalous reading caught her attention, and she frowned. Her eyes darted back across the boards, and her frown deepened. Surely that couldn't be right!

She punched up her traffic files. There was a lot of data, for Centauri was always busy. Every starship to or from Sol had to pass through it, and powerful Home Fleet detachments were permanently on station to support the heavy fortifications guarding The Gateway—the single warp point from Centauri to Sol which was humanity's door to the stars. Despite the apparent confusion of ships moving about the system, its traffic was meticulously regulated . . . yet none of the information in her files explained what a ship would be doing out *there*.

She rubbed her chin, thinking hard. There were Fleet exercises underway—three of them, in fact—but only one involved cloaked units, and she plugged a query into the system, then swore softly as the computers refused to answer. *Well, of course they did,* she scolded herself. *Admiral van der Gelder is supposed to be sneaking up on us, after all.*

Still, there was no good reason for van der Gelder's big, new CVAs to be stooging around out in Theta Quadrant. Which added to her mystification, but didn't offer any answers.

She turned back to the scanner ghost. It wasn't much, but with a little enhancement . . .

She hummed as she worked. Sensor glitch was the most likely explanation, but it was also possible someone had

decided to throw an additional surprise exercise at them—
a sensor shell test, perhaps. Centauri's open warp points
had been plotted three hundred years before, but the TFN
had always worried about closed warp points in strategic
systems, and especially in *this* one. Like all core systems,
it had been provided with a sphere of scansats three light-
hours from the primary to provide warning in the unlikely
event some unfriendly soul *did* find a closed point in—

Nobiki Murakuma's thoughts froze as the computers
beeped. She stared at the analysis of the enhanced datum,
held by shock for just a second, and then a flashing hand
punched a com key.

"CIC, Captain Hammani," a tenor voice said in her
earbug.

"Captain, this is Murakuma in Plotting," Nobiki replied,
and the professionalism of her own voice amazed her in
a distant sort of way. "Sir, according to my board, we have
a cloaked Bug force operating in unknown strength in
Theta Quadrant."

*The survey flotilla slid stealthily in-system. It was a
powerful force, for the Fleet believed in surveying in
strength, yet detection would doom it; that much had
been evident from its first long-range scan. A light cruiser
had been dispatched homeward the instant the entry warp
point was identified as a closed one, fulfilling the most
critical component of its mission, but the Fleet needed
more data. The survey ships' total destruction would be
a paltry price for a strategic prize of this magnitude,
and so the main body swept onward, passive sensors busy.
Eventually, it would be detected, attacked, and—undoubtedly—destroyed, yet it would learn a great deal first.*

The enormous chamber at the heart of Sky Watch
One—officially "Alpha Command," but known to its
denizens simply as "the Pit"—was the Centauri System's
nerve center, and an icy hand squeezed Fleet Admiral
Pederson's heart as an alarm howled. He whirled to Main
Plot's huge tank just as CIC updated it, and his mouth

tightened. A dozen lurid icons flashed crimson, and for just an instant he could only stare at them. Then he punched a stud.

"CIC, Hammani," a harassed voice said in his earbug.

"Gold One," Pederson identified himself tersely. "Talk to me."

"It's confirmed, Sir." Hammani's voice was flat. "We don't have a definitive count. So far, we make it at least six light cruisers, nine or ten battlecruisers, and three superdreadnoughts. From their apparent formation, there are more of them, though. We just haven't seen them yet."

"Jesus Christ, Yassir! How the *hell* did they get this close before we spotted them?"

"Obviously their entry point was too far out for the buoys to pick them up on arrival, and they went into cloak immediately. We didn't even get a sniff till they actually crossed the shell perimeter. On the other hand, I doubt *they* spotted the buoys. The ones we've nailed crossed the line almost perpendicularly, and they wouldn't have given us stern aspects if they could help it."

"Well, thank God for small favors," Pederson muttered, watching the blood-colored icons creep across the tank with near imperceptible speed.

"Yes, Sir. I'd say every credit we ever spent on scansats just justified itself."

"Damn straight. And now what say we blow their asses straight to hell?"

"Sounds good to me, Sir."

"All right." Pederson inhaled deeply, then nodded to himself. "We'll go with Sigma-Three. Send Admiral MacGregor the alert signal and download their loci and vectors. This far in, they'll never be able to outrun her, and—"

"Excuse me, Admiral," a new voice said in his earbug. "I have a Priority One for you."

"Not now, Jeffers," Pederson replied testily. "Tell whoever it is I'll get back. Now, Yassir, as I was—"

"Admiral, I think you'd better take it now. It's Admiral Antonov, Sir."

"*Antonov?*" Pederson looked across the Pit at Hammani, and the captain raised both hands in bafflement. *Damn it, has he added omniscience to his talents? How the devil did even Ivan the Terrible find out about this so fast?*

"Go ahead and alert MacGregor, Yassir," he decided, "but have her hold position until I get back to you. Check?"

"Check, Sir."

"Thanks." Pederson inhaled and sat back down. "All right, Jeffers. Put the Admiral on."

There was a moment of silence, and then an earthquake bass rumbled in his ear.

"Admiral Pederson?"

"Speaking, Sir."

"I understand we have visitors."

"You might put it that way, Sir. I'm just about to send them a welcoming committee."

"I thought as much," Antonov said. "That's why I commed. Admiral, it is imperative that you do nothing—nothing at all—to tell them they've been detected."

Pederson's eyed widened. This was the *Centauri System*—the one, perhaps the only, star system short of Sol itself which humanity simply could not afford to lose—and Antonov wanted him to sit by and do *nothing?*

"Sir," he said, gripping his self-control in both hands, "with all due respect, these ships are already close enough to start getting solid reads on our inner defenses, and even if we hit them as quickly as possible, we won't be able to keep them from getting their drones off. We can't let them amass any more data than they already have!"

"Yes, we can," Antonov replied flatly.

"But, Admiral—"

"I am not in habit of repeating myself." Antonov's voice had gone still deeper, and every senior flag officer knew it was a bad sign when his Standard English started losing definite articles. But Oscar Pederson was the system's commanding officer, and the Admiralty hadn't picked a weakling to run its most critical Fleet Base.

"Admiral Antonov," he said very formally, "I am the

system CO. In my judgment, it is vital to destroy this force as rapidly as possible, and I intend to do so."

"You will *not*." Pederson heard the grumble of shifting tectonic plates in the words. "You will do nothing at all until I reach Alpha Command."

"Sir, I realize you're the *Alliance* Commander-in-Chief, but, again with all due respect, this is a Terran system, and I am responsible for its security."

"Security is relative, Admiral Pederson," Antonov said coldly, "and there is more at stake here than a single star system—even this one. I am not interested in official chains of command, and I will repeat myself one last time. You will take *no action* until I arrive. If you desire, I will have Sky Marshal Avram confirm that order before you and I discuss it personally."

The menace in that last sentence was unmistakable, and more than one TFN officer had brought his career to a catastrophic end by irritating Ivan Antonov. Yet Pederson hovered on the brink of defiance for a long, fulminating moment.

"Very well, Sir," he said at last, in his iciest tone. "I will obey your instructions, but I do so under formal protest and request that you confirm them to me in writing on your arrival."

"As you wish." Antonov's voice was still cold, but there was respect in it as well. Pederson waited for him to say something more, but he heard only the click of a disconnected circuit, and he snarled a silent curse as he turned to glare back down into the tank.

The survey force continued inward, holding its velocity down to .03 c to reduce emissions leakage. Its passive sensors began delivering data on the inner system, and this was the first time the Fleet had encountered such enormous, obviously pre-war fortifications. Combined with the sheer numbers of drive fields swimming about the system's depths and the glaring energy signatures of two habitable planets, their presence amply confirmed the value of its find.

The ships spread wider to cover a greater volume, whispering across the light-seconds to one another with whisker lasers. Each unit's courier drones were configured for continuous download of not only its own sensor data but also that of every ship in communication with it. The priceless information came in slowly, but it came, and the drone memories began to fill up.

"How's your signal strength, Nobiki?" Captain Hammani asked in Nobiki's earbug, and she shrugged, still staring down into her display while her skilled fingers caressed her console.

"Sir, I've got three extra computer sections tied in to help with signal enhancement, but it's still extremely weak. They're moving very slowly, and I'm still hanging onto the ones I had at least-strength three reads on, but two weaker ones have already dropped off the plot. If they get ten or twelve more light-minutes in-system, the buoys are going to lose them completely."

"Understood." There was a moment of silence, and then Hammani spoke gruffly. "You did well, Commander. Very well. Your mother would be proud of you."

Nobiki blinked, but before she had to think of a response, she heard the click of a closed circuit.

Oscar Pederson turned just a bit too quickly as Ivan Antonov entered the Pit, but he managed—somehow—to keep his anger out of his expression as the massive Russian stalked towards him, trailed by Commander Kozlov and Rear Admiral LeBlanc. Kozlov's uniform was immaculate, but the Alliance commander-in-chief's "Bug specialist" looked as though he'd dressed in a hurry. There was nothing sleepy about LeBlanc's expression, however, and he stepped to one side, peering down into the main tank as Pederson greeted Antonov with frigid formality.

"Admiral." He clipped the title off just short of insubordination, and Antonov gave him a very hard look. Then the ex-sky marshal's expression softened micrometrically.

"Admiral Pederson." He studied the Centauri System

CO for a moment longer, then sighed. "I believe I owe you an explanation," he said in the tone of a man clearly unaccustomed to making even oblique apologies. "I have no intention of allowing this force to inflict damage on the Centauri System, and I appreciate your concern over the data they are undoubtedly obtaining. But I have a far more pressing long-term concern: the location of their entry warp point."

Pederson felt his icy fury thaw slightly—very slightly— but it didn't show in his reply.

"I considered that, Sir. Unfortunately, it must be a closed point. That means there's no way we can detect it, and they certainly won't show us where it is."

"Not knowingly, no," Antonov agreed readily, then beckoned. "Admiral LeBlanc, if you please," he rumbled, and Marcus LeBlanc turned from the tank to the two senior officers.

"Yes, Sir?"

"Your evaluation of the enemy's objective?"

"Sir, they're obviously trying to get a fix on the inner system."

"And their probable course of action?"

"They'll keep coming in until they're positive they've been detected," LeBlanc said confidently. "The one thing we know about Bugs is that their units' survival is completely secondary to their missions. They'll hang on until they *know* we see them, then send word back."

"How?" Antonov prompted, watching Pederson's face closely.

"If they've left a picket on the warp point, they *could* use com lasers, Sir. But from what we've seen of them, they'll probably use drones if the range is more than a light-hour or two."

"Precisely," Antonov said.

"Even granting that Admiral LeBlanc is correct, we can't even detect drones at ranges in excess of twelve light-minutes," Pederson objected. "That means we can't possibly track them to their exit warp point." The logic of his own statement was unarguable, yet there was a new note, almost a questioning one, in his voice, and Antonov gave him a sharklike smile.

"Unfortunately for the Bugs, Admiral Pederson, we *will* be able to track them."

"How?" Pederson demanded, and the sharklike smile grew colder.

"I believe Fang Kthaara is coordinating an exercise in which Admiral van der Gelder is tasked to penetrate your defenses?"

"He is," Pederson said slowly.

"Well, I have just been with Fang Kthaara, monitoring the exercise. So unlike you, I know where van der Gelder is at this moment, and Fang Kthaara has already sent her a change of orders. If we can keep these *pizdi* creeping in on us for another four to five hours, she will be able to cut in *behind* them. With a very little luck, her fighters will be able to track any drones the enemy launches. While they will lack the endurance to follow them all the way back to their entry point, we should be able at least to determine its general bearing. If so, we will know which areas to saturate with additional scansats to insure that we *will* detect the next ship to make transit."

"I see," Pederson said in a very different tone. He rubbed an eyebrow for a moment, thinking furiously, then gave a slow nod. "I see," he repeated, smiling back at Antonov for the first time, "and I withdraw my request for written confirmation of your orders, Sir."

"*Korosho!*" Antonov grinned, then nodded to the tank. "In that case, Admiral, let us consider which of your units will make the best beaters when the time comes to start the quarry."

Vice Admiral Jessica van der Gelder stood on TFNS *Thor*'s flag bridge, gray eyes intent as she studied the vectors threaded through the main display. The scansats' tenuous readings were fading, but the Bugs' courses had been plotted with care. Given how steadily they'd held those courses and their clear belief they were still undetected, a direct back plot *should* give a bearing to their warp point. Unfortunately, she couldn't be certain of that.

She frowned and folded her hands behind her, pacing slowly while she wished she had more fighters. Each of her six assault carriers was half again the size of a *Borzoi*-class CV, but they were *assault* carriers, designed to take fighters through defended warp points. Most of that tonnage had gone into tougher defenses, not larger strikegroups, and if she spread her strength too wide watching for courier drones, she wouldn't have much left to help swat Bugs.

Her frown deepened as metronome-steady paces took her up and down, up and down, her flag deck. Examination of enemy wreckage had confirmed that Bug CDs were a tad slower than the Alliance's, with a top speed of just under .2 c. They were faster than any starship, but an F2R recon fighter with two life-support pods could pace them. Unfortunately, even with the pods its endurance would be only seven and a half hours. If the warp point was, say, five light-hours out and the Bugs launched from *two* light-hours out, their drones would take twice that long to reach the point. Her escorting battlecruisers' pinnaces had a month's endurance each, but they could barely hit .12 c. They had *time* to catch the drones, but, unlike her fighters, they lacked the legs.

Lord Talphon's orders indicated Admiral Antonov would settle for a definite bearing, but the firepower the Bugs had brought to bear for *fringe* systems made just thinking about what they would commit against a target like this enough to freeze the blood. Centauri's defenses were massive, but *no* defense could stop an enemy willing to lose enough starships *and* able to get into the system unopposed . . . and mankind's birth world lay one transit away beyond The Gateway.

No, she thought, *we need to know* exactly *where it is. We need to be able to camp on it with the whole damned Home Fleet and blow* anything *that comes through it into dust bunnies. But how do I find it when their drones are either faster or longer ranged than anything I've got to track them with?*

She paused. *Wait a minute. Wait a minute! The pinnaces have plenty of time on their clocks, and the fighters . . .*

"Andrushka!"

Commander Andrei Kulnozov, her ops officer, looked up.

"Yes, Sir?"

"Current range to the enemy?"

"Twenty-six light-minutes," Kulnozov answered, and van der Gelder smiled. They were still far beyond the range at which scanners could detect a target as small as a pinnace drive field.

"All right," she said crisply. "I want every pinnace loaded with fighter scan packs and launched immediately. Get with CIC and work out a conical pattern along the Bugs' backtrack, then assign vectors that will spread the pinnaces to cover it and send them out-system at max."

Kulnozov frowned for a moment, then nodded. "Of course. And we'll hold the fighters until they actually launch."

"Exactly. We use the fighters to track to the limit of their endurance. The drones'll be on a least-time course, so we'll have steady vectors to pass on to the pinnaces. With their head start, they should be able to stay with them out to as much as six light-hours."

"If they've left a picket with gunboats out there, pinnaces will be sitting ducks," Kulnozov pointed out, and van der Gelder nodded.

"Arm them with FM3s. That'll let them shoot back, and the Bugs won't expect the extra range. I know its risky, but locating that warp point is worth losing all of them."

"Agreed." Kulnozov nodded and began giving orders, and she turned back to her plot.

Rear Admiral Hansen Lutz sat in his command chair aboard TFNS *Orinoco*, watching a holo display even more intently than van der Gelder. Unlike van der Gelder's command, Task Group 12 had no carriers, which could prove painful if the Bugs threw in a gunboat attack. But

TG 12 *did* have seventeen SDs, including five *Chimborazo*-class "escort" superdreadnoughts, the first dedicated capital ship anti-missile/anti-fighter platforms the TFN had ever built. BuShips and BuPlans had debated the SDE concept for over five years before the Bugs' use of kamikaze small craft and gunboats provided the final impetus to build them. They carried no energy armament or capital missile launchers, but each could put sixteen standard missiles—or AFHAWKs—into space in a single broadside, and their point defense outfits were massive. If he couldn't have carriers, *Chimborazos* were certainly the next best thing.

He allowed himself a thin smile at the thought while he watched the display. TG 12 and Rear Admiral Wilson's TG 22 had been chosen to play beater because they were conducting routine training ops in the right general positions. Since the alert had come in, they'd altered their headings—as casually as possible—to close on the Bugs. Not directly; their present headings angled to meet well inside the enemy. Hopefully that would encourage the Bugs to assume their maneuvers really were routine, but the enemy was so far in-system that his lower tactical speed would make him easy meat when Lutz and Wilson showed their true intentions.

The survey force noted the approaching enemy and slowed still further. The two groups of starships were obviously headed for a rendezvous well beyond any range at which units in cloak could be detected. Their firepower was more than sufficient to crush the entire survey force, yet it seemed evident the enemy still had no idea the surveyors were there to be crushed. Had he done so, those ships would have rendezvoused outside the survey force to cut it off from retreat, and every other drive source within detection range continued serenely upon its way. Nor was there the least sign of concern from the fixed defenses. Given his apparent blindness, it might even be possible for the survey force to complete its mission and withdraw without losses.

✦   ✦   ✦

Ivan Antonov sat motionless, watching the plot. The last few hours had been nerve-wracking, and the scansats had lost lock on the last enemy unit sixteen minutes ago. CIC had projected their positions based on the last hard data . . . but those positions were *only* projections.

He checked the time. Kthaara had relayed Vice Admiral van der Gelder's decision to deploy her pinnaces three hours ago. Transmission lags meant those pinnaces had been underway for two hours before Kthaara found out about them, and she'd dropped them thirty-one light-minutes out from her present position, so they should be thirty-eight light-minutes out-system from point of launch. That should be far enough . . . and it was going to have to be.

He took one last look at his "beaters." TG 12's super-dreadnoughts were sixteen light-minutes from the Bugs' projected positions; TG 22's four fleet carriers, five superdreadnoughts, and ten battlecruisers were a bit further out, but they were also twenty percent faster than Lutz's command, for all of Wilson's SDs were the new *Athabasca* and *Borneo*-class ships. Antonov still wasn't thoroughly convinced of the concept behind the *Athabascas* and their command ship consorts, yet their speed certainly made them ideal for their present mission.

The class had been conceived as a way to provide heavy escorts which could stay with carrier groups under maximum power. Matching the speed of Gorm battle-line units without using engine tuners had been a technically audacious concept, but the new ships had drawbacks. From a material viewpoint, the worst was cost. Building super-dreadnoughts with battlecruiser speed required a drastic reduction in mass. It had proved possible to design low-mass substitutes for everything except armor, but the new systems were hideously expensive, and drive power still had to rise to unprecedented levels. Which led to the design's major *tactical* drawback: lack of internal volume. For all intents and purposes, the *Athabascas* could mount little more than a battleship's armament simply because of the squeeze effect of those massive drive rooms.

The same research had provided the hulls for the new *Scylla* and *Thor*-class CVAs, but superdreadnoughts were main combatants, not fighter platforms. Antonov would have preferred to give them heavy capital missile outfits and turn them into bigger, tougher versions of the tried and tested *Dunkerque* battlecruisers, but he'd been retired for over ten years when the design was finalized, and BuShips had given them shorter-ranged armaments. There were arguments both ways. Using standard missile launchers had let the designers cram in a decent hetlaser broadside and a missile armament little lighter than the new *Chimborazos*, but only at the expense of conceding the long-ranged missile envelope to any enemy, and—

He shook free of his thoughts and looked at Admiral Pederson.

"Very well, Admiral. You may begin your attack."

The approaching starships abruptly altered course and went to full power. The survey force came to a halt while tactical sections projected the new vectors, but the projections weren't really required, for the enemy's shields were coming up as well. Worse, one group was already launching attack craft. It would never have done that if it had not had a target for them, yet there was no panic. This, after all, was the reaction the survey force had initially anticipated, and sensors had already ascertained that there were new and unfamiliar ship types in both enemy groups. It would be as well to gain data on them before launching courier drones.

It was unfortunate that the survey force's units were so dispersed. Its detachments would be unable to offer one another much support, but at least the closer of the enemy groups appeared to have no attack craft to fend off a gunboat strike.

Just under two hundred gunboats erupted from cloak along a vast arc, heading straight for TG 12, and Admiral Lutz swore as CIC reported the numbers. That many gunboats meant the enemy's strength had been substantially underestimated. They were going to be a handful even for *Chimborazos*, but at least their launch points pinpointed the locations of the starships from which they'd come, and red icons glowed in his plot, marking those locations.

TG 22's fighters altered course, streaking towards the closest enemy starships, and Lutz watched them go. He couldn't fault Erica Wilson's decision. The two task groups were too widely separated for her fighters to intercept the gunboat attack before it hit him, but he was going to miss their support.

"The enemy's launched gunboats at Admiral Lutz, Sir!" Kulnozov said sharply, and van der Gelder nodded. Carrier Group 19 had been able to sneak in closer than she'd dared hope, but she was still too far out to detect drone launches. She drummed on the arm of her command chair, chewing her lower lip, and her thoughts were bleak.

If I launch now, I might distract them—get them to recall their strike to deal with me and leave Hansen alone. But it would also tell them I'm here, and if they know that, they may not launch drones. It's unlikely, but it is possible, and getting them to launch is the whole point.

She chewed harder, fighting the instinct to come to TG 12's assistance, and said nothing.

The enemy's attack craft would reach the survey force well before its gunboats attacked the other enemy force, and there were many of them. It was unlikely the battlecruisers they were about to engage would survive the strike, and so they launched their drones now.

"I have drone separation! Multiple drone separations!" The pilot's taut report crackled from the flag bridge speakers, and Erica Wilson nodded.

"Inform Admiral van der Gelder," she told her com officer sharply.

Thirty-two endless minutes ticked past while van der Gelder and Kulnozov watched the gunboats bearing down on TG 12. The Bugs had covered a third of the original distance to Lutz's ships, and TG 12 was still coming to meet them. It had to, if it was to attack the starships beyond them, and the tension of watching that drawn out approach to carnage had tightened every pair of shoulders on *Thor's* flag bridge. Then van der Gelder's com officer looked up suddenly.

"Admiral Wilson reports drone separation, Sir."

"Time?" van der Gelder snapped.

"Twenty-six minutes ago, Sir."

"CIC has the vectors," Kulnozov reported with a vicious smile. "They're coming right down our throat!"

"Excellent!" van der Gelder's smile matched his. "Launch Captain Ghandra's strike."

Consternation struck the survey force as a fresh, even more powerful wave of attack craft abruptly appeared behind it, but understanding followed instantly. The enemy had known the survey force was here all along! This fresh assault could only mean he had herded the survey force into a trap . . . and that enemy vessels were in position to engage its courier drones.

But the survey force had no way of knowing how many cloaked starships were back there. Two hundred attack craft were already charging to the attack, yet hundreds more might still lurk aboard their mother ships. That many attack craft could easily destroy every drone which had already launched, and it was imperative that at least one get through.

Under these new circumstances, there was only one way to be sure it would, and every survey ship belched its full load of courier drones, sending out such a dense cloud of them as to guarantee saturation of the enemy's ability to engage them.

"Admiral van der Gelder's launched, Sir!"

"How nice," Hansen Lutz said drily. The com message was thirty-four minutes old, and Jessica's launch wouldn't do a thing about the gunboats howling towards him, but he supposed it meant Antonov's plan had worked. At the moment, however, he had other things to worry about. TG 12 was still headed for the enemy at max, closing with the gunboats at a combined speed of over .23 *c*, and the range was down to thirty-six light-seconds.

"There go Admiral Wilson's jocks, Sir," his ops officer reported, and Lutz nodded. He had another two and a half minutes before the Bugs hit him, and he looked at the repeater plot tracking Wilson's strike. Its data was fourteen minutes old, but he felt vengeful pleasure as he watched it. His sensors still couldn't see the cloaked Bug starships, but Erica's pilots could, and fireballs began to glare as the fighter jocks laid into them with the new, longer-ranged FM3.

The bastards won't like that *toy,* he thought, for the new missile had both more range than the AFHAWK *and* better penetration aids than earlier fighter missiles. Its warhead was the same, but more would get through, and pilots didn't have to fly down the Bugs' throat to deliver it.

"Here they come, Sir," the ops officer said grimly, and ten *Matterhorn*-class superdreadnoughts began slamming SBMs into the oncoming gunboats.

"Sixty-one minutes," Kulnozov said, and van der Gelder nodded. Assuming a velocity of .2 *c*, the drones had covered just over twelve light-minutes.

"Roll out the recon fighters," she said, and thirty F2R fighters spat from Carrier Group 19's assault carriers. They carried no weapons, only their internal sensors and a pair of life-support pods, and she and Kulnozov had timed things perfectly. Barely forty seconds after the last recon fighter launched, their scanners picked up the first drones and they swerved in pursuit.

And now, Jessica van der Gelder told herself coldly as she leaned back in her command chair, *we can kill these vermin.*

he supposed it meant Antonov's plan had worked. At the moment, however, he had other things to worry about.

TG 32 was still headed for the enemy at max. closing velocity... and the range was down to fifteen light-seconds.

"There is Admiral Wilson's force, Sir," his ops officer reported. And Lau nodded. He had watched two and a half minutes before the flashing icon he looked at the repeater...

CHAPTER THIRTY-FOUR

Into the Unknown

Kthaara'zarthan was an exceptionally tall Orion, and the species' legs were longer in proportion than those of homo sapiens. Still, he had to hurry to keep up with Antonov as the burly Grand Alliance commander in chief strode along the corridors.

"Why do I have the feeling that we have been through this before, and not so very long ago?" he grumbled.

Antonov gestured dismissively without breaking stride. "The arguments for my taking personal command still apply, Kthaara Kornazhovich. We're just moving things up a little—"

"'A little'!"

"—and launching our offensive from right here, rather than having to go to Zephrain to do it." He grinned over his shoulder. "You must admit the logistics have improved."

"An amusing concept," Kthaara growled. "I trust the inhabitants of this system—and of Sol!—who have suddenly awakened to find themselves on a war front, are equally amused."

"Well, then," Antonov replied serenely as they reached the bottomless-looking abyss of the drop shaft, "we'll just have to push the front away from them, won't we?" Then he addressed the low-grade brain that handled the shaft's routing. "Ground floor."

They stepped off the edge, and the tractor-beam-like

effect took them, lowering them swiftly downward with no sensation of motion. Floor after floor shot upward past them, but Antonov didn't notice, for his thoughts were on the incredible turn of events in Centauri space.

The Bugs had been wiped out, of course, and with little loss. Even Admiral Lutz's BG 12, which had suffered the heaviest damage, hadn't lost a single ship. Best of all, their closed warp point of entry been pinpointed, and that single fact had changed the strategic picture beyond recognition. The universe might have suddenly become an even more dangerous place, but it also offered a new opportunity. And Antonov had all of Terran Home Fleet, plus the beginnings of Second Fleet here at Centauri, with which to take advantage of that opportunity. To have failed to seize the moment was simply not in him.

The drop shaft deposited them on the ground floor with all the impact of falling leaves. Admiral Ellen MacGregor awaited them there, and Antonov nodded to her as she joined him and Kthaara. MacGregor had transferred to Centauri from her position as second in command of Home Fleet to take over the newly designated Allied Fourth Fleet, although calling it a "fleet" at the moment was stretching a point. Along with Oscar Pederson, the short, sturdily built brunette would be responsible for holding the fort here in Centauri, but the enormous warship tonnages already diverted to the fighting front, to various nodal reaction forces, and to bring Antonov's Second Fleet up to strength for "Operation Pesthouse" would leave her shorthanded. The KON had promised to divert at least one heavy task force to support her, yet she couldn't be very happy about her available order of battle, which was why he'd asked her to accompany him to his new flagship for discussions. If she had concerns, he wanted to know about them—just as he wanted any insight she could give him into the capabilities of the squadrons he'd poached from her.

Marine guards fell in around them as they proceeded across the public area towards a side entrance and the skimmer waiting to take Antonov and MacGregor to the space field. They'd covered about half the distance when the commotion began at the main entrance, off to their right.

"Admiral Antonov! Admiral Antonov!" His heart sank at that shrilly nasal voice, and sank even further as its owner broke free of the cluster of arguing flunkies and guards and advanced towards him, trailing a cloud of media types. "As elected representative of the People of Nova Terra, I demand to speak to you!"

It was, he reflected, miserably bad luck that the Bug incursion had come between sessions of the Legislative Assembly. Otherwise Bettina Wister would have been on Old Terra, not tending the farm among her constituents. He firmly suppressed his impulses, for with the holo-cameras whirring away he had to be civil. And he didn't deign to notice Kthaara's amusement.

"Assemblywoman Wister," he greeted mildly. Too mildly. People in the lobby who knew him blanched, although Wister remained oblivious. "As you can see, I'm somewhat rushed just now. But you can contact my public relations officer at—"

"Oh, no!" Wister struck a pose for the cameras. "There'll be no coverup by the Military Establishment this time, Admiral! I am reliably informed that the ravening, genocidal Bug hordes that the Navy *inexcusably* allowed to enter this system launched courier drones, presumably carrying navigational information."

"I seem to recall, Legislative Assemblywoman Wister, that you are on record as objecting vociferously to the 'unenlightened' use of the term 'Bugs' for our opponents in the current unpleasantness. I believe your objections were voiced in the course of the debate in which you opposed reimplementation of General Directive 18."

"Cheap shot!" Wister shot back, face half-turned to the cameras. "Typical of the mean-spirited attacks with which the Navy seeks to divert the People's attention from its failure to totally exterminate these galactic vermin—as I have advocated from the first! But as I was saying, I have it from reliable sources that some of the Bugs' courier drones were allowed to escape!"

"Presumably, Legislative Assemblywoman Wister, your 'reliable sources' are our own press releases, for that has never been a secret. Our first priority was to locate the warp point from which the Bugs had emerged. The need to concentrate on this objective meant that some of the courier drones did, indeed, escape. This was perhaps regrettable, but not disastrous given that we now know where any subsequent attackers must appear and can therefore defend against them."

"Yes," Wister replied with a theatrical sneer, and Antonov's eyes hardened. The fact that self-serving politicos disgusted him didn't mean he didn't understand them, and she clearly had no interest at all in anything he might say. She was proceeding along her own script for the press's benefit, and the sound-byte opportunity of the Navy's "failure" was simply too good for her to pass up. Especially now. Her public stance had undergone a remarkable change from obstructionism to frothing at the mouth enthusiasm when *her* precious constituents found themselves on the front line. It seemed the prospect of hanging could concentrate even Nova Terrans' thoughts. What a pity nothing *short* of that could do the trick!

"I'm aware of the Navy's feeble excuse that the Bugs entered through an unknown warp point," she continued. "I am also aware that you are now departing with large forces, leaving Alpha Centauri undefended, naked before these murderous alien hordes! As a member of the Naval Oversight Committee, I promise you there will be a full investigation of your failure to defend the civilian populace of this system."

If I squash this svolochy *as she deserves, it will only serve her own ends*, Antonov told himself, and forced his deep, rumbling voice to remain calm and reasonable.

"Since you are aware of so much else, Assemblywoman Wister, you must be aware that we have taken steps to secure this system against attack, and that additional reinforcements have already been ordered by Sky Marshal

Avram herself to join Admiral MacGregor—" he indicated the woman beside him "—here in Centauri in my absence."

"Nor will the inquiry stop there," Wister raved on without a break. She was pleased to note the expression on the Orion's face. As a rule, she despised the Orions who had invaded Centauri since the Alliance's activation almost as much as her own militarists, but such a broad, *toothy* smile could only be one of sympathy and encouragement. "We will have answers, Admiral! Answers to the larger question of why the Navy, in well over two years of war, has not wiped out these inhuman monsters to the last foul creature! There will be a thorough housecleaning of—"

"Major Lin!" It wasn't so much Antonov's increased volume that caused Wister to stop short. It was more a kind of subliminal, almost subterranean vibration in his bass voice.

"Sir!" The Marine major in charge of security hurried over and snapped to attention,

"Major, this area is to be cleared at once. The entire building is off-limits to unauthorized personnel until further notice from Lord Talphon. Now, get this *pizda* out of here."

Lin gulped. He'd been around Ivan the Terrible long enough to know that what the admiral had called Wister was the equivalent of an English-speaker's use of the word "asshole." But he also knew that the idiom—used without regard to the gender of the individual in question—translated literally as "cunt." Luckily, Wister's blank look suggested she was unaware of that fact. "Yes, Sir!" he rapped.

Antonov started to turn to go, then paused with the movement half completed. When he spoke, his voice was mild again. "You know, Ms. Wister, there is a mistaken proverb which tells us that those who are ignorant of the past are condemned to repeat it. In fact, they're *lucky* if they're allowed to repeat it. More probably, they're condemned to something even *worse* than the past. This is doubly true of those who believe that their ignorance somehow makes them morally superior to those who don't share it." He turned back and faced Wister squarely, looking at her as he might have looked at something disgusting in a plate of food. "I go now to lead brave men and women into what will be, for many of them, death. They go willingly, out of devotion to a state which unfortunately is not worthy of it. But, as someone once said, it is the quality of the passion that matters, not its object." He turned on his heel and strode away through a thundering silence.

Behind him, Bettina Wister held her head high as she was led away. It was a lovely image for the cameras, she thought: a small, harmless *civilian* woman between two huge, hard-faced Marine guards. It was even more than she'd hoped for, and she hid her triumph behind an expression of outraged dignity, already considering the most effective way for her staffers to cut and edit the recordings.

The type K0v orange primary star of this system (its remote red dwarf companion was quite invisible) reflected feebly from the flanks of Second Fleet's ships. Ivan Antonov stood on TFNS *Colorado*'s flag bridge and gazed at the view screen. One volume of space was much like any other, he supposed. But there was something special about this particular expanse of nothingness. For he was looking at original, pre-war Bug space. He was the first human since Commodore Lloyd Braun to look on such space—and the first ever to look on it as a conqueror.

Admiral van der Gelder's Task Force 22 had led the way through the warp point from Alpha Centauri behind the new fourth generation SBMHAWKs that had blasted a path through the warp point covering force . . . including the gunboats, whose point defense was useless against the sprint-mode missiles the new pods could carry. Raymond Prescott had transited in her wake. His Task Force 21 included his own veteran light carrier force from the Kliean campaign as well as the cream of the new-construction fast superdreadnoughts and refitted battlecruisers. It was like a weapon forged for his hand, and he'd wielded it like a *kendo* master. He'd swept around behind the defenders and driven them into the waiting jaws of van der Gelder's battle-line and Vice Admiral Taathaanahk's fighters, many of them Ophiuchi-piloted and operating from the new assault carriers, and the Bugs hadn't stood a chance. They'd died with their usual horrifying obliviousness to personal survival, inflicting whatever damage they could on an enemy who possessed the prohibitive fire-control advantages of command datalink. And now Antonov stood in the midst of a fleet that was verging on euphoria at the lightness of its losses, waiting for the reports from the drones that had sped on ahead to spy out the system he'd already dubbed Anderson One in honor of his old friend.

"We're getting preliminary readings, Admiral." Blanton Stovall spoke from behind him. "No indication of any habitation—all the planets are useless rockballs or gas giants anyway."

Antonov tried not to show his disappointment. Too bad the first conquered Bug system should turn out to be an undistinguished accumulation of cosmic detritus. *Come, Vanya,* he chided himself. *What did you expect? To transit from Alpha Centauri directly into the capital system of the Tsar of all the Bugs?*

"One lucky break—we think we've already inferred the general location of one warp point," Stovall went on. "It's in the inner system, which is why the drones picked it up so quickly, while looking for life-bearing planets. We're putting it on the display now."

Antonov turned to the holo tank in which the system's features were winking to life as fast as their existence was confirmed. The icon of a warp point had begun to blink off and on, fairly close to the system primary.

"The search for warp points must take first priority," he rumbled. "We must secure this system against counter-attack as quickly as possible."

Stovall nodded in understanding. The Bugs, by fighting to the last ship and not even attempting to flee, had deprived them of any indication of where more of their kind might be expected to appear. This newly discovered warp point might be the gateway to the enemy's heartland, or it might not. And any pickets at other warp points would, of course, have departed by now, before anyone was close enough to detect their departure.

"We'll be prepared to act on any data we receive, Sir," Stovall said confidently. "Now that Admiral Chin's fleet train has transited from Centauri, our post-battle repairs are well in hand."

"Good. Keep me informed of any—"

"Admiral!" Armand de Bertholet's voice came from the flag bridge's com station, where he leaned over an operator's shoulder. "New reports from the inward-bound drones indicate . . . Well , you can see for yourself in the tank."

Antonov did. A short distance outward from the inner-system warp point, but still almost six light-hours from Second Fleet, tiny red icons were popping out like smallpox.

"Bogies," Stovall said unnecessarily.

"Quite a few of them," added Midori Kozlov, joining them. "They can't have already been in this system."

"Of course not," de Bertholet said emphatically. "Their vector shows they've come from that inner warp point. And if their velocity's held constant, they must have emerged from it—" he fiddled with his wrist calculator "—just as we were mopping up the last of the defense force."

"Good timing, from our standpoint," Stovall put in drily.

"But I don't know how valid that constant-velocity assumption is," Kozlov said. "They're moving at what has to be the pace of their slowest ships. They're also keeping a very tight formation, from what we can tell. All in all, I'd say they're advancing very cautiously."

"Wouldn't you, in their place?" De Bertholet's rhetorical question was almost challenging. For reasons doubtless related to his upbringing, he had a way of carrying off remarks that in anyone else would have sounded like sheer bravado. Even his appearance helped; he always kept within grooming and uniform standards, but he still managed to have the kind of looks that had once been called "Byronic," a word whose root no one remembered. He turned to Antonov and Stovall, body language fairly shouting urgency. "Admiral, we must engage them without delay!"

"I think we should amend that to 'Without *unnecessary* delay,' Commander," Stovall spoke in mild reproof. "We've still got some repairs in progress, and I believe we can afford to complete them."

"Get me reports from the ships in question, Commodore Stovall," Antonov ordered. "Also whatever data the drones can provide on this force's composition. Like you, I'd rather complete repairs before we advance. But the important thing is getting those *svolochy* out of this system."

"And so," Midori Kozlov concluded her presentation, "before the Bug force departed through the warp point we were able to make a definitive estimate of its composition, at least by mass equivalents: forty-two superdreadnoughts, ten battlecruisers and thirty light cruisers."

"A considerable force," de Bertholet commented. "Still, distinctly inferior to ours, even without our tech advantages. Small wonder they fell back when we advanced."

"What about the warp point?" Antonov growled.

"Pinpointed, Sir," Stovall reported. "A fast covering force has been dispatched there as per your orders."

"All right." Antonov swept the staff meeting with his eyes. "So we're now sitting on the warp point the Bugs used to enter this system. What about our search for still more warp points?"

"No results as yet, Sir. But there wouldn't be, at this point. We'll need time for some extensive survey work to satisfy ourselves that there are no more open warp points." Stovall paused and gave a wry half-smile. "And of course there's no telling about *closed* warp points; but that's true anywhere—as we've all been reminded lately."

"Very well." Antonov turned to Kozlov. "Commodore,

what is your interpretation of the astrographic and military situation in which we find ourselves?"

"Well, Sir, the military situation is that we've secured this system at very little cost, and that the force the Bugs put into it was so inadequate to face us that it withdrew rather than follow their usual practice of accepting extravagant losses if any appreciable damage can be inflicted in exchange. It seems probable that that force was the only one they *could* put into this system; if they could have deployed enough strength to stop us, they surely would have. This in turn suggests we're in a rather lightly defended area."

"Which won't *remain* lightly defended," Stovall put in grimly.

"Exactly my own conclusions," Antonov stated. "So now I wish to pose the following question: should we proceed deeper into Bug space?" He looked around and decided he'd better recognize the operations officer before he burst. "Commander de Bertholet?"

"I think, Admiral, that we've been given a priceless opportunity." De Bertholet leaned forward as though to physically impart greater force to his words. "But it's an opportunity that won't last. As Commodore Stovall has pointed out, the Bugs must have sent for reinforcements. We've caught them off balance, but we must press on without hesitation before they've had time to regain that balance. This is a crucial moment in history!"

"Now hold on, Commander," Stovall spoke in his slow, deliberate way, rather like a harmonica following a trumpet. "Let's not forget we're in an unsurveyed system. We don't have the slightest idea where we are."

"With great respect, Commodore, we do know one thing, because the Bugs themselves told us." De Bertholet indicated the conference room's small replica of the flag bridge's holo tank. "By falling back through that warp point, they showed us the way to what they consider most vital to defend—which can only be their centers of population and industry."

"That's sheer inference," Kozlov protested.

"But a reasonable one," de Bertholet shot back. "Why would they have withdrawn into some dead-end warp chain? And why would they have been there in the first place? Remember, they emerged from that same warp point."

Stovall shook his head slowly. "I don't know, Admiral. Let's not let success go to our heads. Its's true that we didn't have many outright ship losses, but a fair number of our ships took varying degrees of damage. And Admiral Taathaanahk lost a lot of fighters when they entered the Bugs' defensive envelope. We'll want to replace those losses."

"Of course, Sir," de Bertholet conceded. "But as soon as those matters are seen to, we should advance without further delay. This opportunity is absolutely unique."

"So are the potential dangers," Kozlov argued. "Until we've thoroughly surveyed this system, we can't be sure there are no other warp points. And if there are, there's no guarantee they lead to 'dead-end warp chains,' as some of us are assuming a little too readily. We'd be leaving ourselves vulnerable to being cut off from our base by an attack from an unexpected direction."

De Bertholet's face darkened a half shade, but his self-control was unimpeachable. "I can't deny that what I'm proposing contains an element of risk, Commodore. But if we insist on a total absence of risk, we'll never move at all. As Commodore Stovall intimated, there could be closed warp points here, and no amount of surveying will ever reveal them. It didn't at Centauri—and we've been there almost three hundred years!"

He stopped abruptly, and no one else spoke, for they all knew Antonov well enough to recognize the brooding look he'd assumed. It meant he was through listening to advice or arguments and had assumed the burden of decision that none of them could share.

Well, Vanya, now's when you earn your salary. For a moment he allowed himself to wish he had Kthaara with him. But then he dismissed the thought. After all, he knew exactly what the frosted-sable Orion would say: *Attack!*

And, he thought with growing conviction, Kthaara would be right.

Antonov was far from unaware of the danger of a victorious force letting its *élan* do its thinking for it. And de Bertholet was, by nature, the very voice of *élan*. But his point, stripped of the theatrics, was compelling. For the first time, they had the initiative; it was worth taking terrifying risks to keep it.

And yet . . .

His thoughts came back to the conference room, and his eyes met those of his staff. "Commodore Stovall," he rumbled, "proceed to implement repairs. Make arrangements to begin probing the system beyond this warp point with recon drones. And commence operational planning for a full-scale advance through the warp point after those repairs are completed and our fighter strength is replenished." He studied their reactions. De Bertholet could scarcely contain his elation, and Kozlov looked glum. But Stovall's worried look seemed no more than what he knew was expected of him; he was no more capable of *not* wanting to press on through that beckoning warp point than he was of not voicing all possible objections to it.

"And," Antonov continued, "while we're in the process of ferrying fighters from Alpha Centauri, I myself will be returning there briefly, to put my proposed course of action before the Joint Chiefs." For a moment he let himself enjoy their expressions of almost comical surprise. "Yes, I'm sure it seems out of character. But consider: if Commodore Kozlov's nightmare of a flank attack on this system through an undiscovered warp point comes to pass while Second Fleet is off somewhere deeper in Bug space, the Bugs will be one warp transit away from Centauri, two from Sol—and Old Terra."

He gauged their expressions again. They were surprisingly alike, and he wondered what these disparate people had felt at the words 'Old Terra.' Stovall? Indian summer in the Alleghenies, perhaps. De Bertholet? Surely a montage of images from what historians called the Cavalry Revolution and romanticists knew as the Age of

Chivalry. Kozlov? Hard to say. But for all of them, as for every member of the far-scattered progeny of Adam and Eve, it meant something inexpressibly holy . . . not that anyone would have dreamed of putting it that way.

Antonov shook his head heavily. "No . . . there are some decisions which no one has a right to make alone."

"I gather, Admiral Antonov, that your staff was divided on the question."

"True, Fleet Speaker Noraku," Antonov acknowledged. He permitted himself a tight smile. "It would be remarkable if they hadn't been. I picked them with that in mind. I want lively debate, not sycophancy. My chief of staff, Captain Stovall, is cautious and deliberate by temperament. So I sought out an operations officer with opposite inclinations."

"Ah, yes," Kthaara nodded. "The young commander with the totally unpronounceable name. I like him."

"You would," Hannah Avram remarked. Strictly speaking, she wasn't a member of the Joint Chiefs. But to not invite her to this meeting would have been out of the question. She turned to Antonov. "Yes, your Commander de Bertholet *does* seem to be a firebrand. But I think he—and you, Ivan Nikolayevich—are right about pressing on with Pesthouse. Especially now that Ellen's reinforcements have arrived here at Centauri. Even if the enemy does break into Anderson One behind you, this system will be secure."

"Agreeeeeeed," said Admiral Thaarzhaan. "Ssstill, ittt issss a gaaaaamble. Ssssecond Fffleet would be aaaadvancing into unknownnnnn space, withhhh no notion of the fffffffforces it may fffface."

"Come, we have already been over the arguments." Kthaara's voice was impatient. "Second Fleet's tactical speed advantage should suffice for it to disengage if it finds itself faced with a force too strong to fight. Of course, we cannot ignore the potential threat to this system, and to the Human home world. But Sky Marshal Avraaam is confident she and Ahhhdmiraal MaacGrrregor can guarantee their security. In fact, she and our chairman, both of whom are Human, favor the operation." He paused for the barest heartbeat. "There comes a time when we must not let risks blind us to opportunities, especially when the opportunity is a fleeting one."

"I concur," Noraku stated.

"Asss do I," Thaarzhaan said, a little less emphatically.

Antonov settled back in his chair with a silent sigh. So it was settled. Second Fleet would forge on into the unknown.

"Thank you," he said with unwonted quietness. "I would not have been able to embark wholeheartedly on this without your unanimous support." He rose to his feet. "And now, I must make preparations to return to Anderson One without delay. The offensive must commence as soon as our repair and resupply operations are complete."

Kthaara gave a short growl. "Naturally our chairman is eager as an unleashed *zeget* to return and reassume the command to which he has appointed himself!"

Avram laughed, and Noraku and Thaarzhaan gave their respective races' equivalent indicia of amusement, as the tension evaporated. Antonov smiled, all innocence. "But, Kthaara Kornazhovich, it is *my* plan; surely you must agree that I should be the one to put it into effect."

Kthaara gave him a baleful look. "Trust you to come up with such an argument, Eevaahn'zarthan." He stood and faced his *vilkshatha* brother. "Yes, I understand perfectly. And while you are gone, I shall busy myself thinking of an appropriate way to make you pay for your practice of leaving me behind to handle all the boring administrative work. You have always had a tendency to . . . what is the Human idiom?"

"Pull rank," Avram supplied.

"Now, Kthaasha," Antonov soothed. "There'll be plenty of fighting for everyone before this is over. And don't be like this. It's not as though you're never going to see me again." And, with a jauntiness that was somehow not inappropriate despite his age, Antonov was gone.

CHAPTER THIRTY-FIVE

"What else are we to do?"

Jessica van der Gelder's superdreadnoughts emerged into the new system amid the final reverberations of the SBMHAWK-spawned holocaust among its warp point defenses.

Antonov wasn't advancing into the altogether unknown. RD2s had established that this system was heavily populated, which tended to confirm the conclusions de Bertholet had drawn from the Bugs' avenue of retreat. They'd also provided enough data on the defenders to satisfy Antonov that his fleet train's SBMHAWK inventory would suffice to blast a path through them.

Now he stood on *Colorado*'s flag bridge as the super-dreadnought advanced in van der Gelder's formation (he wasn't about to depart from a tradition which dated back to the First Interstellar War; the supreme commander would go in with the first waves) and saw that view confirmed. Some of the dying glows of SBMHAWK warheads were actually visible to the naked eye in the expanding clouds of vaporized metal they'd wrought, and the holo tank told an ever-elaborating tale of smashed or crippled fortresses. Extensive minefields remained, but Second Fleet's AMBAMs had already cleared paths through them.

TF 22 forged ahead, and Admiral Taathaanahk's TF 23 was already beginning to transit. Soon Raymond

Prescott would bring TF 21 through. But Antonov, staring fixedly at the holo tank, had eyes only for the scarlet icons in Second Fleet's path.

"Commodore Kozlov," he rumbled without shifting his eyes, "have you been able to reach any conclusions regarding the mobile Bug forces?"

"Yes, Sir. Now that our leading elements have begun to exchange fire with them, we're getting harder data. These have to be the same ones that withdrew from Anderson One just ahead of us. The force composition by ship classes is an exact match—too exact for coincidence."

"So they haven't been reinforced yet," de Bertholet breathed. "We've caught them still trying to mobilize against us. This force is still all they can put in our path; it must be under orders to stand and fight this time because this is an inhabited system." He turned to Antonov, his excitement barely under control. "Admiral, this could be the beginning of the end of the war! If we can continue to advance, continue to keep them off balance—"

"Excuse me, Admiral." Kozlov didn't often interrupt de Bertholet, and something in her tone caused even Antonov to turn away from the plot to face her. "We're starting to get some disturbing tactical analyses from the ships most heavily engaged. They're receiving precisely coordinated time-on-target fire from as many as six Bug ships at once."

The silence lasted less than a heartbeat before de Bertholet broke it. "But . . . but that's as many ships as one of our own battlegroups! D'you mean to suggest . . .?"

"I'm not the one suggesting it, Commander. The data speak for themselves." She jerked her chin toward the tank and the midair columns of luminous figures that told the tale of damage well beyond what they'd allowed for at this stage of the engagement. "And," she continued, "why should it be such a surprise? Admiral LeBlanc's been telling anyone who'll listen that it was only a matter of time. The Bugs have seen command datalink in action often enough, and it doesn't require any basic technology beyond their demonstrated horizons. It's just that we've come to take our monopoly for granted, as though it were somehow in the nature of things—"

"Thank you, Commodore," Stovall cut in quietly but authoritatively. He understood her accumulated frustration at the immemorial reluctance of line officers to listen to the intelligence community until after its forecasts had become fact, but this wasn't the time for her to get uncharacteristically worked up about it. "Admiral, we can defer interpreting these data until later. But it's clear that, at a minimum, our projections have erred on the optimistic side where Bug fire control is concerned. Should we implement our contingency plan for breaking off engagement?"

"Nyet." Antonov's voice held absolutely no invitation to debate. "Signal Admiral van der Gelder to press her attack with maximum aggressiveness. And raise Admiral Taathaanahk as soon as he's transited; it is imperative that he begin launching fighter strikes as quickly as possible." He met his staffers' eyes, each in turn. The Theban War lay beyond living memory for their generation, and day-to-day contact tends to rub away the patina of legendry. But all at once the tales they'd grown up on came crowding back, for this was the man who had advanced through every defense like an unstoppable force of nature, grimly disregarding casualties as he gained his objectives . . . and the nickname Ivan the Terrible.

All at once, those tales seemed very real.

"Aye, aye, Sir," Stovall said quietly.

Antonov turned back to the tank and watched van der Gelder's task force advance into a holocaust of fire unprecedented in its intensity. It soon became apparent that at least a dozen of the Bug superdreadnoughts belonged to the missile-heavy *Archer* class. Even with the defensive firepower of her new SDEs, van der Gelder didn't relish missile duels with six-ship battle groups of those behemoths; she ordered her ships to close to beam range while trying to stay outside the zone in which plasma guns were truly deadly. It was a difficult balancing act, performed while nervously awaiting the onset of gunboats on suicide runs.

But no kamikaze attacks came, and the reason became apparent when Taathaanahk's fighters entered the fray. The Bugs, perhaps out of confidence in the way their new datalink technology enhanced their firepower, had held the gunboats back as anti-fighter escorts, adding their loads of AFHAWKs to the tremendous defensive fire from the tight enemy formations.

Losses continued to mount, and periodically *Colorado*, fighting in TF 22's battle-line, shuddered for a sickening instant. Calls for damage control began to reverberate through the great ship, but Antonov never flinched. He held grimly to the rail that surrounded the holo tank and stared at the battle the tank revealed, as though it was a living being with which he was in silent communion, broken only to bark occasional orders.

Finally the balance commenced to tilt. Ships continued to emerge from the warp point, as did the reserve SBMHAWKs, which came under the control of Fleet command. Their firepower, and Second Fleet's overall numerical superiority, began to tell. Almost abruptly, the Bugs broke off in an orderly retreat, and van der Gelder's shaken task force left the job of harrying that retreat to Taathaanahk's already weary fighter pilots and Prescott's newly arrived ones.

"Admirals Taathaanahk and Prescott both report heavy fighter losses," Stovall reported as the fighting receded out of missile range and a palpable air of relief suffused *Colorado*. "The volume of anti-fighter missile fire seems unabated."

"It will abate as the attacks continue to be pressed." Antonov was as impervious to the flagship's new mood as he had been to the earlier tension. "Their magazines aren't infinite. And the attacks *must* be pressed without letup. Make that very clear to Taathaanahk and Prescott. Losses are secondary; we have nearby sources of reinforcement, which they apparently do not."

Stovall swallowed hard. "Aye, aye, Sir."

"Oh, and one other thing, Commodore. As soon as practicable, I want recon drones dispatched sunward. We already know there's a planet here that's a high-energy population center. It must be quite close to a dim sun like this one. We will, of course, proceed there as soon as the Bug forces are cleared from the system."

"You mean, Sir . . . ?"

"Yes." Antonov's expression was absolutely unreadable. "Our orders are clear. We are about to become the first in well over a century to implement General Directive 18."

The staff conference room had a wall screen. Antonov had decreed that it be left on, and eyes kept straying to the planet Harnah—everyone was calling it that by now, even though this system had officially been named Anderson Two. Beyond the world's blue curve was the bone-white crescent of its moon. That moon, like the oxygen-rich atmosphere, represented a triumph over the odds. Harnah orbited just outside the zone in which the orange sun's tidal force would have stopped the planet's rotation and stripped away any natural satellites, but close enough to that relatively feeble fusion furnace for water to exist as a liquid in which life could arise.

And why do you keep letting your mind wander into this astronomical blagadarnost, *Vanya?* Antonov unflinchingly answered his own question: *Because you'd rather think about that, or anything at all, than about what you've found here on this lovely blue planet.*

Things had gone according to plan. Task Forces 21 and 23 had herded the Bugs out of the system with relentless fighter strikes. They'd never broken that dense defensive formation, but the Bugs had withdrawn minus a quarter of their capital ships and most of their light cruisers. Better still, the warp point through which they'd done their withdrawing had been pinpointed and was now heavily guarded against any counterstroke. Meanwhile, TF 22 had proceeded behind a cloud of recon drones, following the spoor of that which the Grand Alliance had condemned to death.

They'd been prepared for swarms of gunboats to rise from the planet in suicidal fury . . . yet none had. There were only orbital defenses—fortresses and the kind of elaborate military/industrial facilities one would expect around a highly developed planet. Antonov had waited until some of the other task forces' carrier formations had joined him, then finished off the orbital works with SBMHAWK bombardments and fighter strikes. And the planet had lain open to them with its two or three billion Bugs . . . and something else.

The wait for the carriers hadn't been a very long one, but it had allowed time for an extensive survey of the surface. In the course of mapping targets, one of Midori Kozlov's subordinates had noticed vast enclosures that were clearly stockyards for meat animals—six-legged vertebrates like all the planet's higher land fauna. But something had bothered him, a wrongness he couldn't quite put his finger on. Kozlov hadn't been able to put her finger on it either, at first. She'd demanded greater and greater magnifications of the imagery . . . .

No one could ever forget the moment when the screen had shown one of the meat animals, the foremost third of its body held erect, making marks on the wall of a shed with a crude implement held in one of its forefeet.

After the planet's sky had been cleared of all opposition, more detailed reconnaissance had commenced, using aural sensors that were the highly evolved descendants of an earlier century's shotgun mikes. And they'd all watched the meat animals, most of them almost reverted to a hexapedal habit, go about their rudimentary socialization under the leadership of the class that had somehow halted their degradation just short of the loss of writing. The computers were still trying to crack the spoken language, and had analyzed a few of the sounds. One of those sounds was "Harnah" for "world," and so it had become in the minds of the horror-stricken humans who gazed at the overgrown ruins of what had clearly been cities, occasionally adorned with sculptures of the proud centauroids who'd built them.

Kozlov's self-consciously flinty voice roused Antonov from his reverie. She hadn't been the only one to turn green around the gills as realization dawned. In retrospect, perhaps, the discovery was inevitable; in every other sense it had been unthinkable. Justin and Kliean had told the Grand Alliance the Bugs regarded them as food sources, yet some deep-seated part of the Alliance's analysts had seen that as an act of opportunity, like the pre-space practices of strip-mining or clear-cutting watersheds. The notion that even Bugs would actually raise sentient beings as a self-sustaining herd of meat animals had not occurred to them . . . *perhaps*, Antonov reflected grimly, *simply because it was so utterly unacceptable*.

"There's no room for doubt," Kozlov was telling the staff and various senior officers. "They're the descendants of the city builders, the original inhabitants of Harnah. Indications are that their civilization was no more advanced than early twentieth-century Earth's. Vacuum tube electronics and hydrocarbon-burning internal combustion engines. They never stood a chance when the Bugs arrived."

Raymond Prescott shook his head slowly. "Are you sure? I mean . . ." He gestured vaguely, and they all knew what he meant, for they'd all watched the occupants of those vast, fetid, dung-choked pens as they shuffled listlessly about.

"Quite sure, Admiral Prescott. Granted, they're incredibly degraded. We have no way of knowing how long they've been . . . livestock. Quite a while, from the condition of the ruins. But they're still sentient—they haven't had time to evolve away from it, even though the capacity to feel such things as rebelliousness must be decidedly contra-survival in their circumstances."

"So," Stovall said in the voice of a man trying to awake from nightmare, "they *know* that they're going to be . . . ?"

"Yes." Kozlov nodded jerkily. Her color was poor, and her voice was that of a machine. "There will have been a strong natural selection in favor of those willing to go on living—and bringing forth offspring—as a domesticated food source."

They were all silent for a few heartbeats, each of them alone in hell with the new-found knowledge that there are worse things than extinction. But they weren't really alone at all, for the human inhabitants of the Bug-occupied worlds seemed to fill the room.

Finally, Antonov cleared his throat. In that silence, it was like a thunderclap. "Thank you, Commodore Kozlov. And now, ladies and gentlemen, we must consider the effect of these findings on our plans to carry out General Directive 18."

De Bertholet's head jerked upward, as though emerging from his private vision of horror. "Ah, Admiral, I don't understand. Surely no one can now doubt the wisdom of reactivating the Directive." The sick look on his face began to give way to one of fury. "The universe must be cleansed of these monsters! We're dealing with an abomination beyond humanity's conception of evil. By comparison, Hitler was a naughty boy, the Rigelians mildly maladjusted!"

"Agreed, Commander. But the Harnahese present a complicating factor. There are, Commodore Kozlov estimates, several million of them scattered among the Bug billions. It isn't always easy to tell just *where* they are, for the 'ranches' where they're bred are interspersed with those devoted to raising other, lower animal species native to this planet." He leaned forward, and his voice dropped to a basso fit for a Mussorgsky chorus. "I am under orders to exterminate the Bugs wherever I find them. But I am neither ordered nor authorized to commit genocide upon *another* sentient race. And I am disinclined to do so—especially in this case." He smiled slightly. "The older one gets, the harder it becomes to believe in any kind of universal ethical balance—divine justice, if you will. But one doesn't like to take chances! And should I happen to be wrong in my skepticism . . . well, if anyone in the universe has suffered enough, the Harnahese have."

Stovall broke the awkward silence that followed. "Admiral, the fact remains that we, like all Alliance forces, are subject to the general order to extirpate all Bug populations. And the Harnahese presence here poses a moral dilemma only if we limit our tactical options to scorching the surface clean of life. Perhaps there are other alternatives."

"I've considered those alternatives, Commodore. General Nagata, please summarize our discussion on the subject."

Brigadier Heinrich Nagata, the senior Marine officer embarked with Second Fleet, came unconsciously to a seated position of attention. "Sir, ever since Justin we've known how tough the Bugs can be in a ground action. And this is the first time we've ever contemplated fighting them on the surface of a long-established planet of theirs, with hundreds of millions of workers available to soak up fire." He paused awkwardly, unaccustomed to presenting arguments *against* going in. But he plowed ahead. "Second Fleet as presently constituted doesn't even incorporate a real landing force. We didn't anticipate needing one. With the reactivation of General Directive 18, it was assumed that any Bug-inhabited worlds would simply be smashed from orbit. All I've got are the ships' regular Marine detachments. There's simply no way I could hope to go down there and selectively wipe out three billion Bugs while preserving the Harnahese."

Kozlov looked up in agony. "We're only two transits from Alpha Centauri, three from Sol. Maybe we could bring in more surface forces—"

"You're talking about Marines, Commodore!" Nagata snapped. "Do you have any conception of how many of them would die, even if we brought in the whole damned Corps?"

"I'm sorry, Brigadier. I know what they'd have to face. But what *else* are we to do?"

Antonov's voice cut the exchange off like a battleaxe. "That cannot be our decision. A policy is going to have to be hammered out for dealing with this world—and others like it. Our surprise is merely a result of wishful thinking; we should have anticipated such situations."

"How coulddd we hhhave, Admiral?" Taathaanahk asked quietly. "Admittedly, we hhhave alll haddd to accusssstom ourselves to whattt the Buggsss do to the inhabitants of conquereddd worrrlds. But the nnnotion of sssentient beingsss rrraised from birthhh as . . ." He couldn't continue. It was the first time any of them had seen the avian lose his composure.

"I suppose," Raymond Prescott grated, "we've simply assumed—*had* to assume—that the Bugs gorged on the conquered human populations until they'd finished them off. We never let ourselves consider that they were keeping some as . . . as breeding stock. Children, probably . . ."

A low sound, more primal than any spoken language, suffused the compartment. Antonov cut it off.

"For present, I have decided how we will proceed." They all noticed the loss of definite articles; a few knew him well enough to realize the stress level that implied. "Commodore Stovall, I want staff to plan surgical strikes aimed at destroying all spaceport facilities and major industrial centers and military installations on surface, as well as any remaining space-based industry. And no, I don't expect you to guarantee these strikes won't kill a single Harnahese; only a politician could be so fatuous. We'll strand Harnah's Bug population on planet, where it can be left to await Alliance's decision. Our next courier drone will inform Centauri of this course of action—and of my assumption of full responsibility for it."

He stood up abruptly and stalked out of the room before the rest of them could rise. They were left staring at the view screen, at the lovely blue planet.

"Yes, Admiral Antonov, the Joint Chiefs—with Sky Marshal Avram's hearty concurrence—fully endorse your handling of the Harnah problem. They wished me to convey that to you in the most emphatic terms." Rear Admiral Jamal Moreno beamed at Antonov. He'd only just arrived at the head of reinforcements that included factory-like repair ships, even more welcome than the warships to a heavily damaged Second Fleet.

"So," Stovall asked, "have they decided what to do about Harnah?" He, de Bertholet and Kozlov sat with the two admirals, bathed in the simulated ruddy light of Anderson Two's primary. One entire bulkhead of *Colorado's* flag lounge was a holo projection, and the cozy compartment seemed open to space in a way that someone from an earlier era would have found disconcerting.

"Not yet," Moreno told him. "They're still thrashing out the problem. It's hoped that genetic engineering may provide the answer: a tailored virus that's deadly to Bugs but harmless to indigenous Harnahese life. They want me to bring back biological samples, which shouldn't be hard to obtain given your absolute control of the planet's sky."

The staffers looked at each other, clearly uncomfortable with the idea. Which, Antonov thought, was a measure of the effect this war was having on its participants. Three years earlier, they wouldn't have been uncomfortable; they would have been glassy-eyed with shock.

The making of microorganisms to order had been a simple matter as far back as the twenty-first century. At first, few had appreciated the horrific potentialities of the djinn crouching within the shiny new bottle. But a few *very* close calls had brought humanity to the realization that, as Howard Anderson had once remarked, "a nuke is just a big bubble-gum pop by comparison." The problem, of course, was microbes' susceptibility to mutation, combined with their eyeblink-brief generations. Tailored bioweapons could evolve out from under whatever limitations had been engineered into them with terrifying speed, and the youthful Federation had decided, with rare unanimity, that the djinn must never be let out. The matter had been beyond debate for centuries, and the Orions, on whose original home world it *had* been let out, were even more emphatic.

"Well," Antonov said gruffly, "with Lord Talphon running the Joint Chiefs, I know any experiments along these lines will be conducted under *extreme* safeguards. We'll send expeditions down to collect your specimens. But now," he continued in a tone that closed the subject, "the Harnah issue is out of our hands. We need to turn to the question of Second Fleet's next move."

De Bertholet looked alarmed. "Surely, Admiral, there can be no question! Once again, we've had our avenue of advance marked out for us by retreating Bugs, and the recon drones have confirmed there are no fortresses guarding the next system. It must be an uninhabited system which doesn't rate large-scale fixed defenses."

"Still," Kozlov said dubiously, "the drones also indicate the Bugs have been surrounding the warp point with minefields and laser buoys. And the mobile forces we drove out of this system have been reinforced up to somewhat more than their original strength."

"In absolute terms, yes," de Bertholet retorted. "But relative to our forces, including the reinforcements Admiral Moreno's brought, they're weaker than they were." He turned back to Antonov with a look of urgency. "Admiral, the enemy can't fail to recognize the threat Operation Pesthouse represents. They would surely have poured in more reinforcements to contest our next transit—*if they could!*"

"This is just more of the same argument you used when we entered *this* system," Kozlov protested.

"And it's just as valid as it was then! Either we're in a poorly defended frontier region, as we originally theorized, or—" a feverish gleam of excitement entered his eyes "—they're so heavily committed on the established fronts that they're coming to the end of their resources! If the former, then we should press on and gain as much ground as possible before reinforcements finally arrive from their main bases, as ours finally arrived in the Romulus Chain. If the latter . . . then they have no massive reserves left to place in our path!"

Stovall spoke in his slow, deliberate way. "I find myself in agreement with Armand, Admiral. In light of what we've seen here, we have a moral responsibility to pursue any course of action that promises a quick end to this war—and to the Bugs!" Kozlov shot him a surprised look, and he smiled with the self-deprecating humor that was so much a part of him. "Yes, I know; we North Americans have always been suckers for anything marketed as a 'moral responsibility.' But look at it from the narrowly tactical standpoint. Here we have a significant force of Bug capital ships which, since they have command datalink, must be among their newest construction or retrofits. And we're in a position to annihilate them!"

"Actually, Commodore," Antonov said in the quiet voice that often surprised people, "I'm less interested in annihilating them than in forcing them to retreat." He smiled into their surprised faces. "You see, I still want to see which *way* they retreat. While I'm not yet prepared to let myself believe in Commander de Bertholet's second possibility, I am firmly convinced the Bugs are in retreat towards their centers of population." He paused, then spoke as much to himself as to the others. "I've made myself remain alert to the possibility of some kind of trap—even more than I ordinarily would, given the alienness of the mind-set we're dealing with. But, damn it, these creatures can build starships! However weird they are, they must be *rational*. That's been true of every technologically advanced race we've encountered. Even those whose philosophies were incomprehensible or repugnant to us, like the Rigellians, were capable of acting rationally in pursuit of those philosophies' goals. But the Bugs have now given up a planet inhabited by over three billion of their own race. I cannot believe rational beings would do such a thing—particularly after *they* initiated the saturation bombardment of planetary populations—if they had *any* other option. And no rational fleet commander would willingly leave this large a force in a position where it didn't stand a chance of survival!"

"Exactly, Sir," de Bertholet urged. "They aren't strong enough to stop us, but sixty-six capital ships and thirty-six light cruisers are too much for *anyone* to consider expendable."

"Still Admiral," Kozlov spoke up, "I'm worried about the possibility of flank attacks. It's a danger that grows as we advance further into enemy space. The latest news from Anderson One should remind us of that."

"What?" Antonov looked up, blinking away his preoccupation. "Oh, yes; the third warp point our survey turned up. They're reasonably certain they've found all the warp points that are there to be found, correct?"

"Yes, Sir."

"Well, then, we'll take most of the ships off survey operations in Anderson One and form them into a flotilla to explore the warp chain beyond this new warp point. We'll make sure we won't be taken by surprise."

Kozlov looked worried. "I'd hoped we could bring some of those ships forward to join us here in Anderson Two, Sir. With all our present survey assets occupied searching this system for warp points, we won't have many survey-equipped craft to take with us into the next one."

De Bertholet waved the point aside. "Let's worry first about fighting our way into it—Anderson Three, I suppose we'll call it. Plenty of time for survey after we're in possession."

"I suppose so," Kozlov said, not sounding altogether convinced.

Antonov only half-heard the exchange. He was examining the problem from every possible angle, seeking any sources of danger he'd missed. For the life of him, he couldn't think of any. Unless . . . but no. Such a mentality was simply inconceivable.

The dark, silent ships hung in space, awaiting the arrival of the enemy who had, unbeknownst to them, named this system "Anderson Three"—this system that the ships were destined never to leave. But that was a matter of no moment to them. That it could even be a consideration was simply inconceivable.

CHAPTER THIRTY-SIX

"I *want* them to escape."

Ivan Antonov's recon drones had told him of the dense minefields that surrounded the emergence warp point in Anderson Three, and of the fifty-seven heavy cruisers that covered those minefields. So he knew how intense an SBMHAWK bombardment was needed to burn a path through those defenses for Second Fleet.

The drones had also confirmed that the enemy's heavy units were being held well back from the warp point. As usual, that placed them outside SBMHAWK range, but Antonov didn't mind, for it allowed him to revive a classic tactic of carrier warfare.

This time, the first ships to enter the hostile system were Admiral Taathaanahk's assault carriers. The instant carbon- and silicon-based brains had reoriented themselves from the wrongness of warp transit, the electromagnetic catapults flung scores of fighters into space. Then the CVAs executed a tight turn and began vanishing back into the warp point from whence they'd come. Once back in Anderson Two they would turn again and re-enter Anderson Three, where their fighters would presumably be ready for rearming after fulfilling their task of covering the emergence of the subsequent assault waves.

It was the sort of maneuver which would have been flatly impossible in the days of reaction drives. Even today, such a turning radius was beyond the capabilities of any other ships in the new super carriers' size range—superdreadnoughts and the very largest freighters. But the maneuver worked, and the superdreadnoughts of Task Force 22 emerged into the unaccustomed environment of friendly-controlled space.

They faced an enemy who was behaving very oddly. Gunboat deployments were promptly detected, and TF 22 braced itself for kamikaze attacks. But none came, and the Bugs hung back in uncharacteristic hesitation while the bulk of van der Gelder's ships—including *Colorado*—transited unmolested. Only then did they close to long missile range.

Antonov had expended almost all his fourth-generation SBMHAWKs to clear the warp point, but he retained a substantial reserve of third-generation pods. These now transited and came under TF 22's control. They went far toward redressing the balance between fifty-six Bug superdreadnoughts and about thirty Terran ones. But the former *did* have command datalink now.

"Admiral," de Bertholet suggested after a time, "should we order the fighters to attack in support of the battle-line?"

"*Nyet*," Antonov answered absently. He knew what was bothering the ops officer. The initial missile exchanges had favored Second Fleet—but those loss ratios included the results of the SBMHAWK increment to TF 22's firepower, and couldn't be expected to continue after the missile pods were gone. Still . . .

"No," he repeated. "For now, we'll continue to hold them back as a shield against gunboat attacks. It's too soon to risk heavy fighter losses. Admiral Taathaanahk's carriers are due back shortly, in conjunction with Admiral Prescott's ships. When we have our entire carrier strength in this system, it will be time to launch a massive, coordinated strike."

Time wore on, and the anticipated gunboat attack failed to materialize. But the shift in the statistics of carnage after the SBMHAWKs ceased to be a factor was as per expectations. The Bugs were playing it very cagily, keeping the missile duel at long range and drawing back gradually as more and more Terran superdreadnoughts emerged. Antonov sensed a mood he didn't like on the flag bridge, a kind of nervous incomprehension of such a radical departure from the Bugs' "normal" suicidal eagerness to close to the shortest possible range. As Taathaanahk's and Prescott's carriers transited one by one, he found himself fretting as well. But the delay gave de Bertholet time to coordinate with TF 23 ops, and it was a very purposeful wave of over seven hundred fighters—Antonov was still holding back his defensive screen—that streaked away towards the silent black ships.

They encountered a nasty surprise: Bug gunboats in a purely defensive stance. The small craft drew as much blood as possible with their externally mounted anti-fighter missiles, then pulled back into a defensive envelope around their capital ships. Strictly defensive formations were rare in space warfare, and this proved to be a very strong one. Frustrated, stung by their losses, and still under orders to avoid excessive losses while still in Anderson Three's outer system, the fighters withdrew for rearming.

That operation reminded Antonov of a possibly decisive advantage that still remained to him, if he only exploited it. He proceeded to do so, ordering Second Fleet to press the missile duel, allowing the Bugs no respite in which to shut down their drives in order to rearm the gunboats. So it was with their internal weaponry alone that those gunboats faced a fresh assault by fighters laden with missiles and freed of their earlier tactical constraints.

Taathaanahk's pilots went relentlessly in, the humans hurling missile strikes at the gunboats while their Ophiuchi comrades covered them against the anticipated counter-attack by those gunboats. But the Bugs stubbornly refused to be drawn out of their defensive hedgehog, and the Ophiuchi were denied the dogfighting at which they were the acknowledged masters. Instead, the fighters pressed their attack home into the defensive envelopes of the Bug capital ships' massive energy weapons and numerous missile launchers, grimly accepting whatever losses it took to blast the gunboats out of the equation.

"And," de Bertholet concluded his report to a hastily convened staff meeting, "the last of the squadrons have reported in or are accounted for. They're all en route back to their carriers, and the loss figures can be regarded as definitive." He indicated the columns of color-coded numbers on the display screen of the small conference room just off *Colorado*'s flag bridge.

Antonov eyed those figures with scant favor. He'd been forced to jettison his original guidelines for what constituted acceptable fighter losses, and he didn't like it. Still less did he like the way the Bugs—*sans* gunboats but still formidable—were continuing to be coy. Their tight formation held back just outside missile range, five and a half light-hours from the K type primary star of this undistinguished binary system whose details the probing RDs were gradually filling in on the plot. They'd already ruled out any high-tech population centers, and Antonov caught himself sighing with relief that there'd be no Harnah here. He shook the thought aside and glared anew at the red icons representing the Bug force, not giving battle but impossible to ignore.

He grew aware that de Bertholet had finished. "Thank you, Commander. Now, Commodore Kozlov, have you been able to form any rationale for the enemy's behavior?"

"We've all been thrashing that one out, Sir. The consensus seems to be that they're being cautious about risking ships equipped with their new datalink technology. Also, they may not have settled yet on a tactical doctrine for utilizing that technology."

"You mean," Stovall queried, "they're still experimenting, and right now they're impressed with its defensive possibilities?"

"That accounts for the observed facts while minimizing assumptions." She gave one of her infrequent smiles. "I'm not sure Bugs shave with Occam's Razor. But it's the best I can do at present."

Antonov continued to glare at those red icons. "If they

won't come to us," he rumbled, "we'll go to them. With our tactical speed advantage, we can force engagement. But before we do, I want our emergency repairs completed. There should be time, because I also want us to wait until the fleet train can rendezvous with us and replenish our depletable munitions."

"Aye, aye, Sir." The relief on Stovall's face was palpable. "Might I suggest that we also consider some organizational adjustment on the battlegroup level? Our losses—especially the five superdreadnoughts—have resulted in some imbalances."

"An excellent suggestion, Commodore. See to it that—"

What brought Antonov up short was the sudden jerk of Midori Kozlov's left forearm. He recognized the reaction of one who was being given an emergency jolt by a wrist communicator—an entirely unexpected jolt, for she'd left orders not to be interrupted. She gave Antonov an embarrassed look.

"Answer it, Commodore Kozlov," he said mildly.

She complied, with the device on minimal volume and held close to her ear. Whatever she was hearing caused the blood to drain from her face. But she reported to Antonov in level tones.

"Admiral, one of our drones has detected hostiles transiting into this system through a warp point located almost directly between us and the system primary—and only about eighty light-minutes from us. CIC designates them Force Two, and they'll be appearing on the display directly."

She'd barely stopped speaking before the fresh icons started blinking into existence. The reporting drone was very close, and data on their force composition began to roll in quickly.

"Lordy," Stovall broke the silence. "This is like Anderson One all over again!"

"Not quite, Sir," Kozlov said, her eyes still fixed on the unfolding data. "There, the second Bug force didn't arrive until we had finished wiping out the system's defenders. *This* force has appeared when we're just *preparing* to do so."

"Precisely, Admiral," de Bertholet said, in rare agreement with the spook. "And on their present vectors the two forces will rendezvous before we can complete the repairs and resupply you've ordered."

Antonov nodded absently as he studied Force Two's composition: eighteen superdreadnoughts and twenty-four battlecruisers. He could continue as planned, and then a rearmed, repaired Second Fleet would face defenders reinforced by those forty-two fresh ships—which, he had to assume, possessed command datalink. Or he could strike now and seek to defeat the two enemy fleets in detail. Given those alternatives, his choice was clear if far from easy.

"Commodore Stovall, as soon as the fighters have rearmed, all elements of Second Fleet will advance to attack Force One. Our objective is to annihilate it before the new arrivals can make contact." He raised a hand in a gesture which foreclosed any discussion. "Yes, I know, we're battered and depleted. Well, they're also battered and depleted. I want there to be nothing but cooling plasma for Force Two to rendezvous with!"

It was a haggard staff that reconvened in the same compartment. Antonov, as usual, seemed elementally impervious to both fatigue and horror, but the others showed the strain of the battle whose reverberations had just died away.

"Are all ships now accounted for?" the admiral asked without preamble.

"Yes, Sir," de Bertholet acknowledged. His left arm hung in a sling; one of Colorado's lurches from a near miss had sent him staggering against a stanchion with shoulder-dislocating force.

"Then report on Fleet's status."

"Aye, aye, Sir. We lost nine superdreadnoughts outright, in addition to the five we lost in the earlier fighting. At that, it could have been worse; as our tactical analysis suggested, they were concentrating their fire on the SDs. Twenty-seven took moderate to heavy damage, but we've only had to order one of them back to Anderson Two—that's *Colima*. *Colorado* got off very lightly, in spite of . . ." He ruefully indicated his arm. "They didn't pay nearly as much attention to our lighter units, but we still lost seven battle-cruisers, with another thirteen damaged."

"And fighter losses?" Antonov had a pretty good idea of what he was going to hear, and he didn't relish it.

"Forty-seven percent of our embarked strength." A chorus of gasps ran around the room. "However, the positive side is that we've fulfilled our objective. All but two of the enemy are confirmed kills, and those two—both battlecruisers—are believed to have withdrawn into cloak."

"What about Force Two?"

"Its status is unchanged, Sir. It completed the course-reversal that it commenced as the battle here reached its final stages, and is continuing to withdraw to its entry warp point at its maximum speed. Your orders as to the pursuit are being carried out: TF 22's faster, relatively undamaged ships are being temporarily reassigned to Admiral Prescott. He and Admiral Taathaanahk probably won't be able to intercept it before it transits, but it's been made clear to them that their first priority is to locate that warp point."

"Good. The rest of us will follow as quickly as possible. And now, Commodore Kozlov, what interpretation do you place on the enemy's actions in this system?"

Midori Kozlov ran a hand through her hair in a characteristic gesture of discomfort. "Admiral, I was discussing this with Commander de Bertholet just before this meeting convened. And while I'm still not altogether comfortable with the conclusion, I can no longer see any reason for *not* concurring with him. A force that powerful—but still manifestly insufficient to stop us—would never have been ordered to stand and fight to the last ship if there were any alternative. It would have either been reinforced or withdrawn to participate in an eventual counterattack, if the resources for such reinforcement or such a counterattack existed. What finally convinced me was the behavior of the reinforcements they *did* put into the system. They tried desperately to come to the aid of the defending force and didn't turn tail until it became unmistakably clear that they couldn't make any difference to the outcome."

"Thank you, Commodore. Does anyone else wish to offer any thoughts?" For once, there was silence, as de Bertholet left well enough alone and no one else sought to disagree.

Antonov examined his own thoughts. Advancing into the unknown like this, overconfidence was the great enemy. From the first, he'd made himself think in terms of the possible trap, the low-probability contingency, the worst-case scenario. But there seemed no rational alternative to the conclusion that they'd broken into the territory of an enemy who was, at least locally, vulnerable. And anything de Bertholet and Kozlov agreed on must be virtually beyond dispute!

"Thank you, Commodore," he said aloud. "I believe your analysis has merit. But for now, we will continue the pursuit."

"The recon drones are beginning to report back, Admiral," Stovall reported.

Antonov grunted. They'd followed the fleeing enemy across Anderson Three's outer system, narrowing the gap but, as he'd more than half expected, unable to overhaul them. The Bugs had transited without slowing down, and Antonov, still wary of ambushes, had ordered recon drones sent ahead to probe the warp point. He wasn't about to charge through in pursuit with no idea of what lay ahead, especially with Second Fleet in a strung-out configuration as the slower ships proceeded towards the warp point even more slowly than usual in order to allow those of their number who'd suffered drive damage to remain in formation.

In a surprisingly short time, Kozlov crossed *Colorado*'s flag bridge and reported to Antonov. Beneath her usual reserve, he thought he could sense a sternly suppressed excitement. But that was typical of the way she'd been acting in this system. She hadn't even come to him with her usual requests for more of their thinly stretched survey resources to explore it for warp points. Doubtless that was why he'd never quite gotten around to ordering it. *Must see to it,* he started to tell himself. But then Kozlov spoke.

"Sir, an unusually large number of drones have reported back—the reason why will become apparent shortly—so we've been able to flesh out our information quickly. What's on the far side of the warp point is a class G single-star system, but with no evidence of habitation. And the Bugs haven't stopped after transiting; they're continuing on across the outer system—the entry warp point is about twenty-three light-minutes from the primary. And . . ." She paused with the air of someone saving the best for last. " . . .the warp point isn't defended. It *isn't even mined.*"

De Bertholet couldn't contain himself. "Admiral! This is the final proof! We *must* have broken through the enemy's defensive shell."

Antonov understood perfectly. Every star nation's defensive doctrine—and there had, God knew, been no indication the Bugs disagreed—called for routinely mining warp points that led inward from the frontier towards the core worlds, turning every system into a barrier to at least delay an invader. Thus the *absence* of mines meant Second Fleet must have entered regions where the Bugs felt entirely safe from attack. They'd burst into a defensive vacuum.

He forced his excitement to heel. "You say they're proceeding across the outer system?"

"Yes, Sir. Their vector takes them even further from the primary, out between two gas-giant orbits. There *can't* be anything out there but another warp point."

"Towards which they're in headlong flight!" Triumph clanged in de Bertholet's voice.

"Still," Stovall cautioned, "we can't rule out the possibility of cloaked enemy units. The drones couldn't have detected them." Antonov knew the chief of staff well enough to recognize the signs of the same predatory excitement that was infecting the rest of them, but being the voice of caution had become a self-imposed duty for him.

"Nevertheless, Commodore, we will transit without delay and proceed in pursuit. But because the point you've raised is a valid one, we'll keep the fleet together as we do so, and not allow the faster ships to open up too much distance between themselves and the main body."

"That will slow us considerably, Sir," de Bertholet pointed out. "Especially given the fact that a number of our superdreadnoughts are even slower than usual due to drive damage."

"I'm aware of that, Commander. But I can accept it." Antonov smiled tightly. "You see, I'm not really interested in catching these Bugs. I want them to escape, showing us the location of the next warp point as they do so."

The last of the Fleet reemerged into normal space-time, leaving behind the swirling combat of gunboats and fighters in the system it had fled.

There had never been any real danger of being overhauled by the enemy's main body in the stern chase across that system. That main body had held tenaciously together, and on at least one occasion the swifter ships had clearly been ordered back as they began to leave their slower sisters too far behind. But the enemy's tiny attack craft had ranged far ahead, and many ships bore the marks of their harassing attacks. The gunboats had been expended to fend off those tormentors, and the remaining ones had been left behind.

The Fleet had been concerned by the possibility that the enemy would, despite everything, overtake it before it could transit, for that would have prevented it from performing that which had been its function from the first: to show the enemy this warp point which he himself wanted so badly to be shown.

But things had gone according to plan. Now nothing must be done to alarm this inscrutable foe into changing his *plan. Which meant, among other things, that no action must be taken against that small exploratory force whose precise location at any given time had proven so annoyingly difficult to pinpoint.*

The disorientation of warp transit subsided, and the heavens stabilized into a pattern bereft of a sun. Rear Admiral Aileen Sommers, commanding Survey Flotilla 19, ordered herself not to be disappointed.

Captain Feridoun Hafezi, her chief of staff, was standing close enough to read her mind. Teeth flashed in his neatly trimmed black beard. "We already knew this was a starless warp nexus, Admiral. The recon drones told us as much."

"Oh, I know. But we've been exploring this worthless warp chain for almost two months, and the only thing to be said for it is that since every system's had just two warp points, there's never been any question where to proceed next. It would've been nice to find something interesting for once. And the fact that our first transit was also into the middle of nowhere makes this almost like rubbing it in."

They'd departed from the conquered system Ivan the Terrible had dubbed Anderson One shortly after its third warp point had been located, entering that first starless warp nexus through a closed warp point. Since then they'd forged on through two systems, both barren—the first a miserable little binary of two red dwarfs, but the second a single star glowing with the yellow light that *ought* to portend life.

"Yes, that last system was a real letdown," Hafezi said, continuing to track her thoughts. "But even if it had had a planet of the right mass at the right orbital radius, it wouldn't have been any good. We knew that star was really young as soon as we got the figures on its rotation rate."

"True. And if there *had* been a life-bearing planet, it probably would've been a solid, writhing mass of Bugs. Still . . ." Sommers started to run a hand through her hair, then remembered that the longish growth—oddly colored, basically dark but with blond streaks—was pulled tightly together at the back of her head. Irritably, she turned away from Hafezi and walked the few steps required to cross the cramped flag bridge of a *Thetis*-class command battlecruiser like *Jamaica*. She stood in front of the view screen and listened as one ship after another reported successful transit.

In her early forties, Aileen Sommers was young for her rank. She was of medium height and had a figure which none of the men in her life—she'd never married—had been able to describe in terms that helped with a certain deeply buried insecurity. It had been self-evident to them that there was absolutely nothing mannish about her, but rather that she looked like exactly what she was: a very strong woman. In fact, this was self-evident to everyone . . . except her.

Hafezi rejoined her, rubbing the tip of his hawklike nose. Sommers had a weakness for historical holodrama, and her mental image of her chief of staff always included a snowy burnoose and flowing white robes. Which was inaccurate, of course. Hafezi's ancestry was Iranian, not Arab, and it was an important part of him. The third son of a highly respected imam, the captain was proud of the role his family had played in rebuilding—and humanizing—Old Terra's Middle East after the carnage of the Great Eastern war.

"I wonder what's happening with Second Fleet?" he asked now, not expecting an answer. It was the flotilla's staple topic of conversation, and had been ever since they'd departed Anderson One in a different direction from that followed by Antonov's fleet. They'd learned of the outcome in Anderson Two and the discovery of Harnah by courier drone while still surveying that first starless warp nexus. Since then . . .

"Too bad we can't still get courier drones," Hafezi resumed.

"True, but there's nothing to be done about it," Sommers replied. "We've gone too far for drones to have a prayer of reaching us without nav buoys at the warp points." *And*, she didn't need to add, *emplacing such buoys*

*would have been like advertising the flotilla's position with
bells and strobe lights for any cloaked Bug pickets that
might be lurking in the systems through which they'd
passed.*

It was an extension of the same consideration which had
led GHQ to issue orders to operate permanently in cloak.
Some of the survey specialists hated the way that slowed
their work, but Sommers, Captain Kabilovic, and the rest
of the "gunslingers" backed it enthusiastically . . . especially
after events in Zephrain.

A report distracted Hafezi's attention for a moment.
Then he turned back. "Everyone's completed transit,
Admiral." An instant later, a status board update verified
his words.

Sommers studied the board. Survey flotillas these days
were weightier than they'd been in prewar days, but SF
19 was even more powerful than usual, since no separate
covering force was available. Besides *Jamaica*, Sommers
commanded three other command battlecruisers to weld
her firepower into datagroups, and that firepower
included five *Dunkerque*-class missile-armed battlecruisers, but the centerpiece of the gunslinger array was
Captain Kabilovic's fleet carrier *Staghound* and the two
attached Ophiuchi *Zirk-Coaalkyr*-class CVLs. Five
Atlanta-class CLEs provided defensive support for the
main combatants, and two *Wayfarer*-class freighters
carried extra ordinance as well as recon drones, maintenance materials and everything else required for long-
term self-sufficiency.

All of the above were along to protect and nurture the
five *Hun*-class cruisers which did the actual survey work
. . . and whose crews could perhaps be excused for
occasional insufferableness about being the *raison d'etre*
for what was, on prewar standards, a not insignificant
fighting force.

"All right, Feridoun," the admiral said briskly. "Let's
recover the drones; waste not, want not. Then we can
commence surveying for warp points. At least we've no
planets to check out."

"That's putting the best possible face on things, Sir," Hafezi muttered. Then he brightened. "Maybe there won't *be* any other warp points, and we'll be able to turn back and report that this is a dead-end warp chain. Then maybe we'll be sent somewhere *interesting*."

CHAPTER THIRTY-SEVEN

"They're not our drones!"

The entire auditoriumlike room rose to attention as Ivan Antonov entered, with Stovall in tow. He took his seat and looked out over the full staff and the senior flag officers and their own chiefs of staff—a sea of TFN black and silver varied by the Ophiuchi and their multicolored feathers. The latter were famous—or infamous, depending on one's viewpoint—for their uncomprehending rejection of military punctilio in all its manifestations, but they'd risen to their feet along with everyone else out of simple courtesy, and respect for the supreme commander.

"As you were," Antonov rumbled. "I trust you've all familiarized yourselves thoroughly with the plan for Operation Xenophon. I realize your time has been limited—as was the time Commander de Bertholet and the rest of the staff had to prepare it." Stovall's face showed satisfaction at the implied compliment even as it showed exhaustion—he had suitcases under his bags. It was certainly true that their time had been limited; Second Fleet had only been here in Anderson Four nineteen standard days, and there had been much else to compete for their attention, notably repairs to battle damage.

"I wish," Antonov continued, "to review the considerations behind our planning. After we secured this system and invested the warp point the Bugs had revealed to us in the course of their withdrawal, we probed that warp point with recon drones. Our probing revealed that the next system has the kind of dense minefields whose absence surprised us in this one. This made it out of the question to press on directly through the warp point. Instead, the decision was made to recoup our strength for a carefully prepared offensive against that system, which clearly is the holding position we've all been expecting to encounter. And subsequent probes have reported that the Bug defenders have been reinforced by eighteen superdreadnoughts, suggesting that the Bugs are frantically trying to shore that position up. We cannot give them any more time to do so.

"It is for this reason that our schedule has been moved up, and the commencement of Operation Xenophon set for tomorrow."

Antonov paused and ran his eyes over the faces. He saw worry on many of them, and he understood it fully. "This decision was not an easy one. I am well aware that Second Fleet is weaker than it was before the last battle; only five fresh superdreadnoughts have arrived to offset the cripples we haven't had time to repair." The concern on Jessica van der Gelder's face intensified, for a disproportionate number of the absent cripples back in Anderson Four with Admiral Chin and the Fleet Train came from her task force. At least she'd gotten Chin's battleships in partial recompense. "But on the positive side," Antonov continued, "our fighter groups have been brought back up to full strength, and our SBMHAWK supplies replenished. Furthermore, the tactical equation should be changed in our favor by the new capital missiles." He saw some of the faces brighten a bit, for they'd all been impressed by the new missile package, with its enhanced penetration aids and evasive maneuvering capabilities. After their experience with datalinked Bug point defense, they were more than willing to accept the tradeoff of some payload capacity.

"Before we take up a detailed discussion of the plan, are there any questions concerning the larger picture?" Antonov scanned the gathering. "Admiral Prescott?"

"Just one thing, Sir. I'm a little concerned about the allocation of our survey assets since SF 24's departure."

There was a murmur of unease. As if they hadn't had enough on their minds here in Anderson Four, a third warp point had come to light, not far, as interplanetary distances went, from the one through which they were preparing to hurl Operation Xenophon. So most of the scout cruisers which had somewhat belatedly set to work in Anderson Three had been rushed forward, and a new flotilla had been organized. It had vanished into the newly discovered warp point only two days before.

"I'm concerned," Prescott repeated, "by the de-emphasis of Anderson Three's warp point survey."

"Commander de Bertholet," Antonov said, turning towards the ops officer, "would you like to respond?"

"Our survey assets are finite, Admiral Prescott, and became even more so when Admiral Sommers' SF 19 was detached in Anderson One. The ones we've got left have become stretched ever more thinly as we've advanced further into enemy space. We've simply had to assign priorities and make choices. When the third warp point turned up here, we had no alternative but to explore beyond it in force. And there may be still others; we haven't completed the survey of this system. I assure you that the search for additional warp points in Anderson Three hasn't been abandoned. We just have fewer ships to do it with."

Prescott said nothing further, for de Bertholet's explanation was unexceptionable. But his face said he wasn't altogether satisfied. *Yes,* Antonov thought, *I too wish we'd started surveying Anderson Three earlier, or had longer to do it before launching Xenophon.* But, he told himself, that was water over the dam. "Thank you, Commander," he said aloud. "And now, if there are no further questions, let us turn to the order in which the first wave's ships will transit."

"General signal from the Flag, Sir. Prepare to execute Xenophon."

"Understood. Anna?" Raymond Prescott glanced at his

chief of staff. Captain Anthea Mandagalla studied her display a moment longer, ebon face intent, then nodded.

"We're ready, Sir—and Admiral Taathaanahk's just confirmed *his* readiness."

"Good." Prescott returned his attention to his plot and the diamond dust of SBMHAWK pods awaiting their brief moment of thunderous splendor. That itchy sense of concern he'd felt since Operation Pesthouse began was back, like the irritating phantom itch of the fingers he no longer had, but that was hardly surprising.

And the bastards are still falling back, he reminded himself, and it was true. Yet he knew a part of him would be happier when Second Fleet finally ran into something so hard it *had* to stop. Considering the wear on its systems, it—

"Execute Xenophon!" the com officer snapped, and hundreds of SBMHAWKs began to vanish.

The waiting gunboats had learned a great deal about the enemy's new missile pods' capabilities, and they knew what to do when the first made transit. Every one of them turned instantly away from the warp point at maximum power, racing to escape the pods' acquisition envelope before the deadly, sprint-mode close assault missiles could launch.

It was the first time they had used the tactic, and it worked for many of them. Those it did not work for were doomed, for all the CAM-armed pods launched against them, and the unstoppable weapons blotted them from the universe. Yet more than half the total CSP survived, and the survivors reversed course as quickly as possible, driving in on the warp point once more.

The heavy cruisers of the warp point defense force fared less well. They were further back, with more time to bring their defensive systems on-line, but they were too slow to evade, and other pods belched standard SBMs against them. Their new datalinked defenses allowed them to destroy hundreds of incoming missiles, and several actually survived. But they were battered and broken, cripples which could inflict little damage upon the enemy. Whatever might be achieved would depend upon the CSP's survivors.

The volume around the warp point was the vestibule of Hell. Bug cruisers blew up, pod-launched AMBAMs streaked outward into the minefields and waiting laser buoys, and TF 23's big, powerful CVAs erupted into an inferno of exploding starships, gunboats, mines, and energy platforms. Surviving laser buoys poured fire into TFNS *Charybdis* and *Succubus*, Vice Admiral Mosby's lead carriers, but this was the sort of attack they'd been *designed* to lead. Their massive armor was rent and buckled, but it held, and Mosby watched her plot stabilize. She felt the whiplash shudder as a full group launch spat from *Thor*'s catapults, more fighter icons erupted from her other carriers, and then—

"Clear decks!" Her ops officer's voice was a bit shriller than usual, but she didn't blame him.

"Turn us around," she replied, and even as *Thor* wheeled to lead the Terran and Ophiuchi carriers back through the warp point, she glanced at her com officer. "Prepare to upload to Admiral Taathaanahk and *Colorado* as soon as we make transit."

She turned back to her plot and winced. The pod-launched AMBAMs had killed most of the Bugs' laser platforms before they could fire; coupled with the CVAs' sheer toughness, that meant most of her ships were going to make it out safely. But the Bugs' new maneuver had saved a lot of their gunboats, and her rearmost units were going to take some heavy hits.

The CSP's own evasion maneuver had carried it beyond immediate striking distance. The nearest gunboat was still far out of range when the big, new carrier vessels made transit, and all of them had launched their attack craft before the defenders could engage them. Nor did the starships linger. Having launched their broods, they wheeled back to the warp point, fleeing with their sensor scans of its environs even as their attack craft howled in to engage the CSP. Dozens of gunboats blew apart, but here and there they broke through, and not all the starships could escape before they were engaged.

Returning carriers spilled from the warp point, transiting with reckless speed and dangerously tight spacing. Most made it safely, but *Dryad* and *Norn*, last in the formation, took a heavy pounding from the gunboats which broke through. Once again, *Dryad's* massive shields and armor stood her in good stead, and she escaped with relatively minor damage. *Norn* was less fortunate, and Ivan Antonov's hard face was expressionless as the shattered, air-streaming wreck staggered from the warp point. A handful of gunboats followed her through, but the massed fighter squadrons covering this side of the warp point made short work of them.

"*Norn's* taken heavy personnel casualties, Sir," de Bertholet reported. He looked up from his console, and his voice was grim. "Commander Lafferty's assumed command. He's her astrogator—third in the chain of command."

Antonov merely nodded, his face betraying none of his own awareness of what a hell the interior of that ship must be just now. Clearly, more of the Bug CSP had survived than anticipated.

"We are fortunate the damage is no worse," he rumbled. "Pass the word, Commander de Bertholet. We will wait ten minutes before sending the next wave through. That should give Mosby's fighters time to clean up the last gunboats."

"Yes, Sir."

"What do we know of their other forces, Commodore Kozlov?"

Kozlov's eyes were locked on her own display, and she didn't look up as she spoke.

"The main body seems to be hanging extremely far back, Sir. They're over seventy light-minutes out, right on the edge of the CVAs' sensor envelope, so our readings are tentative, but it looks like about sixty ships. Plotting and CIC are still trying to refine their data. At the moment, at least seventy percent of them appear to be superdreadnoughts."

"Um." Antonov leaned back in his command chair and rubbed his chin. That would give them near parity with his own battle-line, but they were enormously outnumbered in escorts. *And, of course, they have no carriers. But if they're so far back, why can we see them at all? Why aren't they hiding in cloak?*

De Bertholet sensed his mood. "Sir?"

"I'm simply wondering why they should be so obvious. I don't object to enemies who tell me where they are . . . unless they have something nasty planned for me."

"I was just thinking the same thing, Sir," Stovall said. "It occurs to me that a little caution might be in order."

"Precisely." Antonov shook himself like an irritated bear. "We will take the battle-line through, but we will not advance until we have brought the entire fleet up in support. And we will do so with a fighter shell fifteen light-minutes out in all directions."

The enemy attack craft finished off the last gunboats and crippled heavy cruisers. They took losses of their own, but their casualties were minor compared to the carnage they wreaked. When the enemy's heavy units began to transit at last, the space about the warp point was clear of all save the tattered remnants of minefields which could scarcely even inconvenience him.

The waiting deep space force watched from seventy-one light-minutes as ship after ship streamed from the warp point. The enemy's ship-launched mine-killing missiles completed the task of clearing lanes, and fresh waves of attack craft fanned out to cover his flanks as he began to advance. The deep space force watched . . . and then it began to retreat.

"That's affirmative, Sir," Kozlov announced from her station. "All elements of the enemy main body are withdrawing. They're on a vector which, if unchanged, should take them along this projected course." She made adjustments, and a red line appeared in the flag bridge's holo tank. It was a course that made sense only if the objective was to reach another warp point. *God knows there's nothing else to reach*, Antonov thought; the local primary star was a blue giant, shining palely in a view screen which automatically stepped down its brilliance in deference to human eyes. The recon drones hadn't even bothered scanning for planets.

Maybe the lack of anything to defend explained this unBuglike behavior. Still . . .

"Shall we pursue, Admiral?" de Bertholet asked, breaking into his thoughts.

"*Da*. But we will continue to observe all defensive precautions. Anyone who breaks formation without orders will hear from me!"

"That will hold us down to the speed of the slowest superdreadnoughts." De Bertholet carefully made it an observation, not a protest.

"We will proceed even more slowly than that, Commander. Our drives have been overworked in the course of this campaign, without the opportunity for a proper overhaul. I don't wish to abuse them further. We will pursue at a speed which allows us to keep the Bugs under pressure with fighter strikes. Greater speed than that is neither necessary nor, perhaps, desirable."

"What do you mean, Sir?" Stovall asked.

"Their failure to engage their cloaking ECM still disturbs me. If there's any kind of trap awaiting us, I want to be sure our ships still have their full tactical speed capability available. For this reason, I'd rather not push our drives to their limit just now. If, on the other hand, there's nothing more here than meets the eye—if, that is, it's a simple case of the Bugs retreating because a useless warp nexus like this isn't worth fighting for—then I don't *want* to overtake them before they've shown us the warp point through which they intend to escape."

✧   ✧   ✧

"They're falling back, Sir!" Captain Mandagalla sounded as if she couldn't quite believe her own report. *Crete* and the rest of Prescott's fast superdreadnoughts and battlecruisers led Second Fleet towards the enemy, covered by the smoothly practiced strikegroups of TF 21's CVLs, and Prescott felt his matching surprise as his plot confirmed his chief of staff's report. They *were* falling back, and that itch of worry stirred again.

It wasn't the first time the Bugs had retreated, yet he couldn't quite quash the itch. They *couldn't* retreat fast enough to avoid action forever, and given the massive gunboat force those ships must mother, the logical move would have been to linger just beyond SBMHAWK range, then rush the warp point behind a wall of gunboats and kamikazes. They probably couldn't have *stopped* Second Fleet—especially if Antonov had deployed reserve SBMHAWKs—but it would certainly have been their best chance to hurt it badly. So why hadn't they?

"Anything from the recon fighters, Jacques?" he asked sharply.

"No, Sir," the ops officer replied. "They're over ten light-minutes out already. If there were anything out there, they'd have seen it by now."

The cloaked battlecruisers watched from fifty light-minutes out as the enemy moved to pursue the retreating deep space force. He was not moving at the full speed of which he was capable. That was good; it would take him longer to overtake and destroy his targets.

The battlecruisers waited until the last enemy vessel had cleared the mines, then began their stealthy advance towards the warp point at twenty thousand kilometers per second. It would take them over twelve hours to reach their destination, but that had been calculated from the outset. They were too few in number to affect the outcome of the battle to come, anyway . . . and perfectly sufficient for their mission.

✧   ✧   ✧

Commander Francis Lafferty, acting CO of the brutally wounded CVA *Norn*, let himself sink into the astrogator's command chair with a carefully suppressed groan of exhaustion. He was just as happy Captain Duk's chair had been destroyed by the hit which killed her. He'd liked the captain almost as much as he'd respected her; sitting in her chair would have seemed a slap at her memory, yet Regs and tradition alike would have left him no choice if it had survived her.

At least we've got the command deck pressurized again, he thought bitterly. *That's more than half our compartments can say.*

Norn would fight again, thanks entirely to the engineers who'd designed her for maximum survivability, but Lafferty felt another wrench of anguish as he thought of the hundreds of people who wouldn't be aboard when she did. The anguish only intensified when he added the already confirmed losses her strikegroup had suffered, and he jerked himself away from that painful subject and looked at the visual display. TFNS *Hyacinth*, the *Dunedin*-class CLE detached to stand by the big assault carrier, floated in its depths like a reminder there were still friends in a hostile universe, and just seeing her was an enormous psychological relief.

His com panel chirped, and he pressed the key. "Bridge, Comman—Captain speaking," he corrected himself with a grimace.

"We've got Drive Four and Five back on-line, Sir." Lieutenant Driscoll, *Norn*'s senior surviving engineer, had worked nonstop for twenty hours since the rest of Second Fleet had left the CVA behind to lick her wounds. Her dirty face was etched with deep lines on the com screen, and Lafferty wondered if she would ever look young again.

"Good work, Jeanette," he said sincerely, and was rewarded by a wan smile. *Norn* could make half her designed speed now, and he turned his chair—one of the irritating things about its location was that it *required* him to turn to see his bridge crew—to face his helmsman. "As soon as Lieutenant Driscoll signals readiness, take us to maximum available. I'll feel better with a little more space between us and the warp point."

"Aye, aye, Sir," the helmsman replied.

Lafferty was just turning back to his panel when the acting tac officer spoke.

"Drones transiting the warp point," he announced, then paled. "They're not ours, Sir!"

Lafferty jumped out of his chair and crossed to Tactical, and his face went as pale as the tactical officer's as he saw not simply dozens but scores of drones streaking past his ship.

"Vector?" he snapped.

"They're heading straight up the chain, Sir," the tac officer said grimly, and Lafferty's stomach froze. A few drones passed close enough for *Hyacinth's* point defense to kill, but ninety percent got through, and he could think of only one reason for the Bugs to be sending them.

"How many drones do *we* have left, Com?" he demanded.

"Uh, ten—no, twelve, Sir, but two are damaged. I don't know how reliable they are."

Lafferty's mind raced. With no way to know what course Second Fleet had pursued since his own ship had been detached he couldn't use courier drones to alert the Admiral from here. He could warn the Fleet Train and Alpha Centauri, but to warn Antonov—

He faced the implications squarely, then drew a deep breath. "Stand by to record."

"Standing by, Sir."

"'Enemy courier drones have just been dispatched past this ship,'" Lafferty told the pickup in a flat, overcontrolled voice. "'They are headed up the chain towards Centauri. I repeat, towards Centauri. I will attempt to advise Admiral Antonov.'" He started to say something more, then stopped himself. Anyone who received that message wouldn't need him to tell them the Bugs wouldn't have launched drones unless there was someone to receive them.

Someone lurking along Second Fleet's only line of retreat.

"Got it?" he said instead.

"On the chip, Sir."

"Very well. Append our log and be sure the location and time chops are current, then transmit it to *Hyacinth*. Inform Commander Watanabe that I want him to download it to his drones, then launch half of them for Centauri and the other half to Admiral Chin."

"Aye, aye, Sir. And our own drones?"

"Download the same message and set them for a circular search pattern. Tag their beacons with an all-ships signal and lock in the Code Omega release sequence."

"But—" the com officer began, then closed his mouth as Lafferty met his eyes. He hesitated a moment longer, then nodded. "Aye, Sir," he said quietly, and Lafferty stared down into the plot. He felt the tac officer beside him and tasted the other man's fear as he worked through the logic Lafferty had already followed to its terrifying conclusion.

"We don't have much speed," Lafferty said almost thoughtfully. "If whoever sent those drones is covering the warp point, we'll never be able to outrun them. But if we take *Hyacinth* back through with us, one of us may be able to get a transmission—or at least a drone—off to the Admiral."

He didn't add "before they kill us," but the tac officer swallowed audibly, then nodded. Unless there was time for Plotting to get them a bearing on the rest of Second Fleet, they couldn't even use lasers or give their drones a definite vector. They *might* have time for an omnidirectional transmission, but in twenty hours, Antonov could have moved as much as a hundred light-minutes. That was too far for an omnidirectional message—and if the Bugs who'd launched those drones were directly atop the warp point, it would take far longer than they were likely to have to get the com lasers a bearing. Which meant it would all come down to the twelve drones *Norn* still had, and on a blind search pattern. . . .

"I want as many nonessential personnel as possible off both ships first," Lafferty said quietly. "Tell *Hyacinth* to fill up her small craft, then fill ours, as well. Cram them in as tight as you can without overloading their life support, then get back to me."

"Yes, Sir," the tac officer said just as quietly. "I'll see to it."

The enemy fleet had moved well beyond its sensor range of the warp point in pursuit of the deep space force. It was safe to launch gunboats now, and the battlecruisers deployed one hundred and twenty of them.

TFNS *Norn* and TFNS *Hyacinth* made transit. They survived for twenty-three seconds . . . far too short a time for their sensor systems to stabilize or their transmitters to come on-line.

Even with the auto-launch Omega sequence on-line, only five of *Norn*'s drones got away. Pouncing gunboats killed two, and the other three fled blindly into the depths of the system.

CHAPTER THIRTY-EIGHT

Heralds of Armageddon

Rear Admiral Michael Chin strolled onto the battle-cruiser *Psyche*'s flag bridge with a pleasant sense of repletion. Chin was a small man whose careful tailoring couldn't disguise a slight tubbiness. That caused him the occasional moment of depression, but he was also a cheerful extrovert who liked his simple pleasures, and breakfast had hit the spot nicely. His silver-chased coffee mug bore the crest of TFNS *Prince George*, whose ship's company had presented it to then-Captain Chin on the day he made commodore, and he sipped from it as he ambled across to Commander Maslett, his ops officer.

"Good morning, Sir."

"Morning, Andy." Chin took another sip while he studied the plot. Second Fleet's support ships lay in Anderson Four, near the warp point to Anderson Three, prepared to retreat towards Centauri at need, and a few small craft plied back and forth on routine missions. "Looks quiet," the admiral went on. "Anything more from Admiral Antonov?"

"Not since his initial drones," Maslett replied.

"Huh." Chin lowered his mug and pulled on his nose with his left hand. He was basically Second Fleet's grocer at the moment, but epicurean or not, he was also an experienced—and good—Battle Fleet flag officer, and the enemy's antics puzzled him. There had to be a reason the Bugs were falling back instead of counterattacking, but he was damned if he could think of one. Unless they knew reinforcements were coming and they were trying to rendezvous before Antonov hit them? But if that was the case, why not cloak? A star system was a huge hiding place, and Second Fleet knew the locations of none of Anderson Five's other warp points. If Chin had commanded an inferior system-defense force and known reinforcements were coming, *he* certainly would have stayed cloaked till they got there. He would have taken up a position near the reinforcements' entry warp point and hidden until they arrived to join him—and without carriers, he would have gone right on hiding until he actually engaged the enemy.

Of course, *these* defenders were Bugs, and no one— with the possible exception of Marcus LeBlanc—was prepared even to try to explain how their minds (if any) worked. It was also true the hammering they'd taken over the last five months might have shaken them into panic- born stupidity, he supposed, but it still seemed odd.

Well, that was Antonov's problem, and Chin could think of few people better suited to handle it. His own problems were more prosaic, and he grimaced as he glanced at the icons of the damaged units which had replaced his tried and tested battleships. He'd hated giving up BG 30, but he supposed it would have been churlish to complain when he'd been given eight SDs in exchange. It would have been nice if those SDs hadn't been chosen because they'd been so badly shot up, but whatever shape their armor might be in, his repair ships had gotten most of their *internal* systems back on-line. And, he reminded himself, damaged or not, a superdreadnought was still a superdreadnought.

He smiled at the thought, nodded to Maslett, and headed for the com section to catch up on the day-to- day details of his command.

It was getting on towards lunch, and Admiral Chin was updating reports on his briefing room terminal when a signal warbled at him. His head snapped up as the priority of the two-toned signal registered, and he stabbed at his com key.

"Yes?"

"Sir, we've got drones transiting to Anderson Three." It was Commander Guthrey, his chief of staff, and the report on Chin's display vanished as he opened a window to the com system. Guthrey's face replaced it, and his expression was as tense as his voice. Chin raised an eyebrow, and Guthrey's mouth tightened.

"They weren't ours, Sir," he said quietly, "and we make it at least fifty of them."

"Headed *up* the chain?" Chin's question was sharp, and Guthrey nodded grimly.

Chin felt as if someone had just punched him in the belly. It didn't take a mental giant to realize the Fleet Train was directly in the path of whatever might respond to those drones.

"Did we kill any of them?" he demanded.

"A few, Sir—not many." Guthrey shrugged. "We only had a light CSP out, and they took our pilots completely by surprise and blew past us before anyone could really respond."

"Damn." Chin said the word softly, then closed his eyes and made himself think. If only their survey efforts hadn't fallen so far behind! The Navy still knew virtually nothing about Anderson Three, but the data on One and Two was piling up. If there was an undiscovered Bug warp point back there, and the courier drones said there was, then it was most probably in Three—which put it right on top of Rear Admiral Michael Chin.

He sat for perhaps forty-five seconds, mind flashing through possibilities and options, but he had too little information to assess the former . . . and far too few of the latter.

"Alert the Task Force," he said. "Send the escort to GQ and tell the service ship skippers we're moving out in ten minutes. Then have Astrogation plot a course to take us into Anderson Three and on a sharp dogleg back to Anderson Two."

"A dogleg's going to increase our transit time," Guthrey warned.

"I know. But they wouldn't call in the troops unless they thought they had enough to deal with all of Second Fleet. That means *we* sure as hell can't fight them, but if we make transit quickly enough, we *may* be able to get far enough away from the warp point to hide from them."

"Yes, Sir." Guthrey still didn't like it, but he nodded sharply.

"As soon as you've passed those messages, fire up the com sats to Centauri and—"

"Excuse me, Sir." Andrew Maslett's voice cut into the circuit. "We're picking up more drones, and this time they're ours."

"From Admiral Antonov?"

"No, Sir. Most of them are headed up-chain, but five are coming straight for us, and their beacons say they're from *Hyacinth*. Com is querying them, but they're still six light-minutes out."

"From *Hyacinth?*" Chin's eyes met Guthrey's. The chief of staff shrugged in helpless ignorance, and Chin's jaws clamped tight. *Hyacinth* was only a CLE, so why would *she* dispatch drones to him? If Second Fleet had been engaged, any message should be coming from Antonov or one of his subordinate flag officers, not a light cruiser's skipper!

"All right," he said again. "Pass the rest of those orders, Stan, but hold the message to GHQ until we've had a chance to read *Hyacinth's* drones."

"Yes, Sir."

"I'll see you on Flag Bridge in two minutes," Chin concluded, and cut the circuit.

"We've got the drone download, Sir," Maslett said. Ten dragging minutes had passed since the drone beacons had been picked up. Most of the Fleet Train was already into Anderson Three and headed for Centauri, but *Psyche* had lagged behind to recover the drones, and Chin turned to his ops officer with painfully divided emotions. Part of him burned with impatience for the message's contents, but another part wanted to delay the moment as long as possible, as if not knowing could somehow keep whatever it said from being true.

"Very well, Andy. Let's see it," he said quietly, and the small com screen at his command chair blinked to life with Commander Lafferty's brief message.

Chin watched it with mingled relief and frustration. At least his worst fear—that Second Fleet had been annihilated, leaving *Hyacinth* its sole survivor—had been disproved, but Lafferty's warning had been dispatched two days ago. God only knew what had happened since!

At least Lafferty was in position to see the drones coming, he reminded himself, *and we're tied into the comsat chain to Centauri. From the timing, the bastards waited until Antonov was too far out from the warp point to see them go. That means this probably is an ambush, but Norn saw it coming. By now she's warned Antonov, and we can alert Centauri a hell of a lot faster than if we had to rely on drones of our own.*

"At least we've got some warning," he said quietly.

"Yes, Sir." Guthrey didn't add "for what it's worth," but Chin heard it anyway.

"Update our sitrep, then get it off to Centauri," the admiral went on. "Be sure to append our projected course, and inform Sky Marshal Avram we'll try to evade on our way home."

"Yes, Sir."

A brisk nod dismissed his staffers to their jobs, and the message flashed at light-speed along the chain of satellites Second Fleet had emplaced across Anderson Three. That chain stretched all the way to Centauri, and the message, slowed only briefly at each manned warp point relay station, would reach Centauri within little more than twenty-three hours. Unless, of course, the Bugs had already cut the chain somewhere ahead of the Fleet Train.

Chin leaned back in his command chair, eyes cold as he watched the icons of his command run for safety. His covering force consisted of only eight damaged super-dreadnoughts, eleven battlecruisers, five of them damaged, and five Ophiuchi CVLs, with only a hundred and twenty fighters embarked. That was all he had to cover thirty-three mammoth freighters, transports, and mobile ship-yards, and there were well over a hundred thousand Allied personnel aboard those waddling service ships. If Bug gunboats got loose among them . . .

He made himself push the thought aside, but it was hard. He spared one more moment for a silent prayer for Second Fleet's warships, then turned to face the far grimmer task of trying to save his own command.

The long-anticipated courier drones arrived at last, flicking past the massive warp point fortifications, and the starships stirred as the robotic messengers summoned the Fleet to battle. Ninety-eight warships, fifty of them superdreadnoughts and six the new, more powerful battle-line units which were finally ready for action, streamed through the warp point in a long, sullen chain of destruction and advanced into the enemy's rear.

The attention signal jerked Michael Chin awake. He sat up in his sleeping cabin, rubbing his eyes, and a leaden hammer pounded the back of his forehead. Three exhausting days had passed, and he felt every one of them. A glance at the chronometer told him he'd gotten only about three hours in the sack. It wasn't enough, yet it had taken all his willpower to get even that much. He grimaced and punched the key, accepting the com call audio only.

"Talk to me," he said harshly.

"Plotting's picked something up, Sir." Andrew Maslett sounded grim. "Looks like about two hundred gunboats."

"On an attack vector?" Chin was surprised he could sound so calm when his mouth was suddenly a kiln.

"Not yet, Sir. They're over a light-hour out, and it looks like they're still sweeping for us, but with all these freighters and transports—"

Maslett left the rest unsaid, and Chin swung his feet to the decksole.

"Understood." He rubbed his forehead. A light-hour. Even if the Bugs headed in to the attack, they'd take almost seven hours to reach him. Of course, he wouldn't know they'd even started in for an hour or so after they did, but naval officers were used to thinking in those terms.

His best defense would be his fighters, but they'd be outnumbered something like two-to-one. Some of the Bugs were going to get through. He clenched his jaw and made himself accept that, but his brain was coming fully awake, and he felt it pushing out to other considerations.

Andy was right. He had his warships cloaked, but the gunboats were certain to spot his service ships. When they did, they'd attack . . . and he hoped they would. They wouldn't be here unless there were, indeed, heavy enemy forces somewhere between him and safety, and that meant the *worst* thing they could do was take their time. He had a chance, however slim, against this many gunboats, but he needed another eighty-four hours to make it back into Anderson Two. If the bastards settled for shadowing his starships while one of them went back and whistled up still more gunboats, they could guarantee their ability to swamp his defenses.

"Okay, Andy," he said finally. "Alert the task force and have Commodore Haasnaahr arm his fighters for an anti-gunboat strike. If they head our way, we'll hit them as far out as we can and try to bleed them before they enter the escorts' engagement envelope."

"Yes, Sir. Shall I alter course?"

"No point," Chin sighed. "They know where we're headed. Our only hope was to get far enough off a least-time course they'd miss us entirely, and we didn't make it."

"Yes, Sir," Maslett said very quietly.

"Send an update to Centauri. You'd better get a flight of drones off, too—a heavy one. For all we know, they've already taken out the relay and put a CSP on the Anderson Two warp point. Append our current tac data and inform the Sky Marshal my intentions remain unchanged, and I'll see you on flag bridge in twenty minutes."

"Sir, it might not hurt to get a little more—"

"I appreciate the thought, Andy, but I'm not going to get back to sleep. I might as well sweat it out up there with you." Chin's lips twitched in a parody of a smile Maslett couldn't see. "Ask Chief Reynolds to make sure we've got plenty of coffee. It's going to be a long night."

The units which had detected the enemy's starships represented less than a quarter of the Fleet's total gunboat strength, but that strength was deployed in widely spread search groups, and much could happen in the time it would take to recall and assemble it all. Despite the fifty-light-minute range, the enemy's emissions signatures made it clear these were support ships. They would be unarmed and only weakly shielded, yet it was remotely possible they might somehow slip away. Under the circumstances, there could be only one decision.

One gunboat turned back to the Fleet and a second was sent back to its home system. Six more were detached to keep the enemy under observation, and the remaining hundred and ninety-six altered course sharply towards the enemy.

"Well, they see us now," Commander Guthrey said flatly. Chin simply nodded, then looked at Maslett. "ETA?"

"CIC makes it roughly three and a half hours, Sir."

"Um." Chin folded his hands behind himself and rocked in place. The Bugs' decision to detach some of their number was ominous, but the rest were coming in, and he tried to feel glad he at least had a chance to whittle them down before they called in a really heavy strike.

"Tell Haasnaahr to launch in two hours, Stan," he told Guthrey quietly. "I want them hit fourteen light-minutes out, but we can't afford losses this soon. His pilots are to use FM3s and stand off. Once they launch, their speed will get them back here with thirty minutes to rearm, reorganize, and swap off flight crews before the *Bugs* get here, and their job this time out is to whittle the bastards down, not to stop them dead. Be sure they understand that."

The gunboats continued their run. The enemy had made no attempt to alter course—not that it would have helped—but he had launched attack craft. There were barely half as many of them as there were gunboats, but their presence proved there were warships out there, as well. They were cloaked, not visible on sensors, yet none of the enemy's main fleet could possibly have gotten this far since the summoning drones were launched. No doubt they were no more than the support echelon's escorts, in which case they could not be particularly powerful or numerous. It was likely the gunboats were about to lose heavily, but if the attack craft were foolish enough to close, they would lose, as well. And whatever happened to this strike, others would close in soon.

"There they go."

Chin didn't look up. He was certain whoever had spoken didn't even realize he had, and his own attention was locked to the fourteen-minute-old icons in the plot.

Squadrons began to flash from green to amber as they salvoed their FM3 missiles from just outside the Bugs' point defense envelope. It was like some bloodless simulation . . . or would have been, if every man and woman on *Psyche*'s flag bridge hadn't known what would happen when the "simulation's" survivors reached the task force.

The long launch range didn't help. It reduced accuracy by almost fifty percent, and the fighters needed at least five hits to saturate the Bugs' point defense and guarantee a kill. That took most of a squadron's entire missile load at this range, and he had only twenty squadrons.

Bug icons began to vanish, and he felt the hungry approval of his officers and ratings. The fighters were doing a little better than projected; some of the squadron COs had clearly opted to ignore orders and split their fire between multiple targets—no doubt they'd figured out how unlikely they were to survive to be reprimanded—and this time disobedience was paying off.

The last fighter salvoed its ordnance and broke off, still never having entered the Bugs' range, and he waited while Maslett tallied the results.

"Twenty-seven, Sir," the ops officer announced. "They're down to a hundred sixty-nine. They'll be entering our capital missile envelope in twelve more minutes."

"Turn the support ships away," Chin directed. "Let's slow their overtake."

"And the escorts?"

"We'll stay right where we are, Andy." Chin smiled mirthlessly. "According to the boffins, their gunboats' sensors aren't as good as our recon fighters', and they're probably pretty fixated on the support ships right now. Let's see if we can't play road block."

"It's worth a try, Sir," Maslett agreed with a matching smile.

The enemy changed course at last. There was still no sign of his warships—the attack craft had vanished aboard their cloaked mother ships—but it was likely the escorts were waiting somewhere between the gunboats and their prey. Yet they could not engage the gunboats without revealing their own positions when they fired, and the massed squadrons bored in for the kill.

"Here they come, Sir," Maslett muttered, and Chin glanced at his com link to Commodore Haasnaahr aboard OADCS *Zirk-Cothmyriea*.

"Ready, Haasnaahr?"

"Yesss, Sssir," the fierce-beaked Ophiuchi replied, and Chin nodded.

"Good. Inform Admiral Triam she may engage, Andy."

"Aye, aye, Sir."

Five battlecruisers and five superdreadnoughts began slamming CMs into the gunboats. Their fire control was far better than any fighter's, and their capital missiles were *much* harder to stop. Gunboats tore apart, and Chin watched the fireballs sweep closer. The incoming missiles told the Bugs where the firing ships were, and they altered course to race straight for them.

"Now, Haasnaahr!" Chin snapped, and a hundred and twenty Ophiuchi fighters suddenly launched *behind* the Bugs. Splitting off those carriers and their escorting *Broadswords* had been a gamble, but now the fighters launched at such short range they were already in firing distance—and the gunboats' blind spot—before the Bugs even realized they were there.

Shoals of FM3s streaked out, unopposed by the point defense the Bugs couldn't bring to bear, and the *Broadswords'* heavy broadsides came with them. Over eighty gunboats died in barely forty seconds, and the Bug formation came apart. There were still almost a hundred of them, and half looped back, looking for the carriers. Most of the others continued their runs on the battle-line units, but perhaps twenty ignored carriers and superdreadnoughts alike, racing across the escorts' engagement envelope to pursue the support ships.

The escorts did their best to nail the evaders, but they had to defend themselves, as well, and thirteen Bugs got away clean. Chin swore viciously as he watched them go, but the ones actually engaging his warships were like spiders in a flame. The Ophiuchi pilots fired their last missiles and drove into them with internal lasers, and the close-range plot dissolved into a swirl of dogfighting madness. Ship-launched missiles continued to reach out into the carnage, homing on the more powerful emissions of the gunboats' hybrid drives, and the Bugs were slaughtered.

But some of them closed to FRAM range before they died, and TFNS *Scharnhorst* found herself targeted by at least a dozen. FRAMs smashed the battlecruiser's shields flat, and then, despite her wild evasion maneuvers, two gunboats rammed her cleanly. All three vessels vanished in an intolerable glare, and the last two gunboats swerved to attack her sister *Guam*, only to be bounced and killed barely a thousand kilometers short of target by an Ophiuchi fighter squadron.

And then, suddenly, it was over. *Scharnhorst* was gone, but she was the only warship Chin had lost. It looked like Haasnaahr had lost twenty or thirty irreplaceable fighters, but the rest of the escorts were intact. In fact, none of the survivors reported more than minor damage, and he let himself smile with cold pleasure. They'd massacred the bastards, and badly as *Scharnhorst*'s loss hurt, it could have been far, far worse.

He opened his mouth to congratulate his people, but Maslett spoke before he could.

"Captain Hardiman's just reported, Sir," the ops officer said quietly. "I'm afraid we've lost *Dover*, *Cromarty*, and *Columbine*."

Chin winced, his satisfaction suddenly ashes in his mouth. *Dover* and *Cromarty* were bad enough—the mobile shipyards had each carried a crew of fifteen hundred—but *Columbine* had been a transport, with over five thousand Fleet replacement personnel on board.

"Shit," someone said bitterly behind him. Chin began to turn to see who it was, when a com rating stiffened at her panel, and he looked at her, instead.

"Excuse me, Sir," the young woman said. "Commodore Haasnaahr reports that *Cestus* has just picked up another strike seventy light-minutes astern and closing."

"How many?" the admiral asked Maslett harshly, and the ops officer queried CIC. Chin watched his shoulders tighten before the commander turned his chair to face him.

"Plotting says at least three hundred, Sir—and another group's coming in from port. They're still too far out for a count, but they may be even stronger."

"Christ," someone whispered, and Chin's mouth tightened. Six hundred more—at least. Given the gunboat complements Bug superdreadnoughts mothered, that meant there were *at least* fifty capital ships out there somewhere. Their obvious mission was to close off Second Fleet's retreat, and he doubted they'd let themselves be diverted from that to chase down his task force. But they didn't *need* to divert from it. They could use only their gunboats and destroy every ship he had without even slowing their own progress towards Anderson Five.

"Get the fighters rearmed," he heard himself say, "then bring the service ships back inside our point defense umbrella and have Commodore Hardiman deploy his SBMHAWKs. Stan, you and Astrogation work out a course to take us away from the group to port. We need to tempt them into hitting us as two separate strikes rather than one big one."

"Yes, Sir," Guthrey replied.

"Com, record for transmission to Second Fleet."

"Recording, Sir."

"'Admiral Antonov, this is Rear Admiral Chin. We've engaged and destroyed approximately two hundred enemy gunboats, but we have what appears to be another six hundred on our scanners. I stress that these are how many we've *seen*; there may well be more out there. The numbers we've observed suggest at least fifty capital ships are headed your way. All I can do is try to get my command out; I cannot provide any security for your rear. I've dispatched messages to Centauri and hope and believe a relief force will be organized ASAP, but I can't guarantee even that much.'" He paused, trying to think of some encouraging thing he could add, but there was nothing. "'Good luck, Sir,'" he said softly instead, and nodded to the com officer.

"I want that downloaded to every drone in the task force. Hold back *Psyche*'s own drones, but program all the others for a maximum spread pattern in Anderson Five. And be sure you append full log downloads. Admiral Antonov has to know what's coming up his backside."

"Aye, aye, Sir," the com officer said, and Chin turned back to his staff.

"All right, ladies and gentlemen," he said flatly. "Now we have to find a way out of this. Any suggestions?"

CHAPTER THIRTY-NINE
The Trap Springs

Everyone on TFNS *Xingú's* flag bridge had learned the inadvisability of bothering Sky Marshal Avram—not that most of them would have been inclined to do so in any circumstances. Even now, with the relief force assembled and ready for departure, she still paced in a veritable fury of impatience, occasionally turning to the view screen and glaring at Alpha Centauri A and the distant orange flare of Alpha Centauri B for reminding her by their presence that she hadn't yet departed the system.

Stop being such a goddamned kvetch, she chided herself. Admiral Chin's warnings of disaster had arrived only two standard days before, and this relief force—seventeen superdreadnoughts, ten battleships, eleven battlecruisers and twelve heavy cruisers—had been organized slightly sooner than humanly possible. She would have preferred a heavier force—especially some carriers—but this was all that was available out of the Home Fleet elements immediately at hand. She'd commandeered virtually every one of Admiral MacGregor's mobile units—aside from those currently undergoing scheduled overhauls—and waiting for anything more to arrive from Sol would take time they didn't have. *And*, she thought grimly, *we've already picked Sol so bare for Pesthouse and Fourth Fleet that waiting wouldn't add anything worthwhile to my strength, anyway.*

No, she couldn't really complain about the pace of the preparations. And she'd had to waste less time than she'd feared shouting down various old ladies of both genders who'd gotten their undies in a bunch at the notion of the Sky Marshal taking personal command. No, she wouldn't have been in such a vile mood, except . . .

As though to rub it in, a com rating looked up. "Sky Marshal, Admiral Mukerji sends his apologies for the delay and reports that all elements of his command are ready for departure."

No good deed goes unpunished, Avram philosophized to herself. If she hadn't blocked Agamemnon Waldeck's attempt to put him in command of Fifth Fleet over Vanessa Murakuma's head, Vice Admiral Terence Mukerji would have been shipped off to the Romulus Chain. As it was, he'd been at Centauri in circumstances under which there was no way she could escape having him as her second in command.

"My compliments to Admiral Mukerji," she said through gritted teeth, "and if he's *quite* ready, perhaps we can proceed." Her staff took the hint; orders began to go out, and the ships of the relief force began to swing out of their orbits around the Nova Terra/Eden binary planet and set their courses for the Anderson One warp point.

Avram commanded herself to calmness. There was no way to know what had happened to the Fleet Train since Chin had dispatched his drones. Even less could she know what had happened to Second Fleet. But in all this fog of imponderables, she held fast to one datum. *Norn* had fired off her drones about six standard days ago, and surely she'd sent them to Antonov as well as to Chin. With an ease bred of two days' constant repetition, Avram ran the mental calculations: at their best speed, Bug super-dreadnoughts would take a hundred and ninety hours to cross from one warp point to the other in Anderson Four—*after* transiting from Anderson Three. So Antonov ought to have at least a week's warning. Given that . . . well, if

Ivan Nikolayevich couldn't extricate Second Fleet from
Anderson Five and be well on the way back towards
Centauri, nobody could.

*The enemy's support echelon had proved a much tougher
opponent than anticipated. The first gunboat strike was
annihilated for very little return, and the second suffered
just as badly for even scantier results, for the enemy's
freighters had carried large stores of missile pods. The
support echelon had deployed hundreds of them to cover
its flanks, and the gunboats had not even seen them . . .
until their CAMs launched.*

*The third strike had done much better. The enemy had
exhausted his pods against the second, and the third
destroyed at least six of his warships and a third of his
freighters, but once again it took heavy losses. Indeed,
losses were so severe that the gunboats which had been
detached to seal the warp point through which any enemy
effort to dispatch relief forces to his trapped fleet must
enter the system had been diverted against the stubborn
support ships.*

*The diversion, while irritating, created no problems.
In effect, the Fleet simply exchanged its gunboats for the
blocking force's, which, after striking the enemy's support
ships, would continue on to overtake it before it left the
system. The exchange had delayed blockage of the warp
point by some hundred hours, but the new gunboats had
ample time to reach their position, for the enemy could
not even begin responding until warning drones reached
him.*

*Unfortunately, the support echelon proved a still
dangerous foe when the fourth strike went in. Barely
twenty percent of its support ships survived the attack,
and reports on warship losses—while less definite—
indicated its escorts had been hit equally hard. But before
they died, they killed almost half their attackers. The Fleet
would be going into battle with its gunboats badly
understrength. Even more irritatingly, it had been
impossible to send in a fifth strike without prohibitively*

*delaying either the warp point blocking force or the Fleet,
and the surviving enemy ships had managed to slip away
into the depths of the system.*

*In the long run, it mattered little. Badly damaged, low
on ammunition, and trapped between the blocking force
and the fleet contingents about to annihilate their main
fleet, those ships had nowhere to run. Eventually they
would be hunted down, and the Fleet refused to allow
them to further divert it from its primary mission*

Ivan Antonov's plot flashed with fury as another fighter
strike crashed into the enemy. The Bugs' futile attempt
to evade him had ended in a cataclysm of violence, and
his face was hard as he watched the death toll rise.

It was fortunate he'd decided to bring the battle-line
into action, for the Bug gunboats' AFHAWKs had inflicted
brutal losses on the fighter jocks of the first strike.
Unfortunately for the Bugs, losses hadn't been brutal
enough. Once their AFHAWKs were exhausted, the
gunboats had been easy meat, and while the escort
fighters were exacting their revenge, the battle-line had
closed to SBM range of the main enemy force. Second
Fleet had taken ugly losses of its own, but the second,
FRAM-armed strike had been waiting on the catapults
when the first was launched. Antonov had sent it in along
with the missiles, and the need to stop both fighters *and*
missiles had fatally overloaded the Bugs' point defense.

Not that it had been quick or simple, for Antonov had
declined to close to energy or even standard missile range.
He'd lost his monopoly on command datalink, but he had
more heavy launchers than the enemy this time, and
despite his initial strike's losses, he also had an enormous
fighter strength. He'd used both to batter the enemy for
almost thirty hours at long range before he finally
committed to close action, and his eyes glowed coldly as
the fighters blew through the final gunboats and swept
over what was left of the Bug starships.

"I think it's almost over, Sir," de Bertholet said quietly.
"We only lost about twenty fighters this time."

"*Da*. All that remains is the cleanup," Antonov agreed. He rose from his command chair and stretched hugely. "You did well, Commander." His eyes swept the rest of his flag bridge crew. "You all did. Commodore Stovall, please pass my thanks to the entire Fleet."

"Of course, Sir." Stovall hid a smile. Ivan the Terrible truly had mellowed, he thought.

"Good." Antonov walked closer to the main plot and gazed into it, rubbing his jaw in thought as de Bertholet stepped up beside him. "Still nothing from the recon fighters?"

"Not a word, Sir." The ops officer tugged on an earlobe, then shrugged. "Shall I move them further out?"

"No." Antonov shook his head. The recon fighters watching Second Fleet's flanks were already at fifteen light-minutes. If he pushed them much further out, he'd have to spread them so thin they might miss a cloaked enemy, and fifteen light-minutes would give an hour and a half of warning before even a gunboat launched from cloak could reach attack range. Against *uncloaked* attackers, the warning time jumped to almost ten hours.

He shoved his hands into the pockets of his uniform tunic and thought. He'd lost few ships in the engagement, but several were damaged, and the engineers' reports on drive reliability were even worse now. This particular bunch of Bugs had declined to show him the next outbound warp point and, deep inside, he was just as glad. He needed to regroup, bring up reinforcements, get his rear properly surveyed, and, above all, service his drives before he advanced again.

"We will remain here for seventy-two hours once the enemy has been mopped up, Commander de Bertholet," he said finally. "That will give us time for shipboard resource repairs and to reorganize our strikegroups."

"Yes, Sir."

"We will, of course, be somewhat more vulnerable while we do so," Antonov continued thoughtfully. "So once the strikegroups have reorganized, I think we *will* push the recon shell a bit further out. Inform Admiral Taathaanahk that I want a third of his regular fighters fitted with external sensor packs to expand the shell to twenty light-minutes."

"Yes, Sir."

"Good, Commander," Antonov murmured. "Good."

The dispersed attack groups slowed their advance. The enemy had destroyed the decoy force, but now he sat motionless. His high tactical speed always made him difficult to engage on the Fleet's terms, and the attack groups were grateful for his lack of activity. The longer he sat, the better, for the fourth and final attack group drew closer with every hour. Any one of the four could engage the enemy's total force on terms of near equality; with his retreat sealed and vast numbers of gunboats coming up from adjacent systems, his inferiority would be crushing.

And best of all, he did not even know he was in danger.

"I think you'd better look at this report from Captain Trailman, Sir," Jacques Bichet said.

Raymond Prescott raised a hand at Lieutenant Commander Ruiz, his logistics officer, interrupting their discussion of TF 21's increasingly strained resources, and turned to Bichet with a slight frown. Vincent Trailman, TF 21's *farshathkhanaak*, outranked Bichet, but the two of them had been friends since the Academy. It was unlike the ops officer to refer to him by anything other than his given name, and the ops officer's voice was strained.

"See what, Jacques?"

"One of Vincent's fighters just picked it up," Bichet said grimly. "It's a courier drone beacon." Prescott's eyebrows rose, and Bichet voice went lower. "That's not all, Sir. According to the ID string, it's from *Norn*—and it's Code Omega."

"*Code Omega?*" Prescott snapped upright in his chair, and Bichet jerked a choppy nod.

The stocky admiral stared at his ops officer in horrified disbelief. *Norn* had been left safely behind in Anderson Four—damaged, yes, but in no danger. Unless . . .

"Where *is* this drone?" he demanded, and Bichet consulted his memo pad display.

"According to CIC, it's just under twenty light-minutes out—that's from the fighter shell; it's forty light-minutes from *Crete*—at one-niner-one, zero-three-three, Sir. That puts it right on the very limit for a drone beacon's omnidirectional broadcast range, and signal strength comes and goes. Plotting and Com agree that *could* mean its on a circular search. We lose strength as it heads away from us and pick it up when it closes again."

"A circular search." Something icy crawled down Prescott's spine. He could think of only one explanation for an Omega drone from *Norn*. But that was impossible . . . wasn't it?

"All right," he made himself say. "Pass the information to the Flag and inform Admiral Antonov I'm detaching *Pytor Veliky* and *Ramilles* to recover the drone. Then get hold of Captain Yukon and Captain Shariz. I want them cloaked—this could be some sort of decoy ploy, and I don't want them sucked into anything. After you talk to *them*, tell Vincent I want a fighter sweep in the direction of the drone. If there's anything out there, that may draw its attention away from *Veliky* and *Ramilles*. If they don't, I want them close enough to support the battlecruisers."

"Aye, aye, Sir." Bichet hurried off to give the necessary orders, and Raymond Prescott leaned back in his chair and worried.

Antonov sat facing his three task force commanders on the split-image screen. Prescott had summarized the message of *Norn's* drone, but that was only for the benefit of van der Gelder and Taathaanahk, for its contents had already been downloaded to *Colorado*. So Antonov had already gone beyond what the others were going through now, and could step in quickly to fill the numb silence with his decisive bass.

"Thank you, Admiral Prescott. Now, we must consider the implications of this. Clearly, our information is somewhat out of date, inasmuch as the drone was launched approximately one hundred and eighty hours ago. A lot can happen in almost seven standard days. But we know this much: *Norn* and *Hyacinth* were destroyed here in Anderson Five, so some Bug forces must already be here, doubtless in cloak, in addition to the force—clearly a very powerful one—moving in from somewhere behind us." *From Anderson Three*, he silently corrected himself. *Through some warp point we never found because our survey was too little and too late.* He dismissed the thought; the *pizdi* might have entered some other system through a closed warp point. And self-reproach was hardly the most useful mental exercise just now. "The fact that they've committed this force suggests that there is also a major force waiting ahead of us, intended to be the other jaw of a trap."

"I quite aaaagree, Ssssssir," Taathaanahk said with a calmness drawn from that *naraham*—inadequately translated as "detachment"—that was one of the four pillars of his culture's *Taainohk* philosophy. "I thhhhhhink we musssstttt asssssume they knnnnow their owwwn capabilities—annnd they cccccertainly knnnnow *ours*, fffor thisss cammmpaign hasss given themmm ample opportunity to asssssesss our strength. They woulddd hhhardly hhhave sssprung thisss trapppp unlessss their forrrces were sssuch asss ttto allow a rrrreasonable expectation of sssuccesssss." The Ophiuchi admiral paused as though to invite disagreement. None came. "I therefore sssuggest thatt our firssst priority ssshould be to exxxtricate Sssecond Fleet wiiithout delay."

"I concur," van der Gelder said, blinking the haunted look from her eyes. "We should head back now, hard and fast. With our tactical speed advantage, we can leave whatever's waiting ahead of us eating our dust and blast our way out before the blocking force has had time to settle into a defensive posture behind us."

"Unfortunately, Admiral van der Gelder," Antonov rumbled, "we can take as a given that the blocking force is coming from at least as far back as Anderson Three.

Unless we get out of this system without any sort of observation by the Bug units that destroyed *Norn* and *Hyacinth*—which is sheer wishful thinking—the Bugs will send courier drones through the warp point ahead of us. With that warning, the blocking force will form up and await us on the far side of whichever warp point is most convenient. And without Fleet Train's SBMHAWK stores, we're in no position to mount a warp point assault." He left unspoken the probable fate of the Fleet Train, and watched their reactions. Prescott seemed unfazed—he'd had even longer than Antonov to adjust to the new facts. But he could recognize the signs in van der Gelder, and the subtler ones in Taathaanahk, as the implications began to sink home.

"However," he went on before the silence could stretch too thin, "I agree that we should retire into Anderson Four as promptly as possible, if we can do so without heavy losses. Once there, we'll have the warp point in our rear, as it were; we can hold it against whatever forces are here in Anderson Five while letting the blocking force cross Anderson Four and come to us."

"Alssso, Sssir," Taathaanahk observed, "we'll be able to ussse our fiffghters and AFFFFHAWKs to interdict any courrrier drrrones sssent thhhrough the warrrp pppoint, thusss preventing their ffforcesss from mmmounting a cooooordinated attack."

"Yes!" Van der Gelder leaned forward with new animation. "That would give us the opportunity to defeat them in detail. Especially considering the probability—which I consider high—that Home Fleet has dispatched a relief force."

"They woulddd hhhave had to orrrganize one vvery quickly," Taathaanahk said dubiously.

"If I know the Sky Marshal," van der Gelder rejoined, "she scraped together everything at Centauri that could fly and energize a beam and sent it off—or, more likely, *led* it off—without waiting for reinforcements from Sol. She knows when time is of the essence! So the relief force may not be as big or as well-balanced by ship types as we might like. But if it can hit the Bug blocking force from the rear in Anderson Four while it's heavily engaged with us . . ."

"Even if no such relief force arrives," Prescott put in, "our speed advantage means that all we'd have to do is break through the blocking force to escape. And we may as well face the fact that 'escape' has become our objective." Then a thought seemed to come to him, and he faced Antonov squarely. "But, Sir, I seem to recall that you implied that this is all contingent on our being able to transit from this system back to Anderson Four 'without heavy losses.'"

"Your recollection is correct, Admiral Prescott. You see, we've been assuming that the main threat still lies ahead of us. But there is no justification for such an assumption. What has happened so far suggests a very well-prepared operation with formidable forces behind it. And given the greater numbers of warp points normally associated with massive stars like this one, I consider it entirely possible that there are already one or more large Bug formations here in Anderson Five. Some of them may well be in a position to intercept us as we retire towards Anderson Four, and if we have to fight our way back through this system, those of us who escape to Anderson Four may be too weak to mount a warp point defense against their pursuers."

For several heartbeats, there was silence. The others, even Prescott, had clearly not allowed themselves to explore the full dimensions of the nightmare in which they found themselves.

"Therefore," Antonov finally said, in a voice that only seemed loud, "we will commence our withdrawal to Anderson Four. If we can get back through the warp point with minimal resistance, well and good. But if we detect powerful Bug forces so situated as to be able contest our passage, we will remain here in Anderson Five until the blocking force has been drawn into this system."

"Sssir," Taathaanahk said with uncharacteristic hesitation, "wwwe don't knnnow the sssize of the blllocking ffforccce.

What ifff they cccan divide it, sssending one ffforcccce on into thisss sysssstem and llleaving another in Aaanderson Fffour to hhhold the warrrp pppoint?"

To everyone's astonishment, Antonov actually grinned. "Admiral Taathaanahk, I wouldn't worry about that if I were you. If the Bugs have *that* many ships in the blocking force, then—" a fatalistic Slavic shrug "—we're fucked anyway." Prescott and van der Gelder smothered a guffaw and a giggle respectively. "But assuming that we *do* have a fighting chance, I prefer to take that chance in a war of movement in this system."

No one looked altogether happy, but no one argued. "And now," Antonov resumed, "I wish to announce the following restructuring of our forces for the withdrawal. Admiral Prescott, I am detaching your task force's CVLs; they go to Task Force 23. But in exchange you will get Admiral Taathaanahk's twelve *Borzoi* class fleet carriers."

Prescott and Taathaanahk both looked puzzled. "Hardly an exchange I can complain about, Sir," the former admitted. "But . . . can I keep Captain Trailman, my *farshathkhanaak*?"

"*Nyet*. I think it best that he remain with the strikegroups he knows, and which know him."

"Very well, Sir." Prescott knew better than to argue. "But . . . may I ask the reason for the swap?"

"The reason, Admiral Prescott, is that the *Borzois*, unlike your *Shokakus*, have cloaking ECM. You see, when we begin our withdrawal, I'm going to detach you from our main body. And after being detached, I want your entire command to go into cloak."

The puzzlement on Prescott's face intensified—but only for a moment. Then understanding dawned. And he and Antonov exchanged a grin.

As she'd found herself doing more and more since they'd entered Anderson Two, Hannah Avram let her eyes wander towards the view screen, and thought of the planet, thankfully invisible with distance, that lay within that orange primary's meager liquid-water zone. *We thought we had all the time in the world to figure out a solution to the Harnah problem,* she thought bleakly. So the Bugs were still on that planet, albeit with their space capabilities in ruins. And if the Alliance was forced to give up this system, they'd simply continue to herd their sentient meat-animals for God knew how long.

Her mind recoiled from the thought with disgust, and she turned from the conference room's view screen. Even this meeting, wrestling with the problem of organizing her hastily assembled force while underway, was a welcome refuge from the ghosts of those centauroids.

The staff, with their terminals flanked by untidy stacks of hard copy, filled the compartment. The senior flag officers attended electronically, and had taken up a fair amount of time bickering over who got which ship for which task force. But now Terence Mukerji was striking a new note, and she sighed inwardly as she composed herself to hear him out.

"Of course I can understand your orders to remain in cloak after we transit to Anderson Three, Sky Marshal," he was saying in his unctuous way. "And also your policy of using RD2s to probe the Anderson Three warp point and all subsequent warp points before we transit. After all, this system is the last one we can be certain the Alliance still controls. But we must consider that the Bugs may be—indeed, very probably are—sending blocking forces to bar at least one of these warp points."

"Then what's your point, Admiral?" she demanded, reining in her annoyance. "It's precisely to warn us of such a force that I ordered the probing of the warp points. But in this fluid situation, the blocking forces may not be in place as yet. That's why I insisted on haste in assembling this force."

"Yes, Sir," Mukerji murmured. "And why we didn't wait for additional forces to arrive from Sol."

Avram resolutely held her temper and continued as though the interruption hadn't taken place. "Likewise, remaining cloaked between transits will maximize our chances of advancing up this chain undetected *if* we can make it through the warp points before opposition crystallizes." She had to put up with Mukerji, whose most obvious talent was that of knowing which politicians to cultivate. More than once, she'd listened to Agamemnon Waldeck praise him as "an officer with a sound awareness of the political realities," and somehow refrained from gagging.

"Ah, yes, Sky Marshal. To be sure. At the same time . . . well, I would be derelict in my responsibility as second in command if I failed to point out that such a swift, undetected passage may carry its own risk."

"Precisely what are you talking about, Admiral?"

"Simply this, Sky Marshal. If enemy blocking forces of sufficient strength arrive in position *after* we've transited, and if we find that Second Fleet has already been destroyed or rendered too weak to be of assistance, then we would be trapped ourselves." Mukerji paused and, misinterpreting Avram's silence, pressed on. "So might I suggest that a more deliberate advance, coupled with attempts to ascertain Second Fleet's status, might be in order? This way we could avoid the possibility of, as it were, throwing good money after bad." He paused again, awaiting appreciation of his witticism. But what he saw in Avram's expression decided him against continuing. As the pause stretched and stretched, the noises in *Xingú's* conference room died, one after another, until there was utter silence.

Avram broke it. "Understand me, Admiral Mukerji . . . and everyone else in the sound of my voice. Rescuing Second Fleet is our *only* consideration. We will pursue any course of action that offers a possibility of doing so, and to that end, I'm prepared to risk the loss of this entire force. We are all expendable!" She glared directly at the pickup and noted out of the corner of an eye that Mukerji's face, normally the color of weak coffee, seemed to have acquired an extra dollop of cream. "Is that unmistakably clear, Admiral Mukerji?" *You pusillanimous turd,* she silently added. Without waiting for a reply, she cut the connection. Then she swung her glare towards the staff. With comical abruptness, the hubbub resumed. Avram spared a moment to look back towards the view screen, where the distant stars gave no sense of motion although she knew that they were proceeding towards the Anderson Three warp point with all the speed their drives could provide.

You would've squashed him flat long ago, Ivan Niko-layevich, she thought as she gazed at those frustratingly motionless stars. *But I'm not you. Nobody is. Is that why I'm prepared to risk this force for any chance of getting you out alive? Or is it because Second Fleet is the cream of the TFN, and its loss is unthinkable? Either way, I'm making a logically unexceptionable decision, on the basis of cold calculation. Of course I am. Got to keep telling myself that.*

"Red Seven-Two's picking up something ahead, Skip."

"What?" Commodore Lucinda Chou, officially Special Operations Officer for Fighter Operations but known to one and all as Second Fleet's *farshathkhanaak*, crossed quickly to her assistant's console. Chou would vastly have preferred to be out in her own command fighter, but *Thor*'s CIC was the only logical place for her to be. Simple communications lag would have made it impractical for her too coordinate her recon shell from a point on its periphery.

"Not sure yet, Skip," Commander Ashengi replied. "Looks like a cloaked starship, but it's way out at thirty light-minutes. Seven-Two got dead lucky to pick up anything at that range."

"Maybe they've got a malfunctioning ECM suite," Chou murmured. She turned and looked into the huge holo tank—eight times the size of the one on *Thor*'s flag deck—and rubbed her chin. The tiny light code was barely inside the perimeter of even CIC's plot, but it was almost squarely between Second Fleet and the Anderson Four warp point. That icon might be a sensor ghost, and she wanted to believe it was, but she didn't.

"Inform Admiral Taathaanahk and the Flag, Aucke," she said quietly. "Then set up an armed recon sweep. The

Admiral may just want someone to go take a closer look at this."

Commander Aathmaahr led his mixed Terran-Ophiuchi strikegroup towards the contact. Aathmaahr had been a pilot—one of the elite *Corthohardaa,* whom the Terrans called "the Screaming Eagles" from the stylized *hasfrazi* head of their insignia—for over twenty Terran Standard years, but he'd never seen combat until the Bugs attacked. Now he'd seen more than he'd ever wanted to, and there seemed no end in sight. *Well,* he corrected himself, *there is one possible end, but I will defer it as long as possible.*

He clicked his beak in a grim chuckle and checked his instruments. Like most of his people, he felt disdain for the slower, clumsier gunboats. They were dangerous, yes, but they could never match a fighter's dogfighting maneuverability, and Aathmaahr had made ace (a Human concept the OADC had adopted with enthusiasm) in his very first engagement against them. Of course, that had been before they started carrying AFHAWKs. Trying to go in close now would be even more costly, but squadron for squadron, and despite their point defense, gunboats were still no match for fighters armed with FM3s.

Yet they can *kill us,* he reminded himself, remembering how the human Chou had become Second Fleet's *farshathkhanaak.* That post had been Captain Ythaanhk's . . . until he met one of the gunboat-launched AFHAWKs head on. Not that Chou wasn't a satisfactory replacement. She was less gifted than an Ophiuchi behind the controls, but she certainly understood fighter ops.

He checked his sensors again and shook off his daydreams. His strikegroup was beyond the recon shell perimeter now, and if that sensor ghost was truly a starship, his arrow straight course towards it would draw a response soon.

His fighters streaked onward, laden with three missiles each, and a worm of tension coiled within him. Surely the Bugs realized his purpose, and virtually all Bug starships carried gunboat racks. Only their pure missile platforms retained conventional XO racks, instead, and—

"Talon Leader, Talon Green One," a human voice crackled in his earbug. "Do you see what I see at zero-zero-zero?"

"Affffffirrmatttive, Grrreeen One," Aathmaahr replied. He felt a spike of pique that Lieutenant Brahman had gotten his report in before any of his Ophiuchi pilots, but it was distant and far away. The icons of Bug gunboats were blinking onto his plot in shoals, hundreds of them, with the instantaneous solidity possible only to small craft launching from cloaked starships.

Well, they've seen us, a small voice said deep within him.

"Aaaalphhhha One," he said to his tac officer, and Lieutenant Dahrmaar clicked his beak in assent. Long, strong fingers tapped at his console, flashing the order to the rest of the strikegroup, and Aathmaahr's squadrons closed in around his own fighter. The Bugs had left their launch just too late, he thought grimly. They were launching across a broad arc, which gave an indication of their fleet's deployment, but it also meant they needed time to concentrate. No more than fifty or sixty gunboats could intercept him short of the icon he'd come to examine, and he had forty-eight fighters to throw against them.

Even odds are in our favor, he reminded himself as his pilot rammed the drive to full power, and took his strikegroup straight down the enemy's throat.

Attack Force One had waited eight days for the enemy. His long delay—probably to make repairs—had given the dispersed attack forces ample time to spread out to envelop him, whatever course he finally took, but it was obvious he had detected them at last. Fortunately, he had sent in only a fairly weak force of attack craft; unfortunately, the powerful reinforcements the core systems had sent up to support the attack forces' organic gunboat components were seventy light-minutes astern of Attack Force One . . . and so were the escort cruisers which were most effective against attack craft. Their inability to

*cloak had dictated their deployment, for it had been
essential to hide the attack forces' presence from the
enemy as long as possible.*

*But the enemy knew now, and com lasers sent their
summons flashing astern at the speed of light. Even so,
the message would take over an hour to be received, and
Attack Force One's own gunboats raced to meet the
enemy.*

The fighters held their missiles until the last moment,
then punched every bird straight down the Bugs' throat
at a range of five and a half light-seconds—a half light-
second beyond the range of their AFHAWKs. Aathmaahr
was only peripherally interested in killing gunboats; his
mission was to determine what the enemy had in the way
of starships, and he flung everything he had at the only
foes between him and his objective.

Forty-eight fighters salvoed a hundred and forty-four
missiles. Seventy acquired lock and homed for the kill,
and point defense engaged them as they closed. Thirty-
four were destroyed short of their targets; thirty-six went
home, and fifty-six percent of the gunboats died. But then
the survivors salvoed *their* ordnance, and a hundred and
twelve AFHAWKs came streaking back.

The strikegroup split apart, each squadron maneuvering
hard in the Waldeck Weave and its Ophiuchi equivalent.
There were enough missiles out there to kill the entire
strikegroup twice over, but the Bugs had fired too soon.
Accuracy was poor at that range, and the fighters' evasive
maneuvers made it poorer. "Only" seventeen of Aathmaahr's fighters were blown apart, and the thirty-one
survivors swept back in, drives howling, to tear into the
twenty-eight remaining gunboats with internal lasers. Eight
more fighters died, but they took all of the gunboats with
them, and Aathmaahr led his shrunken group past the
tumbling wreckage of friend and foe alike.

"One passs!" he cautioned his pilots as they swept in
towards the range at which no ECM could hide a starship
from them. There would be time for no more—not with

the other gunboats closing in vengefully from all sides—
but without their missiles, his fighters had a forty-five
percent speed advantage. They could get their look, then
evade and—

His thoughts broke off in disbelief as the Bug starship
appeared suddenly on his sensors. Impossible! *Nothing*
was that big! But the lumbering behemoth refused to
vanish. It hung against the starscape, armored flanks
studded with cavernous weapon bays, and he shook
himself.

"Ffffalll backkk!" he barked over the com. "Tannngo
Two!"

The twenty-three surviving members of SG 371 turned
and fled for their carrier. Behind them, the stupendous
ship they'd come so far to find ground steadily onward
with its consorts.

CHAPTER FORTY

Even Legends Die

TFNS *Colorado*'s flag bridge was deathly silent as the holo of an unbelievable starship hung in the tactical display. It wasn't a real visual, just computer imagery generated from the fighters' sensor data, but that made it no less terrifying. Twice the size of a superdreadnought, it hung there like a curse and chilled every heart with the firepower it must pack.

Too bad LeBlanc isn't here, Ivan Antonov thought distantly. *He keeps insisting Bugs don't think like we do, and here is the proof. Three entire fleets, counting the one we just destroyed. Over five* hundred *starships—a hundred and sixty of them superdreadnoughts—God only knows how many gunboats, and the surrender of a populated star system just to bait a trap, and I walked straight into it.*

He glared at the image, feeling the sickness and self-disgust at his core, then closed his eyes and sucked in a deep breath.

No. It can't all *have been a trick. They would have required omniscience to deliberately let us see them in Centauri just to lure us here. No. They set this up only after we destroyed their covering force in Anderson One, yet that makes it no better. I have led three quarters of Home Fleet into a death trap.*

He opened his eyes once more and made himself think.

"Estimates on firepower?" he asked de Bertholet quietly.

"Impossible to say, Sir." The ops officer seemed almost grateful for the technical question. "We've never even considered building something that size, so I don't have any idea how much mass its engines eat up. At a guess, I'd say it probably has about a sixty or seventy percent edge over a superdreadnought in weapons' tonnage. It can't be a lot more, even as big as it is; the support systems for its crew have to be scaled up, as well."

"So it has *only* a seventy percent individual superiority, eh?"

Antonov's wry voice was poison dry, and de Bertholet surprised himself with a bark of strained laughter. He smoothed any sign of levity from his face instantly, but Antonov only produced a wintry smile without taking his eyes from the display.

"Unless their construction rate is far higher than our own, it must have taken at least two years to build such vessels," he spoke as if only to himself, then nodded. "Yes, that would make sense. Especially since they lacked command datalink at the outset. They couldn't match our datagroups' size, so they built bigger individual units to even the firepower." He frowned, rubbing his chin. "Yet why wait this long to commit them? Unless their breakthrough into modern datalink came as a surprise to them?" He cocked his head, then nodded again. "If that were the case, then they would have had to refit with the new command systems before committing them—possibly even redesign their entire armaments. We know they prefer specialized designs, after all. . . ."

He gazed at the holo a moment longer, then turned away. A raised hand summoned Stovall and Kozlov to join de Bertholet at his side, and he folded his hands behind him as he faced his senior staffers grimly.

"The level of threat has just risen," he said flatly. "We lack even the most imperfect estimate of the firepower this new class represents, nor do we know how many of them the enemy has. We have seen only one. There may be dozens, or they may have only a handful; the only way we can discover which is to engage them."

Stovall nodded with matching grimness. The others simply waited, eyes and mouths tense.

"Unfortunately, we must assume that whatever force their drones summoned *also* has such units. If this is true, a warp point assault against them becomes even more unacceptable. Nor can we risk a head-on engagement with the enemy force we have detected. If we take heavy losses against the single force we *know* about, we weaken ourselves—perhaps fatally—against any additional enemies."

He paused, and Stovall frowned. "You're correct, of course, Sir," he said slowly, "but they're between us and the warp point. To me, that suggests they must have had us under observation the entire time, probably with cloaked light cruisers, or they couldn't have positioned themselves so precisely. Assuming that's true, they have the advantage of knowing where we are. If we let them choose the time and place to hit us—" He shrugged, and Antonov nodded.

"True enough, but we have advantages of our own. Our ships' drives may be less than fully reliable, yet while they last, we retain our speed advantage, and for all we know, this new class is still slower. With a fighter shell posted sufficiently far out, we should be able to detect them—even cloaked—soon enough to evade them."

"While our drives last," Stovall conceded.

"And," Antonov went on, "if they bring up light cruisers to screen their formations against our fighters, they'll become much easier to track, since their fleet-type CLs can't cloak. The same is true of their gunboats, the only vessels with sufficient speed to overhaul us. In short, they cannot force us to commit to close action until and unless we *allow* them to."

"But, Sir," de Bertholet said quietly, "sooner or later, we'll simply run out of supplies, or our drives *will* pack in. All they have to do is sit on our exit warp point long enough, and we'll have no choice but to come to them sooner or later."

"Precisely," Antonov said, and his staff blinked at his icy, armor-plated smile. "And that's why we must keep them from deciding to do just that. We must draw their attention and be certain we hold it—be certain they keep *trying* to overtake us rather than give up and fall back on the warp point—until the final component of their trap makes transit."

"That could take another ten or twelve days, Sir," Stovall said, "and they're going to be throwing every gunboat they can at us the entire time."

"Understood. It will be up to our fighters and escort vessels to hold them off. It will be difficult, and our orders must stress the absolute necessity of conserving ammunition, yet it is the only hope I see. We *must* stay alive long enough for their full force to arrive and then break out at a time of *our* choosing." He paused and swept his eyes slowly from face to face, and his deep voice was a subterranean rumble when he spoke again. "Whatever we may do, our losses will be heavy. Accept that now, for it is inevitable. But we *must* get whatever we can out of this trap."

One by one, his staff nodded. He was right. The task he proposed to accept was virtually impossible—evading multiple enemy fleets while playing matador to all of them would require maneuvers no navy had ever trained for—yet it was the only chance Second Fleet had. And if any flag officer in the Terran Navy could pull it off, the man before them was that officer.

"Very well," Antonov said. "We will alter course, Commander de Bertholet. Turn us away from them and take us above the ecliptic. We will begin by heading away from the warp point."

"Yes, Sir."

"Before altering course, however, detach Admiral Prescott. He knows what I want him to do, but it is essential the Bugs not see him separate from us, so he must go immediately."

"If they *do* have us under observation from cloak, they'll see him drop off their scanners, Sir," Stovall said.

"We'll take the entire Fleet into cloak simultaneously," Antonov replied. "Any scout ships must be outside our present fighter shell, cloaked or not. That means they're too far out to track us in cloak even with known starting positions . . . but they will be able to track our *fighters*. Let them think they've panicked us into a useless attempt at concealment. The picket fighters will maintain their positions relative to the flagship as we move away, and TF 21 will go dead in space. The enemy will track the fighter shell and be drawn after us; once we're well clear, Admiral Prescott will bring up his drives and proceed with his mission."

"And when they send in their first strikes?" the chief of staff asked. "If they have a good count on us now, they're likely to realize someone's missing, Sir."

"A risk we must take, but the Fleet will remain cloaked throughout. Their gunboats shouldn't be surprised if they can't see all of us at any given moment. With luck, they'll assume that's where Prescott is—just out of sight in cloak, but still with the rest of the Fleet."

"Yes, Sir." Stovall nodded. It was a gamble, but, then, so was Antonov's entire plan. And who knew? It might even work.

Clearly the enemy had finally divined the nature of the trap—or a part of it, at least. It was a pity; the Fleet had hoped to keep him in ignorance until the final units arrived. But the possibility had been allowed for. That was why Attack Force One lay directly between him and his escape warp point.

But he appeared even more confused than the Fleet had anticipated. The cloaked light cruisers which had watched cautiously from a light-hour beyond his formation now saw his entire force of starships disappear. ECM had been a matter of some concern when the plan was formulated, for it was possible the enemy might somehow creep past the Fleet to the warp point in cloak. But though his ships might have disappeared, his sphere of attack craft had not. They moved off across the system, swinging away from Attack Force One and—though the enemy could not know it—almost directly towards Attack Force Three. Of course, it was possible he was actually trying to creep away in a totally different direction while his attack craft decoyed the Fleet, but it was unlikely. He persisted in his inexplicable refusal to sacrifice units for tactical advantage, and that shell represented at least a third of his total strength in attack craft.

Attack Force One adjusted its position slightly, swinging to port and climbing above the ecliptic to stay between the enemy and escape, but it made no effort to pursue. There was no need. Eventually Attack Force Three or Attack Force Two would make contact . . . and in the meanwhile, the time had come to commit the gunboats at last.

"Looks like it's working, Sir," Anthea Mandagalla said quietly. "If they knew we were here, they'd be doing something about it."

Raymond Prescott nodded without taking his own gaze from the huge tank. He and his staff were in *Crete's* CIC, not on Flag Bridge, to take advantage of the master plot's size, and he chewed his lower lip as a massive wave of gunboats streaked past his command. The reorganized TF 21—sixteen fast superdreadnoughts, twenty battle-cruisers, and ten fleet carriers—lay motionless, wrapped in the invisibility of their ECM. The nearest gunboat was over twenty light-minutes distant, so the ECM probably wasn't even necessary, but it was impossible to know where the Bugs' cloaked *starships* might be, and he recalled Andy's account of his mission in Justin before Operation Redemption. *This seems to be becoming a Prescott speciality. Let's hope we don't have to do it too often!*

He watched the gunboats streak away after the rest of the fleet, then glanced at Bichet.

"We'll give them another hour, Jacques." His mouth twitched a taut smile. "If this works at all, we've got plenty of time, so let's take it easy and hold those emissions down, shall we?"

❖   ❖   ❖

"Dear God . . . *eleven hundred* gunboats?"

Midori Kozlov had barely spoken above a whisper, but Antonov heard her distinctly in the hush that had fallen over *Colorado's* flag bridge. He ignored her as he studied the holo tank in which the two incoming swarms of gunboats showed as fuzzy amoebas of red light. Any meaningful display of individual craft was out of the question.

They'd detected the first wave-front of six hundred gunboats sweeping in from astern, and everyone had remained steady—it wasn't as though they hadn't been expecting something of the kind. But now the fighter screen had detected this new force approaching on a different bearing. Kozlov's reaction, and the stunned silence from everyone else, told Antonov he needed to dispel the psychologically devastating sensation of being caught between two forces.

"It appears," he said very distinctly, "that the enemy's timing is a little off."

"Sir?" Stovall tore his gaze from the plot.

"Observe, Commodore: the force approaching from astern is so much closer that we should have no trouble dealing with it in detail. Of course," he added thoughtfully, "it won't remain so if the present vectors remain unchanged; in fact, they're probably counting on the rate at which we're closing with the second force." He swung to face Stovall. "We will alter course away from the second gunboat flotilla's bearing. At the same time, have the fighter screen recalled and rearmed with FM3s; the change in course provides an optimum opportunity to do so, and I believe we have sufficient time."

"Aye, aye, Sir." Stovall turned to de Bertholet. "Armand, see to it." As the ops officer busied himself with the necessary orders, the chief of staff turned back to Antonov and spoke more quietly. "Sir, there may be a risk inherent in this evolution. What if they have yet *another* force, waiting in cloak just beyond the fighter shell's detection range? We'll be vulnerable to a gunboat strike launched by such a force while our fighters are away striking the known forces."

Antonov smiled and replied in an equally quiet voice. "I'm glad you're thinking in terms of additional enemy forces, Commodore Stovall, because I haven't wanted to mention the possibility out loud; I don't think it's what most of our people need to hear at the moment. But I'm more and more convinced that the possibility is very real. We know nothing about this system's warp points, or about the forces the Bugs have put through them. Therefore," he continued in a more normal volume, "I intend to hold a quarter of our total fighter strength in reserve to deal with any unexpected threats."

The fighters of the shell returned to their carriers for rearming while the shoals of gunboats continued to crawl across the light-minutes, and Second Fleet turned to meet the closer of them. The carriers still with the fleet's main body were up to about eighty percent of maximum hangar capacity—a total of seven hundred and seven fighters—and five hundred and thirty streaked away, laden with third-generation fighter missiles.

The strain mounted on the flag bridge as the fighters crossed fifteen light minutes to make contact with the Bugs, then ratcheted up to new levels of tension as the report of the strike crept across that distance at the speed of light. Then the messages arrived in a rush, and it was as though an emotional dike had burst.

"Over two hundred and fifty kills!" de Bertholet whooped to make himself heard over the hubbub. "And not a single fighter lost!"

"And," Stovall added more quietly, "they all followed orders and turned tail before they came into AFHAWK range of the enemy." He grinned weakly, looking drained. "Fighter pilots are such hot dogs you can never be sure."

"Yes." Antonov nodded ponderously, standing like a rock amid the jubilation, as impervious to it as he'd been to the earlier stunned apprehension. "They'll have time to return, rearm, and go out for another strike."

"What about the reserve fighters, Sir?" de Bertholet asked, brought back down to earth by the admiral's stolidity.

"Continue to hold them in reserve, Commander. We'll need them soon enough."

The fighters returned, and the flag staff, past its emotional peaks and valleys, coordinated the rearming and the launching of a second strike smoothly. Once again five hundred and thirty fighters went out, and once again they decimated the Bugs from beyond AFHAWK range. This time they returned with the gunboats close behind them, but less than a hundred of those gunboats remained, and swept into AFHAWK range of the screen's escorts with a self-sacrificing futility that would have been appalling in any other species. There was barely time to receive the report of that fact before the last of them had been blasted into oblivion.

"Not a single casualty on our side," de Bertholet breathed, almost reverently.

"And now," Antonov said, still unmoved, "as soon as the fighters have rearmed, I want them launched against the *second* gunboat strike force."

For a moment, silence reigned. No one had been thinking of that other incoming wave of five hundred gunboats.

"Ah, shall we signal the carrier commanders to expedite the rearming, Sir?" Stovall inquired.

"*Nyet,*" Antonov snorted. "They have enough on their minds right now without having pompous admirals and officious staff *zalyotniki* tell them their jobs. They'll get the fighters turned around as fast as it can be done." He scowled. "Unfortunately, by then there won't be time for them to intercept the enemy at long range. So, Commander," he continued without a break, turning to de Bertholet, "I think it's time to launch the reserve fighters. And yes, Commodore Stovall, I know there's a risk involved. But risk avoidance has become a luxury—one which is going to be in shorter and shorter supply." He paused, considering. "On reflection, I think we'll hold back the fighters that are now being rearmed until the reserve fighters have returned, and then send them all out in a combined strike. They've just conducted two long-range attacks without a break, and pilot exhaustion is a factor we don't need."

The hundred and seventy-six fighters of the reserve were off the mark quickly enough to intercept the second wave of gunboats ten light-minutes out, where they killed seventy-five of them with FM3s before returning to their carriers.

"We're only going to have time for one more strike, Sir," Stovall reminded Antonov as the rearming neared completion.

"*Da*," the admiral acknowledged. "And they won't be able to get all the remaining gunboats from outside AFHAWK range." He thought in black abstraction for a heartbeat or two. "After they've expended their FM3s, I authorize one, repeat *one* pass with lasers. Afterwards they're to return directly. We can't afford heavy fighter losses at this stage. There'll be no unrestricted dogfighting, as dearly as I know the young fools would like it." He turned away and gazed into, and beyond, the plot. "The young fools," he repeated in a voice that held infinite sadness.

The gunboats were three light-minutes out when a hurricane of missiles from Antonov's still-undiminished fighter force blasted two hundred and sixty-six of them out of existence. But the others came on, and this time the fighters didn't wheel to flee. They drove in, taking so little time to close that they lost only a few of their number to the AFHAWKs the Bugs were finally able to bring into play. Then the two forces interpenetrated at an unthinkable relative velocity, and that instant of interpenetration was marked by a brief but searingly intense exchange of energy weapon fire in which a hundred and twenty gunboats died. Then, too fast for thought, the fighters were through and commencing the turning maneuver that would take them back to their carriers.

"Sixty-seven fighters lost," Stovall observed grimly as the last squadrons reported in.

"But only thirty-nine gunboats left," de Bertholet breathed. "And *still* they come on!"

It was true. No more discouraged by losses than any other force of nature, the Bugs drove into the warships' defensive envelopes. Five managed to make attacks before the AFHAWKs obliterated them; none of those attacks even penetrated shields to scratch material defenses.

At the moment of the last gunboat's demise, a strange release of emotion swept *Colorado's* flag bridge. Stovall caught himself cheering with the rest, and turned an abashed face to Antonov. Amazingly, the admiral was actually smiling a little. He let the smile linger a second, as though savoring it like the last rose of the season, before relinquishing it.

"They won't make that kind of mistake again in coordinating their attacks," he rumbled, shaking his head slowly.

"But, Sir . . . *eleven hundred gunboats!*"

"True. But to get them, we shot away ninety percent of our FM3s. The remaining ones won't last long when the next gunboat wave comes."

"If there is one, Sir. Maybe they've shot their bolt."

"You believe that about as much as I do, Commodore. No, they'll be back. And when they do, our fighters will have to meet them armed with *short*-ranged munitions. Which means they'll have to get through the gunboats' AFHAWK envelope before they can even use their weapons. And when they do get to fire, they'll be doing it at the gunboats' own most effective range."

Stovall started to open his mouth, then closed it and looked around the flag bridge. The shouting was over, but the cheerful back-slapping and story-comparing was still in progress.

Antonov laid a restraining hand on his arm. "Let them enjoy it while they can, Commodore," he said gently, in a voice no one would ever have expected to hear from Ivan the Terrible. "They'll only have a little while."

The Fleet had not anticipated such savage losses. The new, longer-ranged missiles of the enemy's attack craft offset the gunboats' defensive missile capability, and the timing

*which had sent the first two strikes in separately had denied
them mutual support.*

*But none of the destroyed units had come from the Fleet's
organic gunboat strength; all had come from one of the
adjacent systems, and despite the two botched attacks, a
total of almost three thousand remained.*

The Fleet would use them more wisely henceforth.

"That's a hundred and sixty kills," de Bertholet declared,
looking at the board.

"So," Midori Kozlov said quietly, "that only leaves eleven
hundred and forty."

They'd detected the thirteen hundred incoming gunboats
twenty hours after the destruction of the earlier waves. This
time, Flag Bridge hadn't been blanketed by an aghast silence.
It was as though these people had moved beyond all such
emotions by now. They simply functioned as modular
components of a machine whose purpose was survival.

Antonov's last FM3-armed fighters had gone out and
performed what everyone knew would be their last cost-
free slaughter. Now they were on the way back, to be
rearmed with external laser packs. As they drew closer,
the admiral and his staff held a hurried colloquy.

"We can turn them around in time to launch all six
hundred and forty remaining fighters for another long-
range strike, Sir," de Bertholet reported. "Perhaps we could
simultaneously engage with SBMs. They weren't designed
as gunboat-killers, I know. But it can be done. And keeping
the enemy as busy as possible would help compensate
for the fighters' lack of FM3s."

"I've considered that, Commander, but our stocks of
SBMs are low. We used many of them against the Bug
defensive force that lured me into this system." Antonov's
voice remained level as he implicitly assumed full
responsibility. "Remember also the SBM's greater vulnerability to point defense." The admiral smiled at de
Bertholet's crestfallen look. "Nevertheless, your idea of
coordinated missile and fighter strikes has merit. We will
hold the fighters back until the enemy is within capital

missile range. We still have an abundant supply of those."

So it was that the Bug gunboats approached to within fifteen light-seconds of Second Fleet before the fighters—all that Antonov still possessed—swooped in. The Bugs had a brief time to take advantage of the unaccustomed opportunity to use AFHAWKs, and they made the most of it, killing two hundred and sixteen fighters. But then the deadly little craft were in among them, and swarms of capital missiles came with them, overloading point defense that might otherwise have engaged fighters at what passed for knife range in space combat. The fighters took fearful vengeance, their finely coordinated squadrons going through the serried ranks of gunboats like mowing machines. They slaughtered nine hundred while the missiles that weaved through the defensive laser-lattice claimed another hundred and fifty. On Second Fleet's view screens, as revealed by remote pickups, the rapid-fire immolations resembled a dense swarm of fireflies.

Ninety gunboats got through, and before the fighters could reverse course and catch them they were among the ships. In the brief time left to them, they swarmed around and destroyed two assault carriers, a battleship, two battlecruisers, and . . .

"Sir, *Rio Grande* reports failure of all major systems!" De Bertholet might as well have saved his breath, for another of TF 22's ships was downloading a view of Admiral van der Gelder's flagship, and on a small screen at his station Antonov watched the superdreadnought die.

"*Dosvedania*, Jessica," he breathed as the searing, strobe-like series of explosions seemed to merge into a single transcendent one.

"*Rio Grande* Code Omega," de Bertholet finished, even more unnecessarily.

It was the gunboats' final, dying blow, and a subdued flag bridge watched the damage totals begin to arrive. Cheering, like terror, had seemingly been left behind in some previous life which held room for things besides grim desperation.

✦   ✦   ✦

*The enemy was resilient, but this time he had been hurt.
The distance between the attack forces made coordination
difficult and time consuming, and, once again, losses had
been heavy. But the gunboats were not intended to destroy
the enemy. It would be good if they could, yet their true
function was to wear him down. To batter his starships,
grind away his attack craft, and force him to expend
ammunition before the battle-lines engaged.*

*And they were succeeding. The enemy had lost thirty
percent of his attack craft, and so few of them had attacked
with missiles that his ammunition must be running low.*

*It would be difficult to launch another strike like the
last. Attack Force Three's organic gunboat component
had been effectively eliminated. Attack Force One and
Two retained theirs, but those forces were widely separated, making coordination between them all but impossible.
The last three hundred system-based gunboats would be
committed, but the two attack forces would retain their
integral strength until the decisive moment.*

"That's the last of them, Sir." De Bertholet managed
to make the report fairly crisp, even though, like everyone
else, he'd only been able to catch fitful catnaps during
the sixty hours—it only seemed like an eternity—since
Prescott's task force had split off.

The three hundred gunboats had been detected thirty-
one hours after the last attack. Once again, Antonov's
fighters—four hundred and twenty-three in number now—
had intercepted at close range in coordination with capital
missiles. And again the attackers had been wiped out.
But it had cost seventy-eight fighters as well as the ship
losses beginning to appear on the board.

"Thank you, Commander," the admiral acknowledged,
never removing his eyes from the unfolding toll. A CVA,
five battlecruisers, two light carriers, seven light cruisers
. . . He finally shook himself and turned to assess his staff's
haggardness. Gazing back at him, they saw only bedrock
steadiness.

"You will note," he began, ignoring the losses they'd

just taken and indicating the strategic display of the system, "that since we initially changed course in response to the first gunboat attack our continued course changes have had the net effect of bringing us around in a three-quarter circle, almost two hundred and seventy degrees relative to our original course. I believe it is now time for us to begin working our way back toward that original course."

Midori Kozlov shook herself as though to shake loose from webs of fatigue and despair. "Back toward the Anderson Four warp point, Sir? You think the time has come when . . . ?"

Antonov saw the nascent hope in all their faces. They knew the desperate plan that lay behind the *tottentanz* whose measure they'd been treading. So they knew that the order to set course for the warp point would promise an end to their nightmare . . . one way or another.

"*Nyet.* I'm as certain as I am of anything in the universe that Admiral Prescott is carrying out his orders. But as for the Bug blocking force . . . No. We have a while yet. But it isn't too soon to start working our way onto the heading, very gradually and without being obvious about it."

Raymond Prescott sat on his flag bridge once more as Task Force 21 made its final turn and slunk stealthily towards the warp point. His ships' high designed speed had made this slow, careful approach even more frustrating, yet that slowness had not only reduced the power of his drive signatures, substantially easing his ECM's task, but given his passive sensors ample time to sweep the space before him . . . and the Bugs had been careless.

He bared his teeth as he glanced into his plot once more. The Bugs "knew" where Second Fleet's units were, and so the two battlecruiser datagroups guarding the warp point "knew" they were far beyond any enemy's sensor range. One of them had taken its ECM down—probably only to repair some fault, since it had come back up seventy-one minutes later—but that had been long enough for TF 21 to obtain a firm fix. With that datum in hand,

Prescott had swept a bit wider of the warp point, and his sensor sections, working outward from the ship which had so obligingly revealed itself, had spotted its consorts, as well. It was entirely possible there were other ships watching the warp point, but Prescott was privately certain any others would be light units. He had the battlecruisers, now, and his own *Dunkerques* were cycling continuous targeting updates just in case. When the time came—

"Drones transiting the warp point!" There was an instant of silence, and then, "They're TFN birds!"

Prescott's head jerked up at the sudden announcement, and Anthea Mandagalla's eyes met his, glowing like pools of flame in her space-black face. He looked back into the plot, watching scores—hundreds—of drones fan out in what was obviously a search pattern, and felt his own powerful surge of hope. But—

"They're from Admiral Chin," Com said flatly. "We're reading their beacons clearly."

Chin, Prescott thought, all elation vanished. He made himself sit motionless, refusing to show how terribly he'd hoped they were from an approaching relief force, and a dreadful premonition gripped him. He knew what those drones were going to tell him.

"Are any of them heading our way, Jacques?" he asked quietly.

"Yes, Sir."

"How many?" Prescott kept his eyes on his plot as the cloaked battlecruisers opened fire on the drones. They killed many of them, but they were concentrating on the ones headed in Second Fleet's direction, and Prescott was on the far side of the warp point from the rest of the fleet. The ones which broke out and away from the point were of no concern to the enemy, for no one was out there to receive them . . . they thought.

"About ten, Sir. Some may change vector—there's no way to know what sort of search pattern they're programmed for—but on present headings, at least five will pass within a light-minute or less of the task force."

"Thank you." Prescott thought a moment longer.

Recovering one of those drones was out of the question; he couldn't afford to have one of them simply disappear if the Bugs were tracking it. But it was possible they might shed some light on whatever was coming down the Anderson Chain, and that possibility justified a certain amount of risk. "Commander Hale."

"Yes, Admiral?" *Crete's* senior com officer looked up from her console.

"Can you trigger the com laser on one of those drones and order it to upload to us without terminating its beacon?"

"Without terminating the beacon?" Hale frowned. "I think so, Sir. I'll have to rewrite a couple of lines in the standard interrogation package, though."

"Can you do it before they make their closest approach?"

"No problem, Sir," she said confidently.

"In that case, I want you to trigger the closest drone. Get with Plotting first. Make certain no known enemy positions will be in the transmission paths—from the drone, as well as us—when you do it. It's imperative that the enemy not realize what we've done."

Hannah Avram knew the feeling was irrational. In any real sense, the space here below (arbitrary term!) Anderson Three's primary sun was no more empty than the plane in which its barren planets and ruddy ember of a companion orbited. But she couldn't shake off the feeling of being adrift in a realm of cold dark nothingness where the soul could lose its way.

The relief force had only just left Anderson Two and its tragedy-haunted planet behind and entered Anderson Three when Tracking picked up a massive gunboat formation proceeding from what must be the undiscovered warp point in this system toward the one they'd just transited. Some anxious hours had passed, but the gunboats had proceeded singlemindedly on course, and Avram had breathed a sigh of relief as she realized they were just too late to detect her.

After the last gunboat icon vanished off the edge of

the plot, Admiral Mukerji had shattered the residual silence on *Xingú*'s flag bridge with a request for an electronic conference. "Sky Marshal, in light of what we've just seen, and what it suggests about the sheer scale of Bug activities along the Anderson Chain, may I suggest we send courier drones ahead to alert Admiral Antonov of our estimated time of arrival? This would enable him to plan his operations with a view to being as close to the Anderson Four/Anderson Five warp point as possible at that time. Surely having our two forces in a position to combine their efforts would maximize the chances of success."

And of your personal survival, Avram had thought. But she'd held her tongue. Mukerji's suggestion, whatever motivations lay behind it, wasn't totally irrational. Still . . .

"No, Admiral Mukerji. We have no way of knowing Second Fleet's status, so Admiral Antonov might not be able to act on that information."

"Still, Sky Marshal, what harm can it do?"

"Simply this, Admiral: to reach Admiral Antonov, the drones would have to pass through whatever Bug forces lie ahead of us, and might very well be detected. The enemy's ignorance of our presence is the greatest advantage we possess, and the need to preserve that advantage outweighs the speculative benefits of alerting Second Fleet to our approach. In fact, I'm about to order a course change to take us on a dogleg to the Anderson Four warp point."

"That will add to our flight time, Sky Marshal."

"So it will. But I'm willing to accept that as the price for removing any possibility of random encounters with Bug forces like the gunboat flotilla we just observed."

Her orders had been carried out. Like many—though by no means all—warp points, those connecting Anderson Three to Anderson Two and Four both lay in the same plane as the system's planets. The course change would, indeed, lengthen her passage time. But it would also take her force well outside that plane, keeping it beyond the sensor range of any Bugs shuttling between Anderson Three's known warp points as it proceeded towards the

Anderson Four warp point. She reminded herself of that and tried not to let impatience gnaw holes in her gut.

"That's it, Sir," Stovall reported. "They've all been accounted for."

"And this time our losses are minimal," de Bertholet added, gesturing at the board. "Admiral, this was the weakest gunboat attack we've faced so far. Could it be . . . ?"

All the staffers looked at Antonov, and he read the hunger in their eyes. They wanted him to tell them that this latest attack's feebleness represented a ray of hope in the world of unrelieved blackness they'd inhabited for what seemed as far back as memory could reach.

But he couldn't. *Unless I'm very much mistaken, this wasn't a real attack at all. They were just probing, trying to gauge how much firepower we've got left without expending too many gunboats to do it.* And yet he wouldn't say so aloud, for letting his people have a straw of hope to grasp for couldn't hurt and might possibly help.

So he held his tongue. But gazing at these people, all so much younger than he (*Who isn't?* he thought with a moment's wryness), he saw that it had been a waste of silence. They knew.

As she gazed at the sensor readouts, Hannah Avram thought of Rear Admiral Michael Chin and remembered the *bon vivant* she'd known. Did he still live at all?

The relief force had, on her orders, stayed on full sensor alert even in these regions far outside the system ecliptic, where no Bugs could reasonably be. Her caution had reaped an unexpected reward, for they now had an answer to one of the questions that had been plaguing them since their departure from Centauri: the fate of the Fleet Train.

The further they'd proceeded, the more they'd settled into the glum conclusion that nothing remained of Chin's command except debris dissipating into the void. But the sensors had brushed against what could only be survivors sheltering out here in the deeps far from any warp point— all too few survivors. Avram didn't even let herself think about the personnel losses that the absence of so many repair ships and transports implied. She couldn't, for she had a decision to make.

She made it. "Commodore Borghesi," she addressed her chief of staff, "inform Ops that I want to detach a couple of battlegroups to rendezvous with those survivors while the rest of us continue on course for Anderson Four. They're to convey my orders to Admiral Chin . . . or whoever's in command."

"What orders are those, Sky Marshal?"

"I want them to take up a position, at least ten light-hours from any warp point, and wait for us to return to this system with Second Fleet." Avram pointedly omitted any qualifiers. "At that time, we'll contact them by courier drone—keeping our presence concealed will no longer be a factor then—so they can rejoin us as we retire to Centauri."

"Aye, aye, Sir." Borghesi went to summon the staff and Avram took a last look at the meager tally of fugitives. She didn't really want to divide the none-too-abundant forces she was leading to Second Fleet's rescue. But the tatters of Fleet Train needed additional cover if they were to have any chance at all of surviving. And, unless she was very much mistaken, their morale needed any boost it could get.

"From all the information available to us, it is my judgment that the Bug blocking force will enter this system from Anderson Four in the immediate future."

Ivan Antonov looked at the half-circle of his staffers' faces and watched their reactions as his words sank home through layers of fatigue into their dulled awareness.

Stovall shook his head like a punch-drunk boxer. "You mean . . . ?"

"*Da.* The time has come to set course for the Anderson Four warp point." Antonov quickly raised a forestalling hand. "Let us be in no doubt as to the gravity of our position. Look here." He turned to the system holo display with the tiny icon of the local blue giant star at its center.

In terms of the arbitrary "north" the computer had assigned as a frame of reference, Second Fleet lay about a hundred and forty light-minutes to the south-southeast. The warp point that represented their road home was due east of the star at a distance of slightly over a hundred and ninety light-minutes, placing it somewhat less than three light-hours to their northeast.

"From the vectors of the gunboat strikes we've sustained, Commodore Kozlov and I have been able to infer the approximate configuration of the enemy forces that have been sending them. We believe there are three elements. One has to be about here." He pointed a hand remote and a fuzzy scarlet icon winked to life due south of the star, describing with Second Fleet and the warp point a straight line. "We're less certain about the other two, but they must be in these general areas." A pair of the indeterminate red indicators, oscillating to denote even greater uncertainty, appeared in regions bracketing Second Fleet's present position and the first part of its course to the warp point. "We'll be able to lead the first one a stern chase. The problem will be the other two; they'll try to close in and engage us as we pass."

"Our speed advantage should enable us to slip out of any envelopment, Sir," de Bertholet stated confidently. "Despite the wear and tear our engines have sustained."

"I hope you're right, Commander. However, it can't hurt to throw off the enemy's calculations concerning our capabilities in that area. For this reason, I want to proceed at slightly less than our best speed. Fast enough to prevent the force to our southwest from overhauling, but slow enough to make the Bugs think our engines are in even worse shape than they are."

Midori Kozlov managed a smile. "The technique is called 'disinformation,' Admiral."

Antonov smiled back. "I know, Commodore. My ancestors—and some of yours—were once noted for it."

Attack Force One watched the enemy turn for the warp point at last. He had managed to work his way between

Attack Force Three and Attack Force One, too far distant for either to engage. Attack Force Two was astern of him, and too slow to catch up, and his strategy was now obvious. Badly as he had been hurt, he still hoped to outrun the Fleet and escape through the warp point, and his timing was good—or would have been, if not for Attack Force Four.

But Attack Force Four was almost here. Attack Force One had kept it fully advised with periodic courier drones, and now it sent off another flight. The Fleet's fresh strength would arrive knowing precisely where to look for the enemy . . . and sweep in from the warp point, meeting him head-on. And so Attack Force One let its doomed foes run. It and Attack Force Three closed in from either flank, angling inward while Attack Force Two sealed the rear of the net, and the long, weary pursuit was almost over.

The last three and a half days had been the worst of Raymond Prescott's life, worse even than the desperate days in Telmasa. For eighty-six hours, his ships, a full third of Ivan Antonov's total combat strength, had sat silent and still, watching Bug courier drones come and go but doing *nothing* while their consorts fought for their lives. The battle was far too distant for his sensors to pick up the starships, gunboats, and fighters fighting it, but nuclear and antimatter explosions were glaringly evident, even at extended ranges, and there'd been too many of them.

But at least they mean there's still somebody *left . . . and they're headed this way at last.*

He nodded at the last thought. The Admiral was beginning his run. He was still thirty hours out, but he was coming in, and Prescott felt his inner tension winding still tighter.

And he knew something Antonov didn't. Chin's drones had reported not only the massive strength of the gunboat strikes which had ravaged the Fleet Train but their *timing.*

The Bugs didn't use light-speed communication relays between warp points. Presumably, that—like the cloaked pickets they seemed to leave everywhere—was a security measure, intended to deny any enemy a "bread crumb" trail to their inhabited systems. The fact that they hadn't attempted to destroy the comsat chain Jackson Teller had left in Erebor might also suggest that the notion simply hadn't occurred to them, which might be the best news of this entire disastrous affair. If they didn't realize Second Fleet had established a comsat chain in its rear, they were almost certain to have significantly overestimated the time Centauri would require to respond. If that were so, any relief fleet was likely to arrive long before they expected it. But the important point just now was that the Bugs relied *solely* on courier drones as their only means of coordinating at interstellar distances, and *Chin's* drones had told Prescott how long the Bugs had taken to come within sensor range of the Fleet Train. And *that* data gave him a good idea, given the top speed of courier drones and gunboats, just how far the Bugs' warp point into Anderson Three had been from Chin—and thus from the warp point to Anderson *Four*. Which meant that, unlike Ivan Antonov, he *knew* the Bugs would be arriving within the next fourteen hours . . . and that Ivan Antonov had timed the climactic maneuver of his career perfectly.

Now it was up to TF 21 to be certain it worked.

Ivan Antonov stared fixedly at the plot. It wasn't that he hoped to see anything there that he didn't already know. It was just that it was expected of him: Ivan the Terrible, displaying total, inhuman concentration and impassivity.

So instead of looking for hidden meanings in the display the computer constantly updated—a silicon-based *idiot savant* compulsively pawing its abacus—he let himself covertly contemplate the young people with whom he shared Flag Bridge, and the rest of *Colorado*, and the rest of the fleet.

So young. . . . Those youthful faces truly were from another time, another world, yet if any of them were to live, their survival depended upon him. They trusted him to get it right, and for just an instant, as their trust crushed down upon him like an extra layer of fatigue, he felt the weight of every endless year of his unnaturally extended life and knew he was too old.

He shook free of the thought. Surely all the experience one accumulated in a century and a half must count for something! Anyway, if the antigerone treatments really were a colossal counter-evolutionary mistake, humanity would simply be replaced by something that wouldn't make such errors, for it wouldn't deserve to survive. . . .

"Now don't go Russian-nihilistic on me, EYE-van." Antonov's lips curved in a smile no one else noticed as he heard the voice echoing across the gulf of seven decades. *No, Howard, I won't*, he thought. *I can't afford to just now. I brought these people into this, and it's my duty to get as many of them as possible out of it.*

And, it ought to be possible to get a fair number out . . . if only the timing was right.

Dear God, bozhe-moi, *please let my timing have been right.*

Attack Force Four had reached its final warp point. A fresh shower of courier drones went ahead, announcing its arrival, and its warships prepared for transit. Its losses against the enemy's support echelon left it thirty percent understrength in gunboats, but it still had over four hundred. The ships without gunboat groups would be left behind—someone had to watch the warp point—and the others would join the attack on the enemy's fleet.

"Ships transiting the warp point!"

The announcement from Plotting wasn't loud, yet it cracked like a whip in Flag Bridge's silent tension. Prescott handed his coffee cup to a steward and spun his command chair to face his plot, and his mouth tightened as the deadly stream of Bug warships flowed into existence.

The escorts came first: thirty-six light cruisers, *Cataphracts* and *Carbines* in a tighter transit than any Terran admiral would countenance. They made no effort to

scout—after all, a dozen battlecruisers had been watching
the warp point for over twenty days—but flowed out into
a spherical screen, and then the first of those stupendous
warships followed them. One, two, five—*eighteen* made
transit, and behind them came twenty-four superdreadnoughts, and after them the battlecruisers. One hundred
and three starships burst through the flaw in space and
formed up, and Raymond Prescott realized he was actually
holding his breath as he waited.

Then they began to move, and a fierce exultation flared
within him. Six of the new leviathans and half the
superdreadnoughts remained behind, but the others—
all the others, even the battlecruisers which had picketed
the warp point for so long—headed in-system, and they
were already launching their gunboats.

"All right, Anna, Jacques," he said flatly. "Pass the standby
signal. Those big bastards are the priority targets, then
the SDs."

"Twelve of the new . . . mobile fortresses. At least a
dozen superdreadnoughts. The battlecruiser and light
cruiser totals should be available soon." Midori Kozlov's
voice was an inflectionless drone as she studied the sensor
readouts like a soothsayer peering into the depths of a
crystal ball and read off the tally of the Bug forces sweeping
forward to intercept them.

"How many have been left to cover warp point?"
Antonov's tightly controlled voice might have fooled anyone
who didn't know him well enough to notice the loss of
definite articles.

"Unknown, Sir. We're still too far out."

"No matter. It is time." The admiral swung his bearlike
bulk to face de Bertholet. "Commander, deploy the
fighters."

All the fighters Second Fleet still possessed had been
at alert for hours, their pilots holding exhaustion at bay
with drugs and adrenaline. Now they launched as one
and took up flanking positions against gunboat attacks.

At the maximum speed it could manage and still keep

formation, Second Fleet arrowed directly towards the massed ranks of death coming to meet it.

"All right, people," Prescott murmured, eyes locked to his plot. TF 21 had crept in even closer, moving at glacially slow speed. They were barely half a light-minute from the warp point, directly behind the ships facing the rest of Second Fleet, and any Orion would have envied his fang-baring smile. "This is what we came for. Let's make it count. Are you ready, Jacques?"

"Ready, Sir." The ops officer half-crouched over his console, like a runner in the blocks, and his hands rested lightly, ever so lightly, upon it.

"Execute!" Raymond Prescott snapped.

The ships on the warp point watched the enemy running headlong into the waiting tentacles of the rest of Attack Force Four. Given his speed, some of his units might actually win through the waiting inferno, but the detachment waited to sweep up the broken pieces as they came to it. The attack force's gunboats were two-thirds of the way to the enemy, and—

Four hundred and three SBMs exploded from empty space as TF 21 flushed its external racks. Another hundred belched from the *Dunkerques'* internal launchers, and their targets had had no inkling those ships were there. Thirty seconds passed before light speed sensors even detected TF 21's launch, and there was no time to react, no time to take evasive action or bring active defenses on-line. Raymond Prescott's birds were in terminal acquisition, screaming in on their targets at .8 c, and then the universe blew apart.

All five hundred of those missiles were directed at just six targets, for TF 21 had no idea how much damage those unfamiliar monsters could absorb. But however mighty their shields, however thick their armor, they were no match for that devastating strike. The vortex blazing on the warp point momentarily rivaled the blue giant furnace at the system's heart, and when it cleared, the ships which had been at its core no longer existed.

The Bugs reeled under the totally unexpected blow, and even as they fought to adjust to it, fresh salvos roared in from the *Dunkerques* and ten *Borzoi–C*-class fleet carriers launched three hundred and sixty hoarded fighters. Those strikegroups had been made fully up to strength before they were attached to TF 21, even at the expense of the exhausted, over-strained squadrons which had fought to protect Second Fleet's main body for ten heartbreaking days. Their pilots had sat in their ready rooms, ready for instant launch if TF 21 had been detected yet knowing—for they were veterans all—what their fellow pilots had endured while they sat inviolate in cloak. Now it was their turn, and the key to Second Fleet's survival lay in their hands.

They streaked in, drives howling, vision graying, and behind them came the rest of TF 21. The *Borneo*-class superdreadnoughts had no capital launchers, but they had heterodyne lasers and standard missile launchers, and they were fast. Raymond Prescott brought them in at 30,000 KPS while the *Dunkerques* lay back, pouring in SBMs and capital missiles, and the totally surprised Bug starships fought around in desperate turns to meet them.

It took the fighters three minutes to reach them—three minutes of frantic maneuvers while the *Dunkerques* hammered them with another six hundred missiles. Point defense stopped many of the follow-up birds, but the battlecruisers got two more massive salvoes in virtually unopposed first, and three Bug superdreadnoughts were destroyed and two more damaged before the fighters even arrived.

AFHAWKs roared to meet the strike, but the Bugs had sent their escorts forward with the rest of their attack force. TF 21 lost thirty-seven fighters; the other three hundred and twenty-three, armed with full loads of FRAMs, carried through. There were ten superdreadnoughts and twelve battlecruisers on the warp point when they began their runs; when they finished them, there were three air-streaming, shattered, half-molten wrecks, staggering half-blind towards TF 21 as if in some instinct to hurl themselves bodily upon their enemies.

But they never had the chance, for TF 21's enraged fighter jocks came screaming back. They had no external ordnance, only their internal lasers, but that was sufficient.

The warp point lay half a light-hour behind Attack Force Four; by the time it realized its detached units were under attack, every one of them had been dead for over twenty minutes.

The attack force had no idea how many enemy ships were astern of it. Its sensors showed a horde of attack craft sweeping back from the warp point, disappearing as they rejoined their mother ships to rearm, but no enemy starship had emerged from cloak. There couldn't be many vessels back there—surely the other attack forces would have known if any significant portion of the enemy fleet had eluded them!—and yet there must be a powerful force. The blazing speed of the detachment's destruction, even of the mighty new units, was proof of that, and Attack Force Four dared not be caught between an enemy of unknown strength and the survivors streaming towards it. It must know what it faced, and there was only one way to learn that.

The gunboats which had almost reached Second Fleet arced suddenly away, for they had the speed—and numbers—to reach the warp point once more and spread out, find the enemy, determine the nature of the threat.

Com lasers and courier drones spilled from the attack force to alert the other forces, but it would take yet another half hour for that information to reach the closest addressee. By the time it did, the diverted gunboat strike would be a sixth of the way back to the warp point.

The starships hesitated a moment longer, and then Attack Force Four turned to follow its gunboats. It was still closer to the warp point than the known enemy forces, but given its slower speed, the prey it had come to kill might actually be able to beat it there. Yet it had no choice. The enemy

*had smashed the barricade which was supposed to hold
him pent; if it was not replaced, then* all *of his ships might
yet escape.*

Everyone on *Colorado's* flag bridge had seen photos of
distant nebulas where hot young stars blazed through the
glowing clouds of cosmic dust from which they'd had their
birth. Now they gazed at the main screen where the spectacle at the warp point was displayed: explosions so intense
they must surely gnaw at the fabric of space itself but veiled
by a surrounding haze of superheated gas, a nebula of
man's creation. And there was utter, awed silence in the
presence of a cataclysm that seemed beyond the powers of
any save the Maker of Stars to wreak.

But then, after a time lag that the distance differential
reduced to almost nothing, the four hundred incoming
gunboats swerved away in hundred-and-eighty-degree
turns and began to recede into the blackness. And all at
once the silence shattered into a million fragments as all
the pent-up tension released itself. Such were the cheers
and the weeping that they hardly waxed any further when,
minutes later, the enemy starships also turned back.

"Prescott *did* it, Sir!" Stovall turned exultantly to
Antonov . . . and what he saw stopped him. Boulder-
impervious to the storm of emotion around him, the
admiral was staring at the tank in which the red icons of
the enemy, having completed their turning maneuver, were
racing for the warp point ahead of Second Fleet's green
ones. He consulted his wrist calculator with scowling
concentration, then faced Stovall.

"It appears, Commodore," he said quietly, "that our
speed advantage won't quite suffice to overtake and pass
the blocking force before it gets back to the warp point—
at least not by any significant margin. Note also—" he
indicated another portion of the tank, astern of the green
icons "—that the Bug forces pursuing us have launched
what must be their entire remaining gunboat complement."

"They won't catch us, Sir," Stovall stated emphatically.

"No, they won't . . . unless we slow down as a result

of damage sustained when we catch up with the blocking force just short of the warp point. This leads me to two conclusions, Commodore Stovall, neither of them pleasant."

"Sir?"

"First of all, we will need our fighters to help us fight our way past the blocking force. *All* our fighters; we don't have enough left to send any to Admiral Prescott's assistance when the blocking force's gunboats get back to the warp point."

Stovall swallowed. He hadn't thought that far ahead. But the admiral was right, of course. Prescott would have to stand alone against those four hundred gunboats for as long as it took.

"Ah . . . and the *other* conclusion, Sir?"

"That we *cannot* slow down as we pass the blocking force, for if we do the gunboat waves pursuing us will catch up. Not for *any* reason. Therefore, you will pass the following general order: any ship that falls out of formation from battle damage is to be left behind."

For an instant, it simply didn't register on Stovall. Then he felt his head shaking slowly in mute denial. "Uh, Admiral Antonov, Sir . . . excuse me, but I thought I understood you to say that we are to *abandon our cripples.*"

"That is precisely what I said, Commodore, and I am not in the habit of repeating orders."

Stovall felt a flush spread from his ears and neck, and he didn't care, because before he could even think of stopping himself he blurted out the unsayable. *"No!* By God, Sir, you can't! Every tradition—"

"Commodore Stovall!" Antonov's voice had dropped whole octaves and it seemed to reverberate through the chief of staff's entire body, not just his eardrums. No one else had been able to make out precisely what they were saying; but everyone, in the immemorial manner of subordinates, found something else to be doing with silent concentration. Antonov's voice dropped to a near-whisper. "You will transmit the order, Commodore. Otherwise I will relieve you and order Commander de Bertholet to do so."

"But . . . but, Sir, the crews of those ships! I mean, if we were fighting any normal race—Orions, or even Thebans—it would be different! But—"

"Do you think I like it, Commodore? But understand this: not all of us are going to escape. If we insist on trying to rescue everyone, we will save *no one*. Accept that fact! And let me clarify my order—by 'any ship' I mean to include this one!"

Stovall started to open his mouth again. But then he felt the heat start to recede from his face. For Antonov was right. Oh, maybe not right in a human way . . . but that way offered no hope of survival for any of them.

All at once, for the first time, Stovall truly understood the origin of the nickname "Ivan the Terrible."

"Aye, aye, Sir," he said expressionlessly, and turned towards the com station.

Four hundred gunboats swept towards the warp point. Behind them, the gunboats of Attack Forces One and Three streaked after Second Fleet, fifteen hundred strong, but they would still be over twenty minutes behind Ivan Antonov when his ships made transit.

If they made transit, for Attack Force Four still lay between him and safety, and Raymond Prescott locked his shock frame and sealed his helmet as the gunboats came in. The freshly arrived Bug force had also detached its light cruisers—his sensors had the uncloaked vessels clearly, watching them race towards him behind the gunboats—and CIC reported sensor ghosts which might well be cloaked vessels coming with them. *Battlecruisers,* he thought. *Those have to be battlecruisers. Well, we knew they've used military drives for some of their ships all along; it's about time they tried to produce a "fast wing" to match our Dunkerques.*

"Launch the fighters," he said quietly.

The gunboats roared onward. Their less powerful sensors were beginning to pick up the ghostly traces of cloaked vessels . . . and then there was something besides ghosts on their displays. Three hundred and fifteen attack craft exploded into space, and they knew they were doomed. The enemy's known attack craft strength had been so reduced they had intended to rely on internal weapons to beat off interceptions, and none mounted AFHAWKs.

But there was nowhere else for them to go, and their mission remained unchanged. They must locate and identify the enemy's starships, and they streamed in to the attack.

"Attack sequence X-Ray," Captain Kinkaid announced. Acknowledgments came back, and she altered course slightly, leading her massed strikegroups to meet that phalanx of gunboats. She wasn't driving in as fast as she could have; there was no need, with the enemy coming to her, and so no point in putting the extra wear on her drives. She smiled at the thought—the smile of a hunting wolf—and looked at her tac officer.

"Targeting laid in, Sir," Lieutenant Brancuso announced crisply. "We've got good solutions. Launch range in . . . thirty-one seconds."

Raymond Prescott's fighters salvoed over nine hundred FM3s. Fireballs pocked the Bugs' formation—only a few, at first, but growing in the space of a breath to a forest fire that reached out from the front of that massed wave of gunboats, swept back along its flanks, and ate into its heart. Two hundred and seven died, and the survivors' datanets were shattered. They were no longer squadrons; they were broken bits and pieces, individual craft still charging forward, and Terran and Ophiuchi pilots closed with lasers. They had to enter the Bugs' point defense envelope to engage them, but gunboats were much bigger targets, and, unlike the Bugs, the Allied datanets were intact. Entire squadrons stooped upon their prey, lasers blazing in coordinated attacks on single targets, and Captain Kinkaid, covered by her own carrier's strikegroup and hovering just beyond the melee to coordinate the attack, realized *none* of the bastards mounted AFHAWKs!

"*Kill 'em!*" she snarled, and led SG 211 to join the slaughter.

The cruisers and battlecruisers racing ahead of the rest of Attack Force Four watched their gunboats die, but some of them had gotten far enough in, lasted long enough to pierce the enemy's ECM and get contact reports off. Attack Force Four's detached screen knew what it faced, and the odds were less uneven than it had feared. The enemy had superdreadnoughts and almost as many battlecruisers, but the screen had thirty-six light-cruisers to support the battlecruisers, and the attack craft would have too little time to rearm for an anti-shipping strike. The screen could not kill all those enemy vessels, but it could hurt them badly . . . and that was all it truly had to do, with the rest of Attack Force Four coming up from astern.

"Here they come, Sir," Bichet said through gritted teeth as the fighters' relayed sensor data showed TF 21 the cloaked Bug battlecruisers. Apparently the gunboats had done the same for the enemy, for those battlecruisers began to belch SBMs. Their targeting wasn't perfect, but it was good enough, and point defense began tracking as they streaked in.

"I think we'll codename these 'Antelope,' Jacques. Appropriate, given their speed, don't you think?" Prescott's tone was almost whimsical, however intent his eyes, and Bichet nodded.

"From their salvo densities, they look pretty much like *Dunkerques*, Sir," Lieutenant Commander Ruiz put in. The logistics officer spoke with unnatural calm, refusing to let her admiral out-panache her, but her BuShips background showed in her professional assessment.

"Yes, they do," Prescott agreed as *Crete* began spitting countermissiles. His *Dunkerques* fired back at the Bugs. They could match the enemy's battlecruisers almost one-for-one, and his fighters had nearly completed reforming after the gunboats' massacre, but the Bugs had a solid phalanx of *Cataphract*- and *Carbine*-class CLs. He couldn't send his fighters in against that kind of firepower with only their lasers . . . but he couldn't let the Bugs push him off the warp point, either. He *had* to hold it until the admiral arrived.

"Instruct the fighters to break off, Jacques," he said. "Recover and rearm them ASAP."

"Aye, aye, Sir."

"In the meantime, I believe *we* have an appointment with the Bugs," Prescott added calmly, and TFNS *Crete* led TF 21's superdreadnoughts straight at the enemy.

The enemy came to meet the screen, and the battle-cruisers realized they had erred by concentrating on the enemy's superdreadnoughts. Very few missiles had pene-trated those ships' massed point defense, and the enemy's battlecruisers had used their own immunity to batter the screen painfully. But the superdreadnoughts appeared to mount no capital launchers. They were closing into standard missile range, which would allow even the screen's missile-armed light cruisers to engage them. In the meantime, the battlecruisers shifted fire to the enemy's battlecruisers and prepared to switch from capital missiles to CAMs as the range fell.

At what seemed a crawl in the holo tanks, Second Fleet gradually overhauled the Bug blocking force in their race to the warp point.

Neither Antonov nor any of his officers could avoid a teeth-gritting awareness of the irony involved. If they'd had all the time in the world to kill Bugs, they would have been in an ideal position to close in on those enemy starships from their "blind zones" and eat them alive. But, in the here-and-now, fifteen hundred gunboats would have arrived during the meal. So they had to press on, past those Bug ships.

Nor could they afford the time-wasting course change to give them a wide berth as they passed. No, they had to pass within close range of undamaged, undepleted enemies that included those new behemoths.

They'd just have to take it until they could pull ahead.

TF 21 closed to standard missile range, hammering the Bugs with antimatter warheads, and the superdreadnoughts' powerful hetlasers ignored the battlecruisers. Instead, they swiveled with deadly precision and blew every missile-armed CL apart with a single massed broadside. Then, and only then, did they turn to the battlecruisers— just as the Bugs began firing CAMs.

In ninety-one seconds, twenty-three Bug battlecruisers and seventeen more light cruisers ceased to exist . . . but they took the superdreadnoughts *Erie* and *Koko Nor* and the battlecruisers *California* and *Howe* with them. Only six of Raymond Prescott's SDs escaped totally unscathed, and three more of his battlecruisers were little more than air-streaming wrecks. But he held the warp point, and he looked back at the master plot as the Bug battle-line rumbled down upon him.

One edge of the Bug formation was an incandescent furnace of warheads and energy fire as Antonov's battered ships overtook it. The Bug superdreadnoughts and new, monster ships were forty percent slower than the Allied battle-line, yet it took an agonizingly long time for the Allied ships to begin to draw ahead of them, and Prescott bit his lip as icons flickered and danced with CIC's estimates of damage. The brutal pounding the rest of Second Fleet had endured while TF 21 held station on the warp point was all too evident in the two sides' weight of fire. Ivan Antonov had more ships than his opponent, but his carriers were little more than mobile targets, and many of his capital ships had been beaten into near impotence. Those which could still fight held station on *Colorado*, pounding back at the Bugs with desperate fury, and the hideous firepower of those new, monster ships slaughtered them methodically.

One of the new ships blew up, but the smaller Terran superdreadnoughts were paying at least a two-to-one price to kill them, and the ships Antonov's combat-capable units fought to protect were losing as well. The CVAs *Dragon, Gorgon, Horatious* and *Zirk-Sahaan* blew up or staggered out of formation, and the Bugs seemed to realize it wasn't necessary to *destroy* their enemies outright. As soon as any ship was lamed, they shifted to another target, battering at them, trying to cripple their drives and slow them until their own leviathans could resecure control of the warp point or the other attack forces' pursuing gunboats could overhaul.

The toll of dying ships rose hideously, and Prescott clenched his fists, chained to the warp point by his orders. The faster units of the main Bug formation were close enough to range on his own ships now, and his rearmed fighters launched while his starships bobbed and wove in evasive action and salvoed their own missiles. The battleship *Prince George* blew up in the heart of Antonov's formation, and her sister *Spartiate* lost a drive room and fell back—then turned to join the equally lamed super-dreadnoughts *Sumatra, Kailas,* and *Mount Hood* and engage the enemy more closely. They could no longer escape; all they could do was make their deaths count by covering sisters who could still run, and Prescott's eyes burned as they drove into the enemy.

The battlecruiser *Al-Sabanthu* tore apart, and Vice Admiral Taathaanahk died with his flagship. The CVLs *Arbiter* and *Shangri-La*, a part of Prescott's own task force for so many long months, exploded, and *still* the carnage went on and on and on.

But the Bugs were losing ships, too, he told himself fiercely. Five superdreadnoughts and now three of their new monster ships were gone, and others were damaged. His own fighters arrived, tearing into the enemy, ripple-firing FRAMs, vanishing in hateful spalls of fire as AFHAWKs or energy weapons or point defense snatched them out of space, yet it was working. *It was working!* Hideous as Second Fleet's losses were, some of its units were breaking into the clear, running ahead of the storm, already vanishing through the warp point while Antonov personally coordinated the rearguard and TF 21 engaged the handful of faster Bug ships foolhardy enough to come within its reach. *Crete*'s flag bridge crackled and seethed with combat chatter and orders as Prescott and his staff fought to impose some sort of order on the chaos, and then—

"Sir!"

Prescott's head snapped up at the anguish in Jacques Bichet's voice. He looked at his ops officer, and Bichet's face was white.

"Sir, *Colorado*'s lost three drive rooms!"

Raymond Prescott felt the blood drain from his face. He spun back to his plot and saw the jagged, flashing band that indicated critical damage about the fleet flagship's icon. Somehow, even now, it seemed impossible. It *had* to be a mistake. Ivan Antonov was a legend . . . *but even legends die*, a small, numb corner of Prescott's brain whispered.

"Recall the fighters." He didn't recognize his own voice. "Get them aboard for transit."

"But, Sir, the—"

"*Get them aboard!*" Prescott barked, without even turning his head. And then, "Com, get me the Flag."

Even now the range was sufficient to impose communications lags, and he waited—his heart an ice-wrapped knot—until an image stabilized on his display. He looked past Antonov's helmeted head into the anteroom of Hell. *Colorado*'s flag bridge was a depressurized shambles, littered with bodies—bodies, Prescott was numbly certain, of men and women he'd come to know well—and one side of Antonov's vacsuit was spattered with blood.

"You did well, Admiral," Antonov said quietly. "Thank you."

Prescott wanted to scream, to curse the other for *thanking* him, but he didn't. Instead, he forced his voice to work around the lump which seemed to strangle him.

"Sir, we can hold a little longer," he said. "Keep coming. We can get you out!"

Seconds ticked past while the message sped towards

Colorado, and he saw two more of the cripples covering Second Fleet's retreat wiped from his display before Antonov replied.

"Negative, Admiral Prescott," he said almost calmly. "You are now Second Fleet's commander, and your responsibility is to your people. Recover your fighters and make transit." His eyes stared into Prescott's for a moment, and then he said, very softly, "You can do no more here, Raymond. All you can do is get the rest of our people home. I count on you for that."

The screen went blank as Antonov cut the circuit, and Raymond Prescott bowed his head.

"We can't recover all the fighters before the Bugs get here, Sir," Jacques Bichet said. "Over sixty are too far out to reach us in time."

"We'll have to leave them," Prescott said drearily.

"But—"

"I said we'll have to leave them." Prescott interrupted Bichet's sharp protest, and his voice was so flat with pain the ops officer closed his mouth with a snap.

Prescott felt Bichet's presence, but he couldn't take his eyes from the plot. Not even when his carriers flashed through the warp point, or when his battlecruisers followed. Not even when his own flagship headed into the warp point. He stared into it, watching the last, abandoned units of Second Fleet's rearguard and their tattered umbrella of dying fighters as the pursuing Bugs closed for the kill.

The last thing Raymond Prescott saw before *Crete* vanished into the warp point herself was TFNS *Colorado*, her weapons destroyed, her broken hull trailing atmosphere and water vapor and debris but no life pods—never a life pod—as she redlined her surviving engines . . . and disappeared in an eye-tearing boil of light as she rammed one of those new monster ships head-on.

CHAPTER FORTY-ONE

The Road Home

The enemy had escaped.

It was not possible, yet he had. The Fleet had paid heavily to bait the trap, to close it behind him, to draw him in and expose his core systems to counterattack, and still almost half his warships had escaped.

Attack Force Four turned vengefully on the handful of cripples which remained in the system. The enemy's lamed vessels were no more than wrecks, yet they fought to the last, and when their final weapons were gone, they closed in agonizingly slow ramming attempts. Few succeeded, but each of those who did took yet another starship with it, and so the Fleet stood off and smashed the final units with missile and energy fire.

But when the last died, the Fleet's quandary remained. The plan had called for the enemy to perish here, and he had not. A review of the tactical data indicated that most of his escapees were damaged—many critically—and his losses in attack craft had been even heavier, proportionately, than in starships. Yet those starships remained faster than the Fleet's battle-line, else they had not escaped at all. The handful of new, fast battlecruisers might be able to overtake, as could the light cruisers of the other attack forces, once they reached the warp point, but by that time the enemy's capital ships would have had many hours to make emergency repairs. Superdreadnoughts, even damaged, would be more than a match for such light units, and if the enemy had detached yet another sacrificial rearguard to cover the warp point, the Fleet's starships would pay a hideous price to pursue him.

Yet there might still be an answer. The gunboats of Attack Force One were barely twenty-five minutes from the warp point, with those of Attack Force Two only an hour behind. If Attack Force Four's survivors took those gunboats under command, they could be thrown through the warp point in a single wave fourteen hundred strong. The enemy's decimated attack craft could not stop such a mighty force, and gunboats had the speed to run down any starship.

The decision was made, and Attack Force Four closed on the warp point, licking its wounds and reorganizing its shattered datagroups while it awaited the gunboats.

Crete emerged from the warp point. Too much grief and heartache filled her flag bridge to permit of any sense of elation, but Raymond Prescott dragged himself up from the depths of his own despair. In ten days—no, in twelve *hours*—he'd gone from Second Fleet's most junior task force CO to its commander in chief. That terrible responsibility was his, now, and he felt it grinding down upon him.

"How many fighters made it out, Jacques?"

His voice was quiet, but Bichet flinched. Prescott had no idea how much grief had leaked through his self-control, and the ops officer cleared his throat.

"I'm not certain, Sir. Captain Kinkaid made it—looks like she's *farshathkhanaak* for the fleet now—but I'm not even sure how many of the *carriers* got out. I'm trying to get reports now, but the rest of the fleet's command structure is shot to hell, Sir."

"How many aboard *our* carriers?" Prescott pressed.

"I make it two hundred, Sir," Bichet said softly. "Roughly."

Prescott winced, then drew a deep breath.

"Relaunch half of them immediately. I want them on the warp point as an antigunboat CSP. Rearm the other half with FM3s, if we still have enough. Each strikegroup will have fifteen minutes to reorganize its own squadrons, then I want them in space again. As soon as *they* launch, recall the first half to rearm and reorganize."

Bichet nodded, and Prescott turned to his chief of staff.

"Anna, your job is to find out what's left of the other task forces. I want a head count, and I want to know exactly what munitions—and weapons—everyone has. Sandy," he switched to Ruiz, "I want a complete inventory of what *we* have left, too. Work with Anna to give me a complete picture of the entire fleet ASAP."

The logistics officer nodded, and Prescott turned back to Mandagalla.

"Get me that info fast, Anna," he said with quiet urgency. "The Bugs'll be after us any minute, and I need to know what I have left to fight with."

"Yes, Sir." Mandagalla's ebon face was grim. "What about battlegroup reorganization?"

"That'll have to wait until we know what we've got. Jacques," the ops officer looked up from his console at his name, "for right now, assume whatever TF 21 has left is all we've got. You're authorized to reorganize battlegroups as you see fit. We'll fine tune your OBs later . . . if we get the chance."

"Aye, aye, Sir," Bichet replied, and Prescott turned back to his plot as his staff dived into the frantic effort of discovering how much of Second Fleet had survived.

He already knew the numbers were going to be bad.

The last gunboat had finally arrived. Attack Force Four spent several more minutes rechecking its new battlegroups. Over half its ships had been destroyed, and another ten percent were too damaged to be committed, but it remained a powerful force—and far closer to intact than its enemies could possibly be. It was time.

❖   ❖   ❖

"Gunboats making transit!" *Crete*'s tactical officer snapped.

Prescott's raised hand interrupted Captain Mandagalla's report as he wheeled back to the plot. Icons already spangled it, but the Bugs had given him eighty-one priceless minutes. Every surviving fighter—three hundred and seventy-one of them, barely thirty percent of Second Fleet's original fighter strength—had been rearmed and stationed directly atop the warp point. TF 21's carriers's combined magazines had retained only two hundred and six FM3s. They were mounted aboard a hundred and three fighters; the others had been fitted with three additional laser packs and one life support pod each. Most of those flight crews were exhausted, and every squadron was a scratch-built, jury-rigged improvisation. They were far, far below their usual standards of effectiveness . . . but they were also waiting in ambush.

The gunboats blinked into existence, and the fighters tore into them like demons. Missiles brushed past transit-addled point defense, and the rest of the fighters screamed in with their massive external laser armaments. They killed almost four hundred gunboats in their first pass, and another seventy before the Bugs' systems restabilized . . . but that left almost a thousand.

The fighter jocks wanted to loop back yet again, but Prescott's orders to Captain Kinkaid had been both clear and nondiscretionary. She broke off, using her superior speed to draw clear, and streaked after the rest of Second Fleet.

Prescott watched them come, and his heart was cold. They'd done better than he'd dared hope and lost only twenty-three of their own to do it, but the gunboat force was far stronger than expected. He'd had time for a brief conference with Antonov's exhausted battlegroup COs, and after the enormous hard kills Second Fleet had scored, it had seemed impossible for even Bugs to have that much left.

But they did, and it was coming straight for him.

"All right, Jacques. Go to Ivan Two," he said flatly.

"Aye, aye, Sir." Bichet's orders went out, and TF 21, supported by all the rest of Second Fleet's combat-capable superdreadnoughts and battleships—all twelve of them—dropped further astern of the other survivors. None of those ships' crews expected to survive the next hour . . . but that wasn't their job. All they were supposed to do—all they could *hope* to do, with their depleted magazines and battle damage—was throw up a roadblock. When the fighters reached them, half would peel off to support them; the rest would continue to the fleeing carriers to provide the survivors with whatever frail protection they could after the roadblock died. But Raymond Prescott knew one thing with absolute certainty: if he could draw the Bugs down on his command, few of them would survive his last fight to go after his cripples.

"Enemy ETA forty-seven minutes," Bichet announced quietly, and Prescott nodded.

"Anna, contact Admiral Mosby. I know her. Make absolutely certain that she understands she is not, under any circumstances, to send the other fighters back into this."

The gunboats recognized what the enemy intended, but they were willing to accept his sacrificial gambit, even at the price of their own destruction, for those had to be his last combat-capable units. With them gone, there would be nothing to prevent the other attack forces' new, fast battlecruisers from overhauling and smashing his wounded ships on their long road home.

"ETA twenty minutes," Bichet announced. Prescott nodded acknowledgment without looking away from the plot. *At least it won't take long against this many of them,* he thought. *I wonder—*

"Sir! Admiral Prescott!" The sudden shout jerked his attention to his com officer, and his eyebrows flew up as he saw the wild exultation transfiguring Commander Hale's face. "Sky Marshal Avram!" she blurted. "*Sky Marshal Avram is on the priority channel!*"

❖   ❖   ❖

Hannah Avram's heart twisted as her cloaked starships streaked past the first staggering, broken wrecks. She could feel the agonized exhaustion with which those ships clawed towards home. Second Fleet hadn't been *defeated*; it had been shattered, yet its survivors fought on, and she remembered Second Loreli. This was the second time she'd seen the wreckage of a Terran Fleet, and heartbreak warred with pride as she watched that wreckage which had refused to die.

"I have Admiral Prescott, Sir," her com officer said.

"*Prescott?*"

"Yes, Sir." The com officer sounded stunned, as if he couldn't believe his own words. "Admiral Antonov is dead, Sir."

It hit Hannah like a fist, and even through her shock, she knew it would hit every other Terran officer—and all of their allies—with equal ferocity. But for now she was grateful for her shock. It kept the news from being real while she grappled with what she had to do, and she turned to her com screen as Raymond Prescott's exhausted, harrowed face appeared upon it.

"I'm coming in cloaked from your zero-zero-six, zero-zero-niner," she said flatly. "I have seventeen superdreadnoughts, ten battleships, eleven battlecruisers, and twelve heavy cruisers, but no carriers. Keep coming; I estimate contact in twenty-three minutes. Stay alive, Raymond. Keep them bunched and concentrating on you until I can hit them by surprise, but *stay alive!*"

Raymond Prescott turned away from his com screen. "Jacques, new orders for Kinkaid! *All* of her fighters stay with us."

"Yes, Sir!"

Icons shifted wildly as the fighters which had already passed *Crete* broke back towards her. The gunboats were only sixteen minutes out; he had to survive for five minutes, and without those other fighters, he wouldn't.

Minutes limped into eternity. His own sensors hadn't picked up the Sky Marshal yet, but he knew she was there

. . . and the Bugs didn't. He watched the gunboats sweeping closer. Ten minutes out. Eight. Six. Kinkaid's fighters smashed into them head-on, and the plot was ugly with the fireballs of dying gunboats and allied pilots. His *Dunkerques* began punching SBMs and capital missiles into the Bugs, and the furnace roared hotter. Four minutes. Two. *Crete's* missile batteries began to fire, and then the madness was upon him.

TF 21 and its supporting, scratch-built battlegroups writhed under a tsunami of gunboats. Ships twisted and danced in wild evasion maneuvers, and the visual displays were a kaleidoscope of explosions. The battleship *Timoléon* was the first to die, then the superdreadnoughts *Ellesmere* and *Namcha Barwa*. *Crete's* sisters *Tititcaca* and *Lake Michigan* followed, then the battlecruiser *Arizona* and her squadron mate *Moltke*. But even as they were pounded to pieces, they fired back in an orgy of mutual destruction and hate. It went on and on, seconds stretching into hours and minutes into eternities, and *Crete* staggered again and again. Her shields were down, her armor shattered, her breached hull belching air, but somehow she lived and killed and killed and killed . . .

And then, suddenly, Hannah Avram was there. Her undamaged, unshaken ships slammed into the Bugs like the hammer of God, and they flushed their XO racks as they came. The gunboats had been so intent on their prey they never even saw her coming, and the fresh hurricane of fire took them totally by surprise.

It was the Bug's turn to die, caught between two fires. But they, too, struck back. The superdreadnoughts *Luzon* and *Palawan*, the SDEs *Mercedari*, *Tasmania*, and *Paricutan*, and the battleships *San Genero* and *Terrible* had raced all the way from Centauri to Anderson Four in just fourteen days only to die, but they accomplished their mission. The Bug gunboats burned like a prairie fire, and in their ashes lay the survival of what remained of Second Fleet.

Yet there was one last, agonizing price for the Terran Federation Navy to pay. Even as Hannah Avram's ops officer announced success and she turned to her com link to *Crete*, one last flurry of gunboats evaded every weapon targeted upon them in their death runs. They salvoed their external ordnance and followed it in, tearing deep into TFNS *Xingú*'s armored hull, and Raymond Prescott's com screen went blank with terrible, sudden finality.

The gunboats' destruction was final. The Fleet had no idea how many enemy starships had come to their fellows' rescue, nor of how they could have avoided the blocking gunboat force which should have stopped them, but there was no point in sending battlecruisers and CLs against such heavy units without battle-line support. Courier drones were sent ahead, alerting the forces still between the enemy and home, but although the waiting gunboats might harass them, they were too weak to stop them.

The trap had failed . . . but not completely. The enemy had been decisively crippled, and all four attack forces would pursue as rapidly as possible. The Fleet would arrive on his heels, and this time it would send no mere survey force into the system from whence he had come.

affirmative command to regress and she turned to her own link to Lieutenant Commander Tesla, one last time, so they could [illegible text]

...

CHAPTER FORTY-TWO

Road With No End

"No question about it, Sir," Feridoun Hafezi reported with as much briskness as any of them could manage these days. "They've entered the system in force this time—fourteen battlecruisers."

Rear Admiral Sommers nodded and looked around the haggard faces of Survey Flotilla 19's staff—the faces of people who had, in all probability, just been condemned to death. Irritatingly, at this moment when she had far better uses for it, her mind flew back in space and time to their fourth warp transit from Anderson One, and she couldn't repress a wholly inappropriate smile.

"Well, Feridoun, remember when we'd just transited into that starless warp nexus and you hoped that maybe we could go someplace where things would be more interesting?"

The chief of staff grimaced. "Yes . . . I did, didn't I? Now I finally understand why combat veterans never seem to mind being bored!"

It had been just after that, with their warp point survey of that stretch of space still in progress, when they'd become aware of the Bug forces closing in behind them. Where they could have come from along this barren warp chain, and what their presence implied about the fate of Second Fleet, were questions Sommers hadn't had the luxury of contemplating. Instead, she'd had to make an impossible decision. Trying to fight her way home through enemy forces of unknown size hadn't even been an option; SF 19 was no battle fleet. Forging on into the unknown on the one-in-a-million chance of finding a warp chain that doubled back to Allied space had seemed an equally preposterous alternative. But it had been the only alternative she'd had, and she had ordered the *Huns* to redouble their efforts to find a second warp point.

They'd succeeded . . . just as one of the probing Bug gunboats stumbled onto the cloaked Terran ships. It sounded the alarm before it died, and they'd been unable to prevent the packs of pursuing gunboats from observing them as they fled towards the newly discovered warp point. They'd emerged into the domain of a red giant that had long since incinerated any planets it might have possessed. Without even pausing for breath, Sommers had ordered her *Huns* to spread out in a desperate quest for warp points while the gunslingers turned at bay against the pursuers they'd known would be through the warp point close behind them.

Her fighters had sent the initial wave of gunboats reeling back through the warp point. Then the *real* pursuit burst on them in mass simultaneous transits of gunboats and cruisers, followed by waves of battlecruisers. Sommers' combatants had battered them back through the warp point again, winning priceless time for the scout cruisers' frantic search for a warp point.

TFNS *Inca*, which had found the way out of the last system, had repeated her feat while there was still time. Sommers had ordered the flotilla toward the newly discovered warp point, but fresh Bug gunboats had poured into the system just as the fighter screen she'd left behind had come to the end of its life support and begun to withdraw. A desperate dogfight had swirled across the red giant's sky, and the damaged battle cruiser *Kalinin*, her crew evacuated, had been left behind to an attention-distracting self-immolation. But the flotilla had, in the end, managed to transit undetected, leaving behind the cooling plasma that had been the gunboats which might have pinpointed the escape-hatch warp point. And Sommers had been able to breathe again, in the feeble light of the type M red main-sequence star into whose system they'd materialized.

Ten days had passed before the Bugs found their way into the new system and sent clouds of gunboats probing into it while their battlecruisers sat watchfully on the warp point. Sommers' ships, in cloaked battlegroups built around the *Huns*, had commenced a nerve-racking game of cat and mouse as the search for yet another new warp point went on.

Then, three days after the Bugs' arrival, four of their gunboats blundered into Sommers' carriers and freighters. Hastily launched fighters had blasted them out of space and then rendezvoused with their carriers beyond scanner range. SF 19, reprieved once more, had resumed its cloaked maneuverings. But the Bugs, with their enemies' presence in the system positively confirmed, had intensified their search. And now, three days later, they'd been reinforced, bringing their total in-system strength to thirty-two battlecruisers and God knew how many gunboats. . . .

"Yes," Sommers said, dragging her mind back to the staff meeting, "I believe the situation has ceased to be desperate and become serious." A couple of people smiled. "We now need to decide what changes, if any, to make in our survey procedure." She indicated the display screen. It was no holotank, but two dimensions were all that was required to display the orbital plane of this system's cold, worthless planets. It showed the warp point through which they'd entered and on which the Bug battlecruisers now squatted sullenly, a hundred and twenty light-minutes out from the red star on a bearing about thirty degrees "east" of the display's arbitrary north. Other icons showed the elements into which SF 19 had been divided, probing in regions closer to the system primary. "The floor is now open to suggestions. Yes, Feridoun?"

The chief of staff cleared his throat. "Admiral, in my considered judgment, the arrival of more Bug battlecruisers lends added force to the argument I've made before."

In private, Sommers mentally interjected. Now it seemed he'd decided to go public. "Why is that?" she asked aloud.

"Operating in the inner system, so close to our entry warp point, maximizes our vulnerability to detection by the battlecruisers there. The presence of additional battlecruisers makes the risk we're running an even more unacceptable one."

Sommers decided not to make an issue of Hafezi's arguably improper use of the word *unacceptable*. "You're aware of the basis for my orders."

"Yes, Sir: you're firmly convinced that the warp point we're looking for is a Type Seven, all known examples of which occur within ninety light-minutes of their system primaries." Hafezi drew a deep breath. "Admiral, I have utmost respect for the extensive survey experience on which you base this . . . hunch. But I must point out that only nine percent of all open warp points are Type Sevens. And *all* the other ninety-one percent are located at greater distances from their primaries—usually at considerably greater distances. I therefore recommend that we discontinue our inner-system survey and turn our attention to the outer system, where the probability of finding a warp point is eleven times greater and where we can perform survey operations beyond the enemy battlecruisers' sensor range."

Sommers restrained an angry retort—she *had* opened the floor to suggestions, and Hafezi hadn't quite strayed over the line into insubordination. "There's something in what you say, Commodore. But I would remind you that the Bugs, presumably following the same line of logic as yourself, have sent their gunboats to the system's outer limits and begun a gradual inward sweep. And while gunboat sensors aren't as powerful as those of battlecruisers, there are a lot more of them." She held the chief of staff's eyes. "At any rate, that is all secondary. The central point is that the region we're in now is the place to find a Type Seven. And that, in *my* 'considered judgment,' is precisely what we're looking for."

Hafezi's eyes didn't waver. "I respectfully disagree, Sir."

They continued to lock eyes while the rest of the staffers tried to be inconspicuous and Sommers wondered why the chief of staff was so determined to make this a contest of wills. *Could it be*, came the unwelcome question, *because I'm a woman?*

Feridoun came from a tradition of educated cosmopolitanism; serving under a Westerner wouldn't gall him. But a woman . . .?

It wasn't even that she was a Western woman. There was a strain in Islam which had always equated *Western woman* with *whore*, but he'd no more have any truck with that than Sommers would with the trashier elements of the West's past. Indeed, an Islamic woman might actually have been worse, summoning up from his mental background certain assumptions about the proper roles of the sexes that not even his austere and intellectualized form of Islam had ever entirely exorcised.

But none of that mattered, for Sommers was in command, and she had to *stay* there if they were to have any hope, however forlorn, of survival. Attempts to command by committee—or COs who waffled when decision time came—were a prescription for disaster Aileen Sommers had no intention of following. *And*, she thought grimly, *given that a Type Seven is our only real chance to get out of this system alive, I'm not about to debate logic-versus-instinct with* anyone.

"Your objection is noted, Commodore, and you may have it on record in any form you wish. Nevertheless, we will continue to conduct our survey as per my orders. Is that clear?" Sommers' final question was not just for Hafezi, for her eyes swept over the entire staff.

Only one other pair of eyes wavered under that regard. Commander Arabella Maningo, the logistics officer, looked left and right as though searching for something that wasn't there. When she spoke, her voice was at first quiet to the point of inaudibility and level to the point of expressionlessness, only gradually taking on a high quaver. "What does any of this matter? Even if we do find a warp point and get through it, we'll just be one more system further away from home. And then we'll have to find *another* warp point, and then another, on and on forever, and eventually our ships will wear out and our life-systems will degrade—"

"That will do!" The bullwhip crack in Sommers' voice brought Maningo's head jerking up, eyes blinking, and the fog of incipient hysteria in the compartment seemed to dissipate. "I know that pressing on into the unknown is a bleak option. But it happens to be the only option we've got! And it's *not* hopeless. Remember, the Federation and its allies comprise one hell of a lot of warp nexi. It's not at all out of the question that we'll happen onto one of them. And we're equipped for long-term independent operations. Our maintenance resources won't give out any time soon . . . assuming that *you* manage to do your job."

Maningo's eyes flashed and her jaw clenched. *Good*, Sommers thought. Better anger than the lugubrious despair that would overtake them if they let the nightmare vision of suffocating in their own wastes, lost in an infinity of cold dark emptiness, take up residence in their heads. She found herself half-wishing that the Bugs would find them—this waiting was killing them as dead as combat could, and taking longer about it.

She shook the thought away and met all their eyes again. "We will continue to pursue whatever avenue holds out any hope of survival. That is our minimal obligation to our personnel. Giving up is not an option we are permitted!" She made sure none of those eyes met hers, either in defiance or with a mute plea to let them all lie down and die, before she adjourned the meeting.

The Bugs found them midway into the second watch of the following day.

Sommers and Hafezi were both on the flag bridge, maintaining a mutual politeness which was brittle in its frigidity, when the sensors erupted in electronic panic. A dozen gunboats, sweeping out of the blackness into close sensor range of *Jamaica's* own battlegroup. They were also within missile range of the group's two battlecruisers.

"Get them!" Sommers snapped as the gunboats turned tightly to escape with their news. But missiles were already arrowing forth from *Jamaica* and *Roma* as per standing orders. Nine were blasted apart, yet three got beyond the missiles' reach. Sommers and Hafezi looked at each other wordlessly, all differences forgotten. By unspoken consent, they turned to the system display in which the four tiny battlegroups and the skulking cluster of carriers and freighters swam. Of course there'd be no change in Bug dispositions yet. But as soon as those surviving gunboats' messages could speed across the light-minutes . . .

She stared for a moment at the icon that represented her own little battlegroup—in addition to the battlecruisers she had the *Hun*-class scout cruiser *Uzbek* and the CLE *Marblehead*—and then turned to Hafezi. "Feridoun, I want the battlegroup to proceed on this course." She used her remote, and a string-light grew in the holotank.

"*Away* from the others, Sir?"

"That's right. We're the only ones whose location the Bugs know. I want to draw them away from the rest of the flotilla."

"We'd stand a better chance of defending ourselves if we joined forces, Sir. Especially with the carriers—"

"Negative. Even combined, we wouldn't stand a chance against the Bug forces in this system. No, the other groups' best defense is invisibility. Which means, among other things, that the carriers are *not* to launch their fighters, in support of us or for any other reason. It would maximize the Bugs' chances of detecting them, and their lack of a command ship to datalink their point defense makes them peculiarly vulnerable." She gave the chief of staff a hard look. "Carry out your orders, Commodore."

"Aye, aye, Sir," Hafezi said without a perceptible pause.

Jamaica's battlegroup swung into its new course, and as the minutes crept by the scarlet lights of incoming gunboats began to pop into existence on Sommers' plot like a rash breaking out. *No way*, she thought. *They've got us. No self-deception. And no searching Feridoun's face for reproach.* She straightened her back and gazed at the viewscreen on which the approaching death was, of course, not to be seen. *At least the others will have more time for a search. It's still not impossible that some of them could—*

"Admiral!" The voice from the com station was almost unseemly in its loudness. "Priority signal from *Thémis*. They've found it, Sir!"

"Found it? Found what?" Sommers blinked away her oppressively dark thoughts and fought to shift mental gears.

"A warp point, Sir! A Type Seven, located . . . well, they're downloading it now, Sir."

In the holotank, to the "east-northeast" of the primary star at a distance of about sixty light-minutes from it, the icon of a warp point winked into life like the electric signpost of a doorway out of Hell.

"Admiral! You were right!" It never for an instant occurred to Sommers to suspect Hafezi of brown-nosing. There was nothing in his face but relief and unaffected congratulation. "We can turn around and make it out before any of the gunboats reach us."

"No." Sommers' quiet monosyllable wiped the chief of staff's face clean of every expression but bewilderment. "Our other groups are all closer to it than we are—and we have no knowledge of the Bugs' strength in their vicinity." She shook her head. "No, we'll continue to try to draw the Bugs after us. Order all other elements of the flotilla to clear the system ASAP."

For a moment that stretched, Hafezi stared at her. Then he spoke levelly. "Admiral, have you considered the effect this order will have on our personnel's morale? There's no way we can keep the rumor from circulating through this ship that a warp point's been found."

And that I'm slamming that doorway out of Hell shut in their faces. She forced herself to smile. "Feridoun, you've been a naval officer long enough to know that the only antidote to rumor is forthrightness." (Although, her familiar imp reminded her, some officers *never* learned it.) "I'll address the crew, and have it patched through to the other three ships. I'll tell them the situation, and explain to them that this is the way to maximize the chance of survival for *some* of our people, and that it is therefore our duty."

"With great respect, Admiral, are you *sure* it's our duty? Are you certain this doesn't go just a little beyond it? Is it possible that you're . . . trying to prove something?"

"I'll ignore that last question, Commodore. But as to the nature of our duty . . . yes, this is my interpretation of it. And my interpretation is the one that counts, isn't it?"

"Of course, Admiral. I'll give the necessary orders." Hafezi turned to go, then paused and faced her, and a smile flashed in the beard he'd managed through everything to keep as precisely sculpted as ever. (She recalled the Prophet's admonition to the faithful to grow beards so as not to be mistaken for Romans but to trim them so as not to be mistaken for Jews.) "By the way, I meant it: you were right and I was wrong, and those who *do* get out of this will owe their lives entirely to you." Then he was gone before she could think of a response.

The battlegroups led by *Thémis* and *Belvedera* had transited the newly discovered warp point, and both times *Jamaica* had rung with cheering that had promptly subsided as they'd all gone back to awaiting the approaching gunboats. Finally, the red and green icons crawled together in the holotank, and time seemed to accelerate.

Twenty-odd gunboats swept in from the blackness, sprinkling the battlegroup with missile fire that point defense could deal with. Then they came on through a storm of second-generation close assault missiles, seeking self-immolation. Three of them survived long enough to find it.

A starship's first line of defense against collisions—intended and otherwise—is its electromagnetic shields. Its second line of defense is its space-distorting drive field, without which any physical impact at such velocities would be totally and spectacularly fatal. It is only after both of these are overloaded that the occupants are affected in any way, for any violence—however horrific—that expends itself against them has no physical medium through which to transmit shock waves to the ship itself. Thus Sommers, Hafezi and the rest of the flag bridge's complement sat in their cocooning shock frames and felt no concussion as the gunboat that had approached far too swiftly to be seen was consumed. They also saw nothing, for the viewscreen went black at the moment of impact. When it came back on, a few bits of still white-hot debris could briefly be glimpsed as they spun away and were swallowed by infinity.

"*Roma* got two kamikazes, Sir," Hafezi reported. "Fortunately, there was an interval between them, and there was no physical damage. A near thing, though; she took a lot more shield overload than we did."

"Tell them to get the shields restored as quickly as possible," Sommers ordered. "Same goes for this ship. The next wave—" she waved at the plot "—isn't going to be nearly as easy."

Hafezi moved away. But he was intercepted by the duty com rating. (In a quiet voice; he'd had words with them about blurting things out.) He turned back to Sommers with a frown.

"Admiral, we've gotten a signal from Captain Kabilovic. They've detected a Bug gunboat force vectoring in on the carriers and freighters. In light of the overwhelming probability that they've been detected, he's asking for permission to launch his fighters."

She had to smile. "Yes, that's the way Milos would put it. Permission granted, of course." She sighed deeply. "Well, Feridoun, there's no further point in trying to draw the Bugs off them, is there? Get us headed for the warp point at max. We'll rendezvous with Milos on our way."

For an absurd instant, Hafezi actually looked embarrassed by the fact that the course of action he'd recommended had turned out to be the only viable one. But it only lasted an instant. Then he was off, and Sommers was left looking at the holotank in which the Bug battlecruiser formations at the entry warp point had moved off station and proceeded to intercept this newly detected group of prey.

Even Hafezi was looking a little disheveled—he'd developed a nervous habit of running his fingers through his beard—as they approached their rendezvous with the carriers.

It had been a terrifying chase. For a while it had looked as though the battlecruisers that had been pursuing them—faster than Bug battlecruisers had a right to move—would be able to swerve aside and intercept the carriers at a time when the fighters were otherwise occupied. But then the third survey battlegroup, led by TFNS *Imperieuse*, struggling to reach the warp point, had maneuvered into the Bugs' blind zone and given them a serious load of missiles up the ass. The subsequent degradation in Bug fire control suggested that they'd gotten the command ship—*something* had to go right every now and then—and the subsequent demolition of the unreasonably fast battlecruisers had followed as a matter of course.

Stung, the Bugs had diverted their available gunboats to the new threat, and TFNS *Caio Duilio* had vanished in multiple fireballs of kamikaze attacks. But Sommers had used the time that had been won and was now coming into datalink range of the carriers—

"Incoming gunboats!"

With practiced precision, they all flung themselves into their command chairs and locked their shock frames. Sommers and Hafezi had a chance to make quick eye contact before the flood of data and horror flowed over them.

The gunboats were barely even bothering with extended-range missile fire anymore. With nightmarish persistence, they sought out ramming targets, and this time they came in a wave that swamped the little battlegroup's defenses. With almost physical pain, Sommers watched the readouts that told of *Uzbek's* cataclysmic destruction, of damage to *Roma* and *Marblehead*, of one course after another of *Jamaica's* own shields giving up in showers of sparks and clouds of acrid smoke as their generators overloaded . . .

"*Incoming!*"

As though struck by a war-god's hammer, *Jamaica* shuddered as a gunboat's death agony smashed down the last of her shields and rended hull metal. Sommers barely heard the apocalyptic noise, for her vision began to dim as she was whiplashed back and forth within the life-saving confines of her shock frame. Then came another hammer-stroke, and another, and another . . .

Her next awareness was of shouting that seemed to come from a great distance. She shook her head to clear it, tasting the brassy tang of blood. Vision returned, and she found that the shouts hadn't been coming from so far away after all. In fact, Hafezi's face was only a few inches from hers, and those of the medics crowding in behind him weren't much further. At first she thought the ship was still shuddering, but it was only Hafezi, shaking her.

"Aileen . . . er, Admiral, are you all right?"

Why does he look so frantic? She wondered with a small fraction of her returning consciousness. Most of it took in the fact that she was still on *Jamaica's* flag bridge—a flag bridge that was still functioning. The next fact to register was that Hafezi's faceplate was open, as was hers. So they had air. She tried to sit up, and found she had to shake her head again.

"Yes . . . yes, I'm all right. What about the ship?"

"Damage control has things in hand," Hafezi reported. She wondered why he looked weak with relief, and decided it must be because the ship had come through. "Most of our internal systems are all right, and the rest will be soon. But we haven't much in the way of armor integrity left."

"And the others?"

"You know about *Uzbek*. *Marblehead* isn't much better off; she's got one engine room left, but not much else. *Roma* is in about the same condition we are."

Sommers struggled upright and waved away the medics. "We won't survive the next wave," she muttered. She forced her brain to think and her voice to firm up. "I see we've got a little time left before that next wave's ETA. Let's use it. I want to incorporate the carriers into this ship's datagroup; we can use their point defense. That's our first priority."

"Aye, aye, Sir. But . . . Admiral, you need to let them take you to sickbay and have a look at you."

"No time. Now, our second priority is to get *Marblehead's* survivors evacuated. Send our small craft and *Roma*'s. What's the status of the fighter groups?"

"*Staghound's* squadrons are back aboard the carrier, rearming. Same goes for most of the Ophiuchi. But two of their squadrons got through to *Imperieuse* and her battle group. That's why three of those ships still live, although *Imperieuse* is badly damaged. The Ophiuchi are still there."

"Good. Signal *Imperieuse* and order them to make a beeline for the warp point. Move!" She stood up and smiled at Hafezi and the hovering medics. "See, I'm fine."

They departed, still looking dubious. It was only then that she carefully lowered herself back down into the command chair and closed her eyes to shut out the swirling universe.

The situation was somewhat frustrating. Half the Fleet's available gunboat strength was still in the system's outer reaches, and could not arrive in time to be a factor. And after suffering that costly surprise, the battlecruisers would be kept together—which meant the new fast ones wouldn't be able to take advantage of their speed . . . and that it would take the formation a long time to bring the enemy within missile range.

But did they have that time? The enemy had obviously discovered a warp point; his headlong flight could have no other destination. But where was that warp point? There would be no way of knowing until the enemy ships began to vanish.

So there was no time to organize the gunboats into a single overwhelming wave. The scattered elements must continue to make piecemeal attacks. Even if they couldn't destroy the enemy before he madee transit, they must at all costs stay in contact so as to observe that transit.

"*Nurnberg* is Code Omega, Sir."

Sommers nodded absently, her soul as dulled to pain as her body had become after the repeated kamikaze impacts that had begun to tear *Jamaica's* vitals. The flagship couldn't complain; *Roma* had taken even worse damage.

But the chase was coming to an end—the temporary sort of end that was the only kind that seemed possible for them anymore . . .

"*Boise* has transited, Sir," Hafezi reported quietly.

Sommers nodded again. She couldn't bring herself to rejoice. They'd made it to another warp point, true. But the Bugs would follow them, for they would pinpoint that warp point from her ships' transits. So it would be the same all over again in yet another system. . . .

She straightened. "Get the carriers through as soon as possible. The battlecruisers will form a rearguard. *Jamaica* will, of course, be the last to transit."

"Aye, aye, Sir."

Roma died just short of the warp point. So did the freighter *Voyager,* despite everything the battlecruisers could do to shield her. But then the last battered half-wreck was through, and *Jamaica* was coming up on the hole in spacetime through which she would sail into . . . what?

Hafezi turned to face her. "You did it, Admiral. You got us out of this system."

No one else was in earshot, and she finally let bitterness enter her voice. "Yes . . . for what?" She indicated the plot, with the swarming red icons that would follow them through the warp point.

Hafezi shook his head. "It doesn't matter, Aileen. You did your duty, and a good deal more besides." His eyes held hers, and he reached out a hand and gripped hers, hard, in a motion that his body shielded from all eyes on the flag bridge.

She returned the pressure, wordlessly because there were no words, and smiled tremulously at him.

"Stand by for transit!"

Their hands were still clasped as TFNS *Jamaica* vanished from the system of the red sun.

and the—

CHAPTER FORTY-THREE

"I wish I could spare more."

"I'm afraid that's it, Ellen," Oscar Pederson said wearily.
He ran a hand through his hair and leaned back in his
chair aboard Sky Watch One, gazing into the system
schematic displayed above his desk. It was littered with
the wildly scrambled icons of Fortress Command units,
and Ellen MacGregor sat in the flag briefing room of
TFNS *Amaretsu*, studying its twin from the other end
of their conference link.

"I wish I could spare more," he went on, "but if it
comes apart on you, I'll need everything I've got just to
fend them off Nova Terra and Eden—not to mention
this side of The Gateway."

"I understand, Oscar," MacGregor replied in a sympathetic tone. It was a bit hard, just at the moment, to
sympathize with anyone but herself, yet she didn't envy
Pederson a bit. They held the same rank, but he was
Fortress Command while she was Battle Fleet, and that
gave her command authority in Centauri until Hannah
Avram's return. If she ordered him to give up still more
fortresses, he'd have no recourse but to obey, and part
of her wanted to do just that—especially since she was
busy *leaving* the system at the moment with every warship
she could scrape up. She was also leaving the warp point
mother naked in her absence, but if she *didn't* take those
ships forward into Anderson Two, the gunboats on that

system's warp point to Anderson Three would have a field day against Second Fleet's survivors. Uncovering Centauri didn't make her any happier than it made Pederson. But the very fact that she was leaving only gave added point to his responsibility for all of Centauri, not just the Anderson Two warp point, in her absence, and she refused to second guess his dispositions.

"It ought to be enough," she told him now, lips pursed as she continued her study of the schematic. Alpha Centauri was the second most heavily fortified system in human-held space, with powerful fortress shells and minefields on each of its eleven open warp points. Fortress Command had begun assembling fresh forts to cover the system's newly discovered *twelfth* warp point even before Second Fleet's departure, and a potent shell of eighteen fortresses had been "borrowed" from the other warp points to cover it while its own OWPs were built. Pederson had personally overseen both the siting of the forts and the beginning of the new minefields, and since the new warp point was a closed one, he'd been able to emplace the mines directly atop it. That would deny an attack any clear zone into which it might transit, and he'd ringed the mines with independently deployed energy platforms, including both laser buoys and primary beam platforms, for good measure. With that backing, MacGregor had felt thoroughly confident of even her badly understrength Fourth Fleet's ability to guarantee Centauri's security in Second Fleet's rear.

But that was the critical point: she'd expected to cover Second Fleet's *rear*, and like everyone else, she'd thought she had months to perfect her defenses. Second Fleet was driving the Bugs back, after all, and even if the enemy managed to mount a counterattack, Ivan Antonov's warships would be between him and Centauri. At the very least, Antonov would be able to slow him down and buy time for MacGregor and Pederson to dig in behind him.

That comfortable assumption no longer applied, and Pederson had every minelayer in the system employed in the frantic placement of more mines and platforms. It was going slower than MacGregor would have liked—(*of course,* she thought wryly, *it* couldn't *go fast enough to make me* happy!)—but that wasn't because the weapons weren't available. Mines and energy platforms were being *produced* at a staggering rate by the system's spaceborne industry, and even if they hadn't been, she and Pederson could have raided the other warp points' long established defenses for them. No, the problem was that there were only so many minelayers, and their crews, however skilled, could physically position weapons only so quickly. They were working till they dropped, but the mine densities needed to blunt a Bug attack simply couldn't be built up overnight.

Which was why she was having this conference. Pederson and his staff had stripped ten of Centauri's eleven open warp points of virtually all their OWPs and commandeered every available tug in Centauri and Sol to reposition those forts. Both he and MacGregor were aware that the Grand Alliance was straining every nerve to reinforce Fourth Fleet, and even if MacGregor lost control of the outer system, the forces rushing back towards Centauri would almost certainly regain it in time. But it was Oscar Pederson's job to see to it that there were still live humans on the system's planets when that time came—not to mention his responsibility to protect Centauri's mammoth orbital industrial infrastructure and provide the maximum possible cover for The Gateway. Humanity's home system was even more heavily fortified than Centauri, but Centauri was Sol's buffer and glacis. That had been the bedrock of the TFN's strategic planning ever since there'd *been* a Federation Navy, and that— and Pederson's local concerns here in Centauri—had governed his proposed OWP redistribution. The majority were bound for positions around the system's twin planets to bolster Sky Watch One and the other orbiting space stations. Those not headed there had been divided equally between The Gateway and the closed warp point beyond which Hannah Avram's relief force was—*must* be—leading

Ivan Antonov's survivors towards safety. Once they were all in position, MacGregor would have seventy fortresses, with something like a thousand fighters embarked, to bar the Bugs' passage into Centauri.

And a damned good thing, too, she thought mordantly, *'cause I sure as hell don't have anything else to do the job with!*

She grimaced at the familiar thought. The Federation was enormous, and ships took months to travel from its core to its borders. Those vast distances had always spread the TFN far thinner than raw hull numbers might suggest to the layman, for a starship could be in only one place at a time, and that simple fact was the crux of Ellen MacGregor's problem.

Home Fleet, as the biggest single concentration of Terran warships, had been heavily raided in the war's opening phases. As every available forward-deployed unit had been rushed towards threatened sectors—the Romulus Cluster, originally, and then Kliean—Home Fleet units had been redeployed to fill the vacuum created by their departure. Then the need to build up nodal reaction forces throughout Allied Space had put still more strain on the Alliance's navies, and once again, Home Fleet had been tapped to help make up the required numbers. MacGregor understood the logic behind that. Given Sol's position at the very core of the Federation, it had certainly seemed as unthreatened as any star system was likely to be, and the needed ships had to come from *somewhere*.

But then the Bugs had stumbled into Centauri and Operation Pesthouse had been mounted—from Centauri—ten months before it was scheduled to kick off from Zephrain. Half the units originally earmarked for Second Fleet had already been en route to Zephrain, so the cupboard had been bare when GHQ started looking around for the muscle Pesthouse required, and its eye had fallen yet *again* on Home Fleet. All of which meant that, at this moment, Ellen MacGregor had precisely forty-seven starships, headed by only six superdreadnoughts, nine battleships, and Home Fleet's last eleven carriers and assault carriers, to support those seventy OWPs. More were coming as fast and hard as they could, but they weren't here yet, and she didn't even know precisely how many were on their way. And however many there might be, neither they, nor the forts, nor the minefields were on the warp point *now*.

She shook herself and produced a crooked half-smile for Pederson's benefit.

"It ought to be enough," she repeated. "And it damned well *better* be, hadn't it?"

The attack forces' courier drones confused the blocking force gunboats, for they clearly suggested that the enemy had somehow gotten a relief force through the warp point the gunboats were charged to block. Surely that was impossible. The attacks on the enemy's support echelon had put the blocking force behind schedule, true, but not enough for that. Unless, of course, the Fleet had misjudged the enemy's initial deployments. The Fleet had been unable to scout the intervening systems before attacking, after all. It was possible that the enemy's "relief force" had actually been a routine reinforcement echelon which had already passed through the blocking force's system of responsibility en route to the front when the trap was sprung, and the fact that it had included none of the attack craft mother ships made that seem even more likely.

But whatever had happened, the courier drones had reached the blocking force well before the enemy's survivors, and this time the gunboats would be waiting.

Captain Jeremiah Dillinger, MacGregor's chief of staff, and Commander Fahd Aburish, her operations officer, flanked her as she gazed at the holographic representation of Anderson Two in CIC's holo sphere. The icons representing *Amaretsu* and the core of Fourth Fleet's limited striking power floated in the sphere, and MacGregor felt her staffers' unhappiness—especially Aburish's—at being here. She couldn't blame them, yet she saw no alternative to her deployment. So far, the enemy appeared not to have entered this system. She couldn't be positive of that, but the interstellar comsats were still intact as far as the Anderson *Three* warp point, and the cruisers and destroyers she'd deployed to picket the known warp points in One and Two reported no enemy activity in-system. Unfortunately, she'd also brought along five *Wayfarer*-class freighters with heavy loads of RD2s to mount a watch on the Anderson Three side of the warp point, and the drones had made it clear the enemy was maintaining a massive gunboat screen there. If Antonov and Avram were going to break through that screen with acceptable losses, MacGregor was going to have to help clear their way.

That was why she'd brought Fourth Fleet forward . . . yet she dared not move any *further* forward before Second Fleet arrived. The fact that gunboats were warp-capable prevented her from putting her ships right on top of the warp point, so she had to hold them far enough back to give her time to get her fighters launched before any surprise gunboat strike could reach her. Which, she conceded silently to Aburish, gave her the worst of both worlds. This deep into Anderson Two, she ran a very serious risk of being cut off from her retreat to Centauri if the Bugs managed to run still another ambush force in behind her, yet she was compelled to do nothing constructive until Second Fleet arrived. *If* Second Fleet—

She chopped that thought off and folded her hands behind her while she made herself rethink the strategic situation yet again. If Second Fleet managed to get back more or less intact, Antonov should have an excellent chance—with Fourth Fleet's support—of holding Anderson One. She hoped so, anyway. If he couldn't, then the Navy was going to have to write off all of Survey Flotilla 19, as well. Admiral Sommers might know where Anderson One's third open warp point led by now, but no one else did, and she was much too far out for anyone who hadn't already surveyed the warp line to find her. Yet whatever the future held, what had already happened to Second Fleet was a grimly pointed reminder that there might be other warp points no one knew about, and a part of MacGregor wanted desperately to pull back to One. But her starships would have required seventy-six hours just to cross Anderson Two to the Anderson Three warp point, and that was simply too long a transit time for her pickets to call her forward when the drones indicated Second Fleet's arrival was imminent.

"Time remaining?" she asked after a moment.

"Assuming Sky Marshal Avram had to proceed clear to Anderson Five before turning for home, she should reenter Anderson Three approximately one day from now," Aburish replied. "That would put her on the Anderson Three-Anderson Two warp point in—" he consulted his calculator "—one hundred twenty-six hours."

"I see." MacGregor grimaced at the holo sphere once more. "This waiting is beginning to get just a bit tedious," she observed.

"Sir, I'd like to point out—" Aburish began, but her raised hand stopped him.

"We've already been over it, Fahd," she said, her husky alto quiet but firm, "and the answer's still the same. I recognize the risk I'm running, but we can't know what shape Admiral Antonov's carriers are in . . . or if he's been engaged in a running battle all the way back to us. But the recon drone reports *do* make it clear the Bugs on this warp point are holding tight rather than moving forward to meet him, and we've got almost five hundred fighters aboard *our* carriers. If we hit the bastards from behind while he and Sky Marshal Avram hit them from the front, we should be able to blow the door open before they know which end is up."

"And if they trap us the same way they ambushed Admiral Antonov, Sir?" Aburish wasn't giving up, but his resigned tone said he already knew how his admiral would reply.

"There has to be some limit to even the Bugs' total strength," MacGregor said, "and if *I* were the Bug lord high admiral, I'd've committed everything I had to smashing Second Fleet. The fact that they're using nothing but gunboats to cover this warp point may well indicate that they figured the same way, but even if they do have another ambush force, and even if there *is* an as yet unknown warp point in Two, they'd have a hell of a time coordinating another attack into *our* rear. And let's face it, Fahd: if we don't get Second Fleet back to Centauri, the ships we have with us won't make all that much difference by themselves."

"I suppose not," Aburish sighed. "I just hope we're not throwing good money after bad."

"Well, if I've made the wrong call, I'm sure Antonov or Avram will tell me in no uncertain terms," MacGregor snorted. "In fact, it would probably be something of a relief if I could get them mad enough to replace me!"

Another gunboat squadron had reported still more of those irritating sensor ghosts, but, as with all earlier such reports, they had been unable to run them down. The ghosts' persistent refusal to either go away or let themselves be tracked down was worrisome, for it suggested that the enemy was up to some new technological trick, yet that was a secondary concern for now, for the retreating enemy would reenter this system shortly. The gunboats would have preferred to go to meet him, but that, unfortunately, was impossible. There were still at least some surviving enemy ships in this system, and it seemed extremely likely there were at least some in the next system up the chain. But the ambush which had been supposed to destroy the enemy's entire fleet had skimmed off almost every available gunboat. The eight hundred still guarding the warp point had made the journey from the nearest core system under their own power, operating without tenders or mother ships. That meant the external ordnance they now mounted would be all they had, and they dared not be drawn into wasting that ordnance on any diversionary target. That was why they had not advanced further up the chain towards the enemy's core systems, where they would almost certainly have been engaged and forced to expend their munitions.

But their wait would end shortly, and they began to stir, spreading their outriding squadrons a bit wider to insure that no ship could evade their sensors' sweep.

"They're definitely up to something, Sir," Aburish said tautly. "Look here . . . and over here on the other side of their formation, as well." He jabbed a light pencil at the display generated from the latest RD2 sweep. "Looks like they're expecting company."

"And just about on the button for your time estimate, Fahd," Dillinger noted. "It's got to be the Sky Marshal and Admiral Antonov."

"Agreed." MacGregor rubbed the tip of her nose. "Are the SBMHAWKs ready?"

"Yes, Sir. Standing by and targeted," Aburish said crisply.

"All right," she said. "Given how they're adjusting their position and that no one's turned up to reinforce them, I think we have to proceed on the theory that this force is all they've got." That, as she was painfully aware, could turn out to be a fatal assumption, yet she had no choice but to make it. "I want the probe schedule accelerated. Put a flight through every ten minutes."

"That's going to burn through the available numbers in a hurry," Dillinger pointed out, "and it's also going to increase the chance of their being spotted."

"Those are risks we're just going to have to take, Jeremiah. We've got to know when they get ready to commit, and the probes' sensors are good enough they should see Second Fleet by the time the bad guys do. When they do—"

Ellen MacGregor looked at her senior staffers, and her smile would have chilled a shark.

"There they are, Sir," Anthea Mandagalla said wearily.

"I see them," Raymond Prescott replied. The last week had been as terrible, in its way, as Task Force 21's agonizing wait for Second Fleet to break back towards it in Anderson Five. He and his staff had managed to reorganize the remnants of Ivan Antonov and Hannah Avram's ships into what looked like battlegroups, but they were nothing of the sort. Despite all emergency repairs could do, eighty percent of those ships were totally unfit for combat, their "battlegroups" no more than defensive huddles, tied together by jury-rigged datanets in the hope of fending off at least a few incoming missiles.

But now someone whose ordeal had been even more hideous than Second Fleet's had appeared on their sensors: Michael Chin's surviving support ships, covered by the battlecruisers Hannah had detached on her way through. They were precisely where they were supposed to be, and they moved steadily towards rendezvous with Prescott's tattered command as it headed for the warp point to Anderson Two.

"We've got Admiral Chin's strength report, Admiral," Commander Hale reported, and Prescott looked at her. "He says he has seven fighters to support the Sky Marshal's battlecruisers," the com officer said quietly. "His own escorts are fit only for defensive action."

"Seven," Jacques Bichet repeated softly. "Sweet Jesus, they got hammered even worse than we thought."

"There's been a lot of that going around," Prescott replied with bitter humor, then shook himself. Chin's seven fighters would bring his entire surviving fighter strength up to one hundred and ninety-two. But at least he saw the icons of TFNS *Anchorage* and *Lisbon* in the plot, and those had been two of Antonov's ammunition colliers.

"Inform Admiral Chin that we're critically short of ammunition," he told Bichet. "Tell him we're especially short of fighter munitions and capital missiles. I'm sure the bastards already know we're here, and without the fighter strength to maintain a recon shell, we can't be sure there aren't cloaked fleet units out there. I suspect we'd already have heard from them if they *were* there, but we can't be certain, so I don't want to halt the fleet for very long. On the other hand," he smiled bitterly, "we don't have that many fighters or combat capable ships left. Chin should be able to organize enough shuttles to get what we have resupplied on the fly."

The enemy appeared on the gunboats' own sensors at last. The escapees from the ambush and the survivors of the support echelon had made rendezvous, and they were coming straight for the warp point. Well, it was not as if they had a choice, and the gunboats began to stir. Now that they knew where both the enemy's forces were, they would swarm out and envelop him, spreading themselves too widely for his surviving attack craft to intercept in strength.

"Looks like you called it, Sir," Bichet said. "They're going to wait on the warp point, them come at us on a broad front to spread the fighters."

"And if we send Kinkaid in on a preemptive strike, we guarantee her people will be too far out to support the battle-line when the gunboats she doesn't catch make their runs," Prescott agreed. "Well, we knew it was coming. Let's just be grateful they don't seem to have any regular warships to support them."

"I'm *trying* to feel grateful, Sir," Mandagalla said, "but it doesn't seem to be working."

"That's because—" Prescott began, only to be cut off by a sudden shout from Plotting.

The gunboats' first warning was the sudden emergence of missile pods in their rear. And not just any pods. These were the new type, loaded with close assault missiles, and they seemed to know exactly where each gunboat was. They vomited their deadly cargoes with devastating accuracy, and point defense was useless against the sprint-mode capital missiles.

"*All right!*" It was hardly a professional report, but Prescott felt no inclination to reprimand Bichet, for whoever had planned that attack had demonstrated impeccable timing. He and his command were still five light-minutes out, but the Bugs had been moving away from the warp point when the pods erupted in their rear. Over half of them had been destroyed, and even as they died, the first assault carriers came through the warp point. TFNS *Amaretsu, Ajax, Minotaur,* and *Wizard* led the way, followed by the Ophiuchi *Zirk-Sefmaara* and *Zirk-Siraacan* and five Terran fleet carriers. Missile-armed fighters spat from their catapults, and then the precious carriers wheeled and fled back towards Anderson Two.

The remaining gunboats hesitated, clearly torn between continuing toward Prescott or turning on the fighters in their rear. But their hesitation was brief. They were outnumbered by the newly arrived fighters now, and the carriers' prompt departure deprived them of any starship targets on the warp point. They swerved back onto their original courses, racing for Prescott's command, and he smiled cruelly.

"Launch the fighters, Jacques. Then reverse course."

"Aye, aye, Sir," Bichet said with an answering smile.

The gunboats charged the enemy they had awaited for so long, but that enemy was no longer advancing. Instead, he expelled his own attack craft and then fell back, holding the range open, and the gunboats were doomed. They were slower than the attack craft swarming out from the warp point in pursuit, and they were armed with FRAMs and standard missiles for antishipping attacks, not AFHAWKs.

The attack craft killed the last of them four light-minutes short of their intended victims.

Fifteen days after assuming command of Second Fleet, Raymond Prescott sat still and silent on his flag bridge, eyes burning, as the survivors of Operation Pesthouse limped brokenly back into Centauri. Half of his remaining capital ships were under tow, abused engines crippled beyond repair, and only eight ships—eight, out of Second Fleet's entire initial order of battle and Hannah Avram's relief force—were undamaged. He thought of Hannah and his eyes burned hotter, yet he'd done it. With her help—and Ellen MacGregor's—he'd obeyed Ivan Antonov's last order and gotten his people home.

But the price, he thought. *Dear God, the* price!

His memory replayed Ellen MacGregor's shocked disbelief when he informed her that *he* was Second Fleet's senior surviving officer . . . and that Hannah was dead as well. And her disbelief had turned to horror as his exhausted voice numbly detailed the Navy's losses. Thirty-two superdreadnoughts, eleven assault carriers, six fleet carriers, three light carriers, five battleships, thirty battlecruisers, ten light cruisers, eleven *hundred* fighters, and twenty-eight support ships had been destroyed outright, and the ships which could still fight wouldn't have made three battlegroups. In three hundred years, the Terran Federation had never been more decisively defeated—nor lost so many splendid ships.

And people.

He closed his eyes, clenching himself against the pain. The people. He still didn't have definitive casualty figures, but there were already over two hundred thousand confirmed dead, and all of it—*all* of it!—for a campaign which ended with the Alliance right where it was when it began. The Pesthouse disaster had crippled the offensive capability of the TFN. God only knew how that would affect the strategic balance, yet even more frightening than that was the dreadful firepower of those new, monster ships. GHQ had decided to name them "monitors," for like the original ironclads of Old Terra, they were as slow and clumsy as they were terrifyingly well armored and armed. But slow or not, there was nothing between them and Centauri.

He sat gazing into his plot, drained and exhausted, and fear pulsed deep inside him. They would be coming for Centauri, those monitors. He knew it. And somehow the Alliance would have to stop them without three-quarters of Home Fleet . . . or Hannah Avram or Ivan Antonov.

Somehow.

Chapter Forty-Four

The Black Hole of Centauri

The Fleet made its way back along the warp chain down which the enemy had been lured. There was no opposition, yet even with damaged units under tow, the enemy was too fast to overhaul, and the blocking force had been trapped and expended for minimal results. Its extermination had further weakened the Fleet, but now the survivors of all the attack forces had gathered, joined by the first of the special ramming units. It was the most powerful force the Fleet had ever assembled—not simply in this war, but ever—yet its catastrophic gunboat losses imposed delay. It dared not confront enemy attack craft without a powerful gunboat force, and so all of those massive starships waited while the small craft it needed were rushed to it.

Hundreds of feet scuffed as Ellen MacGregor's senior officers rose, and she crossed the auditorium stage with a brisk, determined stride and her jaw set in a confident jut. Her staff followed, and she deliberately refrained from looking over her shoulder at them. She'd made the public demeanor she expected of them clear in terms no one could possibly have understood.

She reached the lectern between the long conference table and the edge of the stage and turned with parade ground precision to take her place behind it. Her staffers seated themselves at the table behind her, joining her second in command and *his* staff, and she took a moment to turn and smile tightly at Raymond Prescott. He looked less harrowed and exhausted than he had. That still left a lot of room for improvement, but however exhausted he might be, at least he'd evinced none of the bleak despair or outright panic which hovered over Centauri's inhabited planets like an evil fog. *He's got a hell of a lot better right to feel those things than certain other people, too,* she told herself. *Like that son-of-a-bitch Mukerji.*

She allowed herself a fleeting, sharklike grin at the thought of the political admiral. All of Operation Pesthouse's surviving flag officers—except one—had distinguished themselves during Second Fleet's grim retreat. Mukerji hadn't. In fact, an iron-voiced Prescott had been forced to relieve him when he'd revealed the soft, panicky center most of his peers had always suspected was there. Agamemnon Waldeck had, predictably, objected in the strongest terms and even gone so far as to propose Mukerji for command of TF 43, the orbital forts covering the Anderson One warp point. MacGregor, however, had been unimpressed by the Naval Oversight Committee chairman's arguments and, backed to the hilt by the Joint Chiefs of Staff, had confirmed Prescott's decision and sent Mukerji packing with an alacrity she knew would have delighted Hannah Avram. It had certainly delighted *Mukerji* (in the short term, at least), for it had gotten him out of Alpha Centauri and away from the Bug juggernaut he confidently expected to hammer the system flat. It was probable that he would get over his panic once he was certain his own hide was safe, but while it was remotely possible that Waldeck's patronage might be able to find him *some* form of employment one day, MacGregor's scathingly brutal assessment of his state when she approved his relief should keep him from ever again commanding in action.

But her grin faded as she turned back to face the well-filled auditorium, and she scolded herself for dwelling on Mukerji. He'd proven how amply he deserved to be slapped down, yet she knew the savagery with which she'd done that slapping owed even more to her own reaction to the loss of Ivan Antonov and Hannah Avram than to her longstanding contempt for him.

Well, what if it did? she asked herself coldly. *The son-of-a-bitch had it coming, and if kicking his ass is the only thing I do to compensate for my own sheer, howling terror I'm at least in better shape than certain of my esteemed political masters! Or, for that matter,* she added grimly, *than most of my military subordinates.*

"Be seated, ladies and gentlemen," she invited, and feet scuffed once more as her officers—primarily Terran and Ophiuchi, but with a few Tabbies and even a handful of Gorm scattered among them—did whatever their respective species described with the verb "sit."

She let her eyes sweep their tense, silent ranks and felt their anxiety like a barely contained forest fire, probing at the firebreaks she'd labored to erect around it. Ellen MacGregor knew about war, for she'd gone straight from the Academy into the closing stages of the Theban War, yet in all her years of service, she'd never sensed anything quite like this. There was a brittleness to her subordinates, a stunned desperation overlaid by lingering disbelief. That was especially true of the Terrans out there, for it was *their* fleet which had been so savagely mauled, but that same brittle, disbelieving fear—resignation, almost—clung to the nonhumans as well. Hannah Avram had been perhaps the most respected human officer of her generation. Her loss would have been a blow under any circumstances; coupled with Ivan Antonov's death, it had hit the Alliance squarely between the eyes with staggering power. For sixty years, the navies of the Grand Alliance—*all* of them, not just the TFN—had regarded Antonov as the galaxy's greatest living naval commander, the admiral who stood alone as the only true heir to Howard Anderson and Varnik'sheerino. He'd been more than simply the military commander of the Grand Alliance. He'd been its icon, its living war banner. Now that banner had fallen, and with its destruction, the Bugs had destroyed the certitude of the officers who'd followed it into battle.

And the way *they did it only makes it worse,* MacGregor

conceded. *They sucked us in—all of us, not just Antonov—and then jumped us with those godawful monitors. Maybe if we'd really listened to LeBlanc it wouldn't have hit us so hard, but we didn't. Despite the gunboats, despite the Assault Fleet, despite the plasma gun, we never truly believed—not deep down inside—that the Bugs could out-innovate us. We were so sure they'd have to play perpetual technological catch-up that it never occurred to us they might actually produce something that gave them the advantage in hardware, and we were just as confident of our ability to outthink and outfight them. They were simply a huge, unthinking, elemental force, not an opponent capable of analysis and strategic innovation.* She snorted mentally. *Yeah. Sure they were!*

She shook off the thought as she realized her audience had settled into its chairs (or whatever). Ten days had passed since Raymond Prescott led his crippled fleet back to Centauri, and MacGregor sometimes thought she, Kthaara'zarthan, Oscar Pederson, and Prescott were the only four people in the galaxy who realized how priceless those days had been. In addition to her role as Fourth Fleet's CO, she'd found herself tapped as the Federation's acting representative to the Joint Chiefs of Staff, but that responsibility, at least, had been one she could entrust to other hands. She knew enough about Tabbies to recognize how terribly his *vilkshatha* brother's death had hit Lord Talphon, but he'd let neither grief nor his hunger for *vilknarma* divert him from his duties as the Joint Chiefs' new chairman. He and his nonhuman colleagues had worked beyond exhaustion to squeeze out every possible reinforcement for Centauri, but they'd remained tactfully distant from the purely human side of the situation. Especially the political one.

MacGregor deeply appreciated their efforts to bolster Fourth Fleet, and she understood why they'd stepped aside from the political aspects of the crisis. She only wished she could do the same, but that was out of the question. She and Pederson had worn themselves hoarse trying to quell the panic of such notable war leaders as

Bettina Wister (who'd left the very morning after Prescott's return—with indecent haste—for an emergency Assembly session on Old Terra . . . thank God!) without success, yet their own officers were almost worse. They might not run around in circles waving their hands and squealing like that political whore Wister, but their numb lack of anything resembling aggressiveness made MacGregor feel as if she were swimming in tapioca. Perhaps it was only her imagination, but things certainly looked better to *her* than they had ten days ago! Fourth Fleet had acquired sixteen more superdreadnoughts and nine more battleships, counting new arrivals and the combat capable survivors of Second Fleet and Hannah Avram's relief force. Some of those survivors were still being worked on by the repair ships, but all were fit for service under emergency conditions, and if her minefields weren't yet as heavy as she wanted, they were five times heavier than they *had* been. All of that should be evident to every person in this auditorium from Jeremiah Dillinger's daily status reports. Yet try as she might, the bulk of her officers seemed unable to drag themselves out of their slough of despond, and she was getting more than a bit tired of it.

Well, she thought, *if this news doesn't get them off their butts, our morale's in even worse shape than I thought!* She inhaled deeply, propped her forearms on the lectern, and leaned across it to address the assembly in clear, crisp tones.

"Thirtieth Least Fang Harniaar and his task force will arrive in Centauri at approximately 0730 local tomorrow," she told them, and a stir, more sensed than seen, rustled through the auditorium. It wasn't strong enough to call relief, but MacGregor decided to regard it as headed in that direction.

"His arrival will increase our battle-line strength by twenty-seven percent, double our battlecruiser strength, and increase our mobile units' combined fighter strength by eighty-four percent," she went on briskly. "In fact, our order of battle will be stronger in every unit category, except superdreadnoughts, than Second Fleet was for

Pesthouse. And with the additional support of Centauri Sky Watch plus the advantage of a defensive position directly atop a warp point, our effective combat power will be *at least* six times as great!"

She smiled fiercely, but there were no answering smiles from her audience, and she felt her own congeal. That frozen, singing tension remained. It was as if her officers couldn't quite make themselves believe in their own advantages, as if some inner part of them could see anything she said only as an effort to jolly them along. She felt their misgivings mocking her . . . but she felt something else, as well, and a dangerous light flickered in her dark brown eyes. She closed her mouth, firm lips tightening in an ominous line, and glared at the silent rows of officers for a long, smoldering moment. And then, deliberately, she stepped around the lectern. She walked to the very edge of the stage and put her hands behind her, gripping them fiercely together as she glared out at Fourth Fleet's command structure, and her voice was harsh.

"All right, ladies and gentlemen," she half-snapped and half-snarled. "Let's get this out in the open, shall we?" Her hard, contemptuous tone sent another stir through the audience—one of uneasy surprise this time—and she smiled a thin, unpleasant smile. "Oh, come now! *Surely* someone out there would like to address the point so obviously on everyone's mind!"

No one spoke, and she rocked on her toes, bouncing up and down in short, sharp arcs that reminded the humans in her audience of the flick-flick-flicking tail of an irate tigress.

"No? Then *I'll* address it," she told their silence flatly. "We—and by 'we' I mean, specifically, the Terran Federation Navy—got our ass kicked. To date, counting all known losses, the Bugs have destroyed almost three hundred and forty TFN ships. In case some of you haven't run the figures, that's twenty-eight percent of our prewar hulls and over *fifty* percent of our prewar tonnage. Oh, and let's not forget the sixty-four capital ships out of action for major repairs or the 'combat capable' units of our own fleet which still have unrepaired battle damage. Then there's Pesthouse itself. In addition to most of Home Fleet, we've lost Admiral van der Gelder, Admiral Taathaanahk, Sky Marshal Avram, and Admiral Antonov. Worse, we lost all those ships and all those people because we fucked up. We walked right into it—all of us. We and our allies saw what we wanted to see, what the *Bugs* wanted us to see, and we screwed up by the numbers, didn't we? Be honest, ladies and gentlemen," she invited scathingly. "We've just been guests of honor for the biggest cluster-fuck in our mutual histories, and all of us, and especially every *Terran* officer in this auditorium, are scared to death, aren't we?" She glared at the assembled officers, chin jutting aggressively, shoulders squared, eyes snapping, and still no one spoke.

"Well, we've got *reason* to be scared," she went on in a marginally gentler voice. "We've been hammered, we've lost our best commanders and our most experienced units, and we're it—the entire mobile defense force—for Centauri *and* Sol. And just to make things worse, the Bugs have acquired command datalink *and* introduced an entirely new ship type bigger and nastier and lots, *lots* tougher than anything we've got. Does that just about sum it up?"

Again, no one replied from the auditorium seats, but this time a voice spoke up behind her.

"Yes, Sir," Raymond Prescott said with poison-dry wryness. "I guess that *does* sum it up, just about."

MacGregor turned her head, and he smiled crookedly at her. It was a battered and tired smile, but far from a beaten one, and she smiled back.

"I'm glad to hear that, Admiral Prescott," she told him. "I was beginning to think we might have a *serious* problem here." Prescott's smile became a grin, and a few people in the audience actually chuckled. The laughter sounded surprised, as if its authors couldn't quite believe they'd produced it, but it was real, and MacGregor swung back to face the seats.

"All right, people," she said, and her voice had replaced

its brief humor with adamantine determination, "let's cut to the chase. The Bugs are coming. When they get here, they're going to throw a simultaneous assault transit into our faces at a time of their own choosing. They're going to cover that assault with hundreds, probably thousands, of gunboats, and they're going to back it up with superdreadnoughts and these new 'monitors' of theirs, and the bastards will have command datalink. Taking everything into account, this will probably be the most powerful warp point assault in history. And do you know what's going to happen when they launch it?"

Not a voice spoke, and she swiveled her head, sweeping her eyes across them all in slow, remorseless arc, as she let the silence stretch out. Then she snapped it.

"What's going to *happen*, ladies and gentlemen, is that we're going to reduce their fancy new ships, and their gunboats, and their assault fleet—and them—to plasma. We've got the ships, and the forts, and the fighters, and the weapons we need, all backed up by the greatest industrial capacity in the known galaxy, and we are damned well going to turn the Centauri System into a Bug-eating black hole. People, I don't give a good god*damn* what *they* have. All I care about is what *we* have, and we are going to mine that warp point until I can frigging well walk across it! We're going to cover it with energy platforms, and missile pods, and forts, and capital ships, and combat space patrols, and we are fucking well going to *kill* any Bug that sticks its ugly snout through it! And if any of you think we're not going to do those things—or if even *one* of you gives me any less than a one thousand percent effort—being eaten by Bugs will be the *least* of your worries! *Is that perfectly clear?*"

The silence was different now—a ringing stillness, crackling about her, and she nodded.

"Good," she said mildly. "In that case, let's get down to the nuts and bolts of just how we're going to do that, shall we?"

❖   ❖   ❖

Raymond Prescott tipped his chair clear back, stretched and yawned hugely, and propped his heels on the briefing room table to survey his staff wearily.

"Does that just about cover it, Anna?" he asked, and Captain Mandagalla scrolled back through the notes on her own terminal.

"Just about, Sir," she agreed after a moment. "Admiral LeBlanc's agreed to your request to assign Captain Chung as your staff spook—I understand there was quite a bit of competition for his services; Admiral Trevayne even wanted him on Old Terra—and he'll be reporting tomorrow morning. And you've got that com conference with Admiral MacGregor, Admiral Chamhandar, and Fang Harniaar tomorrow, as well. I think we've got most everything nailed down in preparation, but Jacques and I don't have the latest readiness updates yet."

"Um." Prescott rubbed his eyes with his organic hand and wished he could scrub away his fatigue. But it was better than the retreat from Anderson Five had been. He told himself that at least six times a day, and one of these days he was actually going to begin believing it.

He smiled—or grimaced, at least—at the thought, and then again, more naturally, at the memory of how MacGregor had kick-started her officers. He was probably the only other officer in Fourth Fleet who could truly understand how she must feel, given that he was also the only other officer who'd suddenly found himself in the shoes of both Ivan Antonov and Hannah Avram, and he hadn't envied her a bit as she struggled with her subordinates' shattered morale. Her decision to transfer her flag from *Amaretsu* to the hastily repaired *Xingú* had been a statement of her determination to carry on for Hannah, and Prescott had done his dead level best to support her by projecting the confidence she needed from him, but they'd both been fighting a losing battle . . . until she decided to kick ass. *Ivan Antonov couldn't have done it better himself,* he thought, *and if there truly is an afterlife, he and Hannah must be laughing their asses off watching MacGregor. I hope they are, anyway. They deserve it.*

He drew a deep breath, unaware of how his smile had softened, then shook himself.

"All right, then!" he said briskly. "You and Jacques can fine tune the readiness numbers for me before the conference, Anna, but leave it until tomorrow. For right now, I think we can all use some sack time."

The last gunboats arrived under their own power. There were barely two thousand of them, yet the Fleet dared delay no longer. The system beyond the warp point boasted massive industrial capacity. It could undoubtedly build attack craft very quickly and in large numbers. Further delay was thus likely to work in the enemy's favor, despite the new ship types.

"—so as I see it, we've actually got two objectives here, Lord Kolaas," Admiral MacGregor said to Least Fang Harniaar. "First, of course, we have to hold Centauri and protect The Gateway. But just as important, it seems to me, is the need to knock the Bugs back on their heels in a way that every citizen of the Grand Alliance can understand."

She paused, watching the Orion commander of Task Force 42 on her split com screen in *Xingú*'s flag briefing room. The least fang had surrendered twelve superdreadnoughts to Prescott in return for the same number of Terran and Ophiuchi carriers and assault carriers, for it had gone without saying that he would command Fourth Fleet's strikefighters. Now he combed his whiskers with his claws, slowly and thoughtfully, then nodded in a human gesture of agreement.

"You are, of course, correct Ahhhdmiraal Maaac-Gregggorr," he yowled in the Tongue of Tongues. "Your people have been understandably anxious"— MacGregor's lips twitched wryly at the Tabby's choice of words—"since the failure of Operation Pesthouse, but my own have been equally stunned by Second Fleet's losses and their implications for the future conduct of the war."

He paused, and Raymond Prescott and Vice Admiral Ira Chamhandar nodded in grim understanding from their own quadrants of MacGregor's screen. From the outset, the Grand Alliance had tasked the TFN as its primary offensive striking force. The Terran fleet, bigger and more powerful than any of its allies and supported by the most potent industrial machine in the galaxy, had been the only logical choice for the role. But whatever happened when the Bugs attacked Centauri, the TFN would be launching no new offensives any time soon. Simply replacing its lost hulls—and training the personnel to man them—would require at least a full year, and replacement alone wouldn't be enough. The Bugs' now possessed both command datalink and those new, mammoth monitors, and for all MacGregor's brave words, no one really knew if a monitor-led assault *could* be stopped. Even if it could, any sustained offensive would require the Grand Alliance to build vessels of matching weight and power, and that was going to add a minimum of eighteen more months to the wait.

"Given those implications," Harniaar went on levelly, "you are quite correct, Ahhhdmiraal. I do not know if it is possible to damage the *enemy's* morale, but it is imperative to restore our own with a resounding success here. And, of course, it would be most desirable to inflict sufficient losses upon the enemy to induce *him* to abandon further immediate offensives."

"Precisely," MacGregor said, "and that's why—"

The shrill, atonal scream of *Xingú's* General Quarters alarm cut off whatever she'd been about to say.

Two thousand gunboats and a hundred and fifty light cruisers erupted into Centauri space. Fourth Fleet's RD2s had kept a cautious eye on the Bugs in Anderson One, but it appeared the Bugs had realized that. They might not know precisely how it was being accomplished, but they'd allowed for the possibility, and their starships sprang almost instantly from normal standby procedures to all out attack. There was virtually no warning before the gunboats roared off their external racks and the assault fleet's light cruisers lunged for the warp point. Only the fact that the Bugs had been forced to hold their forces beyond SBMHAWK range of the warp point bought Fourth Fleet any time at all, but the first gunboat still burst into Centauri less than fifty seconds after the recon drones which warned of its coming.

Yet Ira Chamhandar's command fort had already sounded the alarm, and the combat space patrol on the warp point was alerted. MacGregor's starships, twenty-five light seconds from the warp point, received the warning fifteen seconds later than Chamhandar, and they were still charging to battle stations when the first Bugs appeared, but the warning was sufficient for the ready duty carriers and Orion battle-line units to launch. Three hundred and twenty fighters streaked towards the warp point, flashing in to join the two hundred forty-strong CSP, and then the mines began to detonate.

Twenty-one light cruisers interpenetrated on transit. That was a somewhat higher percentage than usual, yet it would have been acceptable . . . normally.

But these were not normal conditions, for the Fleet had never encountered such mine densities before, and the new datalink systems' ability to coordinate point defense conferred no advantage. This was a closed warp point. The enemy could place mines directly atop it, and he had. There was no clear zone, no space in which transit-addled electronics could recover. The deadly mines streaked in to blow ship after ship out of space; the fortresses which had been at immediate readiness added their fury to the holocaust; attack craft streaked in, salvoing missiles at the gunboats; and a bright, terrible sphere of flame blazed about the warp point.

"My God, Sir!" Commander Aburish sounded as if he couldn't believe his own readouts. "It looks like— It *is*, by God!" He wheeled to MacGregor with a savage smile. "According to Plotting, Admiral, we've just scored a one hundred percent kill on their cruisers!"

"Outstanding!" MacGregor bared her own teeth, then shook herself. "Gunboats?"

"Harder to say, Sir. Several hundred, at least, but they're much harder mine targets. The CSP caught them with their point defense degraded and nailed a lot of them, and our own strike is on its way in, but—" He shrugged, and MacGregor nodded, then flicked her eyes to Raymond Prescott's portion of her com screen.

"The battle-line will advance to support the forts, Admiral Prescott," she said formally.

The area about the warp point became a wild, swirling melee as fishtailing fighters and gunboats spun and snapped at one another. The standing combat space patrol had exhausted its missiles, but the human and Ophiuchi pilots closed grimly with their internal lasers. The gunboats had suffered terrible losses in the initial strikes, and despite their speed and relatively tiny size a small percentage had been picked off by mines, as well. But half of them had carried AFHAWKs, and all of them had their own internal weapons. Fighters began to die in the vicious, fiery spits of deep-space death, and then the first Bug superdreadnought rumbled through the warp point.

An incandescent halo racked the huge ship's shields as the minefield attacked, but the assault fleet's light cruisers had not died entirely in vain, for they'd drawn in many of the mines directly atop the closed warp point, thinning the field's density. What remained was sufficient to wound the Bug leviathan cruelly, but not to kill it outright, and even as it wallowed in its agony, a second and third superdreadnought followed it into Centauri space. More mines streaked to attack *them*, as well, but with steadily diminishing power, and Ira Chamhandar's eyes were hard.

"Release the pods to local fire control," he told his ops officer coldly. Fresh orders flashed out from his command fort, and the energy-armed Type Three and Four OWPs closest to the warp point acknowledged their instructions. Their fire control activated the shoals of SBMHAWKs slaved to it, firing them in individual, carefully controlled salvos, vomiting sprint-mode capital missiles against the air-bleeding wrecks which had survived the mines' fury, and space itself shuddered as antimatter warheads tore at their targets.

The gunboats realized what was happening, and half of the survivors swerved for the fortresses. But the OWPs' energy weapons flamed in response, and the stupendous "escort" fortresses—two-hundred-thousand-tonne bases designed and armed solely to kill missiles and fighters . . . or gunboats—smashed them by the score even as Allied fighters raced up their wakes. Space was littered with the hideous debris of what once had been gunboats, yet some broke through to hurl themselves bodily upon the forts with full FRAM loads. Shields flashed, armor vaporized, and men and women died as the blast ripped deep into the fortresses' compartments.

"They're getting through to the forts, Sir," Anthea Mandagalla said tautly.

"How bad is it?" Prescott demanded, never taking his eyes from his own plot. His heavy missile ships were almost in range to begin punching SBMs and capital missiles into the holocaust on the warp point, and a sort of deep, visceral horror gnawed at his guts as he watched still more superdreadnoughts transit unflinchingly into the maelstrom. *Nothing* should just keep coming that way, yet they did, and for all its fury, the warp point crucible was less terrible than it had been. The mines were being worn away—not swept, but *absorbed*—and the fortresses had expended most of their missile pods . . . or died.

"It could be worse, but it's not good," Jacques Bichet answered for the chief of staff. "CIC estimates hard kills on forty superdreadnoughts, but they've taken out six forts completely, and a dozen more are badly damaged."

"Admiral Chamhandar's released the Alpha Group energy platforms, Sir!" Commander Hale called out, and then Bichet nodded decisively.

"SBM range, Sir!" he announced sharply.

"Fire as you bear," Raymond Prescott said harshly.

The warp point was a sphere of fiery death, far worse than the Fleet's projections. But the Fleet had allowed for the possibility that its estimates might err. It had sent sixty superdreadnoughts through the invisible hole in space, and courier drones told the tale of destruction which had awaited them. But another fifty superdreadnoughts waited in reserve, backed by the new, larger ships, and those who had led the way had weakened the mines and begun the destruction of the enemy's fortresses.

The attack would continue.

"That's fifty superdreadnoughts confirmed destroyed, Sir," Fahd Aburish said, and Ellen MacGregor nodded silent acknowledgment. *Fifty,* she thought almost calmly. *That's six more than our entire superdreadnought strength, and the bastards are still coming through!*

Xingú staggered as a Bug SBM exploded against her shields. The fleet flagship was a part of Prescott's TF 41, and the Bugs had almost two dozen intact superdreadnoughts—most the missile-heavy *Archers* or the new *Arbalest*-class command ships—in Centauri. Those ships were all damaged to greater or lesser extent, but they were also missile armed, and the survivors had command datalink. Their salvos were as heavy as the ones thundering down upon them, and they were concentrating their fire on Fourth Fleet's battle-line.

Stupid of them, MacGregor thought. *They've got to clear the forts out of their way before they can even think about moving in system, and tonne-for-tonne, an OWP is a hell of a lot more heavily armed than a superdreadnought or a battleship!*

"Admiral Chamhandar's released the Alpha Group platforms, Sir," Aburish said, and MacGregor smiled an ugly smile.

✧   ✧   ✧

The invading Bug starships had absorbed the fury of most of the mines within a half light-second of the warp point, winning at least a limited space in which their consorts could deploy and fight. But the mines had been only a part of Ellen MacGregor and Ira Chamhandar's fixed defenses. Now Chamhandar's command fortress transmitted yet another activation code, and two hundred-plus laser buoys flamed as one. A solid phalanx of X-ray lasers sleeted through the Bugs, ignoring shields to rip deep into armor and alloy, and a baying cheer echoed from *Xingú's* CIC as every single enemy ship on the warp point blew apart.

But the cheer faded almost instantly, for *still* the enemy came on, and he was no longer sending in *Archers*. He was sending through primary-armed *Augers*, force beam-armed *Avalanches*, and deadly, short-ranged *Acids* with their massive plasma gun batteries. TF 41's missiles tore at the new targets, Least Fang Harniaar's TF 42 sent massed fighter strikes screaming down their throats, and Chamhandar's surviving energy-armed fortresses rained fire on them. Yet not even that concentrated torrent of destruction could keep those Bug capital ships from firing back as they died, and Ellen MacGregor's face went white as twenty-one more fortresses—and over a hundred thousand men and women—were wiped out of existence.

"Permission to release the Beta Group platforms?" Chamhandar asked hoarsely, his own expression tight with anguish as he watched his people die, but MacGregor shook her head.

"Denied," she grated, and anger flashed in Chamhandar's eyes. He started to say something more, then clamped his jaw, nodded curtly and turned back to his own staff, and MacGregor understood his rage. But she had no choice, for the Bugs had not yet committed a single monitor. It was possible they wouldn't, that they were saving them, or that they had fewer of them than MacGregor had feared, but she dared not count on that. Any navy which would sacrifice entire fleets and surrender

an entire world inhabited by its own species just to bait
a trap was entirely capable of sacrificing scores of superdreadnoughts just to wear down the defenses before it
launched its decisive blow. And if that was what the Bugs
were doing here, she would need every Beta Group
platform she had.

*The superdreadnoughts' losses continued to mount, and
those losses spelled the probable defeat of the master plan,
for without them, it was unlikely the Fleet would be able
to carry through against the defenses which must have
been erected around the target system's inhabited worlds.
But failure to achieve all of the plan's objectives did not
preclude attaining some of them, and the Fleet appeared
to retain the capacity to at least cripple the forces defending
the warp point. The fragmentary reports from its lead
elements indicated that the enemy's fortress shell had taken
severe losses, and the mines and energy buoys which
covered those fortresses had been sufficiently depleted to
offer a zone in which only the enemy's attack craft and
starships could effectively engage.*

It was time to send in the true attack.

"Oh, *shit!*" Prescott's head snapped around as Bichet
spat the vicious obscenity, and his ops officer looked up
to meet his eyes.

"Here come the monitors, Sir," he said grimly.

"The enemy have committed their monitors, Least
Fang," Harniaar'kolaas' flag captain said in a flat voice,
and the least fang flicked his ears in acknowledgment.

"Understood, Least Claw," he said, and looked at his
operations officer. "What is our fighter status?"

"We retain roughly four hundred of our own and two
hundred Human fighters still aboard ship but tasked for
antishipping strikes," the ops officer replied. "Another two
hundred are returning to rearm, and a strike of approximately three hundred is about to enter attack range. And
we have—" he paused to check a display "—one hundred

and two Ophiuchi fighters armed for gunboat suppression holding just outside the outer minefield shell."

"Hold the present strike and launch the reserve," Harniaar ordered. "We will send them in together, with the Ophiuchi for cover."

"That will delay our attack, Sir," the flag captain pointed out quietly, and Harniaar flicked his ears once more.

"Truth. Yet these are not superdreadnoughts. We will require massed strikes to penetrate their defenses, and I prefer a meaningful blow, even if I must delay its delivery."

"And in the meantime, Sir?"

"And in the meantime, Least Claw, it will be up to Ahhhdmiraal Chaaamhaaandaaar," Harniaar replied softly.

"Activate the Beta Group but do *not* fire!" Ira Chamhandar snapped. He didn't have to ask MacGregor again, for this was the threat against which Fourth Fleet's CO had reserved those energy platforms. The fact that she'd been right to hold them this long didn't make him feel any better about the people he'd lost to the superdreadnoughts, yet his teeth skinned back from his lips as he watched the Bug giants flowing into existence on the warp point. They floated in a hole among the mines—a hole their superdreadnoughts had carved with their own deaths—and their massive batteries began to smash fortresses and Allied capital ships methodically, but still Chamhandar held back. He could only do this once, and he made himself wait . . . and wait . . . and *wait* until no less than two dozen of those mammoth vessels had emerged. Then, and only then, he gave the order, and four hundred more independently deployed energy platforms fired. Not laser buoys, this time, but primary and particle beams that smashed implacably through even monitors' shields and armor. Of the twenty-four monitors on the warp point when they fired, only five survived, and Fourth Fleet closed for the kill.

The lead wave's monitors had been devastated. It was clear now that the system could not be taken, but it was equally clear that the enemy was closing on the warp point. He was approaching with every starship he still possessed, and he would undoubtedly commit his full remaining attack craft strength, as well. The opportunity thus remained to inflict heavy loss upon him, and the Fleet changed its deployment. The second-wave monitors refitted with the new datalink systems were pulled from the assault queue, but the fifteen more expendable monitors still equipped with the old-style datalink moved to the front, accompanied by seventy-six battlecruisers, eighteen light cruisers, and all of the new ramming ships.

"Holy shi——!"

The fighter pilot's exclamation was chopped off by the explosion of his fighter, and Raymond Prescott flinched as his plot changed abruptly. And insanely. Even after Pesthouse, he couldn't believe—not on any deep, emotional level—that *anyone* would do something like *that!*

But the Bugs *had* done it. One moment space about the warp point was all but empty as the fighters and Prescott's own missiles finished off he last Bug cripples. The next moment, over a hundred warships flashed into existence in a stupendous simultaneous transit. Not light cruisers, but *battle*cruisers and even *monitors!* Perhaps a dozen of them interpenetrated and perished, but the others survived, and even with their systems impaired by transit, they belched a hurricane of missiles and beams into Chamhandar's bleeding fortresses.

"Take us in, Jacques!" Prescott heard someone else say with his own voice. "Missile platforms stay back; everything else closes *now!*"

"Fang Pressscott is closing, Sir!" Harniaar's flag captain snapped, and Harniaar bared his fangs. Of course Fang Prescott was closing! His *farshatok* aboard the fortresses were dying, and no holder of the *Ithyrra'doi'khanhaku* would let them die alone. Nor could any officer of the *Zheeerlikou'valkhannaieee* fail to follow where such a one led.

"Send in the fighters, Least Claw," Harniaar said. "Then release our escorts."

Ellen MacGregor sealed her helmet and double checked her shock frame as *Xingú* joined Raymond Prescott's charge. Fleet commander or no, that was all she could do now . . . unless she chose to order Prescott off, and that was unthinkable. A part of her was actually content, for her battle plan had worked. Even for Bugs, this simultaneous transit *had* to be a last gasp by an assault which had failed, yet the carnage had been so vast—and was about to become so much more terrible still—that she could feel no sense of triumph. Later, perhaps, if she lived, she might feel such things. For now, there was only hatred and the need to kill.

She stabbed one last look at her display, saw the faster battlecruisers and *Athabasca*-class superdreadnoughts pulling ahead of their consorts. Bug battlecruisers came to meet them, and a corner of her brain cringed as yet more Bug ships raced straight for Chamhandar's closest surviving forts. Most died in the intervening minefields, but the staggering power of the explosions which killed them came from something far more potent than mines or even the fury of their own antimatter warheads. Only four reached their targets, but for each which did, a Terran fortress died.

Sweet Jesus, MacGregor wondered almost numbly. *What are those things? The bastards must've packed them to the deckhead with antimatter!*

But it was only a passing thought, for *Xingú* had caught up with the madness on the warp point, Harniaar'kolaas' fighters on her heels, and there was no more time. No time for anything but killing.

Pause in the Storm

Kthaara'zarthan rose from the Terran-style chair behind his desk as Ellen MacGregor and Raymond Prescott walked into his office. A week had passed since the Battle of Alpha Centauri, and the RD2s had confirmed what was happening in Anderson One.

The Bugs were digging in. Their minelayers were emplacing their own mines—and, undoubtedly, energy buoys—on their side of the warp point. Powerful mobile forces, including still more of their monitors, hovered watchfully behind the minelayers, but they remained carefully beyond SBMHAWK range of the warp point. No one was prepared to predict that they would stay on the defensive forever, but the implications were clear, and Kthaara bowed to the two officers who had been most responsible for stopping the enemy dead.

"Ahhhdmiraal MaaacGregggorr, Fang Pressscott. Be seated, please," he invited. His guests obeyed the polite command, and he resumed his own seat and regarded them levelly across the desk. "You have done well, both of you," he said quietly. "The Grand Alliance owes you and your *farshatok* more than it can ever hope to repay, and I—" he paused to look directly into Prescott's eyes "—owe a deeply personal debt, for I cannot doubt that among the *chofaki* you and your warriors slew were those responsible for my *vilkshatha* brother's death. There will be more blood balance before this war is over, yet you have exacted the first *vilknarma*, and for that I will be always in your debt."

MacGregor looked a little embarrassed, but Prescott only nodded soberly, and Kthaara flicked his ears twice, then cocked his chair back.

"You have also," he went on in a less emotionally charged voice, "bought the Alliance some additional time. Had the enemy succeeded in taking Centauri, he might well have carried through against Sol. Even if he had not, we would have been forced to retake Centauri at any price, and the losses his monitors might have inflicted against warp point assaults or in deep space could have been devastating. As it is, and despite the losses Fourth Fleet suffered, he has clearly abandoned attacks on this system for the immediate future. By the time he feels secure enough to attempt them once more, we will have three or four times your strength waiting on the warp point for him. I do not think—" he bared his fangs in a lazy, hunter's grin "—that he will enjoy any future attacks on this system even as much as he did his last."

"But that doesn't mean he won't make them, Sir," Prescott pointed out quietly. "And all he has to do is get lucky once."

"Truth, Fang Pressscott," Kthaara acknowledged. "And it will remain true until we are able to take the offensive to *them* once more. Hopefully," a cold, bleak hatred glowed in the Orion's slit-pupilled eyes, "on *our* terms this time."

"You're referring to Zephrain, Sir?" MacGregor asked, and her eyes were troubled when Kthaara nodded. "With all due respect, Sir, I'd think that what happened here—what *almost* happened here—gives even more point to the fears of what might happen to Rehfrak if we attack through Zephrain and fail."

"Truth," Kthaara agreed once more. "There are many who would agree with you, Ahhhdmiraal, and I share your views in great part, as well. There will be no precipitous attacks. This war has lasted for three and a half of your years, almost seven of my people's, and the ghosts of Kliean will not soon be forgotten by any of us. It will take time to prepare our blow, for we must first build our own monitors. Yet I feel it is particularly important that I, as the *Khan'a'khanaaeee*'s representative to the Joint Chiefs, press for the earliest possible date for such an attack. Above all, we dare not allow these creatures leisure to press their own exploration until *they* find the equivalent of Zaaia'pharaan and a blow such as the one you have just stopped falls unopposed upon one of our core systems. I recognize the need to prepare carefully, however hard inactivity comes to one of the *Zheeerlikou'valkhannaieee* in war, yet we must not allow ourselves or our superiors to forget that the breathing space you and your valiant warriors have bought can be only a pause in the storm . . . and that it must be allowed to linger no longer than absolutely necessary."

He gazed at the two human admirals, and they nodded back soberly.

"I am glad you agree," he said after moment, "for you both will have major parts to play. From what I have heard from your admiralty, you, Ahhhdmiraal MaaacGregggorr, will soon be confirmed as Sky Marshal *and* designated as the Federation's permanent representative to the Joint Chiefs." MacGregor hissed in shock, sitting suddenly very straight in her chair, and Kthaara gave another lazy Orion smile. "You have earned it, Ahhhdmiraal," he told her. "Besides, you remind me in many ways of a younger Eevaahn'zarthan . . . although you still have much to learn of the proper way to describe politicians. Still," he permitted himself a purring chuckle, "your new position will no doubt provide sufficient exposure to them to hone your vocabulary."

"I—" MacGregor started to speak, then closed her mouth and settled for a nod, and Kthaara looked at Prescott.

"For you, Raaymmonnd'telmasa, there will be another task," he said quietly. "As you know, our original plan for the Zaaia'pharaan operation would have placed you in command of its battle-line under Ahhhdmiraal Antaanaav while Zhaarnak'telmasa commanded its carriers. That will not now be possible, but after much discussion with my colleagues of the Joint Chiefs, we have decided that *you* will command the entire operation in Eevaahn's place. I believe he would have wished it that way . . . and I can think of no officer whom *I* would prefer to see in that position. Fang Zhaarnak will, of course, be made available to you as your second in command."

"Thank you, Sir," Prescott replied in the Tongue of Tongues, and Kthaara nodded, then inhaled deeply.

"None of that will be happening anytime soon, however," he said more briskly. "In the meantime, I feel confident that we can keep both of you suitably busy right here, overseeing Centauri's defense and helping me kick the *droshokol mizoahaarlesh* of our various research and shipbuilding commands into action. And, I fear," he bared just the tips of his fangs, "making occasional public appearances with our highly respected political leaders."

Prescott groaned aloud, and Kthaara laughed.

"Come now, Raaymmonnd! I can even promise you a special treat this afternoon, for First Fang Ynaathar's personal representative will be passing through Centauri tomorrow, and he has been invited to address your Naval Oversight Committee. I realize how much you dislike interviews and politician's speeches, but I believe you and Ahhhdmiraal MaaacGregggorr will both take particular pleasure from Fang Ulaahkhaa's speech. You see, Fang Ulaahkhaa has served as a member of our equivalent of your Naval Oversight Committee, and I fear he is somewhat of the old school. He is also known to share Eevaahn'zarthan's view of politicians, and he continues to be known for the, ah, *blunt*, plainspoken fashion in which he expresses his views. I mention this only because I understand that both Msss. Wisssterr and Mr. Waaaldeccck will be attending his speech, and—" the big Tabby's smile took on an almost seraphic quality "—I will be most interested to hear how the interpreters render his remarks for them."

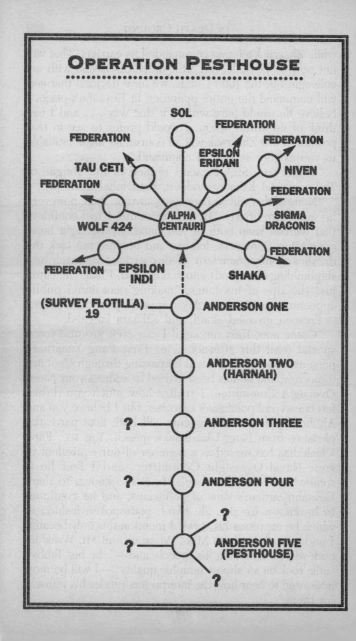

OPERATION PESTHOUSE

SOL

FEDERATION

FEDERATION

EPSILON
ERIDANI

FEDERATION

TAU CETI

NIVEN

FEDERATION

WOLF 424

ALPHA
CENTAURI

FEDERATION

SIGMA
DRACONIS

FEDERATION

FEDERATION

EPSILON
INDI

SHAKA

(SURVEY FLOTILLA)
19

ANDERSON ONE

ANDERSON TWO
(HARNAH)

? — ANDERSON THREE

? — ANDERSON FOUR

? — ANDERSON FIVE
(PESTHOUSE)

?

?

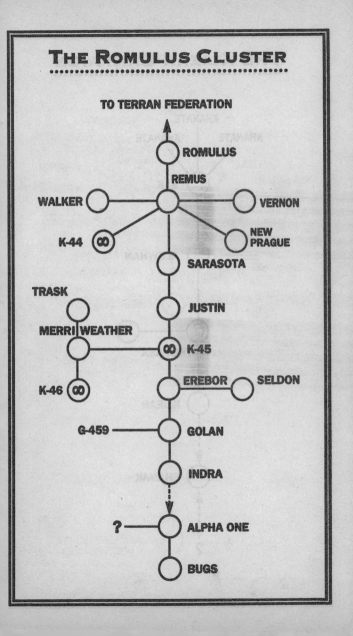

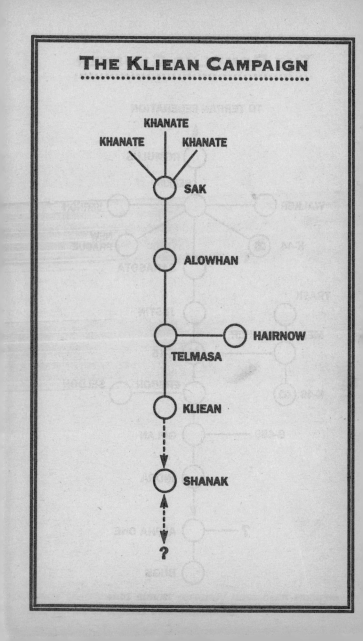

THE KLIEAN CAMPAIGN